# Reel Future

# Reel Future

Edited by

## FORREST J ACKERMAN
## & JEAN STINE

BARNES
&NOBLE
BOOKS
NEW YORK

This edition published by Barnes & Noble, Inc.,
by arrangement with The Ackerman Agency.

1994 Barnes & Noble Books

Book design by Nicola Ferguson

ISBN 1-56619-450-4

Printed and bound in the United States of America

M 9 8 7 6 5 4 3 2 1

# Acknowledgments

Grateful acknowledgment is made to the following for permission to reprint their copyrighted material:

FAREWELL TO THE MASTER by Harry Bates, copyright 1940 Street & Smith Publications, Inc., renewed, reprinted by permission of Forrest J Ackerman, The Ackerman Agency, International, Hollywood, CA 90027; THE ILLUSTRATED MAN by Ray Bradbury, copyright 1951 Esquire Publishing, Inc., renewed, reprinted by permission of Don Congdon Associates, Inc; WHO GOES THERE? by John W. Campbell Jr., copyright 1938 Street & Smith Publications, Inc., renewed, reprinted by permission of Scott Meredith Literary Agency, LP, 845 Third Ave, New York, NY 10022; THE SENTINEL by Arthur C. Clarke, copyright 1951 Avon Periodicals, Inc., renewed, reprinted by permission of the Scott Meredith Literary Agency, LP, 845 Third Ave, New York, NY 10022; WE CAN REMEMBER IT FOR YOU WHOLESALE by Philip K. Dick, copyright 1966 Mercury Press, Inc., renewed, Scott Meredith Literary Agency, LP, 845 Third Ave, New York, NY 10022; THIS ISLAND EARTH by Raymond F. Jones, copyright 1952 Raymond F. Jones, renewed, reprinted by permission of The Ackerman Agency, International, Hollywood, CA 90027; THE FLY by George Langelaan, copyright 1957 H.M.H. Publishing Company, Inc., renewed, reprinted by permission of The Ackerman Agency, International, Hollywood, CA 90027; ENEMY MINE by Barry Longyear, copyright 1979 Barry Longyear, reprinted by permission of the author; THE RACER by Ib Melchior, copyright 1956 by Dee Publishing Company, Inc., renewed, reprinted by permission of The Ackerman Agency, International, Hollywood, CA 90027; EIGHT O'CLOCK IN THE MORNING by Ray Faraday Nelson, copyright 1963 Mercury Press, Inc., reprinted by permission of the author; THE SEVENTH VICTIM by Robert Sheckley, copyright 1953 Galaxy Publishing Corp., renewed, reprinted by permission of The Pimlico Agency,

Inc.; AIR RAID John Varley, copyright 1976 Davis Publications, Inc., reprinted by permission of The Pimlico Agency, Inc.; DAMNATION ALLEY by Roger Zelazny, copyright 1967 by The Galaxy Publishing Co., reprinted by permission of The Pimlico Agency, Inc.

The following stories used in this book are no longer in copyright, but in accordance with long practice, the authors are forwarding honorariums to the author's heirs as they are located:
HERBERT WEST—RE-ANIMATOR by H. P. Lovecraft, copyright Home Brew, Inc. 1921–22; ARMAGEDDON 2419 A.D. by Philip Francis Nowlan, copyright 1928 by Experimenter Publishing, Inc.; THE EMPIRE OF THE ANTS by H. G. Wells, copyright 1905 The Blackwood Publishing Co.

Special thanks to Hollywood Book and Poster for providing materials missing from our own files from their own voluminous stock.

# Contents

# List of Photographs

# Introduction

Cinema and science fiction have a very special relationship. Movies help us envision the wondrous worlds of science fiction, while science fiction allows movies to offer a magical, powerful form of entertainment. And so, in combination, both mediums can realize a greater potential through each other.

Pioneer filmmakers were quick to perceive the possibilities for bringing science fiction to life. Almost as soon as movies were invented, directors and producers understood that these stories provided an ideal vehicle for the astonishing variety of visual effects that this new art form made possible. Motion-picture historians date the birth of the "flickers" at 1895, and by 1901, pioneer cinema magician George Méliès was hard at work on what would become the first classic of science-fiction cinema, *A Trip to the Moon.*

Soon theater goers were able to see amazing worlds in which anything was possible. People pedaled through the air on their personal flying machines; unknown rays rendered a man invisible; robots freed housewives from a life of drudgery; cavemen and -women walked while dinosaurs stalked; finned merfolk swam the sunken halls of Atlantis; scientists isolated the chemicals that triggered passion and produced love; and comets threatened to strike Earth at any moment. The memoirs of author Ray Bradbury and astronaut John Mitchell attest to the fact that seeing these movies, even without the sophistication of sound and color, forever changed the way they perceived the world.

It is hardly surprising that science-fiction films of the silent era had such a profound impact. Throughout that period producers were busy adapting many of the greatest tales the genre possessed. Many film classics, including Stevenson's *Dr. Jekyll and Mr. Hyde* (1908), were unleashed on an unsuspecting public. This movie proved to be so popular with audiences that new versions were filmed in 1912, 1913, and 1914, along with three remakes in 1920 alone. In 1910, Thomas Edison became the first man to film *Frankenstein*; in 1913 (and 1927), *Balaoo, the Demon Baboon* by Gaston Leroux of *Phantom of the Opera* fame, went before the cameras; and in 1916, audiences saw Captain Nemo race "20,000 leagues beneath the sea" in the first of many adaptations of Verne's novel.

However, the three films that would constitute the high points of the science-fiction cinema in the silent era were still to come. In 1925, Arthur Conan Doyle's celebrated adaptation of *Lost World* was made irresistible by the magic "stop-motion" photography of animation pioneer Willis O'Brien. The following year, Fritz Lang brought to the screen his wife's (Thea von Harbou) novel, *Metropolis*, and so produced a vision of the future more vivid, realistic, and complete than anything movie audiences had ever seen before. Then in 1929, just upon the arrival of sound, Lucien Hubbard directed a memorable, atmospheric production of Verne's *Mysterious Island*.

The advent of sound launched a veritable golden age of screen science fiction. These are only some of the distinguished films adapted from novels and stories: *Things to Come, Invasion of the Body Snatchers, When Worlds Collide, Jurassic Park, Village of the Damned, War of the Worlds, The Time Machine, The Andromeda Strain, Planet of the Apes, Fahrenheit 451, The Invisible Man, The Incredible Shrinking Man, Donovan's Brain, A Clockwork Orange, The Dead Zone, Demon Seed, Logan's Run, Dr. Strangelove, Somewhere in Time, Rollerball,* and *On the Beach.*

Most of these films—and the stories on which they were based—were more than mere entertainment. Each offered a cautionary note or pointed to possible new scientific and social trends that, if carried forward, could hold either great promise or great peril for humanity. More than a dozen of these prophetic tales—each the basis of a major science-fiction movie—have been selected for this book.

The first story is H. G. Wells's "The Empire of the Ants." At first glance, it is about insects that become gigantic in size and intellect. However, cloaked beneath lies the question of when and how nature will overwhelm the human species. Many of Wells's novels were adapted for the screen, and these movies were also the inspiration for many other films. His novels discussed invisibility, scientifically evolved or devolved creatures, future prophecy, aliens from space, and, of course, time travel.

Fittingly, "The Empire of the Ants" served as the tale that spawned the giant-insect subgenre, even though the movie version did not arrive on screen until the late 1970s. It is also the first Wells short story, and the only one to date, to have been adapted into a major motion picture. Although the movie has many inadequacies, the basic premise of nature overcoming man still retains its power and significance.

Like Wells's stories, H. P. Lovecraft's are filled with meaning for our time. To Lovecraft (who wrote in the seemingly saner, halcyon days of the twenties and thirties), any sense of security or safety derived from the order and institutions of modern life was illusory. Hailed, condemned, and controversial during his lifetime and afterward, Lovecraft dreamed up a dark new mythology of great archetypal power and persuasiveness. His uneasy iconography of protagonists doomed by destiny—such as those in the haunted, decadent hamlet of Arkham, and in the pantheon of evil, eldritch gods from the *Necronomicon*—have become household words in modern horror. Comprised of a series of loosely knitted stories, and published mostly in the progenitor of all horror magazines, *Weird Tales*, Lovecraft's "Cthulhu Mythos," as it is known, includes such genuine shockers as "The Case of Charles Dexter Ward" and "The Colour Out of Space." Both of these tales were turned into the films *The Haunted Palace* (1963) and *Die, Monster, Die* (1965).

However, one of Lovecraft's most disturbing tales is "Herbert West—Reanimator." The story's inspiration harkens back to our ancestral fears of the dead returning to life. Just as Mary Shelley did in *Frankenstein*, Lovecraft attributed his protagonist's resurrections not to demonic forces or sorcerous spells, but to the awesome forces of the modern scientific laboratory. And, as with other mythic characters who tampered with things "outside humankind's sphere," West's efforts come to an unfortunate end. The R-rated 1986 film version of Herbert West's necromantic misadventures is grisly enough to satisfy the most blood thirsty fan of Lovecraft's canon. The movie is so gory and obscene, it probably would have horrified its notoriously sensitive author.

Less literary, more appealing, and equally prophetic, the work of Lovecraft-contemporary Philip Francis Nowlan is also active today. Nowlan's stories continue to inspire books, games, and movies more than five decades after they were written. Nowlan was raised at the turn of the century, alongside the wonders and miracles brought by the scientific revolution, and his ideas caught fire together with these dreams. By day, Nowlan was a financial reporter for the Philadelphia *Public Record*, but by night he worked away at his vision of a United States not as fortunate in future wars as it had been in the one just concluded.

His voice found a home and a focus in the pages of *Amazing Stories*—the magazine founded by visionary Hugo Gernsback, and the first to be devoted exclusively to the new literature of science fiction. Nowlan's story might have languished forever in the pages of *Amazing* had it not been for the foresight of John Flint Dille, the founder and president of the National Newspaper Syndicate. Dille thought newspaper audiences were ready to have the world of the future delivered to them each morning through the pages of their comic section. When a copy of the August 1928 *Amazing* containing Nowlan's *Armageddon 2419 A.D.* fell into his hands, Dille knew he had struck syndicated pay dirt. He contacted the young financial reporter—and the result was comic-strip, motion-picture, and television history. (Dille made one other contribution that helped insure the new strip's success: He suggested changing the hero's name from the effete "Anthony" Rogers to the more collegiate and manly "Buck.")

Larry "Buster" Crabbe, fresh from his triumphs as Flash Gordon, was the first to bring Buck to the screen, in a 1930s serial still beloved today for its unflagging energy and high-camp visuals. Twenty years later this serial was edited down and released as two separate movies (*Planet Outlaws* and *Destination Saturn*).

Not as dire as the work of Wells and Lovecraft, and more serious than that of Nowlan, the work of John W. Campbell Jr. optimistically portrayed the future as ultimately culminating in the triumph of reason (and by extension, the scientific method) over the savage dangers of nature and our baser passions. Campbell, who is acknowledged as the most influential editor in the history of science fiction, was the editor of *Astounding*. In the beginning *Astounding* was overshadowed by such sensationalistic magazines as *Amazing, Startling Stories, Planet, Super Science, Imagination, Astonishing, Marvel,* and a dozen other science-fiction pulps that featured lurid BEMs (bug-eyed monsters) and metal brassiere covers. It's a miracle that Campbell was successful at all. However, the magazine's quiet persistence; subdued, understated, and doggedly realistic covers; relentless emphasis on logic, reason, and the scientifically plausible; and focus on how technological innovation would impact on the average human life eventually turned the tide away from the pulps. Under Campbell's editorship, *Astounding* spawned a new generation of serious writers who included Asimov and Heinlein.

Campbell was as important and influential a writer as he was editor. In moody, poetic stories such as "Twilight," "Forgetfulness," and "The Elder Gods," he deliberately questioned many of science fiction's underlying assumptions, setting a precedent that has helped the field to continue to thrive ever since.

"Who Goes There?" formed part of that revolution. Although full of suspense and action, it turned science fiction away from stories that were merely suspense and action. It also posed a scientific puzzle: Faced with an alien intelligence that can take over a human body and absorb memories, how do you determine who is a monster and who is human? So persuasive was Campbell's story that it has been filmed twice—once in 1951 and again in 1982.

If Campbell restored science fiction to its original status, Harry Bates single-handedly brought it to the level of pulp fiction. Alternately damned as science fiction's perverter and hailed as its savior, Bates, with the creation of *Astounding*, changed science-fiction magazines from vehicles of scientific and social speculation to marketing tools designed to hook the adolescent male reader.

"Farewell to the Master" is Bates's most celebrated effort. It questions whether or not man's darker instincts can triumph over decency and reason, asking if the deficiencies in man's own brain preclude him from being the best controller of his own destiny. Those who are familiar only with the film version (*The Day the Earth Stood Still*) will discover that the last line of the story adds a wealth of meaning. Although taking scriptural liberties, the movie version does retain the essential elements, subtleties, and charms of Bates's original. From the eerie, convincing design of the robot Klaatu to the immortal words of Pogo—"the enemy is us"—the film remains a classic in science-fiction cinema.

Those who are familiar with only the film version of Raymond F. Jones's *This Island Earth* will also discover depth and meaning in the novel (reprinted here in its entirety for the first time since the early fifties) that was lost when it was adapted for the screen. The reader will also discover that Jones's novel contains an entirely different and far more philosophical plot.

Jones possessed the characteristics that John Campbell prized most—a professional background as a scientist or engineer; a logical mind that could pose fascinating, seemingly insoluble problems; and a stubborn belief that humans really were somehow innately superior to any alien race they might encounter. Not surprisingly, much of Jones's best work appeared in the pages of *Astounding* (*Renaissance*, "The Toymaker," the "Noise Level" trilogy, and "The Model Shop").

Most of Jones's work, like so many *Astounding* stories, concerns itself with conceptual breakthroughs. His stories concern social, psychological, or scientific advances that take place through the destruction of an old paradigm. Perhaps nothing typifies the moment before conceptual breakthrough so well as the scene in *This Island Earth* in which the protagonist, the sole passenger in a remote-controlled airplane whose windows have been completely blacked out, sits awaiting take off to an unknown destination. The fifties film version of "This Island Earth," although departing from Jones's story line half way through the movie, provided the most complete visualization of an alien world and civilization that audiences would see until George Lucas's astonishing *Star Wars*.

The generation of writers who grew up on the works of Campbell and Bates raised equally profound concerns. The first was Ray Bradbury, a dreamy young writer whose science-fiction stories were considered so off track by the genre editors of 1949 that he could only sell them as filler to pulp magazines. Readers who are familiar with Bradbury's work may not believe that such classics of the human dark side as "Mars is Heaven," "The Veldt," and "The Exiles" could ever have been sandwiched between crudely drawn illustrations of monsters and ray guns. Notwithstanding, the young Bradbury, with a family to feed, considered himself lucky to sell a story or two a month for fifty to a hundred dollars.

Only a short year later, in 1950—partly as the result of the championing of such influential mainstream literary critics as Christopher Isherwood, Aldous Huxley, and Martha Foley, and mostly because of the rave reviews of *The Martian Chronicles*—Bradbury was catapulted to bestsellerdom and international fame as one of the supreme science-fiction writers of the age. In the process, he won a vast new audience of readers who had turned up their collective noses at the very magazines that had given Bradbury a living.

The author's swift fame caught Hollywood's fancy, and producers were soon standing in line to option *The Martian Chronicles*, *The Illustrated Man*, and other Bradbury works. However, it would be the less-recognized works, such as "The Foghorn" and "The Meteor," that would take on the form of motion pictures as *The Beast from 20,000 Fathoms* and *It Came from Outer Space*. Audiences would have to wait almost twenty years before television would dramatize *The Martian Chronicles* as a mini-series, and Jack Smight would combine three stories from *The Illustrated Man* in a theatrical feature.

Arthur C. Clarke's readers, like Bradbury's, may be surprised to learn that much of his best work also languished in the pages of the pulps. Yet, despite the nearly forty books and countless short stories he had written, this talented author was virtually unknown outside a select circle of science fiction readers until Stanley Kubrick brought one of his short stories to the screen. The success of *2001: A Space Odyssey* catapulted Clarke to international fame. For the first time, many people who had never read science fiction found themselves seduced by the deeply thoughtful work of this most literate and visionary of modern science-fiction writers.

Oddly enough, "The Sentinel," the brief (3,700 words) original story that inspired *2001*, seems a very slight frame on which to peg such an enormous financial, literary, and cinematic success. This alone is sufficient testimony to director Stanley Kubrick's genius. There is something monumental about the story, for all its briefness. Clarke meant to bring the reader face to face with some ageless, mysterious, and utterly alien force. To expand Clarke's original story to movie length, Kubrick simply asked himself what might have happened before and what might have happened afterward. He was wise enough to leave the central mystery tantalizingly unexplained.

There is considerably less mystery, but equally solid speculation and insight, in Robert Sheckley's "The Seventh Victim." A master satirist, known for his mordant wit and puckish sallies at humanity's many foibles, Sheckley is strongest as a short-story writer. His best work appears in collections like *Can You Feel Anything When I Do This?*, *Citizen in Space*, and *Notions Unlimited*.

One of Sheckley's favorite settings is the futuristic game show in which the participants are pursued across an urban landscape for the entertainment of millions—with life or death as the stakes. The most striking of these stories is "The Seventh Victim," which, like much of Sheckley's work, appeared in H. L. Gold's *Galaxy*—a publication whose determined emphasis on society and psychology reflected its reaction to the doggedly technological orientation of Campbell's *Astounding*.

Sheckley's tale takes place in a world where murder is legal. The only drawback is that the killer must agree that after having taken a victim he, in turn, will then be stalked by a killer. The protagonist is about to take his seventh victim when he discovers that she is female. A chauvinist to the core, the protagonist is dismayed, believing that women do not possess the killer instinct necessary for such a hunt.

On this premise, Sheckley manages to hang a pungent, penetrating satire of the eternal contest between the genders. Fittingly, it was the Italians, those masters of perceptive satires on the gender-wars, who successfully shepherded Sheckley's story to the screen. Sixties in sound, style and verve, and far more farce than suspense, the final result failed to win action-jaded American audiences. However, it did win legendary status as a cult film among smaller, more sophisticated audiences.

An endurance race is also the core of Ib Melchior's "The Racer." Although his name is hardly a familiar one, Melchior has scripted many films that have been broadcasted around the world. Over the course of any given year, *The Time Travelers*, *Reptilicus*, *Robinson Crusoe on Mars*, *Journey to the Seventh Planet*, and others play at least a half-dozen times on local, cable, and satellite channels. However, it is the film adaptation of "The Racer" that has achieved the most fame. Interestingly, *Death Race 2000* was a film that Melchior did not script.

The seeds of this futuristic tale were planted in 1939. Newly arrived in this country from his native Denmark, Melchior had been invited to the Indianapolis Speedway. During the races, he sat with the wives of some of the racers. Suddenly, in the midst of one of the races, there was a disastrous wreck, and one of the drivers was killed. The woman Melchior was seated next to was the dead racer's wife. He then saw a crowd of people begin to push and shove toward the fiery crash site so that they could catch a glimpse of the mangled body. Every pair of field glasses was also trained on the grisly sight;

at the same time, Melchior saw the look of shock and horror on the face of the woman seated beside him.

Years later, when he began to write, Melchior was still haunted by his memories of that bloody accident. From these memories "The Racer" was born. Melchior meant the story as a protest against the mindless fascination that American society has with violence. Some twenty years after its publication, Roger Corman, the legendary king of the "B" filmmakers, acquired the movie rights to "The Racer" for an up-and-coming young actor named Sylvester Stallone. Though the resulting motion-picture version has been criticized as grossly overexaggerated and almost farcical, it was unable to disguise the powerful message that lies at the core of Melchior's story. Ironically, the violence in the film adaptation proved enormously fascinating to the viewing public. *Death Race 2000* became a box-office smash and helped spawn a series of sequels and imitations designed to sate the public's taste for violence with bloody futuristic races, gladiatorial combats, and human hunts.

Literary in tone and serious in treatment and theme, George Langelaan's "The Fly" might seem light-years removed from such tales as "The Seventh Victim" and "The Racer." However, Langelaan's story possesses the classic ingredients of the science fiction/horror film. The idea of man metamorphosing into the form of another earthly creature dates back to myths and legends. His story proved so popular that two film versions were produced, along with a score of sequels.

In many ways the 1958 version of *The Fly* might seem silly, overblown, and far too fervid. However, aficionados find it moodily lit and surprisingly low-key. The movie also has a refreshingly realistic focus. The domestic crisis—the story's central experiment—becomes a metaphor for the estrangements that occur in marriages. It is generally agreed, though, that the remake by David Cronenberg is far superior to the original. His version captures the literary polish, significance, and meaning of Langelaan's original, while keeping at the same time the hero's inevitable transformation as a strong metaphor for the disintegration of the intimate relationship.

Strong metaphor is also at the heart of Ray Faraday Nelson's mordant "Eight O'Clock in the Morning." A hard-core science-fiction fan, cartoonist, and poet with several volumes to his credit, Nelson operates out of a Northern California Bay Area bookshop. Perhaps the most Wellsian of the younger writers, Nelson, whose work includes *Then Beggars Could Ride* and *Ecolog*, is driven by a strong moral core revealing his clear belief in the perfectibility of humanity and human society.

"Eight O'Clock in the Morning" discusses the elusive nature of perception. One morning a man discovers he can see what no one else can see—he realizes that the world is in the control of aliens who have successfully hypnotized everyone but him. Nelson's protagonist is forced to kill when the aliens realize he is no longer under their control. However, the question arises as to whether the narrator is sane or not. Are we simply seeing the delusion from the point of view of the deluded?

Twenty-five years after the story's original publication, producer-director John Carpenter read a comic-book adaptation and knew he had to bring Nelson's work to the screen. The result was *They Live*, in which Carpenter deepened Nelson's central premise into a symbol of the political and social apathy of our times.

Another author whose tales are a complex study of reality is Philip K. Dick. His works are determinedly dystopian and filled with the least appetizing of characters—metaphysical heroes who search for the meaning of truth only to discover that reality is insignificant. Not surprisingly, his stories were seized upon by filmmakers of the disillusioned eighties and nineties.

Starting with *Bladerunner*, a haunting version of the deliciously gothic *Do Androids Dream of Electric Sheep?*, and climaxing with Paul Verhoeven's hyperkinetic adaptation of "We Can Remember It for You Wholesale" (brought to the screen under the title *Total Recall*), these movies helped bring Dick's science-fiction works onto the screen. And for all the liberties taken with the original plot lines, these movies still capture the deeply disturbing way reality manages to remain elusively out of the grasp of the protagonist.

*Bladerunner* and *Total Recall* also manage to capture the essential theme of what it means to be human. The first film is filled with replicants (androids) who feel and humans who are as emotionless as robots; the second is filled with dreamers who seem real and real people who seem dreamlike. Both make the point that human beings who avoid love, empathy, and compassion are no better than robots.

The "message" in Roger Zelazny's "Damnation Alley" is less personal and more universal than Dick's. His story is concerned with the likelihood of ecological disaster. One of the first of the new writers to voice concern about the perils of massive environmental devastation, he tells of a very unpleasant day after tomorrow. "Damnation Alley" appeared first as a novella in *Galaxy* and was later expanded into a novel under the impetus of a movie sale. "Damnation Alley" is very much a tale of its era. It carries rebellious and antiestablishment idioms, with an ecological warning in the subtext, into what had been an almost exclusively bourgeois form of fiction.

The movie version showed substantial alterations in the characters, background, and motivation of the story. Fresh from his work on *The Illustrated Man*, which was not well received by genre critics, Jack Smight transformed Zelazny's antiauthoritarian biker hero, Hell Tanner, into an Air Force officer. His bike was replaced with a futuristic tank/motor home, and instead of a loner, Hell became part of a team. Only the plot of a race against time, across an America ravaged by an ecological disaster, to deliver desperately needed antiplague serum to one of the few groups of survivors remained intact from Zelazny's original tale. In the process Zelazny and Smight unwittingly inaugurated the entire genre of postapocalyptic punk science-fiction films, beginning with *Mad Max*.

Barry Longyear's prizewinning story, "Enemy Mine," is just as philosophical as Zelazny's—but considerably more optimistic. Like "Who Goes There?" and *This Island Earth*, it takes a positive view of humanity and its perfectibility. It also shares the belief in the ultimate triumph of reason over our more primitive impulses.

Longyear's writings burst upon the science-fiction landscape with an issue of *Isaac Asimov's Science Fiction Magazine* and appeared there regularly throughout most of the late seventies and early eighties. When Longyear's deeply moving novella, "Enemy Mine," won both the Hugo and Nebula awards, it was immediately snapped up by the movies and turned into a money-generating, Oscar-nominee motion picture as well as a best-selling book.

The film version of "Enemy Mine" retains the story's passionate humanism. It also presents audiences with the first intelligent, mature look at realistic, sympathetic aliens every bit as civilized, conscious, and worthy of existence as ourselves. The movie was blessed with a quality script, outstanding acting, a sumptuous production, and a moving screenplay directed by one of Europe's most gifted filmmakers. The movie's faithful attempt to preserve the author's message without compromise makes it one of those rarities in science-fiction cinema.

The author's message in the screen adaptation of John Varley's "Air Raid" is also given reverent treatment. As with Wells's "The Empire of the Ants," Varley's tale is a warning of ecological disaster. However, in Varley's story it is not the world, but time itself that faces destruction due to ill-advised tampering by future chrononauts. Like all his work, the story stands on the cutting edge of contemporary science fiction in its ideas and technique. The writing is both fresh and lively, capturing the contemporary cadence of late-twentieth-century idioms.

The movie that resulted from "Air Raid" is unique in many respects. First, the film's producers hired the story's original author to write the script instead of farming it out to a Hollywood hack. Then, when they received a literate script that focused on romantic drama, the producers did not rewrite it to emphasize action and violence. The result was a potent brew that introduced moviegoing audiences to some serious issues.

The stories selected for this book range from science fiction's earliest days to the contemporary blockbusters of the eighties and nineties. Each is guaranteed to provide challenging ideas and thought-provoking reading, as well as absorbing entertainment. Each story represents the way one author (and the filmmakers who adapted his work) saw future possibilities. None is intended to present the only way its writer envisioned our future. Instead, together they represent the many possibilities of our collective futures. These stories, then, are less predictions of "real" futures than speculations on what lies before us.

However, even if the futures herein are more "reel" than "real," the message, warning, or promise at the core of each is genuine. For if there is one lesson the history of science-fiction film has to teach us, it is that these apparently insubstantial dreams can reveal to us profound truths that otherwise we ourselves might never see.

Forrest J Ackerman
Jean Stine
*Hollywood, California*
*1994*

# The Empire of the Ants

## H. G. WELLS

**The Empire of the Ants**

Director/Producer: *Bert I. Gordon*
Screenplay: *Jack Turley*
Music: *Dana Kaproff*
Special Effects: *Roy Downey*
Cast: *Joan Collins, Robert Lansing, John David Carson*
Released by: *American International*
1977, 89 Minutes. Color.

— I —

When Captain Gerilleau received instructions to take his new gunboat, the *Benjamin Constant*, to Badama on the Batemo arm of the Guaramadema and there assist the inhabitants against a plague of ants, he suspected the authorities of mockery. His promotion had been romantic and irregular, the affections of a prominent Brazilian lady and the captain's liquid eyes had played a part in the process, and the *Diario* and *O Futuro* had been lamentably disrespectful in their comments. He felt he was to give further occasion for disrespect.

He was a Creole, his conceptions of etiquette and discipline were pure-blooded Portuguese, and it was only to Holroyd, the Lancashire engineer, who had come over with the boat, and as an exercise in the use of English—his "th" sounds were very uncertain—that he opened his heart.

1

"It is in effect," he said, "to make me absurd! What can a man do against ants? Dey come, dey go."

"They say," said Holroyd, "that these don't go. That chap you said was a Sambo—"

"Zambo—it is a sort of mixture of blood."

"Sambo. He said the people are going!"

The captain smoked fretfully for a time. "Dese tings 'ave to happen," he said at last. "What is it? Plagues of ants and suchlike as God wills. Dere was a plague in Trinidad—the little ants that carry leaves. Orl der orange-trees, all der mangoes! What does it matter? Sometimes ant armies come into your houses—fighting ants; a different sort. You go and they clean the house. Then you come back again;—the house is clean, like new! No cockroaches, no fleas, no jiggers in the floor."

"That Sambo chap," said Holroyd, "says these are a different sort of ant."

The captain shrugged his shoulders, fumed, and gave his attention to a cigarette.

Afterwards he reopened the subject. "My dear 'Olroyd, what am I to do about dese infernal ants?"

The captain reflected. "It is ridiculous," he said. But in the afternoon he put on his full uniform and went ashore, and jars and boxes came back to the ship and subsequently he did. And Holroyd sat on deck in the evening coolness and smoked profoundly and marvelled at Brazil. They were six days up the Amazon, some hundreds of miles from the ocean, and east and west of him there was a horizon like the sea, and to the south nothing but a sand-bank island with some tufts of scrub. The water was always running like a sluice, thick with dirt, animated with crocodiles and hovering birds, and fed by some inexhaustible source of tree trunks; and the waste of it, the headlong waste of it, filled his soul. The town of Alemquer, with its meagre church, its thatched sheds for houses, its discoloured ruins of ampler days, seemed a little thing lost in this wilderness of Nature, a sixpence dropped on Sahara. He was a young man, this was his first sight of the tropics, he came straight from England, where Nature is hedged, ditched, and drained into the perfection of submission, and he had suddenly discovered the insignificance of man. For six days they had been steaming up from the sea by unfrequented channels, and man had been as rare as a rare butterfly. One saw one day a canoe, another day a distant station, the next no men at all. He began to perceive that man is indeed a rare animal, having but a precarious hold upon this land.

He perceived it more clearly as the days passed, and he made his devious way to the Batemo, in the company of this remarkable commander, who ruled over one big gun, and was forbidden to waste his ammunition. Holroyd was learning Spanish industriously, but he was still in the present tense and substantive stage of speech, and the only other person who had any words of English was a negro stoker, who had them all wrong. The second in command was a Portuguese, da Cunha, who spoke French, but it was a different sort of French from the French Holroyd had learned in Southport, and their intercourse was confined to politenesses and simple propositions about the weather. And the weather, like everything else in this amazing new world, the weather had no human aspect, and was hot by night and hot by day, and the air steam, even the wind was hot steam, smelling of vegetation in decay: and the alligators and the strange birds, the flies of many sorts and sizes, the beetles, the ants, the snakes and monkeys seemed to wonder what man was doing in an atmosphere that had no gladness in its sunshine and no coolness in its night. To wear clothing was intolerable, but to cast it aside was to scorch by day, and expose an ampler area to the mosquitoes by night; to go on deck by day was to be blinded by glare and to stay below was to suffocate. And in the daytime came certain flies, extremely clever and noxious about one's wrist and ankle. Captain Gerilleau, who was Holroyd's sole distraction from these physical distresses, developed into a formidable bore, telling the simple story of his heart's affections day by day, a string of anonymous women, as if he was telling beads. Sometimes he suggested sport, and they shot at alligators, and at rare intervals they came to human aggregations in the waste of trees, and stayed for a day or so, and drank and sat about; and, one night, danced with Creole girls, who found Holroyd's poor elements of Spanish, without either past tense or future, amply sufficient for their purposes. But these were mere luminous chinks in the long grey passage of the streaming river, up which the throbbing engines beat. A certain liberal heathen deity, in the shape of a demi-john, held seductive court aft, and, it is probable, forward.

But Gerilleau learned things about the ants, more things and more, at this stopping-place and that, and became interested in his mission.

"Dey are a new sort of ant," he said. "We have got to be—what do you call it?—entomologie Big. Five centimetres! Some bigger! It is ridiculous. We are like the monkeys—sent to pick insects. . . . But dey are eating up the country."

He burst out indignantly. "Suppose—suddenly, there are complications with Europe. Here am I—soon we shall be above the Rio Negro—and my gun, useless!"

He nursed his knee and mused.

"Dose people who were dere at de dancing place, dey 'ave come down. Dey 'ave lost all they got. De ants come to deir house one afternoon. Everyone run out. You know when de ants come one must—everyone runs out and they go over the house. If you stayed they'd eat you. See? Well, presently dey go back; dey say, 'The ants 'ave gone.' . . . De ants 'aven't gone. Dey try to go in—de son, 'e goes in. De ants fight."

"Swarm over him?"

"Bite 'im. Presently he comes out again—screaming and running. He runs past them to the river. See? He get into de water and drowns de ants—yes." Gerilleau paused, brought his liquid eyes close to Holroyd's face, tapped Holroyd's knee with his knuckle. "That night he dies, just as if he was stung by a snake."

"Poisoned—by the ants?"

"Who knows?" Gerilleau shrugged his shoulders, "Perhaps they bit him badly. . . . When I joined dis service I joined to fight men. Dese things, dese ants, dey come and go. It is no business for men."

After that he talked frequently of the ants to Holroyd, and whenever they chanced to drift against any speck of humanity in that waste of water and sunshine and distant trees, Holroyd's improving knowledge of the language enabled him to recognise the ascendant word *Saüba*, more and more completely dominating the whole.

He perceived the ants were becoming interesting, and the nearer he drew to them the more interesting they became. Gerilleau abandoned his old themes almost suddenly, and the Portuguese lieutenant became a conversational figure; he knew something about the leaf-cutting ant, and expanded his knowledge. Gerilleau sometimes rendered what he had to tell to Holroyd. He told of the little workers that swarm and fight, and the big workers that command and rule, and how these latter always crawled to the neck and how their bites drew blood. He told how they cut leaves and made fungus beds, and how their nests in Caracas are sometimes a hundred yards across. Two days the three men spent disputing whether ants have eyes. The discussion grew dangerously heated on the second afternoon, and Holroyd saved the situation by going ashore in a boat to catch ants and see. He captured various specimens and returned and some had eyes and some hadn't. Also, they argued, do ants bite or sting?

"Dese ants," said Gerilleau, after collecting information at a rancho, "have big eyes. They don't run about blind—not as most ants do. No! Dey get in corners and watch what you do."

"And they sting?" asked Holroyd.

"Yes. Dey sting. Dere is poison in the sting." He meditated. "I do not see what men can do against ants. Dey come and go."

"But these don't go."

"They will," said Gerilleau.

Past Tamandu there is a long low coast of eighty miles without any population, and then one comes to the confluence of the main river and the Batemo arm like a great lake, and then the forest came nearer, came at last intimately near. The character of the channel changes, snags abound, and the

*Benjamin Constant* moored by a cable that night, under the very shadow of dark trees. For the first time for many days came a spell of coolness, and Holroyd and Gerilleau sat late, smoking cigars and enjoying this delicious sensation. Gerilleau's mind was full of ants and what they could do. He decided to sleep at last, and lay down on a mattress on deck, a man hopelessly perplexed; his last words, when he already seemed asleep, were to ask, with a flourish of despair: "What can one do with ants?. . . De whole thing is absurd."

Holroyd was left to scratch his bitten wrists, and meditate alone.

He sat on the bulwark and listened to the changes in Gerilleau's breathing until he was fast asleep, and then the ripple and lap of the stream took his mind, and brought back that sense of immensity that had been growing upon him since first he had left Para and come up the river. The monitor showed but one small light, and there was first a little talking forward and then stillness. His eyes went from the dim black outlines of the middle works of the gunboat towards the bank, to the black overwhelming mysteries of forest, lit now and then by a fire-fly, and never still from the murmur of alien and mysterious activities. . . .

It was the inhuman immensity of this land that astonished and oppressed him. He knew the skies were empty of men, the stars were specks in an incredible vastness of space; he knew the ocean was enormous and untamable, but in England he had come to think of the land as man's. In England it is indeed man's, the wild things live by sufferance, grow on lease, everywhere the roads, the fences, and absolute security runs. In an atlas, too, the land is man's, and all coloured to show his claim to it—in vivid contrast to the universal independent blueness of the sea. He had taken it for granted that a day would come when everywhere about the earth, plough and culture, light tramways, and good roads, an ordered security, would prevail. But now, he doubted.

This forest was interminable, it had an air of being invincible, and Man seemed at best an infrequent precarious intruder. One travelled for miles amidst the still, silent struggle of giant trees, of strangulating creepers, of assertive flowers, everywhere the alligator, the turtle, and endless varieties of birds and insects seemed at home, dwelt irreplaceably—but man, man at most held a footing upon resentful clearings, fought weeds, fought beasts and insects for the barest foothold, fell a prey to snake and beast, insect and fever, and was presently carried away. In many places down the river he had been manifestly driven back, this deserted creek or that preserved the name of a *casa*, and here and there ruinous white walls and a shattered tower enforced the lesson. The puma, the jaguar, were more the masters here. . . .

Who were the real masters?

In a few miles of this forest there must be more ants than there are men in the whole world! This seemed to Holroyd a perfectly new idea. In a few thousand years men had emerged from barbarism to a stage of civilisation that made them feel lords of the future and masters of the earth! But what was to prevent the ants evolving also? Such ants as one knew lived in little communities of a few thousand individuals, made no concerted efforts against the greater world. But they had a language, they had an intelligence! Why should things stop at that any more than men had stopped at the barbaric stage? Suppose presently the ants began to store knowledge, just as men had done by means of books and records, use weapons, form great empires, sustain a planned and organised war?

Things came back to him that Gerilleau had gathered about these ants they were approaching. They used a poison like the poison of snakes. They obeyed greater leaders even as the leaf-cutting ants do. They were carnivorous, and where they came they stayed. . . .

The forest was very still. The water lapped incessantly against the side. About the lantern overhead there eddied a noiseless whirl of phantom moths.

Gerilleau stirred in the darkness and sighed. "What can one *do?*" he murmured, and turned over and was still again.

Holroyd was roused from meditations that were becoming sinister by the hum of a mosquito.

— II —

The next morning Holroyd learned they were within forty kilometres of Badama, and his interest in the banks intensified. He came up whenever an opportunity offered to examine his surroundings. He could see no signs of human occupation whatever, save for a weedy ruin of a house and the green-stained façade of the long-deserted monastery at Mojû, with a forest tree growing out of a vacant window space, and great creepers netted across its vacant portals. Several flights of strange yellow butterflies with semi-transparent wings crossed the river that morning, and many alighted on the monitor and were killed by the men. It was towards afternoon that they came upon the derelict cuberta.

She did not at first appear to be derelict; both her sails were set and hanging slack in the afternoon calm, and there was the figure of a man sitting on the fore planking beside the shipped sweeps. Another man appeared to be sleeping face downwards on the sort of longitudinal bridge these big canoes have in the waist. But it was presently apparent, from the sway of her rudder and the way she drifted into the course of the gunboat, that something was out of order with her. Gerilleau surveyed her through a field-glass, and became interested in the queer darkness of the face of the sitting man, a red-faced man he seemed, without a nose—crouching he was rather than sitting, and the longer the captain looked the less he liked to look at him, and the less able he was to take his glasses away.

But he did so at last, and went a little way to call up Holroyd. Then he went back to hail the cuberta. He hailed her again, and so she drove past him. *Santa Rosa* stood out clearly as her name.

As she came by and into the wake of the monitor, she pitched a little, and suddenly the figure of the crouching man collapsed as though all its joints had given way. His hat fell off, his head was not nice to look at, and his body flopped lax and rolled out of sight behind the bulwarks.

"Caramba!" cried Gerilleau, and resorted to Holroyd forthwith.

Holroyd was half-way up the companion. "Did you see dat?" said the captain.

"Dead!" said Holroyd. "Yes. You'd better send a boat aboard. There's something wrong."

"Did you—by any chance—see his face?"

"What was it like?"

"It was—ugh!—I have no words." And the captain suddenly turned his back on Holroyd and became an active and strident commander.

The gunboat came about, steamed parallel to the erratic course of the canoe, and dropped the boat with Lieutenant da Cunha and three sailors to board her. Then the curiosity of the captain made him draw up almost alongside as the lieutenant got aboard, so that the whole of the *Santa Rosa*, deck and hold, was visible to Holroyd.

He saw now clearly that the sole crew of the vessel was these two dead men, and though he could not see their faces, he saw by their outstretched hands, which were all of ragged flesh, that they had been subjected to some strange exceptional process of decay. For a moment his attention, concentrated on these two enigmatical bundles of dirty clothes and laxly flung limbs, and then his eyes went forward to discover the open hold piled high with trunks and cases, and aft, to where the little cabin gaped inexplicably empty. Then he became aware that the planks of the middle decking were dotted with moving black specks.

His attention was riveted by these specks. They were all walking in directions radiating from the fallen man in a manner—the image came unsought to his mind—like the crowd dispersing from a bull-fight.

He became aware of Gerilleau beside him. "Capo," he said, "have you your glasses? Can you focus as closely as those planks there?"

Gerilleau made an effort, grunted, and handed him the glasses.

There followed a moment of scrutiny. "It's ants," said the Englishman, and handed the focused field-glasses back to Gerilleau.

His impression of them was of a crowd of large black ants, very like ordinary ants except for their size, and for the fact that some of the larger of them bore a sort of clothing of grey. But at the time his inspection was too brief for particulars. The head of Lieutenant da Cunha appeared over the side of the cuberta, and a brief colloquy ensued.

"You must go aboard," said Gerilleau.

The lieutenant objected that the boat was full of ants.

"You have your boots," said Gerilleau.

The lieutenant changed the subject. "How did these men die?" he asked.

Captain Gerilleau embarked upon speculations that Holroyd could not follow, and the two men disputed with a certain increasing vehemence. Holroyd took up the field-glass and resumed his scrutiny, first of the ants and then of the dead man amidships.

He has described these ants to me very particularly.

He says they were as large as any ants he has ever seen, black and moving with a steady deliberation very different from the mechanical fussiness of the common ant. About one in twenty was much larger than its fellows, and with an exceptionally large head. These reminded him at once of the master workers who are said to rule over the leaf-cutter ants; like them they seemed to be directing and co-ordinating the general movements. They tilted their bodies back in a manner altogether singular as if they made some use of the fore feet. And he had a curious fancy that he was too far off to verify, that most of these ants of both kinds were wearing accoutrements, had things strapped about their bodies by bright white bands like white metal threads. . . .

He put down the glasses abruptly, realising that the question of discipline between the captain and his subordinate had become acute.

"It is your duty," said the captain, "to go aboard. It is my instructions."

The lieutenant seemed on the verge of refusing. The head of one of the mulatto sailors appeared beside him.

"I believe these men were killed by the ants," said Holroyd abruptly in English.

The captain burst into a rage. He made no answer to Holroyd. "I have commanded you to go aboard," he screamed to his subordinate in Portuguese. "If you do not go aboard forthwith it is mutiny—rank mutiny. Mutiny and cowardice! Where is the courage that should animate us? I will have you in irons, I will have you shot like a dog." He began a torrent of abuse and curses, he danced to and fro. He shook his fists, he behaved as if beside himself with rage, and the lieutenant, white and still, stood looking at him. The crew appeared forward, with amazed faces.

Suddenly, in a pause of this outbreak, the lieutenant came to some heroic decision, saluted, drew himself together and clambered upon the deck of the cuberta.

"Ah!" said Gerilleau, and his mouth shut like a trap. Holroyd saw the ants retreating before da Cunha's boots. The Portuguese walked slowly to the fallen man, stooped down, hesitated, clutched his coat and turned him over. A black swarm of ants rushed out of the clothes, and da Cunha stepped back very quickly and trod two or three times on the deck.

Holroyd put up the glasses. He saw the scattered ants about the invader's feet, and doing what he had never seen ants doing before. They had nothing of the blind movements of the common ant; they were looking at him—as a rallying crowd of men might look at some gigantic monster that had dispersed it.

"How did he die?" the captain shouted.

Holroyd understood the Portuguese to say the body was too much eaten to tell.

"What is there forward?" asked Gerilleau.

The lieutenant walked a few paces, and began his answer in Portuguese. He stopped abruptly and beat off something from his leg. He made some peculiar steps as if he was trying to stamp on something invisible, and went quickly towards the side. Then he controlled himself, turned about, walked deliberately forward to the hold, clambered up to the fore decking, from which the sweeps are worked, stooped for a time over the second man, groaned audibly, and made his way back and aft to the cabin; moving very rigidly. He turned and began a conversation with his captain, cold and respectful in tone on either side, contrasting vividly with the wrath and insult of a few moments before. Holroyd gathered only fragments of its purport.

He reverted to the field-glass, and was surprised to find the ants had vanished from all the exposed surfaces of the deck. He turned towards the shadows beneath the decking, and it seemed to him they were full of watching eyes.

The cuberta, it was agreed, was derelict, but too full of ants to put men aboard to sit and sleep: it must be towed. The lieutenant went forward to take in and adjust the cable, and the men in the boat stood up to be ready to help him. Holroyd's glasses searched the canoe.

He became more and more impressed by the fact that a great if minute and furtive activity was going on. He perceived that a number of gigantic ants— they seemed nearly a couple of inches in length—carrying oddly-shaped burthens for which he could imagine no use—were moving in rushes from one point of obscurity to another. They did not move in columns across the exposed places, but in open, spaced-out lines, oddly suggestive of the rushes of modern infantry advancing under fire. A number were taking cover under the dead man's clothes, and a perfect swarm was gathering along the side over which da Cunha must presently go.

He did not see them actually rush for the lieutenant as he returned, but he has no doubt they did make a concerted rush. Suddenly the lieutenant was shouting and cursing and beating at his legs. "I'm stung!" he shouted, with a face of hate and accusation towards Gerilleau.

Then he vanished over the side, dropped into his boat, and plunged at once into the water. Holroyd heard the splash.

The three men in the boat pulled him out and brought him aboard, and that night he died.

## — III —

Holroyd and the captain came out of the cabin in which the swollen and contorted body of the lieutenant lay, and stood together at the stern of the monitor, staring at the sinister vessel they trailed behind them. It was a close, dark night that had only phantom flickerings of sheet lightning to illuminate it. The cuberta, a vague black triangle, rocked about in the steamer's wake, her sails bobbing and flapping, and the black smoke from the funnels, spark-lit ever and again, streamed over her swaying masts.

Gerilleau's mind was inclined to run on the unkind things the lieutenant had said in the heat of his last fever.

"He says I murdered 'im," he protested. "It is simply absurd. Someone 'ad to go aboard. Are we to run away from these confounded ants whenever they show up?"

Holroyd said nothing. He was thinking of a disciplined rush of little black shapes across bare sunlit planking.

"It was his place to go," harped Gerilleau. "He died in the execution of his duty. What has he to complain of? Murdered! . . . But the poor fellow was— what is it?—demented. He was not in his right mind. The poison swelled him. . . . U'm."

They came to a long silence.

"We will sink that canoe—burn it."

"And then?"

The inquiry irritated Gerilleau. His shoulders went up, his hands flew out at right angles from his body. "What is one to *do*?" he said, his voice going up to an angry squeak.

"Anyhow," he broke out vindictively, "every ant in dat cuberta!—I will burn dem alive!"

Holroyd was not moved to conversation. A distant ululation of howling monkeys filled the sultry night with foreboding sounds, and as the gunboat drew near the black mysterious banks this was reinforced by a depressing clamour of frogs.

"What is one to *do?*" the captain repeated after a vast interval, and suddenly becoming active and savage and blasphemous, decided to burn the *Santa Rosa* without further delay. Everyone aboard was pleased by that idea, everyone helped with zest; they pulled in the cable, cut it, and dropped the boat and fired her with tow and kerosene, and soon the cuberta was crackling and flaring merrily amidst the immensities of the tropical night. Holroyd watched the mounting yellow flare against the blackness, and the livid flashes of sheet lightning that came and went above the forest summits, throwing them into momentary silhouette, and his stoker stood behind him watching also.

The stoker was stirred to the depths of his linguistics. "*Saüba* go pop, pop," he said. "Wahaw!" and laughed richly.

But Holroyd was thinking that these little creatures on the decked canoe had also eyes and brains.

The whole thing impressed him as incredibly foolish and wrong, but—what was one to *do?* This question came back enormously reinforced on the morrow, when at last the gunboat reached Badama.

This place, with its leaf-thatch-covered houses and sheds, its creeper-invaded sugar-mill, its little jetty of timber and canes, was very still in the morning heat, and showed never a sign of living men. Whatever ants there were at that distance were too small to see.

"All the people have gone," said Gerilleau, "but we will do one thing anyhow. We will 'oot and vissel."

So Holroyd hooted and whistled.

Then the captain fell into a doubting fit of the worst kind. "Dere is one thing we can do," he said presently.

"What's that?" said Holroyd.

" 'Oot and vissel again."

So they did.

The captain walked his deck and gesticulated to himself. He seemed to have many things on his mind. Fragments of speeches came from his lips. He appeared to be addressing some imaginary public tribunal either in Spanish or Portuguese. Holroyd's improving ear detected something about ammunition. He came out of these preoccupations suddenly into English. "My dear 'Olroyd!" he cried, and broke off with "But what *can* one do?"

They took the boat and the field-glasses, and went close in to examine the place. They made out a number of big ants, whose still postures had a certain effect of watching them, dotted about the edge of the rude embarkation jetty.

Gerilleau tried ineffectual pistol shots at these. Holroyd thinks he distinguished curious earthworks running between the nearer houses, that may have been the work of the insect conquerors of those human habitations. The explorers pulled past the jetty, and became aware of a human skeleton wearing a loin cloth, and very bright and clean and shining, lying beyond. They came to a pause regarding this. . . .

"I 'ave all dose lives to consider," said Gerilleau suddenly.

Holroyd turned and stared at the captain, realising slowly that he referred to the unappetising mixture of races that constituted his crew.

"To send a landing party—it is impossible—impossible. They will be poisoned, they will swell, they will swell up and abuse me and die. It is totally impossible. . . . If we land, I must land alone, alone, in thick boots and with my life in my hand. Perhaps I should live. Or again—I might not land. I do not know. I do not know."

Holroyd thought he did, but he said nothing.

"De whole thing," said Gerilleau suddenly, " 'as been got up to make me ridiculous. De whole thing!"

They paddled about and regarded the clean white skeleton from various points of view, and then they returned to the gunboat. Then Gerilleau's indecisions became terrible. Steam was got up, and in the afternoon the monitor went on up the river with an air of going to ask somebody something, and by sunset came back again, and anchored. A thunderstorm gathered and broke furiously, and then the night became beautifully cool and quiet and everyone slept on deck. Except Gerilleau, who tossed about and muttered. In the dawn he awakened Holroyd.

"Lord!" said Holroyd, "what now?"

"I have decided," said the captain.

"What—to land?" said Holroyd, sitting up brightly.

"No!" said the captain, and was for a time very reserved. "I have decided," he repeated, and Holroyd manifested symptoms of impatience.

"Well—yes," said the captain. *"I shall fire de big gun!"*

And he did! Heaven knows what the ants thought of it, but he did. He fired it twice with great sternness and ceremony. All the crew had wadding in their ears, and there was an effect of going into action about the whole affair, and first they hit and wrecked the old sugar-mill, and then they smashed the abandoned store behind the jetty. And then Gerilleau experienced the inevitable reaction.

"It is no good," he said to Holroyd; "no good at all. No sort of bally good. We must go back—for instructions. Dere will be de devil of a row about dis ammunition—oh! de *devil* of a row! You don't know, 'Olroyd. . . ."

He stood regarding the world in infinite perplexity for a space.

"But what else was there to *do?*" he cried.

In the afternoon the monitor started downstream again, and in the evening a landing party took the body of the lieutenant and buried it on the bank upon which the new ants have so far not appeared. . . .

— IV —

I heard this story in a fragmentary state from Holroyd not three weeks ago.

These new ants have got into his brain, and he has come back to England with the idea, as he says, of "exciting people" about them "before it is too late." He says they threaten British Guiana, which cannot be much over a trifle of a thousand miles from their present sphere of activity, and that the Colonial Office ought to get to work upon them at once. He declaims with great passion: "These are intelligent ants. Just think what that means!"

There can be no doubt they are a serious pest, and that the Brazilian Government is well advised in offering a prize of five hundred pounds for some effectual method of extirpation. It is certain, too, that since they first appeared in the hills beyond Badama, about three years ago, they have achieved extraordinary conquests. The whole of the south bank of the Batemo River, for nearly sixty miles, they have in their effectual occupation; they have driven men out completely, occupied plantations and settlements, and boarded and captured at least one ship. It is even said they have in some inexplicable way bridged the very considerable Capuarana arm and pushed many miles towards the Amazon itself. There can be little doubt that they are far more reasonable and with a far better social organisation than any previously known ant species; instead of being in dispersed societies they are organised into what is in effect a single nation; but their peculiar and immediate formidableness lies not so much in this as in the intelligent use they make of poison against their larger enemies. It would seem this poison of theirs is closely akin to snake poison, and it is highly probable they actually manufacture it, and that the larger individuals among them carry the needle-like crystals of it in their attacks upon men.

Of course it is extremely difficult to get any detailed information about these new competitors for the sovereignty of the globe. No eye-witnesses of their activity, except for such glimpses as Holroyd's, have survived the encounter. The most extraordinary legends of their prowess and capacity are in circulation in the region of the Upper Amazon, and grow daily as the steady advance of the invader stimulates men's imaginations through their fears. These strange little creatures are credited not only with the use of implements and a knowledge of fire and metals and with organised feats of engineering that stagger our Northern minds—unused as we are to such feats as that of the Saübus of Rio de Janeiro, who, in 1841, drove a tunnel under Parahyba, where it is as wide as the Thames at London Bridge—but with an organised and detailed method of record and communication analogous to our books. So far their action has been a steady progressive settlement, involving the flight or slaughter of every human being in the new areas they invade. They are increasing rapidly in numbers, and Holroyd at least is firmly convinced that they will finally dispossess man over the whole of tropical South America.

And why should they stop at tropical South America?

Well, there they are, anyhow. By 1911 or thereabouts, if they go on as they are going, they ought to strike the Capuarana Extension Railway, and force themselves upon the attention of the European capitalist.

By 1920 they will be half-way down the Amazon. I fix 1950 or '60 at the latest for the discovery of Europe.

Joan Collins struggles helplessly against the attack of The Empire of the Ants.

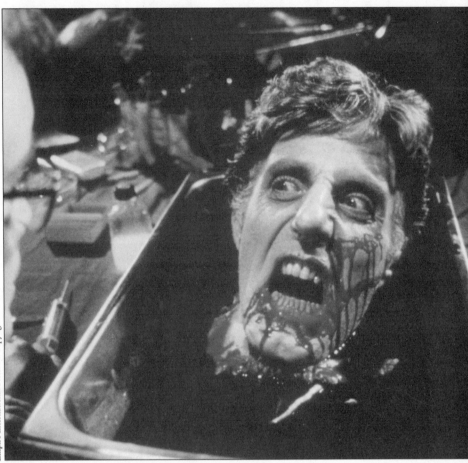

Herbert West (Jeffrey Coombs) has a friendly chat with a re-animated head.

# Herbert West—Re-animator

## H. P. LOVECRAFT

**Re-Animator**

Director: *Stuart Gordon*
Screenplay: *Dennis Paoli*
Producer: *Brian Yuzna*
Music: *Richard Band*
Special Effects: *Anthony Doublin, John Naulin, John Buechler*
Cast: *Jeffrey Combs, Bruce Abbott, Barbara Crampton*
Released by: *Empire International Pictures*
1985, 86 Minutes. Color.

## — I —

### FROM THE DARK

Of Herbert West, who was my friend in college and in after life, I can speak only with extreme terror. This terror is not due altogether to the sinister manner of his recent disappearance, but was engendered by the whole nature of his life-work, and first gained its acute form more than seventeen years ago, when we were in the third year of our course at the Miskatonic University Medical School in Arkham. While he was with me, the wonder and diabolism of his experiments fascinated me utterly, and I was his closest companion. Now that he is gone and the spell is broken, the actual fear is greater. Memories and possibilities are ever more hideous than realities.

The first horrible incident of our acquaintance was the greatest shock I ever experienced, and it is only with reluctance that I repeat it. As I have said, it happened when we were in the medical school, where West had already made himself notorious through his wild theories on the nature of death and the possibility of overcoming it artificially. His views, which were widely ridiculed by the faculty and by his fellow-students, hinged on the essentially mechanistic nature of life; and concerned means for operating the organic machinery of mankind by calculated chemical action after the failure of natural processes. In his experiments with various animating solutions he had killed and treated immense numbers of rabbits, guinea-pigs, cats, dogs, and monkeys, till he had become the prime nuisance of the college. Several times he had actually obtained signs of life in animals supposedly dead; in many cases violent signs; but he soon saw that the perfection of his process, if indeed possible, would necessarily involve a lifetime of research. It likewise became clear that, since the same solution never worked alike on different organic species, he would require human subjects for further and more specialised progress. It was here that he first came into conflict with the college authorities, and was debarred from future experiments by no less a dignitary than the dean of the medical school himself—the learned and benevolent Dr. Allan Halsey, whose work in behalf of the stricken is recalled by every old resident of Arkham.

I had always been exceptionally tolerant of West's pursuits, and we frequently discussed his theories, whose ramifications and corollaries were almost infinite. Holding with Haeckel that all life is a chemical and physical process, and that the so-called "soul" is a myth, my friend believed that artificial reanimation of the dead can depend only on the condition of the tissues; and that unless actual decomposition has set in, a corpse fully equipped with organs may with suitable measures be set going again in the peculiar fashion known as life. That the psychic or intellectual life might be impaired by the slight deterioration of sensitive brain-cells which even a short period of death would be apt to cause, West fully realised. It had at first been his hope to find a reagent which would restore vitality before the actual advent of death, and only repeated failures on animals had shewn him that the natural and artificial life-motions were incompatible. He then sought extreme freshness in his specimens, injecting his solutions into the blood immediately after the extinction of life. It was this circumstance which made the professors so carelessly sceptical, for they felt that true death had not occurred in any case. They did not stop to view the matter closely and reasoningly.

It was not long after the faculty had interdicted his work that West confided to me his resolution to get fresh human bodies in some manner, and continue in secret the experiments he could no longer perform openly. To hear him discussing ways and means was rather ghastly, for at the college we had never procured anatomical specimens ourselves. Whenever the morgue proved inadequate, two local negroes attended to this matter, and they were seldom questioned. West was then a small, slender, spectacled youth with delicate features, yellow hair, pale blue eyes, and a soft voice, and it was uncanny to hear him dwelling on the relative merits of Christchurch Cemetery and the potter's field. We finally decided on the potter's field, because practically every body in Christchurch was embalmed; a thing of course ruinous to West's researches.

I was by this time his active and enthralled assistant, and helped him make all his decisions, not only concerning the source of bodies but concerning a suitable place for our loathsome work. It was I who thought of the deserted Chapman farmhouse beyond Meadow Hill, where we fitted up on the ground floor an operating room and a laboratory, each with dark curtains to conceal our midnight doings. The place was far from any road, and in sight of no other house, yet precautions were none the less necessary; since rumours of strange lights, started by chance nocturnal roamers, would soon bring disaster on our enterprise. It was agreed to call the whole thing a chemical laboratory if discovery should occur. Gradually we equipped our sinister haunt of science with materials either purchased in Boston or quietly borrowed from the college—materials carefully made unrecognisable save to expert eyes—and provided spades and picks for the many burials we should have to make in the cellar. At the college we used an incinerator, but the apparatus was too costly for our unauthorised laboratory. Bodies were always a nuisance—even the small guinea-pig bodies from the slight clandestine experiments in West's room at the boarding-house.

We followed the local death-notices like ghouls, for our specimens demanded particular qualities. What we wanted were corpses interred soon after death and without artificial preservation; preferably free from malforming disease, and certainly with all organs present. Accident victims were our best hope. Not for many weeks did we hear of anything suitable; though we talked with morgue and hospital authorities, ostensibly in the college's interest, as often as we could without exciting suspicion. We found that the college had first choice in every case, so that it might be necessary to remain in Arkham during the summer, when only the limited summer-school classes were held. In the end, though, luck favoured us; for one day we heard of an almost ideal case in the potter's field; a brawny young workman drowned only the morning before in Sumner's Pond, and buried at the town's expense without delay or embalming. That afternoon we found the new grave, and determined to begin work soon after midnight.

It was a repulsive task that we undertook in the black small hours, even though we lacked at that time the special horror of graveyards which later experiences brought to us. We carried spades and oil dark lanterns, for although electric torches were then manufactured, they were not as satisfactory as the tungsten contrivances of today. The process of unearthing was slow and sordid—it might have been gruesomely poetical if we had been artists instead of scientists—and we were glad when our spades struck wood. When the pine box was fully uncovered West scrambled down and removed the lid, dragging out and propping up the contents. I reached down and hauled the contents out of the grave, and then both toiled hard to restore the spot to its former appearance. The affair made us rather nervous, especially the stiff form and vacant face of our first trophy, but we managed to remove all traces of our visit. When we had patted down the last shovelful of earth we put the specimen in a canvas sack and set out for the old Chapman place beyond Meadow Hill.

On an improvised dissecting-table in the old farmhouse, by the light of a powerful acetylene lamp, the specimen was not very spectral looking. It had been a sturdy and apparently unimaginative youth of wholesome plebeian type—large-framed, grey-eyed, and brown-haired—a sound animal without psychological subtleties, and probably having vital processes of the simplest and healthiest sort. Now, with the eyes closed, it looked more asleep than dead; though the expert test of my friend soon left no doubt on that score. We had at last what West had always longed for—a real dead man of the ideal kind, ready for the solution as prepared according to the most careful calculations and theories for human use. The tension on our part became very great. We knew that there was scarcely a chance for anything like complete success, and could not avoid hideous fears at possible grotesque results of partial animation. Especially were we apprehensive concerning the mind and impulses of the creature, since in the space following death some of the more delicate cerebral cells might well have suffered deterioration. I, myself, still held some curious notions about the traditional "soul" of man, and felt an awe at the secrets that might be told by one returning from the dead. I wondered what sights this placid youth might have seen in inaccessible spheres, and what he could relate if fully restored to life. But my wonder was not overwhelming, since for the most part I shared the materialism of my friend. He was calmer than I as he forced a large quantity of his fluid into a vein of the body's arm, immediately binding the incision securely.

The waiting was gruesome, but West never faltered. Every now and then he applied his stethoscope to the specimen, and bore the negative results philosophically. After about three-quarters of an hour without the least sign of life he disappointedly pronounced the solution inadequate, but determined to make the most of his opportunity and try one change in the formula before disposing of his ghastly prize. We had that afternoon dug a grave in the cellar, and would have to fill it by dawn—for although we had fixed a lock on the house we wished to shun even the remotest risk of a ghoulish discovery. Besides, the body would not be even approximately fresh the next night. So taking the solitary acetylene lamp into the adjacent laboratory, we left our silent guest on the slab in the dark, and bent every energy to the mixing of a new solution; the weighing and measuring supervised by West with an almost fanatical care.

The awful event was very sudden, and wholly unexpected. I was pouring something from one test-tube to another, and West was busy over the alcohol blast-lamp which had to answer for a Bunsen burner in this gasless edifice, when from the pitch-black room we had left there burst the most appalling and daemoniac succession of cries that either of us had ever heard. Not more unutterable could have been the chaos of hellish sound if the pit itself had opened to release the agony of the damned, for in one inconceivable cacophony was centred all the supernal terror and unnatural despair of animate nature. Human it could not have been—it is not in man to make such sounds—and without a thought of our late employment or its possible discovery both West and I leaped to the nearest window like stricken animals; overturning tubes, lamp, and retorts, and vaulting madly into the starred abyss of the rural night. I think we screamed ourselves as we stumbled frantically toward the town, though as we reached the outskirts we put on a semblance of restraint—just enough to seem like belated revellers staggering home from a debauch.

We did not separate, but managed to get to West's room, where we whispered with the gas up until dawn. By then we had calmed ourselves a little with rational theories and plans for investigation, so that we could sleep through the day—classes being disregarded. But that evening two items in the paper, wholly unrelated, made it again impossible for us to sleep. The old deserted Chapman house had inexplicably burned to an amorphous heap of ashes; that we could understand because of the upset lamp. Also, an attempt had been made to disturb a new grave in the potter's field, as if by futile and spadeless clawing at the earth. That we could not understand, for we had patted down the mould very carefully.

And for seventeen years after that West would look frequently over his shoulder, and complain of fancied footsteps behind him. Now he had disappeared.

# — II —

## THE PLAGUE-DAEMON

I shall never forget that hideous summer sixteen years ago, when like a noxious afrite from the halls of Eblis typhoid stalked leeringly through Arkham. It is by that satanic scourge that most recall the year, for truly terror brooded with bat-wings over the piles of coffins in the tombs of Christchurch Cemetery; yet for me there is a greater horror in that time—a horror known to me alone now that Herbert West has disappeared.

West and I were doing post-graduate work in summer classes at the medical school of Miskatonic University, and my friend had attained a wide notoriety because of his experiments leading toward the revivification of the dead. After the scientific slaughter of uncounted small animals the freakish work had ostensibly stopped by order of our sceptical dean, Dr. Allan Halsey; though West had continued to perform certain secret tests in his dingy boarding-house room, and had on one terrible and unforgettable occasion taken a human body from its grave in the potter's field to a deserted farmhouse beyond Meadow Hill.

I was with him on that odious occasion, and saw him inject into the still veins the elixir which he thought would to some extent restore life's chemical and physical processes. It had ended horribly—in a delirium of fear which we gradually came to attribute to our own overwrought nerves—and West had never afterward been able to shake off a maddening sensation of being haunted and hunted. The body had not been quite fresh enough; it is obvious that to restore normal mental attributes a body must be very fresh indeed; and the burning of the old house had prevented us from burying the thing. It would have been better if we could have known it was underground.

After that experience West had dropped his researches for some time; but as the zeal of the born scientist slowly returned, he again became importunate with the college faculty, pleading for the use of the dissecting-room and of fresh human specimens for the work he regarded as so overwhelmingly important. His pleas, however, were wholly in vain; for the decision of Dr. Halsey was inflexible, and the other professors all endorsed the verdict of their leader. In the radical theory of reanimation they saw nothing but the immature vagaries of a youthful enthusiast whose slight form, yellow hair, spectacled blue eyes, and soft voice gave no hint of the supernormal—almost diabolical—power of the cold brain within. I can see him now as he was then—and I shiver. He grew sterner of face, but never elderly. And now Sefton Asylum has had the mishap and West has vanished.

West clashed disagreeably with Dr. Halsey near the end of our last undergraduate term in a wordy dispute that did less credit to him than to the kindly dean in point of courtesy. He felt that he was needlessly and irrationally retarded in a supremely great work; a work which he could of course conduct to suit himself in later years, but which he wished to begin while still possessed of the exceptional facilities of the university. That the tradition-bound elders should ignore his singular results on animals, and persist in their denial of the possibility of reanimation, was inexpressibly disgusting and almost incomprehensible to a youth of West's logical temperament. Only greater maturity could help him understand the chronic mental limitations of the "professor-doctor" type—the product of generations of pathetic Puritanism; kindly, conscientious, and sometimes gentle and amiable, yet always narrow, intolerant, custom-ridden, and lacking in perspective. Age has more charity for these incomplete yet high-souled characters, whose worst real vice is timidity, and who are ultimately punished by general ridicule for their intellectual sins—sins like Ptolemaism, Calvinism, anti-Darwinism, anti-Nietzscheism, and every sort of Sabbatarianism and sumptuary legislation. West, young despite his marvellous scientific acquirements, had scant patience with good Dr. Halsey and his erudite colleagues; and nursed an increasing resentment, coupled with a desire to prove his theories to these obtuse worthies in some striking and dramatic fashion. Like most youths, he indulged in elaborate daydreams of revenge, triumph, and final magnanimous forgiveness.

And then had come the scourge, grinning and lethal, from the nightmare caverns of Tartarus. West and I had graduated about the time of its beginning, but had remained for additional work at the summer school, so that we were in Arkham when it broke with full daemoniac fury upon the town. Though not as yet licenced physicians, we now had our degrees, and were pressed frantically into public service as the numbers of the stricken grew. The situation was almost past management, and deaths ensued too frequently for the local undertakers fully to handle. Burials without embalming were made in rapid succession, and even the Christchurch Cemetery receiving tomb was crammed with coffins of the unembalmed dead. This circumstance was not without effect on West, who thought often of the irony of the situation—so many fresh specimens, yet none for his persecuted researches! We were frightfully overworked, and the terrific mental and nervous strain made my friend brood morbidly.

But West's gentle enemies were no less harassed with prostrating duties. College had all but closed, and every doctor of the medical faculty was helping to fight the typhoid plague. Dr. Halsey in particular had distinguished himself in sacrificing service, applying his extreme skill with whole-hearted energy to cases which many others shunned because of danger or apparent hopelessness. Before a month was over the fearless dean had become a popular hero, though he seemed unconscious of his fame as he struggled to keep from collapsing with physical fatigue and nervous exhaustion. West could not withhold admiration for the fortitude of his foe, but because of this was even more determined to prove to him the truth of his amazing doctrines. Taking advantage of the disorganisation of both college work and municipal health regulations, he managed to get a recently deceased body smuggled into the university dissecting-room one night, and in my presence injected a new modification of his solution. The thing actually opened its eyes, but only stared at the ceiling with a look of soul-petrifying horror before collapsing into an inertness from which nothing could rouse it. West said it was not fresh enough—the hot summer air does not favour corpses. That time we were almost caught before we incinerated the thing, and West doubted the advisability of repeating his daring misuse of the college laboratory.

The peak of the epidemic was reached in August. West and I were almost dead, and Dr. Halsey did die on the 14th. The students all attended the hasty funeral on the 15th, and bought an impressive wreath, though the latter was quite overshadowed by the tributes sent by wealthy Arkham citizens and by the municipality itself. It was almost a public affair, for the dean had surely been a public benefactor. After the entombment we were all somewhat depressed, and spent the afternoon at the bar of the Commercial House; where West, though shaken by the death of his chief opponent, chilled the rest of us with references to his notorious theories. Most of the students went home, or to various duties, as the evening advanced; but West persuaded me to aid him in "making a night of it". West's landlady saw us arrive at his room about two in the morning, with a third man between us; and told her husband that we had all evidently dined and wined rather well.

Apparently this acidulous matron was right; for about 3 A.M. the whole house was aroused by cries coming from West's room, where when they broke down the door they found the two of us unconscious on the blood-stained carpet, beaten, scratched, and mauled, and with the broken remnants of West's bottles and instruments around us. Only an open window told what had become of our assailant, and many wondered how he himself had fared after the terrific leap from the second story to the lawn which he must have made. There were some strange garments in the room, but West upon regaining consciousness said they did not belong to the stranger, but were specimens collected for bacteriological analysis in the course of investigations on the transmission of germ diseases. He ordered them burnt as soon as possible in the capacious fireplace. To the police we both declared ignorance of our late companion's identity. He was, West nervously said, a congenial stranger whom we had met at some downtown bar of uncertain location. We had all been rather jovial, and West and I did not wish to have our pugnacious companion hunted down.

That same night saw the beginning of the second Arkham horror—the horror that to me eclipsed the plague itself. Christchurch Cemetery was the scene of a terrible killing; a watchman having been clawed to death in a manner not only too hideous for description, but raising a doubt as to the human agency of the deed. The victim had been seen alive considerably after midnight—the dawn revealed the unutterable thing. The manager of a circus at the neighbouring town of Bolton was questioned, but he swore that no beast had at any time escaped from its cage. Those who found the body noted a trail of blood leading to the receiving tomb, where a small pool of red lay on the concrete just outside the gate. A fainter trail led away toward the woods, but it soon gave out.

The next night devils danced on the roofs of Arkham, and unnatural madness howled in the wind. Through the fevered town had crept a curse which some said was greater than the plague, and which some whispered was the embodied daemon-soul of the plague itself. Eight houses were entered by a nameless thing which strewed red death in its wake—in all, seventeen maimed and shapeless remnants of bodies were left behind by the voiceless, sadistic monster that crept abroad. A few persons had half seen it in the dark, and said it was white and like a malformed ape or anthropomorphic fiend. It had not left behind quite all that it had attacked, for sometimes it had been hungry. The number it had killed was fourteen; three of the bodies had been in stricken homes and had not been alive.

On the third night frantic bands of searchers, led by the police, captured it in a house on Crane Street near the Miskatonic campus. They had organised the quest with care, keeping in touch by means of volunteer telephone stations, and when someone in the college district had reported hearing a scratching at a shuttered window, the net was quickly spread. On account of the general alarm and precautions, there were only two more victims, and the capture was effected without major casualties. The thing was finally stopped by a bullet, though not a fatal one, and was rushed to the local hospital amidst universal excitement and loathing.

For it had been a man. This much was clear despite the nauseous eyes, the voiceless simianism, and the daemoniac savagery. They dressed its wound and carted it to the asylum at Sefton, where it beat its head against the walls of a padded cell for sixteen years—until the recent mishap, when it escaped under circumstances that few like to mention. What had most disgusted the searchers of Arkham was the thing they noticed when the monster's face was cleaned—the mocking, unbelievable resemblance to a learned and self-sacrificing martyr who had been entombed but three days before—the late Dr. Allan Halsey, public benefactor and dean of the medical school of Miskatonic University.

To the vanished Herbert West and to me the disgust and horror were supreme. I shudder tonight as I think of it; shudder even more than I did that morning when West muttered through his bandages,

"Damn it, it wasn't *quite* fresh enough!"

## — III —

## SIX SHOTS BY MOONLIGHT

It is uncommon to fire all six shots of a revolver with great suddenness when one would probably be sufficient, but many things in the life of Herbert West were uncommon. It is, for instance, not often that a young physician leaving college is obliged to conceal the principles which guide his selection of a home and office, yet that was the case with Herbert West. When he and I obtained our degrees at the medical school of Miskatonic University, and sought to relieve our poverty by setting up as general practitioners, we took great care not to say that we chose our house because it was fairly well isolated, and as near as possible to the potter's field.

Reticence such as this is seldom without a cause, nor indeed was ours; for our requirements were those resulting from a life-work distinctly unpopular. Outwardly we were doctors only, but beneath the surface were aims of far greater and more terrible moment—for the essence of Herbert West's existence was a quest amid black and forbidden realms of the unknown, in which he hoped to uncover the secret of life and restore to perpetual animation the graveyard's cold clay. Such a quest demands strange materials, among them fresh human bodies; and in order to keep supplied with these indispensable things one must live quietly and not far from a place of informal interment.

West and I had met in college, and I had been the only one to sympathise with his hideous experiments. Gradually I had come to be his inseparable assistant, and now that we were out of college we had to keep together. It was not easy to find a good opening for two doctors in company, but finally the influence of the university secured us a practice in Bolton—a factory town near Arkham, the seat of the college. The Bolton Worsted Mills are the largest in the Miskatonic Valley, and their polyglot employees are never popular as patients with the local physicians. We chose our house with the greatest care, seizing at last on a rather run-down cottage near the end of Pond Street; five numbers from the closest neighbour, and separated from the local potter's field by only a stretch of meadow land, bisected by a narrow neck of the rather dense forest which lies to the north. The distance was greater than we wished, but we could get no nearer house without going on the other side of the field, wholly out of the factory district. We were not much displeased, however, since there were no people between us and our sinister source of supplies. The walk was a trifle long, but we could haul our silent specimens undisturbed.

Our practice was surprisingly large from the very first—large enough to please most young doctors, and large enough to prove a bore and a burden to students whose real interest lay elsewhere. The mill-hands were of somewhat turbulent inclinations; and besides their many natural needs, their frequent clashes and stabbing affrays gave us plenty to do. But what actually absorbed our minds was the secret laboratory we had fitted up in the cellar—the laboratory with the long table under the electric lights, where in the small hours of the morning we often injected West's various solutions into the veins of the things we dragged from the potter's field. West was experimenting madly to find something which would start man's vital motions anew after they had been stopped by the thing we call death, but had encountered the most ghastly obstacles. The solution had to be differently compounded for different types—what would serve for guinea-pigs would not serve for human beings, and different human specimens required large modifications.

The bodies had to be exceedingly fresh, or the slight decomposition of brain tissue would render perfect reanimation impossible. Indeed, the greatest problem was to get them fresh enough—West had had horrible experiences during his secret college researches with corpses of doubtful vintage. The results of partial or imperfect animation were much more hideous than were the total failures, and we both held fearsome recollections of such things. Ever since our first daemoniac session in the deserted farmhouse on Meadow Hill in Arkham, we had felt a brooding menace; and West, though a calm, blond, blue-eyed scientific automaton in most respects, often confessed to a shuddering sensation of stealthy pursuit. He half felt that he was followed—a psychological delusion of shaken nerves, enhanced by the undeniably disturbing fact that at least one of our reanimated specimens was still alive—a frightful carnivorous thing in a padded cell at Sefton. Then there was another—our first—whose exact fate we had never learned.

We had fair luck with specimens in Bolton—much better than in Arkham. We had not been settled a week before we got an accident victim on the very night of burial, and made it open its eyes with an amazingly rational expression before the solution failed. It had lost an arm—if it had been a perfect body we might have succeeded better. Between then and the next January we secured three more; one total failure, one case of marked muscular motion, and one rather shivery thing—it rose of itself and uttered a sound. Then came a period when luck was poor; interments fell off, and those that did occur were of specimens either too diseased or too maimed for use. We kept track of all the deaths and their circumstances with systematic care.

One March night, however, we unexpectedly obtained a specimen which did not come from the potter's field. In Bolton the prevailing spirit of Puritanism had outlawed the sport of boxing—with the usual result. Surreptitious and ill-conducted bouts among the mill-workers were common, and occasionally professional talent of low grade was imported. This late winter night there had been such a match; evidently with disastrous results, since two timorous Poles had come to us with incoherently whispered entreaties to attend to a very secret and desperate case. We followed them to an abandoned barn, where the remnants of a crowd of frightened foreigners were watching a silent black form on the floor.

The match had been between Kid O'Brien—a lubberly and now quaking youth with a most un-Hibernian hooked nose—and Buck Robinson, "The Harlem Smoke". The negro had been knocked out, and a moment's examination shewed us that he would permanently remain so. He was a loathsome, gorilla-like thing, with abnormally long arms which I could not help calling fore legs, and a face that conjured up thoughts of unspeakable Congo secrets and tom-tom poundings under an eerie moon. The body must have looked even worse in life—but the world holds many ugly things. Fear was upon the whole pitiful crowd, for they did not know what the law would exact of them if the affair were not hushed up; and they were grateful when West, in spite of my involuntary shudders, offered to get rid of the thing quietly—for a purpose I knew too well.

There was bright moonlight over the snowless landscape, but we dressed the thing and carried it home between us through the deserted streets and meadows, as we had carried a similar thing one horrible night in Arkham. We approached the house from the field in the rear, took the specimen in the back door and down the cellar stairs, and prepared it for the usual experiment. Our fear of the police was absurdly great, though we had timed our trip to avoid the solitary patrolman of that section.

The result was wearily anticlimactic. Ghastly as our prize appeared, it was wholly unresponsive to every solution we injected in its black arm; solutions prepared from experience with white specimens only. So as the hour grew dangerously near to dawn, we did as we had done with the others—dragged the thing across the meadows to the neck of the woods near the potter's field, and buried it there in the best sort of grave the frozen ground would furnish.

The grave was not very deep, but fully as good as that of the previous specimen—the thing which had risen of itself and uttered a sound. In the light of our dark lanterns we carefully covered it with leaves and dead vines, fairly certain that the police would never find it in a forest so dim and dense.

The next day I was increasingly apprehensive about the police, for a patient brought rumours of a suspected fight and death. West had still another source of worry, for he had been called in the afternoon to a case which ended very threateningly. An Italian woman had become hysterical over her missing child—a lad of five who had strayed off early in the morning and failed to appear for dinner—and had developed symptoms highly alarming in view of an always weak heart. It was a very foolish hysteria, for the boy had often run away before; but Italian peasants are exceedingly superstitious, and this woman seemed as much harassed by omens as by facts. About seven o'clock in the evening she had died, and her frantic husband had made a frightful scene in his efforts to kill West, whom he wildly blamed for not saving her life. Friends had held him when he drew a stiletto, but West departed amidst his inhuman shrieks, curses, and oaths of vengeance. In his latest affliction the fellow seemed to have forgotten his child, who was still missing as the night advanced. There was some talk of searching the woods, but most of the family's friends were busy with the dead woman and the screaming man. Altogether, the nervous strain upon West must have been tremendous. Thoughts of the police and of the mad Italian both weighed heavily.

We retired about eleven, but I did not sleep well. Bolton had a surprisingly good police force for so small a town, and I could not help fearing the mess which would ensue if the affair of the night before were ever tracked down. It might mean the end of all our local work—and perhaps prison for both West and me. I did not like those rumours of a fight which were floating about. After the clock had struck three the moon shone in my eyes, but I turned over without rising to pull down the shade. Then came the steady rattling at the back door.

I lay still and somewhat dazed, but before long heard West's rap on my door. He was clad in dressing-gown and slippers, and had in his hands a revolver and an electric flashlight. From the revolver I knew that he was thinking more of the crazed Italian than of the police.

"We'd better both go," he whispered. "It wouldn't do not to answer it anyway, and it may be a patient—it would be like one of those fools to try the back door."

So we both went down the stairs on tiptoe, with a fear partly justified and partly that which comes only from the soul of the weird small hours. The rattling continued, growing somewhat louder. When we reached the door I cautiously unbolted it and threw it open, and as the moon streamed revealingly down on the form silhouetted there, West did a peculiar thing. Despite the obvious danger of attracting notice and bringing down on our heads the dreaded police investigation—a thing which after all was mercifully averted by the relative isolation of our cottage—my friend suddenly, excitedly, and unnecessarily emptied all six chambers of his revolver into the nocturnal visitor.

For that visitor was neither Italian nor policeman. Looming hideously against the spectral moon was a gigantic misshapen thing not to be imagined save in nightmares—a glassy-eyed, ink-black apparition nearly on all fours, covered with bits of mould, leaves, and vines, foul with caked blood, and having between its glistening teeth a snow-white, terrible, cylindrical object terminating in a tiny hand.

# — IV —

## THE SCREAM OF THE DEAD

The scream of a dead man gave to me that acute and added horror of Dr. Herbert West which harassed the latter years of our companionship. It is natural that such a thing as a dead man's scream should give horror, for it is obviously not a pleasing or ordinary occurrence; but I was used to similar experiences, hence suffered on this occasion only because of a particular circumstance. And, as I have implied, it was not of the dead man himself that I became afraid.

Herbert West, whose associate and assistant I was, possessed scientific interests far beyond the usual routine of a village physician. That was why, when establishing his practice in Bolton, he had chosen an isolated house near the potter's field. Briefly and brutally stated, West's sole absorbing interest was a secret study of the phenomena of life and its cessation, leading toward the reanimation of the dead through injections of an excitant solution. For this ghastly experimenting it was necessary to have a constant supply of very fresh human bodies; very fresh because even the least decay hopelessly damaged the brain structure, and human because we found that the solution had to be compounded differently for different types of organisms. Scores of rabbits and guinea-pigs had been killed and treated, but their trail was a blind one. West had never fully succeeded because he had never been able to secure a corpse sufficiently fresh. What he wanted were bodies from which vitality had only just departed; bodies with every cell intact and capable of receiving again the impulse toward that mode of motion called life. There was hope that this second and artificial life might be made perpetual by repetitions of the injection, but we had learned that an ordinary natural life would not respond to the action. To establish the artificial motion, natural life must be extinct—the specimens must be very fresh, but genuinely dead.

The awesome quest had begun when West and I were students at the Miskatonic University Medical School in Arkham, vividly conscious for the first time of the thoroughly mechanical nature of life. That was seven years before, but West looked scarcely a day older now—he was small, blond, clean-shaven, soft-voiced, and spectacled, with only an occasional flash of a cold blue eye to tell of the hardening and growing fanaticism of his character under the pressure of his terrible investigations. Our experiences had often been hideous in the extreme; the results of defective reanimation, when lumps of graveyard clay had been galvanised into morbid, unnatural, and brainless motion by various modifications of the vital solution.

One thing had uttered a nerve-shattering scream; another had risen violently, beaten us both to unconsciousness, and run amuck in a shocking way before it could be placed behind asylum bars; still another, a loathsome African monstrosity, had clawed out of its shallow grave and done a deed— West had had to shoot that object. We could not get bodies fresh enough to shew any trace of reason when reanimated, so had perforce created nameless horrors. It was disturbing to think that one, perhaps two, of our monsters still lived—that thought haunted us shadowingly, till finally West disappeared under frightful circumstances. But at the time of the scream in the cellar laboratory of the isolated Bolton cottage, our fears were subordinate to our anxiety for extremely fresh specimens. West was more avid than I, so that it almost seemed to me that he looked half-covetously at any very healthy living physique.

It was in July, 1910, that the bad luck regarding specimens began to turn. I had been on a long visit to my parents in Illinois, and upon my return found West in a state of singular elation. He had, he told me excitedly, in all likelihood solved the problem of freshness through an approach from an entirely new angle—that of artificial preservation. I had known that he was working on a new and highly unusual embalming compound, and was not surprised that it had turned out well; but until he explained the details I was rather puzzled as to how such a compound could help in our work, since the objectionable staleness of the specimens was largely due to delay occurring before we secured them. This, I now saw, West had clearly recognised; creating his embalming compound for future rather than immediate use, and trusting to fate to supply again some very recent and unburied corpse, as it had years before when we obtained the negro killed in the Bolton prize-fight. At last fate had been kind, so that on this occasion there lay in the secret cellar laboratory a corpse whose decay could not by any possibility have begun. What would happen on reanimation, and whether we could hope for a revival of mind and reason, West did not venture to predict. The experiment would be a landmark in our studies, and he had saved the new body for my return, so that both might share the spectacle in accustomed fashion.

West told me how he had obtained the specimen. It had been a vigorous man; a well-dressed stranger just off the train on his way to transact some business with the Bolton Worsted Mills. The walk through the town had been long, and by the time the traveller paused at our cottage to ask the way to the factories his heart had become greatly overtaxed. He had refused a stimulant, and had suddenly dropped dead only a moment later. The body, as might be expected, seemed to West a heaven-sent gift. In his brief conversation the stranger had made it clear that he was unknown in Bolton, and a search of his pockets subsequently revealed him to be one Robert Leavitt of St. Louis, apparently without a family to make instant inquiries about his disappearance. If this man could not be restored to life, no one would know of our experiment. We buried our materials in a dense strip of woods between the house and the potter's field. If, on the other hand, he could be restored, our fame would be brilliantly and perpetually established. So without delay West had injected into the body's wrist the compound which would hold it fresh for use after my arrival. The matter of the presumably weak heart, which to my mind imperilled the success of our experiment, did not appear to trouble West extensively. He hoped at last to obtain what he had never obtained before—a rekindled spark of reason and perhaps a normal, living creature.

So on the night of July 18, 1910, Herbert West and I stood in the cellar laboratory and gazed at a white, silent figure beneath the dazzling arc-light. The embalming compound had worked uncannily well, for as I stared fascinatedly at the sturdy frame which had lain two weeks without stiffening I was moved to seek West's assurance that the thing was really dead. This assurance he gave readily enough; reminding me that the reanimating solution was never used without careful tests as to life; since it could have no effect if any of the original vitality were present. As West proceeded to take preliminary steps, I was impressed by the vast intricacy of the new experiment; an intricacy so vast that he could trust no hand less delicate than his own. Forbidding me to touch the body, he first injected a drug in the wrist just beside the place his needle had punctured when injecting the embalming compound. This, he said, was to neutralise the compound and release the system to a normal relaxation so that the reanimating solution might freely work when injected. Slightly later, when a change and a gentle tremor seemed to affect the dead limbs, West stuffed a pillow-like object violently over the twitching face, not withdrawing it until the corpse appeared quiet and ready for our attempt at reanimation. The pale enthusiast now applied some last perfunctory tests for absolute lifelessness, withdrew satisfied, and finally injected into the left arm an accurately measured amount of the vital elixir, prepared during the afternoon with a greater care than we had used since college days, when our feats were new and groping. I cannot express the wild, breathless suspense with which we waited for results on this first really fresh specimen—the first we could reasonably expect to open its lips in rational speech, perhaps to tell of what it had seen beyond the unfathomable abyss.

West was a materialist, believing in no soul and attributing all the working of consciousness to bodily phenomena; consequently he looked for no revelation of hideous secrets from gulfs and caverns beyond death's barrier. I did not wholly disagree with him theoretically, yet held vague instinctive remnants of the primitive faith of my forefathers; so that I could not help eyeing the corpse with a certain amount of awe and terrible expectation. Besides—I could not extract from my memory that hideous, inhuman shriek we heard on the night we tried our first experiment in the deserted farmhouse at Arkham.

Very little time had elapsed before I saw the attempt was not to be a total failure. A touch of colour came to cheeks hitherto chalk-white, and spread out under the curiously ample stubble of sandy beard. West, who had his hand on the pulse of the left wrist, suddenly nodded significantly; and almost simultaneously a mist appeared on the mirror inclined above the body's mouth. There followed a few spasmodic muscular motions, and then an audible breathing and visible motion of the chest. I looked at the closed eyelids, and thought I detected a quivering. Then the lids opened, shewing eyes which were grey, calm, and alive, but still unintelligent and not even curious.

In a moment of fantastic whim I whispered questions to the reddening ears; questions of other worlds of which the memory might still be present. Subsequent terror drove them from my mind, but I think the last one, which I repeated, was: "Where have you been?" I do not yet know whether I was answered or not, for no sound came from the well-shaped mouth; but I do know that at that moment I firmly thought the thin lips moved silently, forming syllables which I would have vocalised as "only now" if that phrase had possessed any sense or relevancy. At that moment, as I say, I was elated with the conviction that the one great goal had been attained; and that for the first time a reanimated corpse had uttered distinct words impelled by actual reason. In the next moment there was no doubt about the triumph; no doubt that the solution had truly accomplished, at least temporarily, its full mission of restoring rational and articulate life to the dead. But in that triumph there came to me the greatest of all horrors—not horror of the thing that spoke, but of the deed that I had witnessed and of the man with whom my professional fortunes were joined.

For that very fresh body, at last writhing into full and terrifying consciousness with eyes dilated at the memory of its last scene on earth, threw out its
frantic hands in a life and death struggle with the air; and suddenly collapsing
into a second and final dissolution from which there could be no return,
screamed out the cry that will ring eternally in my aching brain:

"Help! Keep off, you cursed little tow-head fiend—keep that damned needle away from me!"

## — V —

## THE HORROR FROM THE SHADOWS

Many men have related hideous things, not mentioned in print, which happened on the battlefields of the Great War. Some of these things have made
me faint, others have convulsed me with devastating nausea, while still others
have made me tremble and look behind me in the dark; yet despite the worst
of them I believe I can myself relate the most hideous thing of all—the shocking, the unnatural, the unbelievable horror from the shadows.

In 1915 I was a physician with the rank of First Lieutenant in a Canadian
regiment in Flanders, one of many Americans to precede the government itself into the gigantic struggle. I had not entered the army on my own initiative, but rather as a natural result of the enlistment of the man whose
indispensable assistant I was—the celebrated Boston surgical specialist,
Dr. Herbert West. Dr. West had been avid for a chance to serve as surgeon
in a great war, and when the chance had come he carried me with him almost
against my will. There were reasons why I would have been glad to let the war
separate us; reasons why I found the practice of medicine and the companionship of West more and more irritating; but when he had gone to Ottawa
and through a colleague's influence secured a medical commission as Major, I
could not resist the imperious persuasion of one determined that I should accompany him in my usual capacity.

When I say that Dr. West was avid to serve in battle, I do not mean to imply that he was either naturally warlike or anxious for the safety of civilisation.
Always an ice-cold intellectual machine; slight, blond, blue-eyed, and spectacled; I think he secretly sneered at my occasional martial enthusiasms and
censures of supine neutrality. There was, however, something he wanted in
embattled Flanders; and in order to secure it he had to assume a military ex-
terior. What he wanted was not a thing which many persons want, but something connected with the peculiar branch of medical science which he had

chosen quite clandestinely to follow, and in which he had achieved amazing and occasionally hideous results. It was, in fact, nothing more or less than an abundant supply of freshly killed men in every stage of dismemberment.

Herbert West needed fresh bodies because his life-work was the reanimation of the dead. This work was not known to the fashionable clientele who had so swiftly built up his fame after his arrival in Boston; but was only too well known to me, who had been his closest friend and sole assistant since the old days in Miskatonic University Medical School at Arkham. It was in those college days that he had begun his terrible experiments, first on small animals and then on human bodies shockingly obtained. There was a solution which he injected into the veins of dead things, and if they were fresh enough they responded in strange ways. He had had much trouble in discovering the proper formula, for each type of organism was found to need a stimulus especially adapted to it. Terror stalked him when he reflected on his partial failures; nameless things resulting from imperfect solutions or from bodies insufficiently fresh. A certain number of these failures had remained alive— one was in an asylum while others had vanished—and as he thought of conceivable yet virtually impossible eventualities he often shivered beneath his usual stolidity.

West had soon learned that absolute freshness was the prime requisite for useful specimens, and had accordingly resorted to frightful and unnatural expedients in body-snatching. In college, and during our early practice together in the factory town of Bolton, my attitude toward him had been largely one of fascinated admiration; but as his boldness in methods grew, I began to develop a gnawing fear. I did not like the way he looked at healthy living bodies; and then there came a nightmarish session in the cellar laboratory when I learned that a certain specimen had been a living body when he secured it. That was the first time he had ever been able to revive the quality of rational thought in a corpse; and his success, obtained at such a loathsome cost, had completely hardened him.

Of his methods in the intervening five years I dare not speak. I was held to him by sheer force of fear, and witnessed sights that no human tongue could repeat. Gradually I came to find Herbert West himself more horrible than anything he did—that was when it dawned on me that his once normal scientific zeal for prolonging life had subtly degenerated into a mere morbid and ghoulish curiosity and secret sense of charnel picturesqueness. His interest became a hellish and perverse addiction to the repellently and fiendishly abnormal; he gloated calmly over artificial monstrosities which would make most healthy men drop dead from fright and disgust; he became, behind his pallid intellectuality, a fastidious Baudelaire of physical experiment—a languid Elagabalus of the tombs.

Dangers he met unflinchingly; crimes he committed unmoved. I think the climax came when he had proved his point that rational life can be restored, and had sought new worlds to conquer by experimenting on the reanimation of detached parts of bodies. He had wild and original ideas on the independent vital properties of organic cells and nerve-tissue separated from natural physiological systems; and achieved some hideous preliminary results in the form of never-dying, artificially nourished tissue obtained from the nearly hatched eggs of an indescribable tropical reptile. Two biological points he was exceedingly anxious to settle—first, whether any amount of consciousness and rational action be possible without the brain, proceeding from the spinal cord and various nerve-centres; and second, whether any kind of ethereal, intangible relation distinct from the material cells may exist to link the surgically separated parts of what has previously been a single living organism. All this research work required a prodigious supply of freshly slaughtered human flesh—and that was why Herbert West had entered the Great War.

The phantasmal, unmentionable thing occurred one midnight late in March, 1915, in a field hospital behind the lines at St. Eloi. I wonder even now if it could have been other than a daemoniac dream of delirium. West had a private laboratory in an east room of the barn-like temporary edifice, assigned him on his plea that he was devising new and radical methods for the treatment of hitherto hopeless cases of maiming. There he worked like a butcher in the midst of his gory wares—I could never get used to the levity with which he handled and classified certain things. At times he actually did perform marvels of surgery for the soldiers; but his chief delights were of a less public and philanthropic kind, requiring many explanations of sounds which seemed peculiar even amidst that babel of the damned. Among these sounds were frequent revolver-shots—surely not uncommon on a battlefield, but distinctly uncommon in an hospital. Dr. West's reanimated specimens were not meant for long existence or a large audience. Besides human tissue, West employed much of the reptile embryo tissue which he had cultivated with such singular results. It was better than human material for maintaining life in organless fragments, and that was now my friend's chief activity. In a dark corner of the laboratory, over a queer incubating burner, he kept a large covered vat full of this reptilian cell-matter; which multiplied and grew puffily and hideously.

On the night of which I speak we had a splendid new specimen—a man at once physically powerful and of such high mentality that a sensitive nervous system was assured. It was rather ironic, for he was the officer who had helped West to his commission, and who was now to have been our associate. Moreover, he had in the past secretly studied the theory of reanimation to some extent under West. Major Sir Eric Moreland Clapham-Lee, D.S.O., was the greatest surgeon in our division, and had been hastily assigned to the St. Eloi sector when news of the heavy fighting reached headquarters. He had come in an aëroplane piloted by the intrepid Lieut. Ronald Hill, only to be shot down when directly over his destination. The fall had been spectacular and awful; Hill was unrecognisable afterward, but the wreck yielded up the great surgeon in a nearly decapitated but otherwise intact condition. West had greedily seized the lifeless thing which had once been his friend and fellow-scholar; and I shuddered when he finished severing the head, placed it in his hellish vat of pulpy reptile-tissue to preserve it for future experiments, and proceeded to treat the decapitated body on the operating table. He injected new blood, joined certain veins, arteries, and nerves at the headless neck, and closed the ghastly aperture with engrafted skin from an unidentified specimen which had borne an officer's uniform. I knew what he wanted—to see if this highly organised body could exhibit, without its head, any of the signs of mental life which had distinguished Sir Eric Moreland Clapham-Lee. Once a student of reanimation, this silent trunk was now gruesomely called upon to exemplify it.

I can still see Herbert West under the sinister electric light as he injected his reanimating solution into the arm of the headless body. The scene I cannot describe—I should faint if I tried it, for there is madness in a room full of classified charnel things, with blood and lesser human debris almost ankle-deep on the slimy floor, and with hideous reptilian abnormalities sprouting, bubbling, and baking over a winking bluish-green spectre of dim flame in a far corner of black shadows.

The specimen, as West repeatedly observed, had a splendid nervous system. Much was expected of it; and as a few twitching motions began to appear, I could see the feverish interest on West's face. He was ready, I think, to see proof of his increasingly strong opinion that consciousness, reason, and personality can exist independently of the brain—that man has no central connective spirit, but is merely a machine of nervous matter, each section more or less complete in itself. In one triumphant demonstration West was about to relegate the mystery of life to the category of myth. The body now twitched more vigorously, and beneath our avid eyes commenced to heave in a frightful way. The arms stirred disquietingly, the legs drew up, and various muscles contracted in a repulsive kind of writhing. Then the headless thing threw out its arms in a gesture which was unmistakably one of desperation—an intelligent desperation apparently sufficient to prove every theory of Herbert West. Certainly, the nerves were recalling the man's last act in life; the struggle to get free of the falling aëroplane.

What followed, I shall never positively know. It may have been wholly an hallucination from the shock caused at that instant by the sudden and complete destruction of the building in a cataclysm of German shell-fire—who can gainsay it, since West and I were the only proved survivors? West liked to think that before his recent disappearance, but there were times when he could not; for it was queer that we both had the same hallucination. The hideous occurrence itself was very simple, notable only for what it implied.

The body on the table had risen with a blind and terrible groping, and we had heard a sound. I should not call that sound a voice, for it was too awful. And yet its timbre was not the most awful thing about it. Neither was its message—it had merely screamed, "Jump, Ronald, for God's sake, jump!" The awful thing was its source.

For it had come from the large covered vat in that ghoulish corner of crawling black shadows.


— VI —


## THE TOMB-LEGIONS

When Dr. Herbert West disappeared a year ago, the Boston police questioned me closely. They suspected that I was holding something back, and perhaps suspected graver things; but I could not tell them the truth because they would not have believed it. They knew, indeed, that West had been connected with activities beyond the credence of ordinary men; for his hideous experiments in the reanimation of dead bodies had long been too extensive to admit of perfect secrecy; but the final soul-shattering catastrophe held elements of daemoniac phantasy which make even me doubt the reality of what I saw.

I was West's closest friend and only confidential assistant. We had met years before, in medical school, and from the first I had shared his terrible researches. He had slowly tried to perfect a solution which, injected into the veins of the newly deceased, would restore life; a labour demanding an abundance of fresh corpses and therefore involving the most unnatural actions. Still more shocking were the products of some of the experiments—grisly masses of flesh that had been dead, but that West waked to a blind, brainless, nauseous animation. These were the usual results, for in order to reawaken the mind it was necessary to have specimens so absolutely fresh that no decay could possibly affect the delicate brain-cells.

This need for very fresh corpses had been West's moral undoing. They were hard to get, and one awful day he had secured his specimen while it was still alive and vigorous. A struggle, a needle, and a powerful alkaloid had transformed it to a very fresh corpse, and the experiment had succeeded for a brief and memorable moment; but West had emerged with a soul calloused and seared, and a hardened eye which sometimes glanced with a kind of hideous and calculating appraisal at men of especially sensitive brain and especially vigorous physique. Toward the last I became acutely afraid of West, for he began to look at me that way. People did not seem to notice his glances, but they noticed my fear; and after his disappearance used that as a basis for some absurd suspicions.

West, in reality, was more afraid than I; for his abominable pursuits entailed a life of furtiveness and dread of every shadow. Partly it was the police he feared; but sometimes his nervousness was deeper and more nebulous, touching on certain indescribable things into which he had injected a morbid life, and from which he had not seen that life depart. He usually finished his experiments with a revolver, but a few times he had not been quick enough. There was that first specimen on whose rifled grave marks of clawing were later seen. There was also that Arkham professor's body which had done cannibal things before it had been captured and thrust unidentified into a madhouse cell at Sefton, where it beat the walls for sixteen years. Most of the other possibly surviving results were things less easy to speak of—for in later years West's scientific zeal had degenerated to an unhealthy and fantastic mania, and he had spent his chief skill in vitalising not entire human bodies but isolated parts of bodies, or parts joined to organic matter other than human. It had become fiendishly disgusting by the time he disappeared; many of the experiments could not even be hinted at in print. The Great War, through which both of us served as surgeons, had intensified this side of West.

In saying that West's fear of his specimens was nebulous, I have in mind particularly its complex nature. Part of it came merely from knowing of the existence of such nameless monsters, while another part arose from apprehension of the bodily harm they might under certain circumstances do him. Their disappearance added horror to the situation—of them all West knew the whereabouts of only one, the pitiful asylum thing. Then there was a more subtle fear—a very fantastic sensation resulting from a curious experiment in the Canadian army in 1915. West, in the midst of a severe battle, had reanimated Major Sir Eric Moreland Clapham-Lee, D.S.O., a fellow-physician who knew about his experiments and could have duplicated them. The head had been removed, so that the possibilities of quasi-intelligent life in the trunk might be investigated. Just as the building was wiped out by a German shell, there had been a success. The trunk had moved intelligently; and, unbelievable to relate, we were both sickeningly sure that articulate sounds had come from the detached head as it lay in a shadowy corner of the laboratory. The shell had been merciful, in a way—but West could never feel as certain as he wished, that we two were the only survivors. He used to make shuddering conjectures about the possible actions of a headless physician with the power of reanimating the dead.

West's last quarters were in a venerable house of much elegance, overlooking one of the oldest burying-grounds in Boston. He had chosen the place for purely symbolic and fantastically aesthetic reasons, since most of the interments were of the colonial period and therefore of little use to a scientist seeking very fresh bodies. The laboratory was in a sub-cellar secretly constructed by imported workmen, and contained a huge incinerator for the quiet and complete disposal of such bodies, or fragments and synthetic mockeries of bodies, as might remain from the morbid experiments and unhallowed amusements of the owner. During the excavation of this cellar the workmen had struck some exceedingly ancient masonry; undoubtedly connected with the old burying-ground, yet far too deep to correspond with any known sepulchre therein. After a number of calculations West decided that it represented some secret chamber beneath the tomb of the Averills, where the last interment had been made in 1768. I was with him when he studied the nitrous, dripping walls laid bare by the spades and mattocks of the men, and was prepared for the gruesome thrill which would attend the uncovering of centuried grave-secrets; but for the first time West's new timidity conquered his natural curiosity, and he betrayed his degenerating fibre by ordering the masonry left intact and plastered over. Thus it remained till that final hellish night; part of the walls of the secret laboratory. I speak of West's decadence, but must add that it was a purely mental and intangible thing. Outwardly he was the same to the last—calm, cold, slight, and yellow-haired, with spectacled blue eyes and a general aspect of youth which years and fears seemed never to change. He seemed calm even when he thought of that clawed grave and looked over his shoulder; even when he thought of the carnivorous thing that gnawed and pawed at Sefton bars.

The end of Herbert West began one evening in our joint study when he was dividing his curious glance between the newspaper and me. A strange headline item had struck at him from the crumpled pages, and a nameless titan claw had seemed to reach down through sixteen years. Something fearsome and incredible had happened at Sefton Asylum fifty miles away, stunning the neighbourhood and baffling the police. In the small hours of the morning a body of silent men had entered the grounds and their leader had aroused the attendants. He was a menacing military figure who talked without moving his lips and whose voice seemed almost ventriloquially connected with an immense black case he carried. His expressionless face was handsome to the point of radiant beauty, but had shocked the superintendent when the hall light fell on it—for it was a wax face with eyes of painted glass. Some nameless accident had befallen this man. A larger man guided his steps; a repellent hulk whose bluish face seemed half eaten away by some unknown malady. The speaker had asked for the custody of the cannibal monster committed from Arkham sixteen years before; and upon being refused, gave a signal which precipitated a shocking riot. The fiends had beaten, trampled, and bitten every attendant who did not flee; killing four and finally succeeding in the liberation of the monster. Those victims who could recall the event without hysteria swore that the creatures had acted less like men than like unthinkable automata guided by the wax-faced leader. By the time help could be summoned, every trace of the men and of their mad charge had vanished.

From the hour of reading this item until midnight, West sat almost paralysed. At midnight the doorbell rang, startling him fearfully. All the servants were asleep in the attic, so I answered the bell. As I have told the police, there was no wagon in the street; but only a group of strange-looking figures bearing a large square box which they deposited in the hallway after one of them had grunted in a highly unnatural voice, "Express—prepaid." They filed out of the house with a jerky tread, and as I watched them go I had an odd idea that they were turning toward the ancient cemetery on which the back of the house abutted. When I slammed the door after them West came downstairs and looked at the box. It was about two feet square, and bore West's correct name and present address. It also bore the inscription, "From Eric Moreland Clapham-Lee, St. Eloi, Flanders". Six years before, in Flanders, a shelled hospital had fallen upon the headless reanimated trunk of Dr. Clapham-Lee, and upon the detached head which—perhaps—had uttered articulate sounds.

West was not even excited now. His condition was more ghastly. Quickly he said, "It's the finish—but let's incinerate—this." We carried the thing down to the laboratory—listening. I do not remember many particulars—you can imagine my state of mind—but it is a vicious lie to say it was Herbert West's body which I put into the incinerator. We both inserted the whole unopened wooden box, closed the door, and started the electricity. Nor did any sound come from the box, after all.

It was West who first noticed the falling plaster on that part of the wall where the ancient tomb masonry had been covered up. I was going to run, but he stopped me. Then I saw a small black aperture, felt a ghoulish wind of ice, and smelled the charnel bowels of a putrescent earth. There was no sound, but just then the electric lights went out and I saw outlined against some phosphorescence of the nether world a horde of silent toiling things which only insanity—or worse—could create. Their outlines were human, semi-human, fractionally human, and not human at all—the horde was grotesquely heterogeneous. They were removing the stones quietly, one by one, from the centuried wall. And then, as the breach became large enough, they came out into the laboratory in single file; led by a stalking thing with a beautiful head made of wax. A sort of mad-eyed monstrosity behind the leader seized on Herbert West. West did not resist or utter a sound. Then they all sprang at him and tore him to pieces before my eyes, bearing the fragments away into that subterranean vault of fabulous abominations. West's head was carried off by the wax-headed leader, who wore a Canadian officer's uniform. As it disappeared I saw that the blue eyes behind the spectacles were hideously blazing with their first touch of frantic, visible emotion.

Servants found me unconscious in the morning. West was gone. The incinerator contained only unidentifiable ashes. Detectives have questioned me, but what can I say? The Sefton tragedy they will not connect with West; not that, nor the men with the box, whose existence they deny. I told them of the vault, and they pointed to the unbroken plaster wall and laughed. So I told them no more. They imply that I am either a madman or a murderer—probably I am mad. But I might not be mad if those accursed tomb-legions had not been so silent.

# Armageddon 2419 A.D.

## PHILIP FRANCIS NOWLAN

**Buck Rogers in the 25th Century**
Directors: *Ford Bebee, Saul A. Goodkind*
Screenplay: *Norman S. Hall, Ray Trampe*
Producer: *Barney Sarecky*
Cast: *Buster Crabbe, Constance Moore*
Released by: *Universal*
1939, Serial, 12 Parts. B&W.

### PROLOGUE

Elsewhere I have set down, for whatever interest they have in this, the 25th Century, my personal recollections of the 20th Century.

Now it occurs to me that my memoirs of the 25th Century may have an equal interest 500 years from now—particularly in view of that unique perspective from which I have seen the 25th Century, entering it as I did, in one leap across a gap of 492 years.

This statement requires elucidation. There are still many in the world who are not familiar with my unique experience. I should state therefore, that I, Anthony Rogers, am, so far as I know the only man alive whose normal span of life has been spread over a period of 573 years. To be precise, I lived the first twenty-nine years of my life between 1898 and 1927; the rest since 2419. The gap between these two, a period of nearly five hundred years, I spent in a state of suspended animation, free from the ravages of catabolic processes, and without any apparent effect on my physical or mental faculties.

When I began my long sleep, man had just begun his real conquest of the air in a sudden series of transoceanic flights in airplanes driven by internal combustion motors. He had barely begun to speculate on the possibilities of harnessing sub-atomic forces, and had made no further practical penetration into the field of ethereal pulsations than the primitive radio and television of that day. The United States of America was the most powerful nation in the world, its political, financial, industrial and scientific influence being supreme.

I awoke to find the America I knew a total wreck—to find Americans a hunted race in their own land, hiding in the dense forests that covered the shattered and leveled ruins of their once magnificent cities, desperately preserving, and struggling to develop in their secret retreats, the remnants of their culture and science—and their independence.

World domination was in the hands of Mongolians, and the center of world power lay in inland China, with Americans one of the few races of mankind unsubdued—and it must be admitted in fairness to the truth, not worth the trouble of subduing in the eyes of the Han Airlords who ruled North America as titular tributaries of the Most Magnificent.

For they needed not the forests in which the Americans lived, nor the resources of the vast territories these forests covered. With the perfection to which they had reduced the synthetic production of necessities and luxuries, their development of scientific processes and mechanical accomplishments of work, they had no economic need for the forests, and no economic desire for the enslaved labor of an unruly race.

They had all they needed for their magnificently luxurious scheme of civilization within the walls of the fifteen cities of sparkling glass they had flung skyward on the sites of ancient American centers, into the bowels of the earth underneath them, and with relatively small surrounding areas of agriculture.

Complete domination of the air rendered communication between these centers a matter of ease and safety. Occasional destructive raids on the wastelands were considered all that was necessary to keep the "wild" Americans on the run within the shelter of their forests, and prevent their becoming a menace to the Han civilization.

But nearly three hundred years of easily maintained security, the last century of which had been nearly sterile in scientific, social and economic progress, had softened them.

It had likewise developed, beneath the protecting foliage of the forest, the growth of a vigorous new American civilization, remarkable in the mobility and flexibility of its organization, in its conquest of almost insuperable obstacles, and in the development and guarding of its industrial and scientific resources. All this was in anticipation of that "Day of Hope" to which Americans had been looking forward for generations, when they would be strong enough to burst from the green chrysalis of the forests, soar into the upper air lanes and destroy the Hans.

At the time I awoke, the "Day of Hope" was almost at hand. I shall not attempt to set forth a detailed history of the Second War of Independence, for that has been recorded already by better historians than I am. Instead I shall confine myself largely to the part I was fortunate enough to play in this struggle and in the events leading up to it.

It all resulted from my interest in radioactive gases. During the latter part of 1927 my company, the American Radioactive Gas Corporation, had been keeping me busy investigating reports of unusual phenomena observed in certain abandoned coal mines near the Wyoming Valley, in Pennsylvania.

With two assistants and a complete equipment of scientific instruments, I began the exploration of a deserted working in a mountainous district, where several weeks before, a number of mining engineers had reported traces of carnotite and what they believed to be radioactive gases. Their report was not without foundation, it was apparent from the outset, for in our examination of the upper levels of the mine, our instruments indicated a vigorous radio activity.

On the morning of December 15th, we descended to one of the lowest levels. To our surprise, we found no water there. Obviously it had drained off through some break in the strata. We noticed too that the rock in the side walls of the shaft was soft, evidently due to the radioactivity, and pieces crumbled under foot rather easily. We made our way cautiously down the shaft, when suddenly the rotted timbers above us gave way.

I jumped ahead, barely escaping the avalanche of coal and soft rock; my companions, who were several paces behind me, were buried under it, and undoubtedly met instant death.

I was trapped. Return was impossible. With my electric torch I explored the shaft to its end, but could find no other way out. The air became increasingly difficult to breathe, probably from the rapid accumulation of the radioactive gas. In a little while my senses reeled and I lost consciousness.

When I awoke, there was a cool and refreshing circulation of air in the shaft. I had not thought that I had been unconscious more than a few hours, although it seems that the radioactive gas had kept me in a state of suspended animation for something like 500 years. My awakening, I figured out later, had been due to some shifting of the strata which reopened the shaft and cleared the atmosphere in the working. This must have been the case, for I was able to struggle back up the shaft over a pile of debris, and stagger up the long incline to the mouth of the mine, where an entirely different world, overgrown with a vast forest and no visible sign of human habitation, met my eyes.

I shall pass over the days of mental agony that followed in my attempt to grasp the meaning of it all. There were times when I felt that I was on the verge of insanity. I roamed the unfamiliar forest like a lost soul. Had it not been for the necessity of improvising traps and crude clubs with which to slay my food, I believe I should have gone mad.

Suffice it to say, however, that I survived this psychic crisis. I shall begin my narrative proper with my first contact with Americans of the year 2419 A.D.

— I —

My first glimpse of a human being of the 25th Century was obtained through a portion of woodland where the trees were thinly scattered, with a dense forest beyond.

I had been wandering along aimlessly, and hopelessly, musing over my strange fate, when I noticed a figure that cautiously backed out of the dense growth across the glade. I was about to call out joyfully, but there was something furtive about the figure that prevented me. The boy's attention (for it seemed to be a lad of fifteen or sixteen) was centered tensely on the heavy growth of the trees from which he had just emerged.

He was clad in rather tight-fitting garments entirely of green, and wore a helmet-like cap of the same color. High around his waist he wore a broad thick belt, which bulked up in the back across the shoulders into something of the proportions of a knapsack.

As I was taking in these details, there came a vivid flash and heavy detonation, like that of a hand grenade, not far to the left of him. He threw up an arm and staggered a bit in a queer, gliding way; then he recovered himself and slipped cautiously away from the place of the explosion, crouching slightly, and still facing the denser part of the forest. Every few steps he would raise his arm, and point into the forest with something he held in his hand. Wherever he pointed there was a terrific explosion, deeper in among the trees. It came to me then that he was shooting with some form of pistol, though there was neither flash nor detonation from the muzzle of the weapon tiself.

After firing several times, he seemed to come to a sudden resolution, and turning in my general direction, leaped—to my amazement sailing through the air between the sparsely scattered trees in such a jump as I had never in my life seen before. That leap must have carried him a full fifty feet, although at the height of his arc, he was not more than ten or twelve feet from the ground.

When he alighted, his foot caught in a projecting root, and he sprawled gently forward. I say "gently" for he did not crash down as I expected him to do. The only thing I could compare it with was a slow-motion cinema, although I have never seen one in which horizontal motions were registered at normal speed and only the vertical movements were slowed down.

Due to my surprise, I suppose my brain did not function with its normal quickness, for I gazed at the prone figure for several seconds before I saw the blood that oozed out from under the tight green cap. Regaining my power of action, I dragged him out of sight back of the big tree. For a few moments I busied myself in an attempt to staunch the flow of blood. The wound was not a deep one. My companion was more dazed than hurt. But what of the pursuers?

I took the weapon from his grasp and examined it hurriedly. It was not unlike the automatic pistol to which I was accustomed, except that it apparently fired with a button instead of a trigger. I inserted several fresh rounds of ammunition into its magazine from my companion's belt as rapidly as I could, for I soon heard near us, the suppressed conversation of his pursuers.

There followed a series of explosions round about us, but none very close. They evidently had not spotted our hiding place, and were firing at random.

I waited tensely, balancing the gun in my hand, to accustom myself to its weight and probable throw.

Then I saw a movement in the green foliage of a tree not far away, and the head and face of a man appeared. Like my companion, he was clad entirely in green, which made his figure difficult to distinguish. But his face could be seen clearly, and had murder in it.

That decided me, I raised the gun and fired. My aim was bad, for there was no kick in the gun, as I had expected; I hit the trunk of the tree several feet below him. It blew him from his perch like a crumpled bit of paper, and he *floated* down to the ground, like some limp, dead thing, gently lowered by an invisible hand. The tree, its trunk blown apart by the explosion, crashed down.

There followed another series of explosions around us. These guns we were using made no sound in the firing, and my opponents were evidently as much at sea as to my position as I was to theirs. So I made no attempt to reply to their fire, contenting myself with keeping a sharp lookout in their general direction. And patience had its reward.

Very soon I saw a cautious movement in the top of another tree. Exposing myself as little as possible, I aimed carefully at the tree trunk and fired again. A shriek followed the explosion. I heard the tree crash down, then a groan.

There was silence for a while. Then I heard a faint sound of boughs swishing. I shot three times in its direction, pressing the button as rapidly as I could. Branches crashed down where my shells had exploded, but there was no body.

Now I saw one of them. He was starting one of those amazing leaps from the bough of one tree to another about forty feet away.

I threw up my gun impulsively and fired. By now I had gotten the feel of the weapon, and my aim was good. I hit him. The "bullet" must have penetrated his body and exploded, for one moment I saw him flying through the air; then the explosion, and he had vanished. He never finished his leap.

How many more of them there were I don't know, but this must have been too much for them. They used a final round of shells on us, all of which exploded harmlessly, and shortly after I heard them swishing and crashing away from us through the tree tops. Not one of them descended to earth.

Now I had time to give some attention to my companion. She was, I found, a girl, and not a boy. Despite her bulky appearance, due to the peculiar belt strapped around her body high up under the arms, she was very slender, and very pretty.

There was a stream not far away, from which I brought water and bathed her face and wound.

Apparently the mystery of these long leaps, the monkey-like ability to jump from bough to bough, and of the bodies that floated gently down instead of falling, lay in the belt. The thing was some sort of anti-gravity belt that almost balanced the weight of the wearer, thereby tremendously multiplying the propulsive power of the leg muscles, and the lifting power of the arms.

When the girl came to, she regarded me as curiously as I did her, and promptly began to quiz me. Her accent and intonation puzzled me a lot, but nevertheless we were able to understand each other fairly well, except for certain words and phrases. I explained what had happened while she lay unconscious, and she thanked me simply for saving her life.

"You are a strange exchange," she said, eying my clothing quizzically. Evidently she found it mirth-provoking by contrast with her own neatly efficient garb. "Don't you understand what I mean by 'exchange?' I mean ah—let me see—a stranger, somebody from some other gang. What gang do you belong to?" (She pronounced it "gan," with only a suspicion of a nasal sound.)

I laughed. "I'm not a gangster," I said. But she evidently did not understand this word. "I don't belong to any gang," I explained, "and never did. Does everybody belong to a gang nowadays?"

"Naturally," she said, frowning. "If you don't belong to a gang, where and how do you live? Why have you not found and joined a gang? How do you eat? Where do you get your clothing?"

"I've been eating wild game for the past two weeks," I explained, "and this clothing I—er—ah—" I paused, wondering how I could explain that it must be many hundred years old.

In the end I saw I would have to tell my story as well as I could, piecing it together with my assumptions as to what had happened. She listened patiently; incredulously at first, but less so as I went on. When I had finished, she sat thinking for a long time.

"That's hard to believe," she said, "but I believe it." She looked me over with frank interest.

"Were you married when you slipped into unconsciousness down in that mine?" she asked me suddenly. I assured her I had never married. "Well, that simplifies matters," she continued. "You see, if you were technically classed as a family man, I could take you back only as an invited exchange and I, being unmarried, and no relation of yours, couldn't do the inviting."

She gave me a brief outline of the very peculiar social and economic system under which her people lived. At least it seemed very peculiar from my 20th Century viewpoint.

I learned with amazement that exactly 492 years had passed over my head as I lay unconscious in the mine.

Wilma Deering, for that was her name, did not profess to be a historian, and so could give me only a sketchy outline of the wars that had been fought, and the manner in which such radical changes had come about. It seemed that another war had followed the First World War, in which nearly all the European nations had banded together to break the financial and industrial power of America. They succeeded in their purpose, though they were beaten, for the war was a terrific one, and left America, like themselves, gasping, bleeding and disorganized, with only the hollow shell of a victory.

This opportunity had been seized by the Russian Soviets, who had made a coalition with the Chinese to sweep over all Europe and reduce it to a state of chaos.

America, industrially geared to world production and the world trade, collapsed economically, and there ensued a long period of stagnation and desperate attempts at economic reconstruction. But it was impossible to stave off war with the Mongolians, who by now had subjugated the Russians, and were aiming at a world empire.

In about 2109, it seems the conflict was finally precipitated. The Mongolians, with overwhelming fleets of great airships, and a science that far outstripped that of crippled America, swept in over the Pacific and Atlantic Coasts, and down from Canada, annihilating American aircraft, armies and cities with their terrific *disintegrator* ray. These rays were projected from a machine not unlike a searchlight in appearance, the reflector of which, however, was not material substance, but a complicated balance of interacting electronic forces. This resulted in a terribly destructive beam. Under its influence, material substance melted into "nothingness"; *i.e.*, into electronic vibrations. It destroyed all then known substances, from air to the most dense metals and stone.

They settled down to the establishment of what became known as the Han dynasty in America, as a sort of province in their World Empire.

Those were terrible days for the Americans. They were hunted like wild beasts. Only those survived who finally found refuge in mountains, canyons and forests. Government was at an end among them. Anarchy prevailed for several generations. Most would have been eager to submit to the Hans, even if it meant slavery. But the Hans did not want them, for they themselves had marvelous machinery and scientific process by which all difficult labor was accomplished.

Ultimately they stopped their active search for, and annihilation of the widely scattered groups of now savage Americans. So long as Americans remained hidden in their forests, and did not venture near the great cities the Hans had built, little attention was paid to them.

Then began the building of the new American civilization. Families and individuals gathered together in clans or "gangs" for mutual protection. For nearly a century they lived a nomadic and primitive life, moving from place to place, in desperate fear of the casual and occasional Han air raids, and the terrible disintegrator ray. As the frequency of these raids decreased, they began to stay permanently in given localities, organizing upon lines which in many respects were similar to those of the military households of the Norman feudal barons. However, instead of gathering together in castles, American defense tactics necessitated a certain scattering of living quarters for families and individuals. They lived virtually in the open air, in the forests, in green tents, resorting to camouflage tactics that would conceal their presence from air observers. They dug underground factories and laboratories that they might better be shielded from the electronic detectors of the Hans. They tapped the radio communication lines of the Hans, with crude instruments at first, better ones later on. They bent every effort toward the redevelopment of science. For many generations they labored as unseen, unknown scholars of the Hans, picking up their knowledge piecemeal.

During the earlier part of this period, there were many deadly wars fought between the various gangs, and occasional courageous but childishly futile attacks upon the Hans, followed by terribly punitive raids.

But as knowledge progressed, the sense of American brotherhood redeveloped. Reciprocal arrangements were made among the gangs over constantly increasing areas. Trade developed, to a certain extent, between one gang and another; but the interchange of knowledge became more important than that of goods as skill in the handling of synthetic processes developed.

Within the gang, an economy was developed that was a compromise between individual liberty and a military socialism. The right of private property was limited practically to personal possessions, but private privileges were many, and sacredly regarded. Stimulation to achievement lay chiefly in the winning of various kinds of leadership and prerogatives. There could be only a very limited degree of owning anything that might be classified as "wealth," and nothing that might be classified as "resources." Resources of every description, for military safety and efficiency, belonged as a matter of public interest to the community as a whole.

In the meantime, through these many generations, the Hans had developed a luxury economy. The Americans were regarded as "wild men of the woods." And since the Hans neither needed nor wanted the woods or the wild men, they treated Americans as beasts, and were conscious of no human brotherhood with them. As time went on, and synthetic processes of producing foods and materials were further developed, less and less ground was needed by the Hans for the purposes of agriculture; finally, even the working of mines was abandoned when it became cheaper to build up metal from electronic vibrations than to dig them out of the ground.

The Han race, devitalized by its vices and luxuries, with machinery and scientific processes to satisfy its every want, with virtually no necessity of labor, began to assume a defensive attitude toward the Americans.

And quite naturally, the Americans regarded the Hans with a deep, grim hatred; they longed desperately for the day when they should be powerful enough to rise and annihilate the Mongolian Blight that lay over the continent.

At the time of my awakening, the gangs were rather loosely organized, but were considering the establishment of a special military force, whose special business it would be to harry the Hans and bring down their air ships whenever possible, without causing general alarm among the Mongolians.

Wilma told me she was a member of the Wyoming Gang, which claimed the entire Wyoming Valley as its territory, under the leadership of Boss Ciardi. Her mother and father were dead, and she was unmarried, so she was not a "family member." She lived in a little group of tents known as Camp 17, under a woman Camp Boss, with seven other girls.

Her duties alternated between military or police scouting and factory work. For the two-week period which would end the next day, she had been on "air patrol." This did not mean, as I first imagined, that she was flying, but rather that she was on the lookout for Han ships over this outlying section of the Wyoming territory, and had spent most of her time perched in the tree tops scanning the skies. Had she seen one she would have fired a "drop flare" several miles off to one side, which would ignite when it was floating vertically toward the earth, so that the direction or point from which it had been fired might not be guessed by the airship and bring a blasting play of the disintegrator ray in her vicinity. Other members of the air patrol would send up rockets on seeing hers, until finally a scout equipped with an ultrophone, which, unlike the ancient radio, operated on the ultronic ethereal vibrations, would pass the warning simultaneously to the headquarters of the Wyoming Gang and other communities within a radius of several hundred miles. This would also alert the few American rocketships that might be in the air, which instantly would duck to cover either through forest clearings or by flattening down to earth in green fields where their coloring would probably protect them from observation.

The favorite American method of propulsion was known as *"rocketing."* The *rocket* is what I would describe, from my 20th Century comprehension of the matter, as an extremely powerful gas blast, atomically produced through the stimulation of chemical action. Scientists of today regard it as a childishly simple reaction, but by that very virtue, most economical and efficient.

But tomorrow, Wilma explained, she would go back to work in the cloth plant, where she would take charge of one of the synthetic processes by which those wonderful substitutes for woven fabrics of wool, cotton and silk are produced. At the end of another two weeks, she would be back on military duty again, perhaps at the same work, or maybe as a "contact guard," on duty where the territory of the Wyomings merged with that of the Delawares, or the "Susquannas" or one of the half dozen other "gangs" in that section of the country which I knew as Pennsylvania and New York States.

Wilma cleared up for me the mystery of those flying leaps which she and her assailants had made, and explained in the following manner the inertron belt balances weight:

*"Jumpers"* were in common use at the time I "awoke," though they were costly, for at that time *inertron* had not been produced in very great quantity. They were very useful in the forest. They were belts, strapped high under the arms, containing an amount of inertron adjusted to the wearer's weight and purposes. In effect they made a man weigh as little as he desired; two pounds if he liked.

*"Floaters"* are a later development of *"jumpers"*—rocket motors encased in *inertron* blocks and strapped to the back in such a way that the wearer floats, when drifting, facing slightly downward. With his motor in operation, he moves like a diver, head-foremost, controlling his direction by twisting his body and by movements of his outstretched arms and hands. Ballast weights locked in the front of the belt adjust weight and lift. Some men

prefer a few ounces of weight in floating, using a slight motor thrust to overcome this. Others prefer a buoyance balance of a few ounces. The inadvertent dropping of weight is not a serious matter. The motor thrust always can be used to descend. But as an extra precaution, in case the motor should fail, for any reason, there are built into every belt a number of detachable sections, one or more of which can be discarded to balance off any loss in weight.

"But who were your assailants," I asked, "and why were you attacked?"

Her assailants, she told me, were members of an outlaw gang, referred to as "Bad Bloods," a group which for several generations had been under the domination of leaders who tried to advance the interests of their clan by tactics which their neighbors had come to regard as unfair, and who in consequence had been virtually boycotted. Their purpose had been to slay Wilma near the Delaware frontier, making it appear that the crime had been committed by Delaware scouts and thus embroil the Delawares and Wyomings in acts of reprisal against each other, or at least cause suspicions.

Fortunately they had not succeeded in surprising her, and she had been successful in dodging them for some two hours before the shooting began, at the moment when I arrived on the scene.

"But we must not stay here talking," Wilma concluded. "I have to take you in, and besides I must report this attack right away. I think we had better slip over to the other side of the mountain. Whoever is on that post will have a phone, and I can make a direct report. But you'll have to have a belt. Mine alone won't help much against our combined weights, and there's little to be gained by jumping heavy. It's almost as bad as walking."

After a little search, we found one of the men I had killed, who had floated down among the trees some distance away and whose belt was not badly damaged. In detaching it from his body, it nearly got away from me and shot up in the air. Wilma caught it, however, and though it reinforced the lift of her own belt so that she had to hook her knee around a branch to hold herself down, she saved it. I climbed the tree, and with my weight added to hers, we floated down easily.

— II —

We were delayed in starting for quite a while since I had to acquire a few crude ideas about the technique of using these belts. I had been sitting down, for instance, with the belt strapped about me, enjoying an ease similar to that of a comfortable armchair; when I stood up with a natural exertion of muscular effort, I shot ten feet into the air, with a wild instinctive thrashing of arms and legs that amused Wilma greatly.

But after some practice, I began to get the trick of gauging muscular effort to a minimum of vertical and a maximum of horizontal. The correct form, I found, was a measure comparable to that of skating. I found, also, that in forest work the arms and hands could be used to great advantage in swinging along from branch to branch, so prolonging leaps almost indefinitely at times.

In going up the side of the mountain, I found that my 20th Century muscles did have an advantage, in spite of lack of skill with the belt; and since the slopes were very sharp, and most of our leaps were upward, I could have outdistanced Wilma, but when we crossed the ridge and descended, she outstripped me with her superior technique. Choosing the steepest slopes, she would crouch in the top of a tree, and propel herself outward, literally diving until, with the loss of horizontal momentum, she would assume a more upright position and float downward. In this manner she would sometimes cover as much as a quarter of a mile in a single leap, while I leaped and scrambled clumsily behind, thoroughly enjoying the sensation.

Halfway down the mountain, we saw another green-clad figure leap out above the tree tops toward us. The three of us perched on an outcropping of rock from which a view for many miles around could be had, while Wilma hastily explained her adventure and my presence to her fellow guard, whose name was Alan. I learned later that this was the modern form of Helen.

"You want to report by phone then, don't you?" Alan took a compact packet about six inches square from a holster attached to her belt and handed it to Wilma.

So far as I could see, it had no special receiver for the ear. Wilma merely threw back a lid, as though she were opening a book, and began to talk. The voice that came back from the machine was as audible as her own.

She was queried closely as to the attack upon her, and at considerable length as to myself, and I could tell from the tone of that voice that its owner was not prepared to take me at my face value as readily as Wilma had. For that matter, neither was the other girl. I could realize it from the suspicious glances she threw my way, when she thought my attention was elsewhere, and the manner in which her hand hovered constantly near her gun holster.

Wilma was ordered to bring me in at once, and informed that another scout would take her place on the other side of the mountain. She closed down the lid of the phone and handed it back to Alan, who seemed relieved to see us departing over the tree tops in the direction of the camps.

We had covered perhaps ten miles, in what still seemed to me a surprisingly easy fashion, when Wilma explained, that from here on we would have to keep to the ground. We were nearing the camps, she said, and there was always the possibility that some small Han scoutship, invisibly high in the sky, might catch sight of us through a projectoscope and thus find the general location of the camps.

Wilma took me to the Scout office, which proved to be a small building of irregular shape, conforming to the trees around it, and substantially constructed of green sheet-like material.

I was received by the assistant Scout Boss, who reported my arrival at once to the historical office, and to officials he called the Psycho Boss and the History Boss, who came in a few minutes later. The attitude of all three men was at first polite but skeptical, and Wilma's ardent advocacy seemed to amuse them.

For the next two hours I talked, explained and answered questions. I had to explain, in detail, the manner of my life in the 20th Century and my understanding of customs, habits, business, science and the history of that period, and about developments in the centuries that had elapsed. Had I been in a classroom, I would have come through the examination with a very poor mark, for I was unable to give any answer to fully half of their questions. But before long I realized that the majority of these questions were designed as traps. Objects, of whose purpose I knew nothing, were casually handed to me, and I was watched keenly as I handled them.

In the end I could see both amazement and belief begin to show in the faces of my inquisitors, and at last the Historical and Psycho Bosses agreed openly that they could find no flaw in my story or reactions, and that my story must be accepted as genuine.

They took me at once to Big Boss Ciardi. He was a portly man with a "poker face." He would probably have been the successful politician even in the 20th Century.

They gave him a brief outline of my story and a report of their examination of me. He made no comment other than to nod his acceptance of it. Then he turned to me.

"How does it feel?" he asked. "Do we look funny to you?"

"A bit strange," I admitted. "But I'm beginning to lose that dazed feeling, though I can see I have an awful lot to learn."

"Maybe we can learn some things from you, too," he said. "So you fought in the First World War. Do you know, we have very little left in the way of records of the details of that war—that is, the precise conditions under which it was fought, and the tactics employed. We forgot many things during the Han terror, and—well, I think you might have a lot of ideas worth thinking over for our raid masters. By the way, now that you're here, and can't go back to your own century, so to speak, what do you want to do? You're welcome to become one of us. Or perhaps you'd just like to visit with us for a while, and then look around among the other gangs. Maybe you'd like some of the others better. Don't make up your mind now. We'll put you down as an exchange for a while. Let's see. You and Dave Berg ought to get along well together. He's Camp Boss of Number 34 when he isn't acting as Raid Boss or Scout Boss. There's a vacancy in his camp. Stay with him and think things over as long as you want to. As soon as you make up your mind to anything, let me know."

We all shook hands, for that was one custom that had not died out in five hundred years, and I set out with Berg.

Dave, like all the others, was clad in green. He was a big man. That is, he was about my own height, five feet eleven. This was considerably above the average now, for the race had lost something in stature, it seemed, through the vicissitudes of five centuries. Most of the women were a bit below five feet, and the men only a trifle above this height.

For a period of two weeks Dave was to confine himself to camp duties, so I had a good chance to familiarize myself with the community life. It was not easy. There were so many marvels to absorb. I never ceased to wonder at the strange combination of rustic social life and feverish industrial activity. At least, it was strange to me. For in my experience, industrial development meant crowded cities, tenements, paved streets, profusion of vehicles, noise, hurrying men and women with strained or dull faces, vast structures and ornate public works.

Here, however, was rustic simplicity, apparently isolated families and groups, living in the heart of the forest, with a quarter of a mile or more between households. There was a total absence of crowds, no means of conveyance other than the belts called jumpers, almost constantly worn by everybody, and an occasional rocket ship—used only for longer journeys—and underground plants or factories that were to my mind more like laboratories and engine rooms. Many of them were excavations as deep as mines, with well finished, lighted and comfortable interiors. These people were adept at camouflage against air observation. Not only would their activity have been unsuspected by an airship passing over the center of the community, but even by an enemy who might happen to drop through the screen of the upper branches to the floor of the forest. The camps, or household structures, were all irregular in shape and of colors that blended with the great trees among which they were hidden.

There were 724 dwellings or "camps" among the Wyomings, located within an area of about fifteen square miles. The total population was 8,688, every man, woman and child, whether member or "exchange," being listed.

The plants were widely scattered through the territory also. Nowhere was anything like congestion permitted. So far as possible, families and individuals were assigned to living quarters, not too far from the plants or offices in which their work lay.

All able-bodied men and women alternated in two-week periods between military and industrial service, except those who were needed for household work. Since working conditions in the plants and offices were ideal, and everybody thus had plenty of healthy outdoor activity in addition, the population was sturdy and active. Laziness was regarded as nearly the greatest of social offenses. Hard work and general merit were variously rewarded with extra privileges, advancement to positions of authority, and with various items of personal equipment for convenience and luxury.

In leisure moments, I got great enjoyment from sitting outside the dwelling in which I was quartered with Dave Berg and ten other men, watching the occasional passers-by, as with leisurely, but swift movements, they swung up and down the forest trail, rising from the ground in long almost-horizontal leaps, occasionally swinging from one convenient branch over head to another before "sliding" back to the ground farther on. Normal traveling pace, where these trails were straight enough, was about twenty miles an hour. Such things as automobiles and railroad trains (the memory of them not more than a month old in my mind) seemed inexpressibly silly and futile compared with such convenience as these belts or jumpers offered.

Dave suggested that I wander around for several days, from plant to plant, to observe and study what I could. The entire community had been apprised of my coming, my rating as an "exchange" reaching every building and post in the community, by means of ultronic broadcast. Everywhere I was welcomed in an interested and helpful spirit.

I visited the plants where ultronic vibrations were isolated from the ether and through slow processes built up into sub-electronic, electronic and atomic forms into the two great synthetic elements, ultron and inertron. I learned something, superficially at least, of the processes of combined chemical and mechanical action through which were produced the various forms of synthetic cloth. I watched the manufacture of the machines which were used at locations of construction to produce the various forms of building materials. But I was particularly interested in the munitions plants and the rocket ship shops.

Ultron is a solid of great molecular density and moderate elasticity, which has the property of being 100 percent conductive to those pulsations known as light, electricity and heat. Since it is completely permeable to light vibrations, it is therefore *absolutely invisible and non-reflective*. Its magnetic response is almost, but not quite, 100 percent also. It is therefore very heavy under normal conditions but extremely responsive to the *repellor* or anti-gravity rays, such as the Hans use as *"legs"* for their airships.

Inertron is the second great triumph of American research and experimentation with ultronic forces. It was developed just a few years before my awakening in the abandoned mine. It is a synthetic element, built up, through a complicated heterodyning of ultronic pulsations, from "infra balanced" subionic forms. It is completely inert to both electric and magnetic forces in all the orders above the *ultronic;* that is to say, the *sub-electronic,* the *electronic,* the *atomic* and the *molecular.* In consequence it has a number of amazing and valuable properties. One of these is *the total lack of weight.* Another is a total lack of heat. It has no molecular vibration whatever. It reflects 100 percent of the heat and light impinging upon it. It does not feel cold to the touch, of course, since it will not absorb the heat of the hand. It is a solid, very dense in molecular structure despite its lack of weight, of great strength and considerable elasticity. It is a perfect shield against the disintegrator rays.

Rocket guns are very simple contrivances so far as the mechanism of launching the bullet is concerned. They are simple light tubes, closed at the rear end with a trigger-actuated pin for piercing the thin skin at the base of the cartridge. This piercing of the skin starts the chemical and atomic reaction. The entire cartridge leaves the tube under its own power, at a very easy initial velocity, just enough to insure accuracy of aim; so the tube does not have to be of heavy construction. The bullet increases in velocity as it goes. It may be solid or explosive. It may explode on contact or on time, or a combination of these two.

Dave and I talked mostly of weapons, military tactics and strategy. Strangely enough he had no idea whatever of the possibilities of the barrage, though the tremendous effect of a "curtain of fire" with such high-explosive projectiles as these modern rocket guns used was obvious to me. But the barrage idea, it seemed, had been lost track of completely in the air wars that followed the First World War, and in the peculiar guerrilla tactics developed by Americans in the later period of operations from the ground against Han airships, and in the gang wars which until a few generations ago I learned, had been almost continuous.

"I wonder," said Dave one day, "if we couldn't work up some form of barrage to spring on the Bad Bloods. The Big Boss told me today that he's been in communication with the other gangs, and all are agreed that the Bad Bloods might as well be wiped out for good. That attempt on Wilma Deering's life and their evident desire to make trouble among the gangs, has stirred up every community east of the Alleghanies. The Boss says that none of the others will object if we go after them. Now show me again how you worked that business in the Argonne forest. The conditions ought to be pretty much the same."

I went over it with him in detail, and gradually we worked out a modified plan that would be better adapted to our more powerful weapons, and the use of jumpers.

"It will be easy," Dave exulted. "I'll slide down and talk it over with the Boss tomorrow."

During the first two weeks of my stay with the Wyomings, Wilma Deering and I saw a great deal of each other. I naturally felt a little closer friendship for her, in view of the fact that she was the first human being I saw after waking from my long sleep.

It was natural enough too, that she should feel an unusual interest in me. In the first place, I was her personal discovery, and I had saved her life. In the second, she was a girl of studious and reflective turn of mind. She never got tired of my stories and descriptions of the 20th Century.

The others of the community, however, seemed to find our friendship a bit amusing. It seemed that Wilma had a reputation for being cold toward the opposite sex, and so others misinterpreted her attitude, much to their own delight. Wilma and I, however, ignored this as much as we could.

There was a girl in Wilma's camp named Gerdi Mann, with whom Dave Berg was desperately in love, and the four of us used to go around a lot together. Gerdi was a distinct type. Whereas Wilma had the usual dark brown hair and hazel eyes that marked nearly every member of the community, Gerdi had red hair, blue eyes and very fair skin. She was a throwback in physical appearance to a certain 20th Century type which I have found very rare among modern Americans. The four of us were engaged one day in a discussion of this very point, when I obtained my first experience of a Han air raid.

We were sitting high on the side of a hill overlooking the valley that teemed with human activity, invisible beneath its blanket of foliage.

The other three, who knew of the Irish but vaguely and indefinitely, as a race on the other side of the globe, which, like ourselves, had succeeded in maintaining a precarious and fugitive existence in rebellion against the Mongolian domination of the earth, were listening with interest to my theory that Gerdi's ancestors of several hundred years ago must have been Irish. I explained that Gerdi was an Irish type, and that her surname might well have been McMann, or McMahan, and still more anciently "mac Mathghamhain." They were interested too in my surmise that "Gerdi" was the same name as that which had been "Gerty" or "Gertrude" in the 20th Century.

In the middle of our discussion, we were startled by an alarm rocket that burst high in the air, far to the north, spreading a pall of red smoke that drifted like a cloud. It was followed by others at scattered points in the northern sky.

"A Han raid!" Dave exclaimed in amazement. "The first in seven years!"

"Maybe it's just one of their ships off its course," I ventured.

"No," said Wilma in some agitation. "That would be green rockets. Red means only one thing, Tony. They're sweeping the countryside with their *dis* beams. Can you see anything, Dave?"

"We had better get under cover," Gerdi said nervously. "The four of us are bunched here in the open. For all we know they may be twelve miles up, out of sight, yet looking at us with a projecto."

Dave had been sweeping the horizon hastily with his glass, but apparently saw nothing.

"We had better scatter, at that," he said finally. "It's orders, you know. See!" He pointed to the valley.

Here and there a tiny human figure shot for a moment above the foliage of the tree tops.

"That's bad," Wilma commented, as she counted the jumpers. "No less than fifteen people visible, and all clearly radiating from a central point. Do they want to give away our location?"

The standard orders covering air raids were that the population was to scatter individually. There should be no grouping, or even pairing, in view of the destructiveness of the disintegrator rays. Experience of generations had proved that if this were done, and everybody remained hidden beneath the tree screens, the Hans would have to sweep mile after mile of territory, foot by foot, to catch more than a small percentage of the community.

Gerdi, however, refused to leave Dave, and Wilma developed an equal obstinacy against quitting my side. I was inexperienced at this sort of thing, she explained, quite ignoring the fact that she was too; she was only thirteen or fourteen years old at the time of the last air raid.

However, since I could not argue her out of it, we leaped together about a quarter of a mile to the right, while Dave and Gerdi disappeared down the hillside among the trees.

Wilma and I both wanted a point of vantage from which we might overlook the valley and the sky to the north, and we found it near the top of the ridge, where, protected from visibility by thick branches, we could look out between the tree trunks, and get a good view of the valley.

No more rockets went up. Except for a few of those warning red clouds, drifting lazily in a blue sky, there was no visible indication of man's past or present existence anywhere in the sky or on the ground.

Then Wilma gripped my arm and pointed. I saw it; away off in the distance; looking like a phantom dirigible in its coat of low-visibility paint.

"Seven thousand feet up," Wilma whispered, crouching close to me. "Watch."

The ship was about the same shape as the great dirigibles of the 20th Century that I had seen, but without the suspended control car, engines, propellors, rudders or elevating planes. As it loomed rapidly nearer, I saw that it was wider and somewhat flatter than I had supposed.

Now I could see the repellor rays that held the ship aloft, like searchlight beams faintly visible in the bright daylight (and still faintly visible to the human eye at night). Actually, I had been informed by my instructors, there were two rays. The visible one was generated by the ship's apparatus, and directed toward the ground as a beam of "carrier" impulses. The true repellor ray, the complement of the other in one sense, induced by the action of the "carrier" reacted in a concentrating upward direction from the mass of the earth. It became successively electronic, atomic and finally molecular, in its nature, according to various ratios of distance between earth mass and "carrier" source, until, in the last analysis, the ship itself actually was supported on an upward rushing column of air, much like a ball continuously supported on a fountain jet.

The raider neared with incredible speed. Its rays were both slanted astern at a sharp angle, so that it slid forward with tremendous momentum.

The ship was operating two disintegrator rays, though only in a casual, intermittent fashion. But whenever they flashed downward with blinding brilliancy, forest, rocks and ground melted instantaneously into nothing where they played upon them.

When later I inspected the scars left by these rays I found them some five feet deep and thirty feet wide, the exposed surfaces being lava-like in texture, but of a pale, iridescent, greenish hue.

No systematic use of the rays was made by the ship, however, until it reached a point over the center of the valley—the center of the community's activities. There it came to a sudden stop by shooting its repellor beams sharply forward and easing them back gradually to the vertical, holding the ship floating and motionless. Then the work of destruction began systematically.

Back and forth traveled the destroying rays, ploughing parallel furrows from hillside to hillside. We gasped in dismay, Wilma and I, as time after time we saw it plough through sections where we knew camps or plants were located.

"This is awful," she moaned, a terrified question in her eyes. "How could they know the location so exactly, Tony? Did you see? They were never in doubt. They stalled at a predetermined spot—and—and it was exactly the right spot."

We did not talk of what might happen if the rays were turned in our direction. We both knew. We would simply be disintegrated in a split second into mere scattered electronic vibrations. Strangely enough, it was this self-reliant girl of the 25th Century, who clung to me—a relatively primitive man of the 20th, less familiar than she with the thought of this terrifying possibility—for moral support.

We knew that many of our companions must have been whisked into absolute non-existence before our eyes in these few moments. The whole thing paralyzed us into mental and physical immobility for I do not know how long.

It couldn't have been long, however, for the rays had not ploughed more than thirty of their twenty-foot furrows or so across the valley, when I regained control of myself, and brought Wilma to herself by shaking her roughly.

"How far will this rocket gun shoot, Wilma?" I demanded, drawing my pistol.

"It depends on your rocket, Tony. It will take even the longest range rocket, but you could shoot more accurately from a longer tube. But why? You couldn't penetrate the shell of that ship with rocket force, even if you could reach it."

I fumbled clumsily with my rocket pouch, for I was excited. I had an idea I wanted to try. With Wilma's help, I selected the longest range explosive rocket in my pouch, and fitted it to my pistol.

"It won't carry seven thousand feet, Tony," Wilma objected. But I took aim carefully. It was another thought that I had in my mind. The supporting repellor ray, I had been told, became molecular in character at what was called a logarithmic level of five (below that it was a purely electronic "flow" or pulsation between the source of the "carrier" and the average mass of the earth). Below that level, if I could project my explosive bullet into this stream where it began to carry material substance upward, might it not rise with the air column, gathering speed and hitting the ship with enough impact to carry it through the shell? It was worth trying anyhow. Wilma became greatly excited, too, when she grasped the nature of my inspiration.

Feverishly I looked around for some formation of branches against which I could rest the pistol, for I had to aim most carefully. At last I found one. Patiently I sighted on the hulk of the ship far above us, aiming at the far side of it, at such an angle as would, so far as I could estimate, bring my bullet path through the forward repellor beam. At last the sights wavered across the point I sought and I pressed the button gently.

For a moment we gazed breathlessly.

Suddenly the ship swung bow down, as on a pivot, and swayed like a pendulum. Wilma screamed in her excitement.

"Oh Tony, you hit it! You hit it! Do it again; bring it down!"

We had only one more rocket of extreme range between us, and we dropped it three times in our excitement in inserting it in my gun. Then, forcing myself to be calm by sheer will power, while Wilma stuffed her little fist into her mouth to keep from shrieking, I sighted carefully again and fired.

The elapsed time of the rocket's invisible flight seemed an age.

Then we saw the ship falling. It seemed to plunge lazily, but actually it fell with terrific acceleration, turning end over end, its disintegrator rays, out of control, describing vast, wild arcs, and once cutting a gash through the forest less than two hundred feet from where we stood.

The crash with which the heavy craft hit the ground reverberated from the hills—the momentum of eighteen or twenty thousand tons, in a sheer drop of seven thousand feet. A mangled mass of metal, it buried itself in the ground, with poetic justice, in the middle of the smoking, semi-molten field of destruction it had been so deliberately ploughing.

The silence, the vacuity of the landscape was oppressive as the last echoes died away.

Then far down the hillside, a single figure leaped exultantly above the foliage screen. And in the distance another, and another.

In a moment the sky was punctured by signal rockets. One after another the little red puffs became drifting clouds.

"Scatter! Scatter!" Wilma exclaimed. "In half an hour there'll be an entire Han fleet here from Nu-Yok, and another from Bah-Flo. They'll get this instantly on their recordographs and location finders. They'll blast the whole valley and the country for miles beyond. Come, Tony. There's no time for the gang to rally. See the signals. We've got to jump. Oh, I'm so proud of you!"

Over the ridge we went, in long leaps towards the east, the country of the Delawares.

From time to time signal rockets puffed in the sky. Most of them were the "red warnings," the "scatter" signals. But from certain of the others, which Wilma identified as Wyoming rockets, she gathered that whoever was in command (we did not know whether the Boss was alive or not) was ordering an ultimate rally toward the south, and so we changed our course.

It was a great pity, I thought, that the clan had not been equipped throughout its membership with ultrophones, but Wilma explained to me that not enough of these had been built for distribution as yet, although general distribution had been contemplated within a couple of months.

We traveled far before nightfall overtook us, trying only to put as much distance as possible between ourselves and the valley.

When gathering dusk made jumping too dangerous, we sought a comfortable spot beneath the trees and consumed part of our emergency rations. It was the first time I had tasted the stuff—a highly nutritive synthetic substance called "concentro," which was, however, a bit bitter and unpalatable. But as only a mouthful or so was needed, it did not matter.

Neither of us had a cloak, but we were both thoroughly tired and happy, so we curled up together for warmth. I remember Wilma making some sleepy remark about our mating, as she cuddled up, as though the matter were all settled, and my surprise at my own instant acceptance of the idea, for I had not consciously thought of her that way before. But we both fell asleep at once.

In the morning we found little time for love making. The practical problem facing us was too great. Wilma felt that the Wyoming plan must be to rally in the Susquanna territory, but she had her doubts about the wisdom of this plan. In my elation at my success in bringing down the Han ship, and my newly found interest in my charming companion, I had forgotten the ominous fact that the Han ship I had destroyed must have known the exact location of the Wyoming Works.

This meant, to Wilma's mind, either that the Hans had perfected new instruments as yet unknown to us, or that somewhere, among the Wyomings or some other nearby gang, there were traitors. In either contingency, she argued, other Han raids would follow, and since the Susquannas had a highly developed organization and more than usually productive plants, the next raid might be expected to strike them.

But at any rate it was clearly our business to get in touch with the other fugitives as quickly as possible, so in spite of muscles that were sore from the excessive leaping of the day before, we continued on our way.

We traveled for only a couple of hours when we saw a multi-colored rocket in the sky, some ten miles ahead of us.

"Bear to the left, Tony," Wilma said, "and listen for the whistle."

"Why?" I asked.

"Haven't they given you the rocket code yet?" she replied. "That's what the green, followed by yellow and purple means: to concentrate five miles east of the rocket position. You know the rocket position itself might draw a play of *dis* rays."

It did not take us long to reach the neighborhood of the indicated rallying, though we were now traveling beneath the trees, with but an occasional leap to a top branch to see if any more rocket smoke was floating above. And soon we heard a distant whistle.

We found about half the Gang already there, in a spot where the trees met high above a little stream. The Big Boss and Raid Bosses were busy reorganizing the remnants.

We reported to Boss Ciardi at once. He was silent, but interested, when he heard our story.

"You two stick close to me," he said, adding grimly, "I'm going back to the valley at once with a hundred picked men, and I'll need you."

— III —

Inside of fifteen minutes we were on our way. A certain amount of caution was sacrificed for the sake of speed, and the men leaped away either across the forest top, or over open spaces of ground, but concentration was forbidden. The Big Boss named the spot on the hillside as the rallying point.

"We'll have to take a chance on being seen, so long as we don't group," he declared, "at least until within five miles of the rallying spot. From then on I want every man to disappear from sight and to travel under cover. And keep your ultrophones open, and turned on ten-four-seven-six."

Wilma and I had received our battle equipment from the Gear Boss. It consisted of a long-gun, a hand-gun, with a special case of ammunition constructed of inertron, which made the load weigh but a few ounces, and a short sword. This gear we strapped over each other's shoulders, on top of our jumping belts. In addition, we each received an ultrophone, and a light inertron blanket rolled into a cylinder about six inches long by two or three in diameter. This fabric was exceedingly thin and light, but it had considerable warmth, because of the mixture of inertron in its composition.

"This looks like business," Wilma remarked to me with sparkling eyes. (And I might mention a curious thing here. The word "business" had survived from the 20th Century American vocabulary, but not with any meaning of "industry" or "trade," for such things being purely community activities were spoken of as "work" and "clearing." Business simply meant fighting, and that was all.)

"Did you bring all this equipment from the valley?" I asked the Gear Boss.

"No," he said. "There was no time to gather anything. All this stuff we cleared from the Susquannas a few hours ago. I was with the Boss on the way down, and he had me jump on ahead and arrange it. But you two had better be moving. He's beckoning you now."

Ciardi was about to call us on our phones when we looked up. As soon as we did so, he leaped away, waving us to follow closely.

He was a powerful man, and he darted ahead in long, swift, low leaps up the banks of the stream, which followed a fairly straight course at this point. By extending ourselves, however, Wilma and I were able to catch up to him.

As we gradually synchronized our leaps with his, he outlined to us, between the grunts that accompanied each leap, his plan of action.

"We have to start the big business—*unh*—sooner or later," he said. "And if—*unh*—the Hans have found any way of locating our positions—*unh*—it's time to start now, although the Council of Bosses—*unh*—had intended waiting a few years until enough rocket ships have been—*unh*—built. But no matter what the sacrifice—*unh*—we can't afford to let them get us on the run—*unh*— We'll set a trap for the yellow devils in the—*unh*—valley if they come back for their wreckage—*unh*—and if they don't, we'll go rocketing for some of their liners—*unh*—on the Nu-yok, Clee-lan, Si-kaga course. We can use—*unh*—that idea of yours of shooting up the repellor—*unh*—beams. Want you to give us a demonstration."

With further admonition to follow him closely, he increased his pace, and Wilma and I were taxed to our utmost to keep up with him. It was only in ascending the slopes that my tougher muscles over-balanced his greater skill, and I was able to set the pace for him, as I had for Wilma.

We slept in greater comfort that night, under our inertron blankets, and were off with the dawn, leaping cautiously to the top of the ridge overlooking the valley which Wilma and I had left.

The Boss scanned the sky with his ultroscope, patiently taking some fifteen minutes to the task, and then swung his phone into use, calling the roll and giving the men their instructions.

His first order was for us all to slip our ear and chest discs into permanent position.

These ultrophones were quite different from the one used by Wilma's companion scout the day I saved her from the attack of the bandit Gang. That one was contained entirely in a small pocket case. These, with which we were now equipped, consisted of a pair of ear discs, each a separate and self-contained receiving set. They slipped into little pockets over our ears in the fabric helmets we wore, and shut out virtually all extraneous sounds. The chest discs were likewise self-contained sending sets, strapped to the chest a few inches below the neck and actuated by the vibrations from the vocal cords through the body tissues. The total range of these sets was about eighteen miles. Reception was remarkably clear, quite free from the static of 20th Century radios, and of a strength in direct proportion to the distance of the speaker.

The Boss' set was triple powered, so that his orders would cut in on any local conversations, which were indulged in, however, with great restraint, and only for the purpose of maintaining contacts.

I marveled at the efficiency of this modern method of battle communication in contrast to the clumsy signaling devices of more ancient times; and also at other military contrasts in which the 20th and 25th Century methods were the reverse of each other in efficiency. These modern Americans, for instance, knew little of hand-to-hand fighting, and nothing, naturally, of trench warfare. And until my recent flash of inspiration, no one among them, apparently, had ever thought of the scheme of shooting a rocket into a repellor beam and letting the beam itself hurl it upward into the most vital part of the Han ship.

Ciardi patiently placed his men, first giving his instructions to the camp-masters, and then remaining silent, while they placed the individuals.

In the end, the hundred men were ringed about the valley, on the hillsides and tops, each in a position from which he had a good view of the wreckage of the Han ship. But not a man had come in view, so far as I could see, in the whole process.

The Boss explained to me that it was his idea that he, Wilma and I should investigate the wreck. If Han ships should appear in the sky, we would leap for the hillsides.

I suggested to him to have the men set up their long-guns trained on an imaginary circle surrounding the wreck. He busied himself with this after the three of us leaped down to the Han ship, serving as a target himself, while he called on the men individually to aim their pieces and lock them in position.

In the meantime Wilma and I climbed into the wreckage, but did not find much. Practically all of the instruments and machinery had been twisted out of all recognizable shape, or utterly destroyed by the ship's disintegrator rays which apparently had continued to operate in the midst of its warped remains for some moments after the crash.

It was unpleasant work searching the mangled bodies of the crew. But it had to be done. The Han clothing, I observed, was quite different from that of the Americans, and more like the garb to which I had been accustomed in the earlier part of my life. It was made of synthetic fabrics like silks, loose and comfortable trousers of knee length, and sleeveless shirts.

No protection, except that against drafts, was needed, Wilma explained to me, for the Han cities were entirely enclosed, with splendid arrangements for ventilation and heating. These arrangements of course were equally adequate in their airships. The Hans, indeed, had quite a distaste for unshaded daylight, since their lighting apparatus diffused a controlled amount of ultraviolet rays, making the unmodified sunlight unnecessary for health, and undesirable for comfort. Since the Hans did not have the secret of inertron, none of them wore anti-gravity belts. Yet in spite of the fact that they had to bear their own full weight at all times, they were physically far inferior to the Americans. They lived lives of physical inertia, having machinery of every description for the performance of all labor, and convenient conveyances for any movement of more than a few steps.

Even from the twisted wreckage of this ship I could see that seats, chairs and couches played an extremely important part in their scheme of existence.

But none of the bodies were overweight. They seemed to have been the bodies of men in good health, but muscularly much underdeveloped. Wilma explained to me that they had mastered the science of gland control, and of course dietetics, to the point where men and women among them not uncommonly reached the age of a hundred years with arteries and general health in splendid condition.

I did not have time to study the ship and its contents as carefully as I would have liked, however. Time pressed, and it was our business to discover some clue to the deadly accuracy with which the ship had spotted the Wyoming Works.

The Boss had hardly finished his arrangements for the ring barrage, when one of the scouts on an eminence to the north, announced the approach of seven Han ships, spread out in a great semicircle.

Ciardi leaped for the hillside, calling to us to do likewise, but Wilma and I had raised the flaps of our helmets and switched off our "speakers" for conversation between ourselves, and by the time we discovered what had happened, the ships were clearly visible, so fast were they approaching.

"Jump!" we heard the Boss order, "Deering to the north. Rogers to the east."

But Wilma looked at me meaningly and pointed to where the twisted plates of the ship, projecting from the ground, offered a shelter.

"Too late, Boss," she said. "They'd see us. Besides I think there's something here we ought to look at. It's probably their magnetic graph."

"You're signing your death warrant," Ciardi warned.

"We'll risk it," said Wilma and I together.

"Good for you," replied the Boss. "Take command then, Rogers, for the present. Do you all know his voice, boys?"

A chorus of assent rang in our ears, and I began to do some fast thinking as the girl and I ducked into the twisted mass of metal.

"Wilma, hunt for that record," I said, knowing that by the simple process of talking I could keep the entire command continuously informed as to the situation. "On the hillsides, keep your guns trained on the circles and stand by. On the hilltops, how many of you are there? Speak in rotation from Bald Knob around to the east, north, west."

In turn the men called their names. There were twenty of them.

I assigned them by name to cover the various Han ships, numbering the latter from left to right.

"Train your rockets on their repellor rays about three-quarters of the way up, between ships and ground. Aim is more important than elevation. Follow those rays with your aim continuously. Shoot when I tell you, not before. Deering has the record. The Hans probably have not seen us, or at least think there are but two of us in the valley, since they're settling without opening up disintegrators. Any opinions?"

My ear discs remained silent.

"Deering and I will remain here until they land and debark. Stand by and keep alert."

Rapidly and easily the largest of the Han ships settled to the earth. Three scouted sharply to the south, rising to a higher level. The others floated motionless about a thousand feet above.

Peeping through a small fissure between two plates, I saw the vast hulk of the ship come to rest full on the line of our prospective ring barrage. A door clanged open a couple of feet from the ground, and one by one the crew emerged.

"They're coming out of the ship." I spoke quietly, with my hand over my mouth, for fear they might hear me. "One—two—three—four—five—six—seven—eight—nine. That seems to be all. Who knows how many men a ship like that is likely to carry?"

"About ten, if there are no passengers," replied one of my men, probably one of those on the hillside.

"How are they armed?" I asked.

"Just knives," came the reply. "They never permit handrays on the ships. Afraid of accidents. Have a ruling against it."

"Leave them to us then," I said, for I had a plan in mind. "You, on the hillsides, take the ships above. Abandon the ring target. Divide up in training on those repellor rays. You on the hilltops, all train on the repellors of the ships to the south. Shoot at the word, but not before.

"Wilma, crawl over to your left where you can make a straight leap for the door in that ship. These men are all walking around the wreck in a bunch. When they're on the far side, I'll give the word and you leap through that door in one bound. I'll follow. Maybe we won't be seen. We'll overpower the guard inside, but don't shoot. We may escape being seen by both this crew and the ships above. They can't see over this wreck."

It was so easy that it seemed too good to be true. The Hans who had emerged from the ship walked round the wreckage lazily, talking in guttural tones, keenly interested in the wreck, but quite unsuspicious.

At last they were on the far side. In a moment they would be picking their way into the wreck.

"Wilma, leap!" I almost whispered the order.

The distance between Wilma's hiding place and the door in the side of the Han ship was not more than fifteen feet. She was already crouched with her feet braced against a metal beam. Taking the lift of the inertron belt into her calculation, she dove headforemost, like a projectile, through the door. I followed in a split second, more clumsily, but no less speedily, bruising my shoulder painfully as I ricocheted from the edge of the opening and brought up sliding against the unconscious girl; for she evidently had hit her head against the partition within the ship into which she had crashed.

We had made some noise within the ship. Shuffling footsteps were approaching down a well-lit gangway.

"Any signs we have been observed?" I asked my men on the hillsides.

"Not yet," I heard the Boss reply. "Ships overhead still standing. No beams have been broken out. Men on ground absorbed in wreck. Most of them have crawled into it out of sight."

"Good," I said quickly. "Deering hit her head. Knocked out. One or more members of the crew approaching. We're not discovered yet. I'll take care of them. Stand a bit longer, but be ready."

I think my last words must have been heard by the man who was approaching, for he stopped suddenly.

I crouched at the far side of the compartment, motionless. I would not draw my sword if there were only one of them.

Apparently reassured at the absence of any further sound, a man came around a sort of bulkhead—and I leaped.

I swung my legs up in front of me as I did so, catching him full in the stomach and knocked him cold.

I ran forward along the keel gangway, searching for the control room. I found it well up in the nose of the ship. And it was deserted. What could I do to jam the controls of the ship that would not register on the recording instruments of the other ships? I gazed at the mass of controls. Levers and wheels galore. In the center of the compartment, on a massively braced universal joint mounting, was what I took for the repellor generator. A dial on it glowed and a faint hum came from within its shielding metallic case. But I had no time to study it.

Above all else, I was afraid that some automatic apparatus existed in the room, through which I might be heard on the other ships. The risk of trying to jam the controls was too great. I abandoned the idea and withdrew softly. I would have to take a chance that there was no other member of the crew aboard.

I ran back to the entrance compartment. Wilma still lay where she had slumped down. I heard the voices of the Hans approaching. It was time to act. The next few seconds would tell whether the ships in the air would try or be able to melt us into nothingness.

"Are you boys all ready?" I asked, creeping to a position opposite the door and drawing my hand-gun.

Again there was a chorus of assent.

"Then on the count of three, shoot up those *rep* rays—all of them—and for God's sake, don't miss." I was beginning to think in the terms the others used generally—*"dis"* for disintegrator, *"rep"* for repellor. And I counted.

I think my "three" was a bit weak. I know it took all the courage I had to utter it.

For an agonizing instant nothing happened, except that the landing party from the ship strolled into my range of vision.

Then startled, they turned their eyes upward. For an instant they stood frozen with horror at whatever they saw.

One hurled his knife at me. It grazed my cheek. Then a couple of them made a break for the doorway. The rest followed. But I fired pointblank with my hand-gun, pressing the button as fast as I could and aiming at their feet to make sure my explosive rockets would make contact and do their work.

The detonations of my rockets were deafening. The spot on which the Hans stood flashed into a blinding glare. Then there was nothing there except their torn and mutilated corpses. They had been fairly bunched, and I got them all.

I ran to the door, expecting any instant to be hurled into infinity by the sweep of a *dis* ray.

Some eighth of a mile away I saw one of the ships crash to earth. A *dis* ray came into my line of vision, wavered uncertainly for a moment and then began to sweep directly toward the ship in which I stood. But it never reached it. Suddenly, like a light switched off, it shot to one side, and a moment later another vast hulk crashed to earth. I looked out, then stepped out on the ground.

The only Han ships in the sky were two of the scouts to the south which were hanging perpendicularly, and sagging slowly down. The others must have crashed down while I was deafened by the sound of the explosion of my own rockets.

Somebody hit the other *rep* ray of one of the two remaining ships and it fell out of sight beyond a hilltop. The other, farther away, drifted down diagonally, its *dis* ray playing viciously over the ground below it.

I shouted with exultation and relief.

"Take back the command, Boss!" I yelled.

His commands, sending out jumpers in pursuit of the descending ship, rang in my ears, but I paid no attention to them. I leaped back into the compartment of the Han ship and knelt beside my Wilma. Her padded helmet had absorbed much of the blow, I thought; otherwise, her skull might have been fractured.

"Oh, my head!" she groaned, coming to as I lifted her gently in my arms and strode out in the open with her. "We must have won, dearest, did we?"

"We most certainly did," I reassured her. "All but one crashed and that one is drifting down toward the south. We've captured this one we're in intact. There was only one member of the crew aboard when we dove in."

Less than an hour afterward the Big Boss ordered the outfit to tune in ultrophones on three-twenty-three to pick up a translated broadcast of the Han intelligence office in Nu-Yok from the Susquanna station. It was in the form of a public warning and news item.

"This is Public Intelligence Office, Nu-Yok, broadcasting warning to navigators of private ships, and news of public interest. The squadron of seven ships which left Nu-Yok this morning to investigate the recent destruction of the GK-984 in the Wyoming Valley, has been destroyed by a series of mysterious explosions similar to those which wrecked the GK-984.

"The phones, viewplates, and all other signaling devices of five of the seven ships ceased operating suddenly at approximately the same moment, about seven-four-nine." (According to the Han system of reckoning time, seven and forty-nine one hundredths after midnight.) "After violent disturbances the location finders went out of operation. Electroactivity registers applied to the territory of the Wyoming Valley remain dead.

"The Intelligence Office has no indication of the kind of disaster which overtook the squadron except certain evidences of the explosive phenomena similar to those in the case of the GK-984, which recently went dead while beaming the valley in a systematic effort to wipe out the works and camps of the tribesmen. The Office considers, as obvious, the deduction that the tribesmen have developed a new, and as yet undetermined, technique of attack on airships, and has recommended to the Heaven-Born that immediate and unlimited authority to be given the Navigation Intelligence Division to make an investigation of this technique and develop a defense against it.

"In the meantime it urges that private navigators avoid this territory in particular, and in general hold as closely as possible to the official inter-city routes, which now are being patrolled by the entire force of the Military Office, which is beaming the routes generously to a width of ten miles. The Military office reports that it is at present considering no retaliatory raids against the tribesmen. With the Navigation Intelligence Division, it holds that unless further evidence of the nature of the disaster is developed in the near future, the public interest will be better served, and at smaller cost of life, by a scientific research than by attempts at retaliation, which may bring destruction on all ships engaging therein. So unless further evidence is developed, or the Heaven-Born orders to the contrary, the Military will hold to a defensive policy.

"Unofficial intimations from Lo-Tan are to the effect that the Heaven-Council has the matter under consideration.

"The Navigation Intelligence Office permits the broadcast of the following condensation of its detailed observations:

"The squadron proceeded to a position above the Wyoming Valley where the wreck of the GK-984 was known to be, from the record of its location finder before it went dead recently. There the bottom projectoscope relays of all ships registered the wreck of the GK-984. Teleprojectoscope views of the wreck and the bowl of the valley showed no evidence of the presence of tribesmen. Neither ship registers nor base registers showed any indication of electroactivity except from the squadron itself. On orders from the Base Squadron Commander, the LD-248, LK-745 and LG-25 scouted southward at 3,000 feet. The GK-43, GK-981 and GK-220 stood above at 2,500 feet, and the GK-18 landed to permit personal inspection of the wreck by the science committee. The party debarked, leaving one man on board in the control cabin. He set all projectoscopes at universal focus except RB-3" (this meant the third projectoscope from the bow of the ship, on the righthand side of the lower deck) "with which he followed the landing group as it walked around the wreck.

"The first abnormal phenomenon recorded by any of the instruments at Base was that relayed automatically from projectoscope RB-4 of the GK-18, which as the party disappeared from view in back of the wreck, recorded two green missiles of roughly cylindrical shape, projected from the wreckage into the landing compartment of the ship. At such close range these were not clearly defined, owing to the universal focus at which the projectoscope was set. The Base Captain of GK-18 at once ordered the man in the control room to investigate, and saw him leave the control room in compliance with this order. An instant later confused sounds reached the control-room electrophone, such as might be made by a man falling heavily, and footsteps reapproached the control room, a figure entering and leaving the control room hurriedly. The Base Captain now believes, and the stills of the photorecord support his belief, that this was not the crew member who had been left in the control room. Before the Base Captain could speak to him he left the room, nor was any response given to the attention signal the Captain flashed throughout the ship.

"At this point projectoscope RB-3 of the ship now out of focus control, dimly showed the landing party walking back toward the ship. RB-4 showed it more clearly. Then on both these instruments, a number of blinding explosives in rapid succession were seen and the electrophone relays registered terrific concussions; the ship's electronic apparatus and projectoscopes apparatus went dead.

"Reports of the other ships' Base Observers and Executives, backed by the photorecords, show the explosions as taking place in the midst of the landing party as it returned, evidently unsuspicious, to the ship. Then in rapid succession they indicate that terrific explosions occurred inside and outside the three ships standing above close to their *rep* ray generators, and all signals from these ships thereupon went dead.

"Of the three ships scouting to the south, the LD-248 suffered an identical fate, at the same moment. Its records add little to the knowledge of the disaster. But with LK-745 and the LG-25 it was different.

"The relay instruments of the LK-745 indicated the destruction by an explosion of the rear *rep* ray generator, and that the ship hung stern down for a short space, swinging like a pendulum. The forward viewplates and indicators did not cease functioning, but their records are chaotic, except for one projectoscope still, which shows the bowl of the valley, and the GK-981 falling, but no visible evidence of tribesmen. The control-room viewplate is also a chaotic record of the ship's crew tumbling and falling to the rear wall. Then the forward *rep* ray generator exploded, and all signals went dead.

"The fate of the LG-25 was somewhat similar, except that this ship hung nose down, and drifted on the wind southward as it slowly descended out of control.

"As its control room was shattered, verbal report from its Action Captain was precluded. The record of the interior rear viewplates shows members of the crew climbing toward the rear *rep* ray generator in an attempt to establish manual control of it, and increase the lift. The projectoscope relays, swinging in wide arcs, recorded little of value except at the ends of their swings. One of these, from a machine which happened to be set in telescopic focus, shows several views of great value in picturing the falls of the other ships, and all of the rear projectoscope records enable the reconstruction in detail of the pendulum and torsional movements of the ship, and its sag toward the earth. But none of the views showing the forest below contain any indication of tribesmen's presence. A final explosion put this ship out of commission at a height of 1,000 feet, and at a point four miles S. by E. of the center of the valley."

The message ended with a repetition of the warning to other airmen to avoid the valley.

# — IV —

After receiving this report, and reassurances of support from the Big Bosses of the neighboring Gangs, Ciardi determined to reestablish the Wyoming Valley community.

A careful survey of the territory showed that it was only the northern sections and slopes that had been "beamed" by the first Han ship.

The synthetic fabrics plant had been partially wiped out, though the lower levels underground had not been reached by the *dis* ray. The forest screen above, however, had been annihilated, and it was determined to abandon it, after removing all usable machinery and evidences of the processes that might be of interest to the Han scientists, should they return to the valley in the future.

The ammunition plant, and the rocketship plant, which had just been about to start operation at the time of the raid, were intact, as were the other important plants.

Ciardi brought the Big Camboss up from the Susquanna Works, and laid out new camp locations, scattering them farther to the south, and avoiding ground which had been seared by the Han beams and the immediate locations of the Han wrecks.

During this period, a sharp check was kept upon Han messages, for the phone plant had been one of the first to be put in operation, and when it became evident that the Hans did not intend any immediate reprisals, the entire membership of the community was summoned back, and normal life was resumed.

Wilma and I had been married the day after the destruction of the ships, and spent this intervening period in a delightful honeymoon, camping high in the mountains. On our return, we had a camp of our own, of course. We were assigned to location 1017. And as might be expected, we had a great deal of banter over which one of us was Camp Boss. The title stood after my name on the Big Boss' records, and those of the Big Camboss, of course, but Wilma airily held that this meant nothing at all—and generally succeeded in making me admit it whenever she chose.

I found myself a full-fledged member of the Gang now, for I had elected to search no farther for a permanent alliance, much as I would have liked to familiarize myself with this 25th Century life in other sections of the country. The Wyomings had a high morale, and had prospered under the rule of Big Boss Ciardi for many years. But many of the gangs, I found, were badly organized, lacked strong hands in authority, and were rife with intrigue. On the whole, I thought I would be wise to stay with a group which had already proved its friendliness, and in which I seemed to have prospects of advancement. Under these modern social and economic conditions, the kind of individual freedom to which I had been accustomed in the 20th Century was impossible.

This entire modern life, it appeared to me, judging from my ancient viewpoint, was organized along what I called "political" lines. And in this connection, it amused me to notice how universal had become the use of the word "boss." There was as little formality in his relations with his followers as there was in the case of the 20th Century political boss, and the same high respect paid him by his followers as well as the same high consideration by him of their interest. He was just as much of an autocrat, and just as much dependent upon the general popularity of his actions for the ability to maintain his autocracy.

The sub-boss who could not command the loyalty of his followers was as quickly deposed, either by them or by his superiors, as the ancient ward leader of the 20th Century who lost control of his votes.

Our victory over the seven Han ships had set the country ablaze. The secret had been carefully communicated to the other gangs, and the country was agog from one end to the other. There was feverish activity in the ammunition plants, and the hunting of stray Han ships became an enthusiastic sport. The results were disastrous to our hereditary enemies.

From the Pacific Coast came the report of a great Transpacific liner of 75,000 tons' "lift" being brought to earth from a position of invisibility above the clouds. A dozen Sacramentos had caught the hazy outlines of its *rep* rays approaching them, head-on, in the twilight, like ghostly pillars reaching into the sky. They had fired rockets into it with ease, whereas they would have had difficulty in hitting it if it had been moving at right angles to their position. They got one *rep* ray. The other was not strong enough to hold it up. It floated to earth, nose down, and since it was unarmed and unarmored, they had no difficulty in shooting it to pieces and massacring its crew and passengers.

From the Jersey Beaches we received news of the destruction of a Nu-Yok–A-lan-a liner. The sand-snippers, practically invisible in their sand colored clothing, and half buried along the beaches, lay in wait for days, risking the play of *dis* beams along the route, and finally registering four hits within a week. The Hans discontinued their service along this route, and as evidence that they were badly shaken by our success, sent no raiders down the Beaches.

It was a few weeks later that Big Boss Ciardi sent for me.

"Tony," he said, "there are two things I want to talk to you about. One of them will become public property in a few days, I think. We aren't going to get any more Han ships by shooting up their *rep* rays unless we use much larger rockets. They are wise to us now. They're putting armor of great thickness in the hulls of their ships below the *rep* ray machines. Near Bah-Flo this morning a party of Eries shot one without success. The explosions staggered her, but did not penetrate. As near as we can gather from their reports, their laboratories have developed a new alloy of great tensile strength and elasticity which nevertheless lets the *rep* rays through like a sieve. Our reports indicate that the Eries' rockets bounced off harmlessly. Most of the party was wiped out as the *dis* rays went into action on them.

"This is going to mean real business for all of the gangs before long. The Big Bosses have just held a national ultrophone council. It was decided that America must organize on a national basis. The first move is to develop sectional organization by Zones. I have been made Superboss of the Midatlantic Zone.

"We're in for it now. The Hans are sure to launch reprisal expeditions, and we've got to keep them away from our camps and plants. I'm thinking of developing a permanent field force, along the lines of the regular armies of the 20th Century you told me about. Its business will be twofold: to carry the warfare as much as possible to the Hans and to serve as a decoy, to keep their attention from our plants. I'm going to need your help in this.

"The other thing I wanted to talk to you about is this: Amazing and impossible as it seems, there is a group, or perhaps an entire gang, somewhere among us, that is betraying us to the Hans. It may be the Bad Bloods, or it may be one of those gangs who live near one of the Han cities. You know, a hundred and fifteen or twenty years ago there were certain of these people's ancestors who mated with the Hans, sometimes serving them as slaves, in the days before they brought all their service machinery to perfection.

"There is such a gang, called the Nagras, up near Bah-flo, and another in Mid-Jersey that men call the Pineys. But I hardly suspect the Pineys. There is little intelligence among them. They wouldn't have the information to give the Hans, nor would they be capable of imparting it. They're absolute savages."

"Just what evidence is there that anybody has been clearing information to the Hans?" I asked.

"Well," he replied, "first of all there was that raid upon us. That first Han ship knew the location of our plants exactly. You remember it floated directly into position above the valley and began a systematic beaming. Then, the Hans quite obviously have learned that we are picking up their electrophone waves, for they've gone back to their old, but extremely accurate, system of directional control. But we've been getting them for the past week by installing automatic rebroadcast units along the scar paths. This is what we call those strips of country directly under the regular ship routes of the Hans, who as a matter of precaution frequently blast them with their *dis* beams to prevent the growth of foliage which might give shelter to us. But they've been beaming those paths so hard, it looks as though they even had information of this strategy. And in addition, they've been using code. Finally, we've picked up three of their messages in which they discuss, with some nervousness, the existence of our 'mysterious' ultrophone."

"But they still have no knowledge of the nature and control of ultronic activity?" I asked.

"No," said the Big Boss thoughtfully, "they don't seem to have a bit of information about it."

"Then it's quite clear," I ventured, "that whoever is 'clearing' us to them is doing it piecemeal. It sounds like a bit of occasional barter, rather than an out and out alliance. They're holding back as much information as possible for future bartering, perhaps."

"Yes," Ciardi said, "and it isn't information the Hans are giving in return, but some form of goods, or privilege. The trick would be to locate the goods. I guess I'll have to make a personal trip around among the Big Bosses."

This conversation set me thinking. All of the Han electrophone inter-communication had been an open record to the Americans for a good many years, and the Hans were just finding it out. For centuries they had not regarded us as any sort of a menace. Unquestionably it had never occurred to them to secrete their own records. Somewhere in Nu-Yok or Bah-Flo, or possibly in Lo-Tan itself, the record of this traitorous transaction would be more or less openly filed. If we could only get at it! I wondered if a raid might not be possible.

David Berg and I talked it over with our Han-affairs Boss and his experts. There ensued several days of research, in which the Han records of the entire decade were scanned and analyzed. In the end they picked out a mass of detail, and fitted it together into a very definite picture of the great central filing office of the Hans in Nu-Yok, where the entire mass of official records was kept, constantly available for instant projectoscoping to any of the city's offices, and of the system by which the information was filed.

The attempt began to look feasible, though Ciardi instantly turned the idea down when I first presented it to him. It was unthinkable, he said. Sheer suicide. But in the end I persuaded him.

"I will need," I said, "Erhart, who is thoroughly familiar with the Han library system; Joyce, who for years has specialized on their military offices; Bill Fabre, the ray specialist, and the best swooper pilot we have." *Swoopers* are one-man and two-man ships, developed by the Americans, with skeleton backbones of inertron (during the war painted green for invisibility against the green forests below) and "bellies" of clear ultron.

"That will be Mort Gibbons," said Ciardi. "We've only got three swoopers left, Tony, but I'll risk one of them if you and the others will voluntarily risk your existences. But mind, I won't urge or order one of you to go. I'll spread the word to every Plant Boss at once to give you anything and everything you need in the way of equipment."

When I told Wilma of the plan, I expected her to raise violent and tearful objections, but she didn't. She was made of far sterner stuff than the women of the 20th Century. Not that she couldn't weep as copiously or be just as whimsical on occasion; but she wouldn't weep for the same reasons.

She just gave me an unfathomable look, in which there seemed to be a bit of pride, and asked eagerly for the details. I confess I was somewhat disappointed that she could so courageously risk my loss.

We were ready to slide off at dawn the next morning. I had kissed Wilma good-bye at our camp, and after a final conference over our plans, we boarded our craft and gently glided away over the tree tops on a course, which, after crossing three routes of the Han ships, would take us out over the Atlantic, off the Jersey coast, whence we would come up on Nu-Yok from the ocean.

Twice we had to nose down and lie motionless on the ground near a route while Han ships passed. Those were tense moments. Had the green back of our ship been observed, we would have been disintegrated in a second. But it wasn't.

Once over the water, however, we climbed in a great spiral, ten miles in diameter, until our altimeter registered ten miles. Here Gibbons shut off his rocket motor, and we floated, far above the level of the Atlantic liners, whose course was well to the north of us anyhow, and waited for nightfall.

Then Gibbons turned from his control long enough to grin at me.

"I have a surprise for you, Tony," he said throwing back the lid of what I had supposed was a big supply case. And with a sigh of relief, Wilma stepped out of the case.

"If you go into zero" (a common expression of the day for being annihilated by the disintegrator ray), "you don't think I'm going to let you go alone, do you, Tony? I couldn't believe my ears last night when you spoke of going without me, until I realized that you are still five hundred years behind the times in lots of ways. Don't you know, dear heart, that you offered me the greatest insult a husband could give a wife? You didn't, of course."

The others, it seemed, had all been in on the secret.

At nightfall, we maneuvered to a position directly above the city. This took some time and calculation on the part of Bill Fabre, who explained to me that he had to determine our point by ultronic bearings. The slightest resort to an electronic instrument, he feared, might be detected by our enemies' locaters. In fact, we did not dare bring our swooper any lower than five miles for fear that its capacity might be reflected in their instruments.

Finally, however, he succeeded in locating above the central tower of the city.

"If my calculations are as much as ten feet off," he remarked with confidence, "I'll eat the tower. Now the rest is up to you, Mort. See what you can do to hold her steady. No—here, watch this indicator—the red beam, not the green one. See—if you keep it exactly centered on the needle, you're O.K. The width of the beam represents seventeen feet. The tower platform is fifty feet square, so we've got a good margin to work on."

For several moments we watched as Gibbons bent over his levers, constantly adjusting them with deft touches of his fingers. After a bit of wavering, the beam remained centered on the needle.

"Now," I said, "let's drop."

I opened the trap and looked down, but quickly shut it again when I felt the air rushing out of the ship into the rarefied atmosphere in a torrent. Gibbons literally yelled a protest from his instrument board.

"I forgot," I mumbled. "Silly of me. Of course, we'll have to drop out of the compartment."

The compartment to which I referred was similar to those in some of the 20th Century submarines. We all entered it. There was barely room for us to stand shoulder to shoulder. With some struggles, we got into our special air helmets and adjusted the pressure. At our signal, Gibbons exhausted the air in the compartment, pumping it into the body of the ship, and as the little signal light flashed, Wilma threw open the hatch.

Setting the ultron wire reel, I climbed through, and began to slide down gently.

We all had our belts on, of course, adjusted to a weight balance of but a few ounces. And the five-mile reel of ultron wire that was to be our guide, was of gossamer fineness, though, anyway, I believe it would have lifted the full weight of the five of us, so strong and tough was this invisible metal. As an extra precaution, since the wire was of the purest metal, and therefore totally invisible, even in daylight, we all had our belts hooked on small rings that slid down the wire.

I went down with the end of the wire. Wilma followed a few feet above me, then Fabre, Erhart, and Joyce. Gibbons, of course, stayed behind to hold the ship in position and control the paying out of the line. We all had our ultro-phones in place inside our air helmets, and so could converse with one another and with Gibbons. But at Wilma's suggestion, although we would have liked to let the Big Boss listen in, we kept them adjusted to short-range work, for fear that those who had been clearing with the Hans, and against whom we were on a raid for evidence, might also pick up our conversation. We had no fear that the Hans would hear us. In fact, we had the added advantage that, even after we landed, we could converse freely without danger of their hearing our voices through our air helmets.

For a while I could see nothing below but utter darkness. Then I realized, from the feel of the air as much as from anything, that we were sinking through a cloud layer. We passed through two more cloud layers before anything was visible to us.

Then there came under my gaze, about two miles below, one of the most beautiful sights I have ever seen: the soft, yet brilliant, radiance of the great Han city of Nu-Yok. Every foot of its structural members seemed to glow with a wonderful incandescence, tower piled upon tower, and all built on the vast base-mass of the city, which, so I had been told, sheered upward from the surface of the rivers to a height of 728 levels.

The city, I noticed with some surprise, did not cover anything like the same area as the New York of the 20th Century. It occupied, as a matter of fact, only the lower half of Manhattan Island, with one section straddling the East River and spreading out sufficiently over what once had been Brooklyn, to provide berths for the great liners and other aircraft.

Straight beneath my feet was a tiny dark patch. It seemed the only spot in the entire city that was not aflame with radiance. This was the central tower, in the top floors of which were housed the vast library of record files and the main projectoscope plant.

"You can shoot the wire now," I ultrophoned Gibbons, and let go the little weighted knob. It dropped like a plummet, and we followed with considerable speed, but braking our descent with gloved hands sufficiently to see whether the knob, on which a faint light glowed as a signal for ourselves, might be observed by any Han guard or night prowler. Apparently it was not, and we again shot down with accelerated speed.

We landed on the roof of the tower without any mishap, and fortunately for our plan, in darkness. Since there was nothing above it on which it would have been worth while to shed illumination, or from which there was any need to observe it, the Hans had neglected to light the tower roof, or indeed to occupy it at all. This was the reason we had selected it as our landing place.

As soon as Gibbons had our word, he extinguished the knob light, and the knob, as well as the wire, became totally invisible. At our ultrophoned word, he would light it again.

"No gun play now," I warned. "Swords only, and then only if absolutely necessary."

Closely bunched, and treading as lightly as only inertron-belted people could, we made our way cautiously through a door and down an inclined plane to the floor below, where Joyce and Erhart assured us the military offices were located.

Twice Fabre cautioned us to stop as we were about to pass in front of mirror-like "windows" in the passage wall, and flattening ourselves to the floor, we crawled past them.

"Projectoscopes" he said. "Probably on automatic record only, at this time of night. Still, we don't want to leave any records for them to study after we're gone."

"Were you ever here before?" I asked.

"No," he replied, "but I haven't been studying their electrophone communications for seven years without being able to recognize these machines when I run across them."

— V —

So far we had not laid eyes on a Han. The tower seemed deserted. Erhart and Joyce, however, assured me that there would be at least one man on "duty" in the military offices, though he would probably be asleep, and two or three in the library proper and the projectoscope plant.

"We've got to put them out of commission," I said. "Did you bring the 'dope' cans, Wilma?"

"Yes," she said, "two for each. Here," and she distributed them.

We were now two levels below the roof, and at the point where we were to separate.

I did not want to let Wilma out of my sight, but it was necessary.

According to our plan, Fabre, was to make his way to the projectoscope plant, Erhart and I to the library, and Wilma and Joyce to the military office.

Erhart and I traversed a long corridor, and paused at the great arched doorway of the library. Cautiously we peered in. Seated at three great switchboards were library operatives. Occasionally one of them would reach lazily for a lever, or sleepily push a button, as little numbered lights winked on and off. They were answering calls for electrograph and viewplate records on all sorts of subjects from all sections of the city.

I apprised my companions of the situation.

"Better wait a bit," Erhart added. "The calls will lessen shortly."

Wilma reported an officer in the military office sound sleep.

"Give him the can, then," I said.

Fabre was to do nothing more than keep watch in the projectoscope plant, and a few moments later he reported himself well concealed, with a splendid view of the floor.

"I think we can take a chance now," Erhart said to me, and at my nod, he opened the lid of his dope can. Of course, the fumes did not affect us through our helmets. They were absolutely without odor or visibility, and in a few seconds the librarians were unconscious. We stepped into the room.

There ensued considerable cautious observation and experiment on the part of Joyce, working from the military office, and Erhart in the library; while Wilma and I, with drawn swords and sharply attuned microphones, stood guard, and occasionally patrolled nearby corridors.

"I hear something approaching," Wilma said after a bit, with excitement in her voice. "It's a soft, gliding sound."

"That's an elevator somewhere," Fabre cut in from the projectoscope floor. "Can you locate it? I can't hear it."

"It's to the east of me," she replied.

"And to my west," said I, faintly catching it. "It's between us, Wilma, and nearer you than me. Be careful. Have you got any information yet, Erhart—Joyce?"

"Getting it now," one of them replied. "Give us two minutes more."

"Keep at it then," I said. "We'll guard."

The soft, gliding sound ceased.

"I think it's very close to me," Wilma almost whispered. "Come closer, Tony. I have a feeling something is going to happen. I've never known my nerves to get taut like this without reason."

In some alarm, I launched myself down the corridor in a great leap toward the intersection whence I knew I could see her.

In the middle of my leap my ultrophone registered her gasp of alarm. The next instant I glided to a stop at the intersection to see Wilma backing toward the door of the military office, her sword red with blood, and an inert form on the corridor floor. Two other Hans were circling to either side of her with wicked-looking knives, while a third, evidently a high officer judging by the resplendence of his garb, tugged desperately to get an electrophone instrument out of a bulky pocket. If he ever gave the alarm, there was no telling what might happen to us.

I was at least seventy feet away, but I crouched low and sprang with every bit of strength in my legs. It would be more correct to say that I dived, for I reached the fellow head on, with no attempt to draw my legs beneath me.

Some instinct must have warned him, for he turned suddenly as I hurtled close to him. But by this time I had sunk close to the floor, and had stiffened myself rigidly, lest a dragging knee or foot might just prevent my reaching him. I brought my blade upward and over. It was a vicious slash that laid him open, bisecting him from groin to chin, and his body toppled down on me as I slid to a tangled stop.

The other two, startled, turned. Wilma leaped at one and struck him down with a side slash. I looked up at this instant, and the dazed fear on his face at the length of her leap, registered vividly. The Hans knew nothing of our inertron belts, it seemed, and these leaps and dives of ours filled them with terror.

As I rose to my feet, a gory mess, Wilma, with a poise and speed which I found time to admire even in this crisis, again leaped. This time she dove head first as I had done, and with a beautifully executed thrust, ran the last Han through the throat.

Uncertainly, she scrambled to her feet, staggered queerly, and then sank gently prone on the corridor. She had fainted.

At this juncture, Erhart and Joyce reported with elation that they had the record we wanted.

"Back to the roof, everybody!" I ordered, as I picked Wilma up in my arms. With her inertron belt, she felt as light as a feather.

Joyce joined me at once from the military office and at the intersection of the corridor, we came upon Erhart waiting for us. Fabre, however, was not in evidence.

"Where are you, Fabre?" I called.

"Go ahead," he replied. "I'll be with you on the roof at once."

We came out in the open without any further mishap, and I instructed Gibbons in the ship to light the knob on the end of the ultron wire. It flashed dully a few feet away from us. Just how he had maneuvered the ship to keep our end of the line in position, without its swinging in a tremendous arc, I have never been able to understand. Had not the night been an unusually still one, he could not have checked the initial pendulum-like movements. As it was, there was considerable air current at certain of the levels, and in different directions too. But Gibbons was an expert of rare ability and sensitivity in the handling of a rocket ship, and he managed, with the aid of his delicate instruments, to sense the drifts almost before they affected the fine ultron wire, and to neutralize them with little shifts in the position of the ship.

Erhart and Joyce fastened their rings to the wire, and I hooked my own and Wilma's on, too. But on looking around, I found that Fabre was still missing.

"Fabre, come!" I called. "We're waiting."

"Coming!" he replied, and indeed, at that instant, his figure appeared up the ramp. He chuckled as he fastened his ring to the wire and said something about a little surprise he had left for the Hans.

"Don't reel in the wire more than a few hundred feet," I instructed Gibbons. "It will take too long to wind it in. We'll float up, and when we're aboard, we can drop it."

In order to float up, we had to dispense with a pound or two of weight apiece. We hurled our swords from us, and kicked off our shoes as Gibbons reeled up the line a bit, and then letting go of the wire, began to hum upward on our rings with increasing velocity.

The rush of air brought Wilma to, and I hastily explained to her that we had been successful. Receding far below us now, I could see our dully shining knob swinging to and fro in an ever-widening arc, as it crossed and recrossed the black square of the tower roof. As an extra precaution, I ordered Gibbons to shut off the light, and to show one from the belly of the ship, for so great was our speed now, that I began to fear we would have difficulty in checking ourselves. We were literally falling upward, and with terrific acceleration.

Fortunately, we had several minutes in which to solve this difficulty, which none of us, strangely enough, had foreseen. It was Gibbons who found the answer.

"You'll be all right if all of you grab the wire tight when I give the word," he said. "First I'll start reeling it in at full speed. You won't get much of a jar, and then I'll decrease its speed again gradually, and its weight will hold you back. Are you ready? One—two—three!"

We all grabbed tightly with our gloved hands as he gave the word. We must have been rising a good bit faster than he figured, however, for it wrenched our arms considerably, and the maneuver set up a sickening pendulum motion.

For a while all we could do was swing there in an arc that may have been a quarter of a mile across, about three and a half miles above the city, and still more than a mile from our ship.

Gibbons skillfully took up the slack as our momentum pulled up the line. Then at last we had ourselves under control again, and continued our upward journey, checking our speed somewhat with our gloves.

There was not one of us who did not breathe a big sigh of relief when we scrambled through the hatch safely into the ship again, cast off the ultron line and slammed the trap shut.

Then we discussed the information that Erhart and Joyce had between them extracted from the Han records, and the advisability of ultrophoning Ciardi at once.

The traitors were, it seemed, a gang located a few miles north of Nu-Yok on the wooded banks of the Hudson, the Sinsings. They had exchanged scraps of information to the Hans in return for several old *rep* ray machines, and the privilege of tuning in on the Han electronic power broadcast for their operation, provided their ships agreed to subject themselves to the orders of the Han traffic office, while aloft.

The rest wanted to ultrophone their news at once, since there was always danger that we might never get back to the gang with it.

I objected, however. The Sinsings would be likely to pick up our message. Even if we used the directional projector, they might have scouts out to the west and south in the big inter-gang stretches of country. They would flee to Nu-Yok and escape the punishment they merited. It seemed to be vitally important that they should not, for the sake of example to other weak groups among the gangs, as well as to prevent a crisis in which they might clear more vital information to the enemy.

"Out to sea again," I ordered Gibbons. "They'll be less likely to look for us in that direction."

"Easy, Boss, easy," he replied. "Wait until we get up a mile or two more. They must have discovered evidences of our raid by now, and their *dis* ray wall may go in operation any moment."

Even as he spoke, the ship lurched downward and to one side.

"There it is!" he shouted. "Hang on, everybody. We're going to nose straight up!" And he flipped the rocket motor control wide open.

Looking through one of the rear ports, I could see a nebulous, luminous ring, and on all sides the atmosphere took on a faint iridescence.

We were almost over the destructive range of the *dis* ray wall, a hollow cylinder of annihilation shooting upward from a solid ring of generators surrounding the city. It was the main defense system of the Hans, which had never been used except in periodic tests. They may or may not have suspected that an American rocket ship was within the cylinder; probably they had turned on their generators more as a precaution to prevent any reaching a position above the city.

But even at our present great height, we were in great danger. It was a question how much we might have been harmed by the rays themselves, for their effective range was not much more than seven or eight miles. The greater danger lay in the terrific downward rush of air within the cylinder to replace that which was being burned into nothingness by the continual play of the disintegrators. The air fell into the cylinder with the force of a gale. It would be rushing toward the wall from the outside with terrific force also, but naturally, the effect was intensified on the interior.

Out ship vibrated and trembled. We had only one chance of escape—to fight our way well above the current. To drift down with it meant ultimately, and inevitably, to be sucked into the annihilating wall at some lower level.

But very gradually and jerkily our upward movement, as shown on the indicators, began to increase; and after an hour of desperate struggle we were free of the maelstrom and into the rarefied upper levels. The terror beneath us was now invisible through several layers of cloud formations.

Gibbons brought the ship back to an even keel, and drove her eastward into one of the most brilliantly gorgeous sunrises I have ever seen.

We described a great circle to the south and west, in a long easy dive, for he had cut out his rocket motors to save them as much as possible. We had drawn terrifically on their fuel reserves in our battle with the elements. For the moment, the atmosphere below cleared, and we could see the Jersey coast far beneath, like a great map.

"We're not through yet," remarked Gibbons suddenly, pointing at his periscope, and adjusting it to telescopic focus. "A Han ship, and a 'drop ship' at that—and he's seen us. If he whips that beam of his on us, we're done."

I gazed, fascinated, at the viewplate. What I saw was a cigar-shaped ship not dissimilar to our own in design, and from the proportional size of its ports, of about the same size as our swoopers. We learned later that they carried crews, for the most part of not more than three or four men. They had streamline hulls and tails that embodied universal-jointed double fish-tail rudders. In operation they rose to great heights on their powerful *rep* rays, then gathered speed either by a straight nose dive, or an inclined dive in which they sometimes used the *rep* ray slanted at a sharp angle. He was already above us, though several miles to the north. He could, of course, try to get on our tail and spear us with his beam as he dropped at us from a great height.

Suddenly his beam blazed forth in a blinding flash, whipping downward slowly to our right. He went through a peculiar corkscrew-like evolution, evidently maneuvering to bring his beam to bear on us with a spiral motion.

Gibbons instantly sent our ship into a series of evolutions that must have looked like those of a frightened hen. Alternately, he used the forward and the reverse rocket blasts, and in varying degree. We fluttered, we shot suddenly to right and left, and dropped like a plummet in uncertain movements. But all the time the Han scout dropped toward us, determinedly whipping the air around us with his beam. Once it sliced across beneath us, not more than a hundred feet, and we dropped with a jar into the pocket formed by the destruction of the air.

He had dropped to within a mile of us, and was coming with the speed of a projectile, when the end came. Gibbons always swore it was sheer luck. Maybe it was, but I like pilots who are lucky that way.

In the midst of a dizzy, fluttering maneuver of our own, with the Han ship enlarging to our gaze with terrifying rapidity, and its beam slowly slicing toward us in what looked like certain destruction within the second, I saw Gibbons' fingers flick at the lever of his rocket gun and a split second later the Han ship flew apart like a clay pigeon.

We staggered, and fluttered crazily for several moments while Gibbons struggled to bring our ship into balance, and a section of about four square feet in the side of the ship near the stern slowly crumbled like rusted metal. His beam actually had touched us, but our explosive rocket had got him a thousandth of a second sooner.

Part of our rudder had been annihilated, and our motor damaged. But we were able to swoop gently back across Jersey, fortunately crossing the ship lanes without sighting any more Han craft, and finally settling to rest in the little glade beneath the trees, near Ciardi's camp.

## — VI —

We had ultrophoned our arrival and the Big Boss himself, surrounded by the Council, was on hand to welcome us and learn our news. In turn we were informed that during the night a band of raiding Bad Bloods, disguised under the insignia of the Altoonas, a gang some distance to the west of us—had destroyed several of our camps before our people had rallied and driven them off. Their purpose, evidently, had been to embroil us with the Altoonas, but fortunately, one of our exchanges recognized the Bad Blood leader, who had been slain.

The Big Boss had mobilized the full raiding force of the Gang, and was on the point of heading an expedition for the extermination of the Bad Bloods.

I looked around the grim circle of the sub-bosses, and realized that the fate of America, at this moment, lay in their hands. Their temper demanded the immediate expenditure of our full effort in revenging ourselves for this raid. But the strategic exigencies, to my mind, quite clearly demanded the instant and absolute extermination of the Sinsings. It might be only a matter of hours, for all we knew, before they would barter clues to the American ultronic secrets to the Hans.

"How large a force have we?" I asked Ciardi.

"Every man and maid who can be spared," he replied. "That gives us seven hundred married and unmarried men, and three hundred girls, more than the entire Bad Blood Gang. Everyone is equipped with belts, ultrophones, rocket guns and swords, and all fighting mad."

I meditated how I might put the matter to these determined men.

Finally I began to speak. I do not remember to this day just what I said. I talked calmly, with due regard over the information we had collected, point by point, building my case logically, and painting a lurid picture of the danger impending in that half-alliance between the Sinsings and the Hans of Nu-Yok. I became impassioned, culminating, I believe, with a vow to proceed single-handed against the hereditary enemies of our race, "if the Wyomings were blindly set on placing a gang feud ahead of the hopes of all America."

As I concluded, a great calm came over me, as of one detached. But it was Ciardi who sensed the temper of the Council more quickly than I did. He arose from the tree trunk on which he had been sitting.

"That settles it," he said, looking around the ring. "I have felt this thing coming on for some time now. I'm sure the Council agrees with me that there is among us a man more capable than I to boss the Wyoming Gang, despite his having had all too short a time in which to familiarize himself with our modern ways and facilities. Whatever I can do to support his effective leadership, at any cost, I pledge myself to do."

As he concluded, he advanced to where I stood, and taking from his head the green-crested helmet that constituted his badge of office, to my surprise he placed it in my mechanically extended hand.

The roar of approval that went up from the Council members left me dazed. Somebody ultrophoned the news to the rest of the Gang, and even though the earflaps of my helmet were turned up, I could hear the cheers with which my invisible followers greeted me, from near and distant hillsides, camps and plants. My first move was to make sure that the Phone Boss, in communicating this news to the members of the Gang, had not re-broadcast my talk nor mentioned my plan of shifting the attack from the Bad Bloods to the Sinsings. I was relieved by his assurance that he had not, so I pledged the Council and my companions to secrecy, and allowed it to be believed that we were about to take to the air and the trees against the Bad Bloods.

That outfit must have been badly scared, the way they were "burning" the ether with ultrophone alibis and propaganda for the benefit of the more distant gangs. It was their old game, these appeals to the spirit of brotherhood, addressed to gangs too far away to have had the sort of experience with them that had fallen to our lot.

I chuckled. Here was another good reason for the shift in my plans. Were we actually to undertake the extermination of the Bad Bloods at once it would have been a hard job to convince some of the gangs that we had not been precipitate and unjustified.

But the extermination of the Sinsings would be another thing. In the first place, there would be no warning of our action until it was all over, I hoped. In the second place, we would have indisputable proof, in the form of their *rep* ray ships and other paraphernalia, of their traffic with the Hans; and the state of American bias, at the time of which I write, held trafficking with the Hans a far more heinous thing than the most vicious gang feud.

I called an executive session of the Council at once. I wanted to inventory our military resources.

I created a new office on the spot, that of "Control Boss," and appointed Ned Sidor to the post, turning over his former responsibility as Plant Boss to his assistant. I needed someone, I felt, to tie in the records of the various functional activities of the campaign, and take over from me the task of keeping the records of them up to the minute.

I received reports from the bosses of the ultrophone unit, and those of food, transportation, fighting gear, chemistry, electronic activity and electrophone intelligence, ultroscopes, air patrol and contact guard.

My ideas for the campaign, of course, were somewhat tinged with my 20th Century experience, and I found myself faced with the task of working out a staff organization that was a composite of the best and most easily applied principles of business and military efficiency, as I knew them from the viewpoint of immediate practicality.

What I wanted was an organization that would be specialized, functionally, not as that indicated above, but from the angles of: intelligence as to the Sinsing activities; intelligence as to Han activities; perfection of communication with my own units; cooperation of field command; and perfect mobilization of emergency supplies and resources.

It took several hours of hard work with the Council to map out the plan. First we assigned functional experts and equipment to each "Division" in accordance with its needs. Then these in turn were reassigned by the new Division Bosses to the Field Commands as needed, or as Independent or Headquarters Units. The two intelligence divisions were named A and M, "A" indicating that one specialized in the American enemy and the other in the Mongolians.

The division in charge of our own communications, the assignment of ultrophone frequencies and strengths, and the maintenance of operators and equipment, I called "Communications."

I named Dave Berg to the post of Field Boss, in charge of the main or undetached fighting units, and to the Resources Division, I assigned all responsibility for what few aircraft we had; and all transportation and supply problems, I assigned to "Resources." The functional bosses stayed with this division.

We finally completed our organization with the assignment of liaison representatives among the various divisions as needed.

Thus I had a "Headquarters Staff" composed of the Division Bosses who reported directly to Ned Sidor as Control Boss, or to Wilma as my personal assistant. And each of the Division Bosses had a small staff of his own.

In the final summing up of our personnel and resources, I found we had roughly a thousand "troops," of whom some three hundred and fifty were, in what I called the Service Divisions, the rest being in Dave Berg's Field Division. This latter number, however, was cut down somewhat by the assignment of numerous small units to detached service. Altogether, the actual available fighting force, I figured, would number about five hundred by the time we actually went into action.

We had only six small swoopers, but I had a plan in mind, as the result of our little raid on Nu-Yok, that would make this sufficient, since the reserves of inertron blocks were larger than I expected to find them. The Resources Division, by packing its supply cases a bit tight, or by slipping in extra blocks of inertron, was able to reduce each to a weight of a few ounces. These easily could be floated and towed by the swoopers in any quantity. Hitched to ultron lines, it would be a virtual impossibility for them to break loose.

The entire personnel, of course, was supplied with jumpers, and if each man and girl was careful to adjust balances properly, the entire number could also be towed along through the air, grasping wires of ultron, swinging below the swoopers, or stringing out behind them.

There would be nothing tiring about this, because the strain would be no greater than that of carrying a one or two pound weight in the hand, except for air friction at high speeds. But to make doubly sure that we should lose none of our personnel, I gave strict orders that the belts and tow lines should be equipped with rings and hooks.

So great was the efficiency of the fundamental organization and discipline of the Gang, that we got under way at nightfall.

One by one the swoopers eased into the air, each followed by its long train or "kite-tail" of humanity and supply cases hanging lightly from its tow line. For convenience, the tow lines were made of an alloy of ultron which, unlike the metal itself, is visible.

At first these "tails" hung downward, but as the ships swung into formation and headed eastward toward the Bad Blood territory, gathering speed, they began to string out behind. And swinging low from each ship on heavily weighted lines, ultroscope, ultrophone, and straight-vision observers keenly scanned the countryside, while intelligence men in the swoopers above bent over their instrument boards and viewplates.

Leaving Control Boss Ned Sidor temporarily in charge of affairs, Wilma and I dropped a weighted line from our ship, and slid down about halfway to the under lookouts—that is to say, about a thousand feet. The sensation of floating swiftly through the air like this, in the absolute security of one's confidence in the inertron belt, was one of never-ending delight to me.

We reascended into the swooper as the expedition approached the territory of the Bad Bloods, and directed the preparations for the Bombardment. It was part of my plan to appear to carry out the attack as originally planned.

About fifteen miles from their camps, our ships came to a halt and maintained their positions for a while with the idling blasts of their rocket motors, to give the ultroscope operators a chance to make a thorough examination of the territory below us. It was vital that this next step in our program should be carried out with all secrecy.

At length they reported the ground below us entirely clear of any appearance of human occupation, and a gun unit of long-range specialists was lowered with a dozen rocket guns, equipped with special automatic devices that the Resources Division had developed at my request a few hours before our departure. These were aiming and timing devices. After calculating the range, elevation and rocket charges carefully, the guns were left, concealed in a ravine, and the men were hauled up into the ship again. At the predetermined hour, those unmanned rocket guns would begin automatically to bombard the Bad Bloods' hillsides, shifting their aim and elevation slightly with each shot, as did many of our artillery pieces in the First World War.

In the meantime, we turned south about twenty miles, and grounded, waiting for the bombardment to begin before we attempted to sneak across the Han ship lane. I was relying for security on the distraction that the bombardment might furnish the Han observers.

It was tense work waiting, but the affair went through as planned, our squadron drifting across the route high enough to enable the ships' tails of troops and supply cases to clear the ground.

In crossing the second ship route, out along the Beaches of Jersey, we were not so successful in escaping observation. A Han ship came speeding along at a very low elevation. We caught it on our electronic location and direction finders, and also located it with our ultroscopes; but it came so fast and so low that I thought it best to remain where we had grounded the second time, and lie quiet, rather than get under way and cross in front of it.

The point was this. While the Hans had no such devices as our ultronoscopes, with which we could see in the dark (within certain limitations of course), and their electronic instruments would be virtually useless in uncovering our presence, since all but natural electronic activities were carefully eliminated from our apparatus, except electrophone receivers (which are not easily spotted), the Hans did have some very highly sensitive sound devices which operated with great efficiency in calm weather, so far as sounds emanating from the air were concerned. But the "ground roar" greatly confused their use of these instruments in the location of specific sounds floating up from the surface of the earth.

This ship must have caught some slight noise of ours, however, in its sensitive instruments, for we heard its electronic devices go into play, and picked up the routine report of the noise to its Base Ship Commander. But from the nature of the conversation, I judged they had not identified it, and were, in fact, more curious about the detonations they were picking up now from the Bad Blood lands some sixty miles to the west.

Immediately after this ship had shot by, we took to the air again, and following much the same route that I had taken the previous night, climbed in a long semi-circle out over the ocean, swung toward the north and finally the west. We set our course, however, for the Sinsing land north of Nu-Yok, instead of for the city itself.

As we crossed the Hudson River, a few miles north of the city, we dropped several units of the M Intelligence Division, with full instrumental equipment. Their apparatus cases were nicely balanced at only a few ounces' weight each, and the men used their chute capes to ease their drops.

We recrossed the river a little distance above and began dropping A Intelligence units and a few long and short range gun units. Then we held our position until we began to get reports. Gradually we ringed the territory of the Sinsings, our observation units working busily and patiently at their locaters and scopes, both aloft and aground, until Sidor finally turned to me with the remark:

"The map circle is complete now, Boss. We've got clear locations all the way around them."

"Let me see it," I replied, and studied the illuminated viewplate map with its little overlapping circles of light that indicated spots proved clear of the enemy by ultroscopic observation.

I nodded to Dave. "Go ahead now, Berg," I said, "and place your barrage men."

He spoke into his ultrophone, and three of the ships began to glide in a wide ring around the enemy territory. Every few seconds, at the word from his Unit Boss, a gunner would drop off the wire, and slipping the clasp of his chute cape, drift down into the darkness below.

Dave formed two lines, parallel to and facing the river, and enclosing the entire territory of the enemy between them. Above and below, straddling the river, were two defensive lines. These latter were merely to hold their positions. The others were to close in toward each other, pushing a high-explosive barrage five miles ahead of them. When the two barrages met, both lines were to switch to short-vision-range barrage and continue to close in on any of the enemy who might have drifted through the previous curtain of fire.

In the meantime, Dave kept his reserves, a picked corps of a hundred men (the same that had accompanied Ciardi and myself in our fight with the Han squadron) in the air, divided about equally among the "kite-tails" of four ships.

A final roll call, by units, companies, divisions and functions, established the fact that all our forces were in position. No Han activity was reported, and no Han broadcasts indicated any suspicion of our expedition. Nor was there any knowledge of the fate in store for them. The idling of *rep* ray generators was reported from the center of their camp, obviously those of the ships the Hans had given them.

Again I gave the word, and Berg passed on the order to his subordinates.

Far below us, and several miles to the right and left, the two barrage lines made their appearance. From the great height to which we had risen, they appeared like lines of brilliant, winking lights, and the detonations were muffled by the distances into a sort of rumbling, distant thunder. Berg and his assistants were very busy measuring, calculating, and snapping out ultrophone orders to unit commanders that resulted in the straightening of lines and the closing of gaps in the barrage.

The A Division Boss reported the utmost confusion in the Sinsing organization (they were an inefficient, loosely disciplined gang), and repeated broadcasts for help to neighboring gangs. Ignoring the fact that the Mongolians had not used explosives for many generations, they nevertheless jumped at the conclusion that they were being raided by the Hans themselves, to whom the sound of the battle was evidently audible, and who were trying to locate the trouble.

At this point, the swooper I had sent south toward the city went into action as a diversion, to keep the Hans at home. Its "kite tail" loaded with long-range gunners, using the most highly explosive rockets we had, hung invisible in the darkness of the sky and bombarded the city from a distance of about five miles. With an entire city to shoot at, and the object of creating as much commotion therein as possible, regardless of actual damage, the gunners had no difficulty in hitting the mark. I could see the glow of the city and the stabbing flashes of exploding rockets. In the end, the Hans, uncertain as to what was going on, fell back on a defensive policy, and shot their "hell cylinder," or wall of upturned disintegrator rays into operation. That, of course, ended our bombardment of them. The rays were a perfect defense, disintegrating our rockets as they were reached.

If they had not sent out ships before turning on the rays, and if they had none within sufficient radius already in the air, all would be well.

I queried Sidor on this, but he assured me M Intelligence reported no indications of Han ships nearer than 800 miles. This would probably give us a free hand for a while, since most of their instruments recorded only imperfectly, or not at all, through the death wall.

Requisitioning one of the viewplates of the headquarters ship, and the services of an expert operator, I instructed him to focus on our lines below. I wanted a close-up of the men in action.

He began to manipulate his controls and chaotic shadows moved rapidly across the plate, fading in and out of focus, until he reached an adjustment that gave me a picture of the forest floor, apparently 100 feet wide, with the intervening branches and foliage of the trees appearing like shadows that melted into reality a few feet above the ground.

I watched one man setting up his long-gun with skillful speed. His lips pursed slightly as though he were whistling, as he adjusted the tall tripod on which the long tube was balanced. Swiftly he twirled the knobs controlling the aim and elevation of his piece. Then, lifting a belt of ammunition from the big box, which itself looked heavy enough to break down the spindly tripod, he inserted the end of it in the lock of his tube and touched the proper combination of buttons.

Then he stepped aside, and occupied himself with peering through the trees ahead. Not even a tremor shook the tube, but I knew that at intervals of something less than a second, it was discharging small projectiles which, traveling under their own continuously reduced power, were arching into the air, to fall precisely five miles ahead and explode with the force of eight-inch shells, such as we used in the First World War.

Another gunner, fifty feet to the right of him, waved a hand and called out something to him. Then, picking up his own tube and tripod, he gauged the distance between the trees ahead of him, and the height of their lowest branches, and bending forward a bit, flexed his muscles and leaped lightly, some twenty-five feet. Another leap took him another twenty feet or so, where he began to set up his piece.

I ordered my observer then to switch to the barrage itself. He got a close focus on it, but this showed little except a continuous series of blinding flashes, which, from the viewplate, lit up the entire interior of the ship. An eight-hundred-foot focus proved better. I had thought that some of our French and American artillery of the 20th Century had achieved the ultimate in mathematical precision of fire, but I had never seen anything to equal the accuracy of that line of terrific explosions as it moved steadily forward, mowing down trees as a scythe cuts grass (or used to 500 years ago), literally churning up the earth and the splintered, blasted remains of the forest giants, to a depth of from ten to twenty feet.

By now the two curtains of fire were nearing each other, lines of vibrant, shimmering, continuous, brilliant destruction, inevitably squeezing the panic-stricken Sinsings between them.

Even as I watched, a group of them, who had been making a futile effort to get their three *rep* ray machines into the air, abandoned their efforts, and rushed forth into the milling mob.

I queried the Control Boss sharply on the futility of this attempt of theirs, and learned that the Hans, apparently in doubt as to what was going on, had continued to "play safe," and broken off their power broadcast, after ordering all their own ships east of the Alleghenies to the ground, for fear these ships they had traded to the Sinsings might be used against them.

Again I turned to my viewplate, which was still focussed on the central section of the Sinsing works. The confusion of the traitors was entirely that of fear, for our barrage had not yet reached them.

Some of them set up their long-guns and fired at random over the barrage line, then gave it up. They realized that they had no target to shoot at, no way of knowing whether our gunners were a few hundred feet or several miles beyond it.

Their ultrophone men, of whom they did not have many, stood around in tense attitudes, their helmet phones strapped around their ears, nervously fingering the tuning controls at their belts. Unquestionably they must have located some of our frequencies, and overheard many of our reports and orders. But they were confused and disorganized. If they had an Ultrophone Boss they evidently were not reporting to him in an organized way.

They were beginning to draw back now before our advancing fire. With intermittent desperation, they began to shoot over our barrage again, and the explosions of their rockets flashed at widely scattered points beyond. A few took distance "pot shots."

Oddly enough it was our own forces that suffered the first casualties in the battle. Some of these distance shots by chance registered hits, while our men were under strict orders not to exceed their barrage distances.

Seen upon the ultroscope viewplate, the battle looked as though it were being fought in daylight, perhaps on a cloudy day, while the explosions of the rockets appeared as flashes of extra brilliance.

The two barrage lines were not more than five hundred feet apart when the Sinsings resorted to tactics we had not foreseen. We noticed first that they began to lighten themselves by throwing away extra equipment. A few of them in their excitement threw away too much, and shot suddenly into the air. Then a scattered few floated up gently, followed by increasing numbers, while still others, preserving a weight balance, jumped toward the closing barrages and leaped high, hoping to clear them. Some succeeded. We saw others blown about like leaves in a windstorm, to crumple and drift slowly down, or else to fall into the barrage, their belts blown from their bodies.

However, it was not part of our plan to allow a single one of them to escape and find his way to the Hans. I quickly passed the word to Dave Berg to have the alternate men in his line raise their barrages and heard him bark out a mathematical formula to the Unit Bosses.

We backed off our ships as the explosions climbed into the air in stagger formation until they reached a height of three miles. I don't believe any of the Sinsings who tried to float away to freedom succeeded.

But we did know later, that a few who leaped the barrage got away and ultimately reached Nu-Yok.

It was those who managed to jump the barrage who gave us the most trouble. With half of our long-guns turned aloft, I foresaw we would not have enough to establish successive ground barrages and so ordered the barrage back two miles, from which positions our "curtains" began to close in again, this time, however, gauged to explode, not on contact, but thirty feet in the air. This left little chance for the Sinsings to leap either over or under it.

Gradually, the two barrages approached each other until they finally met, and in the gray dawn the battle ended.

Our own casualties amounted to forty-seven men in the ground forces, eighteen of whom had been slain in hand-to-hand fighting with the few of the enemy who managed to reach our lines, and sixty-two in the crew and "kite tail" force of swooper No. 4, which had been located by one of the enemy's ultroscopes and brought down with long-gun fire.

Since nearly every member of the Sinsing Gang had, so far as we knew, been killed, we considered the raid a great success.

It had, however, a far greater significance than this. To all of us who took part in the expedition, the effectiveness of our barrage tactics definitely established a confidence in our ability to overcome the Hans.

As I pointed out to Wilma:

"It has been my belief all along, dear, that the American explosive rocket is a far more efficient weapon than the *dis* ray of the Hans, once we can train all our gangs to use it systematically and in co-ordinated fashion. As a weapon in the hands of a single individual, shooting at a mark in direct line of vision, the rocket-gun is inferior in destructive power to the *dis* ray, except as its range may be a little greater. The trouble is that to date it has been used only as we used our rifles and shotguns in the 20th Century. The possibilities of its use as artillery, in laying barrages that advance along the ground, or climb into the air, are tremendous.

"The *dis* ray inevitably reveals its source of emanation. The rocket gun does not. The *dis* ray can reach its target only in a straight line. The rocket may be made to travel in an arc, over intervening obstacles, to an unseen target.

"Nor must we forget that our ultronists now are promising us a perfect shield against the *dis* ray in inertron."

"I tremble though, Tony dear, when I think of the horrors that are ahead of us. The Hans are clever. They will develop defenses against our new tactics. And they are sure to mass against us not only the full force of their power in America, but the united forces of the World Empire."

"Nevertheless," I prophesied, "the Finger of Doom points squarely at them today, and unless you and I are killed in the struggle, we shall live to see America blast the Mongolian Blight from the face of the Earth."

James Arness as The Thing in a publicity shot.

Dr. Copper (Richard Dysart) starts to be ingested by The Thing.

MacReady (Kurt
Russell) waits, cold
and unsure, for
The Thing.

# Who Goes There?

## JOHN W. CAMPBELL JR.

**The Thing (From Another World)**
Director: *Christian Nyby*
Screenplay: *Charles Lederer*
Producer: *Howard Hawks*
Music: *Dimitri Tiomkin*
Special Effects: *Donald Steward*
Cast: *Kenneth Tobey, Margaret Sheridan, James Arness*
Released by: *RKO*
1951, 89 Minutes. B&W.

**The Thing**
Director/Producer: *John Carpenter*
Screenplay: *William Lancaster*
Producer: *David Foster, Lawrence Turman*
Music: *Ennio Morricone*
Special Effects: *Roy Arbogast*
Visual Special Effects: *Albert Whitlock*
Cast: *Kurt Russell, A. Wilford Brimley, T. K. Carter*
Released by: *Universal*
1982, 108 Minutes. Color.

— I —

The place stank. A queer, mingled stench that only the ice-buried cabins of an Antarctic camp know, compounded of reeking human sweat, and the heavy, fish-oil stench of melted seal blubber. An overtone of liniment combated the musty smell of sweat-and-snow-drenched furs. The acrid odor of burnt cooking fat, and the animal, not-unpleasant smell of dogs, diluted by time, hung in the air.

Lingering odors of machine oil contrasted sharply with the taint of harness dressing and leather. Yet, somehow, through all that reek of human beings and their associates—dogs, machines and cooking—came another taint. It was a queer, neck-ruffling thing, a faintest suggestion of an odor alien among the smells of industry and life. And it was a lifesmell. But it came from the thing that lay bound with cord and tarpaulin on the table, dripping slowly, method-ically onto the heavy planks, dank and gaunt under the unshielded glare of the electric light.

Blair, the little bald-pated biologist of the expedition, twitched nervously at the wrappings, exposing clear, dark ice beneath and then pulling the tarpaulin back into place restlessly. His little birdlike motions of suppressed eagerness danced his shadow across the fringe of dingy gray underwear hanging from the low ceiling, the equatorial fringe of stiff, graying hair around his naked skull a comical halo about the shadow's head.

Commander Garry brushed aside the lax legs of a suit of underwear, and stepped toward the table. Slowly his eyes traced around the rings of men sardined into the Administration Building. His tall, stiff body straight-ened finally, and he nodded. "Thirty-seven. All here." His voice was low, yet carried the clear authority of the commander by nature, as well as by title.

"You know the outline of the story back of that find of the Secondary Pole Expedition. I have been conferring with Second-in-Command McReady, and Norris, as well as Blair and Dr. Copper. There is a difference of opinion, and because it involves the entire group, it is only just that the entire Expedition personnel act on it.

"I am going to ask McReady to give you the details of the story, because each of you has been too busy with his own work to follow closely the en-deavors of the others. McReady?"

Moving from the smoke-blued background, McReady was a figure from some forgotten myth, a looming, bronze statue that held life, and walked. Six-feet-four inches he stood as he halted beside the table, and, with a character-istic glance upward to assure himself of room under the low ceiling beams, straightened. His rough, clashingly orange windproof jacket he still had on, yet on his huge frame it did not seem misplaced. Even here, four feet beneath the drift-wind that droned across the Antarctic waste above the ceiling, the cold of the frozen continent leaked in, and gave meaning to the harshness of the man. And he was bronze—his great red-bronze beard, the heavy hair that matched it. The gnarled, corded hands gripping, relaxing, gripping and relaxing on the table planks were bronze. Even the deep-sunken eyes beneath heavy brows were bronzed.

Age-resisting endurance of the metal spoke in the cragged heavy outlines of his face, and the mellow tones of the heavy voice. "Norris and Blair agree on one thing; that animal we found was not—terrestrial in origin. Norris fears there may be danger in that; Blair says there is none.

"But I'll go back to how, and why, we found it. To all that was known before we came here, it appeared that this point was exactly over the South Magnetic Pole of Earth. The compass does point straight down here, as you all know. The more delicate instruments of the physicists, instruments especially designed for this expedition and its study of the magnetic pole, detected a secondary effect, a secondary, less powerful magnetic influence about 80 miles southwest of here.

"The Secondary Magnetic Expedition went out to investigate it. There is no need for details. We found it, but it was not the huge meteorite or magnetic mountain Norris had expected to find. Iron ore is magnetic, of course; iron more so—and certain special steels even more magnetic. From the surface indications, the secondary pole we found was small, so small that the magnetic effect it had was preposterous. No magnetic material conceivable could have that effect. Soundings through the ice indicated it was within one hundred feet of the glacier surface.

"I think you should know the structure of the place. There is a broad plateau, a level sweep that runs more than 150 miles due south from the Secondary station, Van Wall says. He didn't have time or fuel to fly farther, but it was running smoothly due south then. Right there, where that buried thing was, there is an ice-drowned mountain ridge, a granite wall of unshakable strength that has dammed back the ice creeping from the south.

"And four hundred miles due south is the South Polar Plateau. You have asked me at various times why it gets warmer here when the wind rises, and most of you know. As a meteorologist I'd have staked my word that no wind could blow at –70 degrees—that no more than a 5-mile wind could blow at –50—without causing warming due to friction with ground, snow and ice, and the air itself.

"We camped there on the lip of that ice-drowned mountain range for twelve days. We dug our camp into the blue ice that formed the surface, and escaped most of it. But for twelve consecutive days the wind blew at 45 miles an hour. It went as high as 48, and fell to 41 at times. The temperature was –63 degrees. It rose to –60 and fell to –68. It was meteorologically impossible, and it went on uninterruptedly for twelve days and twelve nights.

"Somewhere to the south, the frozen air of the South Polar Plateau slides down from that 18,000-foot bowl, down a mountain pass, over a glacier, and starts north. There must be a funneling mountain chain that directs it, and sweeps it away for four hundred miles to hit that bald plateau where we found the secondary pole, and 350 miles farther north reaches the Antarctic Ocean.

"It's been frozen there since Antarctica froze twenty million years ago. There never has been a thaw there.

"Twenty million years ago Antarctica was beginning to freeze. We've investigated, thought and built speculations. What we believe happened was about like this.

"Something came down out of space, a ship. We saw it there in the blue ice, a thing like a submarine without a conning tower or directive vanes, 280 feet long and 45 feet in diameter at its thickest.

"Eh, Van Wall? Space? Yes, but I'll explain that better later." McReady's steady voice went on.

"It came down from space, driven and lifted by forces men haven't discovered yet, and somehow—perhaps something went wrong then—it tangled with Earth's magnetic field. It came south here, out of control probably, circling the magnetic pole. That's a savage country there, but when Antarctica was still freezing it must have been a thousand times more savage. There must have been blizzard snow, as well as drift, new snow falling as the continent glaciated. The swirl there must have been particularly bad, the wind hurling a solid blanket of white over the lip of that now-buried mountain.

"The ship struck solid granite head-on, and cracked up. Not every one of the passengers in it was killed, but the ship must have been ruined, her driving mechanism locked. It tangled with Earth's field, Norris believes. No thing made by intelligent beings can tangle with the dead immensity of a planet's natural forces and survive.

"One of its passengers stepped out. The wind we saw there never fell below 41, and the temperature never rose above –60. Then—the wind must have been stronger. And there was drift falling in a solid sheet. The *thing* was lost completely in ten paces." He paused for a moment, the deep, steady voice giving way to the drone of wind overhead, and the uneasy, malicious gurgling in the pipe of the galley stove.

Drift—a drift-wind was sweeping by overhead. Right now the snow picked up by the mumbling wind fled in level, blinding lines across the face of the buried camp. If a man stepped out of the tunnels that connected each of the camp buildings beneath the surface, he'd be lost in ten paces. Out there, the slim, black finger of the radio mast lifted 300 feet into the air, and at its peak was the clear night sky. A sky of thin, whining wind rushing steadily from beyond to another beyond under the licking, curling mantle of the aurora. And off north, the horizon flamed with queer, angry colors of the midnight twilight. That was spring 300 feet above Antarctica.

At the surface—it was white death. Death of a needle-fingered cold driven before the wind, sucking heat from any warm thing. Cold—and white mist of endless, everlasting drift, the fine, fine particles of licking snow that obscured all things.

Kinner, the little, scar-faced cook, winced. Five days ago he had stepped out to the surface to reach a cache of frozen beef. He had reached it, started back—and the drift-wind leapt out of the south. Cold, white death that streamed across the ground blinded him in twenty seconds. He stumbled on wildly in circles. It was half an hour before rope-guided men from below found him in the impenetrable murk.

It was easy for man—or *thing*—to get lost in ten paces.

"And the drift-wind then was probably more impenetrable than we know." McReady's voice snapped Kinner's mind back. Back to welcome, dank warmth of the Ad Building. "The passenger of the ship wasn't prepared either, it appears. It froze within ten feet of the ship.

"We dug down to find the ship, and our tunnel happened to find the frozen—animal. Barclay's ice-ax struck its skull.

"When we saw what it was, Barclay went back to the tractor, started the fire up and when the steam pressure built, sent a call for Blair and Dr. Copper. Barclay himself was sick then. Stayed sick for three days, as a matter of fact.

"When Blair and Copper came, we cut out the animal in a block of ice, as you see, wrapped it and loaded it on the tractor for return here. We wanted to get into that ship.

"We reached the side and found the metal was something we didn't know. Our beryllium-bronze, non-magnetic tools wouldn't touch it. Barclay had some tool-steel on the tractor, and that wouldn't scratch it either. We made reasonable tests—even tried some acid from the batteries with no results.

"They must have had a passivating process to make magnesium metal resist acid that way, and the alloy must have been at least 95 per cent magnesium. But we had no way of guessing that, so when we spotted the barely opened lock door, we cut around it. There was clear, hard ice inside the lock, where we couldn't reach it. Through the little crack we could look in and see that only metal and tools were in there, so we decided to loosen the ice with a bomb.

"We had decanite bombs and thermite. Thermite is the ice-softener; decanite might have shattered valuable things, where the thermite's heat would just loosen the ice. Dr. Copper, Norris and I placed a 25-pound thermite bomb, wired it, and took the connector up the tunnel to the surface, where Blair had the steam tractor waiting. A hundred yards the other side of that granite wall we set off the thermite bomb.

"The magnesium metal of the ship caught, of course. The glow of the bomb flared and died, then it began to flare again. We ran back to the tractor, and gradually the glare built up. From where we were we could see the whole ice-field illuminated from beneath with an unbearable light; the ship's shadow was a great, dark cone reaching off toward the north, where the twilight was just about gone. For a moment it lasted, and we counted three other shadow-things that might have been other—passengers—frozen there. Then the ice was crashing down and against the ship.

"That's why I told you about that place. The wind sweeping down from the Pole was at our backs. Steam and hydrogen flame were torn away in white ice-fog; the flaming heat under the ice there was yanked away toward the Antarctic Ocean before it touched us. Otherwise we wouldn't have come back, even with the shelter of that granite ridge that stopped the light.

"Somehow in the blinding inferno we could see great hunched things, black bulks glowing, even so. They shed even the furious incandescence of the magnesium for a time. Those must have been the engines, we knew. Secrets going in blazing glory—secrets that might have given Man the planets. Mysterious things that could lift and hurl that ship—and had soaked in the force of the Earth's magnetic field. I saw Norris' mouth move, and ducked. I couldn't hear him.

"Insulation—something—gave way. All Earth's field they'd soaked up twenty million years before broke loose. The aurora in the sky above licked down, and the whole plateau there was bathed in cold fire that blanketed vision. The ice-ax in my hand got red hot, and hissed on the ice. Metal buttons on my clothes burned into me. And a flash of electric blue seared upward from beyond the granite wall.

"Then the walls of ice crashed down on it. For an instant it squealed the way dry-ice does when it's pressed between metal.

"We were blind and groping in the dark for hours while our eyes recovered. We found every coil within a mile was fused rubbish, the dynamo and every radio set, the earphones and speakers. If we hadn't had the steam tractor, we wouldn't have gotten over to the Secondary Camp.

"Van Wall flew in from Big Magnet at sun-up, as you know. We came home as soon as possible. That is the history of—that." McReady's great bronze beard gestured toward the thing on the table.

— II —

Blair stirred uneasily, his little, bony fingers wriggling under the harsh light. Little brown freckles on his knuckles slid back and forth as the tendons under the skin twitched. He pulled aside a bit of the tarpaulin and looked impatiently at the dark ice-bound thing inside.

McReady's big body straightened somewhat. He'd ridden the rocking, jarring steam tractor forty miles that day, pushing on to Big Magnet here. Even his calm will had been pressed by the anxiety to mix again with humans. It was lone and quiet out there in Secondary Camp, where a wolf-wind howled down from the Pole. Wolf-wind howling in his sleep—winds droning and the evil, unspeakable face of that monster leering up as he'd first seen it through clear, blue ice, with a bronze ice-ax buried in its skull.

The giant meteorologist spoke again. "The problem is this. Blair wants to examine the thing. Thaw it out and make micro slides of its tissues and so forth. Norris doesn't believe that is safe, and Blair does. Dr. Copper agrees pretty much with Blair. Norris is a physicist, of course, not a biologist. But he makes a point I think we should all hear. Blair has described the microscopic life-forms biologists find living, even in this cold and inhospitable place. They freeze every winter, and thaw every summer—for three months— and live.

"The point Norris makes is—they thaw, and live again. There must have been microscopic life associated with this creature. There is with every living thing we know. And Norris is afraid that we may release a plague—some germ disease unknown to Earth—if we thaw those microscopic things that have been frozen there for twenty million years.

"Blair admits that such micro-life might retain the power of living. Such unorganized things as individual cells can retain life for unknown periods, when solidly frozen. The beast itself is as dead as those frozen mammoths they find in Siberia. Organized, highly developed life-forms can't stand that treatment.

"But micro-life could. Norris suggests that we may release some disease-form that man, never having met it before, will be utterly defenseless against.

"Blair's answer is that there may be such still-living germs, but that Norris has the case reversed. They are utterly non-immune to man. Our life-chemistry probably—"

"Probably!" The little biologist's head lifted in a quick, birdlike motion. The halo of gray hair about his bald head ruffled as though angry. "Heh. One look—"

"I know," McReady acknowledged. "The thing is not Earthly. It does not seem likely that it can have a life-chemistry sufficiently like ours to make cross-infection remotely possible. I would say that there is no danger."

McReady looked toward Dr. Copper. The physician shook his head slowly. "None whatever," he asserted confidently. "Man cannot infect or be infected by germs that live in such comparatively close relatives as the snakes. And they are, I assure you," his clean-shaven face grimaced uneasily, "*much* nearer to us than—*that.*"

Vance Norris moved angrily. He was comparatively short in this gathering of big men, some five-feet-eight, and his stocky, powerful build tended to make him seem shorter. His black hair was crisp and hard, like short, steel wires, and his eyes were the gray of fractured steel. If McReady was a man of bronze, Norris was all steel. His movements, his thoughts, his whole bearing had the quick, hard impulse of steel spring. His nerves were steel—hard, quick-acting—swift-corroding.

He was decided on his point now, and he lashed out in its defense with a characteristic quick, clipped flow of words. "Different chemistry be damned. That thing may be dead—or, by God, it may not—but I don't like it. Damn it, Blair, let them see the monstrosity you are petting over there. Let them see the foul thing and decide for themselves whether they want that thing thawed out in this camp.

"Thawed out, by the way. That's got to be thawed out in one of the shacks tonight, if it is thawed out. Somebody—who's watchman tonight? Magnetic—oh, Connant. Cosmic rays tonight. Well, you get to sit up with that twenty-million-year-old mummy of his.

"Unwrap it, Blair. How the hell can they tell what they are buying if they can't see it? It may have a different chemistry. I don't know what else it has, but I know it has something I don't want. If you can judge by the look on its face—it isn't human so maybe you can't—it was annoyed when it froze. Annoyed, in fact, is just about as close an approximation of the way it felt as crazy, mad, insane hatred. Neither one touches the subject.

"How the hell can these birds tell what they are voting on? They haven't seen those three red eyes, and that blue hair like crawling worms. Crawling—damn, it's crawling there in the ice right now!

"Nothing Earth ever spawned had the unutterable sublimation of devastating wrath that thing let loose in its face when it looked around this frozen desolation twenty million years ago. Mad? It was mad clear through—searing, blistering mad!

"Hell, I've had bad dreams ever since I looked at those three red eyes. Nightmares. Dreaming the thing thawed out and came to life—that it wasn't dead, or even wholly unconscious all those twenty million years, but just slowed, waiting—waiting. You'll dream, too, while that damned thing that Earth wouldn't own is dripping, dripping in the Cosmos House tonight.

"And, Connant," Norris whipped toward the cosmic ray specialist, "won't you have fun sitting up all night in the quiet. Wind whining above—and that thing dripping—" He stopped for a moment, and looked around.

"I know. That's not science. But this is, it's psychology. You'll have nightmares for a year to come. Every night since I looked at that thing I've had 'em. That's why I hate it—sure I do—and don't want it around. Put it back where it came from and let it freeze for another twenty million years. I had some swell nightmares—that it wasn't made like we are—which is obvious—but of a different kind of flesh that it can really control. That it can change its shape, and look like a man—and wait to kill and eat—

"That's not a logical argument. I know it isn't. The thing isn't Earth-logic anyway.

"Maybe it has an alien body-chemistry, and maybe its bugs do have a different body-chemistry. A germ might not stand that, but, Blair and Copper, how about a virus? That's just an enzyme molecule, you've said. That wouldn't need anything but a protein molecule of any body to work on.

"And how are you so sure that, of the million varieties of microscopic life it may have, *none* of them are dangerous? How about diseases like hydrophobia—rabies—that attack any warm-blooded creature, whatever its body-chemistry may be? And parrot fever? Have you a body like a parrot, Blair? And plain rot—gangrene—necrosis, do you want? *That* isn't choosy about body-chemistry!"

Blair looked up from his puttering long enough to meet Norris' angry, gray eyes for an instant. "So far the only thing you have said this thing gave off that was catching was dreams. I'll go so far as to admit that." An impish, slightly malignant grin crossed the little man's seamed face. "I had some, too. So. It's dream-infectious. No doubt an exceedingly dangerous malady.

"So far as your other things go, you have a badly mistaken idea about viruses. In the first place, nobody has shown that the enzyme-molecule theory, and that alone, explains them. And in the second place, when you catch tobacco mosaic or wheat rust, let me know. A wheat plant is a lot nearer your body-chemistry than this other-world creature is.

"And your rabies is limited, strictly limited. You can't get it from, nor give it to, a wheat plant or a fish—which is a collateral descendant of a common ancestor of yours. Which this, Norris, is not." Blair nodded pleasantly toward the tarpaulined bulk on the table.

"Well, thaw the damned thing in a tub of formalin if you must thaw it. I've suggested that—"

"And I've said there would be no sense in it. You can't compromise. Why did you and Commander Garry come down here to study magnetism? Why weren't you content to stay at home? There's magnetic force enough in New York. I could no more study the life this thing once had from a formalin-pickled sample than you could get the information you wanted back in New York. And—if this one is so treated, *never in all time to come can there be a duplicate!* The race it came from must have passed away in the twenty million years it lay frozen, so that even if it came from Mars then, we'd never find its like. And—the ship is gone.

"There's only one way to do this—and that is the best possible way. It must be thawed slowly, carefully, and not in formalin."

Commander Garry stood forward again, and Norris stepped back muttering angrily. "I think Blair is right, gentlemen. What do you say?"

Connant grunted. "It sounds right to us, I think—only perhaps he ought to stand watch over it while it's thawing." He grinned ruefully, brushing a stray lock of ripe-cherry hair back from his forehead. "Swell idea, in fact—if he sits up with his jolly little corpse."

Garry smiled slightly. A general chuckle of agreement rippled over the group. "I should think any ghost it may have had would have starved to death if it hung around here that long, Connant," Garry suggested. "And you look capable of taking care of it. 'Ironman' Connant ought to be able to take out any opposing players, still."

Connant shook himself uneasily. "I'm not worrying about ghosts. Let's see that thing. I—"

Eagerly Blair was stripping back the ropes. A single throw of the tarpaulin revealed the thing. The ice had melted somewhat in the heat of the room, and it was clear and blue as thick, good glass. It shone wet and sleek under the harsh light of the unshielded globe above.

The room stiffened abruptly. It was face up there on the plain, greasy planks of the table. The broken half of the bronze ice-ax was still buried in the queer skull. Three mad, hate-filled eyes blazed up with a living fire, bright as fresh-spilled blood, from a face ringed with a writhing, loathsome nest of worms, blue, mobile worms that crawled where hair should grow—

Van Wall, six feet and 200 pounds of ice-nerved pilot, gave a queer, strangled gasp and butted, stumbled his way out to the corridor. Half the company broke for the doors. The others stumbled away from the table.

McReady stood at one end of the table watching them, his great body planted solid on his powerful legs. Norris from the opposite end glowered at the thing with smouldering hate. Outside the door, Garry was talking with half a dozen of the men at once.

Blair had a tack hammer. The ice that cased the thing *schluffed* crisply under its steel claw as it peeled from the thing it had cased for twenty million years—

— III —

"I know you don't like the thing, Connant, but it just has to be thawed out right. You say leave it as it is till we get back to civilization. All right, I'll admit your argument that we could do a better and more complete job there is sound. But—how are we going to get this across the Line? We have to take this through one temperate zone, the equatorial zone, and half way through the other temperate zone before we get it to New York. You don't want to sit with it one night, but you suggest, then, that I hang its corpse in the freezer with the beef?" Blair looked up from his cautious chipping, his bald, freckled skull nodding triumphantly.

Kinner, the stocky, scar-faced cook, saved Connant the trouble of answering. "Hey, you listen, mister. You put that thing in the box with the meat, and by all the gods there ever were, I'll put you in to keep it company. You birds have brought everything movable in this camp in onto my mess tables here already, and I had to stand for that. But you go putting things like that in my meat box or even my meat cache here, and you cook your own damn grub."

"But, Kinner, this is the only table in Big Magnet that's big enough to work on," Blair objected. "Everybody's explained that."

"Yeah, and everybody's brought everything in here. Clark brings his dogs every time there's a fight and sews them up on that table. Ralsen brings in his sledges. Hell, the only thing you haven't had on that table is the Boeing. And you'd 'a' had that in if you coulda figured a way to get it through the tunnels."

Commander Garry chuckled and grinned at Van Wall, the huge Chief Pilot. Van Wall's great blond beard twitched suspiciously as he nodded gravely to Kinner. "You're right, Kinner. The aviation department is the only one that treats you right."

"It does get crowded, Kinner," Garry acknowledged. "But I'm afraid we all find it that way at times. Not much privacy in an Antarctic camp."

"Privacy? What the hell's that? You know, the thing that really made me weep, was when I saw Barclay marchin' through here chantin' 'The last lumber in the camp! The last lumber in the camp!' and carryin' it out to build that house on his tractor. Damn it, I missed that moon cut in the door he carried out more'n I missed the sun when it set. That wasn't just the last lumber

Barclay was walkin' off with. He was carryin' off the last bit of privacy in this blasted place."

A grin rode even on Connant's heavy face as Kinner's perennial good-natured grouch came up again. But it died away quickly as his dark, deep-set eyes turned again to the red-eyed thing Blair was chipping from its cocoon of ice. A big hand ruffed his shoulder-length hair, and tugged at a twisted lock that fell behind his ear in a familiar gesture. "I know that cosmic ray shack's going to be too crowded if I have to sit up with that thing," he growled. "Why can't you go on chipping the ice away from around it—you can do that without anybody butting in, I assure you—and then hang the thing up over the power-plant boiler? That's warm enough. It'll thaw out a chicken, even a whole side of beef, in a few hours."

"I know," Blair protested, dropping the tack hammer to gesture more effectively with his bony, freckled fingers, his small body tense with eagerness, "but this is too important to take any chances. There never was a find like this; there never can be again. It's the only chance men will ever have, and it has to be done exactly right.

"Look, you know how the fish we caught down near the Ross Sea would freeze almost as soon as we got them on deck, and come to life again if we thawed them gently? Low forms of life aren't killed by quick freezing and slow thawing. We have—"

"Hey, for the love of Heaven—you mean that damned thing will come to life!" Connant yelled. "You get the damned thing—Let me at it! That's going to be in so many pieces—"

"NO! No, you fool—" Blair jumped in front of Connant to protect his precious find. "No. Just *low* forms of life. For Pete's sake let me finish. You can't thaw higher forms of life and have them come to. Wait a moment now—hold it! A fish can come to after freezing because it's so low a form of life that the individual cells of its body can revive, and that alone is enough to re-establish life. Any higher forms thawed out that way are dead. Though the individual cells revive, they die because there must be organization and cooperative effort to live. That cooperation cannot be re-established. There is a sort of potential life in any uninjured, quick-frozen animal. But it can't—can't under any circumstances—become active life in higher animals. The higher animals are too complex, too delicate. This is an intelligent creature as high in its evolution as we are in ours. Perhaps higher. It is as dead as a frozen man would be."

"How do you know?" demanded Connant, hefting the ice-ax he had seized a moment before.

Commander Garry laid a restraining hand on his heavy shoulder. "Wait a minute, Connant. I want to get this straight. I agree that there is going to be no thawing of this thing if there is the remotest chance of its revival. I quite agree it is much too unpleasant to have alive, but I had no idea there was the remotest possibility."

Dr. Copper pulled his pipe from between his teeth and heaved his stocky, dark body from the bunk he had been sitting in. "Blair's being technical. That's dead. As dead as the mammoths they find frozen in Siberia. Potential life is like atomic energy—there, but nobody can get it out, and it certainly won't release itself except in rare cases, as rare as radium in the chemical analogy. We have all sorts of proof that things don't live after being frozen—not even fish, generally speaking—and no proof that higher animal life can under any circumstances. What's the point, Blair?"

The little biologist shook himself. The little ruff of hair standing out around his bald pate waved in righteous anger. "The point is," he said in an injured tone, "that the individual cells might show the characteristics they had in life, if it is properly thawed. A man's muscle cells live many hours after he has died. Just because they live, and a few things like hair and fingernail cells still live, you wouldn't accuse a corpse of being a Zombie, or something.

"Now if I thaw this right, I may have a chance to determine what sort of world it's native to. We don't, and can't know by any other means, whether it came from Earth or Mars or Venus or from beyond the stars.

"And just because it looks unlike men, you don't have to accuse it of being evil, or vicious or something. Maybe that expression on its face is its equivalent to a resignation to fate. White is the color of mourning to the Chinese. If men can have different customs, why can't a so-different race have different understandings of facial expressions?"

Connant laughed softly, mirthlessly. "Peaceful resignation! If that is the best it could do in the way of resignation, I should exceedingly dislike seeing it when it was looking mad. That face was never designed to express peace. It just didn't have any philosophical thoughts like peace in its make-up.

"I know it's your pet—but be sane about it. That thing grew up on evil, adolesced slowly roasting alive the local equivalent of kittens, and amused itself through maturity on new and ingenious torture."

"You haven't the slightest right to say that," snapped Blair. "How do you know the first thing about the meaning of a facial expression inherently inhuman? It may well have no human equivalent whatever. That is just a different development of Nature, another example of Nature's wonderful adaptability. Growing on another, perhaps harsher world, it has different form and features. But it is just as much a legitimate child of Nature as you are. You are displaying the childish human weakness of hating the different. On its own world it would probably class you as a fish-belly, white monstrosity with an insufficient number of eyes and a fungoid body pale and bloated with gas.

"Just because its nature is different, you haven't any right to say it's necessarily evil."

Norris burst out a single, explosive, "Haw!" He looked down at the thing. "May be that things from other worlds don't *have* to be evil just because they're different. But that thing *was!* Child of Nature, eh? Well, it was a hell of an evil Nature."

"Aw, will you mugs cut crabbing at each other and get the damned thing off my table?" Kinner growled. "And put a canvas over it. It looks indecent."

"Kinner's gone modest," jeered Connant.

Kinner slanted his eyes up to the big physicist. The scarred cheek twisted to join the line of his tight lips in a twisted grin. "All right, big boy, and what were you grousing about a minute ago? We can set the thing in a chair next to you tonight, if you want."

"I'm not afraid of its face," Connant snapped. "I don't like keeping a wake over its corpse particularly, but I'm going to do it."

Kinner's grin spread. "Uh-huh." He went off to the galley stove and shook down ashes vigorously, drowning the brittle chipping of the ice as Blair fell to work again.

# — IV —

"*Cluck*," reported the cosmic ray counter, "*cluck-brrrp-cluck.*" Connant started and dropped his pencil.

"Damnation." The physicist looked toward the far corner, back at the Geiger counter on the table near that corner, and crawled under the desk at which he had been working to retrieve the pencil. He sat down at his work again, trying to make his writing more even. It tended to have jerks and quavers in it, in time with the abrupt proud-hen noises of the Geiger counter. The muted whoosh of the pressure lamp he was using for illumination, the mingled gargles and bugle calls of a dozen men sleeping down the corridor in Paradise House formed the background sounds for the irregular, clucking noises of the counter, the occasional rustle of falling coal in the copper-bellied stove. And a soft, steady *drip-drip-drip* from the thing in the corner.

Connant jerked a pack of cigarettes from his pocket, snapped it so that a cigarette protruded and jabbed the cylinder into his mouth. The lighter failed to function, and he pawed angrily through the pile of papers in search of a match. He scratched the wheel of the lighter several times, dropped it with a curse and got up to pluck a hot coal from the stove with the coal tongs.

The lighter functioned instantly when he tried it on returning to the desk.

The counter ripped out a series of clucking guffaws as a burst of cosmic rays struck through to it. Connant turned to glower at it, and tried to concentrate on the interpretation of data collected during the past week. The weekly summary—

He gave up and yielded to curiosity, or nervousness. He lifted the pressure lamp from the desk and carried it over to the table in the corner. Then he returned to the stove and picked up the coal tongs. The beast had been thawing for nearly eighteen hours now. He poked at it with an unconscious caution; the flesh was no longer hard as armor plate, but had assumed a rubbery texture. It looked like wet, blue rubber glistening under droplets of water like little round jewels in the glare of the gasoline pressure lantern. Connant felt an unreasoning desire to pour the contents of the lamp's reservoir over the thing in its box and drop the cigarette into it. The three red eyes glared up at him sightlessly, the ruby eyeballs reflecting murky, smoky rays of light.

He realized vaguely that he had been looking at them for a very long time, even vaguely understood that they were no longer sightless. But it did not seem of importance, of no more importance than the labored, slow motion of the tentacular things that sprouted from the base of the scrawny, slowly pulsing neck.

Connant picked up the pressure lamp and returned to his chair. He sat down, staring at the pages of mathematics before him. The clucking of the counter was strangely less disturbing, the rustle of the coals in the stove no longer distracting.

The creak of the floorboards behind him didn't interrupt his thoughts as he went about his weekly report in an automatic manner, filling in columns of data and making brief, summarizing notes.

The creak of the floorboards sounded nearer.

— V —

Blair came up from the nightmare-haunted depths of sleep abruptly. Connant's face floated vaguely above him; for a moment it seemed a continuance of the wild horror of the dream. But Connant's face was angry, and a little frightened. "Blair—Blair you damned log, wake up."

"Uh-eh?" The little biologist rubbed his eyes, his bony, freckled fingers crooked to a mutilated child-fist. From surrounding bunks other faces lifted to stare down at them.

Connant straightened up. "Get up—and get a lift on. Your damned animal's escaped."

"Escaped—what!" Chief Pilot Van Wall's bull voice roared out with a volume that shook the walls. Down the communication tunnels other voices yelled suddenly. The dozen inhabitants of Paradise House tumbled in abruptly, Barclay, stocky and bulbous in long woolen underwear, carrying a fire extinguisher.

"What the hell's the matter?" Barclay demanded.

"Your damned beast got loose. I fell asleep about twenty minutes ago, and when I woke up, the thing was gone. Hey, Doc, the hell you say those things can't come to life. Blair's blasted potential life developed a hell of a lot of potential and walked out on us."

Copper stared blankly. "It wasn't—Earthly," he sighed suddenly. "I—I guess Earthly laws don't apply."

"Well, it applied for leave of absence and took it. We've got to find it and capture it somehow." Connant swore bitterly, his deep-set black eyes sullen and angry. "It's a wonder the hellish creature didn't eat me in my sleep."

Blair stared back, his pale eyes suddenly fear-struck. "Maybe it di—er—uh—we'll have to find it."

"You find it. It's your pet. I've had all I want to do with it, sitting there for seven hours with the counter clucking every few seconds, and you birds in here singing night-music. It's a wonder I got to sleep. I'm going through to the Ad Building."

Commander Garry ducked through the doorway, pulling his belt tight. "You won't have to. Van's roar sounded like the Boeing taking off down wind. So it wasn't dead?"

"I didn't carry it off in my arms, I assure you," Connant snapped. "The last I saw, that split skull was oozing green goo, like a squashed caterpillar. Doc just said our laws don't work—it's unearthly. Well, it's an unearthly monster, with an unearthly disposition, judging by the face, wandering around with a split skull and brains oozing out."

Norris and McReady appeared in the doorway, a doorway filling with other shivering men. "Has anybody seen it coming over here?" Norris asked innocently. "About four feet tall—three red eyes—brains oozing— Hey, has anybody checked to make sure this isn't a cracked idea of humor? If it is, I think we'll unite in tying Blair's pet around Connant's neck like the Ancient Mariner's albatross."

"It's no humor," Connant shivered. "Lord, I wish it were. I'd rather wear—" He stopped. A wild, weird howl shrieked through the corridors. The men stiffened abruptly, and half turned.

"I think it's been located," Connant finished. His dark eyes shifted with a queer unease. He darted back to his bunk in Paradise House, to return almost immediately with a heavy .45 revolver and an ice-ax. He hefted both gently as he started for the corridor toward Dogtown. "It blundered down the wrong corridor—and landed among the huskies. Listen—the dogs have broken their chains—"

The half-terrorized howl of the dog pack changed to a wild hunting melee. The voices of the dogs thundered in the narrow corridors, and through them came a low rippling snarl of distilled hate. A shrill of pain, a dozen snarling yelps.

Connant broke for the door. Close behind him, McReady, then Barclay and Commander Garry came. Other men broke for the Ad Building, and weapons—the sledge house. Pomroy, in charge of Big Magnet's five cows, started down the corridor in the opposite direction—he had a six-foot-handled, long-tined pitchfork in mind.

Barclay slid to a halt, as McReady's giant bulk turned abruptly away from the tunnel leading to Dogtown, and vanished off at an angle. Uncertainly, the mechanician wavered a moment, the fire extinguisher in his hands, hesitating from one side to the other. Then he was racing after Connant's broad back. Whatever McReady had in mind, he could be trusted to make it work.

Connant stopped at the bend in the corridor. His breath hissed suddenly through his throat. "Great God—" The revolver exploded thunderously; three numbing, palpable waves of sound crashed through the confined corridors. Two more. The revolver dropped to the hard-packed snow of the trail, and Barclay saw the ice-ax shift into defensive position. Connant's powerful body blocked his vision, but beyond he heard something mewing, and, insanely, chuckling. The dogs were quieter; there was a deadly seriousness in their low snarls. Taloned feet scratched at hard-packed snow, broken chains were clinking and tangling.

Connant shifted abruptly, and Barclay could see what lay beyond. For a second he stood frozen, then his breath went out in a gusty curse. The Thing launched itself at Connant, the powerful arms of the man swung the ice-ax flatside first at what might have been a hand. It scrunched horribly, and the tattered flesh, ripped by a half-dozen savage huskies, leapt to its feet again. The red eyes blazed with an unearthly hatred, an unearthly, unkillable vitality.

Barclay turned the fire extinguisher on it; the blinding, blistering stream of chemical spray confused it, baffled it, together with the savage attacks of the huskies, not for long afraid of anything that did, or could live, held it at bay.

McReady wedged men out of his way and drove down the narrow corridor packed with men unable to reach the scene. There was a sure fore-planned drive to McReady's attack. One of the giant blow-torches used in warming the plane's engines was in his bronzed hands. It roared gustily as he turned the corner and opened the valve. The mad mewing hissed louder. The dogs scrambled back from the three-foot lance of blue-hot flame.

"Bar, get a power cable, run it in somehow. And a handle. We can electrocute this—monster, if I don't incinerate it." McReady spoke with an authority of planned action. Barclay turned down the long corridor to the power plant, but already before him Norris and Van Wall were racing down.

Barclay found the cable in the electrical cache in the tunnel wall. In a half minute he was hacking at it, walking back. Van Wall's voice rang out in a warning shout of "Power!" as the emergency gasoline-powered dynamo thudded into action. Half a dozen other men were down there now; the coal kindling was going into the firebox of the steam power plant. Norris, cursing in a low, deadly monotone, was working with quick, sure fingers on the other end of Barclay's cable, splicing in a contactor in one of the power leads.

The dogs had fallen back when Barclay reached the corridor bend, fallen back before a furious monstrosity that glared from baleful red eyes, mewing in trapped hatred. The dogs were a semi-circle of red-dipped muzzles with a fringe of glistening white teeth, whining with a vicious eagerness that near matched the fury of the red eyes. McReady stood confidently alert at the corridor bend, the gustily muttering torch held loose and ready for action in his hands. He stepped aside without moving his eyes from the beast as Barclay came up. There was a slight, tight smile on his lean, bronzed face.

Norris' voice called down the corridor, and Barclay stepped forward. The cable was taped to the long handle of a snow-shovel, the two conductors split, and held 18 inches apart by a scrap of lumber lashed at right angles across the far end of the handle. Bare copper conductors, charged with 220 volts, glinted in the light of pressure lamps. The Thing mewed and halted and dodged. McReady advanced to Barclay's side. The dogs beyond sensed the plan with the almost-telepathic intelligence of trained huskies. Their whimpering grew shriller, softer, their mincing steps carried them nearer. Abruptly a huge, night-black Alaskan leapt onto the trapped thing. It turned squalling, saber-clawed feet slashing.

Barclay leapt forward and jabbed. A weird, shrill scream rose and choked out. The smell of burnt flesh in the corridor intensified; greasy smoke curled up. The echoing pound of the gas-electric dynamo down the corridor became a slogging thud.

The red eyes clouded over in a stiffening, jerking travesty of a face. Arm-like, leglike members quivered and jerked. The dogs leapt forward, and Barclay yanked back his shovel-handled weapon. The thing on the snow did not move as gleaming teeth ripped it open.

# — VI —

Garry looked about the crowded room. Thirty-two men, some tensed nervously standing against the wall, some uneasily relaxed, some sitting, most perforce standing, as intimate as sardines. Thirty-two, plus the five engaged in sewing up wounded dogs, made thirty-seven, the total personnel.

Garry started speaking. "All right, I guess we're here. Some of you—three or four at most—saw what happened. All of you have seen that thing on the table, and can get a general idea. Anyone hasn't, I'll lift—" His hand strayed to the tarpaulin bulking over the thing on the table. There was an acrid odor of singed flesh seeping out of it. The men stirred restlessly, hasty denials.

"It looks rather as though Charnauk isn't going to lead any more teams," Garry went on. "Blair wants to get at this thing, and make some more detailed examination. We want to know what happened, and make sure right now that this is permanently, totally dead. Right?"

Connant grinned. "Anybody that doesn't agree can sit up with it tonight."

"All right then, Blair, what can you say about it? What was it?" Garry turned to the little biologist.

"I wonder if we ever saw its natural form." Blair looked at the covered mass. "It may have been imitating the beings that built that ship—but I don't think it was. I think that was its true form. Those of us who were up near the bend saw the thing in action; the thing on the table is the result. When it got loose, apparently, it started looking around. Antarctica still frozen as it was ages ago when the creature first saw it—and froze. From my observations while it was thawing out, and the bits of tissue I cut and hardened then, I think it was native to a hotter planet than Earth. It couldn't, in its natural form, stand the temperature. There is no life-form on Earth that can live in Antarctica during the winter, but the best compromise is the dog. It found the dogs, and somehow got near enough to Charnauk to get him. The others smelled it—heard it—I don't know—anyway they went wild, and broke chains, and attacked it before it was finished. The thing we found was part Charnauk, queerly only half-dead, part Charnauk half-digested by the jellylike protoplasm of that creature, and part the remains of the thing we originally found, sort of melted down to the basic protoplasm.

"When the dogs attacked it, it turned into the best fighting thing it could think of. Some other-world beast apparently."

"Turned," snapped Garry. "How?"

"Every living thing is made up of jelly—protoplasm and minute, submicroscopic things called nuclei, which control the bulk, the protoplasm. This thing was just a modification of that same worldwide plan of Nature; cells made up of protoplasm, controlled by infinitely tinier nuclei. You physicists might compare it—an individual cell of any living thing—with an atom; the bulk of the atom, the space-filling part, is made up of the electron orbits, but the character of the thing is determined by the atomic nucleus.

"This isn't wildly beyond what we already know. It's just a modification we haven't seen before. It's as natural, as logical, as any other manifestation of life. It obeys exactly the same laws. The cells are made of protoplasm, their character determined by the nucleus.

"Only in this creature, the cell-nuclei can control those cells at *will*. It digested Charnauk, and as it digested, studied every cell of his tissue, and shaped its own cells to imitate them exactly. Parts of it—parts that had time to finish changing—are dog-cells. But they don't have dog-cell nuclei." Blair lifted a fraction of the tarpaulin. A torn dog's leg with stiff gray fur protruded. "That, for instance, isn't dog at all; it's imitation. Some parts I'm uncertain about; the nucleus was hiding itself, covering up with dog-cell imitation nucleus. In time, not even a microscope would have shown the difference."

"Suppose," asked Norris bitterly, "it had had lots of time?"

"Then it would have been a dog. The other dogs would have accepted it. We would have accepted it. I don't think anything would have distinguished it, not microscope, nor X-ray, nor any other means. This is a member of a supremely intelligent race, a race that has learned the deepest secrets of biology, and turned them to its use."

"What was it planning to do?" Barclay looked at the humped tarpaulin.

Blair grinned unpleasantly. The wavering halo of thin hair round his bald pate wavered in the stir of air. "Take over the world, I imagine."

"Take over the world! Just it, all by itself?" Connant gasped. "Set itself up as a lone dictator?"

"No," Blair shook his head. The scalpel he had been fumbling in his bony fingers dropped; he bent to pick it up, so that his face was hidden as he spoke. "It would become the population of the world."

"Become—populate the world? Does it reproduce asexually?"

Blair shook his head and gulped. "It's—it doesn't have to. It weighed 85 pounds. Charnauk weighed about 90. It would have become Charnauk, and had 85 pounds left, to become—oh, Jack for instance, or Chinook. It can imitate anything—that is, become anything. If it had reached the Antarctic Sea, it would have become a seal, maybe two seals. They might have attacked a killer whale, and become either killers, or a herd of seals. Or maybe it would have caught an albatross, or a skua gull, and flown to South America."

Norris cursed softly. "And every time it digested something, and imitated it—"

"It would have had its original bulk left, to start again," Blair finished. "Nothing would kill it. It has no natural enemies, because it becomes whatever it wants to. If a killer whale attacked it, it would become a killer whale. If it was an albatross, and an eagle attacked it, it would become an eagle. Lord, it might become a female eagle. Go back—build a nest and lay eggs!"

"Are you sure that thing from hell is dead?" Dr. Copper asked softly.

"Yes, thank Heaven," the little biologist gasped. "After they drove the dogs off, I stood there poking Bar's electrocution thing into it for five minutes. It's dead and—cooked."

"Then we can only give thanks that this is Antarctica, where there is not one, single, solitary, living thing for it to imitate, except these animals in camp."

"Us," Blair giggled. "It can imitate us. Dogs can't make four hundred miles to the sea; there's no food. There aren't any skua gulls to imitate at this season. There aren't any penguins this far inland. There's nothing that can reach the sea from this point—except us. We've got brains. We can do it. Don't you see—*it's got to imitate us—it's got to be one of us—that's the only way it can fly an airplane—fly a plane for two hours, and rule—be—all Earth's inhabitants.* A world for the taking—*if it imitates us!*

"It didn't know yet. It hadn't had a chance to learn. It was rushed—hurried—took the thing nearest its own size. Look—I'm Pandora! I opened the box! And the only hope that can come out is—that nothing can come out. You didn't see me. I did it. I fixed it. I smashed every magneto. Not a plane can fly. Nothing can fly." Blair giggled and lay down on the floor crying.

Chief Pilot Van Wall made a dive for the door. His feet were fading echoes in the corridors as Dr. Copper bent unhurriedly over the little man on the floor. From his office at the end of the room he brought something, and injected a solution into Blair's arm. "He might come out of it when he wakes up," he sighed, rising. McReady helped him lift the biologist onto a nearby bunk. "It all depends on whether we can convince him that thing is dead."

Van Wall ducked into the shack brushing his heavy blond beard absently. "I didn't think a biologist would do a thing like that up thoroughly. He missed the spares in the second cache. It's all right. I smashed them."

Commander Garry nodded. "I was wondering about the radio."

Dr. Copper snorted. "You don't think it can leak out on a radio wave, do you? You'd have five rescue attempts in the next three months if you stop the broadcasts. The thing to do is talk loud and not make a sound. Now I wonder—"

McReady looked speculatively at the doctor. "It might be like an infectious disease. Everything that drank any of its blood—"

Copper shook his head. "Blair missed something. Imitate it may, but it has, to a certain extent, its own body-chemistry, its own metabolism. If it didn't, it would become a dog—and be a dog and nothing more. It has to be an imitation dog. Therefore you can detect it by serum tests. And its chemistry, since it comes from another world, must be so wholly, radically different that a few cells, such as gained by drops of blood, would be treated as disease germs by the dog, or human body."

"Blood—would one of those imitations bleed?" Norris demanded.

"Surely. Nothing mystic about blood. Muscle is about 90 per cent water; blood differs only in having a couple per cent more water, and less connective tissue. They'd bleed all right," Copper assured him.

Blair sat up in his bunk suddenly. "Connant—where's Connant?"

The physicist moved over toward the little biologist. "Here I am. What do you want?"

"Are you?" giggled Blair. He lapsed back into the bunk contorted with silent laughter.

Connant looked at him blankly. "Huh? Am I what?"

"*Are* you there?" Blair burst into gales of laughter. "*Are* you Connant? The beast wanted to be a *man*—not a dog—"


# — VII —


Dr. Copper rose wearily from the bunk, and washed the hypodermic carefully. The little tinkles it made seemed loud in the packed room, now that Blair's gurgling laughter had finally quieted. Copper looked toward Garry and shook his head slowly. "Hopeless, I'm afraid. I don't think we can ever convince him the thing is dead now."

Norris laughed uncertainly. "I'm not sure you can convince me. Oh, damn you, McReady."

"McReady?" Commander Garry turned to look from Norris to McReady curiously.

"The nightmares," Norris explained. "He had a theory about the nightmares we had at the Secondary Station after finding that thing."

"And that was?" Garry looked at McReady levelly.

Norris answered for him, jerkily, uneasily. "That the creature wasn't dead, had a sort of enormously slowed existence, an existence that permitted it, none the less, to be vaguely aware of the passing of time, of our coming, after endless years. I had a dream it could imitate things."

"Well," Copper grunted, "it can."

"Don't be an ass," Norris snapped. "That's not what's bothering me. In the dream it could read minds, read thoughts and ideas and mannerisms."

"What's so bad about that? It seems to be worrying you more than the thought of the joy we're going to have with a mad man in an Antarctic camp." Copper nodded toward Blair's sleeping form.

McReady shook his great head slowly. "You know that Connant is Connant, because he not merely looks like Connant—which we're beginning to believe that beast might be able to do—but he thinks like Connant, talks like Connant, moves himself around as Connant does. That takes more than merely a body that looks like him; that takes Connant's own mind, and thoughts and mannerisms. Therefore, though you know that the thing might make itself *look* like Connant, you aren't much bothered, because you know it has a mind from another world, a totally unhuman mind, that couldn't possibly react and think and talk like a man we know, and do it so well as to fool us for a moment. The idea of the creature imitating one of us is fascinating, but unreal because it is too completely unhuman to deceive us. It doesn't have a human mind."

"As I said before," Norris repeated, looking steadily at McReady, "you can say the damnedest things at the damnedest times. Will you be so good as to finish that thought—one way or the other?"

Kinner, the scar-faced expedition cook, had been standing near Connant. Suddenly he moved down the length of the crowded room toward his familiar galley. He shook the ashes from the galley stove noisily.

"It would do it no good," said Dr. Copper, softly as though thinking out loud, "to merely look like something it was trying to imitate; it would have to understand its feelings, its reaction. It *is* unhuman; it has powers of imitation beyond any conception of man. A good actor, by training himself, can imitate another man, another man's mannerisms, well enough to fool most people. Of course no actor could imitate so perfectly as to deceive men who had been living with the imitated one in the complete lack of privacy of an Antarctic camp. That would take a super-human skill."

"Oh, you've got the bug too?" Norris cursed softly.

Connant, standing alone at one end of the room, looked about him wildly, his face white. A gentle eddying of the men had crowded them slowly down toward the other end of the room, so that he stood quite alone. "My God, will you two Jeremiahs shut up?" Connant's voice shook. "What am I? Some kind of a microscopic specimen you're dissecting? Some unpleasant worm you're discussing in the third person?"

McReady looked up at him; his slowly twisting hands stopped for a moment. "Having a lovely time. Wish you were here. Signed: Everybody.

"Connant, if you think you're having a hell of a time, just move over on the other end for a while. You've got one thing we haven't; you know what the answer is. I'll tell you this, right now you're the most feared and respected man in Big Magnet."

"Lord, I wish you could see your eyes," Connant gasped. "Stop staring, will you! What the hell are you going to do?"

"Have you any suggestions, Dr. Copper?" Commander Garry asked steadily. "The present situation is impossible."

"Oh, is it?" Connant snapped. "Come over here and look at that crowd. By Heaven, they look exactly like that gang of huskies around the corridor bend. Benning, will you stop hefting that damned ice-ax?"

The coppery blade rang on the floor as the aviation mechanic nervously dropped it. He bent over and picked it up instantly, hefting it slowly, turning it in his hands, his brown eyes moving jerkily about the room.

Copper sat down on the bunk beside Blair. The wood creaked noisily in the room. Far down a corridor, a dog yelped in pain, and the dog-drivers' tense voices floated softly back. "Microscopic examination," said the doctor thoughtfully, "would be useless, as Blair pointed out. Considerable time has passed. However, serum tests would be definitive."

"Serum tests? What do you mean exactly?" Commander Garry asked.

"If I had a rabbit that had been injected with human blood—a poison to rabbits, of course, as is the blood of any animal save that of another rabbit—and the injections continued in increasing doses for some time, the rabbit would be human-immune. If a small quantity of its blood were drawn off, allowed to separate in a test-tube, and to the clear serum, a bit of human blood were added, there would be a visible reaction, proving the blood was human. If cow, or dog blood were added—or any protein material other than that one thing, human blood—no reaction would take place. That would prove definitely."

"Can you suggest where I might catch a rabbit for you, Doc?" Norris asked. "That is, nearer than Australia; we don't want to waste time going that far."

"I know there aren't any rabbits in Antarctica," Copper nodded, "but that is simply the usual animal. Any animal except man will do. A dog for instance. But it will take several days, and due to the greater size of the animal, considerable blood. Two of us will have to contribute."

"Would I do?" Garry asked.

"That will make two," Copper nodded. "I'll get to work on it right away."

"What about Connant in the meantime?" Kinner demanded. "I'm going out that door and head off for the Ross Sea before I cook for him."

"He may be human—" Copper started.

Connant burst out in a flood of curses. "Human! *May* be human, you damned saw-bones! What in hell do you think I am?"

"A monster," Copper snapped sharply. "Now shut up and listen." Connant's face drained of color and he sat down heavily as the indictment was put in words. "Until we know—you know as well as we do that we have reason to question the fact, and only you know how that question is to be answered—we may reasonably be expected to lock you up. If you are—unhuman—you're a lot more dangerous than poor Blair there, and I'm going to see that he's locked up thoroughly. I expect that his next stage will be a violent desire to kill you, all the dogs, and probably all of us. When he wakes, he will be convinced we're all unhuman, and nothing on the planet will ever change his conviction. It would be kinder to let him die, but we can't do that, of course. He's going in one shack, and you can stay in Cosmos House with your cosmic ray apparatus. Which is about what you'd do anyway. I've got to fix up a couple of dogs."

Connant nodded bitterly. "I'm human. Hurry that test. Your eyes—Lord, I wish you could see your eyes staring—"

Commander Garry watched anxiously as Clark, the dog-handler, held the big brown Alaskan husky, while Copper began the injection treatment. The dog was not anxious to cooperate; the needle was painful, and already he'd experienced considerable needle work that morning. Five stitches held closed a slash that ran from his shoulder across the ribs half way down his body. One long fang was broken off short; the missing part was to be found half-buried in the shoulder bone of the monstrous thing on the table in the Ad Building.

"How long will that take?" Garry asked, pressing his arm gently. It was sore from the prick of the needle Dr. Copper had used to withdraw blood.

Copper shrugged. "I don't know, to be frank. I know the general method, I've used it on rabbits. But I haven't experimented with dogs. They're big, clumsy animals to work with; naturally rabbits are preferable, and serve ordinarily. In civilized places you can buy a stock of human-immune rabbits from suppliers, and not many investigators take the trouble to prepare their own."

"What do they want with them back there?" Clark asked.

"Criminology is one large field. A says he didn't murder B, but that the blood on his shirt came from killing a chicken. The State makes a test, then it's up to A to explain how it is the blood reacts on human-immune rabbits, but not on chicken-immunes."

"What are we going to do with Blair in the meantime?" Garry asked wearily. "It's all right to let him sleep where he is for a while, but when he wakes up—"

"Barclay and Benning are fitting some bolts on the door of Cosmos House," Copper replied grimly. "Connant's acting like a gentleman. I think perhaps the way the other men look at him makes him rather want privacy. Lord knows, heretofore we've all of us individually prayed for a little privacy."

Clark laughed bitterly. "Not anymore, thank you. The more the merrier."

"Blair," Copper went on, "will also have to have privacy—and locks. He's going to have a pretty definite plan in mind when he wakes up. Ever hear the old story of how to stop hoof-and-mouth disease in cattle?

"If there isn't any hoof-and-mouth disease, there won't be any hoof-and-mouth disease," Copper explained. "You get rid of it by killing every animal that exhibits it, and every animal that's been near the diseased animal. Blair's a biologist, and knows that story. He's afraid of this thing we loosed. The answer is probably pretty clear in his mind now. Kill everybody and everything in this camp before a skua gull or a wandering albatross coming in with the spring chances out this way and—catches the disease."

Clark's lips curled in a twisted grin. "Sounds logical to me. If things get too bad—maybe we'd better let Blair get loose. It would save us committing suicide. We might also make something of a vow that if things get bad, we see that that does happen."

Copper laughed softly. "The last man alive in Big Magnet—wouldn't be a man," he pointed out. "Somebody's got to kill those—creatures that don't desire to kill themselves, you know. We don't have enough thermite to do it all at once, and the decanite explosive wouldn't help much. I have an idea that even small pieces of one of those beings would be self-sufficient."

"If," said Garry thoughtfully, "they can modify their protoplasm at will, won't they simply modify themselves to birds and fly away? They can read all about birds, and imitate their structure without even meeting them. Or imitate, perhaps, birds of their home planet."

Copper shook his head, and helped Clark to free the dog. "Man studied birds for centuries, trying to learn how to make a machine to fly like them. He never did do the trick; his final success came when he broke away entirely and tried new methods. Knowing the general idea, and knowing the detailed structure of wing and bone and nerve-tissue is something far, far different. And as for other-world birds, perhaps, in fact very probably, the atmospheric conditions here are so vastly different that their birds couldn't fly. Perhaps, even, the being came from a planet like Mars with such a thin atmosphere that there were no birds."

Barclay came into the building, trailing a length of airplane control cable.

"It's finished, Doc. Cosmos House can't be opened from the inside. Now where do we put Blair?"

Copper looked toward Garry. "There wasn't any biology building. I don't know where we can isolate him."

"How about East Cache?" Garry said after a moment's thought. "Will Blair be able to look after himself—or need attention?"

"He'll be capable enough. We'll be the ones to watch out," Copper assured him grimly. "Take a stove, a couple of bags of coal, necessary supplies and a few tools to fix it up. Nobody's been out there since last fall, have they?"

Garry shook his head. "If he gets noisy—I thought that might be a good idea."

Barclay hefted the tools he was carrying and looked up at Garry. "If the muttering he's doing now is any sign, he's going to sing away the night hours. And we won't like his song."

"What's he saying?" Copper asked.

Barclay shook his head. "I didn't care to listen much. You can if you want to. But I gathered that the blasted idiot had all the dreams McReady had, and a few more. He slept beside the thing when we stopped on the trail coming in from Secondary Magnetic, remember. He dreamt the thing was alive, and dreamt more details. And—damn his soul—knew it wasn't all dream, or had reason to. He knew it had telepathic powers that were stirring vaguely, and that it could not only read minds, but project thoughts. They weren't dreams, you see. They were stray thoughts that thing was broadcasting, the way Blair's broadcasting his thoughts now—a sort of telepathic muttering in its sleep. That's why he knew so much about its powers. I guess you and I, Doc, weren't so sensitive—if you want to believe in telepathy."

"I have to," Copper sighed. "Dr. Rhine of Duke University has shown that it exists, shown that some are much more sensitive than others."

"Well, if you want to learn a lot of details, go listen in on Blair's broadcast. He's driven most of the boys out of the Ad Building; Kinner's rattling pans like coal going down a chute. When he can't rattle a pan, he shakes ashes.

"By the way, Commander, what are we going to do this spring, now the planes are out of it?"

Garry sighed. "I'm afraid our expedition is going to be a loss. We cannot divide our strength now."

"It won't be a loss—if we continue to live, and come out of this," Copper promised him. "The find we've made, if we can get it under control, is important enough. The cosmic ray data, magnetic work, and atmospheric work won't be greatly hindered."

Garry laughed mirthlessly. "I was just thinking of the radio broadcasts.

Telling half the world about the wonderful results of our exploration flights, trying to fool men like Byrd and Ellsworth back home there that we're doing something."

Copper nodded gravely. "They'll know something's wrong. But men like that have judgment enough to know we wouldn't do tricks without some sort of reason, and will wait for our return to judge us. I think it comes to this: men who know enough to recognize our deception will wait for our return. Men who haven't discretion and faith enough to wait will not have the experience to detect any fraud. We know enough of the conditions here to put through a good bluff."

"Just so they don't send 'rescue' expeditions," Garry prayed. "When—if— we're ever ready to come out, we'll have to send word to Captain Forsythe to bring a stock of magnetos with him when he comes down. But—never mind that."

"You mean if we don't come out?" asked Barclay. "I was wondering if a nice running account of an eruption or an earthquake via radio—with a swell windup by using a stick of decanite under the microphone—would help. Nothing, of course, will entirely keep people out. One of those swell, melodramatic 'last-man-alive-scenes' might make 'em go easy though."

Garry smiled with genuine humor. "Is everybody in camp trying to figure that out too?"

Copper laughed. "What do you think, Garry? We're confident we can win out. But not too easy about it, I guess."

Clark grinned up from the dog he was petting into calmness. "Confident, did you say, Doc?"

— VIII —

Blair moved restlessly around the small shack. His eyes jerked and quivered in vague, fleeting glances at the four men with him; Barclay, six feet tall and weighing over 190 pounds; McReady, a bronze giant of a man; Dr. Copper, short, squatly powerful; and Benning, five-feet-ten of wiry strength.

Blair was huddled up against the far wall of the East Cache cabin, his gear piled in the middle of the floor beside the heating stove, forming an island between him and the four men. His bony hands clenched and fluttered, terrified. His pale eyes wavered uneasily as his bald, freckled head darted about in birdlike motion.

"I don't want anybody coming here. I'll cook my own food," he snapped nervously. "Kinner may be human now, but I don't believe it. I'm going to get out of here, but I'm not going to eat any food you send me. I want cans. Sealed cans."

"O.K., Blair, we'll bring 'em tonight," Barclay promised. "You've got coal, and the fire's started. I'll make a last—" Barclay started forward.

Blair instantly scurried to the farthest corner. "Get out! Keep away from me, you monster!" the little biologist shrieked, and tried to claw his way through the wall of the shack. "Keep away from me—keep away—I won't be absorbed—I won't be—"

Barclay relaxed and moved back. Dr. Copper shook his head. "Leave him alone, Bar. It's easier for him to fix the thing himself. We'll have to fix the door, I think—"

The four men let themselves out. Efficiently, Benning and Barclay fell to work. There were no locks in Antarctica; there wasn't enough privacy to make them needed. But powerful screws had been driven in each side of the door frame, and the spare aviation control cable, immensely strong, woven steel wire, was rapidly caught between them and drawn taut. Barclay went to work with a drill and a keyhole saw. Presently he had a trap cut in the door through which goods could be passed without unlashing the entrance. Three powerful hinges from a stock-crate, two hasps and a pair of three-inch cotter-pins made it proof against opening from the other side.

Blair moved about restlessly inside. He was dragging something over to the door with panting gasps and muttering, frantic curses. Barclay opened the hatch and glanced in, Dr. Copper peering over his shoulder. Blair had moved the heavy bunk against the door. It could not be opened without his cooperation now.

"Don't know but what the poor man's right at that," McReady sighed. "If he gets loose, it is his avowed intention to kill each and all of us as quickly as possible, which is something we don't agree with. But we've something on our side of that door that is worse than a homicidal maniac. If one or the other has to get loose, I think I'll come up and undo those lashings here."

Barclay grinned. "You let me know, and I'll show you how to get these off fast. Let's go back."

The sun was painting the northern horizon in multi-colored rainbows still, though it was two hours below the horizon. The field of drift swept off to the north, sparkling under its flaming colors in a million reflected glories. Low mounds of rounded white on the northern horizon showed the Magnet Range was barely awash above the sweeping drift. Little eddies of wind-lifted snow swirled away from their skis as they set out toward the main encampment two miles away. The spidery finger of the broadcast radiator lifted a gaunt black needle against the white of the Antarctic continent. The snow under their skis was like fine sand, hard and gritty.

"Spring," said Benning bitterly, "is come. Ain't we got fun! I've been looking forward to getting away from this blasted hole in the ice."

"I wouldn't try it now, if I were you." Barclay grunted. "Guys that set out from here in the next few days are going to be marvelously unpopular."

"How is your dog getting along, Dr. Copper?" McReady asked. "Any results yet?"

"In thirty hours? I wish there were. I gave him an injection of my blood today. But I imagine another five days will be needed. I don't know certainly enough to stop sooner."

"I've been wondering—if Connant were—changed, would he have warned us so soon after the animal escaped? Wouldn't he have waited long enough for it to have a real chance to fix itself? Until we woke up naturally?" McReady asked slowly.

"The thing is selfish. You didn't think it looked as though it were possessed of a store of the higher justices, did you?" Dr. Copper pointed out. "Every part of it is all of it, every part of it is all for itself, I imagine. If Connant were changed, to save his skin, he'd have to—but Connant's feelings aren't changed; they're imitated perfectly, or they're his own. Naturally, the imitation, imitating perfectly Connant's feelings, would do exactly what Connant would do."

"Say, couldn't Norris or Van give Connant some kind of a test? If the thing is brighter than men, it might know more physics than Connant should, and they'd catch it out," Barclay suggested.

Copper shook his head wearily. "Not if it reads minds. You can't plan a trap for it. Van suggested that last night. He hoped it would answer some of the questions of physics he'd like to know answers to."

"This expedition-of-four idea is going to make life happy." Benning looked at his companions. "Each of us with an eye on the others to make sure he doesn't do something—peculiar. Man, aren't we going to be a trusting bunch! Each man eyeing his neighbors with the grandest exhibition of faith and trust—I'm beginning to know what Connant meant by 'I wish you could see your eyes.' Every now and then we all have it, I guess. One of you looks around with a sort of 'I-wonder-if-the-other-*three*-are look.' Incidentally, I'm not excepting myself."

"So far as we know, the animal is dead, with a slight question as to Connant. No other is suspected," McReady stated slowly. "The 'always-four' order is merely a precautionary measure."

"I'm waiting for Garry to make it four-in-a-bunk," Barclay sighed. "I thought I didn't have any privacy before, but since that order—"

None watched more tensely than Connant. A little sterile glass test-tube, half-filled with straw-colored fluid. One—two—three—four—five drops of the clear solution Dr. Copper had prepared from the drops of blood from Connant's arm. The tube was shaken carefully, then set in a beaker of clear, warm water. The thermometer read blood heat, a little thermostat clicked noisily, and the electric hotplate began to glow as the lights flickered slightly.

Then—little white flecks of precipitation were forming, snowing down in the clear straw-colored fluid. "Lord," said Connant. He dropped heavily into a bunk, crying like a baby. "Six days—" Connant sobbed, "six days in there— wondering if that damned test would lie—"

Garry moved over silently, and slipped his arm across the physicist's back.

"It couldn't lie," Dr. Copper said. "The dog was human-immune—and the serum reacted."

"He's—all right?" Norris gasped. "Then—the animal is dead—dead for-ever?"

"He is human," Copper spoke definitely, "and the animal is dead."

Kinner burst out laughing, laughing hysterically. McReady turned toward him and slapped his face with a methodical one-two, one-two action. The cook laughed, gulped, cried a moment and sat up rubbing his cheeks, mumbling his thanks vaguely. "I was scared. Lord, I was scared—"

Norris laughed brittlely. "You think we weren't, you ape? You think maybe Connant wasn't?"

The Ad Building stirred with a sudden rejuvenation. Voices laughed, the men clustering around Connant spoke with unnecessarily loud voices, jittery, nervous voices relievedly friendly again. Somebody called out a suggestion, and a dozen started for their skis. Blair. Blair might recover——— Dr. Copper fussed with his test-tubes in nervous relief, trying solutions. The party of relief for Blair's shack started out the door, skis clapping noisily. Down the corridor, the dogs set up a quick yelping howl as the air of excited relief reached them.

Dr. Copper fussed with his tubes. McReady noticed him first, sitting on the edge of the bunk, with two precipitin-whitened test-tubes of straw-colored fluid, his face whiter than the stuff in the tubes, silent tears slipping down from horror-widened eyes.

McReady felt a cold knife of fear pierce through his heart and freeze in his breast. Dr. Copper looked up.

"Garry," he called hoarsely. "Garry, for God's sake, come here."

Commander Garry walked toward him sharply. Silence clapped down on the Ad Building. Connant looked up, rose stiffly from his seat.

"Garry—tissue from the monster—precipitates too. It proves nothing. Nothing but—but the dog was monster-immune too. That one of the two contributing blood—one of us two, you and I, Garry—*one of us is a monster.*"

"Bar, call back those men before they tell Blair," McReady said quietly. Barclay went to the door; faintly his shouts came back to the tensely silent men in the room. Then he was back.

"They're coming," he said. "I didn't tell them why. Just that Dr. Copper said not to go."

"McReady," Garry sighed, "you're in command now. May God help you. I cannot."

The bronzed giant nodded slowly, his deep eyes on Commander Garry.

"I may be the one," Garry added. "I know I'm not, but I cannot prove it to you in any way. Dr. Copper's test has broken down. The fact that he showed it was useless, when it was to the advantage of the monster to have that uselessness not known, would seem to prove he was human."

Copper rocked back and forth slowly on the bunk. "I know I'm human. I can't prove it either. One of us two is a liar, for that test cannot lie, and it says one of us is. I gave proof that the test was wrong, which seems to prove I'm human, and now Garry has given that argument which proves me human—which he, as the monster, should not do. Round and round and round and round and—"

Dr. Copper's head, then his neck and shoulders began circling slowly in time to the words. Suddenly he was lying back on the bunk, roaring with laughter. "It doesn't have to prove one of us is a monster! It doesn't have to prove that at all! Ho-ho. If we're *all* monsters it works the same! We're all monsters—all of us—Connant and Garry and I—and all of you."

"McReady," Van Wall, the blond-bearded Chief Pilot, called softly, "you were on the way to an M.D. when you took up meteorology, weren't you? Can you make some kind of test?"

McReady went over to Copper slowly, took the hypodermic from his hand, and washed it carefully in 95 per cent alcohol. Garry sat on the bunk-edge with wooden face, watching Copper and McReady expressionlessly. "What Copper said is possible," McReady sighed. "Van, will you help here? Thanks." The filled needle jabbed into Copper's thigh. The man's laughter did not stop, but slowly faded into sobs, then sound sleep as the morphia took hold.

McReady turned again. The men who had started for Blair stood at the far end of the room, skis dripping snow, their faces as white as their skis. Connant had a lighted cigarette in each hand; one he was puffing absently, and staring at the floor. The heat of the one in his left hand attracted him and he stared at it, and the one in the other hand, stupidly for a moment. He dropped one and crushed it under his heel slowly.

"Dr. Copper," McReady repeated, "could be right. I know I'm human—but of course can't prove it. I'll repeat the test for my own information. Any of you others who wish to may do the same."

Two minutes later, McReady held a test-tube with white precipitin settling slowly from straw-colored serum. "It reacts to human blood too, so they aren't both monsters."

"I didn't think they were," Van Wall sighed. "That wouldn't suit the monster either; we could have destroyed them if we knew. Why hasn't the monster destroyed us, do you suppose? It seems to be loose."

McReady snorted. Then laughed softly. "Elementary, my dear Watson. The monster wants to have life-forms available. It cannot animate a dead body, apparently. It is just waiting—waiting until the best opportunities come. We who remain human, it is holding in reserve."

Kinner shuddered violently. "Hey. Hey, Mac. Mac, would I know if I was a monster? Would I know if the monster had already got me? Oh Lord, I may be a monster already."

"You'd know," McReady answered.

"But we wouldn't," Norris laughed shortly, half-hysterically.

McReady looked at the vial of serum remaining. "There's one thing this damned stuff is good for, at that," he said thoughtfully. "Clark, will you and Van help me? The rest of the gang better stick together here. Keep an eye on each other," he said bitterly. "See that you don't get into mischief, shall we say?"

McReady started down the tunnel toward Dogtown, with Clark and Van Wall behind him. "You need more serum?" Clark asked.

McReady shook his head. "Tests. There's four cows and a bull, and nearly seventy dogs down there. This stuff reacts only to human blood and—monsters."

McReady came back to the Ad Building and went silently to the wash stand. Clark and Van Wall joined him a moment later. Clark's lips had developed a tic, jerking into sudden, unexpected sneers.

"What did you do?" Connant exploded suddenly. "More immunizing?"

Clark snickered, and stopped with a hiccough. "Immunizing. Haw! Immune all right."

"That monster," said Van Wall steadily, "is quite logical. Our immune dog was quite all right, and we drew a little more serum for the tests. But we won't make any more."

"Can't—can't you use one man's blood on another dog—" Norris began.

"There aren't," said McReady softly, "any more dogs. Nor cattle, I might add."

"No more dogs?" Benning sat down slowly.

"They're very nasty when they start changing," Van Wall said precisely, "but slow. That electrocution iron you made up, Barclay, is very fast. There is only one dog left—our immune. The monster left that for us, so we could play with our little test. The rest—" He shrugged and dried his hands.

"The cattle—" gulped Kinner.

"Also. Reacted very nicely. They look funny as hell when they start melting. The beast hasn't any quick escape, when it's tied in dog chains, or halters, and it had to be to imitate."

Kinner stood up slowly. His eyes darted around the room, and came to rest horribly quivering on a tin bucket in the galley. Slowly, step by step, he retreated toward the door, his mouth opening and closing silently, like a fish out of water.

"The milk—" he gasped. "I milked 'em an hour ago—" His voice broke into a scream as he dived through the door. He was out on the ice cap without windproof or heavy clothing.

Van Wall looked after him for a moment thoughtfully. "He's probably hopelessly mad," he said at length, "but he might be a monster escaping. He hasn't skis. Take a blow-torch—in case."

The physical motion of the chase helped them; something that needed doing. Three of the other men were quietly being sick. Norris was lying flat on his back, his face greenish, looking steadily at the bottom of the bunk above him.

"Mac, how long have the—cows been not—cows—"

McReady shrugged his shoulders hopelessly. He went over to the milk bucket, and with his little tube of serum went to work on it. The milk clouded it, making certainty difficult. Finally he dropped the test-tube in the stand and shook his head. "It tests negatively. Which means either they were cows then, or that, being perfect imitations, they gave perfectly good milk."

Copper stirred restlessly in his sleep and gave a gurgling cross between a snore and a laugh. Silent eyes fastened on him. "Would morphia—a monster—" somebody started to ask.

"Lord knows," McReady shrugged. "It affects every Earthly animal I know of."

Connant suddenly raised his head. "Mac! The dogs must have swallowed pieces of the monster, and the pieces destroyed them! The dogs were where the monster resided. I was locked up. Doesn't that prove—"

Van Wall shook his head. "Sorry. Proves nothing about what you are, only proves what you didn't do."

"It doesn't do that," McReady sighed. "We are helpless. Because we don't know enough, and so jittery we don't think straight. Locked up! Ever watch a white corpuscle of the blood go through the wall of a blood vessel? No? It sticks out a pseudopod. And there it is—on the far side of the wall."

"Oh," said Van Wall unhappily. "The cattle tried to melt down, didn't they? They could have melted down—become just a thread of stuff and leaked under a door to re-collect on the other side. Ropes—no—no, that wouldn't do it. They couldn't live in a sealed tank or—"

"If," said McReady, "you shoot it through the heart, and it doesn't die, it's a monster. That's the best test I can think of, offhand."

"No dogs," said Garry quietly, "and no cattle. It has to imitate men now. And locking up doesn't do any good. Your test might work, Mac, but I'm afraid it would be hard on the men."

## — X —

Clark looked up from the galley stove as Van Wall, Barclay, McReady and Benning came in, brushing the drift from their clothes. The other men jammed into the Ad Building continued studiously to do as they were doing, playing chess, poker, reading. Ralsen was fixing a sledge on the table; Van and Norris had their heads together over magnetic data, while Harvey read tables in a low voice.

Dr. Copper snored softly on the bunk. Garry was working with Dutton over a sheaf of radio messages on the corner of Dutton's bunk and a small fraction of the radio table. Connant was using most of the table for cosmic ray sheets.

Quite plainly through the corridor, despite two closed doors, they could hear Kinner's voice. Clark banged a kettle onto the galley stove and beckoned McReady silently. The meteorologist went over to him.

"I don't mind the cooking so damn much," Clark said nervously, "but isn't there some way to stop that bird? We all agreed that it would be safe to move him into Cosmos House."

"Kinner?" McReady nodded toward the door. "I'm afraid not. I can dope him, I suppose, but we don't have an unlimited supply of morphia, and he's not in danger of losing his mind. Just hysterical."

"Well, we're in danger of losing ours. You've been out for an hour and a half. That's been going on steadily ever since, and it was going for two hours before. There's a limit, you know."

Garry wandered over slowly, apologetically. For an instant, McReady caught the feral spark of fear—horror—in Clark's eyes, and knew at the same instant it was in his own. Garry—Garry or Copper—was certainly a monster.

"If you could stop that, I think it would be a sound policy, Mac," Garry spoke quietly. "There are—tensions enough in this room. We agreed that it would be safe for Kinner in there, because everyone else in camp is under constant eyeing." Garry shivered slightly. "And try, try in God's name, to find some test that will work."

McReady sighed. "Watched or unwatched, everyone's tense. Blair's jammed the trap so it won't open now. Says he's got food enough, and keeps screaming 'Go away, go away—you're monsters. I won't be absorbed. I won't. I'll tell men when they come. Go away.' So—we went away."

"There's no other test?" Garry pleaded.

McReady shrugged his shoulders. "Copper was perfectly right. The serum test could be absolutely definitive if it hadn't been—contaminated. But that's the only dog left, and he's fixed now."

"Chemicals? Chemical tests?"

McReady shook his head. "Our chemistry isn't that good. I tried the microscope, you know."

Garry nodded. "Monster-dog and real dog were identical. But—you've got to go on. What are we going to do after dinner?"

Van Wall had joined them quietly. "Rotation sleeping. Half the crowd asleep; half awake. I wonder how many of us are monsters? All the dogs were. We thought we were safe, but somehow it got Copper—or you." Van Wall's eyes flashed uneasily. "It may have gotten every one of you—all of you but myself may be wondering, looking. No, that's not possible. You'd just spring then. I'd be helpless. We humans must somehow have the greater numbers now. But—" he stopped.

McReady laughed shortly. "You're doing what Norris complained of in me. Leaving it hanging. 'But if one more is changed—that may shift the balance of power.' It doesn't fight. I don't think it ever fights. It must be a peaceable thing, in its own—inimitable—way. It never had to, because it always gained its end—otherwise."

Van Wall's mouth twisted in a sickly grin. "You're suggesting then, that perhaps it already *has* the greater numbers, but is just waiting—waiting, all of them—all of you, for all I know—waiting till I, the last human, drop my wariness in sleep. Mac, did you notice their eyes, all looking at us?"

Garry sighed. "You haven't been sitting here for four straight hours, while all their eyes silently weighed the information that one of us two, Copper or I, is a monster certainly—perhaps both of us."

Clark repeated his request. "Will you stop that bird's noise? He's driving me nuts. Make him tone down, anyway."

"Still praying?" McReady asked.

"Still praying," Clark groaned. "He hasn't stopped for a second. I don't mind his praying if it relieves him, but he yells, he sings psalms and hymns and shouts prayers. He thinks God can't hear well way down here."

"Maybe He can't," Barclay grunted. "Or He'd have done something about this thing loosed from hell."

"Somebody's going to try that test you mentioned, if you don't stop him," Clark stated grimly. "I think a cleaver in the head would be as positive a test as a bullet in the heart."

"Go ahead with the food. I'll see what I can do. There may be something in the cabinets." McReady moved wearily toward the corner Copper had used as his dispensary. Three tall cabinets of rough boards, two locked, were the repositories of the camp's medical supplies. Twelve years ago McReady had graduated, had started for an internship, and been diverted to meteorology. Copper was a picked man, a man who knew his profession thoroughly and modernly. More than half the drugs available were totally unfamiliar to McReady; many of the others he had forgotten. There was no huge medical library here, no series of journals available to learn the things he had forgotten, the elementary, simple things to Copper, things that did not merit inclusion in the small library he had been forced to content himself with. Books are heavy, and every ounce of supplies had been freighted in by air.

McReady picked a barbiturate hopefully. Barclay and Van Wall went with him. One man never went anywhere alone in Big Magnet.

Ralsen had his sledge put away, and the physicists had moved off the table, the poker game broken up when they got back. Clark was putting out the food. The click of spoons and the muffled sounds of eating were the only sign of life in the room. There were no words spoken as the three returned; simply all eyes focused on them questioningly, while the jaws moved methodically.

McReady stiffened suddenly. Kinner was screeching out a hymn in a hoarse, cracked voice. He looked wearily at Van Wall with a twisted grin and shook his head. "Hu-uh."

Van Wall cursed bitterly, and sat down at the table. "We'll just plumb have to take that till his voice wears out. He can't yell like that forever."

"He's got a brass throat and a cast-iron larynx," Norris declared savagely. "Then we could be hopeful, and suggest he's one of our friends. In that case he could go on renewing his throat till doomsday."

Silence clamped down. For twenty minutes they ate without a word. Then Connant jumped up with an angry violence. "You sit as still as a bunch of graven images. You don't say a word, but oh, Lord, what expressive eyes you've got. They roll around like a bunch of glass marbles spilling down a table. They wink and blink and stare—and whisper things. Can you guys look somewhere else for a change, please?

"Listen, Mac, you're in charge here. Let's run movies for the rest of the night. We've been saving those reels to make 'em last. Last for what? Who is it's going to see those last reels, eh? Let's see 'em while we can, and look at something other than each other."

"Sound idea, Connant. I, for one, am quite willing to change this in any way I can."

"Turn the sound up loud, Dutton. Maybe you can drown out the hymns," Clark suggested.

"But don't," Norris said softly, "don't turn off the lights altogether."

"The lights will be out." McReady shook his head. "We'll show all the cartoon movies we have. You won't mind seeing the old cartoons, will you?"

"Goody, goody—a moom pitcher show. I'm just in the mood." McReady turned to look at the speaker, a lean, lanky New Englander, by the name of Caldwell. Caldwell was stuffing his pipe slowly, a sour eye cocked up to McReady.

The bronze giant was forced to laugh. "O.K., Bart, you win. Maybe we aren't quite in the mood for Popeye and trick ducks, but it's something."

"Let's play Classifications," Caldwell suggested slowly. "Or maybe you call it Guggenheim. You draw lines on a piece of paper, and put down classes of things—like animals, you know. One for 'H' and one for 'U' and so on. Like 'Human' and 'Unknown' for instance. I think that would be a hell of a lot better game. Classification, I sort of figure is what we need right now a lot more than movies. Maybe somebody's got a pencil that he can draw lines with, draw lines between the 'U' animals and the 'H' animals for instance."

"McReady's trying to find that kind of a pencil," Van Wall answered quietly, "but we've got three kinds of animals here, you know. One that begins with 'M.' We don't want any more."

"Mad ones, you mean. Uh-huh. Clark, I'll help you with those pans so we can get our little peep-show going." Caldwell got up slowly.

Dutton and Barclay and Benning, in charge of the projector and sound mechanism arrangements, went about their job silently, while the Ad Building was cleared and the dishes and pans disposed of. McReady drifted over toward Van Wall slowly, and leaned back in the bunk beside him. "I've been wondering, Van," he said with a wry grin, "whether or not to report my ideas in advance. I forgot the 'U animals,' as Caldwell named it, could read minds. I've a vague idea of something that might work. It's too vague to bother with though. Go ahead with your show, while I try to figure out the logic of the thing. I'll take this bunk."

Van Wall glanced up, and nodded. The movie screen would be practically on a line with his bunk, hence making the pictures least distracting here, because least intelligible. "Perhaps you should tell us what you have in mind. As it is, only the unknowns know what you plan. You might be—unknown before you got it into operation."

"Won't take long, if I get it figured out right. But I don't want any more all-but-the-test-dog-monsters things. We better move Copper into this bunk directly above me. He won't be watching the screen either." McReady nodded toward Copper's gently snoring bulk. Garry helped them lift and move the doctor.

McReady leaned back against the bunk, and sank into a trance, almost, of concentration, trying to calculate chances, operations, methods. He was scarcely aware as the others distributed themselves silently, and the screen lit up. Vaguely Kinner's hectic, shouted prayers and his rasping hymn-singing annoyed him till the sound accompaniment started. The lights were turned out, but the large, light-colored areas of the screen reflected enough light for ready visibility. It made men's eyes sparkle as they moved restlessly. Kinner was still praying, shouting, his voice a raucous accompaniment to the mechanical sound. Dutton stepped up the amplification.

So long had the voice been going on, that only vaguely at first was McReady aware that something seemed missing. Lying as he was, just across the narrow room from the corridor leading to Cosmos House, Kinner's voice had reached him fairly clearly, despite the sound accompaniment of the pictures. It struck him abruptly that it had stopped.

"Dutton, cut that sound," McReady called as he sat up abruptly. The pictures flickered a moment, soundless and strangely futile in the sudden, deep silence. The rising wind on the surface above bubbled melancholy tears of sound down the stove pipes. "Kinner's stopped," McReady said softly.

"For God's sake start that sound then, he may have stopped to listen," Norris snapped.

McReady rose and went down the corridor. Barclay and Van Wall left their places at the far end of the room to follow him. The flickers bulged and twisted on the back of Barclay's gray underwear as he crossed the still-functioning beam of the projector. Dutton snapped on the lights, and the pictures vanished.

Norris stood at the door as McReady had asked. Garry sat down quietly in the bunk nearest the door, forcing Clark to make room for him. Most of the others had stayed exactly where they were. Only Connant walked slowly up and down the room, in steady, unvarying rhythm.

"If you're going to do that, Connant," Clark spat, "we can get along without you altogether, whether you're human or not. Will you stop that damned rhythm?"

"Sorry." The physicist sat down in a bunk, and watched his toes thoughtfully. It was almost five minutes, five ages while the wind made the only sound, before McReady appeared at the door.

"We," he announced, "haven't got enough grief here already. Somebody's tried to help us out. Kinner has a knife in his throat, which was why he stopped singing, probably. We've got monsters, madmen and murderers. Any more 'M's' you can think of, Caldwell? If there are, we'll probably have 'em before long."

## — XI —

"Is Blair loose?" someone asked.

"Blair is not loose. Or he flew in. If there's any doubt about where our gentle helper came from—this may clear it up." Van Wall held a foot-long, thin-bladed knife in a cloth. The wooden handle was half-burnt, charred with the peculiar pattern of the top of the galley stove.

Clark stared at it. "I did that this afternoon. I forgot the damn thing and left it on the stove."

Van Wall nodded. "I smelled it, if you remember. I knew the knife came from the galley."

"I wonder," said Benning, looking around at the party warily, "how many more monsters have we? If somebody could slip out of his place, go back of the screen to the galley and then down to the Cosmos House and back—he did come back, didn't he? Yes—everybody's here. Well, if one of the gang could do all that—"

"Maybe a monster did it," Garry suggested quietly. "There's that possibility."

"The monster, as you pointed out today, has only men left to imitate. Would he decrease his—supply, shall we say?" Van Wall pointed out. "No, we just have a plain, ordinary louse, a murderer to deal with. Ordinarily we'd call him an 'inhuman murderer' I suppose, but we have to distinguish now. We have inhuman murderers, and now we have human murderers. Or one at least."

"There's one less human," Norris said softly. "Maybe the monsters have the balance of power now."

"Never mind that," McReady sighed and turned to Barclay. "Bar, will you get your electric gadget? I'm going to make certain—"

Barclay turned down the corridor to get the pronged electrocuter, while McReady and Van Wall went back toward Cosmos House. Barclay followed them in some thirty seconds.

The corridor to Cosmos House twisted, as did nearly all corridors in Big Magnet, and Norris stood at the entrance again. But they heard, rather muffled, McReady's sudden shout. There was a savage scurry of blows, dull *ch-thunk, shluff* sounds. "Bar—Bar—" And a curious, savage mewing scream, silenced before even quick-moving Norris had reached the bend.

Kinner—or what had been Kinner—lay on the floor, cut half in two by the great knife McReady had had. The meteorologist stood against the wall, the knife dripping red in his hand. Van Wall was stirring vaguely on the floor, moaning, his hand half-consciously rubbing at his jaw. Barclay, an unutterably savage gleam in his eyes, was methodically leaning on the pronged weapon in his hand, jabbing—jabbing, jabbing.

Kinner's arms had developed a queer, scaly fur, and the flesh had twisted. The fingers had shortened, the hand rounded, the fingernails become three-inch long things of dull red horn, keened to steel-hard razor-sharp talons.

McReady raised his head, looked at the knife in his hand and dropped it. "Well, whoever did it can speak up now. He was an inhuman murderer at that—in that he murdered an inhuman. I swear by all that's holy, Kinner was a lifeless corpse on the floor here when we arrived. But when It found we were going to jab it with the power—It changed."

Norris stared unsteadily. "Oh, Lord, those things can act. Ye gods—sitting in here for hours, mouthing prayers to a God it hated! Shouting hymns in a cracked voice—hymns about a Church it never knew. Driving us mad with its ceaseless howling—"

"Well. Speak up, whoever did it. You didn't know it, but you did the camp a favor. And I want to know how in blazes you got out of that room without anyone seeing you. It might help in guarding ourselves."

"His screaming—his singing. Even the sound projector couldn't drown it." Clark shivered. "It was a monster."

"Oh," said Van Wall in sudden comprehension. "You were sitting right next to the door, weren't you! And almost behind the projection screen already."

Clark nodded dumbly. "He—it's quiet now. It's a dead—Mac, your test's no damn good. It was dead anyway, monster or man, it was dead."

McReady chuckled softly. "Boys, meet Clark, the only one we know is human! Meet Clark, the one who proves he's human by trying to commit murder—and failing. Will the rest of you please refrain from trying to prove you're human for a while? I think we may have another test."

"A test!" Connant snapped joyfully, then his face sagged in disappointment. "I suppose it's another either-way-you-want-it."

"No," said McReady steadily. "Look sharp and be careful. Come into the Ad Building. Barclay, bring your electrocuter. And somebody—Dutton—stand with Barclay to make sure he does it. Watch every neighbor, for by the Hell these monsters came from, I've got something, and they know it. They're going to get dangerous!"

The group tensed abruptly. An air of crushing menace entered into every man's body, sharply they looked at each other. More keenly than ever before—*is that man next to me an inhuman monster?*

"What is it?" Garry asked, as they stood again in the main room. "How long will it take?"

"I don't know, exactly," said McReady, his voice brittle with angry determination. "But I *know* it will work, and no two ways about it. It depends on a basic quality of the *monsters*, not on us. '*Kinner*' just convinced me." He stood heavy and solid in bronzed immobility, completely sure of himself again at last.

"This," said Barclay, hefting the wooden-handled weapon, tipped with its two sharp-pointed, charged conductors, "is going to be rather necessary, I take it. Is the power plant assured?"

Dutton nodded sharply. "The automatic stoker bin is full. The gas power plant is on stand-by. Van Wall and I set it for the movie operation and—we've checked it over rather carefully several times, you know. Anything those wires touch, dies," he assured them grimly. "*I* know that."

Dr. Copper stirred vaguely in his bunk, rubbed his eyes with fumbling hand. He sat up slowly, blinked his eyes blurred with sleep and drugs, widened with an unutterable horror of drug-ridden nightmares. "Garry," he mumbled, "Garry—listen. Selfish—from hell they came, and hellish shell-fish—I mean self— Do I? What do I mean?" He sank back in his bunk, and snored softly.

McReady looked at him thoughtfully. "We'll know presently," he nodded slowly. "But selfish is what you mean all right. You may have thought of that, half-sleeping, dreaming there. I didn't stop to think what dreams you might be having. But that's all right. Selfish is the word. They must be, you see." He turned to the men in the cabin, tense, silent men staring with wolfish eyes each at his neighbor. "Selfish, and as Dr. Copper said *every part is a whole*. Every piece is self-sufficient, an animal in itself.

"That, and one other thing, tell the story. There's nothing mysterious about blood; it's just as normal a body tissue as a piece of muscle, or a piece of liver. But it hasn't so much connective tissue, though it has millions, billions of life-cells."

McReady's great bronze beard ruffled in a grim smile. "This is satisfying, in a way. I'm pretty sure we humans still outnumber you—others. Others standing here. And we have what you, your other-world race, evidently doesn't. Not an imitated, but a bred-in-the-bone instinct, a driving, unquenchable fire that's genuine. We'll fight, fight with a ferocity you may attempt to imitate, but you'll never equal! We're human. We're real. You're imitations, false to the core of your every cell.

"All right. It's a showdown now. You know. You, with your mind reading. You've lifted the idea from my brain. You can't do a thing about it.

"Standing here—

"Let it pass. Blood is tissue. They have to bleed, if they don't bleed when cut, then, by Heaven, they're phony! Phony from hell! If they bleed—then that blood, separated from them, is an individual—*a newly formed individual in its own right, just as they, split, all of them, from one original, are individuals!*

"Get it, Van? See the answer, Bar?"

Van Wall laughed very softly. "The blood—the blood will not obey. It's a new individual, with all the desire to protect its own life that the original—the main mass from which it was split—has. The *blood* will live—and try to crawl away from a hot needle, say!"

McReady picked up the scalpel from the table. From the cabinet, he took a rack of test-tubes, a tiny alcohol lamp, and a length of platinum wire set in a little glass rod. A smile of grim satisfaction rode his lips. For a moment he glanced up at those around him. Barclay and Dutton moved toward him slowly, the wooden-handled electric instrument alert.

"Dutton," said McReady, "suppose you stand over by the splice there where you've connected that in. Just make sure no—thing pulls it loose."

Dutton moved away. "Now, Van, suppose you be first on this."

White-faced, Van Wall stepped forward. With a delicate precision, McReady cut a vein in the base of his thumb. Van Wall winced slightly, then held steady as a half inch of bright blood collected in the tube. McReady put the tube in the rack, gave Van Wall a bit of alum and indicated the iodine bottle.

Van Wall stood motionlessly watching. McReady heated the platinum wire in the alcohol lamp flame, then dipped it into the tube. It hissed softly. Five times he repeated the test. "Human, I'd say." McReady sighed, and straightened. "As yet, my theory hasn't been actually proven—but I have hopes. I have hopes.

"Don't, by the way, get too interested in this. We have with us some unwelcome ones, no doubt. Van, will you relieve Barclay at the switch? Thanks. O.K., Barclay, and may I say I hope you stay with us? You're a damned good guy."

Barclay grinned uncertainly; winced under the keen edge of the scalpel. Presently, smiling widely, he retrieved his long-handled weapon.

"Mr. Samuel Dutt—*Bar!*"

The tensity was released in that second. Whatever of hell the monsters may have had within them, the men in that instant matched it. Barclay had no chance to move his weapon as a score of men poured down on that thing that had seemed Dutton. It mewed, and spat, and tried to grow fangs—and was a hundred broken, torn pieces. Without knives, or any weapon save the brute-given strength of a staff of picked men, the thing was crushed, rent.

Slowly they picked themselves up, their eyes smouldering, very quiet in their emotions. A curious wrinkling of their lips betrayed a species of nervousness.

Barclay went over with the electric weapon. Things smouldered and stank. The caustic acid Van Wall dropped on each spilled drop of blood gave off tickling, cough-provoking fumes.

McReady grinned, his deep-set eyes alight and dancing. "Maybe," he said softly, "I underrated man's abilities when I said nothing human could have the ferocity in the eyes of that thing we found. I wish we could have the opportunity to treat in a more befitting manner these things. Something with boiling oil, or melted lead in it, or maybe slow roasting in the power boiler. When I think what a man Dutton was—

"Never mind. My theory is confirmed by—by one who knew? Well, Van Wall and Barclay are proven. I think, then, that I'll try to show you what I already know. That I too am human." McReady swished the scalpel in absolute alcohol, burned it off the metal blade, and cut the base of his thumb expertly.

Twenty seconds later he looked up from the desk at the waiting men. There were more grins out there now, friendly grins, yet withal, something else in the eyes.

"Connant," McReady laughed softly, "was right. The huskies watching that thing in the corridor bend had nothing on you. Wonder why we think only the wolf blood has the right to ferocity? Maybe on spontaneous viciousness a wolf takes tops, but after these seven days—abandon all hope, ye wolves who enter here!

"Maybe we can save time. Connant, would you step for—"

Again Barclay was too slow. There were more grins, less tensity still, when Barclay and Van Wall finished their work.

Garry spoke in a low, bitter voice. "Connant was one of the finest men we had here—and five minutes ago I'd have sworn he was a man. Those damnable things are more than imitation." Garry shuddered and sat back in his bunk.

And thirty seconds later, Garry's blood shrank from the hot platinum wire, and struggled to escape the tube, struggled as frantically as a suddenly feral, red-eyed, dissolving imitation of Garry struggled to dodge the snake-tongue weapon Barclay advanced at him, white-faced and sweating. The Thing in the test-tube screamed with a tiny, tinny voice as McReady dropped it into the glowing coal of the galley stove.

## — XII —

"The last of it?" Dr. Copper looked down from his bunk with bloodshot, saddened eyes. "Fourteen of them—"

McReady nodded shortly. "In some ways—if only we could have permanently prevented their spreading—I'd like to have even the imitations back. Commander Garry—Connant—Dutton—Clark—"

"Where are they taking those things?" Copper nodded to the stretcher Barclay and Norris were carrying out.

"Outside. Outside on the ice, where they've got fifteen smashed crates, half a ton of coal, and presently will add ten gallons of kerosene. We've dumped acid on every spilled drop, every torn fragment. We're going to incinerate those."

"Sounds like a good plan." Copper nodded wearily. "I wonder, you haven't said whether Blair—"

McReady started. "We forgot him! We had so much else! I wonder—do you suppose we can cure him now?"

"If—" began Dr. Copper, and stopped meaningly.

McReady started a second time. "Even a madman. It imitated Kinner and his praying hysteria—" McReady turned toward Van Wall at the long table. "Van, we've got to make an expedition to Blair's shack."

Van looked up sharply, the frown of worry faded for an instant in surprised remembrance. Then he rose, nodded. "Barclay better go along. He applied the lashings, and may figure how to get in without frightening Blair too much."

Three quarters of an hour, through –37° cold, they hiked while the aurora curtain bellied overhead. The twilight was nearly twelve hours long, flaming in the north on snow like white, crystalline sand under their skis. A 5-mile wind piled it in drift lines pointing off to the northwest. Three quarters of an hour to reach the snow-buried shack. No smoke came from the little shack, and the men hastened.

"Blair!" Barclay roared into the wind when he was still a hundred yards away. "Blair!"

"Shut up," said McReady softly. "And hurry. He may be trying a long hike. If we have to go after him—no planes, the tractors disabled—"

"Would a monster have the stamina a man has?"

"A broken leg wouldn't stop it for more than a minute," McReady pointed out.

Barclay gasped suddenly and pointed aloft. Dim in the twilit sky, a winged thing circled in curves of indescribable grace and ease. Great white wings tipped gently, and the bird swept over them in silent curiosity. "Albatross—" Barclay said softly. "First of the season, and wandering way inland for some reason. If a monster's loose—"

Norris bent down on the ice, and tore hurriedly at his heavy, windproof clothing. He straightened, his coat flapping open, a grim blue-metaled weapon in his hand. It roared a challenge to the white silence of Antarctica.

The thing in the air screamed hoarsely. Its great wings worked frantically as a dozen feathers floated down from its tail. Norris fired again. The bird was moving swiftly now, but in an almost straight line of retreat. It screamed again, more feathers dropped and with beating wings it soared behind a ridge of pressure ice, to vanish.

Norris hurried after the others. "It won't come back," he panted.

Barclay cautioned him to silence, pointing. A curiously, fiercely blue light beat out from the cracks of the shack's door. A very low, soft humming sounded inside, a low, soft humming and a clink and clank of tools, the very sounds somehow bearing a message of frantic haste.

McReady's face paled. "Lord help us if that thing has—" He grabbed Barclay's shoulder, and made snipping motions with his fingers, pointing toward the lacing of control-cables that held the door.

Barclay drew the wire-cutters from his pocket, and kneeled soundlessly at the door. The snap and twang of cut wires made an unbearable racket in the utter quiet of the Antarctic hush. There was only that strange, sweetly soft hum from within the shack, and the queerly, hecticly clipped clicking and rattling of tools to drown their noises.

McReady peered through a crack in the door. His breath sucked in huskily and his great fingers clamped cruelly on Barclay's shoulder. The meteorologist backed down. "It isn't," he explained very softly, "Blair. It's kneeling on something on the bunk—something that keeps lifting. Whatever it's working on is a thing like a knapsack—and it lifts."

"All at once," Barclay said grimly. "No. Norris, hang back, and get that iron of yours out. It may have—weapons."

Together, Barclay's powerful body and McReady's giant strength struck the door. Inside, the bunk jammed against the door, screeched madly and crackled into kindling. The door flung down from broken hinges, the patched lumber of the doorpost dropping inward.

Like a blue-rubber ball, a Thing bounced up. One of its four tentaclelike arms looped out like a striking snake. In a seven-tentacled hand a six-inch pencil of winking, shining metal glinted and swung upward to face them. Its line-thin lips twitched back from snake-fangs in a grin of hate, red eyes blazing.

Norris' revolver thundered in the confined space. The hate-washed face twitched in agony, the looping tentacle snatched back. The silvery thing in its hand a smashed ruin of metal, the seven-tentacled hand became a mass of mangled flesh oozing greenish-yellow ichor. The revolver thundered three times more. Dark holes drilled each of the three eyes before Norris hurled the empty weapon against its face.

The Thing screamed in feral hate, a lashing tentacle wiping at blinded eyes. For a moment it crawled on the floor, savage tentacles lashing out, the body twitching. Then it staggered up again, blinded eyes working, boiling hideously, the crushed flesh sloughing away in sodden gobbets.

Barclay lurched to his feet and dove forward with an ice-ax. The flat of the weighty thing crushed against the side of the head. Again the unkillable monster went down. The tentacles lashed out, and suddenly Barclay fell to his feet in the grip of a living, livid rope. The Thing dissolved as he held it, a white-hot band that ate into the flesh of his hands like living fire. Frantically he tore the stuff from him, held his hands where they could not be reached. The blind Thing felt and ripped at the tough, heavy, windproof cloth, seeking flesh—flesh it could convert—

The huge blow-torch McReady had brought coughed solemnly. Abruptly it rumbled disapproval throatily. Then it laughed gurglingly, and thrust out a blue-white, three-foot tongue. The Thing on the floor shrieked, flailed out blindly with tentacles that writhed and withered in the bubbling wrath of the blow-torch. It crawled and turned on the floor, it shrieked and hobbled madly, but always McReady held the blow-torch on the face, the dead eyes burning and bubbling uselessly. Frantically the Thing crawled and howled.

A tentacle sprouted a savage talon—and crisped in the flame. Steadily McReady moved with a planned, grim campaign. Helpless, maddened, the Thing retreated from the grunting torch, the caressing, licking tongue. For a moment it rebelled, squalling in inhuman hatred at the touch of icy snow. Then it fell back before the charring breath of the torch, the stench of its flesh bathing it. Hopelessly it retreated—on and on across the Antarctic snow. The bitter wind swept over it twisting the torch-tongue; vainly it flopped, a trail of oily, stinking smoke bubbling away from it—

McReady walked back toward the shack silently. Barclay met him at the door. "No more?" the giant meteorologist asked grimly.

Barclay shook his head. "No more. It didn't split?"

"It had other things to think about," McReady assured him. "When I left it, it was a glowing coal. What was it doing?"

Norris laughed shortly. "Wise boys, we are. Smash magnetos, so planes won't work. Rip the boiler tubing out of the tractors. And leave that Thing alone for a week in this shack. Alone and undisturbed."

McReady looked in at the shack more carefully. The air, despite the ripped door, was hot and humid. On a table at the far end of the room rested a thing of coiled wires and small magnets, glass tubing and radio tubes. At the center a block of rough stone rested. From the center of the block came the light that flooded the place, the fiercely blue light bluer than the glare of an electric arc, and from it came the sweetly soft hum. Off to one side was another mechanism of crystal glass, blown with an incredible neatness and delicacy, metal plates and a queer, shimmery sphere of insubstantiality.

"What is that?" McReady moved nearer.

Norris grunted. "Leave it for investigation. But I can guess pretty well. That's atomic power. That stuff to the left—that's a neat little thing for doing what men have been trying to do with 100-ton cyclotrons and so forth. It separates neutrons from heavy water, which he was getting from the surrounding ice."

"Where did he get all—Oh. Of course. A monster couldn't be locked in— or out. He's been through the apparatus caches." McReady stared at the apparatus. "Lord, what minds that race must have—"

"The shimmery sphere—I think it's a sphere of pure force. Neutrons can pass through any matter, and he wanted a supply reservoir of neutrons. Just project neutrons against silica—calcium—beryllium—almost anything, and the atomic energy is released. That thing is the atomic generator."

McReady plucked a thermometer from his coat. "It's 120° in here, despite the open door. Our clothes have kept the heat out to an extent, but I'm sweating now."

Norris nodded. "The light's cold. I found that. But it gives off heat to warm the place through that coil. He had all the power in the world. He could keep it warm and pleasant, as his race thought of warmth and pleasantness. Did you notice the light, the color of it?"

McReady nodded. "Beyond the stars is the answer. From beyond the stars. From a hotter planet that circled a brighter, bluer sun they came."

McReady glanced out the door toward the blasted, smoke-stained trail that flopped and wandered blindly off across the drift. "There won't be any more coming, I guess. Sheer accident it landed here, and that was twenty million years ago. What did it do all that for?" He nodded toward the apparatus.

Barclay laughed softly. "Did you notice what it was working on when we came? Look." He pointed toward the ceiling of the shack.

Like a knapsack made of flattened coffee-tins, with dangling cloth straps and leather belts, the mechanism clung to the ceiling. A tiny, glaring heart of supernal flame burned in it, yet burned through the ceiling's wood without scorching it. Barclay walked over to it, grasped two of the dangling straps in his hands, and pulled it down with an effort. He strapped it about his body. A slight jump carried him in a weirdly slow arc across the room.

"Anti-gravity," said McReady softly.

"Anti-gravity," Norris nodded. "Yes, we had 'em stopped, with no planes, and no birds. The birds hadn't come—but they had coffee-tins and radio parts, and glass and the machine shop at night. And a week—a whole week— all to itself. America in a single jump—with anti-gravity powered by the atomic energy of matter.

"We had 'em stopped. Another half hour—it was just tightening these straps on the device so it could wear it—and we'd have stayed in Antarctica, and shot down any moving thing that came from the rest of the world."

"The albatross—" McReady said softly. "Do you suppose—"

"With this thing almost finished? With that death weapon it held in its hand?

"No, by the grace of God, who evidently does hear very well, even down here, and the margin of half an hour, we keep our world, and the planets of the system too. Anti-gravity, you know, and atomic power. Because *They* came from another sun, a star beyond the stars. *They* came from a world with a bluer sun."

# Farewell to the Master

## HARRY BATES

---

**The Day the Earth Stood Still**

Director: *Robert Wise*
Screenplay: *Edmund H. North*
Producer: *Julian Blaustein*
Music: *Bernard Hermann*
Special Effects: *Fred Sersen*
Cast: *Michael Rennie, Patricia Neal, Billy Grey*
Released by: *20th Century-Fox*
1951, 92 Minutes. B&W.

---

— I —

From his perch high on the ladder above the museum floor, Cliff Sutherland studied carefully each line and shadow of the great robot, then turned and looked thoughtfully down at the rush of visitors come from all over the Solar System to see Gnut and the traveler for themselves and to hear once again their amazing, tragic story.

He himself had come to feel an almost proprietary interest in the exhibit, and with some reason. He had been the only free-lance picture reporter on the Capitol grounds when the visitors from the Unknown had arrived, and had obtained the first professional shots of the ship. He had witnessed at close hand every event of the next mad few days. He had thereafter photographed many times the eight-foot robot, the ship, and the beautiful slain ambassador, Klaatu, and his imposing tomb out in the center of

146

the Tidal Basin, and, such was the continuing news value of the event to the billions of persons throughout habitable space, he was there now once more to get still other shots and, if possible, a new "angle."

This time he was after a picture which showed Gnut as weird and menacing. The shots he had taken the day before had not given quite the effect he wanted, and he hoped to get it today; but the light was not yet right and he had to wait for the afternoon to wane a little.

The last of the crowd admitted in the present group hurried in, exclaiming at the great pure green curves of the mysterious time-space traveler, then completely forgetting the ship at sight of the awesome figure and great head of the giant Gnut. Hinged robots of crude manlike appearance were familiar enough, but never had Earthling eyes lain on one like this. For Gnut had almost exactly the shape of a man—a giant, but a man—with greenish metal for man's covering flesh, and greenish metal for man's bulging muscles. Except for a loin cloth, he was nude. He stood like the powerful god of the machine of some undreamed-of scientific civilization, on his face a look of sullen, brooding thought. Those who looked at him did not make jests or idle remarks, and those nearest him usually did not speak at all. His strange, internally illuminated red eyes were so set that every observer felt they were fixed on himself alone, and he engendered a feeling that he might at any moment step forward in anger and perform unimaginable deeds.

A slight rustling sound came from speakers hidden in the ceiling above, and at once the noises of the crowd lessened. The recorded lecture was about to be given. Cliff sighed. He knew the thing by heart; had even been present when the recording was made, and met the speaker, a young chap named Stillwell.

"Ladies and gentlemen," began a clear and well-modulated voice—but Cliff was no longer attending. The shadows in the hollows of Gnut's face and figure were deeper; it was almost time for his shot. He picked up and examined the proofs of the pictures he had taken the day before and compared them critically with the subject.

As he looked a wrinkle came to his brow. He had not noticed it before, but now, suddenly, he had the feeling that since yesterday something about Gnut was changed. The pose before him was the identical one in the photographs, every detail on comparison seemed the same, but nevertheless the feeling persisted. He took up his viewing glass and more carefully compared subject and photographs, line by line. And then he saw that there *was* a difference.

With sudden excitement, Cliff snapped two pictures at different exposures. He knew he should wait a little and take others, but he was so sure he had stumbled on an important mystery that he had to get going, and quickly fold-ing his accessory equipment he descended the ladder and made his way out. Twenty minutes later, consumed with curiosity, he was developing the new shots in his hotel bedroom.

What Cliff saw when he compared the negatives taken yesterday and today caused his scalp to tingle. Here was a slant indeed! And apparently no one but he knew! Still, what he had discovered, though it would have made the front page of every paper in the Solar System, was after all only a lead. The story, what really had happened, he knew no better than anyone else. It must be his job to find out.

And that meant he would have to secrete himself in the building and stay there all night. That very night; there was still time for him to get back before closing. He would take a small, very fast infrared camera that could see in the dark, and he would get the real picture and the story.

He snatched up the little camera, grabbed an aircab and hurried back to the museum. The place was filled with another section of the ever-present queue, and the lecture was just ending. He thanked Heaven that his arrangement with the museum permitted him to go in and out at will.

He had already decided what to do. First he made his way to the "floating" guard and asked a single question, and anticipation broadened on his face as he heard the expected answer. The second thing was to find a spot where he would be safe from the eyes of the men who would close the floor for the night. There was only one possible place, the laboratory set up behind the ship. Boldly he showed his press credentials to the second guard, stationed at the partitioned passageway leading to it, stating that he had come to interview the scientists; and in a moment was at the laboratory door.

He had been there a number of times and knew the room well. It was a large area roughly partitioned off for the work of the scientists engaged in breaking their way into the ship, and full of a confusion of massive and heavy objects—electric and hot-air ovens, carboys of chemicals, asbestos sheeting, compressors, basins, ladles, a microscope, and a great deal of smaller equipment common to a metallurgical laboratory. Three white-smocked men were deeply engrossed in an experiment at the far end. Cliff, waiting a good moment, slipped inside and hid himself under a table half buried with supplies. He felt reasonably safe from detection there. Very soon now the scientists would be going home for the night.

From beyond the ship he could hear another section of the waiting queue filing in—the last, he hoped, of the day. He settled himself as comfortably as he could. In a moment the lecture would begin. He had to smile when he thought of one thing the recording would say.

Then there it was again—the clear, trained voice of the chap Stillwell. The foot scrapings and whispers of the crowd died away, and Cliff could hear every word in spite of the great bulk of the ship lying interposed.

"Ladies and gentlemen," began the familiar words, "the Smithsonian Institution welcomes you to its new Interplanetary Wing and to the marvelous exhibits at this moment before you."

A slight pause. "All of you must know by now something of what happened here three months ago, if indeed you did not see it for yourself in the telescreen," the voice went on. "The few facts are briefly told. A little after 5:00 P.M. on September 16th, visitors to Washington thronged the grounds outside this building in their usual numbers and no doubt with their usual thoughts. The day was warm and fair. A stream of people was leaving the main entrance of the museum, just outside in the direction you are facing. This wing, of course, was not here at that time. Everyone was homeward bound, tired no doubt from hours on their feet, seeing the exhibits of the museum and visiting the many buildings on the grounds nearby. And then it happened.

"On the area just to your right, just as it is now, appeared the time-space traveler. It appeared in the blink of an eye. It did not come down from the sky; dozens of witnesses swear to that; it just appeared. One moment it was not here, the next it was. It appeared on the very spot it now rests on.

"The people nearest the ship were stricken with panic and ran back with cries and screams. Excitement spread out over Washington in a tidal wave. Radio, television, and newspapermen rushed here at once. Police formed a wide cordon around the ship, and army units appeared and trained guns and ray projectors on it. The direst calamity was feared.

"For it was recognized from the very beginning that this was no spaceship from anywhere in the Solar System. Every child knew that only two spaceships had ever been built on Earth, and none at all on any of the other planets and satellites; and of those two, one had been destroyed when it was pulled into the Sun, and the other had just been reported safely arrived on Mars. Then, the ones made here had a shell of a strong aluminum alloy, while this one, as you see, is of an unknown greenish metal.

"The ship appeared and just sat here. No one emerged, and there was no sign that it contained life of any kind. That, as much as any single thing, caused excitement to sky-rocket. Who, or what, was inside? Were the visitors hostile or friendly? Where did the ship come from? How did it arrive so suddenly right on this spot without dropping from the sky?

"For two days the ship rested here, just as you now see it, without motion or sign that it contained life. Long before the end of that time the scientists had explained that it was not so much a spaceship as a space-time traveler, because only such a ship could arrive as this one did—materialize. They pointed out that such a traveler, while theoretically understandable to us Earthmen, was far beyond attempt at our present state of knowledge, and that this one, activated by relativity principles, might well have come from the far corner of the Universe, from a distance which light itself would require millions of years to cross.

"When this opinion was disseminated, public tension grew until it was almost intolerable. Where had the traveler come from? Who were its occupants? Why had they come to Earth? Above all, why did they not show themselves? Were they perhaps preparing some terrible weapon of destruction?

"And where was the ship's entrance port? Men who dared go look reported that none could be found. No slightest break or crack marred the perfect smoothness of the ship's curving ovoid surface. And a delegation of high-ranking officials who visited the ship could not, by knocking, elicit from its occupants any sign that they had been heard.

"At last, after exactly two days, in full view of tens of thousands of persons assembled and standing well back, and under the muzzles of scores of the army's most powerful guns and ray projectors, an opening appeared in the wall of the ship, and a ramp slid down, and out stepped a man, godlike in appearance and human in form, closely followed by a giant robot. And when they touched the ground the ramp slid back and the entrance closed as before.

"It was immediately apparent to all the assembled thousands that the stranger was friendly. The first thing he did was to raise his right arm high in the universal gesture of peace; but it was not that which impressed those nearest so much as the expression on his face, which radiated kindness, wisdom, the purest nobility. In his delicately tinted robe he looked like a benign god.

"At once, waiting for this appearance, a large committee of high-ranking government officials and army officers advanced to greet the visitor. With graciousness and dignity the man pointed to himself, then to his robot companion, and said in perfect English with a peculiar accent, 'I am Klaatu,' or a name that sounded like that, 'and this is Gnut.' The names were not well understood at the time, but the sight-and-sound film of the television men caught them and they became known to everyone subsequently.

"And then occurred the thing which shall always be to the shame of the human race. From a treetop a hundred yards away came a wink of violet light and Klaatu fell. The assembled multitude stood for a moment stunned, not comprehending what had happened. Gnut, a little behind his master and to one side, slowly turned his body a little toward him, moved his head twice, and stood still, in exactly the position you now see him.

"Then followed pandemonium. The police pulled the slayer of Klaatu out of the tree. They found him mentally unbalanced; he kept crying that the devil had come to kill everyone on Earth. He was taken away, and Klaatu, although obviously dead, was rushed to the nearest hospital to see if anything could be done to revive him. Confused and frightened crowds milled about the Capitol grounds the rest of the afternoon and much of that night. The ship remained as silent and motionless as before. And Gnut, too, never moved from the position he had come to rest in.

"Gnut never moved again. He remained exactly as you see him all that night and for the ensuing days. When the mausoleum in the Tidal Basin was built, Klaatu's burial services took place where you are standing now, attended by the highest functionaries of all the great countries of the world. It was not only the most appropriate but the safest thing to do, for if there should be other living creatures in the traveler, as seemed possible at that time, they had to be impressed by the sincere sorrow of us Earthmen at what had happened. If Gnut was still alive, or perhaps I had better say functionable, there was no sign. He stood as you see him during the entire ceremony. He stood so while his master was floated out to the mausoleum and given to the centuries with the tragically short sight-and-sound record of his historic visit. And he stood so afterward, day after day, night after night, in fair weather and in rain, never moving or showing by any slightest sign that he was aware of what had gone on.

"After the interment, this wing was built out from the museum to cover the traveler and Gnut. Nothing else could very well have been done, it was learned, for both Gnut and the ship were far too heavy to be moved safely by any means at hand.

"You have heard about the efforts of our metallurgists since then to break into the ship, and of their complete failure. Behind the ship now, as you can see from either end, a partitioned workroom has been set up where the attempt still goes on. So far its wonderful greenish metal has proved inviolable. Not only are they unable to get in, but they cannot even find the exact place from which Klaatu and Gnut emerged. The chalk marks you see are the best approximation.

"Many people have feared that Gnut was only temporarily deranged, and that on return to function might be dangerous, so the scientists have completely destroyed all chance of that. The greenish metal of which he is made seemed to be the same as that of the ship and could no more be attacked, they found, nor could they find any way to penetrate to his internals; but they had other means. They sent electrical currents of tremendous voltages and amperages through him. They applied terrific heat to all parts of his metal shell. They immersed him for days in gases and acids and strongly corroding solutions, and they have bombarded him with every known kind of ray. You need have no fear of him now. He cannot possibly have retained the ability to function in any way.

"But—a word of caution. The officials of the government know that visitors will not show any disrespect in this building. It may be that the unknown and unthinkably powerful civilization from which Klaatu and Gnut came may send other emissaries to see what happened to them. Whether or not they do, not one of us must be found amiss in our attitude. None of us could very well anticipate what happened, and we all are immeasurably sorry, but we are still in a sense responsible, and must do what we can to avoid possible retaliations.

"You will be allowed to remain five minutes longer, and then, when the gong sounds, you will please leave promptly. The robot attendants along the wall will answer any questions you may have.

"Look well, for before you stand stark symbols of the achievement, mystery, and frailty of the human race."

The recorded voice ceased speaking. Cliff, carefully moving his cramped limbs, broke out in a wide smile. If they knew what he knew!

For his photographs told a slightly different story from that of the lecturer. In yesterday's a line of the figured floor showed clearly at the outer edge of the robot's near foot; in today's, *that line was covered.* Gnut had moved!

Or been moved, though this was very unlikely. Where was the derrick and other evidence of such activity? It could hardly have been done in one night, and all signs so quickly concealed. And why should it be done at all?

Still, to make sure, he had asked the guard. He could almost remember verbatim his answer:

"No, Gnut has neither moved nor been moved since the death of his master. A special point was made of keeping him in the position he assumed at Klaatu's death. The floor was built in under him, and the scientists who completed his derangement erected their apparatus around him, just as he stands. You need have no fears."

Cliff smiled again. He did not have any fears.

Not yet.

— II —

A moment later the big gong above the entrance doors rang the closing hour, and immediately following it a voice from the speakers called out, "Five o'clock, ladies and gentlemen. Closing time, ladies and gentlemen."

The three scientists, as if surprised it was so late, hurriedly washed their hands, changed to their street clothes and disappeared down the partitioned corridor, oblivious of the young picture man hidden under the table. The slide and scrape of the feet on the exhibition floor rapidly dwindled, until at last there were only the steps of the two guards walking from one point to another, making sure everything was all right for the night. For just a moment one of them glanced in the doorway of the laboratory, then he joined the other at the entrance. Then the great metal doors clanged to, and there was silence.

Cliff waited several minutes, then carefully poked his way out from under the table. As he straightened up, a faint tinkling crash sounded at the floor by his feet. Carefully stooping, he found the shattered remains of a thin glass pipette. He had knocked it off the table.

That caused him to realize something he had not thought of before: A Gnut who had moved might be a Gnut who could see and hear—and really be dangerous. He would have to be very careful.

He looked about him. The room was bounded at the ends by two fiber partitions which at the inner ends followed close under the curving bottom of the ship. The inner side of the room was the ship itself, and the outer was the southern wall of the wing. There were four large high windows. The only entrance was by way of the passage.

Without moving, from his knowledge of the building, he made his plan. The wing was connected with the western end of the museum by a doorway, never used, and extended westward toward the Washington Monument. The ship lay nearest the southern wall, and Gnut stood out in front of it, not far from the northeast corner and at the opposite end of the room from the entrance of the building and the passageway leading to the laboratory. By retracing his steps he would come out on the floor at the point farthest removed from the robot. This was just what he wanted, for on the other side of the entrance, on a low platform, stood a paneled table containing the lecture apparatus, and this table was the only object in the room which afforded a place for him to lie concealed while watching what might go on. The only other objects on the floor were the six manlike robot attendants in fixed stations along the northern wall, placed there to answer visitors' questions. He would have to gain the table.

He turned and began cautiously tiptoeing out of the laboratory and down the passageway. It was already dark there, for what light still entered the exhibition hall was shut off by the great bulk of the ship. He reached the end of the room without making a sound. Very carefully he edged forward and peered around the bottom of the ship at Gnut.

He had a momentary shock. The robot's eyes were right on him!—or so it seemed. Was that only the effect of the set of his eyes, he wondered, or was he already discovered? The position of Gnut's head did not seem to have changed, at any rate. Probably everything was all right, but he wished he did not have to cross that end of the room with the feeling that the robot's eyes were following him.

He drew back and sat down and waited. It would have to be totally dark before he essayed the trip to the table.

He waited a full hour, until the faint beams from the lamps on the grounds outside began to make the room seem to grow lighter; then he got up and peeped around the ship once more. The robot's eyes seemed to pierce right at him as before, only now, due no doubt to the darkness, the strange internal illumination seemed much brighter. This was a chilling thing. Did Gnut know he was there? What were the thoughts of the robot? What *could* be the thoughts of a man-made machine, even so wonderful a one as Gnut?

It was time for the cross, so Cliff slung his camera around on his back, went down on his hands and knees, and carefully moved to the edge of the entrance wall. There he fitted himself as closely as he could into the angle made by it with the floor and started inching ahead. Never pausing, not risking a glance at Gnut's unnerving red eyes, moving an inch at a time, he snaked along. He took ten minutes to cross the space of a hundred feet, and he was wet with perspiration when his fingers at last touched the one-foot rise of the platform on which the table stood. Still slowly, silently as a shadow, he made his way over the edge and melted behind the protection of the table. At last he was there.

He relaxed for a moment, then, anxious to know whether he had been seen, carefully turned and looked around the side of the table.

Gnut's eyes were now full on him! Or so it seemed. Against the general darkness, the robot loomed a mysterious and still darker shadow that, for all his being a hundred and fifty feet away, seemed to dominate the room. Cliff could not tell whether the position of his body was changed or not.

But if Gnut were looking at him, he at least did nothing else. Not by the slightest motion that Cliff could discern did he appear to move. His position was the one he had maintained these last three months, in the darkness, in the rain, and this last week in the museum.

Cliff made up his mind not to give away to fear. He became conscious of his own body. The cautious trip had taken something out of him—his knees and elbows burned and his trousers were no doubt ruined. But these were little things if what he hoped for came to pass. If Gnut so much as moved, and he could catch him with his infrared camera, he would have a story that would buy him fifty suits of clothes. And if on top of that he could learn the purpose of Gnut's moving—provided there was a purpose—that would be a story that would set the world on its ears.

He settled down to a period of waiting; there was no telling when Gnut would move, if indeed he would move that night. Cliff's eyes had long been adjusted to the dark and he could make out the larger objects well enough. From time to time he peered out at the robot—peered long and hard, till his outlines wavered and he seemed to move, and he had to blink and rest his eyes to be sure it was only his imagination.

Again the minute hand of his watch crept around the dial. The inactivity made Cliff careless, and for longer and longer periods he kept his head back out of sight behind the table. And so it was that when Gnut did move he was scared almost out of his wits. Dull and a little bored, he suddenly found the robot out on the floor, halfway in his direction.

But that was not the most frightening thing. It was that when he did see Gnut he did not catch him moving! He was stopped as still as a cat in the middle of stalking a mouse. His eyes were now much brighter, and there was no remaining doubt about their direction: he was looking right at Cliff!

Scarcely breathing, half hypnotized, Cliff looked back. His thoughts tumbled. What was the robot's intention? Why had he stopped so still? Was he being stalked? How could he move with such silence?

In the heavy darkness Gnut's eyes moved nearer. Slowly but in perfect rhythm the almost imperceptible sound of his footsteps beat on Cliff's ears. Cliff, usually resourceful enough, was this time caught flat-footed. Frozen with fear, utterly incapable of fleeing, he lay where he was while the metal monster with the fiery eyes came on.

For a moment Cliff all but fainted, and when he recovered, there was Gnut towering over him, legs almost within reach. He was bending slightly, burning his terrible eyes right into his own!

Too late to try to think of running now. Trembling like any cornered mouse, Cliff waited for the blow that would crush him. For an eternity, it seemed, Gnut scrutinized him without moving. For each second of that eternity Cliff expected annihilation, sudden, quick, complete. And then suddenly and unexpectedly it was over. Gnut's body straightened and he stepped back. He turned. And then, with the almost jerkless rhythm which only he among robots possessed, he started back toward the place from which he came.

Cliff could hardly believe he had been spared. Gnut could have crushed him like a worm—and he had only turned around and gone back. Why? It could not be supposed that a robot was capable of human considerations.

Gnut went straight to the other end of the traveler. At a certain place he stopped and made a curious succession of sounds. At once Cliff saw an opening, blacker than the gloom of the building, appear in the ship's side, and it was followed by a slight sliding sound as a ramp slid out and met the floor. Gnut walked up the ramp and, stooping a little, disappeared inside the ship.

Then, for the first time, Cliff remembered the picture he had come to get.

Gnut had moved, but he had not caught him! But at least now, whatever opportunities there might be later, he could get the shot of the ramp connecting with the opened door; so he twisted his camera into position, set it for the proper exposure, and took a shot.

A long time passed and Gnut did not come out. What could he be doing inside? Cliff wondered. Some of his courage returned to him and he toyed with the idea of creeping forward and peeping through the port, but he found he had not the courage for that. Gnut had spared him, at least for the time, but there was no telling how far his tolerance would go.

An hour passed, then another, Gnut was doing something inside the ship, but what? Cliff could not imagine. If the robot had been a human being, he knew he would have sneaked a look, but, as it was, he was too much of an unknown quantity. Even the simplest of Earth's robots under certain circumstances were inexplicable things; what, then, of this one, come from an unknown and even unthinkable civilization, by far the most wonderful construction ever seen—what superhuman powers might he not possess? All that the scientists of Earth could do had not served to derange him. Acid, heat, rays, terrific crushing blows—he had withstood them all; even his finish had been unmarred. He might be able to see perfectly in the dark. And right where he was, he might be able to hear or in some way sense the least change in Cliff's position.

More time passed, and then, some time after two o'clock in the morning, a simple homely thing happened, but a thing so unexpected that for a moment it quite destroyed Cliff's equilibrium. Suddenly, through the dark and silent building, there was a faint whir of wings, soon followed by the piercing, sweet voice of a bird. A mocking bird. Somewhere in the gloom above his head. Clear and full throated were its notes; a dozen little songs it sang, one after the other without pause between—short insistent calls, twirrings, coaxings, cooings—the spring love song of perhaps the finest singer in the world. Then, as suddenly as it began, the voice was silent.

If an invading army had poured out of the traveler, Cliff would have been less surprised. The month was December; even in Florida the mocking birds had not yet begun their song. How had one gotten into that tight, gloomy museum? How and why was it singing there?

He waited, full of curiosity. Then suddenly he was aware of Gnut, standing just outside the port of the ship. He stood quite still, his glowing eyes turned squarely in Cliff's direction. For a moment the hush in the museum seemed to deepen; then it was broken by a soft thud on the floor near where Cliff was lying.

He wondered. The light in Gnut's eyes changed, and he started his almost jerkless walk in Cliff's direction. When only a little away, the robot stopped, bent over, and picked something from the floor. For some time he stood without motion and looked at a little object he held in his hand. Cliff knew, though he could not see, that it was the mocking bird. Its body, for he was sure that it had lost its song forever. Gnut then turned, and without a glance at Cliff, walked back to the ship and again went inside.

Hours passed while Cliff waited for some sequel to this surprising happening. Perhaps it was because of his curiosity that his fear of the robot began to lessen. Surely if the mechanism was unfriendly, if he intended him any harm, he would have finished him before, when he had such a perfect opportunity. Cliff began to nerve himself for a quick look inside the port. And a picture; he must remember the picture. He kept forgetting the very reason he was there.

It was in the deeper darkness of the false dawn when he got sufficient courage and made the start. He took off his shoes, and in his stockinged feet, his shoes tied together and slung over his shoulder, he moved stiffly but rapidly to a position behind the nearest of the six robot attendants stationed along the wall, then paused for some sign which might indicate that Gnut knew he had moved. Hearing none, he slipped along behind the next robot attendant and paused again. Bolder now, he made in one spurt all the distance to the farthest one, the sixth, fixed just opposite the port of the ship. There he met with a disappointment. No light that he could detect was visible within; there was only darkness and the all-permeating silence. Still, he had better get the picture. He raised his camera, focused it on the dark opening, and gave the film a comparatively long exposure. Then he stood there, at a loss what to do next.

As he paused, a peculiar series of muffled noises reached his ears, apparently from within the ship. Animal noises—first scrapings and pantings, punctuated by several sharp clicks, then deep, rough snarls, interrupted by more scrapings and pantings, as if a struggle of some kind were going on. Then suddenly, before Cliff could even decide to run back to the table, a low, wide, dark shape bounded out of the port and immediately turned and grew to the height of a man. A terrible fear swept over Cliff, even before he knew what the shape was.

In the next second Gnut appeared in the port and stepped unhesitatingly down the ramp toward the shape. As he advanced it backed slowly away for a few feet; but then it stood its ground, and thick arms rose from its sides and began a loud drumming on its chest, while from its throat came a deep roar of defiance. Only one creature in the world beat its chest and made a sound like that. The shape was a gorilla!

And a huge one!

Gnut kept advancing, and when close, charged forward and grappled with the beast. Cliff would not have guessed that Gnut could move so fast. In the darkness he could not see the details of what happened; all he knew was that the two great shapes, the titanic metal Gnut and the squat but terrifically strong gorilla, merged for a moment with silence on the robot's part and terrible, deep, indescribable roars on the other's; then the two separated, and it was as if the gorilla had been flung back and away.

The animal at once rose to its full height and roared deafeningly. Gnut advanced. They closed again, and the separation of before was repeated. The robot continued inexorably, and now the gorilla began to fall back down the building. Suddenly the beast darted at a manlike shape against the wall, and with one rapid side movement dashed the fifth robot attendant to the floor and decapitated it.

Tense with fear, Cliff crouched behind his own robot attendant. He thanked Heaven that Gnut was between him and the gorilla and was continuing his advance. The gorilla backed farther, darted suddenly at the next robot in the row, and with strength almost unbelievable picked it from its roots and hurled it at Gnut. With a sharp metallic clang, robot hit robot, and the one of Earth bounced off to one side and rolled to a stop.

Cliff cursed himself for it afterward, but again he completely forgot the picture. The gorilla kept falling back down the building, demolishing with terrific bursts of rage every robot attendant that he passed and throwing the pieces at the implacable Gnut. Soon they arrived opposite the table, and Cliff now thanked his stars he had come away. There followed a brief silence. Cliff could not make out what was going on, but he imagined that the gorilla had at last reached the corner of the wing and was trapped.

If he was, it was only for a moment. The silence was suddenly shattered by a terrific roar, and the thick, squat shape of the animal came bounding toward Cliff. He came all the way back and turned just between Cliff and the port of the ship. Cliff prayed frantically for Gnut to come back quickly, for there was now only the last remaining robot attendant between him and the madly dangerous brute. Out of the dimness Gnut did appear. The gorilla rose to its full height and again beat its chest and roared its challenge.

And then occurred a curious thing. It fell on all fours and slowly rolled over on its side, as if weak or hurt. Then panting, making frightening noises, it forced itself again to its feet and faced the oncoming Gnut. As it waited, its eye was caught by the last robot attendant and perhaps Cliff, shrunk close behind it. With a surge of terrible destructive rage, the gorilla waddled sideward toward Cliff, but this time, even through his panic, he saw that the animal moved with difficulty, again apparently sick or severely wounded. He jumped back just in time; the gorilla pulled out the last robot attendant and hurled it violently at Gnut, missing him narrowly.

That was its last effort. The weakness caught it again; it dropped heavily on one side, rocked back and forth a few times, and fell to twitching. Then it lay still and did not move again.

The first faint pale light of the dawn was seeping into the room. From the corner where he had taken refuge, Cliff watched closely the great robot. It seemed to him that he behaved very queerly. He stood over the dead gorilla, looking down at him with what in a human would be called sadness. Cliff saw this clearly; Gnut's heavy greenish features bore a thoughtful, grieving expression new to his experience. For some moments he stood so, then as might a father with his sick child, he leaned over, lifted the great animal in his metal arms, and carried it tenderly within the ship.

Cliff flew back to the table, suddenly fearful of yet other dangerous and inexplicable happenings. It struck him that he might be safer in the laboratory, and with trembling knees he made his way there and hid in one of the big ovens. He prayed for full daylight. His thoughts were chaos. Rapidly, one after another, his mind churned up the amazing events of the night, but all was mystery; it seemed there could be no rational explanation for them. That mocking bird. The gorilla. Gnut's sad expression and his tenderness. What could account for a fantastic melange like that!

Gradually full daylight did come. A long time passed. At last he began to believe he might yet get out of that place of mystery and danger alive. At 8:30 there were noises at the entrance, and the good sound of human voices came to his ears. He stepped out of the oven and tiptoed to the passageway.

The noises stopped suddenly and there was a frightened exclamation and then the sound of running feet, and then silence. Stealthily Cliff sneaked down the narrow way and peeped fearfully around the ship.

There Gnut was in his accustomed place, in the identical pose he had taken at the death of his master, brooding sullenly and alone over a space traveler once again closed tight and a room that was a shambles. The entrance doors stood open and, heart in his mouth, Cliff ran out.

A few minutes later, safe in his hotel room, completely done in, he sat down for a second and almost at once fell asleep. Later, still in his clothes and still asleep, he staggered over to the bed. He did not wake up till midafternoon.

Cliff awoke slowly, at first not realizing that the images tumbling in his head were real memories and not a fantastic dream. It was recollection of the pictures which brought him to his feet. Hastily he set about developing the film in his camera.

Then in his hands was proof that the events of the night were real. Both shots turned out well. The first showed clearly the ramp leading up to the port as he had dimly discerned it from his position behind the table. The second, of the open port as snapped from in front, was a disappointment, for a blank wall just back of the opening cut off all view of the interior. That would account for the fact that no light had escaped from the ship while Gnut was inside. Assuming Gnut required light for whatever he did.

Cliff looked at the negatives and was ashamed of himself. What a rotten picture man he was to come back with two ridiculous shots like these! He had had a score of opportunities to get real ones—shots of Gnut in action—Gnut's fight with the gorilla—even Gnut holding the mocking bird—spine-chilling stuff!—and all he had brought back was two stills of a doorway. Oh, sure, they were valuable, but he was a Grade A ass.

And to top this brilliant performance, he had fallen asleep!

Well, he'd better get out on the street and find out what was doing.

Quickly he showered, shaved, and changed his clothes, and soon was entering a nearby restaurant patronized by other picture and newsmen. Sitting alone at the lunch bar, he spotted a friend and competitor.

"Well, what do *you* think?" asked his friend when he took the stool at his side.

"I don't think anything until I've had breakfast," Cliff answered.

"Then haven't you heard?"

"Heard what?" fended Cliff, who knew very well what was coming.

"You're a fine picture man," was the other's remark. "When something really big happens, you are asleep in bed." But then he told him what had been discovered that morning in the museum, and of the world-wide excitement at the news. Cliff did three things at once, successfully—gobbled a substantial breakfast, kept thanking his stars that nothing new had transpired, and showed continuous surprise. Still chewing, he got up and hurried over to the building.

Outside, balked at the door, was a large crowd of the curious, but Cliff had no trouble gaining admittance when he showed his press credentials. Gnut and the ship stood just as he had left them, but the floor had been cleaned up and the pieces of the demolished robot attendants were lined up in one place along the wall. Several other competitor friends of his were there.

"I was away; missed the whole thing," he said to one of them—Gus. "What's supposed to be the explanation for what happened?"

"Ask something easy," was the answer. "Nobody knows. It's thought maybe something came out of the ship, maybe another robot like Gnut. Say—where have you been?"

"Asleep."

"Better catch up. Several billion bipeds are scared stiff. Revenge for the death of Klaatu. Earth about to be invaded."

"But that's—"

"Oh, I know it's all crazy, but that's the story they're being fed; it sells news. But there's a new angle just turned up, very surprising. Come here."

He led Cliff to the table where stood a knot of people looking with great interest at several objects guarded by a technician. Gus pointed to a long slide on which were mounted a number of short dark-brown hairs.

"Those hairs came off a large male gorilla," Gus said with a certain hard-boiled casualness. "Most of them were found among the sweepings of the floor this morning. The rest were found on the robot attendants."

Cliff tried to look astounded. Gus pointed to a test tube partly filled with a light amber fluid.

"And that's blood, diluted—gorilla blood. It was found on Gnut's arms."

"Good Heaven!" Cliff managed to exclaim. "And there's no explanation?"

"Not even a theory. It's your big chance, wonder boy."

Cliff broke away from Gus, unable to maintain his act any longer. He couldn't decide what to do about his story. The press services would bid heavily for it—with all his pictures—but that would take further action out of his hands. In the back of his mind he wanted to stay in the wing again that night, but—well, he simply was afraid. He'd had a pretty stiff dose, and he wanted very much to remain alive.

He walked over and looked a long time at Gnut. No one would ever have guessed that he had moved, or that there had rested on his greenish metal face a look of sadness. Those weird eyes! Cliff wondered if they were really looking at him, as they seemed, recognizing him as the bold intruder of last night. Of what unknown stuff were they made—those materials placed in his eye sockets by one branch of the race of man which all the science of his own could not even serve to disfunction? What was Gnut thinking? What could be the thoughts of a robot—a mechanism of metal poured out of man's clay crucibles? Was he angry at him? Cliff thought not. Gnut had had him at his mercy—and had walked away.

Dared he stay again?

Cliff thought perhaps he did.

He walked about the room, thinking it over. He felt sure Gnut would move again. A Mikton ray gun would protect him from another gorilla—or fifty of them. He did not yet have the real story. He had come back with two miserable architectural stills!

He might have known from the first that he would stay. At dusk that night, armed with his camera and a small Mikton gun, he lay once more under the table of supplies in the laboratory and heard the metal doors of the wing clang to for the night.

This time he would get the story—and the pictures.

If only no guard was posted inside!

— IV —

Cliff listened hard for a long time for any sound which might tell him that a guard had been left, but the silence within the wing remained unbroken. He was thankful for that—but not quite completely. The gathering darkness and the realization that he was now irrevocably committed made the thought of a companion not altogether unpleasant.

About an hour after it reached maximum darkness he took off his shoes, tied them together and slung them around his neck, down his back, and stole quietly down the passageway to where it opened into the exhibition area. All seemed as it had been the preceding night. Gnut looked an ominous, indistinct shadow at the far end of the room, his glowing red eyes again seemingly right on the spot from which Cliff peeped out. As on the previous night, but even more carefully, Cliff went down on his stomach in the angle of the wall and slowly snaked across to the low platform on which stood the table. Once in its shelter, he fixed his shoes so that they straddled one shoulder, and brought his camera and gun holster around, ready on his breast. This time, he told himself, he would get pictures.

He settled down to wait, keeping Gnut in full sight every minute. His vision reached maximum adjustment to the darkness. Eventually he began to feel lonely and a little afraid. Gnut's red-glowing eyes were getting on his nerves; he had to keep assuring himself that the robot would not harm him. He had little doubt but that he himself was being watched.

Hours slowly passed. From time to time he heard slight noises at the entrance, on the outside—a guard, perhaps, or maybe curious visitors.

At about nine o'clock he saw Gnut move. First his head alone; it turned so that the eyes burned stronger in the direction where Cliff lay. For a moment that was all; then the dark metal form stirred slightly and began moving forward—straight toward himself. Cliff had thought he would not be afraid—much—but now his heart stood still. What would happen this time?

With amazing silence, Gnut drew nearer, until he towered an ominous shadow over the spot where Cliff lay. For a long time his red eyes burned down on the prone man. Cliff trembled all over; this was worse than the first time. Without having planned it, he found himself speaking to the creature.

"You would not hurt me," he pleaded. "I was only curious to see what's going on. It's my job. Can you understand me? I would not harm or bother you. I . . . I couldn't if I wanted to! Please!"

The robot never moved, and Cliff could not guess whether his words had been understood or even heard. When he felt he could not bear the suspense any longer, Gnut reached out and took something from a drawer of the table, or perhaps he put something back in; then he stepped back, turned, and retraced his steps. Cliff was safe! Again the robot had spared him!

Beginning then, Cliff lost much of his fear. He felt sure now that this Gnut would do him no harm. Twice he had had him in his power, and each time he had only looked and quietly moved away. Cliff could not imagine what Gnut had done in the drawer of the table. He watched with the greatest curiosity to see what would happen next.

As on the night before, the robot went straight to the end of the ship and made the peculiar sequence of sounds that opened the port, and when the ramp slid out he went inside. After that Cliff was alone in the darkness for a very long time, probably two hours. Not a sound came from the ship.

Cliff knew he should sneak up to the port and peep inside, but he could not quite bring himself to do it. With his gun he could handle another gorilla, but if Gnut caught him it might be the end. Momentarily he expected something fantastic to happen—he knew not what; maybe the mocking bird's sweet song again, maybe a gorilla, maybe—anything. What did at last happen once more caught him with complete surprise.

He heard a sudden muffled sound, then words—human words—every one familiar.

"Gentlemen," was the first, and then there was a very slight pause. "The Smithsonian Institution welcomes you to its new Interplanetary Wing and to the marvelous exhibits at this moment before you."

It was the recorded voice of Stillwell! But it was not coming through the speakers overhead, but much muted, from within the ship.

After a slight pause it went on:

"All of you must . . . must—" Here it stammered and came to a stop. Cliff's hair bristled. That stammering was not in the lecture!

For just a moment there was silence; then came a scream, a hoarse man's scream, muffled, from somewhere within the heart of the ship; and it was followed by muted gasps and cries, as of a man in great fright or distress.

Every nerve tight, Cliff watched the port. He heard a thudding noise within the ship, then out the door flew the shadow of what was surely a human being. Gasping and half stumbling, he ran straight down the room in Cliff's direction. When twenty feet away, the great shadow of Gnut followed him out of the port.

Cliff watched, breathless. The man—it was Stillwell, he saw now—came straight for the table behind which Cliff himself lay, as if to get behind it, but when only a few feet away, his knees buckled and he fell to the floor. Suddenly Gnut was standing over him, but Stillwell did not seem to be aware of it. He appeared very ill, but kept making spasmodic futile efforts to creep on to the protection of the table.

Gnut did not move, so Cliff was emboldened to speak.

"What's the matter, Stillwell?" he asked. "Can I help? Don't be afraid. I'm Cliff Sutherland; you know, the picture man."

Without showing the least surprise at finding Cliff there, and clutching at his presence like a drowning man would a straw, Stillwell gasped out:

"Help me! Gnut . . . Gnut—" He seemed unable to go on.

"Gnut what?" asked Cliff. Very conscious of the fire-eyed robot looming above, and afraid even to move out to the man, Cliff added reassuringly: "Gnut won't hurt you. I'm sure he won't. He doesn't hurt me. What's the matter? What can I do?"

With a sudden accession of energy, Stillwell rose on his elbows.

"Where am I?" he asked.

"In the Interplanetary Wing," Cliff answered. "Don't you know?"

Only Stillwell's hard breathing was heard for a moment. Then hoarsely, weakly, he asked:

"How did I get here?"

"I don't know," said Cliff.

"I was making a lecture recording," Stillwell said, "when suddenly I found myself here . . . or I mean in there—"

He broke off and showed a return of his terror.

"Then what?" asked Cliff gently.

"I was in that box—and there, above me, was Gnut, the robot. Gnut! But they made Gnut harmless! He's never moved!"

"Steady, now," said Cliff. "I don't think Gnut will hurt you."

Stillwell fell back on the floor.

"I'm very weak," he gasped. "Something— Will you get a doctor?"

He was utterly unaware that towering above him, eyes boring down at him through the darkness, was the robot he feared so greatly.

As Cliff hesitated, at a loss what to do, the man's breath began coming in short gasps, as regular as the ticking of a clock. Cliff dared to move out to him, but no act on his part could have helped the man now. His gasps weakened and became spasmodic, then suddenly he was completely silent and still. Cliff felt for his heart, then looked up to the eyes in the shadow above.

"He is dead," he whispered.

The robot seemed to understand, or at least to hear. He bent forward and regarded the still figure.

"What is it, Gnut?" Cliff asked the robot suddenly. "What are you doing? Can I help you in any way? Somehow I don't believe you are unfriendly, and I don't believe you killed this man. But what happened? Can you understand me? Can you speak? What is it you're trying to do?"

Gnut made no sound or motion, but only looked at the still figure at his feet. In the robot's face, now so close, Cliff saw the look of sad contemplation.

Gnut stood so several minutes; then he bent lower, took the limp form carefully—even gently, Cliff thought—in his mighty arms, and carried him to the place along the wall where lay the dismembered pieces of the robot attendants. Carefully he laid him by their side. Then he went back into the ship.

Without fear now, Cliff stole along the wall of the room. He had gotten almost as far as the shattered figures on the floor when he suddenly stopped motionless. Gnut was emerging again.

He was bearing a shape that looked like another body, a larger one. He held it in one arm and placed it carefully by the body of Stillwell. In the hand of his other arm he held something that Cliff could not make out, and this he placed at the side of the body he had just put down. Then he went to the ship and returned once more with a shape which he laid gently by the others; and when this last trip was over he looked down at them all for a moment, then turned slowly back to the ship and stood motionless, as if in deep thought, by the ramp.

Cliff restrained his curiosity as long as he could, then slipped forward and bent over the objects Gnut had placed there. First in the row was the body of Stillwell, as he expected, and next was the great shapeless furry mass of a dead gorilla—the one of last night. By the gorilla lay the object the robot had carried in his free hand—the little body of the mocking bird. These last two had remained in the ship all night, and Gnut, for all his surprising gentleness in handling them, was only cleaning house. But there was a fourth body whose history he did not know. He moved closer and bent very low to look.

What he saw made him catch his breath. Impossible!—he thought; there was some confusion in his directions; he brought his face back, close to the first body. Then his blood ran cold. The first body was that of Stillwell, but the last in the row was Stillwell, too; there were two bodies of Stillwell, both exactly alike, both dead.

Cliff backed away with a cry, and then panic took him and he ran down the room away from Gnut and yelled and beat wildly on the door. There was a noise on the outside.

"Let me out!" he yelled in terror. "Let me out! Let me out! Oh, hurry!"

A crack opened between the two doors and he forced his way through like a wild animal and ran far out on the lawn. A belated couple on a nearby path stared at him with amazement, and this brought some sense to his head and he slowed down and came to a stop. Back at the building, everything looked as usual, and in spite of his terror, Gnut was not chasing him.

He was still in his stockinged feet. Breathing heavily, he sat down on the wet grass and put on his shoes; then he stood and looked at the building, trying to pull himself together. What an incredible melange! The dead Stillwell, the dead gorilla, and the dead mocking bird—all dying before his eyes. And then that last frightening thing, the second dead Stillwell whom he had *not* seen die. And Gnut's strange gentleness, and the sad expression he had twice seen on his face.

As he looked, the grounds about the building came to life. Several people collected at the door of the wing, above sounded the siren of a police copter, then in the distance another, and from all sides people came running, a few at first, then more and more. The police planes landed on the lawn just outside the door of the wing, and he thought he could see the officers peeping inside. Then suddenly the lights of the wing flooded on. In control of himself now, Cliff went back.

He entered. He had left Gnut standing in thought at the side of the ramp, but now he was again in his old familiar pose in the usual place, as if he had never moved. The ship's door was closed, and the ramp gone. But the bodies, the four strangely assorted bodies, were still lying by the demolished robot attendants where he had left them in the dark.

He was startled by a cry behind his back. A uniformed museum guard was pointing at him.

"This is the man!" the guard shouted. "When I opened the door this man forced his way out and ran like the devil!"

The police officers converged on Cliff.

"Who are you? What is all this?" one of them asked him roughly.

"I'm Cliff Sutherland, picture reporter," Cliff answered calmly. "And I was the one who was inside here and ran away, as the guard says."

"What were you doing?" the officer asked, eyeing him. "And where did these bodies come from?"

"Gentlemen, I'd tell you gladly—only business first," Cliff answered. "There's been some fantastic goings on in this room, and I saw them and have the story, but"—he smiled—"I must decline to answer without advice of counsel until I've sold my story to one of the news syndicates. You know how it is. If you'll allow me the use of the radio in your plane—just for a moment, gentlemen—you'll have the whole story right afterward—say in half an hour, when the television men broadcast it. Meanwhile, believe me, there's nothing for you to do, and there'll be no loss by the delay."

The officer who had asked the questions blinked, and one of the others, quicker to react and certainly not a gentleman, stepped toward Cliff with clenched fists. Cliff disarmed him by handing him his press credentials. He glanced at them rapidly and put them in his pocket.

By now half a hundred people were there, and among them were two members of a syndicate crew whom he knew, arrived by copter. The police growled, but they let him whisper in their ears and then go out under escort to the crew's plane. There, by radio, in five minutes, Cliff made a deal which would bring him more money than he had ever before earned in a year. After that he turned over all his pictures and negatives to the crew and gave them the story, and they lost not one second in spinning back to their office with the flash.

More and more people arrived, and the police cleared the building. Ten minutes later a big crew of radio and television men forced their way in, sent there by the syndicate with which he had dealt. And then a few minutes later, under the glaring lights set up by the operators and standing close by the ship and not far from Gnut—he refused to stand underneath him—Cliff gave his story to the cameras and microphones, which in a fraction of a second shot it to every corner of the Solar System.

Immediately afterward the police took him to jail. On general principles and because they were pretty blooming mad.

— V —

Cliff stayed in jail all that night—until eight o'clock the next morning, when the syndicate finally succeeded in digging up a lawyer and got him out. And then, when at last he was leaving, a Federal man caught him by the wrist.

"You're wanted for further questioning over at the Continental Bureau of Investigation," the agent told him. Cliff went along willingly.

Fully thirty-five high-ranking Federal officials and "big names" were waiting for him in an imposing conference room—one of the president's secretaries, the undersecretary of state, the underminister of defense, scientists, a colonel, executives, department heads, and ranking "C" men. Old gray-mustached Sanders, chief of the CBI, was presiding.

They made him tell his story all over again, and then, in parts, all over once more—not because they did not believe him, but because they kept hoping to elicit some fact which would cast significant light on the mystery of Gnut's behavior and the happenings of the last three nights. Patiently Cliff racked his brains for every detail.

Chief Sanders asked most of the questions. After more than an hour, when Cliff thought they had finished, Sanders asked him several more, all involving his personal opinions of what had transpired.

"Do you think Gnut was deranged in any way by the acids, rays, heat, and so forth applied to him by the scientists?"

"I saw no evidence of it."

"Do you think he can see?"

"I'm sure he can see, or else has other powers which are equivalent."

"Do you think he can hear?"

"Yes, sir. That time when I whispered to him that Stillwell was dead, he bent lower, as if to see for himself. I would not be surprised if he also understood what I said."

"At no time did he speak, except those sounds he made to open the ship?"

"Not one word, in English or any other language. Not one sound with his mouth."

"In your opinion, has his strength been impaired in any way by our treatment?" asked one of the scientists.

"I have told you how easily he handled the gorilla. He attacked the animal and threw it back, after which it retreated all the way down the building, afraid of him."

"How would you explain the fact that our autopsies disclosed no mortal wound, no cause of death, in any of the bodies—gorilla, mocking bird, or the two identical Stillwells?"—this from a medical officer.

"I can't."

"You think Gnut is dangerous?"—from Sanders.

"Potentially very dangerous."

"Yet you say you have the feeling he is not hostile."

"To me, I meant. I do have that feeling, and I'm afraid that I can't give any good reason for it, except the way he spared me twice when he had me in his power. I think maybe the gentle way he handled the bodies had something to do with it, and maybe the sad, thoughtful look I twice caught on his face."

"Would you risk staying in the building alone another night?"

"Not for anything." There were smiles.

"Did you get any pictures of what happened last night?"

"No, sir." Cliff, with an effort, held on to his composure, but he was swept by a wave of shame. A man hitherto silent rescued him by saying:

"A while ago you used the word 'purposive' in connection with Gnut's actions. Can you explain that a little?"

"Yes, that was one of the things that struck me: Gnut never seems to waste a motion. He can move with surprising speed when he wants to; I saw that when he attacked the gorilla; but most other times he walks around as if methodically completing some simple task. And that reminds me of a peculiar thing: at times he gets into one position, any position, maybe half bent over, and stays there for minutes at a time. It's as if his scale of time values was eccentric, compared to ours; some things he does surprisingly fast, and others surprisingly slow. This might account for his long periods of immobility."

"That's very interesting," said one of the scientists. "How would you account for the fact that he recently moves only at night?"

"I think he's doing something he wants no one to see, and the night is the only time he is alone."

"But he went ahead even after finding you there."

"I know. But I have no other explanation, unless he considered me harmless or unable to stop him—which was certainly the case."

"Before you arrived, we were considering incasing him in a large block of glasstex. Do you think he would permit it?"

"I don't know. Probably he would; he stood for the acids and rays and heat. But it had better be done in the daytime; night seems to be the time he moves."

"But he moved in the daytime when he emerged from the traveler with Klaatu."

"I know."

That seemed to be all they could think of to ask him. Sanders slapped his hand on the table.

"Well, I guess that's all Mr. Sutherland," he said. "Thank you for your help, and let me congratulate you for being a very foolish, stubborn, brave young man—young businessman." He smiled very faintly. "You are free to go now, but it may be that I'll have to call you back later. We'll see."

"May I remain while you decide about that glasstex?" Cliff asked. "As long as I'm here I'd like to have the tip."

"The decision has already been made—the tip's yours. The pouring will be started at once."

"Thank you, sir," said Cliff—and calmly asked more: "And will you be so kind as to authorize me to be present outside the building tonight? Just outside. I've a feeling something's going to happen."

"You want still another scoop, I see," said Sanders not unkindly, "then you'll let the police wait while you transact your business."

"Not again, sir. If anything happens, they'll get it at once."

The chief hesitated. "I don't know," he said. "I'll tell you what. All the news services will want men there, and we can't have that; but if you can arrange to represent them all yourself, it's a go. Nothing's going to happen, but your reports will help calm the hysterical ones. Let me know."

Cliff thanked him and hurried out and phoned his syndicate the tip—free—then told them Sanders' proposal. Ten minutes later they called him back, said all was arranged, and told him to catch some sleep. They would cover the pouring. With light heart, Cliff hurried over to the museum. The place was surrounded by thousands of the curious, held far back by a strong cordon of police. For once he could not get through; he was recognized, and the police were still sore. But he did not care much; he suddenly felt very tired and needed that nap. He went back to his hotel, left a call, and went to bed.

He had been asleep only a few minutes when his phone rang. Eyes shut, he answered it. It was one of the boys at the syndicate, with peculiar news. Stillwell had just reported, very much alive—the real Stillwell. The two dead ones were some kind of copies; he couldn't imagine how to explain them. He had no brothers.

For a moment Cliff came fully awake, then he went back to bed. Nothing was fantastic any more.

— VI —

At four o'clock, much refreshed and with an infrared viewing magnifier slung over his shoulder, Cliff passed through the cordon and entered the door of the wing. He had been expected and there was no trouble. As his eyes fell on Gnut, an odd feeling went through him, and for some obscure reason he was almost sorry for the giant robot.

Gnut stood exactly as he had always stood, the right foot advanced a little, and the same brooding expression on his face; but now there was something more. He was solidly incased in a huge block of transparent glasstex. From the floor on which he stood to the top of his full eight feet, and from there on up for an equal distance, and for about eight feet to the left, right, back, and front, he was immured in a water-clear prison which confined every inch of his surface and would prevent the slightest twitch of even his amazing muscles.

It was absurd, no doubt, to feel sorry for a robot, a man-made mechanism, but Cliff had come to think of him as being really alive, as a human is alive. He showed purpose and will; he performed complicated and resourceful acts; his face had twice clearly shown the emotion of sadness, and several times what appeared to be deep thought; he had been ruthless with the gorilla, and gentle with the mocking bird and the other two bodies, and he had twice refrained from crushing Cliff when there seemed every reason that he might. Cliff did not doubt for a minute that he was still alive, whatever that "alive" might mean.

But outside were waiting the radio and television men; he had work to do. He turned and went to them and all got busy.

An hour later Cliff sat alone about fifteen feet above the ground in a big tree which, located just across the walk from the building, commanded through a window a clear view of the upper part of Gnut's body. Strapped to the limbs about him were three instruments—his infrared viewing magnifier, a radio mike, and an infrared television eye with sound pickup. The first, the viewing magnifier, would allow him to see in the dark with his own eyes, as if by daylight, a magnified image of the robot, and the others would pick up any sights and sounds, including his own remarks, and transmit them to the several broadcast studios which would fling them millions of miles in all directions through space. Never before had a picture man had such an important assignment, probably—certainly not one who forgot to take pictures. But now that was forgotten, and Cliff was quite proud, and ready.

Far back in a great circle stood a multitude of the curious—and the fearful. Would the plastic glasstex hold Gnut? If it did not, would he come out thirsting for revenge? Would unimaginable beings come out of the traveler and release him, and perhaps exact revenge? Millions at their receivers were jittery; those in the distance hoped nothing awful would happen, yet they hoped something would, and they were prepared to run.

In carefully selected spots not far from Cliff on all sides were mobile ray batteries manned by army units, and in a hollow in back of him, well to his right, there was stationed a huge tank with a large gun. Every weapon was trained on the door of the wing. A row of smaller, faster tanks stood ready fifty yards directly north. Their ray projectors were aimed at the door, but not their guns. The grounds about the building contained only one spot—the hollow where the great tank was—where, by close calculation, a shell directed at the doorway would not cause damage and loss of life to some part of the sprawling capital.

Dusk fell; out streamed the last of the army officers, politicians and other privileged ones; the great metal doors of the wing clanged to and were locked for the night. Soon Cliff was alone, except for the watchers at their weapons scattered around him.

Hours passed. The moon came out. From time to time Cliff reported to the studio crew that all was quiet. His unaided eyes could now see nothing of Gnut but the two faint red points of his eyes, but through the magnifier he stood out as clearly as if in daylight from an apparent distance of only ten feet. Except for his eyes, there was no evidence that he was anything but dead and unfunctionable metal.

Another hour passed. Now and again Cliff thumbed the levels of his tiny radio-television watch—only a few seconds at a time because of its limited battery. The air was full of Gnut and his own face and his own name, and once the tiny screen showed the tree in which he was then sitting and even, minutely, himself. Powerful infrared long-distance television pickups were even then focused on him from nearby points of vantage. It gave him a funny feeling.

Then, suddenly, Cliff saw something and quickly bent his eye to the viewing magnifier. Gnut's eyes were moving; at least the intensity of the light emanating from them varied. It was as if two tiny red flashlights were turned from side to side, their beams at each motion crossing Cliff's eyes.

Thrilling, Cliff signaled the studios, cut in his pickups, and described the phenomenon. Millions resonated to the excitement in his voice. Could Gnut conceivably break out of that terrible prison?

Minutes passed, the eye flashes continued, but Cliff could discern no movement or attempted movement of the robot's body. In brief snatches he described what he saw. Gnut was clearly alive; there could be no doubt he was straining against the transparent prison in which he had at last been locked fast; but unless he could crack it, no motion should show.

Cliff took his eye from the magnifier—and started. His unaided eye, looking at Gnut shrouded in darkness, saw an astonishing thing not yet visible through his instrument. A faint red glow was spreading over the robot's body. With trembling fingers he readjusted the lens of the television eye, but even as he did so the glow grew in intensity. It looked as if Gnut's body was being heated to incandescence!

He described it in excited fragments, for it took most of his attention to keep correcting the lens. Gnut passed from a figure of dull red to one brighter and brighter, clearly glowing now even through the magnifier. And then he moved! Unmistakably he moved!

He had within himself somehow the means to raise his own body temperature, and was exploiting the one limitation of the plastic in which he was locked. For glasstex, Cliff now remembered, was a thermoplastic material, one that set by cooling and conversely would soften again with heat. Gnut was melting his way out!

In three-word snatches, Cliff described this. The robot became cherry-red, the sharp edges of the icelike block rounded, and the whole structure began to sag. The process accelerated. The robot's body moved more widely. The plastic lowered to the crown of his head, then to his neck, then his waist, which was as far as Cliff could see. His body was free! And then, still cherry-red, he moved forward out of sight!

Cliff strained eyes and ears, but caught nothing but the distant roar of the watchers beyond the police lines and a few low, sharp commands from the batteries posted around him. They, too, had heard, and perhaps seen by tele-screen, and were waiting.

Several minutes passed. There was a sharp, ringing crack; the great metal doors of the wing flew open, and out stepped the metal giant, glowing no longer. He stood stock-still, and his red eyes pierced from side to side through the darkness.

Voices out in the dark barked orders and in a twinkling Gnut was bathed in narrow crisscrossing rays of sizzling, colored light. Behind him the metal doors began to melt, but his great green body showed no change at all. Then the world seemed to come to an end; there was a deafening roar, everything before Cliff seemed to explode in smoke and chaos, his tree whipped to one side so that he was nearly thrown out. Pieces of debris rained down. The tank gun had spoken, and Gnut, he was sure, had been hit.

Cliff held on tight and peered into the haze. As it cleared he made out a stirring among the debris at the door, and then dimly but unmistakably he saw the great form of Gnut rise to his feet. He got up slowly, turned toward the tank, and suddenly darted toward it in a wide arc. The big gun swung in an attempt to cover him, but the robot side-stepped and then was upon it. As the crew scattered, he destroyed its breech with one blow of his fist, and then he turned and looked right at Cliff.

He moved toward him, and in a moment was under the tree. Cliff climbed higher. Gnut put his two arms around the tree and gave a lifting push, and the tree tore out at the roots and fell crashing to its side. Before Cliff could scramble away, the robot had lifted him in his metal hands.

Cliff thought his time had come, but strange things were yet in store for him that night. Gnut did not hurt him. He looked at him from arm's length for a moment, then lifted him to a sitting position on his shoulders, legs strad-dling his neck. Then, holding one ankle, he turned and without hesitation started down the path which led westward away from the building.

Cliff rode helpless. Out over the lawns he saw the muzzles of the scattered field pieces move as he moved, Gnut—and himself—their one focus. But they did not fire. Gnut, by placing him on his shoulders, had secured himself against that—Cliff hoped.

The robot bore straight toward the Tidal Basin. Most of the field pieces throbbed slowly after. Far back, Cliff saw a dark tide of confusion roll into the cleared area—the police lines had broken. Ahead, the ring thinned rapidly off to the sides; then, from all directions but the front, the tide rolled in until in-dividual shouts and cries could be made out. It came to a stop about fifty yards off, and few people ventured nearer.

Gnut paid them no attention, and he no more noticed his burden than he might a fly. His neck and shoulders made Cliff a seat hard as steel, but with the difference that their underlying muscles with each movement flexed, just as would those of a human being. To Cliff, this metal musculature became a vivid wonder.

Straight as the flight of a bee, over paths, across lawns, and through thin rows of trees Gnut bore the young man, the roar of thousands of people fol-lowing close. Above droned copters and darting planes, among them police cars with their nerve-shattering sirens. Just ahead lay the still waters of the Tidal Basin, and in its midst the simple marble tomb of the slain ambassador, Klaatu, gleaming black and cold in the light of the dozen searchlights always trained on it at night. Was this a rendezvous with the dead?

Without an instant's hesitation, Gnut strode down the bank and entered the water. It rose to his knees, then waist, until Cliff's feet were under. Straight through the dark waters for the tomb of Klaatu the robot made his inevitable way.

The dark square mass of gleaming marble rose higher as they neared it. Gnut's body began emerging from the water as the bottom shelved upward, until his dripping feet took the first of the rising pyramid of steps. In a mo-ment they were at the top, on the narrow platform in the middle of which rested the simple oblong tomb.

Stark in the blinding searchlights, the giant robot walked once around it, then, bending, he braced himself and gave a mighty push against the top. The marble cracked; the thick cover slipped askew and broke with a loud noise on the far side. Gnut went to his knees and looked within, bringing Cliff well up over the edge.

Inside, in sharp shadow against the converging light beams, lay a transpar-ent plastic coffin, thick walled and sealed against the centuries, and containing all that was mortal of Klaatu, unspoken visitor from the great Unknown. He lay as if asleep, on his face the look of godlike nobility that had caused some of the ignorant to believe him divine. He wore the robe he had arrived in. There were no faded flowers, no jewelry, no ornaments; they would have seemed profane. At the foot of the coffin lay the small sealed box, also of transparent plastic, which contained all of Earth's records of his visit—a description of the events attending his arrival, pictures of Gnut and the traveler, and the little roll of sight-and-sound film which had caught for all time his few brief motions and words.

Cliff sat very still, wishing he could see the face of the robot. Gnut, too, did not move from his position of reverent contemplation—not for a long time. There on the brilliantly lighted pyramid, under the eyes of a fearful, tumultuous multitude, Gnut paid final respect to his beautiful and adored master.

Suddenly, then, it was over. Gnut reached out and took the little box of records, rose to his feet, and started down the steps.

Back through the water, straight back to the building, across lawns and paths as before, he made his irresistible way. Before him the chaotic ring of people melted away, behind they followed as close as they dared, trampling each other in their efforts to keep him in sight. There are no television records of his return. Every pickup was damaged on the way to the tomb.

As they drew near the building, Cliff saw that the tank's projectile had made a hole twenty feet wide extending from the roof to the ground. The door still stood open, and Gnut, hardly varying his almost jerkless rhythm, made his way over the debris and went straight for the port end of the ship. Cliff wondered if he would be set free.

He was. The robot set him down and pointed toward the door; then, turning, he made the sounds that opened the ship. The ramp slid down and he entered.

Then Cliff did the mad, courageous thing which made him famous for a generation. Just as the ramp started sliding back in he skipped over it and himself entered the ship. The port closed.

## — VII —

It was pitch dark, and the silence was absolute. Cliff did not move. He felt that Gnut was close, just ahead, and it was so.

His hard metal hand took him by the waist, pulled him against his cold side, and carried him somewhere ahead. Hidden lamps suddenly bathed the surroundings with bluish light.

He set Cliff down and stood looking at him. The young man already regretted his rash action, but the robot, except for his always unfathomable eyes, did not seem angry. He pointed to a stool in one corner of the room. Cliff quickly obeyed this time and sat meekly, for a while not even venturing to look around.

He saw he was in a small laboratory of some kind. Complicated metal and plastic apparatus lined the walls and filled several small tables; he could not recognize or guess the function of a single piece. Dominating the center of the room was a long metal table on whose top lay a large box, much like a coffin on the outside, connected by many wires to a complicated apparatus at the far end. From close above spread a cone of bright light from a many-tubed lamp.

One thing, half covered on a nearby table, did look familiar—and very much out of place. From where he sat it seemed to be a brief case—an ordinary Earthman's brief case. He wondered.

Gnut paid him no attention, but at once, with the narrow edge of a thick tool, sliced the lid off the little box of records. He lifted out the strip of sight-and-sound film and spent fully half an hour adjusting it within the apparatus at the end of the big table. Cliff watched, fascinated, wondering at the skill with which the robot used his tough metal fingers. This done, Gnut worked for a long time over some accessory apparatus on an adjoining table. Then he paused thoughtfully a moment and pushed inward a long rod.

A voice came out of the coffinlike box—the voice of the slain ambassador.

"I am Klaatu," it said, "and this is Gnut."

From the recording!—flashed through Cliff's mind. The first and only words the ambassador had spoken. But, then, in the very next second he saw that it was not so. There was a man in the box! The man stirred and sat up, and Cliff saw the living face of Klaatu!

Klaatu appeared somewhat surprised and spoke quickly in an unknown tongue to Gnut—and Gnut, for the first time in Cliff's experience, spoke himself in answer. The robot's syllables tumbled out as if born of human emotion, and the expression on Klaatu's face changed from surprise to wonder. They talked for several minutes. Klaatu, apparently fatigued, then began to lie down, but stopped midway, for he saw Cliff. Gnut spoke again, at length. Klaatu beckoned Cliff with his hand, and he went to him.

"Gnut has told me everything," he said in a low, gentle voice, then looked at Cliff for a moment in silence, on his face a faint, tired smile.

Cliff had a hundred questions to ask, but for a moment hardly dared open his mouth.

"But you," he began at last—very respectfully, but with an escaping excitement—"you are not the Klaatu that was in the tomb?"

The man's smile faded and he shook his head.

"No." He turned to the towering Gnut and said something in his own tongue, and at his words the metal features of the robot twisted as if with pain. Then he turned back to Cliff. "I am dying," he announced simply, as if repeating his words for the Earthman. Again to his face came the faint, tired smile.

Cliff's tongue was locked. He just stared, hoping for light. Klaatu seemed to read his mind.

"I see you don't understand," he said. "Although unlike us, Gnut has great powers. When the wing was built and the lectures began, there came to him a striking inspiration. Acting on it at once, in the night, he assembled this apparatus . . . and now he has made me again, from my voice, as recorded by your people. As you must know, a given body makes a characteristic sound. He constructed an apparatus which reversed the recording process, and from the given sound made the characteristic body."

Cliff gasped. So that was it!

"But you needn't die!" Cliff exclaimed suddenly, eagerly. "Your voice recording was taken when you stepped out of the ship, while you were well! You must let me take you to a hospital! Our doctors are very skillful!"

Hardly perceptibly, Klaatu shook his head.

"You still don't understand," he said slowly and more faintly. "Your recording had imperfections. Perhaps very slight ones, but they doom the product. All of Gnut's experiments died in a few minutes, he tells me . . . and so must I."

Suddenly, then, Cliff understood the origin of the "experiments." He remembered that on the day the wing was opened a Smithsonian official had lost a brief case containing film strips recording the speech of various world fauna. There, on that table, was a brief case! And the Stillwells must have been made from strips kept in the table drawer!

But his heart was heavy. He did not want this stranger to die. Slowly there dawned on him an important idea. He explained it with growing excitement.

"You say the recording was imperfect, and of course it was. But the cause of that lay in the use of an imperfect recording apparatus. So if Gnut, in his reversal of the process, had used exactly the same pieces of apparatus that your voice was recorded with, the imperfections could be studied, canceled out, and you'd live, and not die!"

As the last words left his lips, Gnut whipped around like a cat and gripped him tight. A truly human excitement was shining in the metal muscles of his face.

"Get me that apparatus!" he ordered—in clear and perfect English! He started pushing Cliff toward the door, but Klaatu raised his hand.

"There is no hurry," Klaatu said gently; "it is too late for me. What is your name, young man?"

Cliff told him.

"Stay with me to the end," he asked. Klaatu closed his eyes and rested; then, smiling just a little, but not opening his eyes, he added: "And don't be sad, for I shall now perhaps live again . . . and it will be due to you. There is no pain—" His voice was rapidly growing weaker. Cliff, for all the questions he had, could only look on, dumb. Again Klaatu seemed to be aware of his thoughts.

"I know," he said feebly, "I know. We have so much to ask each other. About your civilization . . . and Gnut's—"

"And yours," said Cliff.

"And Gnut's," said the gentle voice again. "Perhaps . . . some day . . . perhaps I will be back—"

He lay without moving. He lay so for a long time, and at last Cliff knew that he was dead. Tears came to his eyes; in only these few minutes he had come to love this man. He looked at Gnut. The robot knew, too, that he was dead, but no tears filled his red-lighted eyes; they were fixed on Cliff, and for once the young man knew what was in his mind.

"Gnut," he announced earnestly, as if taking a sacred oath, "I'll get the original apparatus. I'll get it. Every piece of it, the exact same things."

Without a word, Gnut conducted him to the port. He made the sounds that unlocked it. As it opened, a noisy crowd of Earthmen outside trampled each other in a sudden scramble to get out of the building. The wing was lighted. Cliff stepped down the ramp.

The next two hours always in Cliff's memory had a dreamlike quality. It was as if that mysterious laboratory with the peacefully sleeping dead man was the real and central part of his life, and his scene with the noisy men with whom he talked a gross and barbaric interlude. He stood not far from the ramp. He told only part of his story. He was believed. He waited quietly while all the pressure which the highest officials in the land could exert was directed toward obtaining for him the apparatus the robot had demanded.

When it arrived, he carried it to the floor of the little vestibule behind the port. Gnut was there, as if waiting. In his arms he held the slender body of the second Klaatu. Tenderly he passed him out to Cliff, who took him without a word, as if all this had been arranged. It seemed to be the parting.

Of all the things Cliff had wanted to say to Klaatu, one remained imperatively present in his mind. Now, as the green metal robot stood framed in the great green ship, he seized his chance.

"Gnut," he said earnestly, holding carefully the limp body in his arms, "you must do one thing for me. Listen carefully. I want you to tell your master—the master yet to come—that what happened to the first Klaatu was an accident, for which all Earth is immeasurably sorry. Will you do that?"

"I have known it," the robot answered gently.

"But will you promise to tell your master—just those words—as soon as he is arrived?"

"You misunderstand," said Gnut, still gently, and quietly spoke four more words. As Cliff heard them a mist passed over his eyes and his body went numb.

As he recovered and his eyes came back to focus he saw the great ship disappear. It just suddenly was not there any more. He fell back a step or two. In his ears, like great bells, rang Gnut's last words. Never, never was he to disclose them till the day he came to die.

"You misunderstand," the mighty robot had said. "I am the master."

"Klaatu barrada Niktu!"

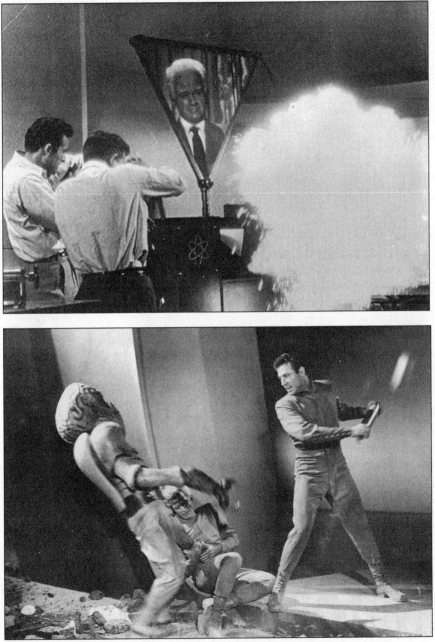

*Top*: Exeter blows up the Interocitor before the eyes of Cal Meacham (Rex Reason) and his assistant.   *Bottom:* Our hero (Rex Reason) attempts to bash in the head of the Mutant in *This Island Earth*.

# This Island Earth

## RAYMOND F. JONES

---

**This Island Earth**

Director: *Joseph Newman*
Screenplay: *Franklin Coen, Edward G. O'Callagan*
Producer: *William Alland*
Music: *Herman Stein*
Special Effects: *Clifford Stine, David S. Horsley*
Cast: *Rex Reason, Faith Domergue, Jeff Morrow, Lance Fuller, Eddie Parker*
Released by: *Universal-International*
1955, 87 Minutes. Color.

---

— I —

The offices of Joe Wilson, purchasing agent for Ryberg Instrument Corporation, looked out over the company's private landing field. Joe stood by the window now, wishing they didn't, because it was an eternal reminder that he'd once had hopes of becoming an engineer instead of an office flunky.

He saw the silver test ship of the radio lab level off at bullet speed, circle once and land. That would be Cal Meacham, Joe thought. Nobody but a radio engineer would fly an airplane that way.

He chomped irritably on his cigar and turned away. From his desk he picked up a letter and read it through slowly for the fourth time. It was in answer to an order he had placed for condensers for Cal's hot transmitter job—Cal's stuff was always hot.

Dear Mr. Wilson:

We were pleased to receive your order of the 8th for samples of our XC-109 condenser. However, we find that our present catalogue lists no such item nor did we ever carry it.

We are, therefore, substituting the AB-619 model, a high-voltage oil-filled transmitting-type condenser. As you specified, it is rated at 10,000 volts with 100% safety factor and has 4 mf. capacity.

We trust these will meet with your approval and that we may look forward to receiving your production order for these items. It is needless, of course, to remind you that we manufacture a complete line of electronic components. We would be glad to furnish samples of any items from our stock which might interest you.

> Respectfully yours,
> A. G. Archmanter
> Electronic Service—Unit 16

Joe Wilson put the letter down slowly and took up the box of beads that had come with it.

He picked up one bead by a lead wire sticking out of it. The bead was about a quarter of an inch in diameter and there seemed to be a smaller concentric shell inside. Between the two was some reddish liquid. Another wire connected to the inner shell, but for the life of him Joe couldn't see how that inner wire came through the outer shell.

It made him dizzy to concentrate on the spot where it came through. The spot seemed to shift and move.

"Ten thousand volts!" he muttered. "Four mikes!"

He tossed the bead back into the box. Cal would be hotter than the transmitter job when he saw these.

Joe heard the door of his secretary's office open and glanced through the glass panel. Cal Meacham burst in with a breeze that ruffled the letters on Joe's desk.

"See that landing I made, Joe? Markus says I ought to be able to get my license to fly that crate in another week."

"I'll bet he added 'if you live that long.' "

"Just because you don't recognize a hot pilot when you see one—what are you so glum about, anyway? And what's happened to those condensers we ordered three days ago? This job's *hot*."

Joe held out the letter silently. Cal scanned the page and flipped it back to the desk.

"We'll try them out. Give me an order and I'll pick them up from receiving on my way to the lab."

"They aren't in receiving. They came in the envelope with the letter."

"What are you talking about? How could they send sixteen mikes of ten kv condensers in an envelope?"

Joe held up one of the beads by a wire. "Guaranteed one hundred percent voltage safety factor."

"What screwball's idea of a joke is this? Did you call Receiving?"

Joe nodded. "I checked *good*. These beads are all that came."

Cal grasped one by the lead wire and held it up to the light. He saw the faint internal structure that Joe had puzzled over.

"It *would* be funny if that's what these things actually were, wouldn't it?" he said.

"You could build a fifty kw transmitter in a suitcase, provided you had other corresponding components."

Cal dropped the rest of the beads in his shirt pocket. "Call them on the teletype. Tell them this job is plenty hot and we've got to have those condensers right away."

"What are you going to do with the beads?"

"I might put ten thousand volts across them and see how long it takes to melt them down. See if you can find out who pulled this gag."

For the rest of the morning Cal checked over the antenna on his new ground transmitter, which wasn't putting out power the way it should. He forgot about the glass beads until late in the afternoon.

Then, as he bent his head down into the framework of the set, one of the sharp leads of the alleged condensers stuck through his shirt.

He jerked sharply and bumped his head on the iron framework. He cursed the refractory transmitter, the missing condensers and the practical joker who had sent the beads. He pulled the things out of his shirt pocket and was about to hurl them across the room.

But a quirk of curiosity halted his hand in midair. Slowly he lowered it and looked again at the beads that seemed to glare at him like eyes in the palm of his hand.

He called across the lab to a junior engineer. "Hey, Max, come here. Put these things on voltage breakdown and see what happens."

"Sure." The junior engineer rolled them over in his palm. "What are they?"

"Just some gadgets we got for test. I forgot about them until now."

He resumed checking the transmitter. Crazy notion, that. As if the beads actually were anything but glass beads. There was only one thing that kept him from forgetting the whole matter. It was the way that one wire seemed to slide around on the bead when you looked at it—

In about five minutes Max was back. "I shot one of your gadgets all to pieces. It held up until thirty-three thousand volts—and not a microamp of leakage. Whatever they are they're *good*. Want to blow the rest?"

Cal turned slowly. He wondered if Max were in on the gag, too. "A few hundred volts would jump right around the glass from wire to wire without bothering to go through!"

"That's what the meter read."

"Come on," said Cal. "Let's check the capacity."

First he tried another on voltage test. He watched it behind the glass shield as he advanced the voltage in steps of five kv. The bead held at thirty—and vanished at thirty-five.

His lips compressed tightly, Cal took the third bead to a standard capacity bridge. He adjusted the plugs until it balanced—at just four microfarads.

Max's eyes were slightly popped. "Four mikes—they *can't* be!"

"No, they can't possibly be, can they?"

Back in the Purchasing Office Cal found Joe Wilson sitting morosely at the desk, staring at a yellow strip of teletype paper.

"Just the man I'm looking for," said Joe. "I called the Continental Electric and they said—"

"I don't care what they said." Cal laid the remaining beads on the desk in front of Joe. "Those are four-mike condensers that don't break down until more than thirty thousand volts. They're everything Continental said they were and more. Where did they get them? Last time I was over there Simon Forrest was in charge of the condenser department. He never—"

"Will you let me tell you?" Joe interrupted. "They didn't come from Continental. Continental says no order for condensers has been received from here in the last six weeks. I sent a recorder by TWX."

"I don't want their order then. I want more of these!" Cal held up a bead. "But where did they come from if not from Continental?"

"That's what I want to know."

"What letterhead came with these? Let's see it again."

"It just says, 'Electronic Service—Unit Sixteen.' I thought that was some subsection of Continental. There's no address on it."

Cal looked intently at the sheet of paper. "You're sure this came back in answer to an order you sent Continental?"

Wearily, Joe flipped over a file. "There's the duplicate of the order I sent."

"Continental always was a screwball outfit, but they must be trying to top themselves. Write them again. Give the reference on this letter. Order a gross of these condensers. While you're at it ask for a new catalogue. Ours may be obsolete. I'd like to see what else they list besides condensers."

"Okay," said Joe. "But I tell you Continental says they didn't even get our order."

"I suppose Santa Claus sent these condensers!"

Three days later Cal was still ironing the bugs out of his transmitter when Joe Wilson called again.

"I just got the condensers—and the catalogue! For the love of Pete, get up here and take a look at it!"

"A whole gross of condensers? That's what I'm interested in."

"Yes—and billed to us for thirty cents apiece."

Cal hung up and walked out towards the Purchasing Office. Thirty cents apiece, he thought. If that outfit should go into the business of radio instruments they could probably sell a radio compass for five bucks.

He found Joe alone, an inch thick manufacturer's catalogue open on the desk in front of him.

"Did this come from Continental?" said Cal.

Joe shook his head and turned over the front cover. It merely said, *Electronic Service Unit 16.*

"We send letters to Continental and stuff comes back," said Cal. "Somebody over there must know about this! What's so exciting about the catalogue?"

Joe arched his eyebrows. "Ever hear of a catherimine tube? One with an endiom complex of plus four, which guarantees it to be the best of its kind on the market?"

"What kind of gibberish is that?"

"I dunno, but this outfit sells them for sixteen dollars each." Joe tossed the catalogue across the desk. "This is absolutely the cockeyedest thing I ever saw. If you hadn't told me those beads were condensers I'd say somebody had gone to a lot of work to pull a pretty elaborate gag. But the condensers were real—and here's a hundred and forty-four more of them."

He picked up a little card with the beads neatly mounted in small holes. "Somebody made these. A pretty doggoned smart somebody, I'd say—but I don't think it was Continental."

Cal was slowly thumbing through the book. Besides the gibberish describing unfamiliar pieces of electronic equipment there was something else gnawing at his mind. Then he grasped it. He rubbed a page of the catalogue between his fingers and thumb.

"Joe, this stuff isn't even paper."

"I know. Try to tear it."

Cal's fingers merely slipped away. "That's as tough as sheet iron!"

"Whoever this Electronic Service outfit is, they've got some pretty bright engineers."

"Bright engineers! This thing reflects a whole electronic culture completely foreign to ours. If it had come from Mars it couldn't be more foreign."

Cal turned the pages, paused to read a description of a *Volterator incorporating an electron sorter based on entirely new principles*. The picture of the thing looked like a cross between a miniature hot air furnace and a backyard incinerator and it sold for six hundred dollars.

He came to an inner dividing cover at the center of the catalogue. *For the first time*, the center cover announced, *Electronic Service—Unit 16 offers a complete line of interocitor components. In the following pages you will find complete descriptions of components which reflect the most modern engineering advances known to interocitor engineers.*

"Ever hear of an interocitor?"

"Sounds like something a surgeon would use to remove gallstones."

"Maybe we should order a kit of parts and build one up," said Cal whimsically.

"That would be like a power engineer trying to build a high-power communications receiver from the *Amateur's Handbook* catalogue section."

"Maybe it could be done." Cal stared at the pages before him. "Do you realize what this means—the extent of the knowledge and electronic culture behind this? It exists right here around us somewhere."

"Maybe some little group of engineers that doesn't believe in exchanging information through the IRE and so on? But are they over at Continental? If so why all the beating about the bush telling us they didn't get our order?"

"It looks bigger than that," said Cal doubtfully. "Regardless, we know their mail goes through Continental."

"What are you going to do about it?"

"Do? I'm going to find out who they are! Mind if I take this catalogue along?"

"It's all right with me," said Joe. "I don't know what it's all about. I'm no engineer—just a dumb purchasing agent around this joint."

"For some things you can be thankful," said Cal.

— II —

The suburb of Mason was a small, moderately concentrated industrial center. Besides Ryberg Instrument there were Eastern Tool and Machine Company, the Metalcrafters, a small die-making plant, and a stapling-machine factory.

This concentration of small industry in the suburb made for an equally concentrated social order of engineers and their families. Most of them did have families but Cal Meacham was not yet among these.

He had been a bachelor for all of his thirty-five years and it looked as if he were going to stay that way. He admitted that he got lonely sometimes but considered it well worth it when he heard Frank Staley up and about at two A.M. in the apartment above his, coaxing the new baby into something resembling silence.

He ate at the company cafeteria and went home to ponder the incredible catalogue that Joe Wilson had obtained. He couldn't understand how such developments could have been kept quiet. And now, why were they being so prosaically announced in an ordinary manufacturer's catalogue? It made absolutely no sense whatever.

He settled down in his easy chair with the catalogue propped on his lap. The section on interocitor components held the greatest fascination for him.

But there was not a single clue as to what the interocitor was, its function or its purpose. To judge from the list of components, however, and some of the sub-assemblies that were shown, it was a terrifically complex piece of equipment.

He picked up the latest copy of the *Amateur's Handbook* and thumbed through the catalogue section. Joe had been right in comparing the job of assembling an interocitor to that of a power engineer trying to build a radio from the *Handbook* catalogue. How much indication would there be to a power engineer as to the purposes of the radio components in the catalogue?

Practically none. He gave up the speculation. He had already made up his mind to go to Continental and find out what this was all about. He *had* to know more about this stuff.

At seven there was a knock on his door. He found Frank Staley and two other engineers from upstairs standing in the hall.

"The wives are having a gabfest," said Frank. "How about a little poker?"

"Sure, I could use a little spending money this week. But are you guys sure you can stand the loss?"

"Ha, loss, he says," said Frank. "Shall we tell him how hot we are tonight, boys?"

"Let him find out the hard way," said Edmunds, one of Eastern's top mechanical engineers.

By nine-thirty Cal had found out the hard way. Even at the diminutive stakes they allowed themselves he was forty-five dollars in the hole.

He threw in his final hand. "That's all for tonight. You can afford to lose your lunch money for a couple of months but nobody will make mine up at home if I can't buy it at the plant."

Edmunds leaned back in his chair and laughed. "I told you we were hot tonight. You look about as glum as Peters, our purchasing agent did today. I had him order some special gears from some outfit a while back and they sent him two perfectly smooth wheels.

"He was about ready to hit the ceiling when he discovered that one wheel rolled against the other would drive it. He couldn't figure it out. Neither could I when I saw it. So I mounted them on shafts and put a motor on one and a pony brake on the other.

"Believe it or not those things would transfer any horsepower I could use and I had up to three hundred and fifty. There was perfect transfer without measureable slippage or backlash. The craziest thing you ever saw."

Like some familiar song in another language Edmunds' story sent a wave of almost frightening recognition through Cal. While Staley and Larsen, the third engineer, listened with polite disbelief, Cal sat in utter stillness, knowing it was all true. He thought of the strange catalogue in his bookcase.

"Did you find out where the gears came from?" he asked.

"No, but we intend to. Believe me, if we can find out the secret of those wheels it's going to revolutionize the entire science of mechanical engineering. They didn't come from the place we ordered them from. We know that much. They came from some place called merely 'Mechanical Service—Unit Eight.' No address. Whoever they are they must be geniuses besides being screwball business people."

Electronic Service—Unit 16, Mechanical Service—Unit 8—they must be bigger than he had supposed, Cal thought.

He went out to the little kitchenette to mix some drinks. From the other room he heard Larsen calling Edmunds a triple-dyed liar. Two perfectly smooth wheels couldn't transmit power of that order merely by friction.

"I didn't say it was friction," Edmunds was saying. "It was something else— we don't know what."

Something else, Cal thought. Couldn't Edmunds see the significance of such wheels? They were as evident of a foreign kind of mechanical culture as the condensers were evidence of a foreign electronic culture.

He went up to the Continental plant the next day, his hopes of finding the solution there considerably dimmed. His old friend, Simon Forrest, was still in charge of condenser development.

He showed Simon the bead and Simon said, "What kind of a gadget is that?"

"A four-mike condenser. You sent it to us. I want to know more about it." Cal watched the engineer's face closely.

Simon shook his head as he took the bead. "You're crazy! A four-mike condenser—we never sent you anything like this!"

He knew Simon was telling the truth.

It was Edmunds' story of the toothless gears that made it easier for Cal to accept the fact that the condensers and catalogue had not come from Continental. This, he decided during the ride home.

But *where* were the engineers responsible for this stuff? *Why* was it impossible to locate them? Mail reached Electronic Service through Continental. He wondered about Mechanical Service. Had Eastern received a catalogue of foreign mechanical components?

Regardless of the fantastic nature of the task, he made up his mind to do what he had suggested at first. He was going to attempt the construction of an interocitor.

But *could* it be done? Now that it was a determined course, the problem had to be analyzed further. In the catalogue were one hundred and six separate components. He knew it was not simply a matter of ordering one of each and putting them together.

That would be like ordering one tuning condenser, one coil, one tube and so on and expecting to build a super-het from them. In the interocitor there would be multiples of some parts, and different electrical values.

And, finally, if he ever got the thing working how would he know if it were performing properly or not?

He quit debating the pros and cons. He had known from the moment he first looked through the catalogue that he was going to try.

He went directly to the Purchasing Office instead of his lab the next morning. Through the glass panels of the outer room he saw Joe Wilson sitting at his desk, his face over a shoe box, staring with an intent and agonized frown.

Cal grinned to himself. It was hard to tell when Joe's mugging was real or not, but he couldn't imagine him sitting there doing it without an audience.

Cal opened the door quietly, and then he caught a glimpse of the contents of the box. It was *wriggling*. He scowled, too.

"What have you got now? An earthworm farm?"

Joe looked up, his face still wearing a bewildered and distant expression. "Oh, hello, Cal. This is a tumbling barrel."

The contents of the box looked like a mass of tiny black worms in perpetual erratic motion. "What's the gag this time? That box of worms doesn't look much like a tumbling barrel."

"It would—if they were metallic worms and just walked around the metal parts that needed tumbling."

"This isn't another Electronics Service—16 product, is it?"

"No. Metalcrafters sent over this sample. Wanted to know if they could sell us any for our mechanical department. The idea is that you just dump whatever needs tumbling into a box of this compound, strain it out in a few minutes and your polishing job is done."

"What makes the stuff wiggle?"

"That's the secret that Metalcrafters won't tell."

"Order five hundred pounds of it," said Cal suddenly. "Call them on the phone and tell them we can use it this afternoon."

"What's the big idea? *You* can't use it."

"Try it."

Dubiously, Joe contacted the order department of Metalcrafters. After a moment he hung up. "They say that due to unexpected technological difficulties in production they are not accepting orders for earlier than thirty day delivery."

"The crazy dopes! They won't get it in thirty days or thirty months."

"What are you talking about?"

"Where do you think they got this stuff? *They* didn't discover it. They got it the same way we got these condensers and they're hoping to cash in on it before they even know what it is. As if they could figure it out in thirty days!"

Then he told Joe about the gears of Edmunds.

"This begins to look like more than accident," said Joe.

Cal nodded slowly. "Samples of products of an incredible technology were apparently missent to three of the industrial plants here in Mason. But I wonder how many times it has happened in other places. It almost looks like a pattern of some sort."

"But who's sending it all and how and why? Who developed this stuff? It couldn't be done on a shoestring, you know. That stuff smells of big money spent in development labs. Those condensers must have cost a half million, I'll bet."

"Make out an order for me," said Cal. "Charge it to my project. There's enough surplus to stand it. I'll take the rap if anybody snoops."

"What do you want?"

"Send it to Continental as before. Just say you want one complete set of components as required for the construction of a single interocitor model. That may get me the right number of duplicate parts unless I get crossed up by something I'm not thinking of."

Joe's eyebrows shot up. "You're going to try to build one by the Chinese method?"

"The Chinese method would be simple," said Cal. "They take a finished cake and reconstruct it. If I had a finished interocitor I'd gladly tackle *that*. This is going to be built by the Cal Meacham original catalogue method."

He worked overtime for the next couple of days to beat out the bugs in the airline ground transmitter and finally turned it over to the production department for processing. There'd still be a lot of work on it because production wouldn't like some of the complex sub-assemblies he'd been forced to design—but he'd have time for the interocitor stuff between jobs.

After two weeks he was almost certain that something had gone wrong and they had lost contact with the mysterious supplier. Then receiving called him and said that fourteen crates had just been delivered for him.

Fourteen crates seemed a reasonable number but he hadn't been prepared for the size of them. They stood seven feet high and were no smaller than four by five feet in cross section.

As he saw them standing on the receiving platform Cal visioned cost sheets with astronomical figures on them. What had he got himself into?

He cleared out one of his screen rooms and ordered the stuff brought in.

In some attempt to classify the components he laid like units together upon the benches around the room. There were plumbing units of seemingly senseless configuration, glass envelopes with innards that looked like nothing he had ever seen in a vacuum tube before. There were boxes containing hundreds of small parts which he supposed must be resistances or condensers—though his memory concerning the glass beads made him cautious about jumping to conclusions regarding anything.

After three hours, the last of the crates had been unpacked and the rubbish carted away. Cal Meacham was left alone in the midst of four thousand, eight hundred and ninety-six—he'd kept a tally of them—unfamiliar gadgets of unknown purposes and characteristics. And he hoped to assemble them into a complete whole—of equally unknown purposes.

He sat down on a lab stool and regarded the stacks of components. In his lap rested the single guide through this impossible maze—the catalogue.

— III —

That evening he had dinner at the plant cafeteria, then returned to the now empty lab. It would take all his nights for months to come.

He hoped there wouldn't be too much curiosity about his project but he could see little chance of keeping it entirely under cover. Most of all he was concerned with keeping Billingsworth, the chief engineer, from complaining about it. This was *big* for a sideline project.

It was obvious that certain parts constituted a framework for the assembly.

He gathered these together and set them up tentatively to get some idea of the size and shape of the finished device.

One thing stood out at once. There was a cube of glass, sixteen inches on a side, filled with a complex mass of elements. Twenty-three terminals were on the outside of the cube. One side of it was coated as if it were a screen. One of the framework panels had an opening exactly the right size to accommodate the face of the cube.

That narrowed the utility of the device, Cal thought. It provided an observer with some kind of intelligence which was viewed in graphic or pictorial form as with a cathoderay tube.

But the complexity of the cube's elements and the multiple leads indicated another necessity. He would have to order duplicates of many parts because these would have to be dissected to destruction in order to determine electrical function.

Nearly all the tubes fell into this classification and he began listing these parts so that Joe could reorder.

He then turned to familiarizing himself with the catalogue name of each part and establishing possible functions from the descriptions and specifications given.

Slowly, through the early morning hours pieces fitted together as if the whole thing were a majestic jigsaw puzzle. At three A.M. Cal locked the screen room and went home for a few hours' sleep, elated by the clues he had discovered.

He was in at eight again and went to Joe's office.

"I see your stuff came," said Joe. "I wanted to come down, but I thought you'd like to work it out alone for a while."

Cal understood Joe's frustrations. "Come down anytime. There's something I'd like you to do. On the crates the stuff came in there was an address of a warehouse in Philadelphia. I wrote it down here. Could you get one of the salesmen to see what kind of a place it is when he's through there? I'd rather not have him know I'm interested. This may be a lead."

"Sure. I think the Sales Office has a regular trip through there next week. I'll see who's on it. What have you found out?"

"Not too much. The thing has a screen for viewing but no clue as to what might be viewed. There's a piece of equipment referred to as a *planetary generator* that seems to be a sort of central unit, something like the oscillator of a transmitter, perhaps. It was mounted in a support that seems to call for mounting on the main frame members.

"This gives me an important dimension so I can finish the framework. But there're about four hundred and ninety terminals—more or less—on that planetary generator. That's what's got me buffaloed but good. These parts seem to be interchangeable in different circuits, otherwise they might be marked for wiring.

"The catalogue refers to various elements, which are named, and gives electrical values for them—but I can't find out which elements are which without tearing into sealed units. So here's a reorder on all the parts I may have to open up."

Joe glanced at it. "Know what that first shipment cost?"

"Don't tell me it cleaned my project out?"

"They billed us this morning for twenty-eight hundred dollars."

Cal whistled softly. "It should have been nearer twenty-eight thousand."

"Say, Cal, why can't we track this outfit down through the patent office? There must be patents on the stuff."

"There's not a patent number on anything. I've already looked."

"Then let's ask them to send us either the number or copies of the patents on some of these things. They wouldn't distribute unpatented items like this, surely. They'd be worth a fortune."

"All right. Put it in the letter with your reorder. I don't think it will do much good."

Cal worked impatiently through the morning on consultations with the production department regarding his transmitter. After lunch he returned to the interocitor. He decided against opening any of the tubes. If anything should happen to their precarious contact with the supplier before they located him—

He began work on identification of the tube elements. Fortunately the catalogue writers had put in all voltage and current data. But there were new units that made no sense to Cal—*albion factors, inverse reduction index, scattering efficiency.*

Slowly he went ahead. Filaments were easy but some of the tubes had nothing resembling filaments or cathodes. When he applied test voltages he didn't know whether anything was happening or not.

Gradually he found out. There was one casual sketch showing a catherimine tube inside a field-generating coil. That gave him a clue to a whole new principle of operation.

After six days he was able to connect proper voltages to more than half his tubes and get the correct responses as indicated by catalogue specifications. With that much information available he was able to go ahead and construct the entire power supply.

Then Joe called him one afternoon. "Hey, Cal! Have you busted any of those tubes yet?"

"No. Why?"

"Don't! They're getting mad or something. They aren't going to send the reorder we asked for and they didn't answer about patents on the stuff. Besides, that address in Philadelphia turned out to be a dud.

"Cramer, the salesman who looked it up, says there's nothing there but an old warehouse that hasn't been used for years. Cal, who can these guys be? I'm beginning to not like the smell of this business."

"Read me their letter."

" 'Dear Mr. Wilson,' they say, 'We cannot understand the necessity of the large amount of reorder which you have submitted to us. We trust that the equipment was not broken or damaged in transit. However, if this is the case please return the damaged parts and we will gladly order replacements for you. Otherwise we fear that, due to the present shortage of interocitor equipment, it will be necessary to return your order unfilled.

" 'Please feel free to call upon us at any time. If you find it possible to function under present circumstances will you please contact us by interocitor at your earliest convenience and we will discuss the matter further.' "

"What was that last line?" Cal asked.

"—'contact us by interocitor—' "

"That's the one! That shows us what the apparatus is—a communication device."

"But from where to where and from whom to whom?"

"That's what I intend to find out!"

They weren't going to let him open up the tubes or other sealed parts. Cal arranged for an X-ray and fluoroscope equipment to obtain some notion of the interior construction of the tubes he could not otherwise analyze. He could trace the terminals back to their internal connections and be fairly sure of not burning things up with improper voltages to the elements.

Besides the power supply, the entire framework with the planetary generator was erected and a bank of eighteen catherimine tubes was fed by it. The output of these went to a nightmare arrangement of plumbing that included unbelievable flares and spirals. Again he found prealigned mounting holes that enabled him to fit most of the plumbing together with only casual reference to the catalogue.

Growing within him was the feeling that the whole thing was some intricately designed puzzle and that clues were deliberately placed there for anyone who would look.

Then one of the catherimine tubes rolled off a table and shattered on the floor.

Cal thought afterwards that he must have stared at the shards for a full five minutes before he moved. He wondered if the whole project were lying there in that shattered heap.

Gently, with tweezers, he picked out the complex tube elements and laid them on a bed of dustless packing material. Then he called Joe.

"Get off another letter to Continental—airmail," he said. "Ask if we can get a catherimine replacement. I just dropped one."

"Aren't you going to send the pieces along as they asked?"

"No. I'm not taking any chances with what I've got. Tell them the remains will be forwarded immediately if they can send a replacement."

"O.K. Mind if I come down tonight and look things over?"

"Not at all."

It was a little before five when Joe Wilson finally entered the screen room. He looked around and whistled softly. "Looks like you're making something out of this, after all."

A neat row of panels nearly fifteen feet long stretched along the center of the room. In the framework behind was a nightmarish assemblage of gadgets and leads. Joe took in the significance of the hundreds of leads that were in place.

"Manufacturers' catalogues are my line," he said. "I see hundreds of them every year. I get so I can almost tell the inside layout just by the cover.

"Catalogue writers aren't very smart, you know. They're mostly forty-fifty-dollar-a-week kids that come out of college with a smattering of journalism but are too dumb to do much about it. So they end up writing catalogues.

"And no catalogue I ever saw would enable you to do this!"

Cal shrugged. "You never saw a catalogue like this before."

"I don't think it's a catalogue."

"What do you think it is?"

"An instruction book. Somebody wanted you to put this together."

Cal laughed. "Why would anyone deliberately plant this stuff so that I would assemble it?"

"Do *you* think it's just a catalogue?"

Cal stopped laughing. "All right, but I still think it's crazy. There *are* things in it that wouldn't be necessary if it were only a catalogue. For instance, this catherimine tube listing.

"It says that with the deflector grid in a four-thousand-gauss field the accelerator plate current will be forty mils. Well, it doesn't matter whether it's in a field or not.

"But that's the only place in the whole book that indicates the normal operation of the tube is in this particular field. There were a bunch of coils with no designation except that they are static field coils.

"On the basis of that one clue I put the tubes and coils together and found an explanation of the unknown 'albion factor' that I've been looking for. It's that way all along. You're right about catalogue writers in general, but the guy that cooked this one up was a genius.

"Yet I still can't quite force myself to the conclusion that I was *supposed* to put this thing together, that I was deliberately led into it."

"Couldn't it be some sort of Trojan Horse gadget?"

"I don't see how it could be. What could it do? As a radiation weapon it wouldn't have a very wide range—I hope."

Joe turned towards the door. "Maybe it's just as well that you broke that tube."

The pile of components whose places in the assembly still were to be determined was astonishingly small, Cal thought, as he left the lab shortly after midnight.

Many of the circuits were complete and had been tested, with a response that might or might not be adequate for their design. At least nothing blew up.

The following afternoon, Joe called again. "We've lost our connection. I just got a TWX from Continental. They want to know what the devil we're talking about in our letter of yesterday—the one asking for a replacement."

There was only a long silence.

"Cal—you still there?"

"Yes, I'm here. Get hold of Oceanic Tube Company for me. Ask them to send one of their best engineers down here—Jerry Lanier if he's in the plant now. We'll see if they can rebuild the tube for us."

"That *is* going to cost money."

"I'll pay it out of my own pocket if I have to. This thing is almost finished."

Why had they cut their connection, Cal wondered? Had they discovered that their contact had been a mistake? And what would happen if he did finish the interocitor? He wondered if there would be anyone to communicate with even if he did complete it.

It was so close to completion now that he was beginning to suffer from the customary engineer's jitters that come when a harebrained scheme is finally about to be tested. Only this was about a thousand times worse because he didn't even know that he would recognize the correct operation of the interocitor if he saw it.

Jerry Lanier finally showed up. Cal gave him only the broken catherimine tube and allowed him to see none of the rest of the equipment.

Jerry scowled at the tube. "Since when did they put squirrel cages in glass envelopes? What is this thing?"

"Top hush-hush," said Cal. "All I want to know is can you duplicate it?"

"Sure. Where did you get it?"

"Military secret."

"It looks simple enough. We could probably duplicate it in three weeks or so."

"Look, Larry, I want that bottle in three days."

"Cal, you know we can't—"

"Oceanic isn't the only tube maker in the business. This might turn out to be pretty hot stuff."

"All right, you horse trader. Guarantee it by air express in five days."

"Good enough."

For two straight nights Cal didn't go home. He grabbed a half hour's snooze on a lab bench in the early morning. And on the second day he was almost caught by the first lab technician who arrived.

But the interocitor was finished.

The realization seemed more like a dream than reality but every one of the nearly five thousand parts had at last been incorporated into the assembly behind the panels—except the broken tube.

He knew it was right. With a nearly obsessive conviction he felt sure that he had constructed the interocitor just as the unknown engineers had designed it.

He locked the screen room and left word with Joe to call him if Jerry sent the tube, then went home to sleep the clock around.

When he finally went back to the lab a dozen production problems on the airline transmitter had turned up and for once he was thankful for them. They helped reduce the tension of waiting.

He was still working on the job of breaking down one of the transmitter sub-assemblies when quitting time came. It was only because Nell Joy, the receptionist in the front hall, was waiting for her boy friend that he received the package at all.

She called him at twenty after five.

"Mr. Meacham? I didn't know whether you'd still be here or not. There's a delivery man here with a package. It looks important. Do you want it tonight?"

"I'll say I do!"

He was out by her desk, signing for the package, almost before she hung up. He tore off the wrappings on the way back to the lab.

# — IV —

It was as beautiful a job of duplication as he could have wished for. Cal could have sworn there was no visual difference between it and the original. But the electrical test would tell the story.

In the lab he put the duplicate tube in the tester he'd devised and checked the albion. That was the critical factor.

He frowned as the meter indicated ten percent deviation, but two of the originals had tolerances that great. It would do.

His hand didn't seem quite steady as he put the tube in its socket. He stood back a moment, viewing the completed instrument.

Then he plunged the master switch on the power panel.

He watched anxiously the flickering hands of two-score meters as he advanced along the panels, energizing the circuits one by one.

Intricate adjustments on the panel controls brought the meter readings into line with the catalogue specifications which he had practically memorized by now—but which were written by the meters for safety.

Then slowly, the grayish screen of the cubical viewing tube brightened. Waves of polychrome hue washed over it. It seemed as if an image were trying to form but it remained out of focus, only a wash of color.

"Turn up the intensifier knob," a masculine voice said suddenly. "That will clear your screen."

To Cal it was like words coming suddenly at midnight in a ghost-ridden house. The sound had come out of the utter unknown into which the interocitor reached—but it was human.

He stepped back to the panel and adjusted the knob. The shapeless color flowed into solid lines, congealed to an image. And Cal stared.

He didn't know what he had expected. But the prosaic color-image of the man who watched him from the plate was too ordinary after the weeks-long effort expended on the interocitor.

Yet there was something of the unknown in the man's eyes too—something akin to the unknown of the interocitor. Cal drew slowly nearer the plate, his eyes unable to leave that face, his breath hard and fast.

"Who are you?" he said almost inaudibly. "What have I built?"

For a moment the man made no answer, as if he hadn't heard. His image was stately, and he appeared of uncertain middle age. He was large and ruggedly attractive of feature. But it was his eyes that held Cal—eyes which seemed to hold an awareness of responsibility to all the people of the world.

"We'd about given you up," the man said at last. "But you've passed. And rather well, too."

"Who are you? What is this—this interocitor I've constructed?"

"The interocitor is simply an instrument of communication. Constructing it was a good deal more.

"I am the employment representative of a group—a certain group who are urgently in need of men, expert technologists. We have a good many stringent requirements for prospective employees. So we require them to take an aptitude test to measure some of those qualifications we desire.

"You have passed that test!"

For a moment Cal stared uncomprehendingly. "What do you mean? I have made no application to work with your—your employers."

A faint trace of a smile crossed the man's face. "No. No one does that. We pick our own applicants and test them, quite without their awareness that they are being tested. You are to be congratulated on your showing."

"What makes you think I'd be interested in working for your employers?"

"You would not have come this far unless you were interested in the job we have to offer."

"I don't understand."

"You have seen the type of technology in our possession. No matter who or what we are, having come this far you would pursue us to the ends of the Earth to find out how we came by that technology and to learn its mastery for yourself. Is it not so?"

The arrogant truth of the man's statement rocked Cal. There was no uncertainty in the man's voice. He *knew* what Cal was going to do more surely than Cal had known himself up to this moment.

"You seem pretty certain of that." Cal found it hard to keep an impulsive hostility out of his voice.

"I am. We pick our applicants carefully. We make offers only to those we are certain will accept. Now, since you are about to join us, I will relieve your mind of some unnecessary tensions.

"It has undoubtedly occurred to you, as to all thinking people of your day, that the scientists have done a particularly abominable job of dispensing the tools they have devised. Like careless and indifferent workmen they have tossed the products of their craft to gibbering apes and baboons. The results have been disastrous, to say the least.

"Not all scientists, however, have been quite so indifferent. There are a group of us who have formed an organization for the purpose of obtaining better and more conservative distribution of these tools. We call ourselves, somewhat dramatically perhaps, but none the less truthfully, *Peace Engineers.*

Our motives are sure to encompass whatever implications you can honestly make of the term.

"But we need men—technicians, men of imagination, men of good will, men of superb engineering abilities—and our method has to be somewhat less than direct. Hence, our approach to you. It involved simply an interception of mail in a manner you would not yet understand.

"You passed your aptitude test and so were more successful than some of your fellow engineers in this community."

Cal thought instantly of Edmunds and the toothless gears and the tumbling barrel compound.

"Those other things—" he said. "They would have led to the same solution?"

"Yes. In a somewhat different way, of course. But that is all the information I can give you at this time. The next consideration is your coming here."

"*Where?* Where are you? How do I come?"

The readiness with which his mind accepted the fact of his going shocked him. Was there no other alternative that he should consider? For what reasons should he ally himself with this unknown band who called themselves *Peace Engineers?* He sought for rational reasons why he should not.

There were few that he could muster up. None, actually. He was alone, without family or obligations. He had no particular professional ties to prevent him from leaving.

As for any potential personal threat that might lie in alliance with the *Peace Engineers*—well, he wasn't much afraid of anything that could happen to him personally.

But in reality none of these factors had any influence. There was only one thing that concerned him. He had to know more about that fantastic technology they possessed.

And they had known that was the one factor capable of drawing him.

The interviewer paused as if sensing what was in Cal's mind. "You will learn the answers to all your questions in proper order," he said. "Can you be ready tomorrow?"

"I'm ready now," Cal said.

"Tomorrow will be soon enough. Our plane will land on your airfield at six P.M. It will remain fifteen minutes. It will take off without you if you are not in it by that time. You will know it by its color. A black ship with a single horizontal orange stripe.

"That is all. Congratulations and good luck to you. I'll be looking forward to seeing you personally.

"Stand back, now. When I cut off, the interocitor will be destroyed. Stand back!"

Cal backed sharply to the far side of the room. He saw the man's head nod, his face smiling a pleasant good-by, then the image vanished from the screen.

Almost instantly there came the hiss of burning insulation, the crack of heat-shattered glass. From the framework of the interocitor rose a blooming bubble of smoke that slowly filled the room as wires melted and insulation became molten and ran.

Cal burst from the screen room and grasped a nearby fire extinguisher, which he played into the blinding smoke pouring from the room. He emptied that one and ran for another.

Slowly the heat and smoke dispelled. He moved back into the room and knew that the interocitor could never be analyzed or duplicated from that ruin. Its destruction had been complete.

It was useless trying to sleep that night. He sat in the park until after midnight, when a suspicious cop chased him off. After that he simply walked the streets until dawn, trying to fathom the implications of what he'd seen and heard.

*Peace Engineers—*

What did the term mean? It could imply a thousand things, a secret group with dictatorial ambitions in possession of a powerful technology—a bunch of crackpots with strange access to genius—or it could be what the term literally implied.

But there was no guarantee that their purposes were altruistic. With his past knowledge of human nature he was more inclined to credit the possibility that he was being led into some Sax Rohmer melodrama.

At dawn he turned towards his apartment. He finally slept a while and cleaned up and ate and left the rent and a note instructing the landlord regarding his belongings. He went to the plant in the midafternoon and resigned amidst a storm of protests from Billingsworth and a forty-percent salary increase offer.

That done, it was nearly evening and he went up to see Joe Wilson.

"I wondered what happened to you this morning," said Joe. "I tried to call you for a couple of hours."

"I slept late," said Cal. "I just came in to resign."

"Resign?" Joe Wilson stared incredulously. "What for? What about the interocitor?"

"It blew up in my face. The whole thing's gone."

"I hoped you would make it," Joe said a little sadly. "I wonder if we will ever find out where that stuff came from."

"Sure," said Cal carelessly. "It was just some shipping mixup. We'll find out about it someday."

"Cal—" Joe Wilson was looking directly into his face. "You found out, didn't you?"

Cal hesitated a moment. He had been put under no bond of secrecy. What could it matter? He understood something of the fascination the problem held for a frustrated engineer turned into a technical purchasing agent.

"Yes," he said. "I found out."

Joe smiled wryly. "I was hoping you would. Can you tell me about it?"

"There's nothing to tell. I don't know where they are. All I know is that I talked to someone. They offered me a job."

They waited together until at last he saw it coming in low and fast, a black and orange ship. Wing flaps down, it slowed and touched the runway. Already it was like the symbol of a vast and important future that had swept him up. Already the familiar surroundings of Ryberg's were something out of a dim and unimportant past.

"I wish we could have learned more about the interocitor," said Joe.

Cal's eyes were still straining towards the ship as it taxied around on the field. Then he shook hands solemnly with Joe. "You and me both," he said. "Believe me—"

Joe Wilson stood by the window and, as Cal went out towards the ship, he knew he'd been correct in that glimpse he'd got of the cockpit canopy silhouetted against the sky.

The ship was pilotless.

Another whispering clue to a mighty, alien technology.

He knew Cal must have seen it, too, but Cal's steps were steady as he walked towards it.

— V —

He must have slept during part of that fantastic night flight. He could remember only the incessant thunder of the engine in front of him and the starlit sky of night above. He remembered the tumultuous flashes of lightning as the ship skirted a vast thunder storm.

Now daylight was racing him out of the east, lighting the cirrus miles above him and shading the desert below. Still the ghostly ship gave no sign of slowing its determined flight.

His hands and feet searched with involuntary constancy for the absent controls. It gave him a sense of helpless imprisonment when he considered that utterly blank cockpit in which he rode. Not a control, not a single instrument—only the thunder of the motor and the propeller and the shriek of the air.

He looked over the edge at the brightening landscape below. About eight thousand feet up, he thought. He strained to recognize familiarity in the terrain below. It looked like cattle country. Oklahoma, Texas, New Mexico or Arizona, perhaps. Distant cliffs of shining vermilion made him fairly certain that it was a Southwest region, probably in one of the latter two states.

While the sun overtook him, Cal watched the passage of tiny towns, the puff of occasional whirlwinds on the desert, the creeping cars that sometimes appeared on a distant highway.

Then, suddenly, the plane dipped. Cal reached for the absent stick, listened critically to the thunder of the motor. Twisting around, he glanced at the elevators. They were depressed to lose altitude.

He scanned the horizon ahead and the vast empty land below. Fat humps of mountains projected from the desert. Then he saw in the distance the haze that hovered over some desert city. The ship seemed to be heading for it.

He did not know this country. As the plane approached the town he saw that he was not headed directly for it but was going north towards a small valley that lay on the other side of low humped mountains.

In the valley were a cluster of buildings. Several hundred houses surrounded a plant composed of four long blank-walled structures and a fifth, much larger, that was in the process of construction.

The plane soared over the plant and circled twice. A small landing field was just west of the four buildings. There was a hangar with a sock hanging limp in the windless air. Nearby was a small building that crouched beneath a giant antenna, a great bowl-like screen that turned slowly on gimbals, ever pointing—straight toward the little plane in which he rode.

The control, he thought— All through those dark hours this mass of metal had been the mysterious beacon that guided the plane.

There were a half dozen men watching the ship from the field but not with any apparent curiosity. They had the appearance of waiting for a routine flight to be completed.

Dust spurted from the earth as the wheels touched. Cal watched the flaps go down and sensed the dragging hand that slowed the ship. It taxied up to the apron before the hangar. The motor died and grunted to a stop in the shadow of the great bowl of the guiding antenna.

It was like the end of a dream in which a sense of sleep still prevails over the senses. He saw the men approaching, saw their mouths move in greeting, but he made no move to stir. One of the mechanics climbed to the wing step and shoved the canopy back. The fresh coolness of the morning desert air brushed his face.

"Did you have a good trip, sir?" The mechanic was smiling. Just a kid in white overalls, he didn't seemed awed by the landing of a ship without controls.

Cal nodded. "No complaint about the trip. But I would like to know where this is."

"That was Phoenix, Arizona, you saw coming in. We're just north of town."

Cal grunted as he rose stiffly and climbed out. "That's something. I was afraid I was going to end up on Calabuluska Island where the meemies eat the white people."

"I don't blame you for getting the willies out of a ride like that. I don't want any of it myself. The beam is used mainly for a lot of other things but I guess the Engineer figured he might as well use it to pick up new employees as well."

"The Engineer?"

"The boss of the whole place. I've never even seen him myself. His name is Jorkovnosnitch or something like that, and he doesn't call himself president, just Engineer. So that's what everybody else calls him too, because they forget how to pronounce his name."

His knees buckled a trifle as Cal jumped from the wing to the ground. He stood a moment to steady himself and looked over the landscape. The people looked human. The plant looked like a lot of other medium sized industrial plants set out near some small city for decentralization purposes.

But the plane behind him, that towering beam director that was now stilled—these belied the appearance of normalcy. These and a director who called himself simply the Engineer and manufactured devices employing a completely strange technology—

There was a stir. Eyes were suddenly directed a short distance down the field. A slim, dark-haired girl was approaching. She wore a white tailored suit whose severity was relieved by the gentle fluffing of her hair as she walked swiftly towards them.

She held out a hand towards Cal as she came up. "I'm Dr. Adams—Ruth Adams," she added as if to invite a more friendly level of acquaintance than the stiff "Dr." would imply.

"I'm Cal Meacham," he said, "but I suppose you know that—"

He stopped awkwardly. The girl's hand felt icy cold. It was firm and competent but—almost imperceptibly—it trembled.

He glanced down. She withdrew it quickly and smiled. "I know quite a bit about you. I'm assistant in the employment department and your files were referred to me for analysis. My doctorate is in psychiatry."

"Yes—yes," he said absently. He was watching her face, narrowing his field of vision to block out the gentle lips, the firm molded cheeks, tinted softly with desert tan—narrowing to her eyes. They were big and soft brown in tone.

And the utter fear that dwelt in them was like an electric shock through his body.

Only when he concentrated on her eyes did he get that intense message of fear she could not hide. But she was so constantly animated that he could not long hold to such a narrow field of vision.

He attempted a smile to break the awkward pause he had created. "This seems to be purely a routine affair to the boys here but it's quite a jolt for me. I'd like to know what this is all about. I spoke to a man over a device called an interocitor. I didn't learn his name but he offered me a job and I took him up on it. He sent this pilotless plane for me and here I am."

"Yes, that was Dr. Warner who spoke with you," said Ruth. Cal found it impossible to think of her as Dr. Adams.

"I work under him," she continued. "He selects all engineers. He was so pleased by your aptitudes and your work that he sent me out personally to bring you to him. Ordinary employees rate only an office boy."

She assumed an attitude of mock regality and they burst out laughing together. Cal almost forgot the fear he had seen in her eyes.

"I appreciate the special attention," he said. "A freckle-faced office boy certainly would have spoiled my day."

"Come with me. I'll take you to Dr. Warner now."

He took her arm lightly as she led the way over the dust-covered apron of the hangar towards the nearest of the four plant buildings. Even in that bright sunlight he felt a faint tremor in her body—as if with cold.

Dr. Warner looked much as he had on the screen of the interocitor tube. A few sparse strands of white hair still adhered to the middle of his pate. A gently protruding paunch was beginning to tell the effects of years at a desk. Yet his face had the tinge of a man used to days out of doors.

He advanced with outstretched hand as soon as Ruth Adams entered his office with Cal in tow. "Mr. Meacham!" He pumped Cal's hand vigorously. "Please sit down. You too, Ruth.

"You want to know all about us, of course," said Dr. Warner. "You want to know our purposes, our means of operation, who we are, why we are, what we intend to do, what we expect of you and in general where you go from here."

"I guess that would just about cover it," said Cal. "You've been asked those questions before."

"Many times. And all of them can be answered in good time. I think you can realize, however, that your initial period here will be in the nature of a probation. The answers to your questions will be given gradually. I'm sure that's reasonable."

"Of course."

"I told you that we believe the world could better utilize the productions of science if scientists themselves placed some restrictions on the use of their talents. In effect, we are on strike against destructive uses. We propose to control the products of our research from here on.

"Already, we have uncovered principles and invented devices that the military cliques of the world would give their eyes for, provided they knew we had them."

"But how can such principles be utilized without being revealed to the military?"

"Some can't. Those are suppressed. Others are released with such controls as will insure their proper use. The interocitor is an example of this."

"How?"

"It is a superb communication device, surpassing common radio principles in a thousand ways. But it can be instantly blanked out or totally destroyed— as you witnessed—the moment it is used for communicating lying propaganda or anything else harmful to the mind of man."

"You consider yourselves censors of all that man does!"

"No—merely of the uses to which our inventions are put. That right of censorship is inherent in the invention or discovery, we submit. Until now it has never been enforced."

"That's a pretty big order."

Warner smiled. "Sometimes we think we are pretty big men. At least we operate on that principle with the silent hope that we just don't get too big for our pants. Somebody had to make the attempt. We are doing it—and rather successfully so far. The militarists would be appalled if they knew the brain power that we have succeeded in draining away from their projects. Including yours—"

"I don't think they will miss me much. I was already—on strike, as you say."

"That's what I mean. So were thousands of others. We are men who are not interested in science for the sake of 'pure' science, whatever that is. We are interested in science as a tool in man's rise from the ape to whatever goal may be possible when his vast potentialities are fully realized. Those who have not come very far from the ape are using that tool with destructive effects which must be curbed. That sums our entire purpose. You are in agreement, of course."

Cal Meacham nodded slowly. "And doubtful of any man's ability to achieve such a purpose—at least in our day."

"We shall try to convince you as we proceed," said Dr. Warner. "But now for your duties here. You have seen the plant under construction. That is nearly completed and is to be an interocitor assembly plant. We want to assign you in charge of that plant."

Cal stared as if he hadn't heard correctly. "In charge—of that plant!"

"Yes. That is correct."

"But I'm just a lab punk. I was only a project engineer at Ryberg. I haven't had a background for that sort of thing."

"We've investigated your background thoroughly. We are satisfied with your qualifications. You will receive an intensive training by the design engineers who produced the interocitor and by the production men now handling it. You will be amply prepared for the job. You will take it, of course."

Cal smiled. "I wish you would put a question mark at the end of one of those statements about me. I get the uncomfortable feeling you know too much about me."

"Not too much—enough. We have to. And that is about all I can tell you at the moment. You will learn other details of our operations as you go along. Eventually, you will meet Mr. Jorgasnovara, Engineer of the entire project, but it may be months. He's an elusive man.

"Dr. Adams will introduce you to the surroundings and your fellow engineers and give you directions in beginning the training which will be necessary. I need not remind you, of course, that your being in charge of interocitor assembly is only a first step in your progress here, but it is an important step."

Warner rose and extended a hand. "It's been a great pleasure to know you. I'll be constantly available for any questions or problems that arise."

— VI —

It was almost a letdown—the contrast between his strange introduction to the Engineers via the interocitor and this seemingly prosaic industrial plant here in the desert. Nothing out of the ordinary seemed to be going on here—nothing, that is, except the manufacture of the interocitor. And a girl whose eyes were haunted with a fear she could not always hide.

She spent the remainder of the morning with him. He learned that her psychiatric work in the employment department was highly essential in testing, judging and training the peculiarly unique individuals required for work in the plant.

They went on a tour of the plant. Two of the buildings, he found, were devoted entirely to development engineering. Over five hundred engineers were employed in scores of projects.

Everything that a researcher could desire was at their disposal. The prodigality of equipment almost made him weak when he thought of the penny-pinching controls imposed at Ryberg, where he'd had to fight tooth and nail for every hundred dollars a project cost.

This was an engineer's paradise!

Ruth Adams sensed what was in his mind as he looked over the beautifully equipped laboratories. "You'll enjoy working here. Anything these men want is theirs for the whistling."

"But it costs heavy money for equipment like this!"

"The company is quite profitable. The Engineer and other heads are not just visionaries."

She introduced him to many of the engineers and section directors. He was not surprised to find a number of professional acquaintances and personal friends among them.

Among them was Ole Swenberg, a big blond fellow he had known very well at college. He had often wondered what had happened to Ole. They had not met since the war.

Ole beamed and ran across the lab to grasp Cal's hand when he recognized him.

"By golly, Cal, I thought it was about time you were showing up here. The way you used to talk when we were in school I expected to find you running the place."

"I hid out. What are you doing here, you big Swede?"

"Any darned thing I please and that's the truth. I don't have to worry about publishing a paper every three weeks in some stinking journal—'for the prestige of the department'—either. I stayed on at college and taught four years before I got fed up. What are you geared up for?"

"They tell me I'm going to direct the interocitor assembly for a while."

"Boy, have *you* got yourself a job! That's hot stuff. They tried to farm it out and no plant in the country could handle it. That's why you've got it. But it's lunch time. Come on. It's on me."

They followed the garrulous Ole to the plant cafeteria, and listened to the account of how he was revolutionizing the world of science with his discoveries—with the small help of the group of Peace Engineers as a whole. But lunchtime was not long enough for him to finish.

"Tell you what," he said, as they finished. "How about a small beer bust in your diggings tonight? You haven't told me a thing about what you've been doing. Ruth and I'll come over and give you the real lowdown on what you're in for. That okay with you, Ruth?"

She smiled tolerantly towards Cal. "The Swede seems to have it all arranged."

"Well, that's fine. Only I don't have any diggings exactly," said Cal. "What do I do in that case?"

"Oh, you have one of the company houses available unless you prefer something in town. It's more convenient out here," said Ruth.

"Suits me."

Cal spent the afternoon unpacking and getting settled in his quarters. He had two comfortable rooms and a kitchenette in case he wanted to do any cooking, but he expected to take his meals at the cafeteria.

Finished with stowing his gear, he sank down on the sofa and looked out the window towards the strange plant where unheard-of technology produced gadgets called interocitors.

It was a weird set-up in some ways, but for the first time in his life he felt completely at ease in his place of work. In the industrial plants he'd known, engineers were constantly shifting from one place to another, moving around, looking for offers, eternally trying to "get somewhere."

None of them could ever define that mystic goal, but they knew the same common sense of deep frustration. They battled each other, trying to make their company's product cheaper, trying to make their electric razor or toaster or radio a bit better than their fellow engineers who worked for other concerns. But, like paid gladiators, they felt no loyalty except that which was inspired by their paychecks.

He had run in that professional rat race for many years. After college he worked for Acme Electric, then he found a better offer at Midwest. Corning had offered a little more money. He had found better working conditions at Colonial. Then Ryberg had seemed to be a better research set-up—

It would have gone on the rest of his life. He'd have landed a department directorship somewhere. Maybe he'd have married. After fifty years they would have given him a gold watch.

It was over. The Engineers were no gold watch outfit. It was too good to be true—too good to last.

Ole and Ruth knocked on his door at eight. Ole had a half dozen brown bottles in his hand and Ruth had a basket of sandwiches.

"We knew you'd be hungry," she said. "You don't look like the cooking type of bachelor."

"Believe me, I'm not."

"See what I told you," said Ole loudly to Ruth. "This is a chance you can't afford to miss."

"Oh, for heaven's sake, Ole!"

Cal smiled and looked from one to the other. He wondered how a serene person like Ruth Adams happened to be going around with the loud-mouthed Ole.

They sat down and Ole became suddenly serious. "We didn't come for just a social call, Cal."

"What, then? I thought you liked my company. Is this place business twenty-four hours a day?"

"Our kind of business is. What kind of an aptitude test did they give you?"

"The interocitor. They teased me into building one from a catalogue."

"Know what mine was? A book that made a page-at-a-glance reader out of me. I ordered some new texts from a company and these things came. I looked at a page—and it stuck. Nothing on it ever left me. Couldn't get rid of it if I wanted to. The most intricate circuit diagrams you can imagine. One glance and they're mine. Pretty neat, eh?"

"Sounds wonderful. I'd like to see some."

"You will. They're used in parts of the training you'll get. You'll get a brainful of stuff you never dreamed was in heaven or earth.

"When I first got those books I tore them apart molecule by molecule to find out what made them tick. I never did find out but I became a biologist, and biochemist as well as an electronics engineer in the process. The Engineers liked my attack, even if it was a failure, so they took me on."

"Do they have a different test for everyone?"

"No. You're the first one, however, that I've known who got the interocitor. That's been top hush-hush stuff. They needed you pretty badly."

"I'd like to know more about how these Peace Engineers operate. I suppose I'll get the dope in time as Warner says, but I wish you could tell me a little more."

Ole looked bleak. "Cal, do you believe that guff?"

"What do you mean, guff?"

"About the Peace Engineers. All this phony window dressing."

Cal sat up straight on the edge of his seat. He felt as if someone had dealt him a blow underneath his ribs. "What are you talking about? You mean this thing isn't on the level?"

"Ole—" Ruth interrupted. "Let me talk."

"Sure. You can make it sound more reasonable."

"When I first came here," she said, "I was appalled by the naïveté of the scientists and engineers who make the wonderful machines of which our civilization boasts.

"Peace Engineers! They knew that half the scientists of the country were sick at heart after the last war because of what had happened through the discoveries of science. It was the most obvious bait they could hold out. And the best brains in the nation bit on it."

"Who are 'they'?"

"That's what we don't know. Ole and I and a dozen or so others of the engineers have become—to put it mildly—suspicious of the whole set-up. And our suspicions have frightened us.

"There is absolutely no organization, no society or fraternal group called 'Peace Engineers' as you might expect. There is nothing but this plant and a group of engineers who work here just as in any other industrial plant—that and the incredible technology that someone possesses. After all the talk about Peace Engineers there is still nothing but—a vacuum.

"Technology in a vacuum. An incredibly advanced technology. You know more about it than either of us do. Under what kind of circumstances would it be produced?"

"Time and money—great quantities of both would be required. But I supposed they had both."

"Ruth has missed an important point," said Ole. "It's more than technology. There's new basic science involved. Science that speaks of a culture almost wholly foreign to anything we know about."

"I'm inclined to agree with that," said Cal thoughtfully. "But does that prohibit the Peace Engineers from originating it, and if so, where did it come from?"

"That's what scares us. Look at what's happening—the cream of the scientific brains of the nation are working for the Engineers. Suppose they aren't so peaceful in spite of their name? Suppose that it is really an enormous camouflage for war preparation? Suppose they are giving us minor secrets in return for the privilege of milking our scientific genius for all they can."

"There are two things wrong with those arguments. You just got through pointing out that these things are not exactly minor. By comparison, we aren't contributing very much for what we get."

"Don't kid yourself. Our best brains being applied to this advanced basic science are producing plenty. And suppose that what we have seen is relatively minor compared with what we haven't seen?"

Cal leaned back heavily. "I can't speak from experience yet but I think you're on the wrong track. An enemy could hardly operate like this under the nose of our own military."

"Who said anything about enemy?" said Ole. "Isn't it just as bad in the long run if our own military has corralled these brains by this deception? In fact, that seems to be the more likely explanation."

"We're not arguing for any one conclusion," said Ruth abruptly. "We don't *know*. We're simply saying that this whole front of Peace Engineer propaganda is false. We want to know what's back of it. It scares us to think what might lie behind this secretly controlled technology.

"But we can't go to any authorities and tell them we're scared and ask them to investigate the place. There is absolutely nothing we can do unless we find out who is behind the Peace Engineers."

"That's where we need your help," said Ole. "You're going to be in a high and responsible place around here. If anyone is in a position to get behind this false front you ought to be able to. Will you help us find out what is going on here?"

"No," said Cal. "The one thing I've looked for all my life is here! I'm willing to grant whoever originated this technology some rights to secrecy regarding the dispersal of it. I'm going to play ball with them until I find out differently and it will take a lot more than these suspicions of yours to change my mind!"

"You don't have to get sore," said Ole. "*Just try to find out.* You'll get curious sooner or later. Then you'll beat your head against the stone wall just like the rest of us are beginning to do. And then maybe you'll begin to get scared, too, when you realize that no one here knows a thing about whose hand is behind all this."

He wasn't sore, Cal thought, as he lay in the darkness vainly trying to sleep long after their departure. He wasn't sore, but he was more than irritated by their jumping him with their suspicions on his first night here.

Certainly, in every organization there were soreheads who didn't like the way things went. He would never have suspected Ole or Ruth of being such, however. But he could scarcely be more generous after what he had heard from them.

And yet—that wasn't the whole story and he knew it. The fear he had seen in those dark eyes of Ruth was a real and tangible thing to her. It was no mere fantasy.

But he would wait. In one respect they were right. In his position he might have opportunity to study the organization as a whole. When he found the answers to their questions he could put their minds at ease. He felt certain the answers would not be what they suspected.

## — VII —

For the next six months his days and nights were spent in the most intensive study he had ever done. The engineering specifications and basic physical principles behind the interocitor were thrown open to him. He pored over the books. He built up components, tore them down again—until he was certain he could build an interocitor blindfolded and with one hand tied behind his back.

In all that time he did not once meet the Engineer, Jorgasnovara, although the man was pointed out to him. Warner had promised that he would be introduced and Cal wondered when the time would come.

It was a wonderful day when he at last saw the assembly lines in full operation and tested the first completed equipment as it came off the line. He had gained skill in executive leadership and he had a smoothly running plant that required only top direction of the most general kind.

It gave him a breathing spell, a measure of freedom to contemplate the significance of what he had accomplished, freedom to review his position, freedom to question—

During those busy months he had found little time to talk to Ruth. At first she'd been his guide in getting him acquainted at the plant, but gradually his entire time had been taken up with other engineers. It had been five weeks, he thought suddenly, since he had even seen her.

He reached for the phone and called her extension.

Her voice was a pleasant sound in his ear. "Ruth! I thought you would be over for the christening. The lines are moving."

"Hello, Cal. I heard about it but I was too busy to get over. Dr. Warner is very pleased with your success, and the Engineer thinks highly of your work. In fact, I was to call you and let you know that he's coming in and wants to talk with you, probably tomorrow."

"Well, how about a little delayed celebration?"

"Such as what?"

"Oh, nothing fancy. A dinner in town, maybe. Then just go for a ride."

For a moment there was no sound from the receiver, then she said hesitantly, "All right, Cal. I'd love to. Pick me up at my place. I live in town, you know."

As he scribbled her address after hanging up he reflected that he hadn't known. He hadn't learned a thing about her in all the time he'd been here. He didn't know where Ole fitted in, but that didn't worry him much. Ole was a good guy but he wasn't for Ruth.

And Cal found himself wondering again about those fears of Ruth. He had found nothing to substantiate them, yet he couldn't forget her eyes as they had looked that first day.

He picked her up at eight. She was dressed in a soft gray evening dress and wore the tiny orchid he had sent. It was utterly impossible to think of an M.D. and Ph.D. in that dress. He didn't try.

There was no hint of distress in her. She was pleasant and gay at dinner and not once did the talk go back to their work at the plant or her feelings about the place.

Afterward he headed the car beyond the outskirts of town. They stopped with the radio on to watch the moon-washed desert.

But her mood seemed to have changed once they left the lights of the restaurant. She settled in silence in the far corner of the seat. A panicky thought occurred to him that he might have offended by stopping. He moved to start the car again.

"Oh, don't, Cal—let's watch it for a while."

"I thought—" he fumbled.

"I got a letter from Ole the other day," said Ruth abruptly.

"Letter? Where is he? I haven't seen him for a couple of months but I thought he was still around the plant."

"No, he's gone." She was looking straight ahead, her voice ending each flat statement with finality as if not willing to volunteer more.

"Why? Where did he go? Was it—what you tried to tell me about—that night six months ago?"

She nodded slowly. "Ole found out. I wanted you to see him and talk to him. Maybe you could have understood what he was trying to say. I made an attempt to call you but you weren't there. And then they came for Ole and took him away. They wouldn't let me see him again—until they had changed him."

"Changed him? What are you talking about, Ruth? Did they do something to Ole?"

She turned slightly towards him so that he could see the moonlight full on her face. It lent a ghostly radiance and heightened the returning fear in her eyes.

"He broke down with hysteria in his lab one day," she said. "His assistants brought him to me. He kept babbling about some fearful thing he'd seen in the sky but I couldn't understand it. And then for just a moment he grew more coherent and said that he'd been working on some interocitor modifications and suddenly he'd heard the Engineer thinking."

"*Thinking!*"

"That's the word he used. He was in such a state of violent terror that I should have given him a quieting hypo immediately, but that was when I tried to get you. I thought maybe you would understand. And then they came and took him away."

"Who?"

"Warner and a couple of his medical assistants. They said they would be able to take care of him, but they wouldn't let me come along. Afraid he'd get too violent, they said."

"What happened?"

"Nothing. I saw Ole the next day. He acted as if very little had occurred. He refused to talk in detail about what had happened and told me he was leaving. That was all he would say."

"Why didn't you tell me this before?"

"I don't know. I thought perhaps I could get more out of Ole later so that I would have proof for you—but I couldn't. I guess I shouldn't have told you tonight except that now that Ole's gone I can't talk to anyone about what I think. The others seem to be too absorbed in their wonderful laboratory privileges to criticize. They're closing their eyes to the suspicions they had."

She turned suddenly and looked into his eyes. "Cal, won't you go and see Ole and try to find out what he learned?"

Cal remained silent. What could they have done to Ole? he wondered. Did they have a method of taking care of disgruntled employees to keep them from talking? Some method that was on a par with the rest of this advanced technology? That would explain how their secret could be so well kept without benefit of military suppression.

"I think I'd like to see Ole," he said. "I wish you had told me this before. Isn't it possible they just sent him away to keep him from disturbing the morale of others with his suspicions?"

"I don't doubt that they did! But that doesn't explain what happened to Ole to make him so deathly frightened."

"Maybe they arranged that, too."

"I could believe that. But what about the interocitor? I don't know anything about the physical science involved in it—but can you honestly say you know *everything* about the device? Ole didn't think so and it was when he was experimenting on it that he had his fit of hysteria."

"Look—nobody can say he knows *everything* about even an ordinary radio set."

"You know what I mean. A radio has a known function and will perform that function when it is properly operating. But are you absolutely certain you know all the proper functions of an interocitor?"

"Well—yeah, sure—hang it all, Ruth, the jigger is so infernally complicated that even while I think I know all about it I still can't say that it might not be capable of something I don't know about. But why should I suspect it?"

"Because the Peace Engineers set-up is a phony."

"That brings us around in a complete circle."

"You forget what happened to Ole. If I'm right—and you don't believe me—I'm putting my life in your hands by telling you this. I'm sure of that."

He reached out and drew her into the curve of his arm. He could feel the tension of her body as he had that first day they met.

"Ruth, you're exaggerating! I'm not saying I won't believe you. Perhaps you are right—engineers are simple-minded folk who can be fooled by almost any kind of make-believe. Armies would still fight with swords and slings if it weren't so.

"On the other hand, because this place is so close to the engineering paradise I've always dreamed about I don't want to get kicked out for going around asking the top guys if they've signed loyalty pledges."

"You're laughing at me," she said bitterly.

"I'm not. I promise I'll do everything I can to find out if you and Ole are right. He was my friend. You shouldn't have kept me from knowing what had happened to him."

"I'm sorry. I didn't think you'd care much, really."

"I'll keep my mouth shut around the plant, but I'll let you know everything I find out."

"Tomorrow you'll see the Engineer," she said prophetically. "Then you'll know."

He had once glimpsed the Engineer from a distance as the plant director climbed into his personal plane on the landing field. From that one glimpse he knew the man was *big*.

Beyond mere physical size, however, there was a *sense* of bigness. This was the first impression that Cal Meacham felt when he stood before the Engineer's desk.

"Sit down." He motioned to Cal.

"I'm Mr. Jorgasnovara," said the man, smiling slowly. "I suppose you can see at once why I'm simply referred to as 'The Engineer.' I rather like the title myself—a vanity, no doubt, but engineering has always seemed about the most important thing in the world to me."

"I can understand that," said Cal. He had almost forgotten Ruth's fears and found himself liking the man. Jorgasnovara appeared to be about sixty. His head had scarcely a speck of fuzz to suggest it had ever grown hair. It was large, a high domed cranium, with deep eyes. His cheek bones were wide, sloping just a little to a square jaw.

"I hope you don't think my actions eccentric in that I haven't asked to meet you until now," he said. "I have been very well satisfied with your progress and have been content to let you proceed at your own pace while I attended to other details of our plants that were not going so smoothly."

"Thanks," said Cal. "The basic science is still pretty far ahead of me but I feel I'm creeping up on it. It still seems rather incredible that such advances as I see can be accounted for by the time you've had available."

The Engineer glanced up sharply from the paperweight on his desk. "How much time do you suppose it has taken?"

"Why, I gathered that you'd just come into existence as an organization since the last war."

He shook his head. "This has been a long time in the making—a long time. The technology you see is largely the work of men long dead. Would it surprise you to know that the history of this society goes back to the seventeenth century?"

"That far!"

"A Frenchman—one Jules de Rande—was the first, as far as we know, to conceive the idea. He published his philosophy for the benefit of a few friends in which he proposed that men of talent determine the use to be made of their genius.

"All about him he saw men given patronage, being bought for their intellects and used like articles of war or commerce. He had the brilliance to glimpse the distant future of our own day in which men of science could be bought like ancient mercenaries.

"De Rande succeeded in persuading many of the learned men of his day to hold back. When he died, his philosophy remained in the minds of a few. Sometimes it all but disappeared, then revived in relatively large groups. But always there was a growing mass of scientific knowledge being withheld from the world in the archives of this group.

"Then, during the American Civil War, the Peace Engineers were organized as a definite society. Their work has been continuous and growing since that time."

"It's almost unbelievable," said Cal. "To think that such a society could exist underground all those years! Were they always ahead of the rest of civilization?"

The Engineer nodded. "Tungsten lamps were available fifteen years before poor Tom Edison began his first carbon filaments. We knew the principles of high-tension power transmission and could have built electric generators as good as any today."

"But withholding all that technology from civilization—"

"Kept the atomic bomb from being used in the First World War instead of the Second. If it had not been so, the Second would perhaps have been the last, and you and I would even now be cowering in caves, snarling over a piece of rotten meat—provided we were alive at all. It was worth it."

Cal sat back weakly in his chair. Slowly he began to perceive the vast panorama of hidden dreams that lay behind the Peace Engineers—

How wrong Ruth and Ole had been in their suspicions!

"What about those who come into the organization and leave? How has the secret been kept? I am thinking of my old friend, Ole Swenberg."

"Ole never knew what I have just told you. Neither do any of the others who leave—and there are many who do. They say little about us because they have little to say. Most of them do not even know as much as you did when they first come here.

"We hire them simply as engineers and advance them as their understanding and personalities develop. I may tell you that there is much yet that I have not revealed—but I have no fear in telling you as much as I have. You will not leave us."

The certainty in the Engineer's voice sent an odd chill through Cal. "How can you be so sure of that?"

The Engineer's smile was enigmatic. "We are quite certain. We know you very well, Mr. Meacham."

The big man seemed to become lost in thought for a moment. The massive lines of his face seemed to slowly shift and form an immobile cast of bleak severity and unknown depth. Cal felt as if he were in the presence of an intellect that had seen the vast stretch of eons of time and light years of space.

Abruptly the man shifted and arose. He extended a massive hand to Cal. "It's been a pleasure talking with you. There is little more that I have for you at this time. Your work is excellent. I shall see you again from time to time and shortly I think we shall have a new assignment for you."

## — VIII —

Cal returned to his own personal laboratory that opened from the executive offices of the interocitor plant. He closed the door and perched on a high lab stool and stared out the windows overlooking the plant buildings.

His feelings churned with doubt and questions he knew not whom to ask. Jorgasnovara's revelation opened up unlimited new channels of speculation.

He had no doubt of the truth of the story. What troubled him was the implication behind the admittedly untold portion of the tale.

The factor that seemed most obviously missing to him was a sense of fraternalism, of organization, a missionary-like zeal to obtain their goal. Perhaps in three hundred years such attitudes of the zealot would normally have been replaced with more practical considerations.

But everything he had heard still left unexplained the resignation of Ole Swenberg. As he thought back Cal had to admit that the Engineer had sidestepped quite completely the direct question of just what had happened to Ole. He couldn't help feeling that it had been deliberate.

At the heart of it all lay the mysterious apparatus, the interocitor. What had Ole learned from it? What had he meant by saying he heard the Engineer thinking? Or had Ruth merely misunderstood him in his incoherence?

Cal moved slowly from the stool to the opposite side of the room, where one of the machines stood. He knew how it was built. He understood the gross electrical characteristics of all its components. He knew that it depended upon a mode of transmission that was not electromagnetic radiation.

It was here that his knowledge broke down. In the intensity of his study to learn how the thing could be produced on an assembly line he had not had the time to burrow into the depths of the mathematical theory on which it was based. That, too, was something wholly beyond conventional technology. An entire new mathematical system had to be absorbed in learning that theory.

Perhaps Ruth was right. He still didn't know *all* the functions of the interocitor.

A sudden knock on the door aroused him. He opened it, admitting Ruth.

"You saw him?" she said.

"We had quite a little chat."

"What do you think?"

"That's a hard question to answer. It has to have so many qualifications. I'll admit he is a strange egg, but he's on the level. As far as he's gone he's not attempting to deceive anyone. I'm sure of that."

"So he won you over that easily."

"Wait a minute. I said there were qualifications. The big factor lies in what he admits he isn't telling, but I honestly can't see any reason for getting the jitters over it."

"Ole did."

"I know. That's what I've been thinking about. I can't understand what he meant when—and if—he said he heard the Engineer thinking—"

"Perhaps he meant just what he said."

"That this thing can pick up thought waves?" Cal rubbed his chin in the cup of his hand. "I should have learned better than to say a thing is impossible around here, but I don't see how. And if so, you'd think Jorgasnovara would protect himself against it."

"Maybe he doesn't know it."

"I'd hate to bet on that. I'm afraid there isn't much that he doesn't know about what goes on around here."

"Well, I hope you find out. I—came in to say good-by, Cal. I'm leaving too. I can't take it any longer, and I don't want to wait until I get the treatment they gave Ole."

"Leaving! No—wait, Ruth. That's not necessary."

"I suppose a psychiatrist should know enough about his own emotions to be able to keep from giving way to the jitters but I just can't any longer. The place is oppressive.

"There's something going on that we don't know anything about. Whatever it is, Ole found out, and it nearly scared him out of his mind. I'd hoped that maybe you could find out, but you've been taken in, just like the rest."

"Look, Ruth—give me a week or a month or whatever it takes. I want to know what happened to Ole just as badly as you do. I promise you that if this interocitor can do any tricks I don't know about I'll find it out."

She hesitated, her brown eyes peering deeply into his. "All right," she agreed. "I'll wait, but there's one more thing I'd like to know. Do you know what is happening to the interocitors you are making, and where they are being sold?"

He laughed. "I've been so doggone busy getting the things off the production line that I haven't worried much about that. I leave it up to the sales and shipping department to get rid of them."

"I went through the shipping department yesterday," she said. "There were six hundred units crated for shipment. They were gone this morning."

"That's our normal production."

"How did they go out?"

"Truck. They tell me the lines generally pick them up after dark on night runs."

"Isn't that a bit unusual?"

"I hadn't thought much about it. What difference does it make anyway?"

"It rained last night. There might be tracks out there even in the asphalt," she said. She turned abruptly and walked to the door, then turned. "How about coming over to my place for dinner tonight? I'm not such a bad cook."

. . .

She disturbed him in more ways than one—and that was all right, he thought. If only they could get this business of her suspicions regarding the Peace Engineers straightened out.

Her remark about the shipping department annoyed him. He *had* wondered about the distribution of the interocitors, but had been too busy to do much inquiring about the sale of them. Certainly a good many of them were being turned out, and he didn't have the faintest idea where they went.

He glanced at the interocitor and at the clock. Lunch time—he should have asked Ruth to go with him. Maybe he'd meet her in the cafeteria.

On the way his curiosity won out. He detoured to the shipping room and dock. Outside the big doors the warmth of the sun was drying the freshly wet landscape. He looked around. He couldn't see any tracks and didn't expect to. The loading area was newly constructed and the asphalt firm.

There was one bad spot, however, that drew his notice. Thirty feet out from the dock a pool of water had collected in a saucerlike depression about twenty feet wide. Have to get that leveled up, he thought.

He didn't see Ruth at lunch, and hurried through the meal to get back to the lab. Once there he settled down again before the interocitor and began work. He got out all the books they had given him on the math behind the machine.

He scarcely moved through the remaining hours of the day as he pored over them. He had to admit that Ruth's fear was slowly convincing him there was something he didn't know about the interocitor—and should.

At nine-thirty that night the phone rang. Even as he picked it up, glancing at the clock, a wave of regret passed over him.

It was Ruth's voice that spoke to him. "Dinner—remember? It's getting pretty cold."

"Ruth! I've been working here ever since you left. I forgot all about it."

"That's a nice compliment. The first time I invite you to dinner you forget it."

"Ruth, I'm awfully sorry!"

"Well, I guessed that's what had happened, so I've packed everything up in an electric warmer. If you're going to be there a while longer I'll bring it over."

"If you're not careful I'm going to be calling you 'darling.' "

"Try it and see what happens."

She hung up before he did.

He returned to his work, but absently. Whatever came of this job, it was worth it to have found her.

It seemed only minutes until he heard her at the door. She bowed formally as he opened it for her. "Your dinner is served, sir."

"Golly, Ruth, I don't know what made me forget. I feel like a heel."

"According to the teachings of psychiatry," she said, as she began spreading out the dinner, "people forget only what they want to forget."

"I can see I've got some rough years ahead of me with a psychiatrist around."

She turned to him with arched eyebrows. "Are you thinking seriously of having one around?"

"Mighty seriously, darling—mighty seriously."

After they had eaten she cleaned up the things and moved towards the door. "At least I hope you'll take me home now."

He ran his fingers through his hair and looked back at the machine in its panels by the wall. "There's just one more thing I want to get through my head. It won't take a minute."

She slumped in a chair and put her elbow on the laboratory bench. "So this is the way it's going to be."

He grinned at her.

For an hour or more he studied the texts on the table in complete silence. Slowly there began to appear a consecutive thread of knowledge that was fundamental in the field employed for communication in the machine. Yet, as it was now built, this basic characteristic seemed to be blanked.

As he nailed down the final factors of it clearly in his mind he straightened up to look at the enigmatic black panels with their shiny indicators and controls. Was this the thing that Ole had stumbled across? He thought of Ruth's description of the boisterous Ole crying hysterically of some vast frightening menace he had seen in the sky, of the thoughts he had heard the Engineer *think*—

If this were it, then perhaps there was something after all in the dread that haunted Ruth and Ole.

Hastily he went over to the interocitor and began removing panels. He reached inside, disconnected a bank of catherimine tubes and reran their input leads. He cut out the visual circuits completely and modified the field strengths in the coils that governed the albion index of the circuits. After half an hour he was finished.

He hesitated a moment before he turned the power into the modified circuits. He glanced at Ruth. Her head was down on the table, her dark hair spilling outward like the leaves of some velvet flower. She was sound asleep. Cal smiled tenderly. Everything was going to be all right.

He threw the switch that energized the altered interocitor. He had no clear conception of what he was looking for, but he knew that the fundamental un-blanked field described in the texts should now be emanating from the machine.

It was hardly perceptible at first, like a haunting memory. It was neither sound nor sight. The only word that leaped to his mind was—*thought*.

He looked about in sudden concern for Ruth. She had raised her head as if suddenly roused from troubled sleep. He couldn't tell whether she perceived it, too.

He shut his eyes momentarily and attempted to blot out the remnant of physical sound that filtered through the quiet night. Faintly, an image was forming in his mind as if he were imagining a picture under his own initiative. But he knew he wasn't thinking it. It was coming from—*outside*.

The image of Jorgasnovara was in his mind and he was speaking—no, thinking, for there were no movements of his lips. His lined, chiseled face was cast in planes of utter weariness and discontent. His thoughts seemed addressed to someone.

". . . report we are doing the best possible under the circumstances. Production of plant C is six hundred units. D is about ready. We have four hundred on hand that you can pick up here tonight. If Secorian outpost goes can we maintain here?"

There was a moment of silence, in which an answer seemed to be coming to the Engineer from some source, but Cal could not get that.

"All right," the Engineer said at last. "Near the outer ring? Give me five minutes."

The thought of Jorgasnovara receded and vanished from Cal's mind. He turned away from the machine.

"That must have been the way it was with Ole," said Ruth in a hushed voice.

"What he heard must have been different, however," said Cal. "This was nothing fearful to drive a man out of his mind."

"But Jorgasnovara knows things that would. Didn't you feel it—the sense that he knows and has been aware of things of utter terror and frightfulness that a normal mind could scarcely endure?"

Cal nodded slowly. He had felt the same.

"Ole must have heard some of those things," said Ruth. "Do you understand what it's all about?"

"No." Cal shook his head. "I don't understand a thing. The interocitor is even more of a mystery than I thought. It is capable of making direct mental contact, yet it is overbuilt with a lot of crude visual and audio circuits.

"Tomorrow we'll go to see Ole. If there's anything sinister that he found we'll get it out of him. I knew him pretty well—he may talk to me. If not, perhaps you can persuade him to submit to pentathol treatment. We'll do what we can.

"Until we know for sure I still won't let go of my paradise. You can't realize what it means to someone who's always wanted to do real engineering and has been bogged down in toaster and electric-razor plants all his life. This technology—it's like breathing pure oxygen."

"And just as likely to make you drunk."

"Perhaps."

"Let's get down to the shipping department," she said. "He said only five minutes."

They had to pass through the section where the long assembly lines were dark and still, and then they came near the shipping department. They heard the sounds together—the rumbling of the great doors that opened to the outside. There were movements and a light inside the shipping room.

"Down here," whispered Ruth.

Reluctantly, Cal crouched behind a foreman's desk with her. He felt a little ridiculous—spying on his own shipping department.

Then Ruth shook his arm fiercely and her voice was almost a tiny scream. "Look at it—out there by the platform—Cal, what is it?"

He saw it then. It had been there all the time but in the darkness it was difficult to distinguish.

A vast ellipsoid that towered above the door, as if it were as tall as the three-story plant. Dim lights were visible in the interior of the thing through the port that was open opposite the platform. A gangplank extended between the two.

Cal thought then of the depression he'd seen that noon after the rain. "So that was the tracks you tried to tell me about!" he said.

Ruth nodded, trembling in the darkness. "I knew that depression hadn't been there long and I wondered if—something—had been pulled up to the door to take away the interocitors. But I didn't dream of anything like this! What is it?"

"I wish I knew." But slowly, there was growing the unbelievable conviction that he *did* know. His mind held it back as long as possible.

The Engineer came into view as they watched. A small instrument like a flashlight was in his hands. With it he was towing a chain of heavy interocitor crates, each of which weighed over nine hundred pounds. They were linked together somehow and followed the tiny beam like obedient dogs.

He disappeared into the depths of the mysterious freighter. The stream of boxes followed for minutes until the last one disappeared into the portal. After moments, the Engineer appeared again.

"Come on!" Cal whispered. "The roof!"

He tugged roughly at Ruth's sleeve. Obediently, she followed, slipping through the darkness, stumbling once or twice on the iron stairway leading to the roof. And then they were outside.

The top of the ellipsoid was still ten feet above the edge of the roof. As they peered over, they heard the sharp clank of the closing doors below.

"We'd better stand back," said Cal. "No telling what—"

The massive object grew suddenly misty. Like a faint, transparent film it seemed suspended fragilely in the air. Then abruptly it was gone.

But Cal had seen its going. It had moved straight up at incredible velocity. For a moment Ruth raised her eyes to follow his gaze out into the distant star field, where a fleeting shadow passed across the Milky Way.

Then she buried her face in his shoulder. "Cal, I'm afraid! What does this mean?"

He made no answer. It was not a thing of terror. A choking sense of awe made it impossible for him to speak. He had witnessed the miracle that he had never dreamed of seeing in his lifetime—and he was part of it! He would know all of it, and make it his.

The Engineers had conquered space.

He understood now the vast secrecy that shrouded their doings, why they held back a knowledge of their motives, their markets, their ultimate ideals.

For how could they tell the fledgling engineers that the interocitors were produced for a market beyond the stars?

## — IX —

The desert was dreamlike in the early morning heat. Cal wished he and Ruth had started a couple of hours earlier than they did. They would have been in the outskirts of Los Angeles now.

He glanced down at the face of his companion, who was curled up in the seat beside him. He smiled tenderly as he watched her sleeping figure. She looked more like a college freshman than a skilled psychiatrist burdened with several degrees.

It was little more than six months since Cal had met her there, he thought. In that short time he had worked harder than ever before in his life. He had put the new plant unit of the Peace Engineers into production in Phoenix. He had seen the first of the complex communicators come off the production lines under his direction—those instruments the Engineers called interocitors.

And he had put his diamond on Ruth's finger.

She stirred as the sunlight brightened the desert. Smiling, she turned her head slowly back and forth.

"Oh-h-h—" she grimaced. "It's going to be stiff for a week."

"Good morning, darling," said Cal. "Breakfast coffee is almost ready—just around the next bend in the road."

Ruth glanced at the straight, miles-long stretch ahead and wrinkled her nose at him. "I'll have mine out of the thermos you didn't want me to bring along."

She reached behind the seat and brought out the bottle. As she sipped the warm coffee she said, "What are you going to say to Ole when we find him? Do you have any idea?"

He shook his head. "It will all depend on how he reacts. If only he could have told us what he knew instead of running away—"

"I wish we were never going back," said Ruth. Her voice was low, almost inaudible above the hum of the engine. "I wish we were never going to hear of Peace Engineers again!"

Cal turned. Her eyes were staring far across the desert to the little fence of mountains beyond. They bore the vision of infinite dread that he had glimpsed the first time he had ever seen her.

It was mid-morning when they reached Los Angeles. The Narcissus Radio Company where Ole worked was one of those small outfits scrabbling for a living on the south side of town. Its single building was a wartime jerry-built shack that looked as if it were now forty years old.

"What a rathole!"

Ruth shook her head in dismay. "I can't imagine an engineer like Ole coming to work here for *any* reason. Did you ever hear of Narcissus Radios?"

"No," said Cal, "and very few people ever will either—except radio service men. I'll bet they really turn out some bloopers in here."

They left the car and entered the building. Two languid typists seemed to be the total office force.

Cal spoke. "We'd like to see Mr. Swenberg of the engineering department."

One of the girls shifted her gum into the far corner of her mouth and laughed. "He *is* the engineering department. Go straight on through to the rear. His office is next to the shipping department."

They passed through a swinging door and found themselves in a dingy assembly room. Twelve girls and a foreman were putting a can full of parts together, which would be boxed and labeled as a car radio.

The foreman came up. Cal said, "We want to see Mr. Swenberg."

"Right back there."

They could see Ole's figure now in the glare of light coming through a door at the rear of the building. He looked up as they approached. His face registered impulsive gladness and then a cold dismay clouded his eyes.

"Hi, Ole!" said Cal. "We finally decided to come over and inspect this rat's nest you left paradise for."

Ole took his hand. "It's a rat's nest, all right. You ought to see our inspection department. The last girl on the line plugs the sets in. If she can tune in KFI the thing goes in a box. I warn you, don't ever buy Narcissus radios—even if I do design them myself."

"Would you be willing to recommend anything else that you've helped design lately?"

"Such as what?"

"Such as interocitors."

Ole hesitated. His face seemed to go slack, and his eyes held a beaten look. "I'd just as soon not talk about *that*."

"It's what we came for, Ole. We've got to talk about it. Ruth and I—we've found out something new for ourselves. We've got to know what made you run away."

"What have you found out?" Ole asked, but his face showed no real interest.

Cal wondered if he should say it, if Ole could understand that he actually meant it. "They've got space flight," he said slowly. "We saw their ships—one of them. It picked up a load of interocitors two nights ago and went off—somewhere. It was a spaceship. I'm absolutely certain of that."

Ole looked narrowly into Cal's eyes. "I suppose it's possible. If it's true, it makes it worse than ever. They'll have their way whenever they come out in the open and let the rest of the world know what they intend to do."

"Did you find out who they are?" said Cal. "Is that why you left?"

Ole shook his head. "It was just like sitting on a time bomb, never knowing when it might go off—or even if it would go off at all while I was there. I had to get out."

Ruth spoke up for the first time. "Ole, don't you remember that day when you came to my office?"

He looked blank, then slowly shook his head. "What do you mean?"

"That day you came in babbling about something that had terrorized you. Warner came right afterwards and wouldn't let me do anything for you, but he took you away. The next time I saw you, you said you were leaving to take this job."

"I don't know what you're talking about. I remember telling you I was leaving, but nothing about the other."

Suddenly, he waved his palm in front of him as if to brush the whole affair away. "I've told you I don't want to talk about any of that ugly business over there. I'm through with it! You can go on thinking what you like about it, but I want nothing to do with it—and as long as you're a part of it I want nothing to do with you either. If that's all you came to talk about you may as well go."

"Ole—!" Ruth began.

Cal touched her arm. "I'm sorry, Ole. We're disturbed about things ourselves and we thought you might be able to help by telling us about that day you came to Ruth's—"

"I don't know what you're talking about! Now, will you please leave?"

They turned and moved slowly back through the dingy assembly room. No one spoke as they went out of the building. In the car, Cal laid a carton on the seat between them.

"Cal—" Ruth said, "we've got to find a way to do something for Ole. He's under terrific tension. He's being torn by some inner conflict that he can't endure much longer."

"Maybe we'll find the answer in this." He tapped the carton as he turned the car out into the stream of traffic.

"What's that? You didn't have anything when we went in there." Then Ruth turned it over and read the printing on the carton. "You took one of their radios! How did you get it?"

"Used to do sleight of hand in college," he said. "I don't think anyone saw me pick it up. I'd rather Ole didn't know it."

"Why did you take it?"

"I don't know for sure, but didn't you notice how anxious Ole was to get us out of there?"

"How could I help notice being ordered out?"

"But did you stop to figure out why?"

"That's obvious. The tension—our bringing up the Peace Engineer trouble again—"

Cal patted her hand. "Look, darling. Sometimes there's a disadvantage in being a very brilliant psychiatrist. You need the talents of a dub who's an old solder slinger from way back. Didn't you notice that back room behind the one we were in?"

"Not particularly."

"He had an interocitor in there."

"An int—! You mean he—?"

"He'd been working on it just before we came in. I could see the rosin vapor rising from his soldering iron. He had parts of it strung all over the bench, but I know an interocitor when I see one."

"He didn't want us to see it!"

"That's why I wanted to get out with one of these things instead of standing around arguing with him. He very definitely didn't want us to see it. Anybody else—it wouldn't matter because they wouldn't know what it was. But our coming really gave him the jitters. Here's a good stopping place."

He swung the car to the curb on a residential dead-end street where little traffic flowed. He turned to the box on the seat and ripped it open. With a screwdriver from the glove compartment he removed a panel from the set and grunted softly. "That's no more a car radio than it is a dishwasher."

"You mean it's something—like an interocitor, maybe? But Ole wouldn't be doing that. He's not *with* them!"

"I don't know. What can we believe? But whatever his purpose, he's certainly lying to us—some pretty fat, bare-faced lies. More than half of these components are the kind of stuff that goes into the interocitor. It's part of the Engineers' technique."

"But, Cal, that can't be. He sounded as bitter towards them as ever. He can't be with them still."

Cal shook his head. "It looks as if instead of leaving them, he has actually been promoted to a job like Jorgasnovara's on a smaller scale. Why he should be lying to us now I don't know. But I'll bet a nickel he runs the whole place back there."

When Ruth finally spoke again her voice was thin with fear. "I suppose you think this means everything is just swell, that Ole has joined them and so it proves that you were right."

"Ruth, please don't talk like that."

"I'm sorry. I'm scared, Cal. You didn't see Ole that day he came babbling to me about what he'd heard the Engineer thinking."

"I don't think everything is all right. I don't see why he lied to us. It makes less sense than ever."

"What are you going to do? Are you going back to see Ole, or tell Jorgasnovara you know about the spaceship?"

He put the box on the back seat and drew her close with his arm about her shoulders. "What do you think I should do?"

"Forget about going back. Let's stay here and never go near the place again. What they've done to Ole they could do to any of us.

"He's not himself. I think they put him under some kind of impressed influence that's made little more than a robot out of him. He's their slave, turning out these devices for whatever purpose they have."

"You don't really believe that, darling. There's a rational explanation that will be perfectly reasonable when we understand it."

He felt the trembling of her shoulders beneath his arm. He stared down the sunny Los Angeles street. A half dozen kids were riding tricycles on the sidewalk.

They could live on a street like this, he thought. They could have a house like one of these, and their kids could be playing here in the sun in a few years.

It was tempting.

He withdrew his arm and turned on the key again. "They've got space flight," he said. "We know it, and that alone would keep me from backing out now. Why, that ship of theirs was so far beyond the clumsy rockets our militarists have been toying with—

"It speaks of a technology in which the pioneering is over. It could make trips to the stars with safety and regularity.

"And, Ruth—*I want to go to the stars.*"

His own sudden vehemence startled him. He looked into her eyes a moment, then spoke more quietly. "It's a dream I had when I was a kid. I thought maybe when I was grown up—I haven't even thought about it for years. And now, suddenly, it's possible. I've got to find out about it. If they're withholding it from the rest of the world I'm going to find out why it can't be given out."

"Yes—of course you will go," she said quietly. "But first you will find out who the Peace Engineers are. You will find out the pieces of the picture that they have kept hidden from us."

He nodded. "That's what makes it so devilishly hard to understand—their elusiveness. Jorgasnovara told me enough so that up to a point I can understand it. But beyond that point it makes no sense at all."

"And you have reached that point?"

"This business with Ole pretty accurately defines it."

"Are you going back there?"

"No." He shook his head slowly. "I think the answer still lies in Phoenix—in the interocitor. Why is Ole using one? I want to know more about this apparent thought reading property the machine has. No. I'm going back to work as if nothing had happened and go on from there."

— **X** —

The long, lonely four-hundred-mile drive back to Phoenix ended in late evening. Cal let Ruth out at her place and kissed her good night.

He turned the car north again and drove slowly toward the mysterious plant beyond town. Crouched on the desert with only a scattering of lights, it was like a sleeping monster that he dared not waken.

He could accept Jorgasnovara's explanation of the Engineers' existence, their purpose and their secrecy, he thought. He could understand their withholding full explanations until he proved himself.

But the one wholly illogical factor was Ole Swenberg. Cal could not comprehend why the engineer, who had so bitterly denounced the organization, who had come to Ruth in such panic over some discovery he'd made concerning it—he could not understand how Ole could now be in obvious charge of a small Peace Engineers' plant.

And, though Ole was still using and working with interocitors, he refused to talk about it with Cal—and with Ruth, who had so keenly shared his distrust of the Peace Engineers. It made no sense whatever.

Before he had seen the Engineers' ship Cal had been so sure that everything was all right, that the Peace Engineers had a legitimate reason for secrecy.

Now nothing seemed right. Ole, who had been so bitter against them, was directing a midget plant for them. And he didn't want Cal or Ruth to know about it.

Wearily, Cal turned into the driveway of his own company-owned house. He felt exhausted beyond endurance. Tomorrow would be time enough for new questions.

In the morning, he returned to the offices and laboratories. It was the same familiar surroundings that he had known for many months, but somehow none of it seemed the same now. He caught himself looking furtively about. He felt watched.

Angrily, he shook off the sensation. He knew it had no basis in reality. It was only the product of his new attitude of suspicion towards the Peace Engineers.

There seemed to be endless details of production to attend to that morning, but by eleven o'clock the assembly lines were rolling smoothly and he managed to get away to his own laboratory.

He locked the door behind him and leaned against it a moment. Would there ever be an end to the questioning in his mind? His doubts fought with his desire to believe that this was the professional paradise he had hoped for—where he could study and work in the freedom that he had always dreamed of—

But Ole had dreamed such dreams—and something had happened to them. With a savage gesture he strode to the interocitor panel he had reconstructed.

He turned on the power and stood in front of the panel, watching the instruments. He closed his eyes, trying to recover the sensation of telepathic eavesdropping he had experienced before, but nothing came except his own threshing, uncertain thoughts. He half-wondered if he had dreamed that he had heard and seen Jorgasnovara through the instrument, but he knew it was real enough. Ruth had seen and heard, too.

Abruptly, a surge of power emanated from the machine like a voice of thunder—but there was no sound.

He shuddered and pressed his eyelids fiercely. In his mind, he thought. Direct contact from mind to mind without sight or sound. He listened to the thoughts that came and watched their elusive images.

But it was not Jorgasnovara, the Engineer. It was someone reporting to him. ". . . six Secorian colonnades lost. General Planners have decided on resurgence in that sector since it has become our weakest area."

And then Jorgasnovara's thoughts surged in.

Cal grasped his head involuntarily at the impact of terrible emotion that was hurled from the machine and buried like a million tiny bolts of flame in the cells of his own brain. The whole spectrum of human feeling seemed alive with tortured, throbbing power.

"When will it end?" the thought came. "When will it ever end?"

Cal searched through the blast for the individual currents of feeling. He sensed a vast homesickness, a longing for peace and confinement to a small spot of land. But strongest of all, a terrifying, overpowering hatred, a hatred reserved only for an enemy whose power has destroyed everything dear. Jorgasnovara hated that kind of enemy, and it seemed to Cal that the power of that hatred alone could destroy life.

Then there came a calmer thought. "You are tired, Jorgasnovara. You should have let yourself be relieved long ago. There are others who could see this facet of the project through to completion. You have done excellently, but you are not indispensable."

"A matter of days now," said the Engineer. "Only a matter of days, and I shall be ready to relinquish my place."

"As you will. But you will soon be needed in another place, I am informed. You will have little chance to rest."

"Rest! Who can rest in the death-struggle of a universe?"

"You are too sensitive. You should have something done about that. You know that our lifetimes will not see the end of the struggle."

"But we can act as if it would be so."

There was no answer, but the vision of Jorgasnovara's thoughts remained.

Jorgasnovara's mind seemed to pass slowly over events of some near or distant past. There were glimpses of strange lands that Cal did not recognize— he wondered momentarily if they might be other planets.

Then, upon a sunny landscape, it seemed, a vast roll of darkness burst out of space and over the whole earth and the planets beyond. From Jorgasnovara, there was the sensation of terror and dismay. And then hate.

The hate grew once again to such mighty intensity that Cal could scarcely endure its presence. Slowly it receded, and there was the vision of ships. Mighty ships of space such as Cal had seen that night by the loading dock.

Ships that went up by the thousands against that roll of darkness out of space—and vanished in the flame of their own consuming. He seemed to see endless days and years of fruitless battle; and then the darkness receded, pressed hard by the vast hordes.

And that was the present, Cal sensed. There was battle, and it was not won, and fleets of ships and endless tons of material were swallowed in the daily gorge of war. There, the thought visions ended.

It was moments before he realized that he was no longer receiving the thoughts of the Engineer. The interocitor was still operating, but nothing came to Cal's mind.

He moved at last from a half-crouching position before the bench. His body was bathed in sweat. His brain felt numb from the pummeling of that wave of impressed thought and emotion. Like a flood, the answers to a thousand mysteries poured through his mind and left a thousand more to be answered.

He moved to the phone and called Ruth. "Come over at once," he said. "I know what it's all about."

He sat down on a laboratory stool while he waited for her coming, and tried to quiet his nerves.

She came, breathless from running. "What is it?" she asked.

Cal nodded to a chair and stared at the interocitor. Slowly he told her what he had just witnessed.

She seemed uncomprehending. "This battle—these ships of space destroying each other—I don't understand."

"War. A more deadly and terrible war than any we could have dreamed of. That's what it means," said Cal soberly. "These Peace Engineers—what a ghastly joke their name turned out to be! They have become involved in a full-scale war.

"Who or what the enemy is, I don't know, but the Engineers are attempting to fight it alone. The Earth at this moment is involved in interstellar warfare, and only this handful of men know it. That explains the secrecy!"

"It's hardly possible," breathed Ruth. "If these Peace Engineers should fail—why don't they come out and enlist the whole world with them? How did it begin? What is the fighting for?"

"I don't know any of those answers," said Cal wearily. In his mind he seemed to see again those flaming ships.

"But it's easy to picture how it might have started. For many years they may have carried on secret flights until their ships came to a high state of perfection. Caught by surprise, perhaps, they encountered the first representatives of another planetary culture. Maybe one of our Solar planets, maybe from across the galaxy. But somebody blundered—and there was conflict.

"And rather than risk revealing their secrets, the Engineers are willing to risk all mankind in their effort to fight it out alone."

Ruth said finally, "What are we going to do?" It was like the sound of a small child in a vast and lonely cavern.

## — XI —

He put his arm around her shoulders, and they stood by the window looking out over the plant and the desert beyond. It was like the last terrible moments before waking from a nightmare, Cal thought. In just a moment now it should be over—

But it wasn't. It never would be as long as he lived. That surging hatred from Jorgasnovara would never leave his mind.

"I keep thinking of Ole," he said. "I wonder if he knows of this? Did they tell him about it that day he came to your office? And is that why he is quietly producing war materials in that broken-down shop of his? That would explain why he threw us out of his place. He couldn't tell us why he'd reversed his violent feelings, or even that he had done so."

"You think that all of this production is war material?"

"What else?" He ran a hand through his thick shock of hair and laughed sharply. "And I was the guy who was so fed up with practising science in the service of the warriors!"

He turned to the interocitor panel and smacked his hand against it. "I wonder what this thing *really* does—destroy armies by turning them into idiots, or something equally beautiful from a militaristic standpoint?"

"Stop it, Cal," said Ruth quietly. "Stop it!"

He faced her. "All right. I promise I won't go off like that again. The immediate problem is what do *we* do? Do we go along and help or do we try to throw wrenches in the machinery?"

"How can we do anything but help if what you say is true? I think we ought to see Jorgasnovara and make him lay all his cards on the table."

"You think he would be willing to do just that?"

"Why not?"

"I don't know. Perhaps if Ole came in this same way they would welcome us. On the other hand, I can't believe he would be very happy about our eavesdropping on his mental processes."

"You said the other night that he must know."

"No, I think not now. I don't believe he would have let us go on this way if he did. I think we've discovered this quite accidentally, and that no one knows anything about it."

"And Ole."

"I wonder—" Cal began. He looked speculatively at the panels surrounding him. "Warner contacted him the first time through the interocitor. I wonder if Ole—"

He advanced to a panel and threw in the power relay again. Ruth watched the familiar glow of the tubes lighting up. Like the candles of some ritual to the gods of science, it seemed to her.

Then Cal started back, his eyes on the meters in sudden fear.

"Someone has activated this—been spying on us while we've talked!"

"Is that possible?"

"Under normal quiescent conditions of the machine—"

There were meaningless flashes of light and color across the bright tube that formed the screen, but nothing recognizable came.

"Do you think you can reach Ole's machine?"

"It's just possible. I may be able to excite his—"

A swirling shape seemed to be growing out of the mist on the screen. Slowly the lines and planes of a room appeared, a vaguely familiar place.

"That's his laboratory!" exclaimed Ruth.

Then, suddenly, there appeared a face, blurred and out of focus. But there was no doubt about whose it was. A harsh voice barked at them.

"Tighten the beam, you fool. Do you want every machine in the plant excited?"

Cal made a quick adjustment and the blurry image came into focus.

On the screen Ole passed a hand wearily over his face. "I'm sorry. I'm pretty well wrought up, I guess. I've been watching you for days. I guess I know which side you're on, now."

"What are you talking about?" said Cal.

"When you came over here I was afraid you might be part of Jorgasnovara's secret police. I couldn't tell whether you were spying on me or not. I had to stay in character as you knew me. I didn't dare say a word. But I've been watching you while you found out what a mess they've got us into. I know now that you're not one of the inner circle yet."

"Did you know about this war all the time?" asked Cal.

"Yes. That's what nearly drove me crazy, and made me leave the plant. Only I saw more of it than you did. I listened in while Jorgasnovara was getting a direct report from one battle sector. Our little wars are like neighborhood kids brawling in the street compared with the way they fight."

"What is it all about? How did it start? Why is it so undercover?"

"I don't know for sure, but I think it's about as you guessed it, a blunder when they first contacted some other world, and now they're trying to carry off the fight without letting the rest of the world in on it. I think I know the why of that. Can't you picture the public response to such information?"

"I don't understand your actions. You're working with them. Why should you be afraid I was spying on you?"

"I'm *not* with them—and I think Jorgasnovara knows it. His spies have been here before. They've got to be stopped. Can't you see that?"

"I'm not so sure—now," said Cal slowly. "Their enemies might wipe out our entire planet. It looks as if only the Engineers stand between us and destruction. I can't see how we can do anything but throw in with them for all we've got—regardless of our feelings about war. We're in it—but good."

"Meacham, the Pacifist!" said Ole bitterly. "There's no reason to believe they'd wipe us out. Maybe they'd like it brought to an end just as much as we would. At least, until we find out, we've no basis for believing otherwise."

"Have you anything but wishful thinking as a basis for believing that?"

"Yes—I was here for a year before you were. I know Jorgasnovara. He would never ask quarter from anybody. Regardless of the rightness of the cause, he'll fight to the complete destruction of his enemy or himself. If it were his own private war I wouldn't care what happened to him, but he's involved the whole human race."

Cal recalled that burning hatred of Jorgasnovara. "It's a question of how we can best get out of this. I can't understand it. It looks like the action of some utter fools, yet they can't be. Their science—"

"It has been pretty well demonstrated that technological sense is not synonymous with social and political acumen."

"That's the whole thesis upon which Jorgasnovara claims the organization is based—and they seem to be living proof of it—but hardly in the way they intended."

"Up to now," said Ole, "I've been alone. I've been waiting and hoping for you to show your hand. I dared not reveal what I knew because of his spies.

"He told me about his secret war when I stumbled onto it through the interocitor. He offered me a chance to go along with them, and I was afraid not to.

"That is why I took over this small outfit for him here. I don't even know what this gadget is we're making. I had to gain time until I could find someone else in the organization whom I could trust—and I was hoping it would be you. You've got to help me find some way to stop this thing before it's too late."

"We're agreed on the ultimate goal of getting out of this mess they've started, but can we compromise on the means for the time being? Let's not try to interfere with their production until we know more. I could do plenty to interrupt production of interocitors—temporarily. But they'd soon replace me when they found out I couldn't keep up," Cal said.

"All right," Ole agreed. "I am coming over for a conference in a couple of days. Since I'm the only one that knows about the war officially let me see what I can do towards pumping Jorgasnovara. You two keep out of the way, and don't say anything until we find out if somebody is liable to get hurt. In the meantime keep glued to your modified interocitor."

"Do you think he knows we're listening in?"

"I don't know. It's possible he does. He's careless about using his own machine on a loose beam. He may be waiting to smack us down like flies as soon as we make a false move, but we've *got to* take that chance."

Cal Meacham did little work the remainder of that day. After Ruth left he paced the floor of his laboratory.

The double identity involved in this whole set-up seemed increasingly fantastic. Altogether there were nearly four thousand persons working at the plant. Most of them were simply assemblers hired in Phoenix who didn't know a resistor from a spark gap in the first place. To them the place was simply an electrical manufacturing plant and a weekly paycheck.

To the engineers hired through the idealistic lures of the group, it was a place of intellectual freedom where a super-technology had flowered and was still growing and developing.

And to Jorgasnovara and his inner circle it was a war center. But who composed the inner circle of the Engineers? Who had complete knowledge of the purpose of the plant?

Of all those Cal had met only Jorgasnovara and Warner had betrayed any such knowledge. Of the others, each man seemed possessed of a single piece of knowledge that was a fragment of the gigantic puzzle. He was given only as much as would fit him into place in that puzzle.

The complacency of his fellow engineers in accepting the place at face value irritated Cal. Yet he almost laughed at his own original willingness to do the same—until he had discovered the unsuspected properties of the interocitor.

It was worse than useless to try to talk to any of the other engineers, he thought. There were several hundred, and to sound them all out would take an endless amount of time that he did not have.

To come face to face with Jorgasnovara and demand information seemed the most foolhardy procedure of all. Yet it seemed the most obvious, since Ole was already in Jorgasnovara's confidence to some degree.

Ole came over in one of the pilotless planes. There were six of these, Cal had learned, and they were in almost constant flight. Besides them, the company used three small planes with conventional controls, and the transport that was Jorgasnovara's private ship.

Ole and Cal went directly to the latter's laboratory. Ruth came in a few moments later. Her face was lined with the strain of having knowledge of the unseen conflict that raged in the heavens.

"Wouldn't it be better for us not to approach Jorgasnovara until we try to find out more by other means?" she asked.

"There's not much chance of it," said Cal. "None of us are what you would call cloak and dagger men and it would take long months of that sort of stuff to get anywhere. I think there is a very good possibility that Jorgasnovara will lay his cards on the table and invite us to have a piece—or else. Particularly since he brought Ole into it as he did."

"Suppose I stowed away," said Ruth. "One of the interocitor packing cases could be fitted out nicely. I'm small enough for one."

"That's nonsense!" said Cal. "It might be possible to learn a good deal—but the chance of getting the information back would be almost zero. We've got to make contact here, where we've got some kind of leverage."

"What do you mean?"

"We've got the whole world on our side—and we can do a pretty quick job of letting it know what information we've got already—provided it comes to that."

"Not if Jorgasnovara decides to throw a quick net around all of us."

"That's why I'm going to see him alone—and you keep out of it," said Ole. "If anything happens to me you had better take what information you've got and head for Washington. It's the only chance I see. I'm due over there in a few minutes. I'll come back as soon as I'm through."

They watched as he crossed the dusty terrain between buildings. Then Cal turned back to his interocitor and switched on the modified circuits. He adjusted it finely, but he could not excite Jorgasnovara's instrument. The Engineer had it blocked against outside excitation.

Ruth sat by the window, staring out at the bleak desert landscape in the distance.

"Penny—" said Cal.

She turned slowly. "Do you trust Ole?" she asked suddenly.

"Trust? What are you talking about?"

"Does it make sense—his being in charge of that small plant over there, and trying to tell us he's opposed to Jorgasnovara? I can't forget how he looked that day after Warner took him away. I can't get over my conviction they did something to put him under their control.

"Isn't it possible that he's just what he said he feared we might be—a spy for Jorgasnovara?"

Cal grinned and put his arms around her. "How about me? Are you sure you can trust me?"

"Cal—I'm serious. I feel we can't trust anybody. Let's gather up some of the evidence that's available. Let's take samples of components, pictures, and so on, and turn them over to Army Intelligence. Let's take them to the White House if necessary. We've got to let someone else know about this. If Ole should be forced to betray us we wouldn't have a chance!"

"Take it easy, darling. We will—if necessary. But we can't go at it blindly. You don't know the Army. I had dealings with the brass during the war. You don't just go up and say, 'Mr. General, some guys out here are running a private war that you ought to know about. They're fighting somebody on another planet.' That would be the quickest way to a private suite in the booby hatch I know of."

"Ole is not the same as he used to be. I know it. And I keep thinking that they can do the same to us that they have done to him."

He took her arm and led her towards the door. "Let's go down to the cafeteria for a snack and forget about it for a while."

"No, I'd better get back to my office. There are two new engineers due this afternoon. If I'm away from my office very long Warner will think something's up. Call me as soon as you hear from Ole."

"Okay—and quit your worrying."

She gave him a faint smile and went out the door.

— XII —

Cal turned to his benches and equipment. It was useless to try to work. His mind spun uncontrollably about the thing they had uncovered. It was like fighting an unknown assailant in the dark. There was nowhere to get a grip on the problem.

He wondered if Ole would blunder in talking with Jorgasnovara. He had his own secret fears that Ruth might be right about Ole. What would the Engineer's reaction be? Cal tried to imagine how the conversation was going, to reconstruct it in his mind—

The desert shadows grew swiftly longer. Cal watched the clock impatiently. At last, with a start, he realized that Ole had been gone nearly four hours. It was almost quitting time at the plant. He went to the phone and buzzed Jorgasnovara's secretary before she left.

"I'd like to know if Mr. Swenberg is still in conference," he said. "I want to see him before I leave."

The girl was silent for a moment as if checking her memory. "Mr. Swenberg left quite some time ago for his own plant. He stayed only ten or fifteen minutes. But he left a message for you that he had to leave right away and would see you next time he came over."

Cal hung up slowly. Outside the window the heat haze on the desert swirled like a copper river. He felt stifled and smothered.

His phone buzzed. It was Ruth.

"Cal? I wanted to call you before I leave. I'm being given a new assignment at another plant, and it's necessary for me to leave right away. I can't tell you anything about it, and I won't be able to see you for some time, but you'll hear from me. I'm sorry it has to be so suddenly. I'll see you soon."

"Ruth! Wait!"

He stopped. It was obvious that she was not alone. She was saying what she had been told to say. They had her trapped.

"It's all right, darling," she said. "Everything's all right. The plane is taking off soon. 'Bye, now."

She hung up.

He stood motionless, staring. Ole's attempt had triggered Jorgasnovara into swift action. They had Ole—now Ruth.

He'd be next, Cal thought. But there wasn't time to consider that. He had to get to Ruth.

He raced down the stairs and through the corridors of the building. His running footsteps echoed on the asphalt walks between buildings.

He entered Ruth's office, and found it empty. Her desk was neatly tidied as if she'd left for the night. Where had she called from, he wondered. Why had they let her call at all?

He turned to the window and looked out at the airfield. In front of the hangar, one of the pilotless ships was being warmed up. Ruth was walking towards it, Warner beside her. Cal choked back an exclamation, and ran from the room. He felt somehow that if she went up in that plane she would be gone from him forever.

She had climbed in, and a mechanic slid the canopy shut as Cal raced along the apron. With a sudden roar the motor was gunned and shot back a sandblast into his face. He ran on, vainly trying to overtake the rolling plane.

It moved to the runway. He ceased his vain running as the plane swiftly grew smaller. It shrank to a dot in the sky.

He turned then at the sound of a footstep behind him. It was Warner.

"Mr. Meacham!" Warner came up and took his hand. "You saved me a trip over your way."

"Ruth—" said Cal.

"Something very special came up this afternoon. Mr. Jorgasnovara asked her to take a special assignment for a time. Sorry it wasn't possible to notify you earlier but you needn't worry. She will be quite all right."

"You wanted to see me?" Cal's mouth felt cottony.

"Yes—we also have something new for you. Mr. Jorgasnovara is very pleased with your work and feels that you can assist us in more complex operations which we have under way. However, I will leave it to him to give you the details. He'd like to see you at nine in the morning in his office. Please be sure to be there on time. I'll be seeing you again."

Warner smiled and walked away.

Cal watched his retreating figure. It was incredible. They were asking him to walk right into it. Did they take him for an utter fool? No. That was not right. They did not underestimate him. They could reach out and take him any moment they chose.

With their damnable technology they could probe his brain and dissect every secret thought. There was no hiding. Why had he supposed for a moment that he and Ole and Ruth could operate in their midst without detection?

He turned again to try to locate that disappearing speck in the sky. It was already gone from sight.

He began walking back towards the plant buildings. Inside, his growing panic turned his stomach into a knot. He wiped his moist hands against his trouser legs. He ought to get out—tonight. He'd have to make a try, at least.

He returned to his lab and drew the venetian blinds. He made doubly sure the interocitors were disconnected, beyond all chance of excitation. Then he began packing. He filled a pair of brief cases with samples of components: some of the incredible ten-thousand-volt condensers the size of a bead—the ones that had first lured him to the Peace Engineers. He took scores of other small-sized components that were wholly foreign to conventional manufacturing techniques. Then he gathered up some of the booklets containing photographs of equipment and some of the textbooks they had given him.

He surveyed the fat cases and crushed them shut. It would have to be enough. Somewhere between the White House and the Pentagon he'd find some brass that would listen to him.

It was dark now. Later there would be a moon, but for the time being the desert was black with night. He moved slowly and quietly along the corridors of the plant and stepped into the shadows outside. Only the watchmen's lights illumined the yard, and he stayed in the dimness of these as much as possible.

He paused a score of times in the shadows to look behind and all about. His heightened fear peopled the dark places with unseen pursuers.

He reached the airfield at last. There were half a dozen mechanics and attendants on night duty, including the operators of the giant target beam that guided the pilotless ships. He swallowed to moisten the cotton dryness of his throat and went into the small, brightly-lit office.

The mechanic in charge looked up. "Hello, Mr. Meacham. Going out tonight?"

"Yes. I want one of the manual ships. I have to take a short trip."

"We could give you one of the automatics, and you could sleep until you get there."

"No. I have quite a number of short stops to make. I'd better have a manual."

"Okay. We'll have it rolled out and warmed up in just a few minutes."

He sat down to wait. Was it his imagination, or were they unnecessarily slow about getting the plane out? He wondered if the mechanic had gone to call Warner or Jorgasnovara for instructions. But it was coming now at last. He heard the rumble of the broad doors of the hangar sliding back and turned to watch them roll the ship out. He picked up his cases and hurried out.

"Warm it up a few minutes for you?" the mechanic asked.

"I'll take it," said Cal. "Thanks a lot."

It was like a dream, he thought afterwards. The white overalled mechanics were like waiting ghosts there in the half-light on the apron. How far were they going to let him go? Which one of them would strike?

But they were starting the engine. It caught suddenly with a hearty roar. He closed the canopy and taxied down to the strip. He gunned the motor and felt the tail lift, then slowly he drew back on the stick and felt the smooth rocking of the airborne ship.

It was unbelievable that he had actually got away. He couldn't believe that he had outwitted the Engineers. They had let him go for some purpose of their own.

But, as the desert merged with mountains and then became desert again, he began to relax and feel the weight of the strain lift from his mind. As he crossed New Mexico, the moon rose and splashed all the earth below with cold light.

He began to think of what he was going to do in Washington, of how he would find someone who would believe his story of a secret group of scientists who had involved Earth in an interstellar war. He began to believe that he would actually get there.

# — XIII —

It was somewhere between Amarillo and Oklahoma City that he first saw the shadow. He was flying almost directly into the moon when the great, semi-transparent silhouette showed up against the silver disc.

His taut nerves forced an involuntary scream from his throat. He knew that shape—that vast, ellipsoid that he had once seen shooting into space faster than the eye could follow.

He leaned the stick and jammed his foot against the pedal. The ship heeled over in a tight turn at right angles to his former course. There was a long low cloud bank a few miles away in the otherwise clear sky. If he could get into that—

He couldn't know whether they had seen him or not, but fear of pursuit and failure swelled within him again.

If they captured him before he revealed his knowledge of the Peace Engineers there would be no one who could warn of the menace their ambitions and blunders had created.

It was foolish, he thought, to suppose that he could get away. If they were really searching for him he could not hide from so simple a thing as a radar beam. And he knew their technology had given them means far more effective than radar.

But the cloud was less than two miles away, and he fled blindly towards it.

Halfway there, the shadow fell over him. It blotted out the moon and the sky of stars, and he screamed again in terror. The great hull was poised almost above, moving silently with his plane. In panic, he jerked on the stick and jabbed the foot pedal.

But the plane did not swerve. And then the motor coughed and died. He gripped the useless controls while the ship continued in the grip of an invisible force from above.

Slowly the distance between the two ships narrowed. And now Cal saw that a wide hatch had opened in the base of the spaceship, a hatch wide enough to swallow his entire plane.

It drew closer. The border of the opening in the spaceship was dropping past him. He shoved back the canopy for a final glimpse of the silvery earth below. Then the hatch closed and he felt the plane drop upon it, resting on its landing gear.

He sat there for a long moment in utter darkness. There was no sound nor sense of motion. It was a void in which all perception had vanished.

It seemed like the suddenness and finality of death. He had blundered, he thought, from first to last. He had been confused by his wanting to believe in the Peace Engineers at their face value. It had taken him too long to believe that they were anything but what they professed to be.

He tried to think of what his failure might mean—to Ruth and Ole and to the whole human race—but he was too tired to put one thought after another in consecutive order. His failure was too great for comprehension.

Abruptly lights came on. Except for his plane, the chamber was completely bare. He climbed down from the cockpit and stood on the metal plating of the hatch door.

A spaceship, he thought. He was actually aboard a spaceship bound for some unknown destination. But there was none of the anticipated boyhood thrill. There was only dull aching despair within him.

His muscles tensed at the sudden faint sound of an opening door. He whirled to face it and saw two men entering. Neither was familiar. Their faces were almost expressionless. There was neither animosity nor greeting.

"Please come with us," said one.

Cal stifled an impulse to let loose a flood of questions. He checked it with the knowledge that it would be useless.

One of them led the way through the door. The other followed Cal. Neither spoke.

They took him down a long metal-walled corridor that reminded him of a battleship. At last they halted before a door.

"Please remain here," said one as he opened the door. "This will be yours until we arrive. If you need anything just press this button by the door and we will attempt to serve you. We would advise that you sleep the remainder of the flight. We arrive early in the morning."

"Where?" Cal could not hold back that one question.

The man looked at his companion, then back at Cal. "Luna," he said. And closed the door.

Cal stood there for a long moment, facing the blank door.

Luna—

He turned about. For the first time he saw that the opposite wall had ports that looked out to space. He walked towards them. There was a single moment of vertigo as he glimpsed the scene outside, and he turned his head away. Then, cautiously, he looked back, his hands gripping tightly the back of a chair by the port.

Below him Earth wheeled, a mottled bowl. About seven or eight hundred miles away, he supposed.

For the first time, the full impact of the gap between the technology of the Engineers and the rest of Earth struck him. Down there at White Sands the Army was fitfully thrusting its feeble rockets one or two hundred miles into the atmosphere. No one had succeeded yet in freeing one from Earth's gravity.

But the Engineers' ships were crossing space with the ease and luxury of liners crossing the Atlantic.

Maybe there was a reason for their not asking help from men who had not succeeded in building anything more than an enlarged firecracker. What help could such men be in a battle that raged across the depths of space?

He slept finally. The bed was as soft and luxurious as he could have asked for.

An alarm wakened him and soon afterwards the guides—or guards—of the previous night entered the room. They carried breakfast on a tray.

"We will arrive within an hour. Please be ready. Jorgasnovara requires your presence for a conference."

"Jorgasnovara! He's aboard?"

"Among others."

They left, and Cal turned again to the ports. They seemed to be coming in for a wide orbit around the Earth side of the moon. Momentarily his awareness of imprisonment retreated and his senses absorbed the beauty of the vision through the porthole. He picked out the old familiar landmarks—Copernicus, Tycho, the Sea of Serenity, Mare Imbrium—

He saw for the first time the other side of the moon with its shadowy, unfamiliar spires and vast craters. The ship began to descend among those unnamed craters.

Cal strained his sight to detect some sign of habitation. Shadowy twilight gave the effect of a fantastic etching, and hid everything that might be familiar.

The ship had almost touched ground before he saw a widespread group of one-story buildings that lay almost perfectly camouflaged on a flat plain between two giant mountain ranges, higher than anything Cal had known existed on the moon.

Beside one section he saw a dozen other ships like the one in which he rode, and four others that were monsters, dwarfing the smaller ships like hens hovering over broods.

The two men came again as the ship touched the surface of the moon. Cal followed them along the same corridor, and then wound through other passages that he sensed were taking him through the width of the ship to the other side. Not once did he see another person.

He observed the airtight causeway that had been extended from the ship to the port, eliminating all need of spacesuits in disembarking.

They came out into the building, and there he saw scores of other people, but none he knew, though he scanned their faces for signs of recognition. The pair who guided him stopped at last before a door.

"Wait here. Mr. Jorgasnovara will be here soon."

He stepped in and closed the door.

Across the room Ole and Ruth were seated.

"*Cal!*" Ruth jumped up and ran towards him. She threw her arms around his neck while he stood rigid, scarcely believing, trying to comprehend what he saw. Then his arms went around her and he held her tight.

Ole came towards them slowly, smiling. "This is about the last place I expected our next meeting to be."

"What have they done to you?" said Cal. "Why are we here? What do they intend to do with us?"

· Ole motioned him to a chair by the small polished table at which they had been sitting.

"We misunderstood some of our data," he said, with sudden bleakness in his face. "Jorgasnovara has straightened Ruth and me out somewhat. In a way the situation is not quite as bad as we thought. From another viewpoint it is much worse, perhaps."

"But they are engaged in a war, aren't they? We weren't mistaken in what we overheard regarding that."

"No—we weren't. They're engaged in a war, all right. Our mistake was the assumption that the Engineers are Earthmen."

Cal stared. "*Mistake!* You mean they are from somewhere else?"

Ole nodded. "The key men. Jorgasnovara and Warner and many of the others. This whole advanced technology was brought by them. It never developed on Earth at all."

Cal stared soundlessly, his entire mental concept of the Peace Engineers shifting slowly to this undreamed of possibility.

"Why? What do they want of us? Are they trying to take Earth over for a war base?"

"No, it's not that. We aren't that important to them. In fact they can get along without us.

"They gave Ruth and me their story yesterday. Jorgasnovara was going to pick you up and bring you to the spaceship after he'd given you the basic facts this morning. He wanted us to see their moon base, and let us use an historical instrument they have here.

"But you fouled it all up by jumping the gun and taking off the way you did.

"I warn you that when Jorgasnovara gets through explaining you'll probably want to punch somebody in the nose or else go out and bat your head against a wall—depending on which way your inferiority complex blows."

"You don't make a bit of sense," said Cal. He turned to Ruth. "What's he talking about?"

She smiled, the same kind of bitter, rueful smile he had seen on Ole's lips. "You'll find out. Here comes Jorgasnovara now."

The Engineer closed the door softly behind him and stood in front of it for a moment. His eyes locked with Cal's, and seemed to peer into the depths of his being as if trying to plumb the hidden knowledge and feelings that he possessed.

— XIV —

Cal understood now the feeling of alienness that diffused from Jorgasnovara. It was not hard to think of him as foreign to Earth. He began walking towards the table and consulted his watch. "I believe our appointment was for nine, Mr. Meacham. Dr. Warner told me he had arranged with you."

"He didn't mean these particular arrangements," said Cal, with faint humor. Somehow he felt a growing sense of ease. He could not erase his initial desire to like Jorgasnovara in spite of the mystery of the man.

"No. We were too busy to pay attention to some of the details of your actions. We did not foresee your attempted escape until you had gone. I'm sorry that it was necessary to subject you to the shock that perhaps resulted from our precipitate method of overtaking you, however, I want to assure you that our purpose is benign."

"You are at war." Cal leaned forward abruptly. "You let us overhear snatches of reports passing between you and others of your group. Why?"

"We wanted you to know about it."

"To what purpose? If you intend to involve Earth or wanted our help in some capacity why didn't you simply say so?"

"We had to find out about you three. We had to know your reaction. We had to know how much you hate war. So we gave you the clues and watched.

Of all those with whom we have worked, your reaction has been most satisfactory. We are ready to ask if you will help us."

"How? And why? Why should we involve ourselves and Earth in something that is no concern of ours?"

Jorgasnovara hesitated, speculating, as if wondering what kind of analysis Cal could comprehend.

"You have had experience during your own recent World War. You saw how the waves of battle washed back and forth over primitive peoples who had little or no comprehension of who was fighting, or to what purpose.

"You saw these primitive peoples sometimes employed or pressed into service by one side or the other. On the islands of your seas they built airfields for you; they sometimes cleared jungles and helped lay airstrips. They had no comprehension of the vast purpose to which they were contributing a meager part, but they helped in a conflict which was ultimately resolved in their favor."

Cal's face had gone white. He half-rose from his seat. "You mean—?"

Jorgasnovara waved him down. "This greater conflict of which I have spoken has existed for hundreds of generations. Your people were barely out of caves when it began. It will not be ended in your generation or mine.

"Its center of origin and the present battle lines are far from your galaxy, far beyond the range of your greatest telescope. The people involved and the principles in dispute are far beyond your powers to comprehend. But we need your help."

"To build an airstrip?"

Jorgasnovara smiled. "These interocitors which you find so interesting are a small item of communication equipment which is used in some of our larger vessels. There are about a score of other, similar devices being made in different parts of the world. They are simple devices, comparable, say, to your pushbuttons. We need you to make some pushbuttons for us."

Cal understood what Ole had meant now. He *did* want to punch somebody in the face. Rage, frustrated and impotent, swirled within him. The insolence of this super-race that would hire Earthmen to make their pushbuttons!

Jorgasnovara saw it and his expression grew cold. "You have a stupid pride that is the greatest hindrance in the progress of your people. Is it of any real importance that there exists a culture to which you can be only makers of pushbuttons? Does that lessen your worth in your own eyes? If it does your values are cheap."

For a moment Cal hated the Engineer. But his rage began to subside, swallowed up by the infinitely greater wisdom that he glimpsed in the man and the culture of Jorgasnovara.

"There is only one question," he said at last. "What is right? Do you have it? Is there any reason we should help you, rather than your enemy, whoever he may be?"

"I think there is," said Jorgasnovara. He slid back a panel in the table top, which Cal had not noticed before. Some kind of instrument panel lay exposed. In a receptacle were several pairs of helmets with cords leading to the panel. Jorgasnovara passed them around the table.

"This is why I brought you three to this base on your moon. You have to see what I am about to show you in order to understand."

They examined the instruments in their hands. Cal noticed a fine mesh network that covered the skull. Fitting over the eyes were a pair of soft opaque pads. They completely blinded him when the helmet was in place.

Jorgasnovara touched a panel of switches and dials and abruptly there was vision. The three of them *felt* that they had been transported across unthinkable vastnesses. There was starry void all about them. They seemed to be moving, and more swiftly than light they approached one star that slowly swelled to a galaxy, its twin spiral arms a pattern of light against the blackness.

The scene shifted and was replaced by the vision of a planet of that galaxy. There were small cities and vast fields of pleasant color, and the world was peopled by creatures not greatly variant from Earthmen. A sense of peace and contentment of mind filled them as they looked upon that scene.

It was midday when the blackness came. A slow blotting out of light that turned the people's faces skyward and froze them with an unnamed terror. The three Earthlings felt that terror as they watched through the instrument of Jorgasnovara. They felt the incalculable evil and death that was in the blackness shrouding the planet.

Time was condensed, and eons became seconds, and they looked upon the world again. This time it was like an anthill in the wake of a flaming torch. Crisped and blackened, everything that represented sentience and growth and living hope had died. Through all time life could never again flourish upon that world.

They could smell death. Destruction and war shrouded them. It seemed more than they could endure. Cal was aware that Ruth had ripped the helmet from her head. He lifted his own and saw her sitting white-faced and trembling.

"Look again," said Jorgasnovara.

Once more they were in space, and their vision encompassed a span of light years. As far as they could see, a line of titanic warships flowed through space beyond the speed of light.

And then there was battle. Like a spark it began and ignited the whole of space. Vast forces that twisted and wove the fabric of space itself engulfed the ships, imprisoning them in webs of impenetrable time and space and turning their crews into screaming things that would live forever.

Cal hurled the set from his head and wiped his sweating face. Ruth was pale and Ole breathed heavily.

"It is possible," said Jorgasnovara slowly, "that the people of your planet would never know that this war had ever raged, regardless of the outcome. You would be of no concern to the enemy. He has higher goals than the conquest of your little world. And my people would never molest you.

"We do not *require* your help, any more than your armies had to have the help of some savage tribe to clear their jungles. You would have won your war. We will win ours.

"But we need you, speaking collectively of all the primitive worlds to whom our emissaries have come. On each of thousands of planets whose people are making whatever items their culture will permit that will be of use to us.

"Some are even building our warships and the mighty generators that warp space about a galaxy. But they do not know to what purpose they are building—only those whom we have commissioned as our agents understand their part in this cosmic effort.

"So that is why I have come to you, Cal Meacham. My predecessors and I have organized the Peace Engineers and carried it on for many decades now. The story I told you was true. Our work spared your planet the devastation of atomic war for many years.

"We have used the products of your greatest men of science. But none have been able to carry on without our direct leadership. We need someone who understands more directly the psychology of Earthmen.

"Will you take charge of our affairs on Earth for the rest of your life?"

Cal had known the question was coming. He had sensed it far ahead of Jorgasnovara's actual voicing of it. Still, it was like a blow that numbed his senses and left him only dimly conscious of the reality about him.

A lifetime of service in a vast effort of war, the whole of which he could never comprehend. He, who had sworn never again to so much as think of an instrument of war, who had hated the scheming and the killing and the designing of scientists for better ways of destroying more of their fellow men. But he thought back to that vision of evil and terror that Jorgasnovara had shown them, and he knew there was only one answer.

"Yes," he said slowly. "I'll help you."

He knew that the things he had seen were true. He knew that Jorgasnovara had not lied, that his people were combating a vast force that would destroy the hope of endless races of sentient life on countless planets.

But that did not assuage his despair.

"When will it ever end?" he said in a voice that was almost a whisper. "Will there ever be a time when sentient beings will not murder their own kind?"

Then he remembered that he had once heard Jorgasnovara thinking that same despairing thought. Their eyes met in a look of common understanding.

"Sometime," the Engineer said. "Sometime there will be an end to the destruction and killing. But come, it is past lunchtime. Let us enjoy a meal together."

It was midnight when the spaceship landed again beside the plant. It paused only long enough for the three to get out of the way of its crushing field and then it vanished into the night sky again.

Cal put his arm about Ruth as they stood there looking up at the moon.

"It didn't happen," said Ole. "I'll swear it didn't."

From somewhere they heard the sound of a car as someone drove in from a late show in Phoenix. All about them the prosaic shadows on the desert and the sounds of night lent unreality to the things that they had seen and heard.

Cal looked up at the stars. He thought of the battle that raged beyond the farthest of them. The light of the suns that illumined that field of battle would not reach Earth for thousands of millennia. Perhaps Earth itself would be cold and dead after those eons had passed. Was such a war any concern of his?

The evil that Jorgasnovara had shown them was timeless. It was the concern of every being in all creation, thought Cal. As long as it existed there would be no absolute freedom for anyone. And his life would be well spent in working with the forces that Jorgasnovara represented.

He took Ruth's hand and started along the walk. "Let's go. It's getting late, and tomorrow we've got to make a lot of—pushbuttons."

— XV —

Two days later Jorgasnovara called Cal from the moon base as he had promised, to give the full story of the group with which Cal had now allied himself. Throughout the morning and well into the afternoon Cal sat before the interocitor letting the flow of thoughts from the Engineer wash through his own mind.

Jorgasnovara belonged to the Llannan Council, an organization of worlds from more than a hundred galaxies. In the Council chambers mutually alien life forms sat to resolve the difficult problems of learning to live together. The greatest problem of all their long history was the one that Jorgasnovara had revealed to Cal, the problem of combating the vast and able enemy who had swept out of the depths of space to conquer all life that stood in its way. There was no telling how many galaxies had been overrun in how many eons of time by that enemy.

The Llanna knew very little of the origin of the creatures they fought. There seemed to be an alliance somewhat like their own between wildly variant members of numerous galaxies. This alliance called itself the Guarra, and it was evident that no one had ever successfully halted its sweep of destruction except the Llannan Council.

A few of the Llannan worlds were inhabited by beings closely resembling Earthmen. Jorgasnovara's own planet was one of these, and from it had been selected the technicians to initiate the work of drawing Earthmen into alliance with the Council.

It was recognized that it would be hopeless to openly invite Earth to participate. The scope of the conflict was too vast. Earth's responsibility was too remote for its people, generally, to grasp the need for participation. It was as Jorgasnovara had said: "Earth is an island, which can be by-passed completely, or temporarily occupied if need be."

In the latter case it would be rocked by the thunder of this mighty intergalactic warfare. But Earthmen, like the islanders of their own seas when Earth's wars swirled about them, had no capacity for understanding the power and depth of the forces involved.

Llannan emissaries and technologists, therefore, had set up manufacturing plants in a score of nations, as they had done on thousands of other worlds which could not participate in open conflict. On each planet they tried to conform to the psychological requirements of the inhabitants. In the case of Earth, they had set up the Peace Engineers ideal, which had attracted Cal.

Jorgasnovara's face was tired as he finished his story over the interocitor. "I don't know whether we have done a very good job or not," he said. "I have often felt that we have not handled this Peace Engineers program as effectively as we might have. It has been very difficult to select any motivation whatever by which we might draw your interest.

"I will be very honest. We do not understand your people. We can't predict what you will do with anything like the degree of accuracy possible among our own. Your irrationalities make it appear as if there is no trustworthiness to be found on your planet, but we know this is not so. We know you have difficulty in understanding yourselves, your own unpredictability, and we have done the best we could to work out a program adapted to it. But I fear that our success has not been exceptional."

"No," said Cal. "When you first came to me with this Peace Engineers ideal I was ready to accept it wholeheartedly, and I am sure that's the case with most of the other engineers. But it was not followed up.

"That was the first thing that really excited our suspicions regarding your organization. The engineers are restless, the whole staff. There needs to be an organization. The psychology of Earthmen requires a fraternal group, meetings, speeches, and slogans. A continual activity along the general theme of Peace Engineers."

"We had something of that nature when we were very small, decades ago. It seemed difficult to continue, and when we grew so much bigger we neglected it, mostly because we didn't know how to handle it properly. Knowing your people, do you think it can be done? Or should the whole idea be dropped and something else supplied to take its place?"

"I don't know," said Cal. "It's difficult working with a false front. Inevitably it blows up in your face. Despite the rigorous tests you gave us, any active organization of that kind will show up crackpots. On the other hand, it can't continue in the half-hearted way it has been conducted so far.

"I'll make a recommendation, if you wish, after I study it further and confer with Ruth and Ole and some of the engineering staff."

"I'll leave it to your judgment," said Jorgasnovara. "I'm going to leave you for a few months, in which you will have time to study the organization and administration.

"Detailed matters will continue to be handled by the Llannan delegates so you will be free. I want you to evaluate the entire program from an Earthman's viewpoint and let me know where we have erred in dealing with people of your psychology."

Jorgasnovara closed his eyes briefly and passed a hand over his lined face. "I have to go to confer with the General Council," he continued. "I am going to try to take a rest, but I fear there will be little time for that.

"You may as well know that the war is going very badly. Our reverses in recent months have been terrible. Production of weapons and equipment must be increased. That will be your main objective, to get a greatly increased production of all the various instruments being manufactured on Earth."

"Could the war be lost?" said Cal.

The Llannan nodded slowly. "It could—but it won't. Civilizations in countless galaxies of the universe are depending on us to see that it is not."

Looking upon the great, tired features of the emissary, Cal felt regret for his doubts about the wisdom of committing himself and Earth's resources to the Llannan battle cause.

Jorgasnovara affected him like that. In the man's presence he understood instinctively what was right and what was wrong. It was only when he was alone with his fears and doubts that questions entered his mind about the propriety of what he had done.

"Do your best," said Jorgasnovara, after a moment's pause. "If any real emergency arises you can call my subordinates here at moon base. Also, the administrators of the other manufacturing plants know of your appointment. When I return I will take you on a tour of all Llannan properties.

"Until then I will say good-by."

Cal smiled wistfully and nodded as the screen of the interocitor went dark. For a long time he continued to sit in the Engineer's office staring at the dark screen and the factories visible in the desert haze beyond the window.

The Llanna were right, he thought. It was beyond the capacity of Earthmen to comprehend the scope of that great intergalactic battle. But he wondered how great was the capacity of the Llanna themselves to understand all that was taking place. Could any sentient mind think in terms of galaxies by the hundreds, of a conflict involving an enemy from beyond the farthest reaches of Earth's telescopes?

And, he thought bitterly, having conquered such vastness in space and time, why did sentient creatures have to devote their energies to conquest and war and destruction?

Could any of them find the answer to that question?

It was almost dusk when his reverie was broken by Ole's approach from the outer office. Ole had spent the last two days investigating his own new duties as director of the interocitor assembly plant.

He entered the office and sat down across from Cal and wiped a hand across his moist face.

"How did it go?" said Cal. "Can you handle the production bugs?"

"The Llannan boys can handle those. They don't need any help from us. Sometimes I wonder why they dragged us into this at all on the engineering level."

"Manpower. They haven't got enough people of their own to do the job. They'll pull out as soon as we're completely ready to take over."

"I'm beginning to wonder if we can handle the labor end of it."

"Why?"

Ole shook his head. "I'm not sure. Probably I'm just worrying about the necessary secrecy of the whole deal—this keeping our own people from knowing where the stuff is going.

"But it seemed like there was something more in the plant today as I walked through it. Maybe it's because I've been away from interocitor assembly for so long that I thought I noticed a difference."

"What kind of a difference?"

"A feeling. You know how it is when you come into a room where people have been quarreling. I can't put a finger on it. It's ugly, like a mutiny. It smells like strike to me."

"Strike? What the devil would they want to strike about?"

Ole shrugged. "What do people ever strike about? Restlessness. A need to express their own importance. We're ripe for it here. They don't know what's going on. It pricks their ego. They can prick back by pulling a walkout.

"I think it's coming, and if it does, this whole thing will be blown wide open. Government officials will be brought into it. It will be impossible to maintain the secrecy of our delivery destination and what we're making here.

"I tell you, Cal, this whole thing has grown too big. It can't be handled the way Jorgasnovara wants to do it. Maybe they can do it that way on most of the other planets where they operate, but not on Earth. Earthmen are too dog-goned nosey about something that even smells like mystery or secrecy."

"Have you talked with the union?" said Cal.

"It hasn't gone that far—yet. I tell you it's just a feeling I've got, but I know it's coming. It's going to blow up in our faces."

"Figure out some kind of production bonus," said Cal, "before they have a chance to complain openly. We hold the upper hand there. We don't have to show a financial profit. The Llanna can pour all the money we need into this project."

"There'll be some other excuse, then," said Ole gloomily. "It won't matter how much money you give them. They just have to strike periodically to show things are still done the democratic way around here, and they're just as good as the next guy."

"It'll stall them a while, and we need that. I've got to get my feet on the ground. I want to take a tour of all the plants with Jorgasnovara, but it might be two months away. Maybe we can figure out a way to handle it after that, but let's try to stall that long."

Cal took a tour through the interocitor plant himself the following day. He walked along the huge assembly lines and stopped to chat with the foremen and the girl assemblers. He visited the engineering section, looking over the shoulders of the draftsmen, checking details with the designers who were striving to meet new specifications on the interocitors and other devices.

By noon he had reached his own conclusions. Ole was unquestionably right. Something unpleasant was in the air. He felt it emanate from the working force as he moved among them. The engineers' discontent over the Peace Engineers setup, he understood, but he should have noticed the atmosphere of the production lines long before. It hadn't built up overnight.

He called a conference with Dr. Warner and Ruth Adams the next morning. Warner was a Llannan, a psychologist among his own race, but he was wholly dependent on Ruth for his understanding of Terrestrian psychology. Even Ruth had not known that fact until after Jorgasnovara's revelation.

Warner had relied wholly on her knowledge and advice in choosing the recruits for the engineering staff, at the same time concealing from her his dependence. Now that she understood fully what her position had been, she felt bewildered and a little helpless at its magnitude.

Cal outlined to them Ole's suspicions and his own feelings about the plant.

"It's almost as if the whole thing is on the verge of breakdown," he said, "just as Jorgasnovara has turned it over to us. At the moment I've got to admit, Dr. Warner, that I don't see how the secrecy of the project can be maintained much longer. When the break comes, the knowledge of what we are doing will spread in every direction."

"I think not," said Dr. Warner. "Take a glance at this, Cal."

He passed forward a sheet of paper. Cal glanced down and began reading. It was a standard resignation form prepared for those leaving Peace Engineers. Cal scanned through it, then looked up with a blank stare on his face. He looked helplessly from Ruth to Warner.

The Llannan psychologist pressed a button at the base of the desk lamp beside him. "Read it again," he said.

Cal glanced down once more. The sudden gap that had appeared in his mind seemed to close with a swift, rushing flow of knowledge.

"What—what did you do?" he said. "What happened to me?"

"Selective, induced amnesia. Presentation of this page for a workman or engineer to sign will wipe from his mind all recollection of the things he has learned and done while here. It has been used quite a number of times so far, with very good success. It is a reverse of the process used in the training manuals. I didn't think you had been shown this before."

"No, I hadn't!" said Cal faintly. The memory of that sudden gap in his mind was appalling. "It's a neat gimmick, but I don't believe it's going to solve our problems if we get a mass strike. You can't line everybody up and flash one of those things in front of his face before he gets away."

"There are other applications of the same principle." Warner smiled without humor. "But you are right. It will not solve the problem of getting the production we need.

"It is all very difficult. Dealing with Earthmen is very difficult. You have an imagination, and an inquisitiveness which we have seldom encountered elsewhere. These are wonderful qualities for the young and growing planet, but they make our dealings with you extremely difficult."

He turned to Ruth. "Do you see any answer to this problem that they suspect is beginning to exist?"

"If I had known the true nature of your work from the beginning," said Ruth, "I would have done many things differently. It will take days of work to see how serious the situation really is. I suspect what the final solution may be, however, and I need not tell you now how drastic it appears."

## — XVI —

It was April when Jorgasnovara turned the Llannan properties over to Cal's supervision. In June, Cal and Ruth were married, and Jorgasnovara returned for his promised instruction tour of all Llannan properties on Earth.

Cal and Ruth laid their plans for the trip to do double duty as a honeymoon as well as a technical orientation tour. But the strain of the responsibilities toward the Llannan Council and toward Earth itself were too great to permit conventional honeymoon gaiety.

Only gradually did the darkness of the shadow under which they had agreed to live become apparent.

As Cal sweated over the delicate problems of the secrecy of the Peace Engineers there continued to unfold vast areas of knowledge which he knew his own people would not encounter for many decades, or even centuries. He felt almost a sense of guilt at possession of the great treasure of knowledge, and at the same time an overwhelming gratitude that it was his good fortune to possess it.

But the purpose of that possession still rankled in his mind. He accepted the righteousness of the Llannan cause; he accepted himself as a warrior mercenary. Only now, however, was there a full awareness of the extent to which he had committed not only himself, but all mankind.

He had not understood this at first. Not until he stood night after night at the great loading docks watching the ships of the Llanna carrying away into space the materials and substance of Earth itself.

The science and technology that had created those instruments belonged to the Llanna, but the substance and the labor belonged to Earth. There was significance in this. The materials that were being hurled into the great conflict were, in a sense, the possession and property of each man of Earth. By dedicating them to the Llannan cause, Cal Meacham knew that he had in effect dedicated each man of Earth to that same cause.

Jorgasnovara came at the end of June, after Cal and Ruth had been married for two weeks. To them, the Engineer looked more tired than before he left, as if his vacation had been devoted to even heavier duties. His massive hands trembled almost visibly as he sat across from them in his office at the plant.

"We've got to have more interocitors," he said. "There are only a dozen worlds on which these instruments can be effectively produced, and Earth is one of the best of these. Production has got to double and triple here, and we've got to find new worlds where they can be made."

"It can't be done here," said Cal. "Not by simply expanding the size of the productive facilities we already have."

Then he told Jorgasnovara about the labor unrest.

"You've got to solve that problem," said the Llannan. "That's your job. That's the thing you have agreed to do."

"Then you will have to let us do it in our own way. Increasing the size of this plant is not the way."

"What is the way?" Jorgasnovara demanded.

"We've figured out what we think is a solution. I'll let Ruth tell it."

"Decentralization. Cybernetic control—those are the answers," said Ruth. "The only ones we can see now."

Jorgasnovara shook his head. "It has taken too long to build this up here. We haven't time. And the plants would not be any less conspicuous if they were operated by negligible manpower."

"We would not be threatened by strikes," said Cal, "which is our immediate problem. That will cost us more time than if we broke up the plant into scattered units. If we did that, we could eventually become as big as you like, but this plant is impossible to operate under the secrecy requirements you have. The question of strike is the thing that will defeat it."

The Llannan Engineer shook his head. "That's among the most curious customs I have found on Earth. I have never found another planet where it operates. Must it be allowed to run its course? Is there no way of preventing it?"

"I have done what I can, but your requirements place too much strain on our peculiar human nature. It's like a reactor building to critical mass."

"Can you explain why?"

"It's fairly simple," Cal said. "Out of necessity a man assigns control of his life to whatever employment he is engaged in. Nine times out of ten it is not the thing he would be doing if he had free choice. When he loses control of himself in such a manner anger builds up. When the accumulated anger of a mass of workmen reaches its critical peak it is expressed. They strike.

"After such a period of dramatization, the anger subsides, they go back to work, and the cycle begins building again. It's virtually inevitable unless suppression of the individual is practised to the point where they cannot strike.

"During most of the history of Earth such suppression has been the case. Only recently has it become possible to strike, and on the whole it is probably a healthy thing—but not conducive to high interocitor production. Where it is unknown, I would guess that there is either no need to work, or complete suppression."

"Do you think it safe to take the tour at this time?" said Jorgasnovara. "Would it be better to stay here and attend to these matters?"

"I've got to become acquainted with the other plants if I'm going to administer them. I think we should leave at once, and gamble on getting back and reaching a solution before it explodes—which it will do if we cannot persuade you to permit drastic changes."

They left by commercial airline the same afternoon in order to avoid tying up a Llannan ship needed in more urgent freight service.

They rushed across the desert, the great wheatlands, and above the smoke-crowned industrial centers. It was all the same and yet so different. No one would suspect it as part of the arsenal of the Guarra-Llannan struggle. It gave Cal a chill as he thought of it. Their efforts were so puny. But multiplied by tens of thousands of other worlds similarly engaged, perhaps it was not so.

On the way to Gander they stopped at a Canadian paper mill. A tiny place which turned out a few tons a day of the special kind of paper used in the memory imprinting textbooks of the Llanna.

In England they visited a textile mill. The purpose of its product was incomprehensible to Cal. Jorgasnovara gave up trying to explain it to him. In France, they saw a die making shop where skilled craftsmen turned out structures like weird, surrealistic sculpture. Jorgasnovara explained that they were actually three dimensional projections of certain intricate equations and were used as control templates in some of the war computers of the Llannan Council.

Swiss instrument shops. Italian ceramic factories. They visited a score of such where workmen busily turned out devices whose purposes were unknown to them. Cal felt stunned by the actual contact with the far-flung enterprise he had agreed to administer. For the first time, he began to understand its vastness, even on Earth.

All the places they saw were comparatively small shops, each one supervised by a Llannan technologist, whom Jorgasnovara wanted to replace as quickly as possible. None of the plants were of the scope of the interocitor plant in Phoenix.

Cal and Ruth were startled when the Llannan set the course of their tour for the African coast. But there they found a small settlement of native craftsmen skillfully turning objects in ivory. The purpose of these, too, was inexplicable to the Earth mind.

And then from Dakar they took a plane to Rio. They were in Peru, at the shops where skilled gold- and silversmiths hammered intricate patterns in the precious metals, and Cal and Ruth wondered why it couldn't have been done a thousand times more efficiently by machine shop and assembly line methods.

There, word from Ole caught up with them. The interocitor plant was closed down. The union had struck.

"This is it," said Cal as he handed the radio message to Jorgasnovara. "I was wrong. We should have stayed. We'll have to catch the next plane."

Jorgasnovara glanced somberly at the message. "Have you an immediate plan?"

"We've told you what we advise. Why didn't you follow the plan of the small European plants when you built the American one?" he said. "Most of them are secure. You won't have trouble there."

"I don't see the difference. We couldn't build them alike. Interocitor production is a big thing. It demands an enormous factory. To break it up would have seemed senseless. Just why are the European plants better?"

"Simply because they're smaller," said Cal. "Somewhere there must be a natural limit of size in which the secrecy of these projects can be maintained. I don't know what that limit may be. Perhaps we can find it mathematically. It's what we've got to do.

"We must manufacture parts in decentralized locations, ship them to one assembly plant controlled cybernetically by a very few employees on the engineer level."

Jorgasnovara continued to shake his head. "No. It would mean starting the entire project over again. We haven't the time for that in this critical stage."

On arriving in Phoenix, they found the pattern of the strike was a familiar one. Ole had been forced to discharge an obviously incompetent assembler. The union seized upon this opportunity they had long awaited.

The same afternoon they arrived, they met with the union representatives in Cal's office. Cushman, the shop steward, was a squat, defiant little man who reminded Cal very much of a bantam rooster. Biggers, the union negotiator, on the other hand, was tall and suave, and needed only a Homburg to complete his diplomatic bearing.

"You've got to put Smithers back on," said Cushman bluntly as he sat down across the desk from Cal, "or we don't go back. That's final."

"I understand the complaint," said Cal, "was that Smithers was unable to perform the assembly operation assigned to him. Our contract with your union clearly states that the required level of competence shall exist in an employee or he shall not be retained."

"You switched jobs on Smithers," said Cushman. "He was doing all right as a screw and nut man which was what you hired him for. Then you switched him to soldering operations. They've been laying for him for weeks at the plant. I've seen it. When they couldn't get anything else on him, his assignment was switched. We won't stand for it."

Cal sighed. "How about this, Ole?"

Ole shrugged and spread his hands in resignation. "We changed the fastening operation on a sub-assembly and soldering lugs were substituted for previous nut and bolt fastenings. Smithers' old assembly operation never existed. We assigned him the new one. He couldn't tell a soldering iron from a burned out cigar stub. He held up the entire assembly line. We had to let him go."

"It was a deliberate trick," said Cushman. "We won't stand for it, I tell you. We're here to defend the rights of this boy, and we don't go back to work until he's back on."

Biggers cleared his throat lightly and spoke for the first time. "It would certainly seem, gentlemen, that some sort of compromise could be reached. It may well be that the—ah—intellectual qualifications of Mr. Smithers are somewhat limited. That, I think, however, should not prevent him from achieving full and honest employment. There must be numerous menial tasks which he could adequately perform."

"They are already being performed," snapped Cal. "Our janitorial force is filled with union men, and we have no position with any standard of competency lower than that of an assembler. If Smithers can't handle a soldering iron he'd better find a location somewhere on the end of a shovel."

"Then it appears that we shall have to resort to—ah—mediation," said Biggers. "And, of course, in the meantime we shall be obliged to picket."

Cal looked steadily at the two men without speaking. He wondered what would happen if he told them about the conflict being fought across a few hundred million light years of space. How would they react to the information that the interocitors were contributing to that cosmic struggle?

They wouldn't understand it, of course. They'd laugh in his face. And it was obvious that the Llanna had been wise in one regard, not coming into the open and inviting Earth to contribute.

There were too many little fires to be kept burning here. Ones like this. He wondered what parallel might exist between the little struggle here and the bigger one out in space. Was life so constituted that its common denominator from one end of eternity to the other was to strive with other life?

"Picket all you like," said Cal. "We may not open the plant again at all."

Jorgasnovara was not at the conference, considering it beyond the scope of his own ability to comprehend the wrangle over labor details. While Ruth, Ole, and Dr. Warner remained to try working out some basis for mediation, Cal went to report personally to Jorgasnovara.

He found the Engineer seated at his desk, his head bowed in his hands. The interocitor at the side of the room was activated, but its screen was blank.

He looked up slowly as Cal entered. The deep set eyes gave a momentary frightening impression of being burned out. Then he rubbed them vigorously and straightened in the chair.

"I'm glad you came," he said. "I've just talked with our moon base."

"What is it?"

Jorgasnovara hesitated, glancing towards the huge rolls of star charts that could be unfolded against one wall. "I hardly know how to tell you this," he said slowly. "I hadn't supposed that it would happen."

He walked over to the wall and unrolled one of the great charts, spreading it to cover the entire wall and fastening it at the opposite corner.

His finger traced along a thick red line that ran in a jagged diagonal across the chart. "This is a picture of a billion light years of space. Here is the present battle line. The report I have just received indicates that the entire lower quarter of the line has collapsed."

With colored chalk he drew a new line to show the change. "Here," he said. "Here is your galaxy."

Cal's breath sucked in. He stared at the little white dot almost at the bottom of the chart, and at the jagged red line that was like a trail of blood across it.

"We had not foreseen this development," said Jorgasnovara. "The entire effort of the enemy has been on the opposite end of the line. You must understand that this is not merely a line but represents a plane in three dimensional space. The whole Guarra effort has been to extend that plane upward on the chart. Now that effort has been shifted and he is sweeping inward on the lower end. Sweeping toward this galaxy in which you Earthmen live."

## — XVII —

"What does it mean for Earth?" said Cal in a tight voice. "Can the Llannan Council hold that line?"

"I think so. We're shifting forces to meet the threat. Somehow we should have been able to predict this. You can't fight a war you can't predict—" His head shook in dismay.

Cal ignored the question that surged in his mind—how could you predict war at all? He was staring again at the narrow gap between the battle line and his own galaxy.

"The line is important," Jorgasnovara went on. "The Guarra are only a few hundred light years from our largest engine factory. We cannot permit such a position to fall."

He rolled the chart back again. "But it is serious," he said. "Very serious. Every production center has to be called upon to make increased output. I tell you this not to frighten you with a threat to Earth—which I think is remote as ever—but to impress upon you the urgency of our needs.

"Tell me. What was the solution arrived at with the union?"

"There was no solution," said Cal. "And there can't be. We've got to change our program regardless of how urgent the need for production is. As a matter of fact, urgency is all the more reason for changing."

Jorgasnovara turned away and faced the window toward the main plant building. Cal could see his head was moving slowly in a negative gesture.

"No," the Llannan said, "I will not permit that to be done in spite of what has happened. There have to be other answers. In a sense, our work here is expendable. If it becomes impossible to hold the present battle line in some future time we can always retreat and find another civilization to do the work we have chosen yours to do.

"But at this precise moment in time continued production is urgent. We will continue it along present lines until it collapses of its own weight—if that is inevitable.

"Elsewhere, other Engineers will already be setting up new plants on new worlds in case of our withdrawal here. You will please go ahead as the program has been outlined."

Expendable.

The word chilled Cal. He thought of green jungle islands during the war, native villages smashed and people driven aside only to be ignored in pain and misery when the tide of battle swept past.

One thing Jorgasnovara had never understood was the tragic magnitude of the decision that had changed Cal Meacham from a pacifist to a war maker, but if that decision could not be recognized for what it was by the Llannan it had better not have been made.

Cal faced Jorgasnovara, his voice shaking as he spoke. "I'll manage the project in the manner I consider necessary, or not at all. I know my own people, and what they will do."

For a moment the two stood looking silently at each other. Cal felt an intimation of the terrible power latent behind the Engineer's eyes, and wondered if that power were going to be turned against him.

Jorgasnovara shifted his weight. He stepped toward Cal. "We can compromise," he said gently. "I chose you because I knew you had the strength and the ability to tell us what we need to know. We will begin the process of building up the diffused assembly centers as you have suggested, but let us not close down here until they are completed and in operation. Do you think that will be satisfactory?"

"It won't be. Every minute that this plant is in operation we are running risks of exposure."

"We'll take it. In the meantime, the other half of the program will get under way."

"And you will have to get some new boys to take over when Ruth and Ole and I are doing a ten year stretch for un-American activities."

"I don't understand."

"Skip it. I've got to run down with my hat in my hand and ask the union boys to please go back to their jobs."

It was late, and he was not able to find Biggers or Cushman that day. He thought afterwards that he might have been able to do it if he had not given way to his feelings of frustration in the face of Jorgasnovara's conflicting demands. He should have exerted himself to run them down, to get the plant in operation to avoid losing a day's production.

But he did not.

At four o'clock the next morning he was awakened by a call from the plant. It was Peterson, the temporary watchman, coming on at change of shifts. There was the sound of tears and terror in his voice.

"They wrecked the place, Mr. Meacham," he bawled. "They wrecked the place!"

"What are you talking about?"

"The strikers! They wrecked the place. George must have been drugged. He didn't hear a thing."

Cal's mind seemed to wait in a condition of stasis while his body went through the mechanical motions of donning his clothes.

Maybe it's the way it should be, he thought. We'll let them get away with it. We'll let them go, and they'll be too scared to talk. And Jorgasnovara will have to do things the right way.

He called Ole, who met him and Ruth at the main gate.

When they arrived, there was no one there except the custodial employees, and the plant was mostly dark. He was glad for that. He wanted this quiet as yet.

Peterson, a conscientious old man, let them in at the side door. His hand trembled so greatly he could scarcely manipulate the lock.

"They may still be around the plant," he said nervously. "You shouldn't have come without the police, Mr. Meacham."

"I don't think they'll do us any harm," said Cal. "And they probably beat it long ago. You keep watch at the door. Don't let anyone else in until I give the word. We'll take a look."

The three passed on into the corridor leading to the main assembly room. The extent of the damage was obvious. It was not merely the overturning of furniture and scattering of parts that could have been restored with comparative ease. At each station along the assembly line all valuable and some almost irreplaceable metering and test equipment had been methodically smashed.

Cal marched at a slow pace the full length of the assembly line, Ruth at his side. Ole paused here and there, poking into the shards of shattered equipment, then hurrying to catch up with Cal and Ruth, stopping once more to investigate another station of disaster like a frightened ant whose tunnels have been destroyed by a boy with a stick.

In an adjoining wing of the building they examined the screen rooms of the test department. Here the damage was even greater. The complex instruments required to make final tests of the interocitor assemblies were smashed beyond repair.

"You could hardly ask for a more thorough job," said Cal bitterly. "We ought to invite all the strikers through here to take a look. Let them have a piece for a souvenir. It ought to make them feel very good."

"Don't blame the union," said Ruth. "They don't support this kind of thing. It's the crackpot morons who get in that are responsible for this."

"The union is responsible!" said Cal. "It's responsible because it admits and upholds and goes on strike in behalf of the crackpots and morons. Each individual member of the organization is responsible for this as long as he votes and strikes in support of a sub-normal moron we need to remove in order to run a factory. There's no way on Earth they can escape that responsibility."

Ole joined them abruptly. "What do you suppose Jorgasnovara will do now? Do you think he'll make us rebuild this place or go ahead with the dispersal?"

"It would be insane to rebuild here," said Cal. "If he insists on that I'm through. The raw part of this whole deal is that we can't publicly or legally lay the blame on the union. All we can do is take it. If we tried to sue them for damages that would blow the whole enterprise wide open.

"The only satisfaction possible would be the flattening of Biggers' nose, but probably we'd better not allow ourselves even that small pleasure. At least I think we have a club we can hold over the union's head that may be even better than a punch in the nose."

He went into the office and put in a call for Biggers and Cushman. They showed up within a half hour and Cal led them without warning into the assembly room.

The two union men stared with mouths agape, and Biggers paled so genuinely that Cal was almost disturbed about their guilt until he realized that these two were professionals. Undoubtedly they had expected this call and were prepared to act their parts.

"It's a good job your goon squad did," he said. "So good that this plant simply isn't going to run any more."

"Our boys never done nothing like this!" Cushman said. "What do you think we are—a bunch of lousy Red saboteurs? You try to hang this one on us, and we'll really show you what we can do. As a matter of fact, I'll bet you arranged this yourself just to lay it on the union."

Biggers turned more calmly to Cal. "I assure you, Mr. Meacham, our men had nothing to do with the affair. I am sure that, in view of the high priority secrecy of your project, there are other explanations. Communist sabotage, as my companion suggested, is the most likely. We shall do all we can to assist you in running down the culprits."

"Look," said Cal. "We know who did this and we know why it was done. We're taking this plant out of production completely and making substitute assembly by cybernetic techniques. That means we don't intend to have anything to do with your union now or ever. If you try to molest or organize one of our plants again a complete record of this sabotage and a suit for full damages will be thrown into court.

"We'd do it now, except that it would be of no value to us except as an act of revenge, and we are not interested in that. You could not repay the monetary damage, and nothing would be accomplished by trying to avenge ourselves on you. What we do have is a good thick club, and we'll let you have it if your union ever approaches one of our plants again."

"We won't stand for it," said Biggers. "You can't smear our record that way. We want it cleared—now! This is blackmail."

Ole grunted harshly and swept a hand over the wreckage. "Blackmail, the man says!"

Biggers and Cushman left without further argument, but with a promise to see Cal later.

"We'll never see those birds again," Cal prophesied. "I'll bet they're glad to get off so easy."

"I don't think they did it," said Ruth quietly. "I think they were honestly as shocked as we were when they came in."

"I suppose you're going to tell me now that it's some subtle Llannan scheme of Jorgasnovara's," Cal snapped irritably.

"No, I just don't think the union did. I've studied human beings long enough to know genuine surprise when I see it. I don't know who did this, but we may be very greatly surprised when we find out."

Jorgasnovara expected to leave within a short time, and was preparing his office for his final departure when Cal entered with news of the disaster.

"The plant's useless," he said. "There's no point at all in rebuilding here. I told the union that we would not reopen."

Jorgasnovara sat unmoving. His massive arms spread the width of the broad desk clenching each side with white knuckled hands.

"It isn't possible, is it," he said slowly, "that you had something to do with the arrangement of this in order to assure the carrying out of your program rather than mine?"

Cal continued to look at him without changing expression or offering to speak.

"I just wanted to make sure," said Jorgasnovara. "I don't understand Earthmen very well. This destruction—it's the work of an enemy, not of members of your own kind."

"The enemy out there—" Cal nodded to the war charts, "—that is no different. Life fighting life—it's no more understandable than this stupid act of the union."

"Perhaps you're right." Jorgasnovara rose. "I can't give you an immediate answer. I'll have to consult with my superiors for further instructions. Let me call you later in the day."

Cal nodded agreement and left the offices. Suddenly, outside the door, he realized that there was nowhere to go. There was no factory to be run. There were no interocitors to be made.

He returned to his own office and called Ruth and Ole. "School's out, kids," he said. "Let's make it a holiday."

It was an insane thing, but they were all just a little insane, he thought. You don't work and sleep with an intergalactic conflict and remain entirely sane.

They gathered picnic things and set out along one of the desert roads. Recent spring rains had sent long dormant flowers bursting from the desert floor. The wasteland was a garden as far as they could see.

At the edge of a low hill they gathered dry cactus and added packing case lumber they had brought from the plant. Within a few minutes the comforting sizzle of frying steaks merged with the desert silence. Ruth sat on a rock, her knees drawn up.

"It would be easy to forget all about Jorgasnovara, and all his Llannan Council now," she said.

"Are you suggesting we do that?" said Ole.

"I don't know whether I am or not. It's just that there's no end to it. Anything else that people do has a logical and reasonable end either in their own lifetime or they can pass it on to their children, but this—There's nothing to end it, and no goal to pass on with assurance of its being achieved. Everything connected with it seems so purposeless and endless."

"Anything connected with war," said Cal, "is always useless except at the very moment you are defending your own life. You never know quite what it's all about until that moment comes. And when it does, you wish you could go back a year, a decade, a century maybe and kill not merely the one who attacks you but the blunderers who brought you to that moment."

"That sounds a lot different from the Cal Meacham of some months ago," said Ole.

Cal shook his head. "No. It's the same one. I knew such moments during the war. I'm just convinced that I've been brought to such a moment again, and I wish with all my heart that I could go back a century or a millenium and face the ones who have brought it."

At that moment they were interrupted by the alarm of the portable set in the car. It was Jorgasnovara.

"Please return to my office as soon as possible," he said. "I have contacted the Planning Committee for Earth. They have given a decision on the present matter. In addition, they wish to know what your feelings are regarding the possibility of leaving Earth and taking up residence in the same work on a similar planet in another solar system."

## — XVIII —

The three of them were almost mute on the trip back to the plant. It was not until they were again in the office that Ruth burst out, "Another planet! Why?"

"There's nothing definite yet," said Jorgasnovara. "But the Committee is seriously considering the possibility of transferring the whole project to a more suitable location in case of necessity.

"I have recommended to them that if such should be necessary you three would be very desirable to continue with the project, if you would consider it."

"You can't ask for an answer to that," said Cal, "until the time comes absolutely and definitely. Why should they consider removal of operations from Earth, anyway?"

"The Committee is disturbed by this strike situation. It is something they never anticipated. They understood the customs of your people, but it was supposed that your administration could see that such an emergency did not arise, particularly since you are authorized for unlimited use of funds, and that appeared to be the cause of strikes."

Cal knew that his face was deepening in color and he tried to keep his breath from coming faster in rage. "I've told you before that money is the last thing that men strike for. And I warned you that it was coming long before it did. My only error was in estimating the time. But if my warnings had been given attention, we might have been able to prevent the whole thing.

"But what about the program now? Are we to go ahead?"

Jorgasnovara shook his head. "The Committee has reversed my decision to build decentralized plants to run parallel to this one. You might suppose that they would abandon this one completely. The answer is no.

"They demand restoration of the present plant. Their computers show this can be done in less than sixty percent of the time required to get your plan for dispersed centers into operation."

"Then I refuse to have any more to do with it," flared Cal. "I was supposed to administer this program, and it turns out that the Llannan Council believes it knows more about Earthmen than we do ourselves. You see the results! They can continue running it."

He stalked out of the office and returned to his own. There was for a moment a tremendous sense of freedom that he had not known since first hearing of the Peace Engineers. He gave a short laugh of disgust as he thought of the starry-eyed wonder with which they had fished him in. Supermen—who didn't have sense enough to come in out of the rain.

But suddenly he stopped laughing. That was right. They *were* supermen, from a technological standpoint. And they *didn't* know enough to come in out of the rain, from a psychological standpoint. Why, he wondered? What was lacking that made them unable to understand what was necessary in dealing properly with Earthmen? The organization had been around for a couple of hundred years, Jorgasnovara said. And they had learned so little!

He tried to make the first move to gather his papers and personal belongings, but he continued to sit there, his hands motionless on the desk top as he considered the imponderable behavior of the Llanna.

How did the Llannan Council manage to keep tens of thousands of manufacturing plants in line with such tactics as these? He didn't know, but maybe it was important to find out—to find out this and a good number of other things about the Llanna.

He glanced down at the drawers which he ought to be emptying. He wasn't going to empty them, he thought. The Llannan Council actually needed much more help than he had supposed—more than they even realized themselves! And he had committed himself to their aid as long as the Guarra legions were rampant in the depths of space.

At that moment the door opened and Ruth walked in. "Over your mad?" she said casually.

Cal permitted a wry grin. "Yeah, I guess so. What did he say?"

"He was pretty upset, but I told him you didn't mean it. I was surprised at you. I thought you had discovered a long time ago that there was no walking out on this."

"I just discovered it now."

"Good. Then we won't have any more nonsense like this. Jorgasnovara says that a shipment of replacement equipment for the plant will be on its way from the sub-storage base serving this area. It should be ready for the beginning of installation tomorrow."

He spent the remainder of the day with Ole supervising the removal of debris and making ready for re-installation. Contacting the union, he re-established relations with them—to the point of backing down on the accusations he had made.

This enabled him to get a few key men back on the job that afternoon.

Standard Earth equipment was ordered by wire and flown in from distant parts of the country. Most of these arrived by the next morning. The Llannan ship docked during the night and deposited its load of emergency replacement parts so that by the following afternoon the plant was stocked with many of the necessary components to restore operation.

When quitting time came that day, Ruth was with Cal surveying the stacks of crates and the long assembly lines now cleared of wreckage and waiting for installation of the complex test and assembly tools.

"Suppose it happens again," said Ruth quietly.

Cal jerked his head to look at her. "Suppose what happens again? You think those crazy union goons would be dumb enough to break in here again?"

"So you still think it was the union?"

"Who else?"

"I don't know. All I know is the way Biggers and Cushman looked when they first saw the wreckage. They understood who would get the blame."

"You bet they did!"

"But if the union didn't do it, it's liable to happen again." She glanced at the stacks of crates whose value was undetermined in Earth figures, but which they knew were worth more than a couple of million dollars at best.

"It might even happen tonight with all this brand new equipment standing around inviting trouble."

"There'll be guards, as usual."

"Let's you and I stand watch in the plant tonight," said Ruth, "to guard the guards, as it were."

"That's the craziest idea I've heard of since I first met an interocitor," said Cal.

"Just for the heck of it, huh?"

He spread his hands helplessly.

"I'll make some sandwiches and sneak them into the office in a brief case and we'll just stay after hours. Set up an interocitor somewhere in the plant so that it can be energized and we can pick up the thoughts of whoever is down there."

"It should be highly entertaining to learn what mice think about in the middle of the night," said Cal.

With grumbling reluctance he agreed to humor Ruth and spend the night in the plant. He prepared to do some work at his desk until Ruth reminded him that they shouldn't show a light. Then he reclined full length on his back on the carpeted floor and stared up into the blackness of the ceiling shadows.

Ruth sat by the window. The interocitor headpiece partially covered her ears.

"I wish I knew what the devil you expect to find," Cal muttered repeatedly.

"I wish I did, too."

It was futile trying to get any other kind of answer out of her. Cal shut his eyes while he worried over the problem of how to get the dispersed facilities constructed over the heads of the Llanna.

As the hours passed, Ruth glanced repeatedly at the dial of her watch which glowed faintly in the dim light of a waning moon. She wondered if it had been a fool's hunch, after all. There was no reason to believe the sabotage would be repeated on this particular night. But there were other nights, she thought philosophically—

Of course, she would have to do any further watching alone. Cal would stand for no more nonsense of this kind. But she felt certain the attack would come again, and when it did they ought to be prepared to find the source of it.

It was just after midnight when the first alien whispering touched her senses. She had to stop an instant and think what it was that caught her attention.

"Cal," she whispered. "Cal!"

"Huh? Yeah—what is it?" He yawned in audible sleepiness.

"Cal—there aren't any ships due from the moon tonight, are there?"

"No. They brought everything belonging to this batch in the shipment last night. Why?"

"I just saw a shadow out there. It passed over us. Just a little shadow."

"Probably some fool night owl looking for the airport," he muttered in disgust. "Let's go home and go to bed, Ruth. We've got work to do tomorrow."

"No, wait. Did you hear that?"

He sat up sharply and jumped to his feet, suddenly wide awake and alert. There had been just the faintest tremor pass through the building. Something so far below the threshold of sound that it was totally inaudible. There had been a distant impact that affected some deep sense besides that of hearing.

"It landed on the roof," whispered Ruth. "We can get up there if we hurry, and see who gets out."

Cal's hand stopped her impulsive flight toward the door. "This doesn't make sense. I don't think anybody landed on the roof."

But he knew it wasn't true.

"Let's try the interocitor." He stepped to the controls that Ruth had temporarily abandoned. He energized the instrument he had left down in the plant near the assembly lines.

Standing in the darkness with the headpieces on, they slowly became aware of faint impulses and images like some strange, other-world thoughts. Ruth was suddenly trembling as if hit by an emotional blast she could not withstand. Cal felt the back of his neck turn cold. He swore softly.

"Cal, what is it?" Ruth murmured.

"What kind of men are they?"

"That's it! They're not men—"

They attuned their thoughts to the flowing mental waves that came through the interocitor, but there was nothing recognizable in terms of human words or ideas. It was a flowing stream of sheer evil.

Ruth threw off the headpiece. "I can't stand that anymore. What are we going to do, Cal?"

He turned up the illumination of the instrument, but there were only shapeless shadows visible in the darkened plant. Abruptly there was a faint crunching sound followed by the clatter of metal and glass.

"They're smashing things," said Ruth. "But how can they keep the noise so muffled?"

"I don't know. You stay here. I'm going to try to make it down to the watchman's locker. Mac has a gun around there somewhere. If I'm not back in twenty minutes call Ole to bring help."

"No, I'm going with you."

"You stay here!" Cal ordered with sudden hardness in his voice. "This is no two-bit movie drama. We've got to find out who they are, and I need your help up here."

In darkness, Cal moved into the corridor. He felt his way along the wall until he reached the stairway leading to the main assembly floor below. Moving down slowly he could hear more plainly the sounds of destruction as cases were ripped open and their contents smashed.

Then he was aware of an odor that filled him with sudden nausea. He stifled a sudden choking agony in his throat. He grabbed a handkerchief and wadded it against his nose, cautiously drawing short breaths through it.

The smell was like that of some age-old jungle where slimy things crept and crawled in darkness. He knew of no source within the plant that could have released such a gas upon being smashed. Momentarily, he wondered if the saboteurs had released some anesthetic to protect themselves while they worked. But it didn't have that kind of effect. It was merely nauseating.

Holding his breath for a large part of the time and breathing cautiously, he gained a degree of conditioning towards the odor. At last he reached the watchman's closet. He wondered what had become of the men on duty, if the invaders had killed them—

He did not think the union would stoop to murder. But was he sure now that these were union goons? They weren't, he told himself. He didn't know who or what they were, but they represented nothing that he had ever experienced before in his life.

He found the gun he was looking for and checked it by touch. He wet his handkerchief in the washbowl in the small room and applied it again to his nose as he moved back toward the assembly room. He carried a large flashlight in one coat pocket and the gun in the other, moving slowly along by finger touch.

The noise of demolition increased. He moved forward even more cautiously as he approached it, trying to orient the sound by ear. Then he had it placed.

They were working in one of the screen rooms where a few pieces had been uncrated and tentatively set up. Not a ray of light shone anywhere. They were working somehow in complete darkness, as if they could see without light.

But that was fantastic. Yet if it were true, the darkness was no protection at all to him—

He tried to keep behind the protection of the assembly line storage cabinets, waiting for the sound of the saboteurs to emerge from the screen room. He had grown accustomed to the nauseous odor so that he could abandon the handkerchief now as long as he confined his breath to short intakes.

With one hand he held the flashlight in front of him and the gun in the other. A tremor of apprehension went through him as a sound of shuffling, dragging feet came near the door and passed out of the screen room. He flicked the switch on the light.

He knew he must have screamed aloud at the sight. Two figures faced him, clad in suits that completely covered them from head to foot. The upper half was semi-transparent, and through the covering he could see grotesque features that he knew belonged nowhere upon Earth.

They were green and minutely scaly and spoke of alien swamp lands. Tiny puffs of greenish atmosphere with the overpowering odor exuded from the vents in the suits.

Cal raised the gun to fire. He watched it come up as if observing a distant, slow motion film. He saw his finger begin to squeeze the trigger. In the instant of doing so, a crushing blow smashed against his skull from behind.

His body twisted half around and he collapsed against the floor. His last vision was of the two alien creatures looking with a kind of unbelievable satisfaction beyond him to one who stood behind.

# — XIX —

The light made a blinding sheet of the green walls that surrounded him. He closed his eyes against its hurt. He guessed vaguely that he was in the single hospital room of the plant dispensary.

The people around him would be Ruth and Ole and Jorgasnovara. Maybe Doc Howard and one of the nurses, but he was too tired to open his eyes again to make sure.

He felt cool hands touching his own and resting against his cheek. That would be Ruth. He smiled a little in appreciation of her presence.

"He's coming around now," he heard someone say. It was Doc Howard, all right. "We'd better go out now, and leave him alone."

Cal opened his eyes again and moved a hand.

"No," he murmured. "No."

Ruth glanced at the Doctor, who shrugged permission and left her with Cal. Ole and Jorgasnovara remained for a moment.

"What happened?" said Ole. "Can you tell us what happened to you?"

What had happened? Cal thought dully. He'd given up the ideals he had once lived by because he became convinced he no longer lived in a world where they applied. Now he was face to face with the thing he had undertaken to combat. He turned to Jorgasnovara, his lips silent, but his eyes seeking confirmation.

The Llannan engineer nodded as if understanding Cal's unspoken question.

"Yes, they were Guarra agents," he said. "We should have suspected from the first. The pattern has occurred elsewhere. What did they look like? Did you get to see?"

Reconstruct all your childhood nightmares, and then you'll know, Cal thought. He tried to picture to Jorgasnovara the moment of horror when he flashed his light on the scaly, suited creatures.

"Suoinard," said Jorgasnovara. "I don't understand why they were picked for this job. Other species among the Guarra are almost identical with Earthmen. Perhaps they are rather desperate to accomplish this particular piece of work."

"What work?" said Cal. "What are they doing?"

"Trying to destroy interocitor production. It's much easier to do it by sending a couple of agents for sabotage than it is to send a fleet to devastate an entire planet."

The words of the Llannan seemed to roll against the walls of the room and echo thunderously in his ears. He tried to shut out the sound and closed his eyes against the light that was too bright again.

He hadn't faced the risk before. He had just imagined that he had. The risk of putting himself and all mankind face to face with an enemy out of space, whose technology could wipe the planet clean of life.

"What will they do, now that we know about them?" said Cal. "They got away, didn't they?"

"Yes—they got away. I don't know what they'll do next. Don't you worry about that. We'll talk about it when the time comes. For the next two or three days Ole and I will continue the work of rebuilding the assembly lines."

They left in a little while, leaving him and Ruth alone. Ruth put her head against his chest, both of her hands clasping one of his.

"We should never have taken it on," she murmured. "It's too big for us. We are like the jungle islanders trying to fight with poisoned arrows against an enemy who has atomic bombs. If those arrows annoy the enemy enough he might blast the whole island out of existence."

"There's no danger." Cal patted her hand. "The Llanna will see to it that the Guarra make no real threat to Earth. They promised that this would be so."

But to him his voice sounded hollow as it echoed from the bare plaster walls.

"They haven't! The Guarra are here—and look what they've done to you," cried Ruth. "Cal, don't you know who it was that struck you?"

"One of the Guarra, of course! There must have been at least three of them. I thought they were all in the screen room, but one must have been waiting for me. They can probably see in the dark—by infra-red, I suppose."

"Cal—I heard them talking through the interocitor. Not all of them were so alien as the ones you saw. I could understand the thoughts of one of them."

He could feel the almost uncontrollable shaking of her body now, and raised her head so that he could look into her eyes. They were wide with terror.

"It was Ole, Cal—! It was Ole Swenberg who struck you!"

Cal half raised his head from the pillow in spite of the pain.

"Ole! You're crazy—Ole and I have known each other since he went to college. How could he be guiding the Guarra agents?"

"He's not only their guide, he *is* a Guarra agent." Ruth's voice was low and she glanced about the bare room as if fearful of being overheard. "I know it's crazy, but I wasn't mistaken. I heard him."

Cal's head sank back on the pillow wearily. "You know you're mistaken, Ruth. How can you insist on such a fantastic thing?"

"I don't know what it all means, but you've got to believe I'm right. Ole's just waiting for a chance to stab you in the back. He meant to kill you. He was disappointed that he didn't succeed. He'll try again."

"The strain of all this has been more than you could take," said Cal gently. "You're believing the impossible. I lived with Ole for months. We swapped ties and shirts and girl friends at college. Go home and get some sleep and then come back and tell me it's a nightmare we've both been having."

"It's a nightmare, but not the kind you have asleep. I'm not going to leave you. I'll sleep on the cot in the first aid room. I'm not going to give Ole a chance again."

She kissed him quickly and fled from the room before he could protest. In a way he was glad. His throat felt too tired to answer. His head seemed to burn from hot fires somewhere deep within it. There was no use arguing with Ruth over this fantastic thing at this time. She would get over it when morning came.

But grey dawn was painful when it came. He was aware of little all that day. He knew that people came in to talk, but he was too tired to talk. His temperature was checked and he was fed, and Ruth sat by the bed and put her hand in his. And this brought back a nightmare where she said something about Ole trying to kill him. He wished he could wake up from it.

During the night he slept well, and on the following morning the nightmare was gone. He awoke with clear vision, and the fuzziness had gone out of his head. Some of the pain remained, but it didn't overshadow everything else now.

He struggled to sit up as dawn of the second morning lighted the room. His head spun and he had to hold it for a moment to dispel the feeling that it was entirely disconnected from his shoulders.

The feeling passed, and he was remembering. He had to see Jorgasnovara. He had to see Ole. He had to find out what was being done about the Guarra agents.

Ruth came in while he was getting his clothes out of the closet.

"Cal! You're not able to get up yet."

"Both willing and able," he said, tottering slightly as he sorted the clothes. "Help me with these things."

They ate breakfast from the meager supplies Ruth had brought to supply her through her own vigil. Cal called Jorgasnovara with word that he was coming over. The Llannan offered to come to him, but Cal insisted he was able to get up.

There was a strange silence about the plant and over the entire desert surroundings as Cal and Ruth walked to the office. There seemed no activity at all in the direction of restoration of the plant.

"It looks like the place is being allowed to die a natural death," Cal muttered.

When they walked into the Engineer's office, Cal felt a sudden shock. Jorgasnovara's bony features seemed even more gaunt, verging on the cadaverous. He looked up from the papers scattered about the desk. There was no smile in the greeting he offered.

"I hope there will be no permanent results of this injury," he said.

Cal slid into a chair. "I'm O.K. I want to know where we go from here. The place looks dead. What goes on?"

For a long time Jorgasnovara simply looked at them, his hands resting on the desk as if in complete resignation. He spoke finally.

"Nothing goes on. We're moving out."

"Out?" Cal's face was blank. "Where—?"

"Out of Earth. Out of this solar system. Out of the galaxy."

For a wild moment Cal had a fleeting vision of two green beings with inhuman expressions upon their faces.

"What do you mean? Tell me what this is all about!"

"Our intelligence reports," said Jorgasnovara very slowly, "show that the Guarra have shifted their line of offense and are moving rapidly towards this solar system with this planet as their specific objective.

"This is the direct result of the failure of their agents to maintain a steady pressure of sabotage upon our production of interocitors. I told you we had seen the pattern before and that they considered it economical warfare to stop the flow of supplies at their source.

"We were unable to predict, however—and the error is wholly ours—that the Guarra would move their line so far in order to attack this source if their sabotage program failed. But they have moved. Therefore, our entire line is moving back. Our personnel and all salvageable equipment are being transferred as rapidly as possible."

"But the Guarra will invade Earth!" Ruth cried. "You've drawn them here and you promised we'd be safe if we helped you. You've got to hold them back!"

The Engineer's face grew even whiter as he spoke again. "This is the decision of the Llannan Council," he said. "It is the result of error in our computations. Believe me, I am sorry. If I had foreseen a thing like this I would have turned down this assignment. I would not have willingly brought this upon you."

"You are sorry! Sorry that you have drawn us into a conflict we can't fight—and then turn your back upon us—!"

"Though I realize it is small comfort for the loss of your home planet," said Jorgasnovara, "I can offer you personal safety. You will be transferred immediately to one of the other worlds suitable for your habitation. My own home planet is one of these. I would welcome you there, though I would not be so stupid as to suppose I could ever compensate for the loss of your own world."

Only dimly, it seemed to Cal later, did he hear Ruth's almost hysterical outburst and Jorgasnovara's repeated sympathy.

So this is where it had led to, he thought. He remembered the long gone day when he first saw the strange bead-like condensers that were the beginning of his aptitude test for Peace Engineers. He wanted to laugh now at that phrase, but there was not left in him either humor or bitterness enough to ridicule those tragic words.

When had it begun? There was no way of knowing. It had been inevitable from the beginning. He had wanted something better for himself, and for all sentient life in the universe. He had been no more than a fish acting on a simple stimulus-response mechanism. The Llanna had only to hold out the brightly colored lure, and he was hooked.

He thought again of Earth, the island Earth, which he had gambled as a base for Llannan activities. And he thought of all those other islands he had seen where striving armies had fought and blasted and left desolation.

"Why?" he asked at last, in the vacuum of silence that had fallen over them. "Why have we been left alone?

"We agreed to assist in this because we thought it was good to support life in the whole universe, wherever it might be. We need not have engaged in the war, you told us. The Guarra would not have come. Now you tell us they will come and the Llanna will make no move in our defense. Why?"

Jorgasnovara spread his hands. "I have told you my personal feeling. There is no answer to 'why,' really. Our war computers say that we should not defend at this point. That is the only answer I can give you. Your world is not a world to those machines. It is only a pinpoint in space.

"I can give you only another day to prepare to leave. By tomorrow night we must have evacuated all we intend to take from Earth. Please be reasonable in the amount of baggage you wish to take with you. You will be allowed an almost unlimited amount within the bounds of prudence. The ship will leave about midnight tomorrow."

Ruth's eyes blazed. "What makes you think we're going?" she demanded. "Do you think we could ever live with ourselves knowing we had betrayed Earth and fled from the thing we had brought upon it? You have said you did not understand Earthmen. You have never spoken a truer statement. When your ship leaves, it will be without us!"

Jorgasnovara's head bowed. "I had supposed that's the way it would be. I will not try to dissuade you, but if you change your mind let me know. You will be welcome to the very last moment."

## — XX —

Ruth's eyes were on a distant vision, as if she were already seeing that death out of space. "What will it be like?" she said. "What will it be like for us here on Earth?"

"If there is no defense it will be as easy and as merciful as any death can be," said Jorgasnovara. "A fleet will circle the Earth, pushing a wave of fire ahead of it. There will be a terrible panic for a few hours and then it will be over. The Guarra are very efficient in this respect. We have seen it many times."

"You said, if there were no defense," said Cal questioningly.

The Engineer nodded. "Any defense near an inhabited planet causes a prolonged agony due to the fields set up by the opposing forces which interact and produce interdimensional spatial strains.

"For this reason we have always tried to establish lines of defense that do not approach inhabited planets. If the Llanna were to defend Earth it would have to be done outside the galaxy."

They left the room after the interview, and went out into the sunlight. The desert heat was oppressive already, a burning reminder of the Guarra doom.

Cal sought the shade at the side of the building as a wave of weakness swept over him.

"We'd better go home," said Ruth, "where you can lie down."

He nodded absently, staring into the distance. He felt caught up in some eternal now of space and time. The world was covered with the dusty sunlight that had existed forever here on this desert. The buildings of the Llanna, new under their dust coating, the mountains beyond the city to the south—all of this was eternal in this moment.

He shifted his weight and started walking and his movement broke that eternal now as he had broken the destiny of all the Earth.

"Where are you going?" said Ruth.

"Ole. I forgot about Ole. We've got to tell him. Maybe he'll want to go with Jorgasnovara."

"No!" cried Ruth. "Don't go near him, please! Won't you believe what I learned about him—"

There was a feeling of dullness—almost of stupidity—in Cal's mind at the doubled burden, which he had almost forgotten, Ruth's accusation of Ole added to the Llannan desertion.

There was something tremendously important at stake in this. He was aware that in these final days there would be only one thing of importance, the trust and fellowship of his own kind. Ole was important to him. Ole's understanding and respect was important. Ruth's accusation irritated him beyond endurance. Rudely, he ignored her.

The housing project was somewhat deserted. Many of the people had gone away for a few days pending settlement of the strike. Here and there a few kids rode tricycles in the dust of the streets, and housewives hung washing in their back yards. And in his mind Cal had a vision of a wave of fire sweeping all of this into blackness and darkness forever—because of him.

Ole's car was in the driveway as they drove up to his place. Through the window they glimpsed him moving rapidly about inside.

"I wonder why he wasn't down to the plant this morning," said Cal. "Maybe Jorgasnovara has already told him."

Then Ole was opening the door. Unfamiliar, tight lines in his face shaped it like a mask. The sight of it was a shock to Cal.

Beyond, the room was littered and upset. Books and suitcases and papers cluttered the chairs and floor.

"You've heard?" said Cal.

Ole nodded. "I'm getting out. You're going with Jorgasnovara, I suppose?"

"If it would do any good we would go along. This way, we haven't any right to."

"I've got a right to!" snapped Ole. Then his tension eased and he spoke more normally. "I thought you'd make that decision, but you've got to come along. Turn it around: what good is it staying behind? You can accomplish nothing by your deaths. Out there we'll have a chance again. We can join the Llannan forces and fight the Guarra as long as we live. That's all there is left to us, but we haven't the right to back down on *that*."

"Revenge is no worthwhile purpose," said Cal, "if it's that and nothing more. With Earth gone, there's nothing for any of us. But you go ahead and do what you think best. I'm not trying to change your mind."

Ole's eyes lowered. He put his hands in his pockets and scuffed a toe against the pile of the rug. He opened his mouth as if to say something and then shut it without speaking.

Ruth glanced about and took a step toward the kitchen door. "It smells as if you have a can of something very badly spoiled out here," she said lightly. But Cal could see that she was trembling. He had to get her out of here before she blurted out some stupid accusation about Ole.

"Refrigerator went haywire," grunted Ole. "It was off a couple of days. I haven't cleaned up everything yet."

He turned to piles of books and journals and made a business of shuffling through them. Ruth moved on through the door to the kitchen.

Cal moved a step closer. He started to ask her to come on out and let Ole finish packing. Then he caught a whiff of the odor Ruth had mentioned. He almost held his breath to keep from inhaling it. To keep from recognizing the associations that poured upon him.

When he moved, his foot made a shuffle on the floor. Ole was faster. He whirled from the books with a gun in his hand.

Cal lurched forward then drew back stunned by the sight of the gun and Ole's distorted face.

"Don't warn her," Ole said, nodding toward the kitchen. "Call her back in here."

Cal was prepared to shout to Ruth to run out the back door, but she was already back in the room facing them.

She screamed at the sight of the gun. "I told you, Cal!"

"Over here together." Ole gestured with the gun.

"Why?" Said Cal evenly. "Just who are you, Ole?"

"Does it make any difference now? If it does, you may know that I am Martolan, chief Guarra agent for Earth."

"Aren't you the Ole Swenberg that went to Central Tech with me?"

"Sure," Ole grinned maliciously. "There has been no mysterious switching of personalities. My entire life has been devoted to evaluating and combating the Llannan program on Earth. We hoped that it would not be necessary to spend our forces in wiping out this civilization of yours because the Llanna had leeched on to it, but their program has gone too far. The actual crisis was our failure to stop interocitor production without resort to sabotage. I did all I could to discourage you; now you will have to suffer the consequences of my failure."

He suddenly raised his voice and snapped a string of guttural sounds in some alien tongue. Immediately, the bedroom door opened behind them and out strode the two creatures Cal had confronted in the plant. With them came the increase of nauseous exudate in the air.

"The boys are a little smelly," said Ole wryly. "I knew you'd recognize it the moment you stepped in. It was too much to hope that Ruth could get it passed off as spoiled food."

"What are you going to do?" said Ruth thinly. "What is to become of us?"

"I'm leaving. Our work is done. You know what I *ought* to do with you." His hand tightened on the gun. "I ought to make sure there is no further risk of your causing me trouble. But actually I can't see any way that you can.

"So I'm going to take just a little risk because I don't want either of you to miss the opportunity of witnessing and experiencing what you have brought to all of Earth by your meddling. I find it very curious that you refuse to go with Jorgasnovara, but I know your people well enough to know you will stand by that decision.

"In there, quickly." He gestured once more with the gun in the direction of the bedroom.

"In the closet there. It's a stout door, and I don't think you'll be able to break through it for several hours, and if you don't break through at all it will be rather sad. You'll probably find there is air enough if you don't expend too much of it trying to break out."

The room was filled with the sickening odor of the two aliens. Ruth gagged and struggled for a clean breath, but Ole pushed her on into the shallow closet. They heard the click of the lock. Ole's footsteps died away, leaving them in silence and darkness except for a narrow crack of light at the bottom of the door.

Ruth was crying now. Cal put his arms about her, but did not try to stop her sobbing. From the other parts of the house, there was the violent sound of Ole's departure, the hasty gathering of belongings and slamming of doors.

And then it was abruptly quiet. Ruth's low sobbing ceased and she stirred in Cal's arms.

"Thanks, darling," she murmured. "I'm sorry I let go—How are we going to get out of here? Can you break the door open?"

Cal patted her arm and released her. He moved to the door and leaned his shoulder hard against it.

"I think I could do it if there was room to get a good shove, but it's hopeless inside this closet. The Llanna didn't put up ordinary sub-division houses when they built this development. These doors are good and the locks are better."

Ruth touched her foot along the bottom of the wall. "This is plaster. Maybe it would be easier to break through that."

"The outside wall of the house is over there," said Cal. "And here is a bunch of shelving in the linen closet of the bathroom, and the other side is tiled. The best way out is probably through the ceiling!"

Ruth helped him make a heap of the remaining clothing and other articles in the room. When he stood on this he could just reach the ceiling with his pocket knife in hand. Rapidly, he twisted the blade against the rough plaster. They shielded their faces against the fine shower that drifted down.

"It'll take you forever," protested Ruth, "if you drill enough holes that way to get through."

"I don't intend to." Cal continued twisting, while his arms began to ache with the awkward exertion. He stopped to rest for a moment.

"I wonder why we didn't suspect Ole before," said Cal. "His efforts to discredit Jorgasnovara when I first came—the breakdown of the plant as soon as he took over. Obviously, he arranged that firing to incite the union. We should have known."

"We couldn't have," said Ruth. "We didn't have the data. He and Jorgasnovara both belong to races of supermen. Either of them could twist us around their fingers. All they need of us is manpower. Otherwise, we're nothing to either of them but chessmen to be won or lost by chance."

"Jorgasnovara isn't that way."

"Personally, no—but his race is of that attitude. We never had a chance."

Cal resumed the slow drilling. At last the blade pierced the plaster board backing and went all the way through to free space in the attic beyond. He made the hole as large as he could with the knife and then lifted the metal clothes pole out of its sockets. He forced this upward against the hole he had made and twisted from side to side.

Chunks of plaster began to fall. Cal withdrew the pole and forced it upward against one edge of the small hole. A sizable chunk of plaster cracked and slid to the floor.

He stood on the pile of articles again and hung on the edge of broken plaster with all his weight. A two foot square broke loose.

"That does it."

With one foot on the doorknob and the other against the back wall of the closet he wedged himself upward until he could draw his body through the hole to the attic.

"Stand on the pile of junk," he called to Ruth. "I can pull you up."

She gave him her hand. In a few moments they were sitting together on the edge of the joists breathing hard and covered with plaster dust. In the sunlight streaming through the ventilation louvres they caught a glimpse of each other and laughed shakily.

After a brief rest, Cal reached over and raised the trap door in the ceiling of the bathroom. He jumped down and helped Ruth through the opening. Silently, they listened for sounds elsewhere in the house, but there were none.

The nauseating odor of the Guarra agents was still present, but fainter than before. The house was a shambles in the wake of Ole's departure, but no one was in it except themselves.

"What shall we do now?" said Ruth. "Do you suppose they have left Earth?"

"If they didn't smash up the interocitor Ole had here we'll call Jorgasnovara. Maybe there's a way to stop them."

They went to the rear bedroom which Ole had used as a study and the interocitor was still there and intact.

Cal adjusted the controls as they put on the head pieces for direct mental communication with the Llannan Engineer. For a moment the machine buzzed with the random noise of its thermionic elements. Then abruptly it cleared, and into the minds of Ruth and Cal there came a desperate cry of extreme agony.

"Cal, help me! Help me—wherever you are!" It was the cry of Jorgasnovara, the Llannan Engineer.

# — XXI —

Almost instantly, upon that frantic cry from the Llannan, Cal understood the thing he had never recognized before. The purpose of the interocitor.

The instrument was not a mere communication device as he had been told. It was a weapon. An incredible weapon by which one mind could reach out and seize another to twist it, guide it, or destroy it.

Instinctively, Cal understood the strength of that terrible weapon as he witnessed its use. It could reach through force fields and armor plate that no radiation engines could destroy. This was the supreme Llannan weapon, and now the Guarra had seized it for their own, and were destroying the Llannan capacity to produce it.

A thousand awry factors suddenly fell into place. He understood the desperate Llannan need of interocitors, the Guarran theft of the instrument and sabotage.

He understood because he felt it. Felt the force of the weapon being directed against Jorgasnovara now by the Guarra agents.

But he was seized with a moment of panic as that cry came from the Llannan. He knew nothing of how to operate the machine as a weapon, and then he looked deeper, penetrating the Engineer's mind, sending out the questions and finding the answers almost as rapidly as if they were his own thoughts.

There were added circuits here, circuits which had not been put in on the assembly line. They had been made on some other world for addition to the Earth-made instruments in order to make these great weapons out of them.

Cal was one with Jorgasnovara, and Ruth joined him. They understood the meanings and operations of those additional circuits. And in the same instant they felt the flood of terrible force being hurled by the Guarra from somewhere out in space.

Cal saw Ruth pale before the onslaught. He motioned her away, but she shook her head and remained to add her strength to that of Cal and Jorgasnovara.

A wave of gratitude swelled from the mind of the Llannan. He poured out instructions directing them to let him guide their concerted attack. They agreed to follow his lead.

Alone, the machine was useless. Powered by the direct impulses of the human mind, it was like a giant amplifier multiplying the telepathic and telekinetic powers a billion fold and hurling them against the enemy.

Cal waded out into the sea of fire, but there had to be more than mere passive resistance to that flood. It had to be turned back and sent upon the Guarra, and he could not force it from him.

"It's not Ole!" Jorgasnovara said savagely.

And Cal understood. He had thought still of the Ole he had known at college, his room mate who had borrowed ties and shirts and girls. He shut out that remembrance and thought of the Ole who would attack from behind, hoping to kill. He understood then what was required to operate the interocitor weapon.

It was powered by the desire of the operator. That desire had to be for the death of the enemy. In Cal and in Ruth that desire had never been present until this moment.

Jorgasnovara helped them. He showed them what Earth would be like when the Guarra came—and for the moment they forgot there was no preventing that coming. He showed the flames sweeping round the world.

"You can't stop that," he reminded them. "But you can stop those who have helped bring it about. Kill them!"

They fled forth on wings of fire. They were aware of the interior of the Guarra ship. Cal understood fully the thing that Ole was, and the aspirations of the alien Guarra mind.

He hurled himself upon his former friend. Ole laughed and a livid flame sprang at Cal, throwing him down with its searing wave. He gasped amid the suffocating fire and for an instant tried to tear himself from the machine.

There was a taunting ease in the effort of Ole. The Guarra trio worked as a team with skills established by experience.

Cal knew it could not be matched. Then there was a new and deeper contact with the mind of the Llannan.

"This is it, Cal and Ruth," said Jorgasnovara quietly. "Follow me closely. Let me lead you, and give me all the strength you have."

Cal had no time to wonder what the Llannan planned. Immediately, his outpouring of force battered down and washed away the wall that the Guarra had built. Cal and Ruth were carried along and added to it with all their beings.

The attack struck with living flame against the vessel in which the aliens moved. Cal had a vision of the interior again. He saw Ole and the scaly creatures. There was a moment's insight into the mind of Ole, and an instant of pity for him who had been his friend for so long. But pity died with that insight. Cal saw that in this moment of death there was no regret in Ole. His purpose had not changed. The purpose of death to all who opposed the Guarra.

The vision cut off, and Cal retreated knowing that somewhere high above the Earth a molten ball of flame plummeted to destruction.

He stood in silence and darkness then, utterly alone in all the universe. At last he opened his eyes and took off the headpiece of the interocitor. Beside him, Ruth was slumped on the floor in exhaustion. Her face was white and bitter as she looked up and slowly removed her own headpiece.

"We've got to get Jorgasnovara," she said. "We've got to see what happened to him."

There had been a separation of the three of them at the moment of the vessel's destruction. Cal turned to the panel and called, but the Llannan made no answer.

Ruth got to her feet. "Come on. We've got to hurry."

They left the house and went out to the car. The landscape about them seemed a dim reality overshadowed by the nightmare through which they had just passed.

They drove between the neat rows of houses again to the administration building. There, they raced up the steps and through the corridor leading to Jorgasnovara's office.

Cal hesitated a moment before the closed door. Ruth brushed past him and twisted the knob impulsively. Against the far wall was mounted the interocitor, and at its base lay the inert figure of the Llannan Engineer.

The massive form was lying prone upon the floor. Cal and Ruth turned him gently over. He was still breathing, but something seemed to have gone out of him, something carrying all but a fraction of his life.

The great cranium seemed even more cadaverous. The skin was waxy on the hand that clutched impulsively at Cal's sleeve.

"Maybe it wasn't worth it," he murmured. "We could have let him get away. But I hated him! I knew that one of them was in our midst, but I didn't know it was Ole until now."

"We've got to get help for you," said Ruth.

Jorgasnovara stopped her with a wave of his hand. "No. There is no help for one who is the victor in such an interocitor contest as I am. One can fight but a single such battle. As in all war, he who wins is also the vanquished."

Cal understood. He had felt it. The very life substance of Jorgasnovara being converted into pure energy and hurled through space to destroy the Guarran spies.

"You have to go, now—" said Jorgasnovara, looking from one to the other of them. "Only you are left to go before the Council and plead for Earth as I intended to do.

"You were right. Earth does not deserve to be left to the mercy of the Guarra. Perhaps I have learned to think too much like an Earthman in the time I have been here. But I had planned to plead with the Council to defend Earth.

"Now I cannot go. Take my papers. Go before the Llanna and show them the things I believed. Tell them I believed that perhaps a war cannot be fought with justice by a machine, after all. That it takes heart, and courage, and faith. These are strange words. They will not wholly understand them, but you can explain. That is the thing you must do—help them understand once again what compassion means, for they have been at war so long in its defense that they scarcely understand it anymore.

"The ship will be here as I promised. I want them to take me back to my home world. I will not be alive when they come. You will have to do this for me, Cal and Ruth. I wish that you—"

The sentence was not finished. Slowly, the great head turned to one side, and Cal felt the life go out of the hand that still held him by the arm.

They stared for a long moment at the dead form before they dared look at each other again. Then they rose from beside the body and went out of the building into the sunlight.

Cal held his wife's hand and looked across the familiar desert. The gray and purple mountains were vague beyond the copper haze in the sky.

It may be the last time, he thought. Maybe this is the last time that we will ever see it, but there is no choice. Jorgasnovara gave them none. Their own decision long ago gave them none.

They saw Warner later in the afternoon to discuss arrangements for leaving and caring for Jorgasnovara's body. The death of his leader seemed to have done something to Warner. It had put a shell about him. A cracked and brittle shell that left Cal with the feeling that the Llannan regretted his whole part in the Terrestrian project.

Packing, that afternoon, was like something done in a dream. They inventoried all their possessions, and estimated all possible needs in the long future and began assembling nearly everything they owned.

At once they saw the futility of trying to prepare for indefinite existence on the unknown world to which they were going.

"We're going to live there, so we'll have to use what is available there. Let's cut this down," said Cal.

They ended by taking a minimum, what they could carry in a half dozen suit cases. When they were through, it was still mid-afternoon, and the ship would not come until midnight. Warner was taking care of the body of Jorgasnovara, and there was nothing of importance left for Cal and Ruth to do.

They went out of the house and over to the plant where they walked through the empty corridors and passed the assembly lines, still half demolished. They encountered only an occasional watchman or maintenance engineer.

The plant would become a great mystery, Cal thought. The salaries of these men would stop, and suddenly there would be found no one at all in authority over the plant. The Government would investigate and its agents would wonder what strange sabotage was brewed here. They would if there were time enough for such wonder before the Guarra legions swept it from the face of the Earth.

He wondered why he kept thinking with such complete certainty that this was going to happen. If he had so completely accepted this in his own mind there was no use going before the Llannan Council. He would have no chance at all to make a plea for Earth.

In the hot afternoon sunlight, he tried to shake that conviction out of him. He tried to let the clean light of the desert burn the infection of that thought from his mind.

Walking beside him, Ruth felt the tensions as he struggled to shed his apprehensions. They were not in her, yet she knew she could not help him. She could not absorb his conviction or drive it out of him.

For herself, she knew that this land was never going to be swept by the Guarra fire. These buildings and these people were not going to vanish in a puff of flame at the whim of the invader. It would not have helped Cal for her to say these things. Yet she knew that this was the way it was going to be. They were going to turn aside the Guarran horde.

She did not know how this was going to come about. She only knew that it was going to be so.

## — XXII —

The spaceship came at midnight. It landed at the same place, at the great doors of the shipping platform, where they had first seen it in all its mystery and grandeur.

As they went aboard this time, Ruth thought of that day in Los Angeles when Cal had said, *"I want to see space."* She wondered what he was thinking now as they were embarking upon this first journey to deep space.

There was no joy in his face, only grim determination. He seemed wholly oblivious to the journey they were about to undertake.

The Commander of the ship welcomed them, and was saddened by the news of Jorgasnovara's death. That news seemed to pervade the whole vessel within moments of its landing and made of it a funeral barge.

As they heard the faint thud of the hatches being sealed, Cal and Ruth sat by the port of their stateroom. They saw the Earth begin its long retreat, without feeling the effects of the vast acceleration. In a matter of minutes, it seemed, the moon swung past their vision and they knew they were beyond its orbit.

Jorgasnovara had never told them clearly where the center of government of the Llannan Council lay. It was a voyage of sixteen Earth days, the Commander later told them. In the chart room he pointed out the great trajectory over which the ship was hurtling at many times the speed of light.

He made no comment on the purpose of their journey. They had presented Jorgasnovara's papers to him as the Engineer had instructed. As the journey progressed, Cal felt that a faint, invisible wall between him and the Llanna was slowly thickening.

Its increasing pressure forced him to attempt a way through it. He cornered Warner in the chart room when they were half way out.

"Why don't any of you believe Ruth and I should try to carry out the mission Jorgasnovara planned?"

Warner's face lost some of the austerity it had held since his leader's death. "We can understand you, and why you would want to do such a thing. It is Jorgasnovara whom we do not understand. He knew the insignificance of Earth in the broad scope of our military plans. Why he should have allowed his sentimentality to overwhelm him in the face of that knowledge is beyond our understanding."

"I'll bet you could understand it if it were your own world that was being overrun," said Ruth with fury in her voice.

"I have seen that very thing," said Warner quietly. "Thirty years ago. I watched while my own planet was burned and our fleet stood helplessly by."

"I'm sorry," said Ruth humbly. "I didn't know."

"We're glad you're with us," said Warner. "We will make a place for you, but we wish you would give up this foolish and vain hope. It can only lead to disappointment and perhaps the establishment of enmity between us if that disappointment is great enough."

"Perhaps," said Cal. "But we have to try."

It gave Cal no overall understanding of the Llannan military problem, but he began to feel an understanding of what it was like to be a people who had been at war all their lives. He could understand just a little how they could be struggling for the survival of good will among sentient creatures of the universe and yet consider the sacrifice of a world as a small thing in itself.

The landing of the vessel was made on Jorgasnovara's home world. It was, as he had told them, a place not unlike Earth. The light of its sun burned down with familiar warmth and color. The grasp of its gravity and the texture of its sod beneath their feet were no different, and the air they breathed might have been blowing through a cool familiar valley upon Earth itself.

They watched the solemn rites that accompanied the chemical dissolution of Jorgasnovara's body and its dispersal into the seas as was customary among his people.

For the first time they realized how high he must have been in the Council of the Llanna, and how revered on his home world. They were called upon time after time to repeat the story of his final struggle with the Guarra agents. It would become a legend to add to the endless annals of heroic deeds accumulated by this people in their long struggle for security.

Warner took it upon himself to act as their host and ambassador, as if recognizing that he had been unnecessarily harsh during the first days of the journey. The day after Jorgasnovara's rites he came to them in the plain quarters that had been assigned to them.

"The papers have been presented to the Council," he said. "They have accepted Jorgasnovara's report, and have agreed to listen to your message."

Cal had already discovered that the governing body of the Llannan worlds was an almost unbelievable thing. The Council was not concentrated on any one planet nor was it composed of any single race.

There were representatives of more than a hundred races. Each met in their own Council chambers on planets of many galaxies. These chambers were linked by the faster than light communications that welded them as closely as if they had met about a single conference table.

Cal understood that he would meet with only a comparatively small sub-council. There was scarcely any problem of sufficient magnitude to demand the attention of the whole Council, but his would be acted upon by the larger body, upon recommendation by the sub-council.

Warner led him through the corridors of the Council building in the center of the city. There, high on an upper floor, he entered the local chambers where a score of representatives of this world were seated about a table.

Overhead, and on panels surrounding them were the intricate communication devices linking them with numerous and similar chambers in other galaxies where the rulers of the Llanna would give brief audience to his plea for Earth.

Those about the table were as man-like as Jorgasnovara had been. For this he was grateful. If he had been among a Council of nightmare creatures like the two Guarra, he could not have endured it, he thought.

The group leader spoke from the head of the table. His voice was kindly as Jorgasnovara's had been, but it carried the same incisive determination, an assurance that his audience would be brief but courteously heard—and decided with a finality from which there would be no appeal.

They waited then for Cal to speak.

"I have asked to come before you," he said slowly, "to make a personal appeal for my planet. You know the nature of that appeal. You have the papers of your agent, Jorgasnovara, before you.

"Through him, you prevailed upon us to cooperate in the manufacture of interocitors and other instruments. Now, through the accident of the Guarra attack, which this assistance drew upon us, you have abandoned us to the enemy.

"I protest this abandonment!"

Cal shifted his eyes about the group. They were listening politely—and with pre-determined decision. He could read it in their faces, the admission that his cause was just, and resignation to its hopelessness.

His voice grew edgy with anger. He checked himself, and went on more deliberately. "I was told by Jorgasnovara that the great cause for which you have sustained this conflict is the preservation of cooperative, sentient life in the universe. I represent two and a half billion members of one species of that life.

"Almost none of them have any knowledge of this attack which is coming. I was led to involve them upon the assurance that Earth lay far beyond the bounds of any Guarran activity. By deception, we were led into cooperation in the initial belief that we were promoting peace. When we discovered it was an effort of war we continued that cooperation in the belief that your goals were righteous and deserved our support.

"Your betrayal of our cooperative effort cannot be overbalanced by ten thousand victories. If you feel no obligation to defend this island Earth against the unexpected Guarran invasion you are not worthy to seek the goal you are fighting for. You are worthy only of defeat, and if you betray my people to the Guarra you are already defeated.

"You do not understand the meaning of your goal. You do not understand that no victory, however great, can compensate for a single betrayal of those who have an investment of trust in you.

"I ask for a defense of my planet Earth by the forces of the Llannan Council!"

Abruptly, Cal finished and returned to his seat. Right and left, about that circle of faces surrounding the table, he saw no politeness now. There was agitation in every face, but he could not read the expressions. There were one or two short whispered conferences, but most of the members were silent and grim.

He sensed the similar results that he had produced on the many other worlds of the Llannan Council. Presently, the evaluations of all of them would be transmitted to the central computer and swiftly integrated into a single final answer.

A small light glowed in the table panel in front of the group leader. He punched at the small keyboard there and his eyes scanned the sheet that appeared. After a long silence, he arose slowly and began speaking.

"Cal Meacham, of Earth, it is a momentous indictment which you bring against the Llannan Council for their interference in the affairs of your world.

"We came to you originally because the interocitor is our prime weapon, and of all the races with which we have contact, yours is one of the best equipped to assist in the production of the weapon. You understand that your production was but a drop of the total we required, but it was to have been increased many fold and become one of our major supply centers. This, the Guarra knew through their agent who infiltrated into the project.

"For your help we are grateful. We wish with all our beings that there might be a way for justice to answer your request. But there is none.

"We have learned by long and very sad experience that war cannot be fought by whim or even by mercy. It can be fought only by cold computation which can predict accurately the outcome of any projected action. We can predict the outcome of a retreat from your section. The defense of Earth cannot be predicted except as a random factor totally unrelated to the final objectives. To send a large force on such a mission would expose it to defeat for a purpose wholly unrelated to the ultimate goal of our military maneuvers.

"We know the emotions with which you accompany this charge against us. To this we must be blind. Perhaps you are right—that we have already lost the goal. We learned long ago that it may have been lost at the very moment when creatures first essayed such a conflict as this one in which we and our ancestors have been engaged. We do not know. We know only that it is to go on, even at the risk of the goals for which it is being fought.

"You do not understand, of course, the military requirements which have led to the decision to abandon your island, Earth. We grant, if you wish it, the privilege of examining our military computers by which these decisions are made. We would grant, even, that if you could better the ultimate plan and show how military expediency could be served by the defense of Earth, that such defense might be undertaken. But we know, of course, that this is an impossibility, and we do not place such a burden upon you.

"All we can say is that your request cannot be granted, Cal Meacham of Earth."

## — XXIII —

He returned to the house where Ruth waited and reported what had happened. She remained as still and silent as a portrait while he told her the words of the group leader.

It was like turning around in the middle of a life and discovering all that had gone before was a dream, she thought.

"There's another answer, somewhere, somehow—" she said. There was movement only of her lips as she continued staring through the window at the distant landscape that might have been of Earth—almost.

"We ought to go back," said Cal. He was staring out the window, too. "If they would take us back, we ought to go. We have no right to stay here."

"What was it they said, Cal—That if you could find a military reason for defending Earth they would do it? That's our answer. You've got to find a military advantage in it for them. A real one—or make one up! It doesn't matter any more!"

She turned suddenly, her eyes blazing. "They tricked us. They lied to us. It doesn't matter any more what we do to them! Find a lie that they will believe—and make them save Earth!"

He watched her slump forward, her hands over her face. He listened to her cry without moving to comfort her.

*You* find a lie—*You*—Even Ruth knew that the responsibility was his. He couldn't put it anywhere else. He tried to think that it was as much the fault of the scores of other engineers and workmen who had fallen for the Peace Engineers deception. But it wasn't. The Guarra had kept them in check, and all the Llannan emissaries. Only when Cal had tried to persuade Jorgasnovara there was one proper way to get the production he wanted had the Guarra taken the steps to attack.

The offer of the Council was a farce, of course. He could not hope to beat their vast computers in thinking out a war plan. If the computers could find no military expediency in defending Earth, he could not. The only grounds were those of mercy and justice. And you couldn't put those into a computer!

He crossed the room and sat down in a deep chair. He closed his eyes and looked down the years ahead of them. There was nothing. The Llanna wouldn't return them to Earth, of course.

"The only thing we can do is volunteer for some kind of assignment to help them carry on," he said. "It's the only way we can hope to make up even a little bit."

She watched his face misshapen by regret. His defeat had taken him completely from her. He was like a hollow man now and would never be anything else if he found no answer.

She felt relief after her tears. She wished that Cal would break, too, and let the dammed up misery flow out of him. But she knew he would not.

"You've got to try what they offered." She approached and sat down beside him. "Maybe it's a wild, foolish chance, but so was this whole trip. They gave you their word. Maybe they would not break it if you could show them *something*."

Later in the day Warner came to see them again. Cal asked about the possibility of going back. Warner shook his head. "You knew this was a one way trip when you started."

"Will you let us visit the computers, as the Council suggested?" asked Ruth.

Warner smiled faintly. "That was an idle suggestion, you understand. There is nothing you could do to alter the general program of the war."

"You'll take us there?" Ruth persisted.

"If that's what you want."

The great building of the military computing engines was one of a multitude on many planets. It housed receptor and transmission units. The computer and library was actually on another planet, but all data and computations were available to each world through similar units as this one.

They went about the many floors of the building. Warner patiently showed them the intricate workings. At first Cal was almost indifferent to those things and Ruth did most of the questioning. But in the central planning room where the final digestion of data was interpreted on the great star charts he took increased interest.

He saw a duplicate of the chart Jorgasnovara had shown him days before. He saw how the plan of action and the battle lines had shifted—closer to his own galaxy. He wondered exactly why the computers had given out the answer that the line should not be held beyond that galaxy. Abruptly, the whole machinery of the computer took on meaning. There *was* something he wanted to know here!

Even if Earth could not be saved, he wanted to know why. He bent over the chart and began an examination of the equations adjacent to it. With the help of the Llannan technician in charge, he began tracing his way through, conversing by means of the interpreting instrument provided for him.

He became oblivious to the presence of Ruth and Warner. Only hours later did he realize what he had done, that Ruth and Warner were no longer with him. In that time, however, he had established close communication with the Llannan technician, Rakopt.

When he reached home he was still preoccupied. Ruth asked, "How much longer is there—?"

"About two weeks." The question irritated him. He was restless during dinner and avoided Ruth's glance. After the meal he arose.

"I'm going down there again for a few hours. You won't mind?"

She shook her head, holding back the questions that were on her lips. She dared not ask if he had found anything.

He was there the next day, and shortly, all his waking hours were being spent at the computer building. He was restless when he came home, and slept fitfully during the night. There was something that Ruth could sense building to the point of detonation within him, but she dared not risk setting it off by asking questions.

The fifth night after his initial visit to the computer, Cal did not get to bed at all when he came home. He slumped in the deep chair by the window that looked out over the sparsely lit city in the night. Ruth put a robe about her and came out to sit by him.

"Can I help?" she said.

He turned as if seeing her for the first time in several days. He smiled wanly. "Time," he said. "If there were time, something might show up. I can see something, but I don't know what it is. Something is wrong with the whole basis of Llannan calculations. I can't put my finger on it. And there's only another week—"

"How about a good sleep, and putting the whole thing out of your mind for one night?"

"No." He leaned his head back and stared up at the ceiling. "There was something that Jorgasnovara was always saying—predictability. He had a phobia about things that were not predictable. On the plant dispersal plan, you remember, he wouldn't take a chance without getting a check on the predictability of its results. Without a crystal ball, he was lost. I've noticed the same thing about the rest of them here. Nobody will so much as spit without being able to predict within three decimal places where they will hit."

He sat up suddenly. "That's it! That's the answer to their whole failure in this war. They've got to throw away their crystal balls! If I could only make them see it—"

"I don't understand—"

He kissed her suddenly and stood up. "Get some sleep, honey. I don't know when I'll be back."

Before he left he put in a call to Rakopt, who agreed to meet him at the computer building.

The computer was attended around the clock, but Rakopt worked days only. The young Llannan technician, however, had become so absorbed by Cal's problem that he hoped almost as much as the Earthman that the problem would be solved. But he had no understanding of how this might be done.

His eyes were eager as he met Cal in the chart room. "Have you got it?" he said.

"If I understand your operations thoroughly enough," said Cal, "the purpose of the computer is chiefly that of prediction."

"Of course," said Rakopt. "That is obvious."

"You predict what the Guarra will do on the basis of their strength, and also what you should do to best counter and attack their forces?"

"Yes."

"But the Guarra also have computers."

Rakopt nodded. "Theirs are very good. It is almost a battle of computers rather than armies. And that is the reason why no non-computable factors are allowed to enter as far as we are able to control them."

"But what do you do to lower your own predictability to the Guarra?" said

Cal. "If they know the logic of your computers, the strength of your forces, and your ultimate goals they know almost exactly what you will do from day to day."

"We try to keep their knowledge of our forces as incomplete as possible," said Rakopt. "What else can we do?"

"Throw away your computers!" said Cal.

Warner was surprised by Cal's request for an immediate audience with the Council again, but he agreed to arrange it. Cal had no sleep that night. He went home to shave for the first time in four days, and to eat and change clothes.

"You come along this time," he said to Ruth. "We've either got it or we haven't."

The Council chamber was filled with an atmosphere of unbelieving expectancy. No one in the room or in any of the galaxy-distant chambers believed that Cal would ask for another appearance. There was unrest mingled with irritation that he should approach them with matters already decided.

"I have studied the history of your wars," he said in beginning. "For a long time you have been engaged in a calculated retreat before the Guarran forces. Retreat is not victory. I know what your long-term goals are, of course, but even though you face your goals you do not approach them by walking backwards.

"From Jorgasnovara I learned the one thing the Llanna demand of themselves and the universe—predictability. You even demand it of your enemies, the Guarra. With your great computers, you determine exactly what a course should be in view of the known forces and objectives.

"And the Guarra do the same. They predict you almost down to the seventeenth decimal place. And you carefully oblige them by carrying forth as expected!"

The group leader interrupted. "If you please, our time is limited."

"All right, then. Here is what you have done: You line yourselves up like sitting ducks with your incredibly accurate predicting computers and the Guarra pick you off at will. For a generation you have operated with a technique in which defeat is inevitable!"

A half dozen Councilors were on their feet. "We have no obligation to endure this nonsense—!"

The group leader motioned for order. "We have promised to hear this out," he reminded them.

"It should have been obvious to you long ago," said Cal, "why you have been in constant retreat."

"The Guarran forces have been measurably greater," said the Councilor on his left. "We have been forced to be prudent with our own resources."

"That is sheer nonsense!" said Cal. "The secret is that the Guarra know how to break the predictability equations. Think about it: You were all ready to set up a major supply point on Earth. At *no* point until the very last did you know that the Guarra were going to attack. Where were your fine computers then?

"I remember the dismay with which Jorgasnovara told me of the shift in the line. I thought he was concerned with Earth, then. Now I know what a blow it was to him to contemplate this surprise move of the Guarra.

"But why did your computers fail to show you that Earth would be attacked if you set up an interocitor center there?"

"There are many factors—" said the group leader.

"But the most important factor is that the Guarra are better computermen than you. They know how to deliberately make themselves unpredictable to your machines. It has happened before. It will happen again as long as you, yourselves, remain so completely predictable.

"Their method is to operate under certain circumstances by a completely random thrust. Such is their strike toward Earth—random. The attack had no predicating factors. Jorgasnovara believed it was due to the failure of the Guarran agents to hold down production without an attack. Such was not true. I felt it was not a valid answer then. I know now that it was not. The Guarra picked Earth as their target at complete random.

"They'll do it again, combining it with brute force attacks against your main fleets, but in the end it will be the random attacks that win—for the Guarra."

The Councilors were silent, sitting as if sudden recognition of a long dreaded ghost had come upon them. Cal knew that they sensed the truth of what he said. In their great pride of accomplishment in precision warfare, they had not looked to this ghost that haunted them.

"We've seen it happen on Earth," said Cal gently now. "Troops trained and drilled and marched through forests to be slaughtered by random attacking aborigines. When you fight such an enemy you use his own tactics against him."

"And that is—" said the group leader.

"Send every ship you can spare to the defense of the failing line. Yes, defend my Earth. The Guarra *know* you won't. Your computers tell you not to, and they know it. So do it. I don't know if you'll win. Intelligence is too incomplete to show the balance of forces available. But one thing you will do is throw off the Guarran predictability and let them know they've been in one hell of a fight. And that, I assure you, will bring your own final victory much closer to possibility. You will no longer be sitting ducks, no longer finely drilled troops marching through a forest of random fighters!"

The hours that passed next were long. It was night again when Warner finally brought the news. Rakopt was with him and the eyes of both men were glowing with excitement.

"The Council has agreed," said Warner. "Earth will be defended." Then he extended his hand and took Cal's and Ruth's warmly, in turn. "And I'm very glad," he said.

Ruth cried then. She put her head against Cal's shoulder and let the long days of apprehension release.

"We won," she sobbed. "I knew it would be this way—"

"No," Warner reminded her soberly. "We haven't won, but we've got a chance now, and maybe Cal is right—the whole war may be nearer its end because of this."

Word went out to the fleets that night. Ships were transferred to the new battle zone. On one of these Ruth and Cal and Warner were picked up.

Through the port, while the battleship was still in primary drive, Cal and Ruth watched the receding home of Jorgasnovara as it disappeared among the pinpoints of light. Whether the battle were won or lost, he supposed they would not see it again.

With the shifting to secondary drive, the whole starscape vanished and he turned away. He thought of all he had done since the Llanna had first approached him. He wondered if he would do it again the same way. And suddenly he knew that he would. Like it or not, Earth was a member of the community of worlds. That there was no established commerce, and the fact that Earthmen did not know of the existence of the Llanna or the Guarra made no difference whatever. What happened between the Llanna and the Guarra now would affect the destiny of unborn generations of Earthmen. The present generation should have a word as to what that destiny might be.

The Llanna had made foolish blunders. They had fought the war in their own set way so long that they had forgotten there were other ways. They were on the road to defeat. Of this, Cal was certain.

Whether his introduction of guerrilla fighting tactics in space war would change that, he didn't know, but at least it would make the Llanna less vulnerable.

Ruth watched him from the chair by the port. "Is it the way you thought it would be, as fine and wonderful as you hoped?" she said.

"What?"

"Space, that you wanted to see so badly."

He glanced at the port, blackened by the secondary drive. "I guess I haven't had time to think much about it." His thoughts scanned the romantic yearning he'd once had toward the stars, the aching urge with which he had once looked up at the sky. It would be good to look up at it again—from Earth—he thought.

"Must be getting old for that sort of thing," he said. "I think I'm ready for the little house with a lawn around it—and kids riding tricycles on the sidewalk."

# The Illustrated Man

## RAY BRADBURY

**The Illustrated Man**

Director: *Jack Smight*
Screenplay: *Howard B. Kreitsek*
Producers: *Ted Mann, Howard B. Kreitsek*
Music: *Jerry Goldsmith*
Special Effects: *Ralph Webb*
Tattoo Designs: *James Reynolds*
Cast: *Rod Steiger, Claire Bloom, Robert Drivas*
Released by: *Warner/Seven Arts*
1969, 103 Minutes. Color.

"Hey, the Illustrated Man!"

A calliope screamed, and Mr. William Philippus Phelps stood, arms folded, high on the summer-night platform, a crowd unto himself.

He was an entire civilization. In the Main Country, his chest, the Vasties lived—nipple-eyed dragons swirling over his fleshpot, his almost feminine breasts. His navel was the mouth of a slit-eyed monster—an obscene, in-sucked mouth, toothless as a witch. And there were secret caves where Darklings lurked, his armpits, adrip with slow subterranean liquors, where the Darklings, eyes jealously ablaze, peered out through rank creeper and hanging vine.

Mr. William Philippus Phelps leered down from his freak platform with a thousand peacock eyes. Across the sawdust meadow he saw his wife, Lisabeth, far away, ripping tickets in half, staring at the silver belt buckles of passing men.

Mr. William Philippus Phelps' hands were tattooed roses. At the sight of his wife's interest, the roses shriveled, as with the passing of sunlight.

A year before, when he had led Lisabeth to the marriage bureau to watch her work her name in ink, slowly, on the form, his skin had been pure and white and clean. He glanced down at himself in sudden horror. Now he was like a great painted canvas, shaken in the night wind! How had it happened? Where had it all begun?

It had started with the arguments, and then the flesh, and then the pictures. They had fought deep into the summer nights, she like a brass trumpet forever blaring at him. And he had gone out to eat five thousand steaming hot dogs, ten million hamburgers, and a forest of green onions, and to drink vast red seas of orange juice. Peppermint candy formed his brontosaur bones, the hamburgers shaped his balloon flesh, and strawberry pop pumped in and out of his heart valves sickeningly, until he weighed three hundred pounds.

"William Philippus Phelps," Lisabeth said to him in the eleventh month of their marriage, "you're dumb and fat."

That was the day the carnival boss handed him the blue envelope. "Sorry, Phelps. You're no good to me with all that gut on you."

"Wasn't I always your best tent man, boss?"

"Once. Not anymore. Now you sit, you don't get the work out."

"Let me be your Fat Man."

"I *got* a Fat Man. Dime a dozen." The boss eyed him up and down. "Tell you what, though. We ain't had a Tattooed Man since Gallery Smith died last year. . . ."

That had been a month ago. Four short weeks. From someone, he had learned of a tattoo artist far out in the rolling Wisconsin country, an old woman, they said, who knew her trade. If he took the dirt road and turned right at the river and then left. . . .

He had walked out across a yellow meadow, which was crisp from the sun. Red flowers blew and bent in the wind as he walked, and he came to the old shack, which looked as if it had stood in a million rains.

Inside the door was a silent, bare room, and in the center of the bare room sat an ancient woman.

Her eyes were stitched with red resin-thread. Her nose was sealed with black wax-twine. Her ears were sewn, too, as if a darning-needle dragonfly had stitched all her senses shut. She sat, not moving, in the vacant room. Dust lay in a yellow flour all about, unfoot-printed in many weeks; if she had moved it would have shown, but she had not moved. Her hands touched each other like thin, rusted instruments. Her feet were naked and obscene as rain rubbers, and near them sat vials of tattoo milk—red, lightning-blue, brown, cat-yellow. She was a thing sewn tight into whispers and silence.

Only her mouth moved, unsewn: "Come in. Sit down. I'm lonely here."

He did not obey.

"You came for the pictures," she said in a high voice. "I have a picture to show you, first."

She tapped a blind finger to her thrust-out palm. "See!" she cried.

It was a tattoo-portrait of William Philippus Phelps.

"Me!" he said.

Her cry stopped him at the door. "Don't run."

He held to the edges of the door, his back to her. "That's me, that's me on your hand!"

"It's been there fifty years." She stroked it like a cat, over and over.

He turned. "It's an *old* tattoo." He drew slowly nearer. He edged forward and bent to blink at it. He put out a trembling finger to brush the picture. "Old. That's impossible! You don't know *me*. I don't know *you*. Your eyes, all sewed shut."

"I've been waiting for you," she said. "And many people." She displayed her arms and legs, like the spindles of an antique chair. "I have pictures on me of people who have already come here to see me. And there are other pictures of other people who are coming to see me in the next one hundred years. And you, you have come."

"How do you know it's me? You can't see!"

"You *feel* like the lions, the elephants, and the tigers, to me. Unbutton your shirt. You need me. Don't be afraid. My needles are as clean as a doctor's fingers. When I'm finished with illustrating you, I'll wait for someone else to walk along out here and find me. And someday, a hundred summers from now, perhaps, I'll just go lie down in the forest under some white mushrooms, and in the spring you won't find anything but a small blue cornflower. . . ."

He began to unbutton his sleeves.

"I know the Deep Past and the Clear Present and the even Deeper Future," she whispered, eyes knotted into blindness, face lifted to this unseen man. "It is on my flesh. I will paint it on yours, too. You will be the only *real* Illustrated Man in the universe. I'll give you special pictures you will never forget. Pictures of the Future on your skin."

She pricked him with a needle.

He ran back to the carnival that night in a drunken terror and elation. Oh, how quickly the old dust-witch had stitched him with color and design. At the end of a long afternoon of being bitten by a silver snake, his body was alive with portraiture. He looked as if he had dropped and been crushed between the steel rollers of a print press, and come out like an incredible rotogravure. He was clothed in a garment of trolls and scarlet dinosaurs.

"Look!" he cried to Lisabeth. She glanced up from her cosmetic table as he tore his shirt away. He stood in the naked bulb-light of their car-trailer, expanding his impossible chest. Here, the Tremblies, half-maiden, half-goat, leaping when his biceps flexed. Here, the Country of Lost Souls, his chins. In so many accordion pleats of fat, numerous small scorpions, beetles, and mice were crushed, held, hid, darting into view, vanishing, as he raised or lowered his chins.

"My God," said Lisabeth. "My husband's a freak."

She ran from the trailer and he was left alone to pose before the mirror. Why had he done it? To have a job, yes, but, most of all, to cover the fat that had larded itself impossibly over his bones. To hide the fat under a layer of color and fantasy, to hide it from his wife, but most of all from himself.

He thought of the old woman's last words. She had needled him two *special* tattoos, one on his chest, another for his back, which she would not let him see. She covered each with cloth and adhesive.

"You are not to look at these two," she had said.

"Why?"

"Later, you may look. The Future is in these pictures. You can't look now or it may spoil them. They are not quite finished. I put ink on your flesh and the sweat of you forms the rest of the picture, the Future—your sweat and your thought." Her empty mouth grinned. "Next Saturday night, you may advertise! The Big Unveiling! Come see the Illustrated Man unveil his picture! You can make money in that way. You can charge admission to the Unveiling, like to an Art Gallery. Tell them you have a picture that even *you* never have seen, that *nobody* has seen yet. The most unusual picture ever painted. Almost alive. And it tells the Future. Roll the drums and blow the trumpets. And you can stand there and unveil at the Big Unveiling."

"That's a good idea," he said.

"But only unveil the picture on your chest," she said. "That is first. You must save the picture on your back, under the adhesive, for the following week. Understand?"

"How much do I owe you?"

"Nothing," she said. "If you walk with these pictures on you, I will be repaid with my own satisfaction. I will sit here for the next two weeks and think how clever my pictures are, for I make them to fit each man himself and what is inside him. Now, walk out of this house and never come back. Good-bye."

"Hey! The Big Unveiling!"

The red signs blew in the night wind: NO ORDINARY TATTOOED MAN! THIS ONE IS "ILLUSTRATED"! GREATER THAN MICHELANGELO! TONIGHT! ADMISSION 10 CENTS!

Now the hour had come. Saturday night, the crowd stirring their animal feet in the hot sawdust.

"In one minute—" the carny boss pointed his cardboard megaphone—"in the tent immediately to my rear, we will unveil the Mysterious Portrait upon the Illustrated Man's chest! Next Saturday night, the same hour, same location, we'll unveil the Picture upon the Illustrated Man's *back!* Bring your friends!"

There was a stuttering roll of drums.

Mr. William Philippus Phelps jumped back and vanished; the crowd poured into the tent, and, once inside, found him reestablished upon another platform, the band brassing out a jig-time melody.

He looked for his wife and saw her, lost in the crowd, like a stranger, come to watch a freakish thing, a look of contemptuous curiosity upon her face. For, after all, he was her husband, and this was a thing she didn't know about him herself. It gave him a feeling of great height and warmness and light to find himself the center of the jangling universe, the carnival world, for one night. Even the other freaks—the Skeleton, the Seal Boy, the Yoga, the Magician, and the Balloon—were scattered through the crowd.

"Ladies and gentlemen, the great moment!"

A trumpet flourish, a hum of drumsticks on tight cowhide.

Mr. William Philippus Phelps let his cape fall. Dinosaurs, trolls, and half-women-half-snakes writhed on his skin in the stark light.

Ah, murmured the crowd, for surely there had never been a tattooed man like this! The beast eyes seemed to take red fire and blue fire, blinking and twisting. The roses on his fingers seemed to expel a sweet pink bouquet. The tyrannosaurus rex reared up along his leg, and the sound of the brass trumpet in the hot tent heavens was a prehistoric cry from the red monster throat. Mr. William Philippus Phelps was a museum jolted to life. Fish swam in seas of electric-blue ink. Fountains sparkled under yellow suns. Ancient buildings stood in meadows of harvest wheat. Rockets burned across spaces of muscle and flesh. The slightest inhalation of his breath threatened to make chaos of the entire printed universe. He seemed afire, the creatures flinching from the flame, drawing back from the great heat of his pride, as he expanded under the audience's rapt contemplation.

The carny boss laid his fingers to the adhesive. The audience rushed forward, silent in the oven vastness of the night tent.

"You ain't seen nothing yet!" cried the carny boss.

The adhesive ripped free.

There was an instant in which nothing happened. An instant in which the Illustrated Man thought that the Unveiling was a terrible and irrevocable failure.

But then the audience gave a low moan.

The carny boss drew back, his eyes fixed.

Far out at the edge of the crowd, a woman, after a moment, began to cry, began to sob, and did not stop.

Slowly, the Illustrated Man looked down at his naked chest and stomach.

The thing that he saw made the roses on his hands discolor and die. All of his creatures seemed to wither, turn inward, shrivel with the arctic coldness that pumped from his heart outward to freeze and destroy them. He stood trembling. His hands floated up to touch that incredible picture, which lived, moved and shivered with life. It was like gazing into a small room, seeing a thing of someone else's life, so intimate, so impossible that one could not believe and one could not long stand to watch without turning away.

It was a picture of his wife, Lisabeth, and himself.

And he was killing her.

Before the eyes of a thousand people in a dark tent in the center of a black-forested Wisconsin land, he was killing his wife.

His great flowered hands were upon her throat, and her face was turning dark and he killed her and he killed her and did not ever in the next minute stop killing her. It was real. While the crowd watched, she died, and he turned very sick. He was about to fall straight down into the crowd. The tent whirled like a monster bat wing, flapping grotesquely. The last thing he heard was a woman, sobbing, far out on the shore of the silent crowd.

And the crying woman was Lisabeth, his wife.

In the night, his bed was moist with perspiration. The carnival sounds had melted away, and his wife, in her own bed, was quiet now, too. He fumbled with his chest. The adhesive was smooth. They had made him put it back.

He had fainted. When he revived, the carny boss had yelled at him, "Why didn't you *say* what that picture was like?"

"I didn't know, I didn't," said the Illustrated Man.

"Good God!" said the boss. "Scare hell outa everyone. Scared hell outa Lizzie, scared hell outa me. Christ, where'd you *get* that damn tattoo?" He shuddered. "Apologize to Lizzie, now."

His wife stood over him.

"I'm sorry, Lisabeth," he said, weakly, his eyes closed. "I didn't know."

"You did it on purpose," she said. "To scare me."

"I'm sorry."

"Either it goes or I go," she said.

"Lisabeth."

"You heard me. That picture comes off or I quit this show."

"Yeah, Phil," said the boss. "That's how it is."

"Did you lose money? Did the crowd demand refunds?"

"It ain't the money, Phil. For that matter, once the word got around, hundreds of people wanted in. But I'm runnin' a clean show. That tattoo comes off! Was this your idea of a practical joke, Phil?"

He turned in the warm bed. No, not a joke. Not a joke at all. He had been as terrified as anyone. Not a joke. That little old dust-witch, what had she *done* to him and how had she done it? Had she put the picture there? No; she had said that the picture was unfinished, and that he himself, with his thoughts and his perspiration, would finish it. Well, he had done the job all right.

But what, if anything, was the significance? He didn't want to kill anyone. He didn't want to kill Lisabeth. Why should such a silly picture burn here on his flesh in the dark?

He crawled his fingers softly, cautiously down to touch the quivering place where the hidden portrait lay. He pressed tight, and the temperature of that spot was enormous. He could almost feel that little evil picture killing and killing and killing all through the night.

*I don't wish to kill her,* he thought, insistently, looking over at her bed. And then, five minutes later, he whispered aloud: "Or *do* I?"

"What?" she cried, awake.

"Nothing," he said, after a pause. "Go to sleep."

The man bent forward, a buzzing instrument in his hand. "This costs five bucks an inch. Costs more to peel tattoos off than put 'em on. Okay, jerk the adhesive."

The Illustrated Man obeyed.

The skin man sat back. "Christ! No wonder you want that off! That's ghastly. *I* don't even want to look at it." He flicked his machine. "Ready? This won't hurt."

The carny boss stood in the tent flap, watching. After five minutes, the skin man changed the instrument head, cursing. Ten minutes later he scraped his chair back and scratched his head. Half an hour passed and he got up, told Mr. William Philippus Phelps to dress, and packed his kit.

"Wait a minute," said the carny boss. "You ain't done the job."

"And I ain't going to," said the skin man.

"I'm paying good money. What's wrong?"

"Nothing, except that damn picture just won't come off. Damn thing must go right down to the bone."

"You're crazy."

"Mister, I'm in business thirty years and never seen a tattoo like this. An inch deep, if it's anything."

"But I've got to get it off!" cried the Illustrated Man.

The skin man shook his head. "Only one way to get rid of that."

"How?"

"Take a knife and cut off your chest. You won't live long, but the picture'll be gone."

"Come back here!"

But the skin man walked away.

They could hear the big Sunday-night crowd, waiting.

"That's a big crowd," said the Illustrated Man.

"But they ain't going to see what they came to see," said the carny boss. "You ain't going out there, except with the adhesive. Hold still now, I'm curious about this *other* picture, on your back. We might be able to give 'em an Unveiling on this one instead."

"She said it wouldn't be ready for a week or so. The old woman said it would take time to set, make a pattern."

There was a soft ripping as the carny boss pulled aside a flap of white tape on the Illustrated Man's spine.

"What do you see?" gasped Mr. Phelps, bent over.

The carny boss replaced the tape. "Buster, as a Tattooed Man, you're a washout, ain't you? Why'd you let that old dame fix you up this way?"

"I didn't know who she was."

"She sure cheated you on this one. No design to it. Nothing. No picture at all."

"It'll come clear. You wait and see."

The boss laughed. "Okay. Come on. We'll show the crowd part of you, anyway."

They walked out into an explosion of brassy music.

He stood monstrous in the middle of the night, putting out his hands like a blind man to balance himself in a world now tilted, now rushing, now threatening to spin him over and down into the mirror before which he raised his hands. Upon the flat, dimly lighted table top were peroxides, acids, silver razors, and squares of sandpaper. He took each of them in turn. He soaked the vicious tattoo upon his chest, he scraped at it. He worked steadily for an hour.

He was aware, suddenly, that someone stood in the trailer door behind him. It was three in the morning. There was a faint odor of beer. She had come home from town. He heard her slow breathing. He did not turn. "Lisabeth?" he said.

"You'd better get rid of it," she said, watching his hands move the sandpaper. She stepped into the trailer.

"I didn't want the picture this way," he said.

"You did," she said. "You planned it."

"I didn't."

"I know you," she said. "Oh, I know you hate me. Well, that's nothing. I hate you, I've hated you a long time now. Good God, when you started putting on the fat, you think anyone could love you then? I could teach you some things about hate. Why don't you ask me?"

"Leave me alone," he said.

"In front of that crowd, making a spectacle out of me!"

"I didn't know what was under the tape."

She walked around the table, hands fitted to her hips, talking to the beds, the walls, the table, talking it all out of her. And he thought: *Or did I know? Who made this picture, me or the witch? Who formed it? How? Do I really want her dead? No! And yet. . . .* He watched his wife draw nearer, nearer, he saw the ropy strings of her throat vibrate to her shouting. This and this and *this* was wrong with him! That and that and *that* was unspeakable about him! He was a liar, a schemer, a fat, lazy, ugly man, a child. Did he think he could compete with the carny boss or the tent-peggers? Did he think he was sylphine and graceful, did he think he was a framed El Greco? Da Vinci, huh! Michelangelo, my eye! She brayed. She showed her teeth. "Well, you can't scare me into staying with someone I don't want touching me with their slobby paws!" she finished, triumphantly.

"Lisabeth," he said.

"Don't Lisabeth me!" she shrieked. "I know your plan. You had that picture put on to scare me. You thought I wouldn't *dare* leave you. Well!"

"Next Saturday night, the Second Unveiling," he said. "You'll be proud of me."

"Proud! You're silly and pitiful. God, you're like a whale. You ever see a beached whale? I saw one when I was a kid. There it was, and they came and shot it. Some lifeguards shot it. Jesus, a whale!"

"Lisabeth."

"I'm leaving, that's all, and getting a divorce."

"Don't."

"And I'm marrying a man, not a fat woman—that's what you are, so much fat on you there ain't no sex!"

"You can't leave me," he said.

"Just watch!"

"I love you," he said.

"Oh," she said. "Go look at your pictures."

He reached out.

"Keep your hands off," she said.

"Lisabeth."

"Don't come near. You turn my stomach."

"Lisabeth."

All the eyes of his body seemed to fire, all the snakes to move, all the monsters to seethe, all the mouths to widen and rage. He moved toward her—not like a man, but a crowd.

He felt the great blooded reservoir of orangeade pump through him now, the sluice of cola and rich lemon pop pulse in sickening sweet anger through his wrists, his legs, his heart. All of it, the oceans of mustard and relish and all the million drinks he had drowned himself in in the last year were aboil; his face was the color of a steamed beef. And the pink roses of his hands became those hungry, carnivorous flowers kept long years in tepid jungle and now let free to find their way on the night air before him.

He gathered her to him, like a great beast gathering in a struggling animal. It was a frantic gesture of love, quickening and demanding, which, as she struggled, hardened to another thing. She beat and clawed at the picture on his chest.

"You've got to love me, Lisabeth."

"Let go!" she screamed. She beat at the picture that burned under her fists. She slashed at it with her fingernails.

"Oh, Lisabeth," he said, his hands moving up her arms.

"I'll scream," she said, seeing his eyes.

"Lisabeth." The hand moved up to her shoulders, to her neck. "Don't go away."

"Help!" she screamed. The blood ran from the picture on his chest.

He put his fingers about her neck and squeezed.

She was a calliope cut in mid-shriek.

Outside, the grass rustled. There was the sound of running feet.

Mr. William Philippus Phelps opened the trailer door and stepped out.

They were waiting for him. Skeleton, Midget, Balloon, Yoga, Electra, Popeye, Seal Boy. The freaks, waiting in the middle of the night, in the dry grass.

He walked toward them. He moved with a feeling that he must get away; these people would understand nothing, they were not thinking people. And because he did not flee, because he only walked, balanced, stunned, between the tents, slowly, the freaks moved to let him pass. They watched him, because their watching guaranteed that he would not escape. He walked out across the black meadow, moths fluttering in his face. He walked steadily as long as he was visible, not knowing where he was going. They watched him go, and then they turned and all of them shuffled to the silent car-trailer together and pushed the door slowly wide. . . .

The Illustrated Man walked steadily in the dry meadows beyond the town.

"He went that way!" a faint voice cried. Flashlights bobbled over the hills. There were dim shapes, running.

Mr. William Philippus Phelps waved to them. He was tired. He wanted only to be found now. He was tired of running away. He waved again.

"There he is!" The flashlights changed direction. "Come on! We'll get the bastard!"

When it was time, the Illustrated Man ran again. He was careful to run slowly. He deliberately fell down twice. Looking back, he saw the tent stakes they held in their hands.

He ran toward a far crossroads lantern, where all the summer night seemed to gather; merry-go-rounds of fireflies whirling, crickets moving their song toward that light, everything rushing, as if by some midnight attraction, toward that one high-hung lantern—the Illustrated Man first, the others close at his heels.

As he reached the light and passed a few yards under and beyond it, he did not need to look back. On the road ahead, in silhouette, he saw the upraised tent stakes sweep violently up, up, and then *down!*

A minute passed.

In the country ravines, the crickets sang. The freaks stood over the sprawled Illustrated Man, holding their tent stakes loosely.

Finally they rolled him over on his stomach. Blood ran from his mouth.

They ripped the adhesive from his back. They stared down for a long moment at the freshly revealed picture. Someone whispered. Someone else swore, softly. The Thin Man pushed back and walked away and was sick. Another and another of the freaks stared, their mouths trembling, and moved away, leaving the Illustrated Man on the deserted road, the blood running from his mouth.

In the dim light, the unveiled Illustration was easily seen.

It showed a crowd of freaks bending over a dying fat man on a dark and lonely road, looking at a tattoo on his back which illustrated a crowd of freaks bending over a dying fat man on a. . . .

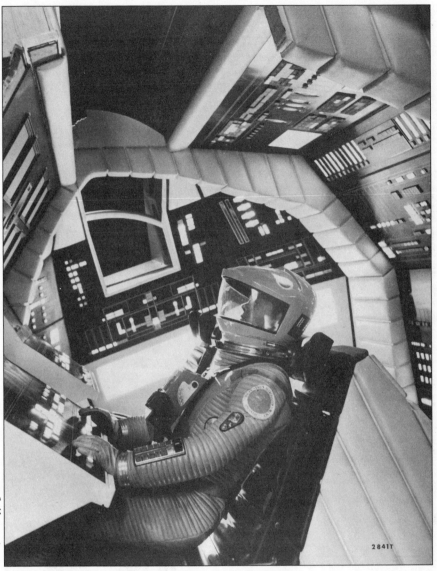

2841T

In *2001*, astronaut Frank Poole (Gary Lockwood) monitors the Command Module aboard the *Discovery*.

Astronaut Frank Poole, left (Gary Lockwood) and Mission Commander David Bowman (Keir Dullea) attempt to correct a malfunction in the *Discovery*'s antenna, which threatens to sever their only link with Earth.

# The Sentinel

## ARTHUR C. CLARKE

**2001: A Space Odyssey**

Director/Producer: *Stanley Kubrick*
Screenplay: *Stanley Kubrick, Arthur C. Clarke*
Special Effects: *Wally Veevers, Douglas Trumbull, Con Pederson, Tom Howard*
Cast: *Keir Dullea, Gary Lockwood, Douglas Rain*
Released by: *MGM*
1968, 160 Minutes. [Picture was cut to 139 minutes by Director after its premiere.] Color.

The next time you see the full moon high in the South, look carefully at its right-hand edge and let your eye travel upwards along the curve of the disc. Round about 2 o'clock you will notice a small, dark oval: anyone with normal eyesight can find it quite easily. It is the great walled plain, one of the finest on the Moon, known as the Mare Crisium—the Sea of Crises. Three hundred miles in diameter, and almost completely surrounded by a ring of magnificent mountains, it had never been explored until we entered it in the late summer of 1996.

Our expedition was a large one. We had two heavy freighters which had flown our supplies and equipment from the main lunar base in the Mare Serenitatis, five hundred miles away. There were also three small rockets which were intended for short-range transport over regions which our surface vehicles couldn't cross. Luckily, most of the Mare Crisium is very flat. There are none of the great crevasses so common and so dangerous elsewhere, and very few craters or mountains of any size. As far as we could tell, our powerful caterpillar tractors would have no difficulty in taking us wherever we wished.

I was geologist—or selenologist, if you want to be pedantic—in charge of the group exploring the southern region of the Mare. We had crossed a hundred miles of it in a week, skirting the foothills of the mountains along the shore of what was once the ancient sea, some thousand million years before. When life was beginning on Earth, it was already dying here. The waters were retreating down the flanks of those stupendous cliffs, retreating into the empty heart of the Moon. Over the land which we were crossing, the tideless ocean had once been half a mile deep, and now the only trace of moisture was the hoarfrost one could sometimes find in caves which the searing sunlight never penetrated.

We had begun our journey early in the slow lunar dawn, and still had almost a week of Earth-time before nightfall. Half a dozen times a day we would leave our vehicle and go outside in the spacesuits to hunt for interesting minerals, or to place markers for the guidance of future travellers. It was an uneventful routine. There is nothing hazardous or even particularly exciting about lunar exploration. We could live comfortably for a month in our pressurized tractors, and if we ran into trouble we could always radio for help and sit tight until one of the spaceships came to our rescue. When that happened there was always a frightful outcry about the waste of rocket fuel, so a tractor sent out an SOS only in a real emergency.

I said just now that there was nothing exciting about lunar exploration, but of course that isn't true. One could never grow tired of those incredible mountains, so much steeper and more rugged than the gentle hills of Earth. We never knew, as we rounded the capes and promontories of that vanished sea, what new splendors would be revealed to us. The whole southern curve of the Mare Crisium is a vast delta where a score of rivers had once found their way into the ocean, fed perhaps by the torrential rains that must have lashed the mountains in the brief volcanic age when the Moon was young. Each of these ancient valleys was an invitation, challenging us to climb into the unknown uplands beyond. But we had a hundred miles still to cover, and could only look longingly at the heights which others must scale.

We kept Earth-time aboard the tractor, and precisely at 22.00 hours the final radio message would be sent out to Base and we would close down for the day. Outside, the rocks would still be burning beneath the almost vertical sun, but to us it was night until we awoke again eight hours later. Then one of us would prepare breakfast, there would be a great buzzing of electric shavers, and someone would switch on the short-wave radio from Earth. Indeed, when the smell of frying bacon began to fill the cabin, it was sometimes hard to believe that we were not back on our own world—everything was so normal and homey, apart from the feeling of decreased weight and the unnatural slowness with which objects fell.

It was my turn to prepare breakfast in the corner of the main cabin that served as a galley. I can remember that moment quite vividly after all these years, for the radio had just played one of my favorite melodies, the old Welsh air *David of the White Rock*. Our driver was already outside in his spacesuit, inspecting our caterpillar treads. My assistant, Louis Garnett, was up forward in the control position, making some belated entries in yesterday's log.

As I stood by the frying pan, waiting, like any terrestrial housewife, for the sausages to brown, I let my gaze wander idly over the mountain walls which covered the whole of the southern horizon, marching out of sight to east and west below the curve of the Moon. They seemed only a mile or two from the tractor, but I knew that the nearest was twenty miles away. On the Moon, of course, there is no loss of detail with distance—none of that almost imperceptible haziness which softens and sometimes transfigures all far-off things on Earth.

Those mountains were ten thousand feet high, and they climbed steeply out of the plain as if ages ago some subterranean eruption had smashed them skywards through the molten crust. The base of even the nearest was hidden from sight by the steeply curving surface of the plain, for the Moon is a very little world, and from where I was standing the optical horizon was only two miles away.

I lifted my eyes towards the peaks which no man had ever climbed, the peaks which, before the coming of terrestrial life, had watched the retreating oceans sink sullenly into their graves, taking with them the hope and the morning promise of a world. The sunlight was beating against those ramparts with a glare that hurt the eyes, yet only a little way above them the stars were shining steadily in a sky blacker than a winter midnight on Earth.

I was turning away when my eye caught a metallic glitter high on the ridge of a great promontory thrusting out into the sea thirty miles to the west. It was a dimensionless point of light, as if a star had been clawed from the sky by one of those cruel peaks, and I imagined that some smooth rock surface was catching the sunlight and heliographing it straight into my eyes. Such things were not uncommon. When the Moon is in her second quarter, observers on Earth can sometimes see the great ranges in the Oceanus Procellarum burning with a blue-white iridescence as the sunlight flashes from their slopes and leaps again from world to world. But I was curious to know what kind of rock could be shining so brightly up there, and I climbed into the observation turret and swung our four-inch telescope round to the west.

I could see just enough to tantalize me. Clear and sharp in the field of vision, the mountain peaks seemed only half a mile away, but whatever was catching the sunlight was still too small to be resolved. Yet it seemed to have an elusive symmetry, and the summit upon which it rested was curiously flat. I stared for a long time at that glittering enigma, straining my eyes into space, until presently a smell of burning from the galley told me that our breakfast sausages had made their quarter-million-mile journey in vain.

All that morning we argued our way across the Mare Crisium while the western mountains reared higher in the sky. Even when we were out prospecting in the spacesuits, the discussion would continue over the radio. It was absolutely certain, my companions argued, that there had never been any form of intelligent life on the Moon. The only living things that had ever existed there were a few primitive plants and their slightly less degenerate ancestors. I knew that as well as anyone, but there are times when a scientist must not be afraid to make a fool of himself.

"Listen," I said at last, "I'm going up there, if only for my own peace of mind. That mountain's less than twelve thousand feet high—that's only two thousand under Earth gravity—and I can make the trip in twenty hours at the outside. I've always wanted to go up into those hills, anyway, and this gives me an excellent excuse."

"If you don't break your neck," said Garnett, "you'll be the laughingstock of the expedition when we get back to Base. That mountain will probably be called Wilson's Folly from now on."

"I *won't* break my neck," I said firmly. "Who was the first man to climb Pico and Helicon?"

"But weren't you rather younger in those days?" asked Louis gently.

"That," I said with great dignity, "is as good a reason as any for going."

We went to bed early that night, after driving the tractor to within half a mile of the promontory. Garnett was coming with me in the morning; he was a good climber, and had often been with me on such exploits before. Our driver was only too glad to be left in charge of the machine.

At first sight, those cliffs seemed completely unscalable, but to anyone with a good head for heights, climbing is easy on a world where all weights are only a sixth of their normal value. The real danger in lunar mountaineering lies in overconfidence; a six-hundred-foot drop on the Moon can kill you just as thoroughly as a hundred-foot fall on Earth.

We made our first halt on a wide ledge about four thousand feet above the plain. Climbing had not been very difficult, but my limbs were stiff with the unaccustomed effort, and I was glad of the rest. We could still see the tractor as a tiny metal insect far down at the foot of the cliff, and we reported our progress to the driver before starting on the next ascent.

Hour by hour the horizon widened and more and more of the great plain came into sight. Now we could look for fifty miles out across the Mare, and could even see the peaks of the mountains on the opposite coast more than a hundred miles away. Few of the great lunar plains are as smooth as the Mare Crisium, and we could almost imagine that a sea of water and not of rock was lying there two miles below. Only a group of crater-pits low down on the sky-line spoilt the illusion.

Our goal was still invisible over the crest of the mountain, and we were steering by maps, using the Earth as a guide. Almost due east of us, that great silver crescent hung low over the plain, already well into its first quarter. The sun and the stars would make their slow march across the sky and would sink presently from sight, but Earth would always be there, never moving from her appointed place, waxing and waning as the years and seasons passed. In ten days' time she would be a blinding disc bathing these rocks with her midnight radiance, fifty-fold brighter than the full moon. But we must be out of the mountains long before night, or else we would remain among them forever.

Inside our suits it was comfortably cool, for the refrigeration units were fighting the fierce sun and carrying away the body-heat of our exertions. We seldom spoke to each other, except to pass climbing instructions and to discuss our best plan of ascent. I do not know what Garnett was thinking, probably that this was the craziest goose-chase he had ever embarked upon. I more than half agreed with him, but the joy of climbing, the knowledge that no man had ever gone this way before and the exhilaration of the steadily widening landscape gave me all the reward I needed.

I don't think I was particularly excited when I saw in front of us the wall of rock I had first inspected through the telescope from thirty miles away. It would level off about fifty feet above our heads, and there on the plateau would be the thing that had lured me over these barren wastes. It was, almost certainly, nothing more than a boulder splintered ages ago by a falling meteor, and with its cleavage planes still fresh and bright in this incorruptible unchanging silence.

There were no hand-holds on the rock face, and we had to use a grapnel. My tired arms seemed to gain new strength as I swung the three-pronged metal anchor round my head and sent it sailing up towards the stars. The first time, it broke loose and came falling slowly back when we pulled the rope. On the third attempt, the prongs gripped firmly and our combined weights could not shift it.

Garnett looked at me anxiously. I could tell that he wanted to go first, but I smiled back at him through the glass of my helmet and shook my head. Slowly, taking my time, I began the final ascent.

Even with my spacesuit, I weighed only forty pounds here, so I pulled myself up hand over hand without bothering to use my feet. At the rim I paused and waved to my companion, then I scrambled over the edge and stood upright, staring ahead of me.

You must understand that until this very moment I had been almost completely convinced that there could be nothing strange or unusual for me to find here. Almost, but not quite; it was that haunting doubt that had driven me forwards. Well, it was a doubt no longer, but the haunting had scarcely begun.

I was standing on a plateau perhaps a hundred feet across. It had once been smooth—too smooth to be natural—but falling meteors had pitted and scored its surface through immeasurable aeons. It had been levelled to support a glittering, roughly pyramidal structure, twice as high as a man, that was set in the rock like a gigantic, many-faceted jewel.

Probably no emotion at all filled my mind in those first few seconds. Then I felt a great lifting of my heart, and a strange, inexpressible joy. For I loved the Moon, and now I knew that the creeping moss of Aristarchus and Eratosthenes was not the only life she had brought forth in her youth. The old, discredited dream of the first explorers was true. There had, after all, been a lunar civilization—and I was the first to find it. That I had come perhaps a hundred million years too late did not distress me; it was enough to have come at all.

My mind was beginning to function normally, to analyze and to ask questions. Was this a building, a shrine—or something for which my language had no name? If a building, then why was it erected in so uniquely inaccessible a spot? I wondered if it might be a temple, and I could picture the adepts of some strange priesthood calling on their gods to preserve them as the life of the Moon ebbed with the dying oceans, and calling on their gods in vain.

I took a dozen steps forward to examine the thing more closely, but some sense of caution kept me from going too near. I knew a little of archaeology, and tried to guess the cultural level of the civilization that must have smoothed this mountain and raised the glittering mirror surfaces that still dazzled my eyes.

The Egyptians could have done it, I thought, if their workmen had possessed whatever strange materials these far more ancient architects had used. Because of the thing's smallness, it did not occur to me that I might be looking at the handiwork of a race more advanced than my own. The idea that the Moon had possessed intelligence at all was still almost too tremendous to grasp, and my pride would not let me take the final, humiliating plunge.

And then I noticed something that set the scalp crawling at the back of my neck—something so trivial and so innocent that many would never have noticed it at all. I have said that the plateau was scarred by meteors; it was also coated inches deep with the cosmic dust that is always filtering down upon the surface of any world where there are no winds to disturb it. Yet the dust and the meteor scratches ended quite abruptly in a wide circle enclosing the little pyramid, as though an invisible wall was protecting it from the ravages of time and the slow but ceaseless bombardment from space.

There was someone shouting in my earphones, and I realized that Garnett had been calling me for some time. I walked unsteadily to the edge of the cliff and signalled him to join me, not trusting myself to speak. Then I went back towards that circle in the dust. I picked up a fragment of splintered rock and tossed it gently towards the shining enigma. If the pebble had vanished at that invisible barrier I should not have been surprised, but it seemed to hit a smooth, hemispherical surface and slid gently to the ground.

I knew then that I was looking at nothing that could be matched in the antiquity of my own race. This was not a building, but a machine, protecting itself with forces that had challenged Eternity. Those forces, whatever they might be, were still operating, and perhaps I had already come too close. I thought of all the radiations man had trapped and tamed in the past century. For all I knew, I might be as irrevocably doomed as if I had stepped into the deadly, silent aura of an unshielded atomic pile.

I remember turning then towards Garnett, who had joined me and was now standing motionless at my side. He seemed quite oblivious to me, so I did not disturb him but walked to the edge of the cliff in an effort to marshal my thoughts. There below me lay the Mare Crisium—Sea of Crises, indeed—strange and weird to most men, but reassuringly familiar to me. I lifted my eyes towards the crescent Earth, lying in her cradle of stars, and I wondered what her clouds had covered when these unknown builders had finished their work. Was it the steaming jungle of the Carboniferous, the bleak shoreline over which the first amphibians must crawl to conquer the land—or, earlier still, the long loneliness before the coming of life?

Do not ask me why I did not guess the truth sooner—the truth that seems so obvious now. In the first excitement of my discovery, I had assumed without question that this crystalline apparition had been built by some race belonging to the Moon's remote past, but suddenly, and with overwhelming force, the belief came to me that it was as alien to the Moon as I myself.

In twenty years we had found no trace of life but a few degenerate plants. No lunar civilization, whatever its doom, could have left but a single token of its existence.

I looked at the shining pyramid again, and the more remote it seemed from anything that had to do with the Moon. And suddenly I felt myself shaking with a foolish, hysterical laughter, brought on by excitement and over-exertion: for I had imagined that the little pyramid was speaking to me and was saying: "Sorry, I'm a stranger here myself."

It has taken us twenty years to crack that invisible shield and to reach the machine inside those crystal walls. What we could not understand, we broke at last with the savage might of atomic power and now I have seen the fragments of the lovely, glittering thing I found up there on the mountain.

They are meaningless. The mechanisms—if indeed they are mechanisms—of the pyramid belong to a technology that lies far beyond our horizon, perhaps to the technology of para-physical forces.

The mystery haunts us all the more now that the other planets have been reached and we know that only Earth has ever been the home of intelligent life. Nor could any lost civilization of our own world have built that machine, for the thickness of the meteoric dust on the plateau has enabled us to measure its age. It was set there upon its mountain before life had emerged from the seas of Earth.

When our world was half its present age, *something* from the stars swept through the Solar System, left this token of its passage, and went again upon its way. Until we destroyed it, that machine was still fulfilling the purpose of its builders; and as to that purpose, here is my guess.

Nearly a hundred thousand million stars are turning in the circle of the Milky Way, and long ago other races on the worlds of other suns must have scaled and passed the heights that we have reached. Think of such civilizations, far back in time against the fading afterglow of Creation, masters of a universe so young that life as yet had come only to a handful of worlds. Theirs would have been a loneliness we cannot imagine, the loneliness of gods looking out across infinity and finding none to share their thoughts.

They must have searched the star-clusters as we have searched the planets. Everywhere there would be worlds, but they would be empty or peopled with crawling, mindless things. Such was our own Earth, the smoke of the great volcanoes still staining its skies, when that first ship of the peoples of the dawn came sliding in from the abyss beyond Pluto. It passed the frozen outer worlds, knowing that life could play no part in their destinies. It came to rest among the inner planets, warming themselves around the fire of the Sun and waiting for their stories to begin.

Those wanderers must have looked on Earth, circling safely in the narrow zone between fire and ice, and must have guessed that it was the favorite of the Sun's children. Here, in the distant future, would be intelligence; but there were countless stars before them still, and they might never come this way again.

So they left a sentinel, one of millions they have scattered throughout the universe, watching over all worlds with the promise of life. It was a beacon that down the ages has been patiently signalling that fact that no one had discovered it.

Perhaps you understand now why that crystal pyramid was set upon the Moon instead of on the Earth. Its builders were not concerned with races still struggling up from savagery. They would be interested in our civilization only if we proved our fitness to survive—by crossing space and so escaping from the Earth, our cradle. That is the challenge that all intelligent races must meet, sooner or later. It is a double challenge, for it depends in turn upon the conquest of atomic energy and the last choice between life and death.

Once we had passed that crisis, it was only a matter of time before we found the pyramid and forced it open. Now its signals have ceased, and those whose duty it is will be turning their minds upon Earth. Perhaps they wish to help our infant civilization. But they must be very, very old, and the old are often insanely jealous of the young.

I can never look now at the Milky Way without wondering from which of those banked clouds of stars the emissaries are coming. If you will pardon so commonplace a simile, we have broken the glass of the fire-alarm and have nothing to do but to wait.

I do not think we will have to wait for long.

# The Seventh Victim

## ROBERT SHECKLEY

---

**The Tenth Victim**

Director: *Elio Petri*
Screenplay: *Tonino Guerra, Giorgio Salvioni, Ennio Flaiano, Elio Petri*
Producers: *Joseph E. Levine, Carlo Ponti*
Music: *Piero Piccioni*
Cast: *Marcello Mastroianni, Ursula Andress, Elsa Martinelli*
Released by: *Embassy*
1965, 92 Minutes. Color.

---

Stanton Frelaine sat at his desk, trying to look as busy as an executive should at nine-thirty in the morning. It was impossible. He couldn't concentrate on the advertisement he had written the previous night, couldn't think about business. All he could do was wait until the mail came.

He had been expecting his notification for two weeks now. The government was behind schedule, as usual.

The glass door of his office was marked *Morger and Frelaine, Clothiers.* It opened, and E. J. Morger walked in, limping slightly from his old gunshot wound. His shoulders were bent; but at the age of seventy-three, he wasn't worrying much about his posture.

"Well, Stan?" Morger asked. "What about that ad?"

Frelaine had joined Morger sixteen years ago, when he was twenty-seven. Together they had built Protec-Clothes into a million-dollar concern.

"I suppose you can run it," Frelaine said, handing the slip of paper to Morger. If only the mail would come earlier, he thought.

" 'Do you own a Protec-Suit?' " Morger read aloud, holding the paper close to his eyes. " 'The finest tailoring in the world has gone into Morger and Frelaine's Protec-Suit, to make it the leader in men's fashions.' "

Morger cleared his throat and glanced at Frelaine. He smiled and read on.

" 'Protec-Suit is the safest as well as the smartest. Every Protec-Suit comes with a special built-in gun pocket, guaranteed not to bulge. No one will know you are carrying a gun—except you. The gun pocket is exceptionally easy to get at, permitting fast, unhindered draw. Choice of hip or breast pocket.' Very nice," Morger commented.

Frelaine nodded morosely.

" 'The Protec-Suit Special has the fling-out gun pocket, the greatest modern advance in personal protection. A touch of the concealed button throws the gun into your hand, cocked, safeties off. Why not drop into the Protec-Store nearest you? *Why not be safe?*'

"That's fine," Morger said. "That's a very nice, dignified ad." He thought for a moment, fingering his white mustache. "Shouldn't you mention that Protec-Suits come in a variety of styles, single and double-breasted, one- and two-button rolls, deep and shallow flares?"

"Right. I forgot."

Frelaine took back the sheet and jotted a note on the edge of it. Then he stood up, smoothing his jacket over his prominent stomach. Frelaine was forty-three, a little overweight, a little bald on top. He was an amiable-looking man with cold eyes.

"Relax," Morger said. "It'll come in today's mail."

Frelaine forced himself to smile. He felt like pacing the floor, but instead sat on the edge of the desk.

"You'd think it was my first kill," he said, with a deprecating smile.

"I know how it is," Morger said. "Before I hung up my gun, I couldn't sleep for a month, waiting for a notification. I know."

The two men waited. Just as the silence was becoming unbearable, the door opened. A clerk walked in and deposited the mail on Frelaine's desk.

Frelaine swung around and gathered up the letters. He thumbed through them rapidly and found what he had been waiting for—the long white envelope from ECB, with the official government seal on it.

"That's it!" Frelaine said, and broke into a grin. "That's the baby!"

"Fine." Morger eyed the envelope with interest, but didn't ask Frelaine to open it. It would be a breach of etiquette, as well as a violation in the eyes of the law. No one was supposed to know a Victim's name except his Hunter. "Have a good hunt."

"I expect to," Frelaine replied confidently. His desk was in order—had been for a week. He picked up his briefcase.

"A good kill will do you a world of good," Morger said, putting his hand lightly on Frelaine's padded shoulder. "You've been keyed up."

"I know," Frelaine grinned again and shook Morger's hand.

"Wish I was a kid again," Morger said, glancing down at his crippled leg with wryly humorous eyes. "Makes me want to pick up a gun again."

The old man had been quite a Hunter in his day. Ten successful hunts had qualified him for the exclusive Tens Club. And, of course, for each hunt Morger had had to act as Victim, so he had twenty kills to his credit.

"I sure hope my Victim isn't anyone like you," Frelaine said, half in jest.

"Don't worry about it. What number will this be?"

"The seventh."

"Lucky seven. Go to it," Morger said. "We'll get you into the Tens yet."

Frelaine waved his hand and started out the door.

"Just don't get careless," warned Morger. "All it takes is a single slip and I'll need a new partner. If you don't mind, I like the one I've got now."

"I'll be careful," Frelaine promised.

Instead of taking a bus, Frelaine walked to his apartment. He wanted time to cool off. There was no sense in acting like a kid on his first kill.

As he walked, Frelaine kept his eyes strictly to the front. Staring at anyone was practically asking for a bullet, if the man happened to be serving as Victim. Some Victims shot if you just glanced at them. Nervous fellows. Frelaine prudently looked above the heads of the people he passed.

Ahead of him was a huge billboard, offering J. F. O'Donovan's services to the public.

"Victims!" the sign proclaimed in huge red letters. "Why take chances? Use an O'Donovan accredited Spotter. Let us locate your assigned killer. Pay *after* you get him!"

The sign reminded Frelaine. He would call Ed Morrow as soon as he reached his apartment.

He crossed the street, quickening his stride. He could hardly wait to get home now, to open the envelope and discover who his victim was. Would he be clever or stupid? Rich, like Frelaine's fourth Victim, or poor, like the first and second? Would he have an organized spotter service, or try to go it on his own?

The excitement of the chase was wonderful, coursing through his veins, quickening his heartbeat. From a block or so away, he heard gunfire. Two quick shots, and then a final one.

Somebody got his man, Frelaine thought. Good for him.

It was a superb feeling, he told himself. He was *alive* again.

At his one-room apartment, the first thing Frelaine did was call Ed Morrow, his spotter. The man worked as a garage attendant between calls.

"Hello, Ed? Frelaine."

"Oh, hi, Mr. Frelaine." He could see the man's thin, grease-stained face, grinning flat-lipped at the telephone.

"I'm going out on one, Ed."

"Good luck, Mr. Frelaine," Ed Morrow said. "I suppose you'll want me to stand by?"

"That's right. I don't expect to be gone more than a week or two. I'll probably get my notification of Victim Status within three months of the kill."

"I'll be standing by. Good hunting, Mr. Frelaine."

"Thanks. So long." He hung up. It was a wise safety measure to reserve a first-class spotter. After his kill, it would be Frelaine's turn as Victim. Then, once again, Ed Morrow would be his life insurance.

And what a marvelous spotter Morrow was! Uneducated—stupid, really. But what an eye for people! Morrow was a natural. His pale eyes could tell an out-of-towner at a glance. He was diabolically clever at rigging an ambush. An indispensable man.

Frelaine took out the envelope, chuckling to himself, remembering some of the tricks Morrow had turned for the Hunters. Still smiling, he glanced at the data inside the envelope.

*Janet-Marie Patzig.*

His Victim was a female!

Frelaine stood up and paced for a few moments. Then he read the letter again. Janet-Marie Patzig. No mistake. A girl. Three photographs were enclosed, her address, and the usual descriptive data.

Frelaine frowned. He had never killed a female.

He hesitated for a moment, then picked up the telephone and dialed ECB.

"Emotional Catharsis Bureau, Information Section," a man's voice answered.

"Say, look," Frelaine said. "I just got my notification and I pulled a girl. Is that in order?" He gave the clerk the girl's name.

"It's all in order, sir," the clerk replied after a minute of checking microfiles. "The girl registered with the board under her own free will. The law says she has the same rights and privileges as a man."

"Could you tell me how many kills she has?"

"I'm sorry, sir. The only information you're allowed is the Victim's legal status and the descriptive data you have received."

"I see." Frelaine paused. "Could I draw another?"

"You can refuse the hunt, of course. That is your legal right. But you will not be allowed another Victim until you have served. Do you wish to refuse?"

"Oh, no," Frelaine said hastily. "I was just wondering. Thank you."

He hung up and sat down in his largest armchair, loosening his belt. This required some thought.

Damn women, he grumbled to himself, always trying to horn in on a man's game. Why can't they stay home?

But they were free citizens, he reminded himself. Still, it just didn't seem *feminine*.

He knew that, historically speaking, the Emotional Catharsis Board had been established for men and men only. The board had been formed at the end of the fourth world war—or sixth, as some historians counted it.

At that time there had been a driving need for permanent, lasting peace. The reason was practical, as were the men who engineered it.

Simply—annihilation was just around the corner.

In the world wars, weapons increased in magnitude, efficiency and exterminating power. Soldiers became accustomed to them, less and less reluctant to use them.

But the saturation point had been reached. Another war would truly be the war to end all wars. There would be no one left to start another.

So this peace *had* to last for all time, but the men who engineered it were practical. They recognized the tensions and dislocations still present, the cauldrons in which wars are brewed. They asked themselves why peace had never lasted in the past.

"Because men like to fight," was their answer.

"Oh, no!" screamed the idealists.

But the men who engineered the peace were forced to postulate, regretfully, the presence of a need for violence in a large percentage of mankind.

Men aren't angels. They aren't fiends, either. They are just very human beings, with a high degree of combativeness.

With the scientific knowledge and the power they had at that moment, the practical men could have gone a long way toward breeding this trait out of the race. Many thought this was the answer.

The practical men didn't. They recognized the validity of competition, love of battle, courage in the face of overwhelming odds. These, they felt, were admirable traits for a race, and insurance toward its perpetuity. Without them, the race would be bound to retrogress.

The tendency toward violence, they found, was inextricably linked with ingenuity, flexibility, drive.

The problem, then: To arrange a peace that would last after they were gone. To stop the race from destroying itself, without removing the responsible traits.

The way to do this, they decided, was to rechannel Man's violence.

Provide him with an outlet, an expression.

The first big step was the legalization of gladiatorial events, complete with blood and thunder. But more was needed. Sublimations worked only up to a point. Then people demanded the real thing.

There is no substitute for murder.

So murder was legalized, on a strictly individual basis, and only for those who wanted it. The governments were directed to create Emotional Catharsis Boards.

After a period of experimentation, uniform rules were adopted.

Anyone who wanted to murder could sign up at the ECB. Giving certain data and assurances, he would be granted a Victim.

Anyone who signed up to murder, under the government rules, had to take his turn a few months later as Victim—if he survived.

That, in essence, was the setup. The individual could commit as many murders as he wanted. But between each, he had to be a Victim. If he successfully killed his Hunter, he could stop, or sign up for another murder.

At the end of ten years, an estimated third of the world's civilized population had applied for at least one murder. The number slid to a fourth, and stayed there.

Philosophers shook their heads, but the practical men were satisfied. War was where it belonged—in the hands of the individual.

Of course, there were ramifications to the game, and elaborations. Once its existence had been accepted it became big business. There were services for Victim and Hunter alike.

The Emotional Catharsis Board picked the Victims' names at random. A Hunter was allowed two weeks in which to make his kill. This had to be done by his own ingenuity, unaided. He was given the name of his Victim, address and description, and allowed to use a standard-caliber pistol. He could wear no armor of any sort.

The Victim was notified a week before the Hunter. He was told only that he was a Victim. He did not know the name of his Hunter. He was allowed his choice of armor. He could hire spotters. A spotter couldn't kill; only Victim and Hunter could do that. But he could detect a stranger in town, or ferret out a nervous gunman.

The Victim could arrange any kind of ambush in his power to kill the Hunter.

There were stiff penalties for killing or wounding the wrong man, for no other murder was allowed. Grudge killings and gain killings were punishable by death.

The beauty of the system was that the people who wanted to kill could do so. Those who didn't—the bulk of the population—didn't have to.

At least, there weren't any more big wars. Not even the imminence of one. Just hundreds of thousands of small ones.

Frelaine didn't especially like the idea of killing a woman; but she *had* signed up. It wasn't his fault. And he wasn't going to lose out on his seventh hunt.

He spent the rest of the morning memorizing the data on his Victim, then filed the letter.

Janet Patzig lived in New York. That was good. He enjoyed hunting in a big city, and he had always wanted to see New York. Her age wasn't given, but to judge from her photographs, she was in her early twenties.

Frelaine phoned for his jet reservations to New York, then took a shower. He dressed with care in a new Protec-Suit Special made for the occasion. From his collection he selected a gun, cleaned and oiled it, and fitted it into the fling-out pocket of the suit. Then he packed his suitcase.

A pulse of excitement was pounding in his veins. Strange, he thought, how each killing was a new thrill. It was something you just didn't tire of, the way you did of French pastry or women or drinking or anything else. It was always new and different.

Finally, he looked over his books to see which he would take.

His library contained all the good books on the subject. He wouldn't need any of his Victim books, like L. Fred Tracy's *Tactics for the Victim*, with its insistence on a rigidly controlled environment, or Dr. Frisch's *Don't Think Like a Victim!*

He would be very interested in those in a few months, when he was a Victim again. Now he wanted hunting books.

*Tactics for Hunting Humans* was the standard and definitive work, but he had it almost memorized. *Development of the Ambush* was not adapted to his present needs.

He chose *Hunting in Cities*, by Mitwell and Clark, *Spotting the Spotter*, by Algreen, and *The Victim's In-group*, by the same author.

Everything was in order. He left a note for the milkman, locked his apartment and took a cab to the airport.

In New York, he checked into a hotel in the midtown area, not too far from his Victim's address. The clerks were smiling and attentive, which bothered Frelaine. He didn't like to be recognized so easily as an out-of-town killer.

The first thing he saw in his room was a pamphlet on his bed-table. *How to Get the Most Out of Your Emotional Catharsis*, it was called, with the compliments of the management. Frelaine smiled and thumbed through it.

Since it was his first visit to New York, he spent the afternoon just walking the streets in his Victim's neighborhood. After that, he wandered through a few stores.

Martinson and Black was a fascinating place. He went through their Hunter-Hunted room. There were lightweight bulletproof vests for Victims, and Richard Arlington hats, with bulletproof crowns.

On one side was a large display of a new .38 caliber sidearm.

"Use the Malvern Strait-shot!" the ad proclaimed. "ECB-approved. Carries a load of twelve shots. Tested deviation less than .001 inches per 1000 feet. Don't miss your Victim! Don't risk your life without the best! Be safe with Malvern!"

Frelaine smiled. The ad was good, and the small black weapon looked ultimately efficient. But he was satisfied with the one he had.

There was a special sale on trick canes, with concealed four-shot magazine, promising safety and concealment. As a young man, Frelaine had gone in heavily for novelties. But now he knew that the old-fashioned ways were usually best.

Outside the store, four men from the Department of Sanitation were carting away a freshly killed corpse. Frelaine regretted missing the take.

He ate dinner in a good restaurant and went to bed early.

Tomorrow he had a lot to do.

The next day, with the face of his Victim before him, Frelaine walked through her neighborhood. He didn't look closely at anyone. Instead, he moved rapidly, as though he were really going somewhere, the way an old Hunter should walk.

He passed several bars and dropped into one for a drink. Then he went on, down a side street off Lexington Avenue.

There was a pleasant sidewalk cafe there. Frelaine walked past it.

And there she was! He could never mistake the face. It was Janet Patzig, seated at a table, staring into a drink. She didn't look up as he passed.

Frelaine walked to the end of the block. He turned the corner and stopped, hands trembling.

Was the girl crazy, exposing herself in the open? Did she think she had a charmed life?

He hailed a taxi and had the man drive around the block. Sure enough, she was just sitting there. Frelaine took a careful look.

She seemed younger than her pictures, but he couldn't be sure. He would guess her to be not much over twenty. Her dark hair was parted in the middle and combed above her ears, giving her a nunlike appearance. Her expression, as far as Frelaine could tell, was one of resigned sadness.

Wasn't she even going to make an attempt to defend herself?

Frelaine paid the driver and hurried to a drugstore. Finding a vacant telephone booth, he called ECB.

"Are you sure that a Victim named Janet-Marie Patzig has been notified?"

"Hold on, sir." Frelaine tapped on the door while the clerk looked up the information. "Yes, sir. We have her personal confirmation. Is there anything wrong, sir?"

"No," Frelaine said. "Just wanted to check."

After all, it was no one's business if the girl didn't want to defend herself.

He was still entitled to kill her.

It was his turn.

He postponed it for that day, however, and went to a movie. After dinner, he returned to his room and read the ECB pamphlet. Then he lay on his bed and glared at the ceiling.

All he had to do was pump a bullet into her. Just ride by in a cab and kill her.

She was being a very bad sport about it, he decided resentfully, and went to sleep.

The next afternoon, Frelaine walked by the cafe again. The girl was back, sitting at the same table. Frelaine caught a cab.

"Drive around the block very slowly," he told the driver.

"Sure," the driver said, grinning with sardonic wisdom.

From the cab, Frelaine watched for spotters. As far as he could tell, the girl had none. Both her hands were in sight upon the table.

An easy, stationary target.

Frelaine touched the button of his double-breasted jacket. A fold flew open and the gun was in his hand. He broke it open and checked the cartridges, then closed it with a snap.

"Slowly, now," he told the driver.

The taxi crawled by the cafe. Frelaine took careful aim, centering the girl in his sights. His finger tightened on the trigger.

"Damn it!" he said.

A waiter had passed by the girl. He didn't want to chance winging someone else.

"Around the block again," he told the driver.

The man gave him another grin and hunched down in his seat. Frelaine wondered if the driver would feel so happy if he knew that Frelaine was gunning for a woman.

This time there was no waiter around. The girl was lighting a cigarette, her mournful face intent on her lighter. Frelaine centered her in his sights, squarely above the eyes, and held his breath.

Then he shook his head and put the gun back in his pocket.

The idiotic girl was robbing him of the full benefit of his catharsis.

He paid the driver and started to walk.

It's too easy, he told himself. He was used to a real chase. Most of the other six kills had been quite difficult. The Victims had tried every dodge. One had hired at least a dozen spotters. But Frelaine had reached them all by altering his tactics to meet the situation.

Once he had dressed as a milkman, another time as a bill collector. The sixth Victim he had had to chase through the Sierra Nevadas. The man had clipped him, too. But Frelaine had done better.

How could he be proud of this one? What would the Tens Club say?

That brought Frelaine up with a start. He wanted to get into the club. Even if he passed up this girl he would have to defend himself against a Hunter. If he survived, he would still be four hunts away from membership. At that rate, he might never get in.

He began to pass the cafe again, then, on impulse, stopped abruptly.

"Hello," he said.

Janet Patzig looked at him out of sad blue eyes, but said nothing.

"Say, look," he said, sitting down. "If I'm being fresh, just tell me and I'll go. I'm an out-of-towner. Here on a convention. And I'd just like someone feminine to talk to. If you'd rather I didn't—"

"I don't care," Janet Patzig said tonelessly.

"A brandy," Frelaine told the waiter. Janet Patzig's glass was still half full.

Frelaine looked at the girl and he could feel his heart throbbing against his ribs. This was more like it—having a drink with your Victim!

"My name's Stanton Frelaine," he said, knowing it didn't matter.

"Janet."

"Janet what?"

"Janet Patzig."

"Nice to know you," Frelaine said, in a perfectly natural voice. "Are you doing anything tonight, Janet?"

"I'm probably being killed tonight," she said quietly.

Frelaine looked at her carefully. Did she realize who he was? For all he knew, she had a gun leveled at him under the table.

He kept his hand close to the fling-out button.

"Are you a Victim?" he asked.

"You guessed it," she said sardonically. "If I were you, I'd stay out of the way. No sense getting hit by mistake."

Frelaine couldn't understand the girl's calm. Was she a suicide? Perhaps she just didn't care. Perhaps she wanted to die.

"Haven't you got any spotters?" he asked, with the right expression of amazement.

"No." She looked at him, full in the face, and Frelaine saw something he hadn't noticed before.

She was very lovely.

"I am a bad, bad girl," she said lightly. "I got the idea I'd like to commit a murder, so I signed for ECB. Then—I couldn't do it."

Frelaine shook his head, sympathizing with her.

"But I'm still in, of course. Even if I didn't shoot, I still have to be a Victim."

"But why don't you hire some spotters?" he asked.

"I couldn't kill anyone," she said. "I just couldn't. I don't even have a gun."

"You've got a lot of courage," Frelaine said, "coming out in the open this way." Secretly, he was amazed at her stupidity.

"What can I do?" she asked listlessly. "You can't hide from a Hunter. Not a real one. And I don't have enough money to make a good disappearance."

"Since it's in your own defense, I should think—" Frelaine began, but she interrupted.

"No. I've made up my mind on that. This whole thing is wrong, the whole system. When I had my Victim in the sights—when I saw how easily I could—I could—"

She pulled herself together quickly.

"Oh, let's forget it," she said and smiled.

Frelaine found her smile dazzling.

After that, they talked of other things. Frelaine told her of his business, and she told him about New York. She was twenty-two, an unsuccessful actress.

They had supper together. When she accepted Frelaine's invitation to go to the Gladiatorials, he felt absurdly elated.

He called a cab—he seemed to be spending his entire time in New York in cabs—and opened the door for her. She started in. Frelaine hesitated. He could have pumped a shot into her at that moment. It would have been very easy.

But he held back. Just for the moment, he told himself.

The Gladiatorials were about the same as those held anywhere else, except that the talent was a little better. There were the usual historical events, swordsmen and netmen, duels with saber and foil.

Most of these, naturally, were fought to the death.

Then bull fighting, lion fighting and rhino fighting, followed by the more modern events. Fights from behind barricades with bow and arrow. Dueling on a high wire.

The evening passed pleasantly.

Frelaine escorted the girl home, the palms of his hands sticky with sweat. He had never found a woman he liked better. And yet she was his legitimate kill.

He didn't know what he was going to do.

She invited him in and they sat together on the couch. The girl lighted a cigarette for herself with a large lighter, then settled back.

"Are you leaving soon?" she asked him.

"I suppose so," Frelaine said. "The convention is only lasting another day."

She was silent for a moment. "I'll be sorry to see you go."

They were quiet for a while. Then Janet went to fix him a drink. Frelaine eyed her retreating back. Now was the time. He placed his hand near the button.

But the moment had passed for him, irrevocably. He wasn't going to kill her. You don't kill the girl you love.

The realization that he loved her was shocking. He'd come to kill, not to find a wife.

She came back with the drink and sat down opposite him, staring at emptiness.

"Janet," he said. "I love you."

She sat, just looking at him. There were tears in her eyes.

"You can't," she protested. "I'm a Victim. I won't live long enough to—"

"You won't be killed. I'm your Hunter."

She stared at him a moment, then laughed uncertainly.

"Are you going to kill me?" she asked.

"Don't be ridiculous," he said. "I'm going to marry you."

Suddenly she was in his arms.

"Oh, Lord!" she gasped. "The waiting—I've been so frightened—"

"It's all over," he told her. "Think what a story it'll make for our kids. How I came to murder you and left marrying you."

She kissed him, then sat back and lighted another cigarette.

"Let's start packing," Frelaine said. "I want—"

"Wait," Janet interrupted. "You haven't asked if *I* love *you*."

"What?"

She was still smiling, and the cigarette lighter was pointed at him. In the bottom of it was a black hole. A hole just large enough for a .38 caliber bullet.

"Don't kid around," he objected, getting to his feet.

"I'm not being funny, darling," she said.

In a fraction of a second, Frelaine had time to wonder how he could ever have thought she was not much over twenty. Looking at her now—*really* looking at her—he knew she couldn't be much less than thirty. Every minute of her strained, tense existence showed on her face.

"I don't love you, Stanton," she said very softly, the cigarette lighter poised.

Frelaine struggled for breath. One part of him was able to realize detachedly what a marvelous actress she really was. She must have known all along.

Frelaine pushed the button, and the gun was in his hand, cocked and ready.

The blow that struck him in the chest knocked him over a coffee table. The gun fell out of his hand. Gasping, half-conscious, he watched her take careful aim for the *coup de grâce*.

"Now I can join the Tens," he heard her say elatedly as she squeezed the trigger.

# The Racer

## IB MELCHIOR

**Death Race 2000**

Director: *Paul Bartel*
Screenplay: *Robert Thom, Charles B. Griffith*
Producer: *Roger Corman*
Music: *Paul Chihara*
Special Effects: *Richard Maclean*
Cars: *James Power, Dean Jefferies*
Cast: *David Carradine, Simone Griffeth, Sylvester Stallone*
Released by: *New World*
1975, 78 Minutes. Color.

Willie felt the familiar intoxicating excitement. His mouth was dry; his heart beat faster, all his senses seemed more aware than ever. It was a few minutes before 0800 hours—his time to start.

This was the day. From all the Long Island Starting Fields the Racers were taking off at 15-minute intervals. The sputter and roar of cars warming up were everywhere. The smell of oil and fuel fumes permeated the air. The hubbub of the great crowd was a steady din. This was the biggest race of the year—New York to Los Angeles—100,000 bucks to the winner! Willie was determined to better his winning record of last year: 33 hours, 27 minutes, 12 seconds in Time. And although it was becoming increasingly difficult he'd do his damnedest to better his Score too!

He took a last walk of inspection around his car. Sleek, low-slung, dark brown, the practically indestructible plastiglass top looking deceptively fragile, like a soap bubble. Not bad for an old-fashioned diesel job. He kicked the solid plastirubber tires in the time-honored fashion of all drivers. Hank was giving a last-minute shine to the needle-sharp durasteel horns protruding from the front fenders. Willie's car wasn't nicknamed "The Bull" without reason. The front of the car was built like a streamlined bull's head complete with bloodshot, evil-looking eyes, iron ring through flaring nostrils—and the horns. Although most of the racing cars were built to look like tigers, or sharks, or eagles, there *were* a few bulls—but Willie's horns were unequalled.

"Car 79 ready for Start in five minutes," the loudspeaker blared. "Car 79. Willie Connors, driver. Hank Morowski, mechanic. Ready your car for Start in five minutes."

Willie and Hank took their places in "The Bull." At a touch by Willie on the starter the powerful diesel engine began a low purr. They drove slowly to the starting line.

"Last Check!" said Willie.

"Right," came Hank's answer.

"Oil and Fuel?"

"40 hours."

"Cooling Fluid?"

"Sealed."

"No-Sleeps?"

"Check."

"Energene Tabs?"

"Check."

"Thermo Drink?"

"Check."

The Starter held the checkered flag high over his head. The crowds packing the grandstands were on their feet. Hushed. Waiting.

"Here we go!" whispered Willie.

The flag fell. A tremendous cry rose from the crowd. But Willie hardly heard it. Accelerating furiously he pushed his car to its top speed of 190 miles an hour within seconds—shooting like a bullet along the straightaway toward Manhattan. He was elated; exhilarated. He was a Racer. And full of tricks!

Willie shot through the Tunnel directly to Jersey.

"Well?" grumbled Hank. "Can you tell me now?"

"Toledo," said Willie. "Toledo, Ohio. On the Thruway. We should make it in under three hours."

He felt a slight annoyance with Hank. There was no reason for the man to be touchy. He knew a driver didn't tell *anyone* the racing route he'd selected. News like that had a habit of getting around. It could cost a Racer his Score.

"There's not much chance of anything coming up until after we hit Toledo," Willie said, "but keep your eyes peeled. You never know."

Hank merely grunted.

It was exactly 1048 hours when "The Bull" streaked into the deserted streets of Toledo.

"O.K.—what now?" asked Hank.

"Grand Rapids, Michigan," said Willie laconically.

"Grand Rapids! But that's—that's an easy 300 miles detour!"

"I know."

"Are you crazy? It'll cost us a couple of hours."

"So Grand Rapids is all the way up between the Lakes. So who'll be expecting us up there?"

"Oh! Oh, yeah, I see," said Hank.

"The *Time* isn't everything, my friend. Whoever said the shortest distance between two points is a straight line? The *Score* counts too. And here's where we pick up *our* Score!"

The first Tragi-Acc never even knew the Racer had arrived. "The Bull" struck him squarely, threw him up in the air and let him slide off its plastiglass back, leaving a red smear behind and somewhat to the left of Willie—all in a split second. . . .

Near Calvin College an imprudent coed found herself too far from cover when the Racer suddenly came streaking down the campus. Frantically she sprinted for safety, but she didn't have a chance with a driver like Willie behind the wheel. The razor sharp horn on the right fender sliced through her spine so cleanly that the jar wasn't even felt inside the car.

Leaving town the Racer was in luck again. An elderly woman had left the sanctuary of her stone-walled garden to rescue a straying cat. She was so easy to hit that Willie felt a little cheated.

At 1232 hours they were on the speedway headed for Kansas City.

Hank looked in awe at Willie. "Three!" he murmured dreamily, "a Score of three already. And all of them Kills—for sure. You *really* know how to drive!"

Hank settled back contentedly as if he could already feel his 25,000 dollar cut in his pocket. He began to whistle "*The Racers Are Roaring*" off key.

Even after his good Score it annoyed Willie. And for some reason he kept remembering the belatedly pleading look in the old woman's eyes as he struck her. Funny *that* should stay with him . . .

He estimated they'd hit Kansas City at around 1815 hours, CST. Hank turned on the radio. Peoria, Illinois, was warning its citizens of the approach of a Racer. All spectators should watch from safety places. Willie grinned. That would be him. Well—he wasn't looking for any Score in Peoria.

Dayton, Ohio, told of a Racer having made a Tragic Accident Score of one, and Fort Wayne, Indiana, was crowing over the fact that three Racers had passed through without scoring once. From what he heard it seemed to Willie he had a comfortable lead, both in Time and Score.

They were receiving Kansas City now. An oily-voiced announcer was filling in the time between Racing Scores with what appeared to be a brief history of Racing.

". . . and the most popular spectator sports of the latter half of the 20th Century were such mildly exciting pursuits as boxing and wrestling. Of course the spectators enjoyed seeing the combatants trying to maim each other, and there was always the chance of the hoped-for fatal accident.

"Motor Racing, however, gave a much greater opportunity for the Tragic Accidents so exciting to the spectator. One of the most famed old speedways, Indianapolis, where many drivers and spectators alike ended as bloody Tragi-Accs, is today the nation's racing shrine. Motor Racing was already then held all over the world, sometimes with Scores reaching the hundred mark, and long-distance races were popular.

"The modern Race makes it possible for the entire population to . . ."

Willie switched off the radio. Why did they always have to stress the *Score?* *Time* was important too. The *speed*—and the *endurance.* That was part of an Ace Racer as well as his scoring ability. He took an Energene Tab. They were entering Kansas City.

The check point officials told Willie that there were three Racers with better Time than he, and one had tied his Score. "The Bull" stayed just long enough in the check point pit for Hank to make a quick engine inspection—then they took off again. It was 1818 hours, CST, when they left the city limits behind. They'd been driving over nine hours.

About 50 miles along the Thruway to Denver, just after passing through a little town called Lawrence, Willie suddenly slowed down. Hank, who'd been dozing, sat up in alarm.

"What's the matter?" he cried, "what's wrong?"

"Nothing's wrong," Willie said irritably. "Relax. You seem to be good at that."

"But why are you slowing down?"

"You heard the check point record. Our Score's already been tied. We've got to better it," Willie answered grimly.

The plastirubber tires screeched on the concrete speedway as Willie turned down an exit leading to a Class II road.

"Why down here?" asked Hank. "You can only go about 80 MPH."

A large lumi-sign appeared on the side of the road ahead—

it announced.

Willie pointed. "That's why," he said curtly.

In a few minutes Lone Star came into view. It was a small village. Willie was traveling as fast as he could on the secondary road. He plowed through a flock of chickens, hurtled over a little mongrel dog, which crawled yelping towards the safety of a house and the waiting arms of a little girl, and managed to graze the leg of a husky youth who vaulted a high wooden fence—then they were through Lone Star.

Hank activated the little dashboard screen which gave them a rear view.

"That's not going to do much for our Score," he remarked sourly.

"Oh, shut up!" Willie exploded, surprising both himself and Hank.

What was the *matter* with him? He couldn't be getting tired already. He swallowed a No-Sleep. That'd help.

Hank was quiet as they sped through Topeka and took the Thruway to Oklahoma City, but out of the corner of his eyes he was looking speculatively at Willie, hunched over the wheel.

It was getting dusk. Willie switched on his powerful headbeams. They had a faint reddish tint because of the coloring of "The Bull's" eyes. They had just whizzed through a little burg named Perry, when there was a series of sharp cracks. Willie started.

"There they go again!" chortled Hank. "Those dumb hinterland hicks will never learn they can't hurt us with their fly-poppers." He knocked the plastiglass dome affectionately. "Takes atomic pellets to get through this baby."

Of course! He *must* be on edge to be taken by surprise like that. He'd run into the Anti-Racers before. Just a handful of malcontents. The Racing Commission had already declared them illegal. Still—at every race they took pot shots at the Racers; a sort of pathetic defiance. Why should anyone want to do away with Racing?

They were entering the outskirts of Oklahoma City. Willie killed his headbeams. No need to advertise.

Suddenly Hank grabbed his arm. Wordlessly he pointed. There—garish and gaudy—gleamed the neon sign of a theater. . . .

Willie slowed to a crawl. He pulled over to the curb and the dark car melted into the shadows. He glanced at the clock. 2203 hours. Perhaps . . .

Down the street a man cautiously stuck his head out from the theater entrance. Warily he emerged completely, looking up and down the street carefully. He did not see "The Bull." Presently he ventured out into the center of the roadway. He stood still listening for a moment. Then he turned and beckoned towards the theater. Immediately a small group of people emerged at a run.

Now!

The acceleration slammed the Racers back in their seats. "The Bull" shot forward and bore down on the little knot of petrified people with appalling speed.

This time there was no mistaking the hits. A quick succession of pars had Willie calling upon all his driving skill to keep from losing control. Hank pressed the Clean-Spray button to wash the blood off the front of the dome. He sat with eyes glued to the rear view screen.

"Man, oh man," he murmured. "What a record! What a Score!" He turned to Willie. "Please," he said, "please stop. Let's get out. I know it's against regulations, but I've just gotta see how we did. It won't take long. We can afford a couple of minutes' Time now!"

Suddenly Willie felt he had to get out too. This was the biggest Tragi-Acc he'd ever had. He had a vague feeling there was something he wanted to do. He brought the car to a stop. They stepped out.

Within seconds the deserted street was swarming with people. Now the Racers were out of their car they felt safe. And curious. A few of them pressed forward to take a look at Willie. Naturally he was recognized. His photo had been seen in one way or another by everyone.

Willie was gratified by this obvious adulation. He looked about him. There were many people in the street now. But—but they were not all fawning and beaming upon him. Willie frowned. Most of them looked grim—even hostile. Why? What was wrong? Wasn't he one of their greatest Racers? And hadn't he just made a record Score? Given them a Tragi-Acc they wouldn't soon forget? What was the matter with those hicks?

Suddenly the crowd parted. Slowly a young girl walked up to Willie. She was beautiful—even with the terrible anger burning on her face. In her arms she held the still body of a child. She looked straight at Willie with loathing in her eyes. Her voice was low but steady when she said:

"*Butcher!*"

Someone in the crowd called: "Careful, Muriel!" but she paid no heed. Turning from him she walked on through the crowd, parting for her.

Willie was stunned.

"Come on, let's get out of here," Hank said anxiously.

Willie didn't answer. He was looking back through the crowd to the scene of his Tragi-Acc. Never before had he stopped. Never before had he been this close. He could hear the moaning and sobbing of the Maims over the low murmur of the crowd. It made him uneasy. Back there they worked hurriedly

to get the Tragi-Accs off the street. *There were so many of them....*
Butcher ... ?

All at once he was conscious of Hank pulling at him.

"Let's get roaring! Let's go!"

Quickly he turned and entered the car. Almost at once the street was empty. He turned on his headbeams and started up. Faster—and faster. The street was dead—empty. . . .

No! There! Someone! Holding a . . .

It was butcher—no, *Muriel.* She stood rooted to the spot in the middle of the street holding the child in her arms. In the glaring headlights her face was white, her eyes terrible, burning, dark . . .

Willie did not let up. The car hurtled down upon the lone figure—and passed. . . .

They'd lost 13 minutes. Now they were on their way to El Paso, Texas. The nagging headache Willie'd suffered the whole week of planning before the race had returned. He reached for a No-Sleep, hesitated a second, then took another.

Hank glanced at him, worriedly. "Easy, boy!"

Willie didn't answer.

"That Anti-Racer get under your skin?" Hank suggested. "Don't let it bother you."

*"Butcher," she'd said. "Butcher!"*

Willie was staring through the plastiglass dome at the racing pool of light from the headbeams. "The Bull" was tearing along the Thruway at almost 180 MPH.

What was that? There—in the light? It was a face—terrible, dark eyes—getting larger—larger—*Muriel!* It was butcher—no, Muriel! No—it was a Racer—a Racing Car with Muriel's face, shrieking down upon him—closer—closer . . .

He threw his arms in front of his face. Dimly he heard Hank shout "Willie!" He felt the car lurch. Automatically he tightened his grip on the wheel. They had careened close to the shoulder of the speedway. Willie sat up. Ahead of him the road was clear—and empty.

It was still dark when they hit El Paso. The radio told them their Oklahoma Score. Five and eight. Five Kills—eight Maims! Hank was delighted. They were close to setting a record. He'd already begun to spend his $25,000.

Willie was uneasy. His headache was worse. His hands were clammy. He kept hearing Muriel's voice saying: "Butcher"—"Butcher"—"Butcher!" . . .

But he was *not* a butcher. He was a Racer! He'd show them. He'd win this race.

El Paso was a disappointment. Not a soul in sight. Phoenix next.

The clock said 0658 hours, MST, when they roared into Phoenix. The streets were clear. Willie had to slow down to take a corner. As he sped into the new street he saw her. She was running to cross the roadway. Hank whooped.

"Go, Willie! Go!"

The girl looked up an instant in terror.

*Her face!*

It was the old woman with the cat! No!—it was Muriel. Muriel with the big, dark eyes. . . .

In the last split second Willie touched the power steering. "The Bull" responded immediately, and shot past the girl as she scampered to safety.

"What the hell is the matter with you?" Hank roared at Willie. "You could've scored! Are you out of your head?"

"We don't need her. We'll win without her. I—I—"

Yes, why hadn't he scored? It wasn't Muriel. Muriel was back in butcher—in—Oklahoma City. Damn this headache!

"Maybe so," said Hank angrily. "But I wanna be sure. And what about the bonus for setting a record? Ten thousand apiece. And we're close." He looked slyly at Willie. "Or—maybe you've lost your nerve. Wonder what the Commission will say to that?"

"I've got plenty of nerve," Willie snapped.

"Prove it!" said Hank quickly. He pointed to the dashboard map slowly tracing their progress. "There. See that village? With the screwy name? *Wikieup!* Off the Thruway. Let's see you score there!"

Willie said nothing. He hadn't lost his nerve, he knew that. He was the best of the Racers. No one could drive like he could; constant top speed, and the stamina it took, the split-second timing, the unerring judgment—

"Well?"

"All right," Willie agreed.

They hadn't even reached Wikieup when they spotted the farmer. He didn't have a chance. "The Bull" came charging down upon him. But in the last moment the car veered slightly. One of the horns ripped the man's hip open. In the rear view screen Willie saw him get up and hobble off the road.

"You could've made it a Kill," Hank growled accusingly. "Why didn't you?"

"Bad road," Willie said. "The wheel slipped on a stone."

That's what must have happened, he thought. He didn't consciously veer away from the man. He was a good Racer. He couldn't help a bad road.

Needles was left behind at 1045 hours, PST. No one had been out. Hank turned on the radio to a Needles station:

". . . has just left the city going West. No other Racer is reported within twenty minutes of the city. We repeat: A Racer has just left. . . ."

Hank clicked it off. "Hear that?" he said excitedly. "Twenty minutes. They don't expect anyone for twenty minutes!" He took hold of Willie's arm. "Turn around! Here's where we can get ourselves that Record Score. Turn around, Willie!"

"We don't need it."

"I do! *I want that bonus!*"

Willie made no answer.

"Listen to me, you two-bit Racer!" Hank's tone was menacing. "You or nobody else is going to cheat me out of that bonus. You've been acting mighty peculiar. More like an Anti-Racer! Ever since you stopped at that Tragi-Acc back there. Yeah! That girl—that Anti-Racer who called you a—a butcher. Listen! You get that Record Score, or I'll report you to the Commission for having snooped around a Tragi-Acc. You'll never race again!"

Never race again! Willie's brain was whirling. But he *was* a Racer. Not a butcher. *A Racer.* Record Score? Yes—that's what he had to do. Set a record. Be the best damned Racer of them all.

Without a word he turned the car. In minutes they were back at the Needles suburbs. That building. A school house. And there—marching orderly in two rows with their teacher, a class, a whole class of children. . . .

"The Bull" came charging down the street. Only a couple of hundred feet now to that Record Score. . . .

But what was that—it was . . . they were *Muriel*—they were all Muriel. Terrible, dark eyes. No!—they were children—the child in Muriel's arms. *They were all the child in Muriel's arms!* Were they already moaning and screaming? Butcher! *Butcher!* No! He couldn't butcher them—he was a *Racer*—not a *butcher. Not a butcher!* Deliberately he swung the car to the empty side of the street.

Suddenly he felt Hank's hands up on the wheel. "You—dirty—lousy—Anti-Racer!" the mechanic snarled as he struggled for the wheel.

The car lurched. The two men fought savagely for control. They were only yards from the fleeing children.

With a violent wrench Willie turned the wheel sharply. The car was going 165 miles an hour when it struck the school house and crashed through the wall into the empty building.

The voices came to Willie through thick wads of cotton—and they kept fading in and out.

". . . *dead instantaneously. But the Racer is still* . . ."

It sounded like the voice of Muriel. Muriel . . .

". . . *keeps calling for* . . ."

Willie tried to open his eyes. Everything was milky white. Why was there so much fog? A face was bending over him. Muriel? No—it was not Muriel. He lost consciousness again.

When he opened his eyes once more he knew he was not alone. He turned his head. A girl was sitting at his bedside. Muriel . . .

It *was* Muriel.

He tried to sit up.

"It's you! But—but, how . . . ?"

The girl put her hand on his arm.

"The radio. They said you kept calling for 'Muriel.' I knew. Never mind that now."

She looked steadily at him. Her eyes were not terrible—not burning—only dark, and puzzled.

"Why did you call for *me?*" she asked earnestly.

Willie struggled to sit up.

"I wanted to tell you," he said, "to tell you—I—I am not a butcher!"

The girl looked at him for a long moment. Then she leaned down and whispered to him:

*"Nor a Racer!"*

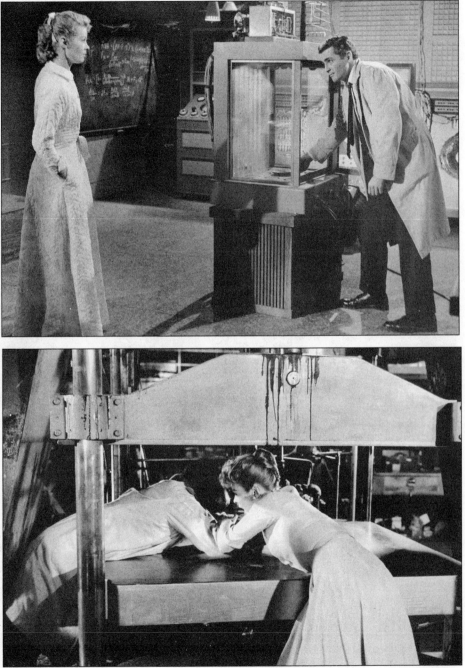

The star-crossed lovers (Al Hedison and Patricia Owens) in *The Fly* (1958) soon realize that their romance must end tragically.

Seth Brundle (Jeff Goldblum) realizes that his teleportation is causing a troubling metamorphosis in *The Fly* (1986).

# The Fly

## GEORGE LANGELAAN

**THE FLY**

Director/Producer: *Kurt Neumann*
Screenplay: *James Clavell*
Music: *Paul Sawtell*
Special Effects: *L. B. Abbott*
Cast: *Vincent Price, Al "David" Hedison, Patricia Owens*
Released by: *20th Century-Fox*
1958, 94 Minutes. B&W.

**THE FLY**

Director: *David Cronenberg*
Screenplay: *Charles Edward Pogue, David Cronenberg*
Producer: *Stuart Cornfeld*
Music: *Howard Shore*
Special Effects: *ILM*
Cast: *Jeff Goldblum, Geena Davis*
Released by: *20th Century-Fox*
1986, 100 Minutes. Color.

Telephones and telephone bells have always made me uneasy. Years ago, when they were mostly wall fixtures, I disliked them, but nowadays, when they are planted in every nook and corner, they are a downright intrusion. We have a saying in France that a coalman is master in his own house; with the telephone that is no longer true, and I suspect that even the Englishman is no longer king in his own castle.

At the office, the sudden ringing of the telephone annoys me. It means that, no matter what I am doing, in spite of the switchboard operator, in spite of my secretary, in spite of doors and walls, some unknown person is coming into the room and onto my desk to talk right into my very ear, confidentially—whether I like it or not. At home, the feeling is still more disagreeable, but the worst is when the telephone rings in the dead of night. If anyone could see me turn on the light and get up blinking to answer it, I suppose I would look like any other sleepy man annoyed at being disturbed. The truth in such a case, however, is that I am struggling against panic, fighting down a feeling that a stranger has broken into the house and is in my bedroom. By the time I manage to grab the receiver and say: *"Ici Monsieur Delambre. Je vous écoute,"* I am outwardly calm, but I only get back to a more normal state when I recognize the voice at the other end and when I know what is wanted of me.

This effort at dominating a purely animal reaction and fear had become so effective that when my sister-in-law called me at two in the morning, asking me to come over, but first to warn the police that she had just killed my brother, I quietly asked her how and why she had killed André.

"But, François! . . . I can't explain all that over the telephone. Please call the police and come quickly."

"Maybe I had better see you first, Hélène?"

"No, you'd better call the police first; otherwise they will start asking you all sorts of awkward questions. They'll have enough trouble as it is to believe that I did it alone . . . And, by the way, I suppose you ought to tell them that André . . . André's body, is down at the factory. They may want to go there first."

"Did you say that André is at the factory?"

"Yes . . . under the steam-hammer."

"Under the what!"

"The steam-hammer! But don't ask so many questions. Please come quickly François! Please understand that I'm afraid . . . that my nerves won't stand it much longer!"

Have you ever tried to explain to a sleepy police officer that your sister-in-law has just phoned to say that she has killed your brother with a steam-hammer? I repeated my explanation, but he would not let me.

*"Qui, monsieur, oui,* I hear . . . but who are you? What is your name? Where do you live? I said, where do you live!"

It was then that Commissaire Charas took over the line and the whole business. He at least seemed to understand everything. Would I wait for him? Yes, he would pick me up and take me over to my brother's house. When? In five or ten minutes.

I had just managed to pull on my trousers, wriggle into a sweater and grab a hat and coat, when a black Citroën, headlights blazing, pulled up at the door.

"I assume you have a night watchman at your factory, Monsieur Delambre. Has he called you?" asked Commissaire Charas, letting in the clutch as I sat down beside him and slammed the door of the car.

"No, he hasn't. Though of course my brother could have entered the factory through his laboratory where he often works late at night . . . all night sometimes."

"Is Professor Delambre's work connected with your business?"

"No, my brother is, or was, doing research work for the Ministère de l'Air. As he wanted to be away from Paris and yet within reach of where skilled workmen could fix up or make gadgets big and small for his experiments, I offered him one of the old workshops of the factory and he came to live in the first house built by our grandfather on the top of the hill at the back of the factory."

"Yes, I see. Did he talk about his work? What sort of research work?"

"He rarely talked about it, you know; I suppose the Air Ministry could tell you. I only know that he was about to carry out a number of experiments he had been preparing for some months, something to do with the disintegration of matter, he told me."

Barely slowing down, the Commissaire swung the car off the road, slid it through the open factory gate and pulled up sharp by a policeman apparently expecting him.

I did not need to hear the policeman's confirmation. I knew now that my brother was dead, it seemed that I had been told years ago. Shaking like a leaf, I scrambled out after the Commissaire.

Another policeman stepped out of a doorway and led us towards one of the shops where all the lights had been turned on. More policemen were standing by the hammer, watching two men setting up a camera. It was tilted downwards, and I made an effort to look.

It was far less horrid than I had expected. Though I had never seen my brother drunk, he looked just as if he were sleeping off a terrific binge, flat on his stomach across the narrow line on which the white-hot slabs of metal were rolled up to the hammer. I saw at a glance that his head and arm could only be a flattened mess, but that seemed quite impossible; it looked as if he had somehow pushed his head and arms right into the metallic mass of the hammer.

Having talked to his colleagues, the Commissaire turned towards me:

"How can we raise the hammer, Monsieur Delambre?"

"I'll raise it for you."

"Would you like us to get one of your men over?"

"No, I'll be all right. Look, here is the switchboard. It was originally a steam-hammer, but everything is worked electrically here now. Look, Commissaire, the hammer has been set at fifty tons and its impact at zero."

"At zero . . . ?"

"Yes, level with the ground if you prefer. It is also set for single strokes, which means that it has to be raised after each blow. I don't know what Hélène, my sister-in-law, will have to say about all this, but one thing I am sure of: she certainly did not know how to set and operate the hammer."

"Perhaps it was set that way last night when work stopped?"

"Certainly not. The drop is never set at zero, Monsieur le Commissaire."

"I see. Can it be raised gently?"

"No. The speed of the upstroke cannot be regulated. But in any case it is not very fast when the hammer is set for single strokes."

"Right. Will you show me what to do? It won't be very nice to watch, you know."

"No, no, Monsieur le Commissaire. I'll be all right."

"All set?" asked the Commissaire of the others. "All right then, Monsieur Delambre. Whenever you like."

Watching my brother's back, I slowly but firmly pushed the upstroke button.

The unusual silence of the factory was broken by the sigh of compressed air rushing into the cylinders, a sigh that always makes me think of a giant taking a deep breath before solemnly socking another giant, and the steel mass of the hammer shuddered and then rose swiftly. I also heard the sucking sound as it left the metal base and thought I was going to panic when I saw André's body heave forward as a sickly gush of blood poured all over the ghastly mess bared by the hammer.

"No danger of it coming down again, Monsieur Delambre?"

"No, none whatever," I mumbled as I threw the safety switch and, turning around, I was violently sick in front of a young green-faced policeman.

For weeks after, Commissaire Charas worked on the case, listening, questioning, running all over the place, making out reports, telegraphing and telephoning right and left. Later, we became quite friendly and he owned that he had for a long time considered me as suspect number one, but had finally given up that idea because, not only was there no clue of any sort, but not even a motive.

Hélène, my sister-in-law, was so calm throughout the whole business that the doctors finally confirmed what I had long considered the only possible solution: that she was mad. That being the case, there was of course no trial.

My brother's wife never tried to defend herself in any way and even got quite annoyed when she realized that people thought her mad, and this of course was considered proof that she was indeed mad. She owned up to the murder of her husband and proved easily that she knew how to handle the hammer; but she would never say why, exactly how, or under what circumstances she had killed my brother. The great mystery was how and why had my brother so obligingly stuck his head under the hammer, the only possible explanation for his part in the drama.

The night watchman had heard the hammer all right; he had even heard it twice, he claimed. This was very strange, and the stroke-counter which was always set back to nought after a job, seemed to prove him right, since it marked the figure two. Also, the foreman in charge of the hammer confirmed that after cleaning up the day before the murder, he had as usual turned the stroke-counter back to nought. In spite of this, Hélène maintained that she had only used the hammer once, and this seemed just another proof of her insanity.

Commissaire Charas, who had been put in charge of the case, at first wondered if the victim were really my brother. But of that there was no possible doubt, if only because of the great scar running from his knee to his thigh, the result of a shell that had landed within a few feet of him during the retreat in 1940; and there were also the fingerprints of his left hand which corresponded to those found all over his laboratory and his personal belongings up at the house.

A guard had been put on his laboratory and the next day half-a-dozen officials came down from the Air Ministry. They went through all his papers and took away some of his instruments, but before leaving, they told the Commissaire that the most interesting documents and instruments had been destroyed.

The Lyons police laboratory, one of the most famous in the world, reported that André's head had been wrapped up in a piece of velvet when it was crushed by the hammer, and one day Commissaire Charas showed me a tattered drapery which I immediately recognized as the brown velvet cloth I had seen on a table in my brother's laboratory, the one on which his meals were served when he could not leave his work.

After only a very few days in prison, Hélène had been transferred to a nearby asylum, one of the three in France where insane criminals are taken care of. My nephew Henri, a boy of six, the very image of his father, was entrusted to me, and eventually all legal arrangements were made for me to become his guardian and tutor.

Hélène, one of the quietest patients of the asylum, was allowed visitors and I went to see her on Sundays. Once or twice the Commissaire had accompanied me and, later, I learned that he had also visited Hélène alone. But we were never able to obtain any information from my sister-in-law, who seemed to have become utterly indifferent. She rarely answered my questions and hardly ever those of the Commissaire. She spent a lot of her time sewing, but her favorite pastime seemed to be catching flies, which she invariably released unharmed after having examined them carefully.

Hélène only had one fit of raving—more like a nervous breakdown than a fit, said the doctor who had administered morphia to quieten her—the day she saw a nurse swatting flies.

The day after Hélène's one and only fit, Commissaire Charas came to see me.

"I have a strange feeling that there lies the key to the whole business, Monsieur Delambre," he said.

I did not ask him how it was that he already knew all about Hélène's fit.

"I do not follow you, Commissaire. Poor Madame Delambre could have shown an exceptional interest for anything else, really. Don't you think that flies just happen to be the border-subject of her tendency to raving?"

"Do you believe she is really mad?" he asked.

"My dear Commissaire, I don't see how there can be any doubt. Do you doubt it?"

"I don't know. In spite of all the doctors say, I have the impression that Madame Delambre has a very clear brain . . . even when catching flies."

"Supposing you were right, how would you explain her attitude with regard to her little boy? She never seems to consider him as her own child."

"You know, Monsieur Delambre, I have thought about that also. She may be trying to protect him. Perhaps she fears the boy or, for all we know, hates him?"

"I'm afraid I don't understand, my dear Commissaire."

"Have you noticed, for instance, that she never catches flies when the boy is there?"

"No. But come to think of it, you are quite right. Yes, that is strange. . . . Still, I fail to understand."

"So do I, Monsieur Delambre. And I'm very much afraid that we shall never understand, unless perhaps your sister-in-law should *get better.*"

"The doctors seem to think that there is no hope of any sort you know."

"Yes. Do you know if your brother ever experimented with flies?"

"I really don't know, but I shouldn't think so. Have you asked the Air Ministry people? They knew all about the work."

"Yes, and they laughed at me."

"I can understand that."

"You are very fortunate to understand anything, Monsieur Delambre. I do not . . . but I hope to some day."

"Tell me, Uncle, do flies live a long time?"

We were just finishing our lunch and, following an established tradition between us, I was just pouring some wine into Henri's glass for him to dip a biscuit in.

Had Henri not been staring at his glass gradually being filled to the brim, something in my look might have frightened him.

This was the first time that he had ever mentioned flies, and I shuddered at the thought that Commissaire Charas might quite easily have been present. I could imagine the glint in his eye as he would have answered my nephew's question with another question. I could almost hear him saying:

"I don't know, Henri. Why do you ask?"

"Because I have again seen the fly that *Maman* was looking for."

And it was only after drinking off Henri's own glass of wine that I realized that he had answered my spoken thought.

"I did not know that your mother was looking for a fly."

"Yes, she was. It has grown quite a lot, but I recognized it all right."

"Where did you see this fly, Henri, and . . . how did you recognize it?"

"This morning on your desk, Uncle François. Its head is white instead of black, and it has a funny sort of leg."

Feeling more and more like Commissaire Charas, but trying to look unconcerned, I went on:

"And when did you see this fly for the first time?"

"The day that Papa went away. I had caught it, but *Maman* made me let it go. And then after, she wanted me to find it again. She'd changed her mind," and shrugging his shoulders just as my brother used to, he added, "You know what women are."

"I think that fly must have died long ago, and you must be mistaken, Henri," I said, getting up and walking to the door.

But as soon as I was out of the dining room, I ran up the stairs to my study. There was no fly anywhere to be seen.

I was bothered, far more than I cared to even think about. Henri had just proved that Charas was really closer to a clue than had seemed when he told me about his thoughts concerning Hélène's pastime.

For the first time I wondered if Charas did not really know much more than he let on. For the first time also, I wondered about Hélène. Was she really insane? A strange, horrid feeling was growing on me, and the more I thought about it, the more I felt that, somehow, Charas was right: Hélène was *getting away with it!*

What could possibly have been the reason for such a monstrous crime? What had led up to it? Just what had happened?

I thought of all the hundreds of questions that Charas had put to Hélène, sometimes gently like a nurse trying to soothe, sometimes stern and cold, sometimes barking them furiously. Hélène had answered very few, always in a calm quiet voice and never seeming to pay any attention to the way in which the question had been put. Though dazed, she had seemed perfectly sane then.

Refined, well-bred and well-read, Charas was more than just an intelligent police official. He was a keen psychologist and had an amazing way of smelling out a fib or an erroneous statement even before it was uttered. I knew that he had accepted as true the few answers she had given him. But then there had been all those questions which she had never answered: the most direct and important ones. From the very beginning, Hélène had adopted a very simple system. "I cannot answer that question," she would say in her low quiet voice. And that was that! The repetition of the same question never seemed to annoy her. In all the hours of questioning that she underwent, Hélène did not once point out to the Commissaire that he had already asked her this or that. She would simply say, "I cannot answer that question," as though it was the very first time that that particular question had been asked and the very first time she had made that answer.

This cliché had become the formidable barrier beyond which Commissaire Charas could not even get a glimpse, an idea of what Hélène might be thinking. She had very willingly answered all questions about her life with my brother—which seemed a happy and uneventful one—up to the time of his end. About his death, however, all that she would say was that she had killed him with the steam-hammer, but she refused to say why, what had led up to the drama and how she got my brother to put his head under it. She never actually refused outright; she would just go blank and, with no apparent emotion, would switch over to, "I cannot answer that question for you."

Hélène, as I have said, had shown the Commissaire that she knew how to set and operate the steam-hammer.

Charas could only find one single fact which did not coincide with Hélène's declarations, the fact that the hammer had been used twice. Charas was no longer willing to attribute this to insanity. That evident flaw in Hélène's stonewall defense seemed a crack which the Commissaire might possibly enlarge. But my sister-in-law finally cemented it by acknowledging:

"All right, I lied to you. I did use the hammer twice. But do not ask me why, because I cannot tell you."

"Is that your only ... misstatement, Madame Delambre?" had asked the Commissaire, trying to follow up what looked at last like an advantage.

"It is ... and you know it, Monsieur le Commissaire."

And, annoyed, Charas had seen that Hélène could read him like an open book.

I had thought of calling on the Commissaire, but the knowledge that he would inevitably start questioning Henri made me hesitate. Another reason also made me hesitate, a vague sort of fear that he would look for and find the fly Henri had talked of. And that annoyed me a good deal because I could find no satisfactory explanation for that particular fear.

André was definitely not the absent-minded sort of professor who walks about in pouring rain with a rolled umbrella under his arm. He was human, had a keen sense of humor, loved children and animals and could not bear to see anyone suffer. I had often seen him drop his work to watch a parade of the local fire brigade, or see the Tour de France cyclists go by, or even follow a circus parade all around the village. He liked games of logic and precision, such as billiards and tennis, bridge and chess.

How was it then possible to explain his death? What could have made him put his head under that hammer? It could hardly have been the result of some stupid bet or a test of his courage. He hated betting and had no patience with those who indulged in it. Whenever he heard a bet proposed, he would invariably remind all present that, after all, a bet was but a contract between a fool and a swindler, even if it turned out to be a toss-up as to which was which.

It seemed there were only two possible explanations to André's death. Either he had gone mad, or else he had a reason for letting his wife kill him in such a strange and terrible way. And just what could have been his wife's role in all this? They surely could not have been both insane?

Having finally decided not to tell Charas about my nephew's innocent revelations, I thought I myself would try to question Hélène.

She seemed to have been expecting my visit for she came into the parlor almost as soon as I had made myself known to the matron and been allowed inside.

"I wanted to show you my garden," explained Hélène as I looked at the coat slung over her shoulders.

As one of the "reasonable" inmates, she was allowed to go into the garden during certain hours of the day. She had asked for and obtained the right to a little patch of ground where she could grow flowers, and I had sent her seeds and some rosebushes out of my garden.

She took me straight to a rustic wooden bench which had been in the men's workshop and only just set up under a tree close to her little patch of ground.

Searching for the right way to broach the subject of André's death, I sat for a while tracing vague designs on the ground with the end of my umbrella.

"François, I want to ask you something," said Hélène after a while.

"Anything I can do for you, Hélène?"

"No, just something I want to know. Do flies live very long?"

Staring at her, I was about to say that her boy had asked the very same question a few hours earlier when I suddenly realized that here was the opening I had been searching for and perhaps even the possibility of striking a great blow, a blow perhaps powerful enough to shatter her stonewall defense, be it sane or insane.

Watching her carefully, I replied:

"I don't really know, Hélène; but the fly you were looking for was in my study this morning."

No doubt about it I had struck a shattering blow. She swung her head round with such force that I heard the bones crack in her neck. She opened her mouth, but said not a word; only her eyes seemed to be screaming with fear.

Yes, it was evident that I had crashed through something, but what? Undoubtedly, the Commissaire would have known what to do with such an advantage; I did not. All I knew was that he would never have given her time to think, to recuperate, but all I could do, and even that was a strain, was to maintain my best poker-face, hoping against hope that Hélène's defenses would go on crumbling.

She must have been quite a while without breathing, because she suddenly gasped and put both her hands over her still open mouth.

"François . . . did you kill it?" she whispered, her eyes no longer fixed, but searching every inch of my face.

"No."

"You have it then. . . . You have it on you! Give it to me!" she almost shouted, touching me with both her hands, and I knew that had she felt strong enough, she would have tried to search me.

"No, Hélène, I haven't got it."

"But you know now. . . . You have guessed, haven't you?"

"No, Hélène. I only know one thing, and that is that you are not insane. But I mean to know all, Hélène, and, somehow, I am going to find out. You can choose: either you tell me everything and I'll see what is to be done, or . . ."

"Or what? Say it!"

"I was going to say it, Hélène . . . or I assure you that your friend the Commissaire will have that fly first thing tomorrow morning."

She remained quite still, looking down at the palms of her hands on her lap and, although it was getting chilly, her forehead and hands were moist.

Without even brushing aside a wisp of long brown hair blown across her mouth by the breeze, she murmured:

"If I tell you . . . will you promise to destroy that fly before doing anything else?"

"No, Hélène. I can make no such promise before knowing."

"But, François, you must understand. I promised André that fly would be destroyed. That promise must be kept and I can say nothing until it is."

I could sense the deadlock ahead. I was not yet losing ground, but I was losing the initiative. I tried a shot in the dark:

"Hélène, of course you understand that as soon as the police examine that fly, they will know that you are not insane, and then . . ."

"François, no! For Henri's sake! Don't you see? I was expecting that fly; I was hoping it would find me here but it couldn't know what had become of me. What else could it do but go to others it loves, to Henri, to you . . . you who might know and understand what was to be done!"

Was she really mad, or was she simulating again? But mad or not, she was cornered. Wondering how to follow up and how to land the knockout blow without running the risk of seeing her slip away out of reach, I said very quietly:

"Tell me all, Hélène. I can then protect your boy."

"Protect my boy from what? Don't you understand that if I am here, it is merely so that Henri won't be the son of a woman who was guillotined for having murdered his father? Don't you understand that I would by far prefer the guillotine to the living death of this lunatic asylum?"

"I understand, Hélène, and I'll do my best for the boy whether you tell me or not. If you refuse to tell me, I'll still do the best I can to protect Henri, but you must understand that the game will be out of my hands, because Commissaire Charas will have the fly."

"But why must you know?" said, rather than asked, my sister-in-law, struggling to control her temper.

"Because I must and will know how and why my brother died, Hélène."

"All right. Take me back to the . . . house. I'll give you what your Commissaire would call my 'Confession.' "

"Do you mean to say that you have written it!"

"Yes. It was not really meant for you, but more likely for *your friend*, the Commissaire. I had foreseen that, sooner or later, he would get too close to the truth."

"You then have no objection to his reading it?"

"You will act as you think fit, François. Wait for me a minute."

Leaving me at the door of the parlor, Hélène ran upstairs to her room. In less than a minute she was back with a large brown envelope.

"Listen, François; you are not nearly as bright as was your poor brother, but you are not unintelligent. All I ask is that you read this alone. After that, you may do as you wish."

"That I promise you, Hélène," I said, taking the precious envelope. "I'll read it tonight and although tomorrow is not a visiting day, I'll come down to see you."

"Just as you like," said my sister-in-law without even saying good-bye as she went back upstairs.

It was only on reaching home, as I walked from the garage to the house, that I read the inscription on the envelope:

TO WHOM IT MAY CONCERN

(Probably Commissaire Charas)

Having told the servants that I would have only a light supper to be served immediately in my study and that I was not to be disturbed after, I ran upstairs, threw Hélène's envelope on my desk and made another careful search of the room before closing the shutters and drawing the curtains. All I could find was a long since dead mosquito stuck to the wall near the ceiling.

Having motioned to the servant to put her tray down on a table by the fireplace, I poured myself a glass of wine and locked the door behind her. I then disconnected the telephone—I always did this now at night—and turned out all the lights but the lamp on my desk.

Slitting open Hélène's fat envelope, I extracted a thick wad of closely written pages. I read the following lines neatly centered in the middle of the top page:

*This is not a confession because, although I killed my husband, I am not a murderess. I simply and very faithfully carried out his last wish by crushing his head and right arm under the steam-hammer of his brother's factory.*

Without even touching the glass of wine by my elbow, I turned the page and started reading.

For very nearly a year before his death *(the manuscript began)*, my husband had told me of some of his experiments. He knew full well that his colleagues of the Air Ministry would have forbidden some of them as too dangerous, but he was keen on obtaining positive results before reporting his discovery.

Whereas only sound and pictures had been, so far, transmitted through space by radio and television, André claimed to have discovered a way of transmitting matter. Matter, any solid object, placed in his "transmitter" was instantly disintegrated and reintegrated in a special receiving set.

André considered his discovery as perhaps the most important since that of the wheel sawn off the end of a tree trunk. He reckoned that the transmission of matter by instantaneous "disintegration-reintegration" would completely change life as we had known it so far. It would mean the end of all means of transport, not only of goods including food, but also of human beings. André, the practical scientist who never allowed theories or daydreams to get the better of him, already foresaw the time when there would no longer be any airplanes, ships, trains or cars and, therefore, no longer any roads or railway lines, ports, airports or stations. All that would be replaced by matter-transmitting and -receiving stations throughout the world. Travelers and goods would be placed in special cabins and, at a given signal, would simply disappear and reappear almost immediately at the chosen receiving station.

André's receiving set was only a few feet away from his transmitter, in an adjoining room of his laboratory, and he at first ran into all sorts of snags. His first successful experiment was carried out with an ash tray taken from his desk, a souvenir we had brought back from a trip to London.

That was the first time he told me about his experiments and I had no idea of what he was talking about the day he came dashing into the house and threw the ash tray in my lap.

"Hélène, look! For a fraction of a second, a bare ten-millionth of a second, that ash tray had been completely disintegrated. For one little moment it no longer existed! Gone! Nothing left, absolutely nothing! Only atoms traveling through space at the speed of light! And the moment after, the atoms were once more gathered together in the shape of an ash tray!"

"André, please . . . please! What on earth are you raving about?"

He started sketching all over a letter I had been writing. He laughed at my wry face, swept all my letters off the table and said:

"You don't understand? Right. Let's start all over again. Hélène, do you remember I once read you an article about the mysterious flying stones that seem to come from nowhere in particular, and which are said to occasionally fall in certain houses in India? They come flying in as though thrown from outside and that in spite of closed doors and windows."

"Yes, I remember. I also remember that Professor Augier, your friend of the Collège de France, who had come down for a few days, remarked that if there was no trickery about it, the only possible explanation was that the stones had been disintegrated after having been thrown from outside, come through the walls, and then been reintegrated before hitting the floor or the opposite walls."

"That's right. And I added that there was, of course, one other possibility, namely the momentary and partial disintegration of the walls as the stone or stones came through."

"Yes, André. I remember all that, and I suppose you also remember that I failed to understand, and that you got quite annoyed. Well, I still do not understand why and how, even disintegrated, stones should be able to come through a wall or a closed door."

"But it is possible, Hélène, because the atoms that go to make up matter are not close together like the bricks of a wall. They are separated by relative immensities of space."

"Do you mean to say that you have disintegrated that ash tray, and then put it together again after pushing it through something?"

"Precisely, Hélène. I projected it through the wall that separates my transmitter from my receiving set."

"And would it be foolish to ask how humanity is to benefit from ash trays that can go through walls?"

André seemed quite offended, but he soon saw that I was only teasing, and again waxing enthusiastic, he told me of some of the possibilities of his discovery.

"Isn't it wonderful, Hélène?" he finally gasped, out of breath.

"Yes, André. But I hope you won't ever transmit me; I'd be too much afraid of coming out at the other end like your ash tray."

"What do you mean?"

"Do you remember what was written under that ash tray?"

"Yes, of course: MADE IN JAPAN. That was the great joke of our typically British souvenir."

"The words are still there, André; but . . . look!"

He took the ash tray out of my hands, frowned, and walked over to the window. Then he went quite pale, and I knew that he had seen what had proved to me that he had indeed carried out a strange experiment.

The three words were still there, but reversed and reading:

ᴎ∀ꟼ∀ꞁ ᴎI Ǝᗡ∀M

Without a word, having completely forgotten me, André rushed off to his laboratory. I only saw him the next morning, tired and unshaven after a whole night's work.

A few days later, André had a new reverse which put him out of sorts and made him fussy and grumpy for several weeks. I stood it patiently enough for a while, but being myself bad tempered one evening, we had a silly row over some futile thing, and I reproached him for his moroseness.

"I'm sorry, *chérie*. I've been working my way through a maze of problems and have given you all a very rough time. You see, my very first experiment with a live animal proved a complete fiasco."

"André! You tried that experiment with Dandelo, didn't you?"

"Yes. How did you know?" he answered sheepishly. "He disintegrated perfectly, but he never reappeared in the receiving set."

"Oh, André! What became of him then?"

"Nothing . . . there is just no more Dandelo; only the dispersed atoms of a cat wandering, God knows where, in the universe."

Dandelo was a small white cat the cook had found one morning in the garden and which we had promptly adopted. Now I knew how it had disappeared and was quite angry about the whole thing, but my husband was so miserable over it all that I said nothing.

I saw little of my husband during the next few weeks. He had most of his meals sent down to the laboratory. I would often wake up in the morning and find his bed unslept in. Sometimes, if he had come in very late, I would find that storm-swept appearance which only a man can give a bedroom by getting up very early and fumbling around in the dark.

One evening he came home to dinner all smiles, and I knew that his troubles were over. His face dropped, however, when he saw I was dressed for going out.

"Oh. Were you going out, Hélène?"

"Yes, the Drillons invited me for a game of bridge, but I can easily phone them and put it off."

"No, it's all right."

"It isn't all right. Out with it, dear!"

"Well, I've at last got everything perfect and I wanted you to be the first to see the miracle."

"*Magnifique*, André! Of course I'll be delighted."

Having telephoned our neighbors to say how sorry I was and so forth, I ran down to the kitchen and told the cook that she had exactly ten minutes in which to prepare a "celebration dinner."

"An excellent idea, Hélène," said my husband when the maid appeared with the champagne after our candlelight dinner. "We'll celebrate with reintegrated champagne!" and taking the tray from the maid's hands, he led the way down to the laboratory.

"Do you think it will be as good as before its disintegration?" I asked, holding the tray while he opened the door and switched on the lights.

"Have no fear. You'll see! Just bring it here, will you," he said, opening the door of a telephone call-box he had bought and which had been transformed into what he called a transmitter. "Put it down on that now," he added, putting a stool inside the box.

Having carefully closed the door, he took me to the other end of the room and handed me a pair of very dark sun glasses. He put on another pair and walked back to a switchboard by the transmitter.

"Ready, Hélène?" said my husband, turning out all the lights. "Don't remove your glasses till I give the word."

"I won't budge, André, go on," I told him, my eyes fixed on the tray which I could just see in a greenish shimmering light through the glass-paneled door of the telephone booth.

"Right," said André, throwing a switch.

The whole room was brilliantly illuminated by an orange flash. Inside the cabin I had seen a crackling ball of fire and felt its heat on my face, neck and hands. The whole thing lasted but the fraction of a second, and I found myself blinking at green-edged black holes like those one sees after having stared at the sun.

"*Et voilà!* You can take off your glasses, Hélène."

A little theatrically perhaps, my husband opened the door of the cabin. Though André had told me what to expect, I was astonished to find that the champagne, glasses, tray and stool were no longer there.

André ceremoniously led me by the hand into the next room, in a corner of which stood a second telephone booth. Opening the door wide, he triumphantly lifted the champagne tray off the stool.

Feeling somewhat like the good-natured kind-member-of-the-audience that has been dragged onto the music hall stage by the magician, I repressed from saying, "All done with mirrors," which I knew would have annoyed my husband.

"Sure it's not dangerous to drink?" I asked as the cork popped.

"Absolutely sure, Hélène," he said, handing me a glass. "But that was nothing. Drink this off and I'll show you something much more astounding."

We went back into the other room.

"Oh, André! Remember poor Dandelo!"

"This is only a guinea pig, Hélène. But I'm positive it will go through all right."

He set the furry little beast down on the green enameled floor of the booth and quickly closed the door. I again put on my dark glasses and saw and felt the vivid crackling flash.

Without waiting for André to open the door, I rushed into the next room where the lights were still on and looked into the receiving booth.

"Oh, André! *Chéri!* He's there all right!" I shouted excitedly, watching the little animal trotting round and round. "It's wonderful, André. It works! You've succeeded!"

"I hope so, but I must be patient. I'll know for sure in a few weeks' time."

"What do you mean? Look! He's as full of life as when you put him in the other cabin."

"Yes, so he seems. But we'll have to see if all his organs are intact, and that will take some time. If that little beast is still full of life in a month's time, we then consider the experiment a success."

I begged André to let me take care of the guinea pig.

"All right, but don't kill it by over-feeding," he agreed with a grin for my enthusiasm.

Though not allowed to take Hop-là—the name I had given the guinea pig—out of its box in the laboratory, I had tied a pink ribbon round its neck and was allowed to feed it twice a day.

Hop-là soon got used to its pink ribbon and became quite a tame little pet, but that month of waiting seemed a year.

And then one day, André put Miquette, our cocker spaniel, into his "transmitter." He had not told me beforehand, knowing full well that I would never have agreed to such an experiment with our dog. But when he did tell me, Miquette had been successfully transmitted half-a-dozen times and seemed to be enjoying the operation thoroughly; no sooner was she let out of the "reintegrator" than she dashed madly into the next room, scratching at the "transmitter" door to have "another go," as André called it.

I now expected that my husband would invite some of his colleagues and Air Ministry specialists to come down. He usually did this when he had finished a research job and, before handing them long detailed reports which he always typed himself, he would carry out an experiment or two before them. But this time, he just went on working. One morning I finally asked him when he intended throwing his usual "surprise party," as we called it.

"No, Hélène; not for a long while yet. This discovery is much too important. I have an awful lot of work to do on it still. Do you realize that there are some parts of the transmission proper which I do not yet myself fully understand? It works all right, but you see, I can't just say to all these eminent professors that I do this and that and, poof, it works! I must be able to explain how and why it works. And what is even more important, I must be ready and able to refute every destructive argument they will not fail to trot out, as they usually do when faced with anything really good."

I was occasionally invited down to the laboratory to witness some new experiment, but I never went unless André invited me, and only talked about his work if he broached the subject first. Of course it never occurred to me that he would, at that stage at least, have tried an experiment with a human being; though, had I thought about it—knowing André—it would have been obvious that he would never have allowed anyone into the "transmitter" before he had been through to test it first. It was only after the accident that I discovered he had duplicated all his switches inside the disintegration booth, so that he could try it out by himself.

The morning André tried this terrible experiment, he did not show up for lunch. I sent the maid down with a tray, but she brought it back with a note she had found pinned outside the laboratory door: "Do not disturb me, I am working."

He did occasionally pin such notes on his door and, though I noticed it, I paid no particular attention to the unusually large handwriting of his note.

It was just after that, as I was drinking my coffee, that Henri came bouncing into the room to say that he had caught a funny fly, and would I like to see it. Refusing even to look at his closed fist, I ordered him to release it immediately.

"But, *Maman*, it has such a funny white head!"

Marching the boy over to the open window, I told him to release the fly immediately, which he did. I knew that Henri had caught the fly merely because he thought it looked curious or different from other flies, but I also knew that his father would never stand for any form of cruelty to animals, and that there would be a fuss should he discover that our son had put a fly in a box or a bottle.

At dinner time that evening, André had still not shown up and, a little worried, I ran down to the laboratory and knocked at the door.

He did not answer my knock, but I heard him moving around and a moment later he slipped a note under the door. It was typewritten:

HÉLÈNE, I AM HAVING TROUBLE. PUT THE BOY TO BED AND COME BACK IN AN HOUR'S TIME.   A.

Frightened, I knocked and called, but André did not seem to pay any attention and, vaguely reassured by the familiar noise of his typewriter, I went back to the house.

Having put Henri to bed, I returned to the laboratory, where I found another note slipped under the door. My hand shook as I picked it up because I knew by then that something must be radically wrong. I read:

HÉLÈNE, FIRST OF ALL I COUNT ON YOU NOT TO LOSE YOUR NERVE OR DO ANYTHING RASH BECAUSE YOU ALONE CAN HELP ME. I HAVE HAD A SERIOUS ACCIDENT. I AM NOT IN ANY PARTICULAR DANGER FOR THE TIME BEING THOUGH IT IS A MATTER OF LIFE AND DEATH. IT IS USELESS CALLING TO ME OR SAYING ANYTHING. I CANNOT ANSWER, I CANNOT SPEAK. I WANT YOU TO DO EXACTLY AND VERY CAREFULLY ALL THAT I ASK. AFTER HAVING KNOCKED THREE TIMES TO SHOW THAT YOU UN-DERSTAND AND AGREE, FETCH ME A BOWL OF MILK LACED WITH RUM. I HAVE HAD NOTHING ALL DAY AND CAN DO WITH IT.

Shaking with fear, not knowing what to think and repressing a furious de-sire to call André and bang away until he opened, I knocked three times as re-quested and ran all the way home to fetch what he wanted.

In less than five minutes I was back. Another note had been slipped under the door:

HÉLÈNE, FOLLOW THESE INSTRUCTIONS CAREFULLY. WHEN YOU KNOCK I'LL OPEN THE DOOR. YOU ARE TO WALK OVER TO MY DESK AND PUT DOWN THE BOWL OF MILK. YOU WILL THEN GO INTO THE OTHER ROOM WHERE THE RECEIVER IS. LOOK CAREFULLY AND TRY TO FIND A FLY WHICH OUGHT TO BE THERE BUT WHICH I AM UNABLE TO FIND. UNFOR-TUNATELY I CANNOT SEE SMALL THINGS VERY EASILY.
BEFORE YOU COME IN YOU MUST PROMISE TO OBEY ME IMPLICITLY. DO NOT LOOK AT ME AND REMEMBER THAT TALKING IS QUITE USELESS. I CANNOT ANSWER. KNOCK AGAIN THREE TIMES AND THAT WILL MEAN I HAVE YOUR PROMISE. MY LIFE DEPENDS ENTIRELY ON THE HELP YOU CAN GIVE ME.

I had to wait a while to pull myself together, and then I knocked slowly three times.

I heard André shuffling behind the door, then his hand fumbling with the lock, and the door opened.

Out of the corner of my eye, I saw that he was standing behind the door, but without looking round, I carried the bowl of milk to his desk. He was ev-idently watching me and I must at all costs appear calm and collected.

"*Chéri*, you can count on me," I said gently, and putting the bowl down un-der his desk lamp, the only one alight, I walked into the next room where all the lights were blazing.

My first impression was that some sort of hurricane must have blown out of the receiving booth. Papers were scattered in every direction, a whole row of test tubes lay smashed in a corner, chairs and stools were upset and one of the window curtains hung half torn from its bent rod. In a large enamel basin on the floor a heap of burned documents was still smoldering.

I knew that I would not find the fly André wanted me to look for. Women know things that men only suppose by reasoning and deduction; it is a form of knowledge very rarely accessible to them and which they disparagingly call intuition. I already knew that the fly André wanted was the one which Henri had caught and which I had made him release.

I heard André shuffling around in the next room, and then a strange gurgling and sucking as though he had trouble in drinking his milk.

"André, there is no fly here. Can you give me any sort of indication that might help? If you can't speak, rap or something . . . you know: once for yes, twice for no."

I had tried to control my voice and speak as though perfectly calm, but I had to choke down a sob of desperation when he rapped twice for "no."

"May I come to you, André? I don't know what can have happened, but whatever it is, I'll be courageous, dear."

After a moment of silent hesitation, he tapped once on his desk.

At the door I stopped aghast at the sight of André standing with his head and shoulders covered by the brown velvet cloth he had taken from a table by his desk, the table on which he usually ate when he did not want to leave his work. Suppressing a laugh that might easily have turned to sobbing, I said:

"André, we'll search thoroughly tomorrow, by daylight. Why don't you go to bed? I'll lead you to the guest room if you like, and won't let anyone else see you."

His left hand tapped the desk twice.

"Do you need a doctor, André?"

"No," he rapped.

"Would you like me to call up Professor Augier? He might be of more help. . . ."

Twice he rapped "no" sharply. I did not know what to do or say. And then I told him:

"Henri caught a fly this morning which he wanted to show me, but I made him release it. Could it have been the one you are looking for? I didn't see it, but the boy said its head was white."

André emitted a strange metallic sigh, and I just had time to bite my fingers fiercely in order not to scream. He had let his right arm drop, and instead of his long-fingered muscular hand, a gray stick with little buds on it like the branch of a tree, hung out of his sleeve almost down to his knee.

"André, *mon chéri*, tell me what happened. I might be of more help to you if I knew. André . . . oh, it's terrible!" I sobbed, unable to control myself.

Having rapped once for yes, he pointed to the door with his left hand.

I stepped out and sank down crying as he locked the door behind me. He was typing again and I waited. At last he shuffled to the door and slid a sheet of paper under it.

HÉLÈNE, COME BACK IN THE MORNING. I MUST THINK AND WILL HAVE TYPED OUT AN EXPLANATION FOR YOU. TAKE ONE OF MY SLEEPING TABLETS AND GO STRAIGHT TO BED. I NEED YOU FRESH AND STRONG TOMORROW, MA PAUVRE CHÉRIE. A.

"Do you want anything for the night, André?" I shouted through the door.

He knocked twice for no, and a little later I heard the typewriter again.

The sun full on my face woke me up with a start. I had set the alarm-clock for five but had not heard it, probably because of the sleeping tablets. I had indeed slept like a log, without a dream. Now I was back in my living nightmare and crying like a child I sprang out of bed. It was just on seven!

Rushing into the kitchen, without a word for the startled servants, I rapidly prepared a trayload of coffee, bread and butter with which I ran down to the laboratory.

André opened the door as soon as I knocked and closed it again as I carried the tray to his desk. His head was still covered, but I saw from his crumpled suit and his open camp-bed that he must have at least tried to rest.

On his desk lay a typewritten sheet for me which I picked up. André opened the other door, and taking this to mean that he wanted to be left alone, I walked into the next room. He pushed the door to and I heard him pouring out the coffee as I read:

DO YOU REMEMBER THE ASH TRAY EXPERIMENT? I HAVE HAD A SIMILAR ACCIDENT. I "TRANSMITTED" MYSELF SUCCESSFULLY THE NIGHT BE-FORE LAST. DURING A SECOND EXPERIMENT YESTERDAY A FLY WHICH I DID NOT SEE MUST HAVE GOT INTO THE "DISINTEGRATOR." MY ONLY HOPE IS TO FIND THAT FLY AND GO THROUGH AGAIN WITH IT. PLEASE SEARCH FOR IT CAREFULLY SINCE, IF IT IS NOT FOUND, I SHALL HAVE TO FIND A WAY OF PUTTING AN END TO ALL THIS.

If only André had been more explicit! I shuddered at the thought that he must be terribly disfigured and then cried softly as I imagined his face inside-out, or perhaps his eyes in place of his ears, or his mouth at the back of his neck, or worse!

André must be saved! For that, the fly must be found!

Pulling myself together, I said:

"André, may I come in?"

He opened the door.

"André, don't despair; I am going to find that fly. It is no longer in the laboratory, but it cannot be very far. I suppose you're disfigured, perhaps terribly so, but there can be no question of putting an end to all this, as you say in your note; that I will never stand for. If necessary, if you do not wish to be seen, I'll make you a mask or a cowl so that you can go on with your work until you get well again. If you cannot work, I'll call Professor Augier, and he and all your other friends will save you, André."

Again I heard that curious metallic sigh as he rapped violently on his desk.

"André, don't be annoyed; please be calm. I won't do anything without first consulting you, but you must rely on me, have faith in me and let me help you as best I can. Are you terribly disfigured, dear? Can't you let me see your face? I won't be afraid . . . I am your wife, you know."

But my husband again rapped a decisive "no" and pointed to the door.

"All right. I am going to search for the fly now, but promise me you won't do anything foolish; promise you won't do anything rash or dangerous without first letting me know all about it!"

He extended his left hand, and I knew I had his promise.

I will never forget that ceaseless day-long hunt for a fly. Back home, I turned the house inside-out and made all the servants join in the search. I told them that a fly had escaped from the Professor's laboratory and that it must be captured alive, but it was evident they already thought me crazy. They said so to the police later, and that day's hunt for a fly most probably saved me from the guillotine later.

I questioned Henri and as he failed to understand right away what I was talking about, I shook him and slapped him, and made him cry in front of the round-eyed maids. Realizing that I must not let myself go, I kissed and petted the poor boy and at last made him understand what I wanted of him. Yes, he remembered, he had found the fly just by the kitchen window; yes, he had released it immediately as told to.

Even in summer time we had very few flies because our house is on the top of a hill and the slightest breeze coming across the valley blows round it. In spite of that, I managed to catch dozens of flies that day. On all the window sills and all over the garden I had put saucers of milk, sugar, jam, meat—all the things likely to attract flies. Of all those we caught, and many others which we failed to catch but which I saw, none resembled the one Henri had caught the day before. One by one, with a magnifying glass, I examined every unusual fly, but none had anything like a white head.

At lunch time, I ran down to André with some milk and mashed potatoes. I also took some of the flies we had caught, but he gave me to understand that they could be of no possible use to him.

"If that fly has not been found tonight, André, we'll have to see what is to be done. And this is what I propose: I'll sit in the next room. When you can't answer by the yes-no method of rapping, you'll type out whatever you want to say and then slip it under the door. Agreed?"

"Yes," rapped André.

By nightfall we had still not found the fly. At dinner time, as I prepared André's tray, I broke down and sobbed in the kitchen in front of the silent servants. My maid thought that I had had a row with my husband, probably about the mislaid fly, but I learned later that the cook was already quite sure that I was out of my mind.

Without a word, I picked up the tray and then put it down again as I stopped by the telephone. That this was really a matter of life and death for André, I had no doubt. Neither did I doubt that he fully intended committing suicide, unless I could make him change his mind, or at least put off such a drastic decision. Would I be strong enough? He would never forgive me for not keeping a promise, but under the circumstances, did that really matter? To the devil with promises and honor! At all costs André must be saved! And having thus made up my mind, I looked up and dialed Professor Augier's number.

"The Professor is away and will not be back before the end of the week," said a polite neutral voice at the other end of the line.

That was that! I would have to fight alone and fight I would. I would save André come what may.

All my nervousness had disappeared as André let me in and, after putting the tray of food down on his desk, I went into the other room, as agreed.

"The first thing I want to know," I said as he closed the door behind me, "is what happened exactly. Can you please tell me, André?"

I waited patiently while he typed an answer which he pushed under the door a little later.

HÉLÈNE, I WOULD RATHER NOT TELL YOU, SINCE GO I MUST, I WOULD RATHER YOU REMEMBER ME AS I WAS BEFORE. I MUST DESTROY MYSELF IN SUCH A WAY THAT NONE CAN POSSIBLY KNOW WHAT HAS HAPPENED TO ME. I HAVE OF COURSE THOUGHT OF SIMPLY DISINTEGRATING MYSELF IN MY TRANSMITTER, BUT I HAD BETTER NOT BECAUSE, SOONER OR LATER, I MIGHT FIND MYSELF REINTEGRATED. SOME DAY, SOMEWHERE, SOME SCIENTIST IS SURE TO MAKE THE SAME DISCOVERY. I HAVE THEREFORE THOUGHT OF A WAY WHICH IS NEITHER SIMPLE NOR EASY, BUT YOU CAN AND WILL HELP ME.

For several minutes I wondered if André had not simply gone stark raving mad.

"André," I said at last, "whatever you may have chosen or thought of, I cannot and will never accept such a cowardly solution. No matter how awful the result of your experiment or accident, you are alive, you are a man, a brain . . . and you have a soul. You have no right to destroy yourself! You know that!"

The answer was soon typed and pushed under the door.

I AM ALIVE ALL RIGHT, BUT I AM ALREADY NO LONGER A MAN. AS TO MY BRAIN OR INTELLIGENCE, IT MAY DISAPPEAR AT ANY MOMENT. AS IT IS, IT IS NO LONGER INTACT. AND THERE CAN BE NO SOUL WITHOUT INTELLIGENCE . . . AND YOU KNOW THAT!

"Then you must tell the other scientists about your discovery. They will help you and save you, André!"

I staggered back frightened as he angrily thumped the door twice.

"André . . . why? Why do you refuse the aid you know they would give you with all their hearts?"

A dozen furious knocks shook the door and made me understand that my husband would never accept such a solution. I had to find other arguments.

For hours, it seemed, I talked to him about our boy, about me, about his family, about his duty to us and to the rest of humanity. He made no reply of any sort. At last I cried:

"André . . . do you hear me?"

"Yes," he knocked very gently.

"Well, listen then. I have another idea. You remember your first experiment with the ash tray? . . . Well, do you think that if you had put it through again a second time, it might possibly have come out with the letters turned back the right way?"

Before I had finished speaking, André was busily typing and a moment later I read his answer:

I HAVE ALREADY THOUGHT OF THAT. AND THAT WAS WHY I NEEDED THE FLY. IT HAS GOT TO GO THROUGH WITH ME. THERE IS NO HOPE OTHER- WISE.

"Try all the same, André. You never know!"

I HAVE TRIED SEVEN TIMES ALREADY

was the typewritten reply I got to that.

"André! Try again, please!"

The answer this time gave me a flutter of hope, because no woman has ever understood, or will ever understand, how a man about to die can possibly consider anything funny.

I DEEPLY ADMIRE YOUR DELICIOUS FEMININE LOGIC. WE COULD GO ON DOING THIS EXPERIMENT UNTIL DOOMSDAY. HOWEVER, JUST TO GIVE YOU THAT PLEASURE, PROBABLY THE VERY LAST I SHALL EVER BE ABLE TO GIVE YOU, I WILL TRY ONCE MORE. IF YOU CANNOT FIND THE DARK GLASSES, TURN YOUR BACK TO THE MACHINE AND PRESS YOUR HANDS OVER YOUR EYES. LET ME KNOW WHEN YOU ARE READY.

"Ready, André!" I shouted without even looking for the glasses and following his instructions.

I heard him moving around and then open and close the door of his "disintegrator." After what seemed a very long wait, but probably was not more than a minute or so, I heard a violent crackling noise and perceived a bright flash through my eyelids and fingers.

I turned around as the cabin door opened.

His head and shoulders still covered with the brown velvet carpet, André was gingerly stepping out of it.

"How do you feel, André? Any difference?" I asked touching his arm.

He tried to step away from me and caught his foot in one of the stools which I had not troubled to pick up. He made a violent effort to regain his balance, and the velvet carpet slowly slid off his shoulders and head as he fell heavily backwards.

The horror was too much for me, too unexpected. As a matter of fact, I am sure that, even had I known, the horror-impact could hardly have been less powerful. Trying to push both hands into my mouth to stifle my screams and although my fingers were bleeding, I screamed again and again. I could not take my eyes off him, I could not even close them, and yet I knew that if I looked at the horror much longer, I would go on screaming for the rest of my life.

Slowly, the monster, the thing that had been my husband, covered its head, got up and groped its way to the door and passed it. Though still screaming, I was able to close my eyes.

I who had ever been a true Catholic, who believed in God and another, better life hereafter, have today but one hope: that when I die, I really die, and that there may be no afterlife of any sort because, if there is, then I shall never forget! Day and night, awake or asleep, I see it, and I know that I am condemned to see it forever, even perhaps into oblivion!

Until I am totally extinct, nothing can, nothing will ever make me forget that dreadful white hairy head with its low flat skull and its two pointed ears. Pink and moist, the nose was also that of a cat, a huge cat. But the eyes! Or rather, where the eyes should have been were two brown bumps the size of saucers. Instead of a mouth, animal or human, was a long hairy vertical slit from which hung a black quivering trunk that widened at the end, trumpet-like, and from which saliva kept dripping.

I must have fainted, because I found myself flat on my stomach on the cold cement floor of the laboratory, staring at the closed door behind which I could hear the noise of André's typewriter.

Numb, numb and empty, I must have looked as people do immediately after a terrible accident, before they fully understand what has happened. I could only think of a man I had once seen on the platform of a railway station, quite conscious, and looking stupidly at his leg still on the line where the train had just passed.

My throat was aching terribly, and that made me wonder if my vocal cords had not perhaps been torn, and whether I would ever be able to speak again.

The noise of the typewriter suddenly stopped and I felt I was going to scream again as something touched the door and a sheet of paper slid from under it.

Shivering with fear and disgust, I crawled over to where I could read it without touching it:

NOW YOU UNDERSTAND. THAT LAST EXPERIMENT WAS A NEW DISAS-TER, MY POOR HÉLÈNE. I SUPPOSE YOU RECOGNIZED PART OF DANDELO'S HEAD. WHEN I WENT INTO THE DISINTEGRATOR JUST NOW, MY HEAD WAS ONLY THAT OF A FLY. I NOW ONLY HAVE ITS EYES AND MOUTH LEFT. THE REST HAS BEEN REPLACED BY PARTS OF THE CAT'S HEAD. POOR DANDELO WHOSE ATOMS HAD NEVER COME TOGETHER. YOU SEE NOW THAT THERE CAN ONLY BE ONE POSSIBLE SOLUTION, DON'T YOU? I MUST DISAPPEAR. KNOCK ON THE DOOR WHEN YOU ARE READY AND I SHALL EXPLAIN WHAT YOU HAVE TO DO.  A.

Of course he was right, and it had been wrong and cruel of me to insist on a new experiment. And I knew that there was now no possible hope, that any further experiments could only bring about worse results.

Getting up dazed, I went to the door and tried to speak, but no sound came out of my throat . . . so I knocked once!

You can of course guess the rest. He explained his plan in short typewritten notes, and I agreed, I agreed to everything!

My head on fire, but shivering with cold, like an automaton, I followed him into the silent factory. In my hand was a full page of explanations: what I had to know about the steam-hammer.

Without stopping or looking back, he pointed to the switchboard that controlled the steam-hammer as he passed it. I went no further and watched him come to a halt before the terrible instrument.

He knelt down, carefully wrapped the carpet round his head, and then stretched out flat on the ground.

It was not difficult. I was not killing my husband. André, poor André, had gone long ago, years ago it seemed. I was merely carrying out his last wish . . . and mine.

Without hesitating, my eyes on the long still body, I firmly pushed the "stroke" button right in. The great metallic mass seemed to drop slowly. It was not so much the resounding clang of the hammer that made me jump as the sharp cracking which I had distinctly heard at the same time. My hus . . . the thing's body shook a second and then lay still.

It was then I noticed that he had forgotten to put his right arm, his fly-leg, under the hammer. The police would never understand but the scientists would, and they must not! That had been André's last wish, also!

I had to do it and quickly, too; the night watchman must have heard the hammer and would be round any moment. I pushed the other button and the hammer slowly rose. Seeing but trying not to look, I ran up, leaned down, lifted and moved forward the right arm which seemed terribly light. Back at the switchboard, again I pushed the red button, and down came the hammer a second time. Then I ran all the way home.

You know the rest and can now do whatever you think right.

*So ended Hélène's manuscript.*

The following day I telephoned Commissaire Charas to invite him to dinner.

"With pleasure, Monsieur Delambre. Allow me, however, to ask: is it the Commissaire you are inviting, or just Monsieur Charas?"

"Have you any preference?"

"No, not at the present moment."

"Well then, make it whichever you like. Will eight o'clock suit you?"

Although it was raining, the Commissaire arrived on foot that evening.

"Since you did not come tearing up to the door in your black Citroën, I take it you have opted for Monsieur Charas, off duty?"

"I left the car up a side-street," mumbled the Commissaire with a grin as the maid staggered under the weight of his raincoat.

"*Merci,*" he said a minute later as I handed him a glass of Pernod into which he tipped a few drops of water, watching it turn the golden amber liquid to pale blue milk.

"You heard about my poor sister-in-law?"

"Yes, shortly after you telephoned me this morning. I am sorry, but perhaps it was all for the best. Being already in charge of your brother's case, the inquiry automatically comes to me."

"I suppose it was suicide."

"Without a doubt. Cyanide, the doctors say quite rightly; I found a second tablet in the unstitched hem of her dress."

"*Monsieur est servi,*" announced the maid.

"I would like to show you a very curious document afterwards, Charas."

"Ah, yes. I heard that Madame Delambre had been writing a lot, but we could find nothing beyond the short note informing us that she was committing suicide."

During our tête-à-tête dinner, we talked politics, books and films, and the local football club of which the Commissaire was a keen supporter.

After dinner, I took him up to my study, where a bright fire—a habit I had picked up in England during the war—was burning.

Without even asking him, I handed him his brandy and mixed myself what he called "crushed-bug juice in soda water"—his appreciation of whiskey.

"I would like you to read this, Charas; first, because it was partly intended for you and, secondly, because it will interest you. If you think Commissaire Charas has no objection, I would like to burn it after."

Without a word, he took the wad of sheets Hélène had given me the day before and settled down to read them.

"What do you think of it all?" I asked some twenty minutes later as he carefully folded Hélène's manuscript, slipped it into the brown envelope, and put it into the fire.

Charas watched the flames licking the envelope, from which wisps of gray smoke were escaping, and it was only when it burst into flames that he said, slowly raising his eyes to mine:

"I think it proves very definitely that Madame Delambre was quite insane."

For a long while we watched the fire eating up Hélène's "confession."

"A funny thing happened to me this morning, Charas. I went to the cemetery, where my brother is buried. It was quite empty and I was alone."

"Not quite, Monsieur Delambre. I was there, but I did not want to disturb you."

"Then you saw me . . ."

"Yes. I saw you bury a matchbox."

"Do you know what was in it?"

"A fly, I suppose."

"Yes. I had found it early this morning, caught in a spider's web in the garden."

"Was it dead?"

"No, not quite. I . . . crushed it . . . between two stones. Its head was . . . white . . . all white."

# Eight O'Clock in the Morning

## RAY FARADAY NELSON

---

**They Live**

Director: *John Carpenter*
Screenplay: *Frank Armitage*
Producer: *Larry Franco*
Music: *John Carpenter*
Cast: *Roddy Piper, Keith David, Meg Foster*
Released by: *Carolco/Alive*
1988, 98 Minutes. Color.

---

At the end of the show the hypnotist told his subjects, "Awake."

Something unusual happened.

One of the subjects awoke all the way. This had never happened before. His name was George Nada and he blinked out at the sea of faces in the theatre, at first unaware of anything out of the ordinary. Then he noticed, spotted here and there in the crowd, the non-human faces, the faces of the Fascinators. They had been there all along, of course, but only George was really awake, so only George recognized them for what they were. He understood everything in a flash, including the fact that if he were to give any outward sign, the Fascinators would instantly command him to return to his former state, and he would obey.

He left the theatre, pushing out into the neon night, carefully avoiding giving any indication that he saw the green, reptilian flesh or the multiple yellow eyes of the rulers of earth. One of them asked him, "Got a light buddy?" George gave him a light, then moved on.

At intervals along the street George saw the posters hanging with photographs of the Fascinators' multiple eyes and various commands printed under them, such as, "Work eight hours, play eight hours, sleep eight hours," and "Marry and Reproduce." A TV set in the window of a store caught George's eye, but he looked away in the nick of time. When he didn't look at the Fascinator in the screen, he could resist the command, "Stay tuned to this station."

George lived alone in a little sleeping room, and as soon as he got home, the first thing he did was to disconnect the TV set. In other rooms he could hear the TV sets of his neighbors, though. Most of the time the voices were human, but now and then he heard the arrogant, strangely bird-like croaks of the aliens. "Obey the government," said one croak. "We are the government," said another. "We are your friends, you'd do anything for a friend, wouldn't you?"

"Obey!"

"Work!"

Suddenly the phone rang.

George picked it up. It was one of the Fascinators.

"Hello," it squawked. "This is your control, Chief of Police Robinson. You are an old man, George Nada. Tomorrow morning at eight o'clock, your heart will stop. Please repeat."

"I am an old man," said George. "Tomorrow morning at eight o'clock, my heart will stop."

The control hung up.

"No, it won't," whispered George. He wondered why they wanted him dead. Did they suspect that he was awake? Probably. Someone might have spotted him, noticed that he didn't respond the way the others did. If George were alive at one minute after eight tomorrow morning, then they would be sure.

"No use waiting here for the end," he thought.

He went out again. The posters, the TV, the occasional commands from passing aliens did not seem to have absolute power over him, though he still felt strongly tempted to obey, to see these things the way his master wanted him to see them. He passed an alley and stopped. One of the aliens was alone there, leaning against the wall. George walked up to him.

"Move on," grunted the thing, focusing his deadly eyes on George.

George felt his grasp on awareness waver. For a moment the reptilian head dissolved into the face of a lovable old drunk. Of course the drunk would be lovable. George picked up a brick and smashed it down on the old drunk's head with all his strength. For a moment the image blurred, then the blue-green blood oozed out of the face and the lizard fell, twitching and writhing. After a moment it was dead.

George dragged the body into the shadows and searched it. There was a tiny radio in its pocket and a curiously shaped knife and fork in another. The tiny radio said something in an incomprehensible language. George put it down beside the body, but kept the eating utensils.

"I can't possibly escape," thought George. "Why fight them?"

But maybe he could.

What if he could awaken others? That might be worth a try.

He walked twelve blocks to the apartment of his girl friend, Lil, and knocked on her door. She came to the door in her bathrobe.

"I want you to wake up," he said.

"I'm awake," she said. "Come on in."

He went in. The TV was playing. He turned it off.

"No," he said. "I mean really wake up." She looked at him without comprehension, so he snapped his fingers and shouted, *"Wake up!* The masters command that you wake up!"

"Are you off your rocker, George?" she asked suspiciously. "You sure are acting funny." He slapped her face. "Cut that out!" she cried, "What the hell are you up to anyway?"

"Nothing," said George, defeated. "I was just kidding around."

"Slapping my face wasn't just kidding around!" she cried.

There was a knock at the door.

George opened it.

It was one of the aliens.

"Can't you keep the noise down to a dull roar?" it said.

The eyes and reptilian flesh faded a little and George saw the flickering image of a fat middle-aged man in shirtsleeves. It was still a man when George slashed its throat with the eating knife, but it was an alien before it hit the floor. He dragged it into the apartment and kicked the door shut.

"What do you see there?" he asked Lil, pointing to the many-eyed snake thing on the floor.

"Mister . . . Mister Coney," she whispered, her eyes wide with horror. "You . . . just killed him, like it was nothing at all."

"Don't scream," warned George, advancing on her.

"I won't George. I swear I won't, only please, for the love of God, put down that knife." She backed away until she had her shoulder blades pressed to the wall.

George saw that it was no use.

"I'm going to tie you up," said George. "First tell me which room Mister Coney lived in."

"The first door on your left as you go toward the stairs," she said. "Georgie . . . Georgie. Don't torture me. If you're going to kill me, do it clean. Please, Georgie, please."

He tied her up with bedsheets and gagged her, then searched the body of the Fascinator. There was another one of the little radios that talked a foreign language, another set of eating utensils, and nothing else.

George went next door.

When he knocked, one of the snake-things answered, "Who is it?"

"Friend of Mister Coney. I wanna see him," said George.

"He went out for a second, but he'll be right back." The door opened a crack, and four yellow eyes peeped out. "You wanna come in and wait?"

"Okay," said George, not looking at the eyes.

"You alone here?" he asked, as it closed the door, its back to George.

"Yeah, why?"

He slit its throat from behind, then searched the apartment.

He found human bones and skulls, a half-eaten hand.

He found tanks with huge fat slugs floating in them.

"The children," he thought, and killed them all.

There were guns too, of a sort he had never seen before. He discharged one by accident, but fortunately it was noiseless. It seemed to fire little poisoned darts.

He pocketed the gun and as many boxes of darts as he could and went back to Lil's place. When she saw him she writhed in helpless terror.

"Relax, honey," he said, opening her purse, "I just want to borrow your car keys."

He took the keys and went downstairs to the street.

Her car was still parked in the same general area in which she always parked it. He recognized it by the dent in the right fender. He got in, started it, and began driving aimlessly. He drove for hours, thinking—desperately searching for some way out. He turned on the car radio to see if he could get some music, but there was nothing but news and it was all about him, George Nada, the homicidal maniac. The announcer was one of the masters, but he sounded a little scared. Why should he be? What could one man do?

George wasn't surprised when he saw the road block, and he turned off on a side street before he reached it. No little trip to the country for you, Georgie boy, he thought to himself.

They had just discovered what he had done back at Lil's place, so they would probably be looking for Lil's car. He parked it in an alley and took the subway. There were no aliens on the subway, for some reason. Maybe they were too good for such things, or maybe it was just because it was so late at night.

When one finally did get on, George got off.

He went up to the street and went into a bar. One of the Fascinators was on the TV, saying over and over again, "We are your friends. We are your friends. We are your friends." The stupid lizard sounded scared. Why? What could one man do against all of them?

George ordered a beer, then it suddenly struck him that the Fascinator on the TV no longer seemed to have any power over him. He looked at it again and thought, "It has to believe it can master me to do it. The slightest hint of fear on its part and the power to hypnotize is lost." They flashed George's picture on the TV screen and George retreated to the phone booth. He called his control, the Chief of Police.

"Hello, Robinson?" he asked.

"Speaking."

"This is George Nada. I've figured out how to wake people up."

"What? George, hang on. Where are you?" Robinson sounded almost hysterical.

He hung up and paid and left the bar. They would probably trace his call.

He caught another subway and went downtown.

It was dawn when he entered the building housing the biggest of the city's TV studios. He consulted the building directory and then went up in the elevator. The cop in front of the studio entrance recognized him. "Why, you're Nada!" he gasped.

George didn't like to shoot him with the poison dart gun, but he had to.

He had to kill several more before he got into the studio itself, including all the engineers on duty. There were a lot of police sirens outside, excited shouts, and running footsteps on the stairs. The alien was sitting before the TV camera saying, "We are your friends. We are your friends," and didn't see George come in. When George shot him with the needle gun he simply stopped in mid-sentence and sat there, dead. George stood near him and said, imitating the alien croak, "Wake up. Wake up. See us as we are and kill us!"

It was George's voice the city heard that morning, but it was the Fascinator's image, and the city did awake for the very first time and the war began.

George did not live to see the victory that finally came. He died of a heart attack at exactly eight o'clock.

In *They Live*, Roddy Piper (top photo, left) and Keith David realize that the world is secretly being taken over by aliens who can only be seen with special glasses (as those worn by David) which reveal the aliens' skeletal faces (bottom photo).

Quaid (Arnold Schwarzenegger), while trying to flee from killers, realizes that his disguise has been detected in *Total Recall*.

# We Can Remember It For You Wholesale

## PHILIP K. DICK

---

**Total Recall**

Director: *Paul Verhoeven*
Screenplay: *Ronald Shusett, Dan O'Bannon, Gary Goldman*
Producer: *Ronald Shusett*
Music: *Jerry Goldsmith*
Special Effects: *Thomas Fisher, Eric Revig*
Cast: *Arnold Schwarzenegger, Rachel Ticotin, Sharon Stone, Ronny Cox*
Released by: *Carolco*
1989, 120 Minutes. Color.

---

He awoke—and wanted Mars. The valleys, he thought. What would it be like to trudge among them? Great and greater yet: the dream grew as he became fully conscious, the dream and the yearning. He could almost feel the enveloping presence of the other world, which only Government agents and high officials had seen. A clerk like himself? Not likely.

"Are you getting up or not?" his wife Kirsten asked drowsily, with her usual hint of fierce crossness. "If you are, push the hot coffee button on the darn stove."

"Okay," Douglas Quail said, and made his way barefoot from the bedroom of their conapt to the kitchen. There, having dutifully pressed the hot coffee button, he seated himself at the kitchen table, brought out a yellow, small tin of fine Dean Swift snuff. He inhaled briskly, and the Beau Nash mixture stung his nose, burned the roof of his mouth. But still he inhaled; it woke him up and allowed his dreams, his noctural desires and random wishes, to condense into a semblance of rationality.

I will go, he said to himself. Before I die I'll see Mars.

It was, of course, impossible, and he knew this even as he dreamed. But the daylight, the mundane noise of his wife now brushing her hair before the bedroom mirror—everything conspired to remind him of what he was. A miserable little salaried employee, he said to himself with bitterness. Kirsten reminded him of this at least once a day and he did not blame her; it was a wife's job to bring her husband down to Earth. Down to Earth, he thought, and laughed. The figure of speech in this was literally apt.

"What are you sniggering about?" his wife asked as she swept into the kitchen, her long busy-pink robe wagging after her. "A dream, I bet. You're always full of them."

"Yes," he said, and gazed out the kitchen window at the hovercars and traffic runnels, and all the little energetic people hurrying to work. In a little while he would be among them. As always.

"I'll bet it has to do with some woman," Kirsten said witheringly.

"No," he said. "A god. The god of war. He has wonderful craters with every kind of plant-life growing deep down in them."

"Listen." Kirsten crouched down beside him and spoke earnestly, the harsh quality momentarily gone from her voice. "The bottom of the ocean—*our* ocean is much more, an infinity of times more beautiful. You know that; everyone knows that. Rent an artificial gill-outfit for both of us, take a week off from work, and we can descend and live down there at one of those year-round aquatic resorts. And in addition—" She broke off. "You're not listening. You should be. Here is something a lot better than that compulsion, that obsession you have about Mars, and you don't even listen!" Her voice rose piercingly. "God in heaven, you're doomed, Doug! What's going to become of you?"

"I'm going to work," he said, rising to his feet, his breakfast forgotten. "That's what's going to become of me."

She eyed him. "You're getting worse. More fanatical every day. Where's it going to lead?"

"To Mars," he said, and opened the door to the closet to get down a fresh shirt to wear to work.

Having descended from the taxi Douglas Quail slowly walked across three densely-populated foot runnels and to the modern, attractively inviting doorway. There he halted, impeding mid-morning traffic, and with caution read the shifting-color neon sign. He had, in the past, scrutinized this sign before . . . but never had he come so close. This was very different; what he did now was something else. Something which sooner or later had to happen.

REKAL, INCORPORATED

Was this the answer? After all, an illusion, no matter how convincing, remained nothing more than an illusion. At least objectively. But subjectively—quite the opposite entirely.

And anyhow he had an appointment. Within the next five minutes.

Taking a deep breath of mildly smog-infested Chicago air, he walked through the dazzling polychromatic shimmer of the doorway and up to the receptionist's counter.

The nicely-articulated blonde at the counter, bare-bosomed and tidy, said pleasantly, "Good morning, Mr. Quail."

"Yes," he said. "I'm here to see about a Rekal course. As I guess you know."

"Not 'rekal' but *re*call," the receptionist corrected him. She picked up the receiver of the vidphone by her smooth elbow and said into it, "Mr. Douglas Quail is here, Mr. McClane. May he come inside, now? Or is it too soon?"

"Giz wetwa wum-wum wamp," the phone mumbled.

"Yes, Mr. Quail," she said. "You may go on in; Mr. McClane is expecting you." As he started off uncertainly she called after him, "Room D, Mr. Quail. To your right."

After a frustrating but brief moment of being lost he found the proper room. The door hung open and inside, at a big genuine walnut desk, sat a genial-looking man, middle-aged, wearing the latest Martian frog-pelt gray suit; his attire alone would have told Quail that he had come to the right person.

"Sit down, Douglas," McClane said, waving his plump hand toward a chair which faced the desk. "So you want to have gone to Mars. Very good."

Quail seated himself, feeling tense. "I'm not so sure this is worth the fee," he said. "It costs a lot and as far as I can see I really get nothing." Costs almost as much as going, he thought.

"You get tangible proof of your trip," McClane disagreed emphatically. "All the proof you'll need. Here; I'll show you." He dug within a drawer of his impressive desk. "Ticket stub." Reaching into a manila folder he produced a small square of embossed cardboard. "It proves you went—and returned. Postcards." He laid out four franked picture 3-D full-color postcards in a neatly-arranged row on the desk for Quail to see. "Film. Shots you took of local sights on Mars with a rented movie camera." To Quail he displayed those, too. "Plus the names of people you met, two hundred poscreds worth of souvenirs, which will arrive—from Mars—within the following month. And passport, certificates listing the shots you received. And more." He glanced up keenly at Quail. "You'll know you went, all right," he said. "You won't remember us, won't remember me or ever having been here. It'll be a real trip in your mind; we guarantee that. A full two weeks of recall; every last piddling detail. Remember this: if at any time you doubt that you really took an extensive trip to Mars you can return here and get a full refund. You see?"

"But I didn't go," Quail said. "I won't have gone, no matter what proofs you provide me with." He took a deep, unsteady breath. "And I never was a secret agent with Interplan." It seemed impossible to him that Rekal, Incorporated's extra-factual memory implant would do its job—despite what he had heard people say.

"Mr. Quail," McClane said patiently. "As you explained in your letter to us, you have no chance, no possibility in the slightest, of ever actually getting to Mars; you can't afford it, and what is much more important, you could never qualify as an undercover agent for Interplan or anybody else. This is the only way you can achieve your, ahem, life-long dream; am I not correct, sir? You can't be this; you can't actually do this." He chuckled. "But you can *have been* and *have done*. We see to that. And our fee is reasonable; no hidden charges." He smiled encouragingly.

"Is an extra-factual memory that convincing?" Quail asked.

"More than the real thing, sir. Had you really gone to Mars as an Interplan agent, you would by now have forgotten a great deal; our analysis of true-mem systems—authentic recollections of major events in a person's life—shows that a variety of details are very quickly lost to the person. Forever. Part of the package we offer you is such deep implantation of recall that nothing is forgotten. The packet which is fed to you while you're comatose is the creation of trained experts, men who have spent years on Mars; in every case we verify details down to the last iota. And you've picked a rather easy extra-factual system; had you picked Pluto or wanted to be Emperor of the Inner Planet Alliance we'd have much more difficulty . . . and the charges would be considerably greater."

Reaching into his coat for his wallet, Quail said, "Okay. It's been my life-long ambition and I can see I'll never really do it. So I guess I'll have to settle for this."

"Don't think of it that way," McClane said severely. "You're not accepting second-best. The actual memory, with all its vagueness, omissions and ellipses, not to say distortions—that's second best." He accepted the money and pressed a button on his desk. "All right, Mr. Quail," he said, as the door of his office opened and two burly men swiftly entered. "You're on your way to

Mars as a secret agent." He rose, came over to shake Quail's nervous, moist hand. "Or rather, you have been on your way. This afternoon at four-thirty you will, um, arrive back here on Terra; a cab will leave you off at your conapt and as I say you will never remember seeing me or coming here; you won't, in fact, even remember having heard of our existence."

His mouth dry with nervousness, Quail followed the two technicians from the office; what happened next depended on them.

Will I actually believe I've been on Mars? he wondered. That I managed to fulfill my lifetime ambition? He had a strange, lingering intuition that something would go wrong. But just what—he did not know.

He would have to wait to find out.

The intercom on McClane's desk, which connected him with the work-area of the firm, buzzed and a voice said, "Mr. Quail is under sedation now, sir. Do you want to supervise this one, or shall we go ahead?"

"It's routine," McClane observed. "You may go ahead, Lowe; I don't think you'll run into any trouble." Programming an artificial memory of a trip to another planet—with or without the added fillip of being a secret agent—showed up on the firm's work-schedule with monotonous regularity. In one month, he calculated wryly, we must do twenty of these . . . ersatz interplanetary travel has become our bread and butter.

"Whatever you say, Mr. McClane," Lowe's voice came, and thereupon the intercom shut off.

Going to the vault section in the chamber behind his office, McClane searched about for a Three packet—trip to Mars—and a Sixty-two packet: secret Interplan spy. Finding the two packets, he returned with them to his desk, seated himself comfortably, poured out the contents—merchandise which would be planted in Quail's conapt while the lab technicians busied themselves installing the false memory.

A one-poscred sneaky-pete side arm, McClane reflected; that's the largest item. Sets us back financially the most. Then a pellet-sized transmitter, which could be swallowed if the agent were caught. Code book that astonishingly resembled the real thing . . . the firm's models were highly accurate: based, whenever possible, on actual U.S. military issue. Odd bits which made no intrinsic sense but which would be woven into the warp and woof of Quail's imaginary trip, would coincide with his memory: half an ancient silver fifty cent piece, several quotations from John Donne's sermons written incorrectly, each on a separate piece of transparent tissue-thin paper, several match folders from bars on Mars, a stainless steel spoon engraved PROPERTY OF DOME-MARS NATIONAL KIBBUZIM, a wire tapping coil which—

The intercom buzzed. "Mr. McClane, I'm sorry to bother you but something rather ominous has come up. Maybe it would be better if you were in here after all. Quail is already under sedation; he reacted well to the narkidrine; he's completely unconscious and receptive. But—"

"I'll be in." Sensing trouble, McClane left his office; a moment later he emerged in the work area.

On a hygienic bed lay Douglas Quail, breathing slowly and regularly, his eyes virtually shut; he seemed dimly—but only dimly—aware of the two technicians and now McClane himself.

"There's no space to insert false memory-patterns?" McClane felt irritation. "Merely drop out two work weeks; he's employed as a clerk at the West Coast Emigration Bureau, which is a government agency, so he undoubtedly has or had two weeks vacation within the last year. That ought to do it." Petty details annoyed him. And always would.

"Our problem," Lowe said sharply, "is something quite different." He bent over the bed, said to Quail, "Tell Mr. McClane what you told us." To McClane he said, "Listen closely."

The gray-green eyes of the man lying supine in the bed focussed on McClane's face. The eyes, he observed uneasily, had become hard; they had a polished, inorganic quality, like semi-precious tumbled stones. He was not sure that he liked what he saw; the brilliance was too cold. "What do you want now?" Quail said harshly. "You've broken my cover. Get out of here before I take you all apart." He studied McClane. "Especially you," he continued. "You're in charge of this counter-operation."

Lowe said, "How long were you on Mars?"

"One month," Quail said gratingly.

"And your purpose there?" Lowe demanded.

The meager lips twisted; Quail eyed him and did not speak. At last, drawling the words out so that they dripped with hostility, he said, "Agent for Interplan. As I already told you. Don't you record everything that's said? Play your vid-aud tape back for your boss and leave me alone." He shut his eyes, then; the hard brilliance ceased. McClane felt, instantly, a rushing splurge of relief.

Lowe said quietly, "This is a tough man, Mr. McClane."

"He won't be," McClane said, "After we arrange for him to lose his memory-chain again. He'll be as meek as before." To Quail he said, "So *this* is why you wanted to go to Mars so terribly badly."

Without opening his eyes Quail said, "I never wanted to go to Mars. I was assigned it—they handed it to me and there I was: stuck. Oh yeah, I admit I was curious about it; who wouldn't be?" Again he opened his eyes and surveyed the three of them, McClane in particular. "Quite a truth drug you've got here; it brought up things I had absolutely no memory of." He pondered. "I wonder about Kirsten," he said, half to himself. "Could she be in on it? An Interplan contact keeping an eye on me . . . to be certain I didn't regain my memory? No wonder she's been so derisive about my wanting to go there." Faintly, he smiled; the smile—one of understanding—disappeared almost at once.

McClane said, "Please believe me, Mr. Quail; we stumbled onto this entirely by accident. In the work we do—"

"I believe you," Quail said. He seemed tired, now; the drug was continuing to pull him under, deeper and deeper. "Where did I say I'd been?" he murmured. "Mars? Hard to remember—I know I'd like to see it; so would everybody else. But me—" His voice trailed off. "Just a clerk, a nothing clerk."

Straightening up, Lowe said to his superior, "He wants a false memory implanted that corresponds to a trip he actually took. And a false reason which is the real reason. He's telling the truth; he's a long way down in the narkidrine. The trip is very vivid in his mind—at least under sedation. But apparently he doesn't recall it otherwise. Someone, probably at a government military-sciences lab, erased his conscious memories; all he knew was that going to Mars meant something special to him, and so did being a secret agent. They couldn't erase that; it's not a memory but a desire, undoubtedly the same one that motivated him to volunteer for the assignment in the first place."

The other technician, Keeler, said to McClane, "What do we do? Graft a false memory-pattern over the real memory? There's no telling what the results would be; he might remember some of the genuine trip, and the confusion might bring on a psychotic interlude. He'd have to hold two opposite premises in his mind simultaneously: that he went to Mars and that he didn't. That he's a genuine agent for Interplan and he's not, that it's spurious. I think we ought to revive him without any false memory implantation and send him out of here; this is hot."

"Agreed," McClane said. A thought came to him. "Can you predict what he'll remember when he comes out of sedation?"

"Impossible to tell," Lowe said. "He probably will have some dim, diffuse memory of his actual trip, now. And he'd probably be in grave doubt as to its validity; he'd probably decide our programming slipped a gear-tooth. And he'd remember coming here; that wouldn't be erased—unless you want it erased."

"The less we mess with this man," McClane said, "the better I like it. This is nothing for us to fool around with; we've been foolish enough to— or unlucky enough to—uncover a genuine Interplan spy who has a cover so perfect that up to now even he didn't know what he was—or rather is." The sooner they washed their hands of the man calling himself Douglas Quail the better.

"Are you going to plant packets Three and Sixty-two in his conapt?" Lowe said.

"No," McClane said. "And we're going to return half his fee."

" 'Half'! Why half?"

McClane said lamely, "It seems to be a good compromise."

As the cab carried him back to his conapt at the residential end of Chicago, Douglas Quail said to himself, It's sure good to be back on Terra.

Already the month-long period on Mars had begun to waver in his memory; he had only an image of profound gaping craters, an ever-present ancient erosion of hills, of vitality, of motion itself. A world of dust where little happened, where a good part of the day was spent checking and rechecking one's portable oxygen source. And then the life forms, the unassuming and modest gray-brown cacti and maw-worms.

As a matter of fact he had brought back several moribund examples of Martian fauna; he had smuggled them through customs. After all, they posed no menace; they couldn't survive in Earth's heavy atmosphere.

Reaching into his coat pocket he rummaged for the container of Martian maw-worms—

And found an envelope instead.

Lifting it out he discovered, to his perplexity, that it contained five hundred and seventy poscreds, in cred bills of low denomination.

Where'd I get this? he asked himself. Didn't I spend every 'cred I had on my trip?

With the money came a slip of paper marked: *one-half fee ret'd. By McClane.* And then the date. Today's date.

"Recall," he said aloud.

"Recall what, sir or madam?" the robot driver of the cab inquired respectfully.

"Do you have a phone book?" Quail demanded.

"Certainly, sir or madam." A slot opened; from it slid a microtape phone book for Cook County.

"It's spelled oddly," Quail said as he leafed through the pages of the yellow section. He felt fear, then; abiding fear. "Here it is," he said. "Take me there, to Rekal, Incorporated. I've changed my mind; I don't want to go home."

"Yes sir, or madam, as the case may be," the driver said. A moment later the cab was zipping back in the opposite direction.

"May I make use of your phone?" he asked.

"Be my guest," the robot driver said. And presented a shiny new emperor 3-D color phone to him.

He dialed his own conapt. And after a pause found himself confronted by a miniature but chillingly realistic image of Kirsten on the small screen. "I've been to Mars," he said to her.

"You're drunk." Her lips writhed scornfully. "Or worse."

"'S god's truth."

"When?" she demanded.

"I don't know." He felt confused. "A simulated trip, I think. By means of one of those artificial or extra-factual or whatever it is memory places. It didn't take."

Kirsten said witheringly, "You *are* drunk." And broke the connection at her end. He hung up, then, feeling his face flush. Always the same tone, he said hotly to himself. Always the retort, as if she knows everything and I know nothing. What a marriage. Keerist, he thought dismally.

A moment later the cab stopped at the curb before a modern, very attractive little pink building, over which a shifting, poly-chromatic neon sign read: REKAL, INCORPORATED.

The receptionist, chic and bare from the waist up, started in surprise, then gained masterful control of herself. "Oh hello Mr. Quail," she said nervously. "H-how are you? Did you forget something?"

"The rest of my fee back," he said.

More composed now the receptionist said, "Fee? I think you are mistaken, Mr. Quail. You were here discussing the feasibility of an extrafactual trip for you, but—" She shrugged her smooth pale shoulders. "As I understand it, no trip was taken."

Quail said, "I remember everything, miss. My letter to Rekal, Incorporated, which started this whole business off. I remember my arrival here, my visit with Mr. McClane. Then the two lab technicians taking me in tow and administering a drug to put me out." No wonder the firm had returned half his fee. The false memory of his "trip to Mars" hadn't taken—at least not entirely, not as he had been assured.

"Mr. Quail," the girl said, "although you are a minor clerk you are a good-looking man and it spoils your features to become angry. If it would make you feel any better, I might, ahem, let you take me out. . . ."

He felt furious, then. "I remember you," he said savagely. "For instance the fact that your breasts are sprayed blue; that stuck in my mind. And I remember Mr. McClane's promise that if I remembered my visit to Rekal, Incorporated I'd receive my money back in full. Where is Mr. McClane?"

After a delay—probably as long as they could manage—he found himself once more seated facing the imposing walnut desk, exactly as he had been an hour or so earlier in the day.

"Some technique you have," Quail said sardonically. His disappointment—and resentment—were enormous, by now. "My so-called 'memory' of a trip to Mars as an undercover agent for Interplan is hazy and vague and shot full of contradictions. And I clearly remember my dealings here with you people. I ought to take this to the Better Business Bureau." He was burning angry, at this point; his sense of being cheated had overwhelmed him, had destroyed his customary aversion to participating in a public squabble.

Looking morose, as well as cautious, McClane said, "We capitulate, Quail. We'll refund the balance of your fee. I fully concede the fact that we did absolutely nothing for you." His tone was resigned.

Quail said accusingly, "You didn't even provide me with the various artifacts that you claimed would 'prove' to me I had been on Mars. All that song-and-dance you went into—it hasn't materialized into a damn thing. Not even a ticket stub. Nor postcards. Nor passport. Nor proof of immunization shots. Nor—"

"Listen, Quail," McClane said. "Suppose I told you—" He broke off. "Let it go." He pressed a button on his intercom. "Shirley, will you disburse five hundred and seventy more 'creds in the form of a cashier's check made out to Douglas Quail? Thank you." He released the button, then glared at Quail.

Presently the check appeared; the receptionist placed it before McClane and once more vanished out of sight, leaving the two men alone, still facing each other across the surface of the massive walnut desk.

"Let me give you a word of advice," McClane said as he signed the check and passed it over. "Don't discuss your, ahem, recent trip to Mars with anyone."

"What trip?"

"Well, that's the thing." Doggedly, McClane said, "The trip you partially remember. Act as if you don't remember; pretend it never took place. Don't ask me why; just take my advice: it'll be better for all of us." He had begun to perspire. Freely. "Now, Mr. Quail, I have other business, other clients to see." He rose, showed Quail to the door.

Quail said, as he opened the door, "A firm that turns out such bad work shouldn't have any clients at all." He shut the door behind him.

On the way home in the cab Quail pondered the wording of his letter of complaint to the Better Business Bureau, Terra Division. As soon as he could get to his typewriter he'd get started; it was clearly his duty to warn other people away from Rekal, Incorporated.

When he got back to his conapt he seated himself before his Hermes

Rocket portable, opened the drawers and rummaged for carbon paper—and noticed a small, familiar box. A box which he had carefully filled on Mars with Martian fauna and later smuggled through customs.

Opening the box he saw, to his disbelief, six dead maw-worms and several varieties of the unicellular life on which the Martian worms fed. The proto-zoa were dried-up, dusty, but he recognized them; it had taken him an entire day picking among the vast dark alien boulders to find them. A wonderful, il-luminated journey of discovery.

But I didn't go to Mars, he realized.

Yet on the other hand—

Kirsten appeared at the doorway to the room, an armload of pale brown groceries gripped. "Why are you home in the middle of the day?" Her voice, in an eternity of sameness, was accusing.

"*Did I go to Mars?*" he asked her. "You would know."

"No, of course you didn't go to Mars; *you* would know that, I would think. Aren't you always bleating about going?"

He said, "By God, I think I went." After a pause he added, "And simulta-neously I think I didn't go."

"Make up your mind."

"How can I?" He gestured. "I have both memory-tracks grafted inside my head; one is real and one isn't but I can't tell which is which. Why can't I rely on you? They haven't tinkered with you." She could do this much for him at least—even if she never did anything else.

Kirsten said in a level, controlled voice, "Doug, if you don't pull yourself together, we're through. I'm going to leave you."

"I'm in trouble." His voice came out husky and coarse. And shaking. "Prob-ably I'm heading into a psychotic episode; I hope not, but—maybe that's it. It would explain everything, anyhow."

Setting down the bag of groceries, Kirsten stalked to the closet. "I was not kidding," she said to him quietly. She brought out a coat, got it on, walked back to the door of the conapt. "I'll phone you one of these days soon," she said tonelessly. "This is goodbye, Doug. I hope you pull out of this eventually; I really pray you do. For your sake."

"Wait," he said desperately. "Just tell me and make it absolute; I did go or I didn't—tell me which one." But they may have altered your memory-track also, he realized.

The door closed. His wife had left. Finally!

A voice behind him said, "Well, that's that. Now put up your hands, Quail. And also please turn around and face this way."

He turned, instinctively, without raising his hands.

The man who faced him wore the plum uniform of the Interplan Police

Agency, and his gun appeared to be UN issue. And, for some odd reason, he seemed familiar to Quail; familiar in a blurred, distorted fashion which he could not pin down. So, jerkily, he raised his hands.

"You remember," the policeman said, "your trip to Mars. We know all your actions today and all your thoughts—in particular your very important thoughts on the trip home from Rekal, Incorporated." He explained, "We have a telep-transmitter wired within your skull; it keeps us constantly informed."

A telepathic transmitter; use of a living plasma that had been discovered on Luna. He shuddered with self-aversion. The thing lived inside him, within his own brain, feeding, listening, feeding. But the Interplan police used them; that had come out even in the homeopapes. So this was probably true, dismal as it was.

"Why me?" Quail said huskily. What had he done—or thought? And what did this have to do with Rekal, Incorporated?

"Fundamentally" the Interplan cop said, "this has nothing to do with Rekal; it's between you and us." He tapped his right ear. "I'm still picking up your mentational processes by way of your cephalic transmitter." In the man's ear Quail saw a small white-plastic plug. "So I have to warn you: anything you think may be held against you." He smiled. "Not that it matters now; you've already thought and spoken yourself into oblivion. What's annoying is the fact that under narkidrine at Rekal, Incorporated you told them, their technicians and the owner, Mr. McClane, about your trip; where you went, for whom, some of what you did. They're very frightened. They wish they had never laid eyes on you." He added reflectively, "They're right."

Quail said, "I never made any trip. It's a false memory-chain improperly planted in me by McClane's technicians." But then he thought of the box, in his desk drawer, containing the Martian life forms. And the trouble and hardship he had had gathering them. The memory seemed real. And the box of life forms; that certainly was real. Unless McClane had planted it. Perhaps this was one of the "proofs" which McClane had talked glibly about.

The memory of my trip to Mars, he thought, doesn't convince me—but unfortunately it has convinced the Interplan Police Agency. They think I really went to Mars and they think I at least partially realize it.

"We not only know you went to Mars," the Interplan cop agreed, in answer to his thoughts, "but we know that you now remember enough to be difficult for us. And there's no use expunging your conscious memory of all this, because if we do you'll simply show up at Rekal, Incorporated again and start over. And we can't do anything about McClane and his operation because we have no jurisdiction over anyone except our own people. Anyhow, McClane hasn't committed any crime." He eyed Quail. "Nor, technically, have you. You didn't go to Rekal, Incorporated with the idea of regaining your memory; you went, as we realize, for the usual reason people go there—a love by plain, dull people for adventure." He added, "Unfortunately you're not plain, not dull, and you've already had too much excitement; the last thing in the universe you needed was a course from Rekal, Incorporated. Nothing could have been more lethal for you or for us. And, for that matter, for McClane."

Quail said, "Why is it 'difficult' for you if I remember my trip—my alleged trip—and what I did there?"

"Because," the Interplan harness bull said, "what you did is not in accord with our great white all-protecting father public image. You did, for us, what we never do. As you'll presently remember—thanks to narkidrine. That box of dead worms and algae has been sitting in your desk drawer for six months, ever since you got back. And at no time have you shown the slightest curiosity about it. We didn't even know you had it until you remembered it on your way home from Rekal; then we came here on the double to look for it." He added, unnecessarily, "Without any luck; there wasn't enough time."

A second Interplan cop joined the first one; the two briefly conferred. Meanwhile, Quail thought rapidly. He did remember more, now; the cop had been right about narkidrine. They—Interplan—probably used it themselves. Probably? He knew darn well they did; he had seen them putting a prisoner on it. Where would *that* be? Somewhere on Terra? More likely Luna, he decided, viewing the image rising from his highly defective—but rapidly less so—memory.

And he remembered something else. Their reason for sending him to Mars; the job he had done.

No wonder they had expunged his memory.

"Oh god," the first of the two Interplan cops said, breaking off his conversation with his companion. Obviously, he had picked up Quail's thoughts. "Well, this is a far worse problem, now; as bad as it can get." He walked toward Quail, again covering him with his gun. "We've got to kill you," he said. "And right away."

Nervously, his fellow officer said, "Why right away? Can't we simply cart him off to Interplan New York and let them—"

"*He* knows why it has to be right away," the first cop said; he too looked nervous, now, but Quail realized that it was for an entirely different reason. His memory had been brought back almost entirely, now. And he fully understood the officer's tension.

"On Mars," Quail said hoarsely, "I killed a man. After getting past fifteen bodyguards. Some armed with sneaky-pete guns, the way you are." He had been trained, by Interplan, over a five year period to be an assassin. A professional killer. He knew ways to take out armed adversaries . . . such as these two officers; and the one with the ear-receiver knew it, too.

If he moved swiftly enough—

The gun fired. But he had already moved to one side, and at the same time he chopped down the gun-carrying officer. In an instant he had possession of the gun and was covering the other, confused, officer.

"Picked my thoughts up," Quail said, panting for breath. "He knew what I was going to do, but I did it anyhow."

Half sitting up, the injured officer grated, "He won't use that gun on you, Sam; I pick that up, too. He knows he's finished, and he knows we know it, too. Come on, Quail." Laboriously, grunting with pain, he got shakily to his feet. He held out his hand. "The gun," he said to Quail. "You can't use it, and if you turn it over to me I'll guarantee not to kill you; you'll be given a hearing, and someone higher up in Interplan will decide, not me. Maybe they can erase your memory once more; I don't know. But you know the thing I was going to kill you for; I couldn't keep you from remembering it. So my reason for wanting to kill you is in a sense past."

Quail, clutching the gun, bolted from the conapt, sprinted for the elevator. If you follow me, he thought, I'll kill you. So don't. He jabbed at the elevator button and, a moment later, the doors slid back.

The police hadn't followed him. Obviously they had picked up his terse, tense thoughts and had decided not to take the chance.

With him inside the elevator descended. He had gotten away—for a time. But what next? Where could he go?

The elevator reached the ground floor; a moment later Quail had joined the mob of peds hurrying along the runnels. His head ached and he felt sick. But at least he had evaded death; they had come very close to shooting him on the spot, back in his own conapt.

And they probably will again, he decided. When they find me. And with this transmitter inside me, that won't take too long.

Ironically, he had gotten exactly what he had asked Rekal, Incorporated for. Adventure, peril, Interplan police at work, a secret and dangerous trip to Mars in which his life was at stake—everything he had wanted as a false memory.

The advantages of it being a memory—and nothing more—could now be appreciated.

On a park bench, alone, he sat dully watching a flock of perts: a semi-bird imported from Mars' two moons, capable of soaring flight, even against Earth's huge gravity.

Maybe I can find my way back to Mars, he pondered. But then what? It would be worse on Mars; the political organization whose leader he had assassinated would spot him the moment he stepped from the ship; he would have Interplan and *them* after him, there.

Can you hear me thinking? he wondered. Easy avenue to paranoia; sitting here alone he felt them tuning in on him, monitoring, recording, discussing ... he shivered, rose to his feet, walked aimlessly, his hands deep in his pockets. No matter where I go, he realized. You'll always be with me. As long as I have this device inside my head.

I'll make a deal with you, he thought to himself—and to them. Can't you imprint a false-memory template on me again, as you did before, that I lived an average, routine life, never went to Mars? Never saw an Interplan uniform up close and never handled a gun?

A voice inside his brain answered, "As has been carefully explained to you: that would not be enough."

Astonished, he halted.

"We formerly communicated with you in this manner," the voice continued. "When you were operating in the field, on Mars. It's been months since we've done it; we assumed, in fact, that we'd never have to do so again. Where are you?"

"Walking," Quail said, "to my death." By your officers' guns, he added as an afterthought. "How can you be sure it wouldn't be enough?" he demanded. "Don't the Rekal techniques work?"

"As we said. If you're given a set of standard, average memories you get— restless. You'd inevitably seek out Rekal or one of its competitors again. We can't go through this a second time."

"Suppose," Quail said, "once my authentic memories have been cancelled, something more vital than standard memories are implanted. Something which would act to satisfy my craving." he said. "That's been proved; that's probably why you initially hired me. But you ought to be able to come up with something else—something equal. I was the richest man on Terra but I finally gave all my money to educational foundations. Or I was a famous deep-space explorer. Anything of that sort; wouldn't one of those do?"

Silence.

"Try it," he said desperately. "Get some of your top-notch military psychiatrists; explore my mind. Find out what my most expansive daydream is." He tried to think. "Women," he said. "Thousands of them, like Don Juan had. An interplanetary playboy—a mistress in every city on Earth, Luna and Mars. Only I gave that up, out of exhaustion. Please," he begged. "Try it."

"You'd voluntarily surrender, then?" the voice inside his head asked. "If we agreed to arrange such a solution? *If* it's possible?"

After an interval of hesitation he said, "Yes." I'll take the risk, he said to himself. That you don't simply kill me.

"You make the first move," the voice said presently. "Turn yourself over to us. And we'll investigate that line of possibility. If we can't do it, however, if your authentic memories begin to crop up again as they've done at this time, then—" There was silence and then the voice finished, "We'll have to destroy you. As you must understand. Well, Quail, you still want to try?"

"Yes," he said. Because the alternative was death now—and for certain. At least this way he had a chance, slim as it was.

"You present yourself at our main barracks in New York," the voice of the Interplan cop resumed. "At 580 Fifth Avenue, floor twelve. Once you've surrendered yourself we'll have our psychiatrists begin on you; we'll have personality-profile tests made. We'll attempt to determine your absolute, ultimate fantasy wish—and then we'll bring you back to Rekal, Incorporated, here; get them in on it, fulfilling that wish in vicarious surrogate retrospection. And—good luck. We do owe you something; you acted as a capable instrument for us." The voice lacked malice; if anything, they—the organization—felt sympathy toward him.

"Thanks," Quail said. And began searching for a robot cab.

"Mr. Quail," the stern-faced, elderly Interplan psychiatrist said, "you possess a most interesting wish-fulfillment dream fantasy. Probably nothing such as you consciously entertain or suppose. This is commonly the way; I hope it won't upset you too much to hear about it."

The senior ranking Interplan officer present said briskly, "He better not be too much upset to hear about it, not if he expects not to get shot."

"Unlike the fantasy of wanting to be an Interplan undercover agent," the psychiatrist continued, "which, being relatively speaking a product of maturity, had a certain plausibility to it, this production is a grotesque dream of your childhood; it is no wonder you fail to recall it. Your fantasy is this: you are nine years old, walking alone down a rustic lane. An unfamiliar variety of space vessel from another star system lands directly in front of you. No one on Earth but you, Mr. Quail, sees it. The creatures within are very small and helpless, somewhat on the order of field mice, although they are attempting to invade Earth; tens of thousands of other such ships will soon be on their way, when this advance party gives the go-ahead signal."

"And I suppose I stop them," Quail said, experiencing a mixture of amusement and disgust. "Single-handed I wipe them out. Probably by stepping on them with my foot."

"No," the psychiatrist said patiently. "You halt the invasion, but not by destroying them. Instead, you show them kindness and mercy, even though by telepathy—their mode of communication—you know why they have come. They have never seen such humane traits exhibited by any sentient organism, and to show their appreciation they make a covenant with you."

Quail said, "They won't invade Earth as long as I'm alive."

"Exactly." To the Interplan officer the psychiatrist said, "You can see it does fit his personality, despite his feigned scorn."

"So by merely existing," Quail said, feeling a growing pleasure, "by simply being alive, I keep Earth safe from alien rule. I'm in effect, then, the most important person on Terra. Without lifting a finger."

"Yes indeed, sir," the psychiatrist said. "And this is bedrock in your psyche; this is a life-long childhood fantasy. Which, without depth and drug therapy, you never would have recalled. But it has always existed in you; it went underneath, but never ceased."

To McClane, who sat intently listening, the senior police official said, "Can you implant an extrafactual memory pattern that extreme in him?"

"We get handed every possible type of wish-fantasy there is," McClane said. "Frankly, I've heard a lot worse than this. Certainly we can handle it. Twenty-four hours from now he won't just *wish* he'd saved Earth; he'll devoutly believe it really happened."

The senior police official said, "You can start the job, then. In preparation we've already once again erased the memory in him of his trip to Mars."

Quail said, "What trip to Mars?"

No one answered him, so, reluctantly, he shelved the question. And anyhow a police vehicle had now put in its appearance; he, McClane and the senior police officer crowded into it, and presently they were on their way to Chicago and Rekal, Incorporated.

"You had better make no errors this time," the police officer said to heavyset, nervous-looking McClane.

"I can't see what could go wrong," McClane mumbled, perspiring. "This has nothing to do with Mars or Interplan. Single-handedly stopping an invasion of Earth from another star-system." He shook his head at that. "Wow, what a kid dreams up. And by pious virtue, too; not by force. It's sort of quaint." He dabbed at his forehead with a large linen pocket handkerchief.

Nobody said anything.

"In fact," McClane said, "it's touching."

"But arrogant," the police official said starkly. "Inasmuch as when he dies the invasion will resume. No wonder he doesn't recall it; it's the most grandiose fantasy I ever ran across." He eyed Quail with disapproval. "And to think we put this man on our payroll."

When they reached Rekal, Incorporated the receptionist, Shirley, met them breathlessly in the outer office. "Welcome back, Mr. Quail," she fluttered, her melon-shaped breasts—today painted an incandescent orange—bobbing with agitation. "I'm sorry everything worked out so badly before; I'm sure this time it'll go better."

Still repeatedly dabbing at his shiny forehead with his neatly-folded Irish linen handkerchief, McClane said, "It better." Moving with rapidity he rounded up Lowe and Keeler, escorted them and Douglas Quail to the work area, and then, with Shirley and the senior police officer, returned to his familiar office. To wait.

"Do we have a packet made up for this, Mr. McClane?" Shirley asked, bumping against him in her agitation, then coloring modestly.

"I think we do." He tried to recall; then gave up and consulted the formal chart. "A combination," he decided aloud, "of packets Eighty-one, Twenty, and Six." From the vault section of the chamber behind his desk he fished out the appropriate packets, carried them to his desk for inspection. "From Eighty-one," he explained, "a magic healing rod given him—the client in question, this time Mr. Quail—by the race of beings from another system. A token of their gratitude."

"Does it work?" the police officer asked curiously.

"It did once," McClane explained. "But he, ahem, you see, used it up years ago, healing right and left. Now it's only a momento. But he remembers it working spectacularly." He chuckled, then opened packet Twenty. "Document from the UN Secretary General thanking him for saving Earth; this isn't precisely appropriate, because part of Quail's fantasy is that no one knows of the invasion except himself, but for the sake of verisimilitude we'll throw it in." He inspected packet Six, then. What came from this? He couldn't recall; frowning, he dug into the plastic bag as Shirley and the Interplan police officer watched intently.

"Writing," Shirley said. "In a funny language."

"This tells who they were," McClane said, "and where they came from. Including a detailed star map logging their flight here and the system of origin. Of course it's in *their* script, so he can't read it. But he remembers them reading it to him in his own tongue." He placed the three artifacts in the center of the desk. "These should be taken to Quail's conapt," he said to the police officer. "So that when he gets home he'll find them. And it'll confirm his fantasy. SOP—standard operating procedure." He chuckled apprehensively, wondering how matters were going with Lowe and Keeler.

The intercom buzzed. "Mr. McClane, I'm sorry to bother you." It was

Lowe's voice; he froze as he recognized it, froze and became mute. "But something's come up. Maybe it would be better if you came in here and supervised. Like before, Quail reacted well to the narkidrine; he's unconscious, relaxed and receptive. But—"

McClane sprinted for the work area.

On a hygienic bed Douglas Quail lay breathing slowly and regularly, eyes half-shut, dimly conscious of those around him.

"We started interrogating him," Lowe said, white-faced. "To find out exactly when to place the fantasy-memory of him single-handedly having saved Earth. And strangely enough—"

"They told me not to tell," Douglas Quail mumbled in a dull drug-saturated voice. "That was the agreement. I wasn't even supposed to remember. But how could I forget an event like that?"

I guess it would be hard, McClane reflected. But you did—until now.

"They even gave me a scroll," Quail mumbled. "of gratitude. I have it hidden in my conapt; I'll show it to you."

To the Interplan officer who had followed after him, McClane said, "Well, I offer the suggestion that you better not kill him. If you do they'll return."

"They also gave me a magic invisible destroying rod," Quail mumbled, eyes totally shut, now. "That's how I killed that man on Mars you sent me to take out. It's in my drawer along with the box of Martian maw-worms and dried-up plant life."

Wordlessly, the Interplan officer turned and stalked from the work area.

I might as well put those packets of proof-artifacts away, McClane said to himself resignedly. He walked, step by step, back to his office. Including the citation from the UN Secretary General. After all—

The real one probably would not be long in coming.

# Damnation Alley

## ROGER ZELAZNY

---

**Damnation Alley**

Director: *Jack Smight*
Screenplay: *Alan Sharpe, Lukas Heller*
Music: *Jerry Goldsmith*
Special Effects: *Milt Rice*
Cast: *Jan-Michael Vincent, George Peppard, Dominique Sands,
Paul Winfield*
Released by: *20th Century-Fox*
1977, 95 Minutes. Color.

---

— I —

The gull swooped by, seemed to hover a moment on unmoving wings.

Hell Tanner flipped his cigar butt at it and scored a lucky hit. The bird uttered a hoarse cry and beat suddenly at the air. It climbed about fifty feet, and whether it shrieked a second time, he would never know.

It was gone.

A single gray feather rocked in the violet sky, drifted out over the edge of the cliff and descended, swinging, toward the ocean. Tanner chuckled through his beard, between the steady roar of the wind and the pounding of the surf. Then he took his feet down from the handlebars, kicked up the stand and gunned his bike to life.

He took the slope slowly till he came to the trail, then picked up speed and was doing fifty when he hit the highway.

He leaned forward and gunned it. He had the road all to himself, and he laid on the gas pedal till there was no place left for it to go. He raised his goggles and looked at the world through crud-colored glasses, which was pretty much the way he looked at it without them, too.

All the old irons were gone from his jacket, and he missed the swastika, the hammer and sickle and the upright finger, especially. He missed his old emblem, too. Maybe he could pick one up in Tijuana and have some broad sew it on and. . . . No. It wouldn't do. All that was dead and gone. It would be a giveaway, and he wouldn't last a day. What he *would* do was sell the Harley, work his way down the coast, clean and square and see what he could find in the other America.

He coasted down one hill and roared up another. He tore through Laguna Beach, Capistrano Beach, San Clemente and San Onofre. He made it down to Oceanside, where he refueled, and he passed on through Carlsbad and all those dead little beaches that fill the shore space before Solana Beach Del Mar. It was outside San Diego that they were waiting for him.

He saw the roadblock and turned. They were not sure how he had managed it that quickly, at that speed. But now he was heading away from them. He heard the gunshots and kept going. Then he heard the sirens.

He blew his horn twice in reply and leaned far forward. The Harley leaped ahead, and he wondered whether they were radioing to someone further on up the line.

He ran for ten minutes and couldn't shake them. Then fifteen.

He topped another hill, and far ahead he saw the second block. He was bottled in.

He looked all around him for side roads, saw none.

Then he bore a straight course toward the second block. Might as well try to run it.

No good!

There were cars lined up across the entire road. They were even off the road on the shoulders.

He braked at the last possible minute, and when his speed was right he reared up on the back wheel, spun it and headed back toward his pursuers.

There were six of them coming toward him, and at his back new siren calls arose.

He braked again, pulled to the left, kicked the gas and leaped out of the seat. The bike kept going, and he hit the ground rolling, got to his feet and started running.

He heard the screeching of their tires. He heard a crash. Then there were more gunshots, and he kept going. They were aiming over his head, but he didn't know it. They wanted him alive.

After fifteen minutes he was backed against a wall of rock, and they were fanned out in front of him, and several had rifles, and they were all pointed in the wrong direction.

He dropped the tire iron he held and raised his hands.

"You got it, citizens," he said. "Take it away."

And they did.

They handcuffed him and took him back to the cars. They pushed him into the rear seat of one, and an officer got in on either side of him. Another got into the front beside the driver, and this one held a sawed-off shotgun across his knees.

The driver started the engine and put the car into gear, heading back up 101.

The man with the shotgun turned and stared through bifocals that made his eyes look like hourglasses filled with green sand as he lowered his head. He stared for perhaps ten seconds, then said, "That was a stupid thing to do."

Hell Tanner stared back until the man said, "Very stupid, Tanner."

"Oh, I didn't know you were talking to me."

"I'm looking at you, son."

"And I'm looking at you. Hello, there."

Then the driver said, without taking his eyes off the road, "You know, it's too bad we've got to deliver him in good shape—after the way he smashed up the other car with that damn bike."

"He could still have an accident. Fall and crack a couple ribs, say," said the man to Tanner's left.

The man to the right didn't say anything, but the man with the shotgun shook his head slowly. "Not unless he tries to escape," he said. "L.A. wants him in good shape."

"Why'd you try to skip out, buddy? You might have known we'd pick you up."

Tanner shrugged.

"Why'd you pick me up? I didn't do anything?"

The driver chuckled.

"That's why," he said. "You didn't do anything, and there's something you were supposed to do. Remember?"

"I don't owe anybody anything. They gave me a pardon and let me go."

"You got a lousy memory, kid. You made the nation of California a promise when they turned you loose yesterday. Now you've had more than the twenty-four hours you asked for to settle your affairs. You can tell them 'no' if you want and get your pardon revoked. Nobody's forcing you. Then you can spend the rest of your life making little rocks out of big ones. We couldn't care less. I heard they got somebody else lined up already."

"Give me a cigarette," Tanner said.

The man on his right lit one and passed it to him.

He raised both hands, accepted it. As he smoked, he flicked the ashes onto the floor.

They sped along the highway, and when they went through towns or encountered traffic the driver would hit the siren and overhead the red light would begin winking. When this occurred, the sirens of the two other patrol cars that followed behind them would also wail. The driver never touched the brake, all the way up to L.A., and he kept radioing ahead every few minutes.

There came a sound like a sonic boom, and a cloud of dust and gravel descended upon them like hail. A tiny crack appeared in the lower right-hand corner of the bullet-proof windshield, and stones the size of marbles bounced on the hood and the roof. The tires made a crunching noise as they passed over the gravel that now lay scattered upon the road surface. The dust hung like a heavy fog, but ten seconds later they had passed out of it.

The men in the car leaned forward and stared upward.

The sky had become purple, and black lines crossed it, moving from west to east. These swelled, narrowed, moved from side to side, sometimes merged. The driver had turned on his lights by then.

"Could be a bad one coming," said the man with the shotgun.

The driver nodded, and, "Looks worse further north, too," he said.

A wailing began, high in the air above them, and the dark bands continued to widen. The sound increased in volume, lost its treble quality, became a steady roar.

The bands consolidated, and the sky grew dark as a starless, moonless night and the dust fell about them in heavy clouds. Occasionally, there sounded a *ping* as a heavier fragment struck against the car.

The driver switched on his country lights, hit the siren again and sped ahead. The roaring and the sound of the siren fought with one another above them, and far to the north a blue aurora began to spread, pulsing.

Tanner finished his cigarette, and the man gave him another. They were all smoking by then.

"You know, you're lucky we picked you up, boy," said the man to his left. "How'd you like to be pushing your bike through that stuff?"

"I'd like it," Tanner said.

"You're nuts."

"No. I'd make it. It wouldn't be the first time."

By the time they reached Los Angeles, the blue aurora filled half the sky, and it was tinged with pink and shot through with smoky, yellow streaks that reached like spider legs into the south. The roar was a deafening, physical thing that beat upon their eardrums and caused their skin to tingle. As they left the car and crossed the parking lot, heading toward the big, pillared building with the frieze across its forehead, they had to shout at one another in order to be heard.

"Lucky we got here when we did!" said the man with the shotgun. "Step it up!" Their pace increased as they moved toward the stairway, and, "It could break any minute now!" screamed the driver.

— II —

As they had pulled into the lot, the building had had the appearance of a piece of ice-sculpture, with the shifting lights in the sky playing upon its surfaces and casting cold shadows. Now, though, it seemed as if it were a thing out of wax, ready to melt in an instant's flash of heat.

Their faces and the flesh of their hands took on a bloodless, corpse-like appearance.

They hurried up the stairs, and a State Patrolman let them in through the small door to the right of the heavy metal double doors that were the main entrance to the building. He locked and chained the door behind them, after snapping open his holster when he saw Tanner.

"Which way?" asked the man with the shotgun.

"Second floor," said the trooper, nodding toward a stairway to their right. "Go straight back when you get to the top. It's the big office at the end of the hall."

"Thanks."

The roaring was considerably muffled, and objects achieved an appearance of natural existence once more in the artificial light of the building.

They climbed the curving stairway and moved along the corridor that led back into the building. When they reached the final office, the man with the shotgun nodded to his driver. "Knock," he said.

A woman opened the door, started to say something, then stopped and nodded when she saw Tanner. She stepped aside and held the door. "This way," she said, and they moved past her into the office, and she pressed a button on her desk and told the voice that said, "Yes, Mrs. Fiske?": "They're here, with that man, sir."

"Send them in."

She led the to the dark, paneled door in the back of the room and opened it before them.

They entered, and the husky man behind the glass-topped desk leaned backward in his chair and wove his short fingers together in front of his chins and peered over them through eyes just a shade darker than the gray of his hair. His voice was soft and rasped just slightly. "Have a seat," he said to Tanner, and to the others, "Wait outside."

"You know this guy's dangerous, Mister Denton," said the man with the shotgun as Tanner seated himself in a chair situated five feet in front of the desk.

Steel shutters covered the room's three windows, and though the men could not see outside they could guess at the possible furies that stalked there as a sound like machine-gun fire suddenly rang through the room.

"I know."

"Well, he's handcuffed, anyway. Do you want a gun?"

"I've got one."

"Okay, then. We'll be outside."

They left the room.

The two men stared at one another until the door closed, then the man called Denton said, "Are all your affairs settled now?" and the other shrugged. Then, "What the hell *is* your first name, really? Even the records show—"

"Hell," said Tanner. "That's my name. I was the seventh kid in our family, and when I was born the nurse held me up and said to my old man, 'What name do you want on the birth certificate?' and Dad said, 'Hell!' and walked away. So she put it down like that. That's what my brother told me. I never saw my old man to ask if that's how it was. He copped out the same day. Sounds right, though."

"So your mother raised all seven of you?"

"No. She croaked a couple weeks later, and different relatives took us kids."

"I see," said Denton. "You've still got a choice, you know. Do you want to try it or don't you?"

"What's your job, anyway?" asked Tanner.

"I'm the Secretary of Traffic for the nation of California."

"What's that got to do with it?"

"I'm coordinating this thing. It could as easily have been the Surgeon General or the Postmaster General, but more of it really falls into my area of responsibility. I know the hardware best. I know the odds—"

"What are the odds?" asked Tanner.

For the first time, Denton dropped his eyes.

"Well, it's risky. . . ."

"Nobody's ever done it before, except for that nut who ran it to bring the news, and he's dead. How can you get odds out of that?"

"I know," said Denton slowly. "You're thinking it's a suicide job, and you're probably right. We're sending three cars, with two drivers in each. If any one just makes it close enough, its broadcast signals may serve to guide in a Boston driver. You don't have to go though, you know."

"I know. I'm free to spend the rest of my life in prison."

"You killed three people. You could have gotten the death penalty."

"I didn't, so why talk about it? Look, mister, I don't want to die and I don't want the other bit either."

"Drive or don't drive. Take your choice. But remember, if you drive and you make it, all will be forgiven and you can go your own way. The nation of California will even pay for that motorcycle you appropriated and smashed up, not to mention the damage to that police car."

"Thanks a lot," and the winds boomed on the other side of the wall, and the steady staccato from the window shields filled the room.

"You're a very good driver," said Denton, after a time. "You've driven just about every vehicle there is to drive. You've even raced. Back when you were smuggling, you used to make a monthly run to Salt Lake City. There are very few drivers who'll try that, even today."

Hell Tanner smiled, remembering something.

". . . And in the only legitimate job you ever held, you were the only man who'd make the mail run to Albuquerque. There've only been a few others since you were fired."

"That wasn't my fault."

"You were the best man on the Seattle run, too," Denton continued. "Your supervisor said so. What I'm trying to say is that, of anybody we could pick, you've probably got the best chance of getting through. That's why we've been indulgent with you, but we can't afford to wait any longer. It's yes or no right now, and you'll leave within the hour if it's yes."

Tanner raised his cuffed hands and gestured toward the window.

"In all this crap?" he asked.

"The cars can take this storm," said Denton.

"Man, you're crazy."

"People are dying even while we're talking," said Denton.

"So a few more ain't about to make that much difference. Can't we wait till tomorrow?"

"No! A man gave his life to bring us the news! And we've got to get across the continent as fast as possible now or it won't matter! Storm or no storm, the cars leave now! Your feelings on the matter don't mean a good goddamn in the face of this! All I want out of you, Hell, is one word: Which one will it be?"

"I'd like something to eat. I haven't. . . ."

"There's food in the car. What's your answer?"

Hell stared at the dark window.

"Okay," he said, "I'll run Damnation Alley for you. I won't leave without a piece of paper with some writing on it, though."

"I've got it here."

Denton opened a drawer and withdrew a heavy cardboard envelope from which he extracted a piece of stationery bearing the Great Seal of the nation of California. He stood and rounded the desk and handed it to Hell Tanner.

Hell studied it for several minutes, then said, "This says that if I make it to Boston I receive a full pardon for every criminal action I've ever committed within the nation of California. . . ."

"That's right."

"Does that include ones you might not know about now, if someone should come up with them later?"

"That's what it says, Hell—'every criminal action.' "

"Okay, you're on, fat boy. Get these bracelets off me and show me my car."

The man called Denton moved back to his seat on the other side of his desk.

"Let me tell you something else, Hell," he said. "If you try to cop out anywhere along the route, the other drivers have their orders, and they've agreed to follow them. They will open fire on you and burn you into little bitty ashes. Get the picture?"

"I get the picture," said Hell. "I take it I'm supposed to do them the same favor?"

"That is correct."

"Good enough. That might be fun."

"I thought you'd like it."

"Now, if you'll unhook me, I'll make the scene for you."

"Not till I've told you what I think of you," Denton said.

"Okay, if you want to waste time calling me names, while people are dying—"

"Shut up! You don't care about them and you know it! I just want to tell you that I think you are the lowest, most reprehensible human being I have ever encountered. You have killed men and raped women. You once gouged out a man's eyes, just for fun. You've been indicted twice for pushing dope and three times as a pimp. You're a drunk and a degenerate, and I don't think you've had a bath since the day you were born. You and your hoodlums terrorized decent people when they were trying to pull their lives together after the war. You stole from them and you assaulted them, and you extorted money and the necessaries of life with the threat of physical violence. I wish you had died in the Big Raid, that night, like all the rest of them. You are not a human being, except from a biological standpoint. You have a big dead spot somewhere inside you where other people have something that lets them live together in society and be neighbors. The only virtue that you possess—if you want to call it that—is that your reflexes may be a little faster, your muscles a little stronger, your eye a bit more wary than the rest of us, so that you can sit behind a wheel and drive through anything that has a way through it. It is for this that the nation of California is willing to pardon your inhumanity if you will use that one virtue to help rather than hurt. I don't approve. I don't want to depend on you, because you're not the type. I'd like to see you die in this thing, and while I hope that somebody makes it through, I hope that it will be somebody else. I hate your bloody guts. You've got your pardon now. The car's ready. Let's go."

Denton stood, at a height of about five feet eight inches, and Tanner stood and looked down at him and chuckled.

"I'll make it," he said. "If that citizen from Boston made it through and died, I'll make it through and live. I've been as far as the Missus Hip."

"You're lying."

"No, I ain't either, and if you ever find out that's straight, remember I got this piece of paper in my pocket—'every criminal action' and like that. It wasn't easy, and I was lucky, too. But I made it that far and, nobody else you know can say that. So I figure that's about halfway, and I can make the other half if I can get that far."

They moved toward the door.

"I don't like to say it and mean it," said Denton, "but good luck. Not for your sake, though."

"Yeah, I know."

Denton opened the door, and, "Turn him loose," he said. "He's driving."

The officer with the shotgun handed it to the man who had given Tanner the cigarettes, and he fished in his pockets for the key. When he found it, he unlocked the cuffs, stepped back, and hung them at his belt; and, "I'll come with you," said Denton. "The motor pool is downstairs."

They left the office, and Mrs. Fiske opened her purse and took a rosary into her hands and bowed her head. She prayed for Boston and she prayed for the soul of its departed messenger. She even threw in a couple for Hell Tanner.

— III —

They descended to the basement, the sub-basement and the sub-sub-basement.

When they got there, Tanner saw three cars, ready to go; and he saw five men seated on benches along the wall. One of them he recognized.

"Denny," he said, "come here," and he moved forward, and a slim, blond youth who held a crash helmet in his right hand stood and walked toward him.

"What the hell are you doing?" he asked him.

"I'm second driver in car three."

"You've got your own garage and you've kept your nose clean. What's the thought on this?"

"Denton offered me fifty grand," said Denny, and Hell turned away his face.

"Forget it! It's no good if you're dead!"

"I need the money."

"Why?"

"I want to get married and I can use it."

"I thought you were making out okay."

"I am, but I'd like to buy a house."

"Does your girl know what you've got in mind?"

"No."

"I didn't think so. Listen, I've got to do it—it's the only way out for me. You don't have to—"

"That's for me to say."

"—so I'm going to tell you something: You drive out to Pasadena to that place where we used to play when we were kids—with the rocks and the three big trees—you know where I mean?"

"Yeah, I sure do remember."

"Go back of the big tree in the middle, on the side where I carved my initials. Step off seven steps and dig down around four feet. Got that?"

"Yeah. What's there?"

"That's my legacy, Denny. You'll find one of those old strong boxes, probably all rusted out by now. Bust it open. It'll be full of excelsior, and there'll be a six-inch joint of pipe inside. It's threaded, and there's caps on both ends. There's a little over five grand rolled up inside it, and all the bills are clean."

"Why you telling me this?"

"Because it's yours now," he said, and hit him in the jaw.

When Denny fell, he kicked him in the ribs, three times, before the cops grabbed him and dragged him away.

"You fool!" said Denton as they held him. "You crazy, damned fool!"

"Uh-uh," said Tanner. "No brother of mine is going to run Damnation Alley while I'm around to stomp him and keep him out of the game. Better find another driver quick, because he's got cracked ribs. Or else let me drive alone."

"Then you'll drive alone," said Denton, "because we can't afford to wait around any longer. There's pills in the compartment, to keep you awake, and you'd better use them, because if you fall back they'll burn you up. Remember that."

"I won't forget you, mister, if I'm ever back in town. Don't fret about that."

"Then you'd better get into car number two and start heading up the ramp. The vehicles are all loaded. The cargo compartment is under the rear seat."

"Yeah, I know."

". . . And if I ever see you again, it'll be too soon. Get out of my sight, scum!"

Tanner spat on the floor and turned his back on the Secretary of Traffic. Several cops were giving first aid to his brother, and one had dashed off in search of a doctor. Denton made two teams of the remaining four drivers and assigned them to cars one and three. Tanner climbed into the cab of his own, started the engine and waited. He stared up the ramp and considered what lay ahead. He searched the compartments until he found cigarettes. He lit one and leaned back.

The other drivers moved forward and mounted their own heavily shielded vehicles. The radio crackled, crackled, hummed, crackled again, and then a voice came through as he heard the other engines come to life.

"Car one—ready!" came the voice.

There was a pause, then, "Car three—ready!" said a different voice. Tanner lifted the microphone and mashed the button on its side. "Car two ready," he said.

"Move out," came the order, and they headed up the ramp.

The door rolled upward before them, and they entered the storm.

## — IV —

It was a nightmare, getting out of L.A. and onto Route 91. The waters came down in sheets and rocks the size of baseballs banged against the armor plating of his car. Tanner smoked and turned on the special lights. He wore infrared goggles, and the night and the storm stalked him.

The radio crackled, many times, and it seemed that he heard the murmur of a distant voice, but he could never quite make out what it was trying to say.

They followed the road for as far as it went, and as their big tires sighed over the rugged terrain that began where the road ended, Tanner took the lead and the others were content to follow. He knew the way; they didn't.

He followed the old smugglers' route he'd used to run candy to the Mormons. It was possible that he was the only one left alive that knew it. Possible, but then there was always someone looking for a fast buck. So, in all of L.A., there might be somebody else.

The lightning began to fall, not in bolts, but sheets. The car was insulated, but after a time his hair stood on end. He might have seen a giant Gila Monster once, but he couldn't be sure. He kept his fingers away from the fire-control board. He'd save his teeth till menaces were imminent. From the rearview scanners it seemed that one of the cars behind him had discharged a rocket, but he couldn't be sure, since he had lost all radio contact with them immediately upon leaving the building.

Waters rushed toward him, splashed about his car. The sky sounded like an artillery range. A boulder the size of a tombstone fell in front of him, and he swerved about it. Red lights flashed across the sky from north to south. In their passing, he detected many black bands going from west to east. It was not an encouraging spectacle. The storm could go on for days.

He continued to move forward, skirting a pocket of radiation that had not died in the four years since last he had come this way.

They came upon a place where the sands were fused into a glassy sea, and he slowed as he began its passage, peering ahead after the craters and chasms it contained.

Three more rockfalls assailed him before the heavens split themselves open and revealed a bright blue light, edged with violet. The dark curtains rolled back toward the Poles, and the roaring and the gunfire reports diminished. A lavender glow remained in the north, and a green sun dipped toward the horizon.

They had ridden it out. He killed the infras, pushed back his goggles and switched on the normal night lamps.

The desert would be bad enough, all by itself.

Something big and bat-like swooped through the tunnel of his lights and was gone. He ignored its passage. Five minutes later it made a second pass, this time much closer, and he fired a magnesium flare. A black shape, perhaps forty feet across, was illuminated, and he gave it two five-second bursts from the fifty-calibers and it fell to the ground and did not return again.

To the squares, this was Damnation Alley. To Hell Tanner, this was still the parking lot. He'd been this way thirty-two times, and so far as he was concerned the Alley started in the place that was once called Colorado.

He led, and they followed, and the night wore on like an abrasive.

No airplane could make it. Not since the war. None could venture above a couple hundred feet, the place where the winds began. The winds. The mighty winds that circled the globe, tearing off the tops of mountains, Sequoia trees, wrecked buildings, gathering up birds, bats, insects and anything else that moved, up into the dead belt; the winds that swirled about the world, lacing the skies with dark lines of debris, occasionally meeting, merging, clashing, dropping tons of carnage wherever they came together and formed too great a mass. Air transportation was definitely out, to anywhere in the world. For these winds circled, and they never ceased. Not in all the twenty-five years of Tanner's memory had they let up.

Tanner pushed ahead, cutting a diagonal by the green sunset. Dust continued to fall about him, great clouds of it, and the sky was violet, then purple once more. Then the sun went down and the night came on, and the stars were very faint points of light somewhere above it all. After a time, the moon rose, and the half-face that it showed that night was the color of a glass of chianti wine held before a candle.

He lit another cigarette and began to curse, slowly, softly and without emotion.

They threaded their way amid heaps of rubble: rock, metal, fragments of machinery, the prow of a boat. A snake, as big around as a garbage can and dark green in the cast light, slithered across Tanner's path, and he braked the vehicle as it continued and continued and continued. Perhaps a hundred and twenty feet of snake passed by before Tanner removed his foot from the brake and touched gently upon the gas pedal once again.

Glancing at the left-hand screen, which held an infrared version of the view to the left, it seemed that he saw two eyes glowing within the shadow of a heap of girders and masonry. Tanner kept one hand near the fire-control button and did not move it for a distance of several miles.

There were no windows in the vehicle, only screens which reflected views in every direction including straight up and the ground beneath the car. Tanner sat within an illuminated box which shielded him against radiation. The "car" that he drove had eight heavily treaded tires and was thirty-two feet in length. It mounted eight fifty-caliber automatic guns and four grenade throwers. It carried thirty armor-piercing rockets which could be discharged straight ahead or at any elevation up to forty degrees from the plane. Each of the four sides, as well as the roof of the vehicle, housed a flame thrower. Razor-sharp "wings" of tempered steel—eighteen inches wide at their bases and tapering to points, an inch and a quarter thick where they ridged—could be moved through a complete hundred-eighty-degree arc along the sides of the car and parallel to the ground, at a height of two feet and eight inches. When standing at a right angle to the body of the vehicle—eight feet to the rear of the front bumper—they extended out to a distance of six feet on either side of the car. They could be couched like lances for a charge. They could be held but slightly out from the sides for purposes of slashing whatever was sideswiped. The car was bullet-proof, air-conditioned and had its own food locker and sanitation facilities. A long-barreled .357 Magnum was held by a clip on the door near the driver's left hand. A 30.06, a .45 caliber automatic and six hand grenades occupied the rack immediately above the front seat.

But Tanner kept his own counsel, in the form of a long, slim SS dagger inside his right boot.

He removed his gloves and wiped his palms on the knees of his denims. The pierced heart that was tattooed on the back of his right hand was red in the light from the dashboard. The knife that went through it was dark blue, and his first name was tattooed in the same color beneath it, one letter on each knuckle, beginning with that at the base of his little finger.

He opened and explored the two near compartments but could find no cigars. So he crushed out his cigarette butt on the floor and lit another.

The forward screen showed vegetation, and he slowed. He tried using the radio but couldn't tell whether anyone heard him, receiving only static in reply.

He slowed, staring ahead and up. He halted once again.

He turned his forward lights up to full intensity and studied the situation.

A heavy wall of thorn bushes stood before him, reaching to a height of perhaps twelve feet. It swept on to his right and off to his left, vanishing out of sight in both directions. How dense, how deep a pit might be, he could not tell. It had not been there a few years before.

He moved forward slowly and activated the flame throwers. In the rearview screen, he could see that the other vehicles had halted a hundred yards behind him and dimmed their lights.

He drove till he could go no further, then pressed the button for the forward flame.

It shot forth, a tongue of fire, licking fifty feet into the bramble. He held it for five seconds and withdrew it. Then he extended it a second time and backed away quickly as the flames caught.

Beginning with a tiny glow, they worked their way upward and spread slowly to the right and the left. Then they grew in size and brightness.

As Tanner backed away, he had to dim his screen, for they'd spread fifty feet before he'd backed more than a hundred, and they leapt thirty and forty feet into the air.

The blaze widened, to a hundred feet, two, three. . . . As Tanner backed away, he could see a river of fire flowing off into the distance, and the night was bright about him.

He watched it burn, until it seemed that he looked upon a molten sea. Then he searched the refrigerator, but there was no beer. He opened a soft drink and sipped it while he watched the burning. After about ten minutes, the air conditioner whined and shook itself to life. Hordes of dark, four-footed creatures, the size of rats or cats, fled from the inferno, their coats smouldering. They flowed by. At one point, they covered his forward screen, and he could hear the scratching of their claws upon the fenders and the roof.

He switched off the lights and killed the engine, tossed the empty can into the waste box. He pushed the "Recline" button on the side of the seat, leaned back, and closed his eyes.

# — V —

He was awakened by the blowing of horns. It was still night, and the panel clock showed him that he had slept for a little over three hours.

He stretched, sat up, adjusted the seat. The other cars had moved up, and one stood to either side of him. He leaned on his own horn twice and started his engine. He switched on the forward lights and considered the prospect before him as he drew on his gloves.

Smoke still rose from the blackened field, and far off to his right there was a glow, as if the fire still continued somewhere in the distance. They were in the place that had once been known as Nevada.

He rubbed his eyes and scratched his nose, then blew the horn once and engaged the gears.

He moved forward slowly. The burnt-out area seemed fairly level and his tires were thick.

He entered the black field, and his screens were immediately obscured by the rush of ashes and smoke which arose on all sides.

He continued, hearing the tires crunching through the brittle remains. He set his screens at maximum and switched his headlamps up to full brightness.

The vehicles that flanked him dropped back perhaps eighty feet, and he dimmed the screens that reflected the glare of their lights.

He released a flare, and as it hung there, burning, cold, white and high, he saw a charred plain that swept on to the edges of his eyes' horizon.

He pushed down on the accelerator, and the cars behind him swung far out to the sides to avoid the clouds that he raised. His radio crackled, and he heard a faint voice but could not make out its words.

He blew his horn and rolled ahead even faster. The other vehicles kept pace.

He drove for an hour and a half before he saw the end of the ash and the beginning of clean sand up ahead.

Within five minutes, he was moving across desert once more, and he checked his compass and bore slightly to the west. Cars one and three followed, speeding up to match his new pace, and he drove with one hand and ate a corned beef sandwich.

When morning came, many hours later, he took a pill to keep himself alert and listened to the screaming of the wind. The sun rose up like molten silver to his right, and a third of the sky grew amber and was laced with fine lines like cobwebs. The desert was topaz beneath it, and the brown curtain of dust that hung continuously at his back, pierced only by the eight shafts of the other cars' lights, took on a pinkish tone as the sun grew a bright red corona and the shadows fled into the west. He dimmed his lights as he passed an orange cactus shaped like a toadstool and perhaps fifty feet in diameter.

Giant bats fled south, and far ahead he saw a wide waterfall descending from the heavens. It was gone by the time he reached the damp sand of that place, but a dead shark lay to his left, and there was seaweed, seaweed, seaweed, fishes, driftwood all about.

The sky pinked over from east to west and remained that color. He gulped a bottle of ice water and felt it go into his stomach. He passed more cacti, and a pair of coyotes sat at the base of one and watched him drive by. They seemed to be laughing. Their tongues were very red.

As the sun brightened, he dimmed the screen. He smoked, and he found a button that produced music. He swore at the soft, stringy sounds that filled the cabin, but he didn't turn them off.

He checked the radiation level outside, and it was only a little above normal. The last time he had passed this way, it had been considerably higher.

He passed several wrecked vehicles such as his own. He ran across another plain of silicon, and in the middle was a huge crater which he skirted. The pinkness in the sky faded and faded and faded, and a bluish tone came to replace it. The dark lines were still there, and occasionally one widened into a black river as it flowed away into the east. At noon, one such river partly eclipsed the sun for a period of eleven minutes. With its departure, there came a brief dust storm, and Tanner turned on the radar and his lights. He knew there was a chasm somewhere ahead, and when he came to it he bore to the left and ran along its edge for close to two miles before it narrowed and vanished. The other vehicles followed, and Tanner took his bearings from the compass once more. The dust had subsided with the brief wind, and even with the screen dimmed Tanner had to don his dark goggles against the glare of reflected sunlight from the faceted field he now negotiated.

He passed towering formations which seemed to be quartz. He had never stopped to investigate them in the past, and he had no desire to do it now. The spectrum danced at their bases, and patches of such light occurred for some distance about them.

Speeding away from the crater, he came again upon sand, clean, brown, white dun and red. There were more cacti, and huge dunes lay all about him. The sky continued to change, until finally it was as blue as a baby's eyes. Tanner hummed along with the music for a time, and then he saw the Monster.

. . .

It was a Gila, bigger than his car, and it moved in fast. It sprang from out the sheltering shade of a valley filled with cacti and it raced toward him, its beaded body bright with many colors beneath the sun, its dark, dark eyes unblinking as it bounded forward on its lizard-fast legs, sable fountains rising behind its upheld tail that was wide as a sail and pointed like a tent.

He couldn't use the rockets because it was coming in from the side.

He opened up with his fifty-calibers and spread his "wings" and stamped the accelerator to the floor. As it neared, he sent forth a cloud of fire in its direction. By then, the other cars were firing, too.

It swung its tail and opened and closed its jaws, and its blood came forth and fell upon the ground. Then a rocket struck it. It turned; it leaped.

There came a booming, crunching sound as it fell upon the vehicle identified as car number one and lay there.

Tanner hit the brakes, turned, and headed back.

Car number three came up beside it and parked. Tanner did the same.

He jumped down from the cab and crossed to the smashed car. He had the rifle in his hands and he put six rounds into the creature's head before he approached the car.

The door had come open, and it hung from a single hinge, the bottom one.

Inside, Tanner could see the two men sprawled, and there was some blood upon the dashboard and the seat.

The other two drivers came up beside him and stared within. Then the shorter of the two crawled inside and listened for the heartbeat and the pulse and felt for breathing.

"Mike's dead," he called out, "but Greg's starting to come around."

A wet spot that began at the car's rear and spread and continued to spread, and the smell of gasoline filled the air.

Tanner took out a cigarette, thought better of it and replaced it in the pack. He could hear the gurgle of the huge gas tanks as they emptied themselves upon the ground.

The man who stood at Tanner's side said, "I never saw anything like it. . . . I've seen pictures, but—I never saw anything like it. . . ."

"I have," said Tanner, and then the other driver emerged from the wreck, partly supporting the man he'd referred to as Greg.

The man called out, "Greg's all right. He just hit his head on the dash."

The man who stood at Tanner's side said, "You can take him, Hell. He can back you up when he's feeling better," and Tanner shrugged and turned his back on the scene and lit a cigarette.

"I don't think you should do—" the man began, and Tanner blew smoke in his face. He turned to regard the two approaching men and saw that Greg was dark-eyed and deeply tanned. Part Indian, possibly. His skin seemed smooth, save for a couple pockmarks beneath his right eye, and his cheekbones were high and his hair very dark. He was as big as Tanner, which was six-two, though not quite so heavy. He was dressed in overalls; and his carriage, now that he had had a few deep breaths of air, became very erect, and he moved with a quick, graceful stride.

"We'll have to bury Mike," the short man said.

"I hate to lose the time," said his companion, "but—" and then Tanner flipped his cigarette and threw himself to the ground as it landed in the pool at the rear of the car.

There was an explosion, flames, then more explosions. Tanner heard the rockets as they tore off toward the east, inscribing dark furrows in the hot afternoon's air. The ammo for the fifty-calibers exploded, and the hand grenades went off, and Tanner burrowed deeper and deeper into the sand, covering his head and blocking his ears.

As soon as things grew quiet, he grabbed for the rifle. But they were already coming at him, and he saw the muzzle of a pistol. He raised his hands slowly and stood.

"Why the goddamn hell did you do a stupid thing like that?" said the other driver, the man who held the pistol.

Tanner smiled, and, "Now we don't have to bury him," he said. "Cremation's just as good, and it's already over."

"You could have killed us all, if those guns or those rocket launchers had been aimed this way!"

"They weren't. I looked."

"The flying metal could've—Oh. . . . I see. Pick up your damn rifle, buddy, and keep it pointed at the ground. Eject the rounds it's still got in it and put 'em in your pocket."

Tanner did this thing while the other talked.

"You wanted to kill us all, didn't you? Then you could have cut out and gone your way, like you tried to do yesterday. Isn't that right?"

"You said it, mister, not me."

"It's true, though. You don't give a good goddamn if everybody in Boston croaks, do you?"

"My gun's unloaded now," said Tanner.

"Then get back in your bloody buggy and get going! I'll be behind you all the way!"

Tanner walked back toward his car. He heard the others arguing behind him, but he didn't think they'd shoot him. As he was about to climb up into the cab, he saw a shadow out of the corner of his eye and turned quickly.

The man named Greg was standing behind him, tall and quiet as a ghost.

"Want me to drive awhile?" he asked Tanner, without expression.

"No, you rest up. I'm still in good shape. Later on this afternoon, maybe, if you feel up to it."

The man nodded and rounded the cab. He entered from the other side and immediately reclined his chair.

Tanner slammed his door and started the engine. He heard the air conditioner come to life.

"Want to reload this?" he asked. "And put it back on the rack?" And he handed the rifle and the ammo to the other, who had nodded. He drew on his gloves then and said, "There's plenty of soft drinks in the 'frig. Nothing much else, though," and the other nodded again. Then he heard car three start and said, "Might as well roll," and he put it into gear and took his foot off the clutch.

— VI —

After they had driven for about half an hour, the man called Greg said to him, "Is it true what Marlowe said?"

"What's a Marlowe?"

"He's driving the other car. Were you trying to kill us? Do you really want to skip out?"

Hell laughed, then, "That's right," he said. "You named it."

"Why?"

Hell let it hang there for a minute, then said, "Why shouldn't I? I'm not anxious to die. I'd like to wait a long time before I try that bit."

Greg said, "If we don't make it, the population of the continent may be cut in half."

"If it's a question of them or me, I'd rather it was them."

"I sometimes wonder how people like you happen."

"The same way as anybody else, mister, and it's fun for a couple people for awhile, and then the trouble starts."

"What did they ever do to you, Hell?"

"Nothing. What did they ever do *for* me? Nothing. Nothing. What do I owe them? The same."

"Why'd you stomp your brother back at the Hall?"

"Because I didn't want him doing a damfool thing like this and getting himself killed. Cracked ribs he can get over. Death is a more permanent ailment."

"That's not what I asked you. I mean, what do you care whether he croaks?"

"He's a good kid, that's why. He's got a thing for this chick, though, and he can't see straight."

"So what's it to you?"

"Like I said, he's my brother and he's a good kid. I like him."

"How come?"

"Oh, hell! We've been through a lot together, that's all! What are you trying to do? Psychoanalyze me?"

"I was just curious, that's all."

"So now you know. Talk about something else if you want to talk, okay?"

"Okay. You've been this way before, right?"

"That's right."

"You been any further east?"

"I've been all the way to the Missus Hip."

"Do you know a way to get across it?"

"I think so. The bridge is still up at Saint Louis."

"Why didn't you go across it the last time you were there?"

"Are you kidding? The thing's packed with cars full of bones. It wasn't worth the trouble to try and clear it."

"Why'd you go that far in the first place?"

"Just to see what it was like. I heard all these stories—"

"What was it like?"

"A lot of crap. Burnt down towns, big craters, crazy animals, some people—"

"People? People still live there?"

"If you want to call them that. They're all wild and screwed up. They wear rags or animal skins or they go naked. They threw rocks at me till I shot a couple. Then they let me alone."

"How long ago was that?"

"Six—maybe seven years ago. I was just a kid then."

"How come you never told anybody about it?"

"I did. A coupla my friends. Nobody else ever asked me. We were going to go out there and grab off a couple of the girls and bring them back, but everybody chickened out."

"What would you have done with them?"

Tanner shrugged. "I dunno. Sell 'em, I guess."

"You guys used to do that, down on the Barbary Coast—sell people, I mean—didn't you?"

Tanner shrugged again.

"Used to," he said, "before the Big Raid."

"How'd you manage to live through that? I thought they'd cleaned the whole place out?"

"I was doing time," he said. "A.D.W."

"What's that?"

"Assault with a deadly weapon."

"What'd you do after they let you go?"

"I let them rehabilitate me. They got me a job running the mail."

"Oh yeah, I heard about that. Didn't realize it was you, though. You were supposed to be pretty good—doing all right and ready for a promotion. Then you kicked your boss around and lost your job. How come?"

"He was always riding me about my record and about my old gang down on the Coast. Finally, one day I told him to lay off, and he laughed at me, so I hit him with a chain. Knocked out the bastard's front teeth. I'd do it again."

"Too bad."

"I was the best driver he had. It was his loss. Nobody else will make the Albuquerque run, not even today. Not unless they really need the money."

"Did you like the work, though, while you were doing it?"

"Yeah, I like to drive."

"You should probably have asked for a transfer when the guy started bugging you."

"I know. If it was happening today, that's probably what I'd do. I was mad, though, and I used to get mad a lot faster than I do now. I think I'm smarter these days than I was before."

"If you make it on this run and you go home afterwards, you'll probably be able to get your job back. Think you'd take it?"

"In the first place," said Tanner, "I don't think we'll make it. And in the second, if we do make it and there's still people around that town, I think I'd rather stay there than go back."

Greg nodded. "Might be smart. You'd be a hero. Nobody'd know much about your record. Somebody'd turn you on to something good."

"The hell with heroes," said Tanner.

"Me, though, I'll go back if we make it."

"Sail 'round Cape Horn?"

"That's right."

"Might be fun. But why go back?"

"I've got an old mother and a mess of brothers and sisters I take care of, and I've got a girl back there."

Tanner brightened the screen as the sky began to darken.

"What's your mother like?"

"Nice old lady. Raised the eight of us. Got arthritis bad now, though."

"What was she like when you were a kid?"

"She used to work during the day, but she cooked our meals and sometimes brought us candy. She made a lot of our clothes. She used to tell us stories, like about how things were before the war. She played games with us and sometimes she gave us toys."

"How about your old man?" Tanner asked him, after awhile.

"He drank pretty heavy and he had a lot of jobs, but he never beat us too much. He was all right. He got run over by a car when I was around twelve."

"And you take care of everybody now?"

"Yeah. I'm the oldest."

"What is it that you do?"

"I've got your old job. I run the mail to Albuquerque."

"Are you kidding?"

"No."

"I'll be damned! Is Gorman still the supervisor?"

"He retired last year, on disability."

"I'll be damned! That's funny. Listen, down in Albuquerque do you ever go to a bar called Pedro's?"

"I've been there."

"Have they still got a little blonde girl plays the piano? Named Margaret?"

"No."

"Oh."

"They've got some guy now. Fat fellow. Wears a big ring on his left hand."

Tanner nodded and downshifted as he began the ascent of a steep hill.

"How's your head now?" he asked, when they'd reached the top and started down the opposite slope.

"Feels pretty good. I took a couple of your aspirins with that soda I had."

"Feel up to driving for awhile?"

"Sure, I could do that."

"Okay, then." Tanner leaned on the horn and braked the car. "Just follow the compass for a hundred miles or so and wake me up. All right?"

"Okay. Anything special I should watch out for?"

"The snakes. You'll probably see a few. Don't hit them, whatever you do."

"Right."

They changed seats, and Tanner reclined the one, lit a cigarette, smoked half of it, crushed it out and went to sleep.

— VII —

When Greg awakened him, it was night. Tanner coughed and drank a mouthful of ice water and crawled back to the latrine. When he emerged, he took the driver's seat and checked the mileage and looked at the compass. He corrected their course and, "We'll be in Salt Lake City before morning," he said, "if we're lucky.—Did you run into any trouble?"

"No, it was pretty easy. I saw some snakes and I let them go by. That was about it."

Tanner grunted and engaged the gears.

"What was that guy's name that brought the news about the plague?" Tanner asked.

"Brady or Brody or something like that," said Greg.

"What was it that killed him? He might have brought the plague to L.A., you know."

Greg shook his head.

"No. His car had been damaged, and he was all broken up—and he'd been exposed to radiation a lot of the way. They burnt his body and his car, and anybody who'd been anywhere near him got shots of Haffikine."

"What's that?"

"That's the stuff we're carrying—Haffikine antiserum. It's the only cure for the plague. Since we had a bout of it around twenty years ago, we've kept it on hand and maintained the facilities for making more in a hurry. Boston never did, and now they're hurting."

"Seems kind of silly for the only other nation on the continent—maybe in the world—not to take better care of itself, when they knew we'd had a dose of it."

Greg shrugged.

"Probably, but there it is. Did they give you any shots before they released you?"

"Yeah."

"That's what it was, then."

"I wonder where their driver crossed the Missus Hip? He didn't say, did he?"

"He hardly said anything at all. They got most of the story from the letter he carried."

"Must have been one hell of a driver, to run the Alley."

"Yeah. Nobody's ever done it before, have they?"

"Not that I know of."

"I'd like to have met the guy."

"Me too, at least I guess."

"It's a shame we can't radio across country, like in the old days."

"Why?"

"Then he wouldn't of had to do it, and we could find out along the way whether it's really worth making the run. They might all be dead by now, you know."

"You've got a point there, mister, and in a day or so we'll be to a place where going back will be harder than going ahead."

Tanner adjusted the screen as dark shapes passed.

"Look at that, will you!"

"I don't see anything."

"Put on your infras."

Greg did this and stared upward at the screen.

Bats. Enormous bats cavorted overhead, swept by in dark clouds.

"There must be hundreds of them, maybe thousands. . . ."

"Guess so. Seems there are more than there used to be when I came this way a few years back. They must be screwing their heads off in Carlsbad."

"We never see them in L.A. Maybe they're pretty much harmless."

"Last time I was up to Salt Lake, I heard talk that a lot of them were rabid. Some day someone's got to go—them or us."

"You're a cheerful guy to ride with, you know?"

Tanner chuckled and lit a cigarette, and, "Why don't you make us some coffee?" he said. "As for the bats, that's something our kids can worry about, if there are any."

Greg filled the coffee pot and plugged it into the dashboard. After a time, it began to grumble and hiss.

"What the hell's that?" said Tanner, and he hit the brakes. The other car halted, several hundred yards behind his own, and he turned on his microphone and said, "Car three! What's that look like to you?" and waited.

He watched them: towering, tapered tops that spun between the ground and the sky, wobbling from side to side, sweeping back and forth, about a mile ahead. It seemed there were fourteen or fifteen of the things. Now they stood like pillars, now they danced. They bored into the ground and sucked up yellow dust. There was a haze all about them. The stars were dim or absent above or behind them.

Greg stared ahead and said, "I've heard of whirlwinds, tornadoes—big, spinning things. I've never seen one, but that's the way they were described to me."

And then the radio crackled, and the muffled voice of the man called Marlowe came through:

"Giant dust devils," he said. "Big, rotary sand storms. I think they're sucking stuff up into the dead belt, because I don't see anything coming down—"

"You ever see one before?"

"No, but my partner says he did. He says the best thing might be to shoot our anchoring columns and stay put."

Tanner did not answer immediately. He stared ahead, and the tornadoes seemed to grow larger.

"They're coming this way," he finally said. "I'm not about to park here and be a target. I want to be able to maneuver. I'm going ahead through them."

"I don't think you should."

"Nobody asked you, mister, but if you've got any brains you'll do the same thing."

"I've got rockets aimed at your tail, Hell."

"You won't fire them—not for a thing like this, where I could be right and you could be wrong—and not with Greg in here, too."

There was silence within the static, then, "Okay, you win, Hell. Go ahead, and we'll watch. If you make it, we'll follow. If you don't, we'll stay put."

"I'll shoot a flare when I get to the other side," Tanner said. "When you see it, you do the same. Okay?"

Tanner broke the connection and looked ahead, studying the great black columns, swollen at their tops. There fell a few layers of light from the storm which they supported, and the air was foggy between the blacknesses of their revolving trunks. "Here goes," said Tanner, switching his lights as bright as they would beam. "Strap yourself in, boy," and Greg obeyed him as the vehicle crunched forward.

Tanner buckled his own safety belt as they slowly edged ahead.

The columns grew and swayed as he advanced, and he could now hear a rushing, singing sound, as of a chorus of the winds.

He skirted the first by three hundred yards and continued to the left to avoid the one which stood before him and grew and grew. As he got by it, there was another, and he moved further to the left. Then there was an open area of perhaps a quarter of a mile leading ahead and toward his right.

He swiftly sped across it and passed between two of the towers that stood like ebony pillars a hundred yards apart. As he passed them, the wheel was almost torn from his grip, and he seemed to inhabit the center of an eternal thunderclap. He swerved to the right then and skirted another, speeding.

Then he saw seven more and cut between two and passed about another. As he did, the one behind him moved rapidly, crossing the path he had just taken. He exhaled heavily and turned to the left.

He was surrounded by the final four, and he braked so that he was thrown forward and the straps cut into his shoulder, as two of the whirlwinds shook violently and moved in terrible spurts of speed. One passed before him, and the front end of his car was raised from off the ground.

Then he floored the gas pedal and shot between the final two, and they were all behind him.

He continued on for about a quarter of a mile, turned the car about, mounted a small rise and parked.

He released the flare.

It hovered, like a dying star, for about half a minute.

He lit a cigarette as he stared back, and he waited.

He finished the cigarette.

Then, "Nothing," he said. "Maybe they couldn't spot it through the storm. Or maybe we couldn't see theirs."

"I hope so," said Greg.

"How long do you want to wait?"

"Let's have that coffee."

An hour passed, then two. The pillars began to collapse until there were only three of the slimmer ones. They moved off toward the east and were gone from sight.

Tanner released another flare, and still there was no response.

"We'd better go back and look for them," said Greg.

"Okay."

And they did.

There was nothing there, though, nothing to indicate the fate of car three.

Dawn occurred in the east before they had finished with their searching, and Tanner turned the car around, checked the compass, and moved north.

"When do you think we'll hit Salt Lake?" Greg asked him, after a long silence.

"Maybe two hours."

"Were you scared, back when you ran those things?"

"No. Afterwards, though, I didn't feel so good."

Greg nodded.

"You want me to drive again?"

"No. I won't be able to sleep if I stop now. We'll take in more gas in Salt Lake, and we can get something to eat while a mechanic checks over the car. Then I'll put us on the right road, and you can take over while I sack out."

The sky was purple again and the black bands had widened. Tanner cursed and drove faster. He fired his ventral flame at two bats who decided to survey the car. They fell back, and he accepted the mug of coffee Greg offered him.

## — VIII —

The sky was as dark as evening when they pulled into Salt Lake City. John Brady—that was his name—had passed that way but days before, and the city was ready for the responding vehicle. Most of its ten thousand inhabitants appeared along the street, and before Hell and Greg had jumped down from the cab after pulling into the first garage they saw, the hood of car number two was opened and three mechanics were peering at the engine.

They abandoned the idea of eating in the little diner across the street. Too many people hit them with too many questions as soon as they set foot outside the garage. They retreated and sent someone after eggs, bacon and toast.

There was cheering as they rolled forth onto the street and sped away into the east.

"Could have used a beer," said Tanner. "Damn it!"

And they rushed along beside the remains of what had once been U.S. Route 40.

Tanner relinquished the driver's seat and stretched out on the passenger side of the cab. The sky continued to darken above them, taking upon it the appearance it had had in L.A. the day before.

"Maybe we can outrun it," Greg said.

"Hope so."

The blue pulse began in the north, flared into a brilliant aurora. The sky was almost black directly overhead.

"Run!" cried Tanner. "Run! Those are hills up ahead! Maybe we can find an overhang or a cave!"

But it broke upon them before they reached the hills. First came the hail, then the flak. The big stones followed, and the scanner on the right went dead. The sands blasted them, and they rode beneath a celestial waterfall that caused the engine to sputter and cough.

They reached the shelter of the hills, though, and found a place within a rocky valley where the walls jutted steeply forward and broke the main force of the wind/sand/dust/rock/water storm. They sat there as the winds screamed and boomed about them. They smoked and they listened.

"We won't make it," said Greg. "You were right. I thought we had a chance. We don't. Everything's against us, even the weather."

"We've got a chance," said Tanner. "Maybe not a real good one. But we've been lucky so far. Remember that."

Greg spat into the waste container.

"Why the sudden optimism? From you?"

"I was mad before and shooting off my mouth. Well, I'm still mad—but I got me a feeling now: I feel lucky. That's all."

Greg laughed. "The hell with luck. Look out there," he said.

"I see it," said Tanner. "This buggy is built to take it, and it's doing it. Also, we're only getting about ten per cent of its full strength."

"Okay, but what difference does it make? It could last for a couple days."

"So we wait it out."

"Wait too long, and even that ten per cent can smash us. Wait too long, and even if it doesn't there'll be no reason left to go ahead. Try driving, though, and it'll flatten us."

"It'll take me ten or fifteen minutes to finish that scanner. We've got spare 'eyes.' If the storm lasts more than six hours, we'll start out anyway."

"Says who?"

"Me."

"Why? You're the one who was so hot on saving his own neck. How come all of a sudden you're willing to risk it, not to mention mine too?"

Tanner smoked awhile, then said, "I've been thinking," and then he didn't say anything else.

"About what?" Greg asked him.

"Those folks in Boston," Tanner said. "Maybe it is worth it. I don't know. They never did anything for me. But hell, I like action and I'd hate to see the whole world get dead. I think I'd like to see Boston, too, just to see what it's like. It might even be fun being a hero, just to see what that's like. Don't get me wrong. I don't give a damn about anybody up there. It's just that I don't like the idea of everything being like the Alley here—all burnt-out and screwed up and full of crap. When we lost the other car back in those torna-does, it made me start thinking. . . . I'd hate to see everybody go that way—everything. I might still cop out if I get a real good chance, but I'm just telling you how I feel now. That's all."

Greg looked away and laughed, a little more heartily than usual.

"I never suspected you contained such philosophic depths."

"Me neither. I'm tired. Tell me about your brothers and sisters, huh?"

"Okay."

Four hours later when the storm slackened and the rocks became dust and the rain fog, Tanner replaced the right scanner; and they moved on out, pass-ing later through Rocky Mountain National Park. The dust and the fog com-bined to limit visibility throughout the day. That evening they skirted the ruin that was Denver, and Tanner took over as they headed toward the place that had once been called Kansas.

He drove all night, and in the morning the sky was clearer than it had been in days. He let Greg snore on and sorted through his thoughts while he sipped his coffee.

It was a strange feeling that came over him as he sat there with his par-don in his pocket and his hands upon the wheel. The dust fumed at his back. The sky was the color of rosebuds, and the dark trails had shrunken once again. He recalled the stories of the days when the missiles came down, burning everything but the northeast and the southwest; the day when the winds arose and the clouds vanished and the sky had lost its blue; the days when the Panama Canal had been shattered and radios had ceased to function; the days when the planes could no longer fly. He regretted this, for he had always wanted to fly, high, birdlike, swooping and soaring. He felt slightly cold, and the screens now seemed to possess a crystal clarity, like pools of tinted water. Somewhere ahead, far, far ahead lay what might be the only other sizeable pocket of humanity that remained on the shoul-ders of the world. He might be able to save it, if he could reach it in time. He looked about him at the rocks and the sand and the side of a broken garage that had somehow come to occupy the slope of a mountain. It re-mained within his mind long after he had passed it. Shattered, fallen down, half covered with debris, it took on a stark and monstrous form, like a de-caying skull which had once occupied the shoulders of a giant; and he pressed down hard on the accelerator, although it could go no further. He began to tremble. The sky brightened, but he did not touch the screen con-trols. Why did he have to be the one? He saw a mass of smoke ahead and to the right. As he drew nearer, he saw that it rose from a mountain which had lost its top and now held a nest of fires in its place. He cut to the left, going miles, many miles, out of the way he had intended. Occasionally, the ground shook beneath his wheels. Ashes fell about him, but now the smouldering cone was far to the rear of the right-hand screen. He wondered after the days that had gone before and the few things that he actually knew about them. If he made it through, he decided he'd learn more about history. He threaded his way through painted canyons and forded a shallow river. Nobody had ever asked him to do anything important before, and he hoped that nobody ever would again. Now, though, he was taken by the feeling that he could do it. He wanted to do it. Damnation Alley lay all about him, burning, fuming, shaking, and if he could not run it then half the world would die, and the chances would be doubled that one day all the world would be part of the Alley. His tattoo stood stark on his whitened knuckles, saying "Hell," and he knew that it was true. Greg still slept, the sleep of exhaustion, and Tanner narrowed his eyes and chewed his beard and never touched the brake, not even when he saw the rockslide beginning. He made it by and sighed. That pass was closed to him forever, but he had shot through without a scratch. His mind was an expanding bubble, its surfaces like the viewscreens, registering everything about him. He felt the flow of the air within the cab and the upward pressure of the pedal upon his foot. His throat seemed dry, but it didn't matter. His eyes felt gooey at their inside corners, but he didn't wipe them. He roared across the pocked plains of Kansas, and he knew now that he had been sucked into the role completely and that he wanted it that way. Damn-his-eyes Denton had been right. It had to be done. He halted when he came to the lip of a chasm and headed north. Thirty miles later it ended, and he turned again to the south. Greg muttered in his sleep. It sounded like a curse. Tanner repeated it softly a couple times and turned toward the east as soon as a level stretch occurred. The sun stood in high heaven, and Tanner felt as though he were drifting bodiless beneath it, above the brown ground flaked with green spikes of growth. He clenched his teeth and his mind went back to Denny, doubtless now in a hospital. Better than being where the others had gone. He hoped the money he'd told him about was still there. Then he felt the ache begin, in the places between his neck and his shoulders. It spread down into his arms, and he realized how tightly he was gripping the wheel. He blinked and took a deep breath and realized that his eyeballs hurt. He lit a cigarette and it tasted foul, but he kept puffing at it. He drank some water and he dimmed the rear view-screen as the sun fell behind him. Then he heard a sound like a distant rumble of thunder and was fully alert once more. He sat up straight and took his foot off the accelerator.

He slowed. He braked and stopped. Then he saw them. He sat there and watched them as they passed, about a half-mile ahead.

A monstrous herd of bison crossed before him. It took the better part of an hour before they had passed. Huge, heavy, dark, heads down, hooves scoring the soil, they ran without slowing until the thunder was great and then rolled off toward the north, diminishing, softening, dying, gone. The screen of their dust still hung before him, and he plunged into it, turning on his lights.

He considered taking a pill, decided against it. Greg might be waking soon, he wanted to be able to get some sleep after they'd switched over.

He came up beside a highway, and its surface looked pretty good, so he crossed onto it and sped ahead. After a time, he passed a faded, sagging sign that said "TOPEKA—110 MILES."

Greg yawned and stretched. He rubbed his eyes with his knuckles and then rubbed his forehead, the right side of which was swollen and dark.

"What time is it?" he asked.

Tanner gestured toward the clock in the dashboard.

"Morning or is it afternoon?"

"Afternoon."

"My God! I must have slept around fifteen hours!"

"That's about right."

"You been driving all that time?"

"That's right."

"You must be done in. You look like hell. Let me just hit the head. I'll take over in a few minutes."

"Good idea."

Greg crawled toward the rear of the vehicle.

After about five minutes, Tanner came upon the outskirts of a dead town. He drove up the main street, and there were rusted-out hulks of cars all along it. Most of the buildings had fallen in upon themselves, and some of the opened cellars that he saw were filled with scummy water. Skeletons lay about the town square. There were no trees standing above the weeds that grew there. Three telephone poles still stood, one of them leaning forward and trailing wires like a handful of black spaghetti. Several benches were visible within the weeds beside the cracked sidewalks, and a skeleton lay stretched out upon the second one Tanner passed. He found his way barred by a fallen telephone pole, and he detoured around the block. The next street was somewhat better preserved, but all its storefront windows were broken, and a nude mannikin posed fetchingly with her left arm missing from the elbow down.

The traffic light at the corner stared blindly as Tanner passed through its intersection.

Tanner heard Greg coming forward as he turned at the next corner.

"I'll take over now," he said.

"I want to get out of this place first," and they both watched in silence for the next fifteen minutes until the dead town was gone from around them.

Tanner pulled to a halt then and said, "We're a couple hours away from a place that used to be called Topeka. Wake me if you run into anything hairy."

"How did it go while I was asleep? Did you have any trouble?"

"No," said Tanner, and he closed his eyes and began to snore.

Greg drove away from the sunset, and he ate three ham sandwiches and drank a quart of milk before Topeka.

— IX —

Tanner was awakened by the firing of the rockets. He rubbed the sleep from his eyes and stared dumbly ahead for almost half a minute.

Like gigantic dried leaves, great clouds fell about them. Bats, bats, bats. The air was filled with bats. Tanner could hear a chittering, squeaking, scratching sound, and the car was buffeted by their dark bodies.

"Where are we?" he asked.

"Kansas City. The place seems full of them," and Greg released another rocket, which cut a fiery path through the swooping, spinning horde.

"Save the rockets. Use the fire," said Tanner, switching the nearest gun to manual and bringing cross-hairs into focus upon the screen. "Blast 'em in all directions—for five, six seconds—then I'll come in."

The flame shot forth, orange and cream blossoms of combustion. When they folded, Tanner sighted in the screen and squeezed the trigger. He swung the gun, and they fell. Their charred bodies lay all about him, and he added new ones to the smouldering heaps.

"Roll it!" he cried, and the car moved forward, swaying, bat-bodies crunching beneath its tires.

Tanner laced the heavens with gunfire, and when they swooped again he strafed them and fired a flare.

In the sudden magnesium glow from overhead, it seemed that millions of vampire-faced forms were circling, spiraling down toward them.

He switched from gun to gun, and they fell about him like fruit. Then he called out, "Brake, and hit the topside flame!" and Greg did this thing.

"Now the sides! Front and rear next!"

Bodies were burning all about them, heaped as high as the hood, and Greg put the car into low gear when Tanner cried "Forward!" And they pushed their way through the wall of charred flesh.

Tanner fired another flare.

The bats were still there, but circling higher now. Tanner primed the guns and waited, but they did not attack again in any great number. A few swept about them, and he took pot-shots at them as they passed.

Ten minutes later he said, "That's the Missouri River to our left. If we just follow alongside it now, we'll hit Saint Louis."

"I know. Do you think it'll be full of bats, too?"

"Probably. But if we take our time and arrive with daylight, they shouldn't bother us. Then we can figure a way to get across the Missus Hip."

Then their eyes fell upon the rearview screen, where the dark skyline of Kansas City with bats was silhouetted by pale stars and touched by the light of the bloody moon.

After a time, Tanner slept once more. He dreamt he was riding his bike, slowly, down the center of a wide street, and people lined the sidewalks and began to cheer as he passed. They threw confetti, but by the time it reached him it was garbage, wet and stinking. He stepped on the gas then, but his bike slowed even more and now they were screaming at him. They shouted obscenities. They cried out his name, over and over, and again. The Harley began to wobble, but his feet seemed to be glued in place. In a moment, he knew, he would fall. The bike came to a halt then, and he began to topple over toward the right side. They rushed toward him as he fell, and he knew it was just about all over. . . .

He awoke with a jolt and saw the morning spread out before him: a bright coin in the middle of a dark blue tablecloth and a row of glasses along the edge.

"That's it," said Greg. "The Missus Hip."

Tanner was suddenly very hungry.

After they had refreshed themselves, they sought the bridge.

"I didn't see any of your naked people with spears," said Greg. "Of course, we might have passed their way after dark—if there are any of them still around."

"Good thing, too," said Tanner. "Saved us some ammo."

The bridge came into view, sagging and dark save for the places where the sun gilded its cables, and it stretched unbroken across the bright expanse of waters. They moved slowly toward it, threading their way through streets gorged with rubble, detouring when it became completely blocked by the rows of broken machines, fallen walls, sewer-deep abysses in the burst pavement.

It took them two hours to travel half a mile, and it was noon before they reached the foot of the bridge, and, "It looks as if Brady might have crossed here," said Greg, eying what appeared to be a cleared passageway amidst the wrecks that filled the span. "How do you think he did it?"

"Maybe he had something with him to hoist them and swing them out over the edge. There are some wrecks below, down where the water is shallow."

"Were they there last time you passed by?"

"I don't know. I wasn't right down here by the bridge. I topped that hill back there," and he gestured at the rearview screen.

"Well, from here it looks like we might be able to make it. Let's roll."

They moved upward and forward onto the bridge and began their slow passage across the mighty Missus Hip. There were times when the bridge creaked beneath them, sighed, groaned, and they felt it move.

The sun began to climb, and still they moved forward, scraping their fenders against the edges of the wrecks, using their wings like plows. They were on the bridge for three hours before its end came into sight through a rift in the junkstacks.

When their wheels finally touched the opposite shore, Greg sat there breathing heavily and then lit a cigarette.

"You want to drive awhile, Hell?"

"Yeah. Let's switch over."

He did, and, "God! I'm bushed!" he said as he sprawled out.

Tanner drove forward through the ruins of East Saint Louis, hurrying to clear the town before nightfall. The radiation level began to mount as he advanced, and the streets were cluttered and broken. He checked the inside of the cab for radioactivity, but it was still clean.

It took him hours, and as the sun fell at his back he saw the blue aurora begin once more in the north. But the sky stayed clear, filled with its stars, and there were no black lines that he could see. After a long while, a rose-colored moon appeared and hung before him. He turned on the music, softly, and glanced at Greg. It didn't seem to bother him, so he let it continue.

The instrument panel caught his eye. The radiation level was still climbing. Then, in the forward screen, he saw the crater and he stopped.

It must have been over half a mile across, and he couldn't tell its depth.

He fired a flare, and in its light he used the telescopic lenses to examine it to the right and to the left.

The way seemed smoother to the right, and he turned in that direction and began to negotiate it.

The place was hot! So very, very hot! He hurried. And he wondered as he sped, the gauge rising before him: What had it been like on that day, Whenever? That day when a tiny sun had lain upon this spot and fought with, and for a time beaten, the brightness of the other in the sky, before it sank slowly into its sudden burrow? He tried to imagine it, succeeded, then tried to put it out of his mind and couldn't. How do you put out the fires that burn forever? He wished that he knew. There'd been so many places to go then, and he liked to move around.

What had it been like in the old days, when a man could just jump on his bike and cut out for a new town whenever he wanted? And nobody emptying buckets of crap on you from out of the sky? He felt cheated, which was not a new feeling for him, but it made him curse even longer than usual.

He lit a cigarette when he'd finally rounded the crater, and he smiled for the first time in months as the radiation gauge began to fall once more. Before many miles, he saw tall grasses swaying about him, and not too long after that he began to see trees.

Trees short and twisted, at first, but the further he fled from the place of carnage, the taller and straighter they became. They were trees such as he had never seen before—fifty, sixty feet in height—and graceful, and gathering stars, there on the plains of Illinois.

He was moving along a clean, hard, wide road, and just then he wanted to travel it forever—to Floridee, of the swamps and Spanish moss and citrus groves and fine beaches and the Gulf; and up to the cold, rocky Cape, where everything is gray and brown and the waves break below the lighthouses and the salt burns in your nose and there are graveyards where bones have lain for centuries and you can still read the names they bore, chiseled there into the stones above them; down through the nation where they say the grass is blue; then follow the mighty Missus Hip to the place where she spreads and comes and there's the Gulf again, full of little islands where the old boosters stashed their loot; and through the shag-topped mountains he'd heard about: the Smokies, Ozarks, Poconos, Catskills; drive through the forest of Shenandoah; park, and take a boat out over Chesapeake Bay; see the big lakes and the place where the water falls, Niagara. To drive forever along the big road, to see everything, to eat the world. Yes. Maybe it wasn't all Damnation Alley. Some of the legendary places must still be clean, like the countryside about him now. He wanted it with a hunger, with a fire like that which always burned in his loins. He laughed then, just one short, sharp bark, because now it seemed like maybe he could have it.

The music played softly, too sweetly perhaps, and it filled him.

# — X —

By morning he was into the place called Indiana and still following the road. He passed farmhouses which seemed in good repair. There could even be people living in them. He longed to investigate, but he didn't dare to stop. Then after an hour, it was all countryside again, and degenerating.

The grasses grew shorter, shriveled, were gone. An occasional twisted tree clung to the bare earth. The radiation level began to rise once more. The signs told him he was nearing Indianapolis, which he guessed was a big city that had received a bomb and was now gone away.

Nor was he mistaken.

He had to detour far to the south to get around it, backtracking to a place called Martinsville in order to cross over the White River. Then as he headed east once more, his radio crackled and came to life. There was a faint voice, repeating, "Unidentified vehicle, halt!" and he switched all the scanners to telescopic range. Far ahead, on a hilltop, he saw a standing man with binoculars and a walkie-talkie. He did not acknowledge receipt of the transmission, but kept driving.

He was hitting forty miles an hour along a halfway decent section of roadway, and he gradually increased his speed to fifty-five, though the protesting of his tires upon the cracked pavement was sufficient to awaken Greg.

Tanner stared ahead, ready for an attack, and the radio kept repeating the order, louder now as he neared the hill, and called upon him to acknowledge the message.

He touched the brake as he rounded a long curve, and he did not reply to Greg's "What's the matter?"

When he saw it there, blocking the way, ready to fire, he acted instantly.

The tank filled the road, and its big gun was pointed directly at him.

As his eye sought for and found passage around it, his right hand slapped the switches that sent three armor-piercing rockets screaming ahead and his left spun the wheel counter-clockwise and his foot fell heavy on the accelerator.

He was half off the road then, bouncing along the ditch at its side, when the tank discharged one fiery belch which missed him and then caved in upon itself and blossomed.

There came the sound of rifle fire as he pulled back onto the road on the other side of the tank and sped ahead. Greg launched a single grenade to the right and the left and then hit the fifty calibers. They tore on ahead, and after about a quarter of a mile Tanner picked up his microphone and said,

"Sorry about that. My brakes don't work," and hung it up again. There was no response.

As soon as they reached a level plain, commanding a good view in all directions, Tanner halted the vehicle and Greg moved into the driver's seat.

"Where do you think they got hold of that armor?"

"Who knows?"

"And why stop us?"

"They didn't know what we were carrying—and maybe they just wanted the car."

"Blasting, it's a helluva way to get it."

"If they can't have it, why should they let us keep it?"

"You know just how they think, don't you?"

"Yes."

"Have a cigarette."

Tanner nodded, accepted.

"It's been pretty bad, you know?"

"I can't argue with that."

". . . And we've still got a long way to go."

"Yeah, so let's get rolling."

"You said before that you didn't think we'd make it."

"I've revised my opinion. Now I think we will."

"After all we've been through?"

"After all we've been through."

"What more do we have to fight with?"

"I don't know all that yet."

"But on the other hand, we know everything there is behind us. We know how to avoid a lot of it now."

Tanner nodded.

"You tried to cut out once. Now I don't blame you."

"You getting scared, Greg?"

"I'm no good to my family if I'm dead."

"Then why'd you agree to come along?"

"I didn't know it would be like this. You had better sense, because you had an idea what it would be like."

"I had an idea."

"Nobody can blame us if we fail. After all, we've tried."

"What about all those people in Boston you made me a speech about?"

"They're probably dead by now. The plague isn't a thing that takes its time, you know?"

"What about that guy Brady? He died to get us the news."

"He tried, and God knows I respect the attempt. But we've already lost four guys. Now should we make it six, just to show that everybody tried?"

"Greg, we're a lot closer to Boston than we are to L.A. now. The tanks should have enough fuel in them to get us where we're going, but not to take us back from here."

"We can refuel in Salt Lake."

"I'm not even sure we could make it back to Salt Lake."

"Well, it'll only take a minute to figure it out. For that matter, though, we could take the bikes for the last hundred or so. They use a lot less gas."

"And you're the guy was calling me names. You're the citizen was wondering how people like me happen. You asked me what they ever did to me. I told you, too: Nothing. Now maybe I want to do something for them, just because I feel like it. I've been doing a lot of thinking."

"You ain't supporting any family, Hell. I've got other people to worry about beside myself.

"You've got a nice way of putting things when you want to chicken out. You say I'm not really scared, but I've got my mother and my brothers and sisters to worry about, and I got a chick I'm hot on. That's why I'm backing down. No other reason.

"And that's right, too! I don't understand you, Hell! I don't understand you at all! You're the one who put this idea in my head in the first place!"

"So give it back, and let's get moving."

He saw Greg's hand slither toward the gun on the door, so he flipped his cigarette into his face and managed to hit him once, in the stomach—a weak, left-handed blow, but it was the best he could manage from that position.

Then Greg threw himself upon him, and he felt himself borne back into his seat. They wrestled, and Greg's fingers clawed their way up his face toward his eyes.

Tanner got his arms free above the elbows, seized Greg's head, twisted and shoved with all his strength.

Greg hit the dashboard, went stiff, then went slack.

Tanner banged his head against it twice more, just to be sure he wasn't faking. Then he pushed him away and moved back into the driver's seat. He checked all the screens while he caught his breath. There was nothing menacing approaching.

He fetched cord from the utility chest and bound Greg's hands behind his back. He tied his ankles together and ran a line from them to his wrists.

Then he positioned him in the seat, reclined it part way and tied him in place within it.

He put the car into gear and headed toward Ohio.

Two hours later Greg began to moan, and Tanner turned the music up to drown him out. Landscape had appeared once more: grass and trees, fields of green, orchards of apples, apples still small and green, white farm houses and brown barns and red barns far removed from the roadway he raced along; rows of corn, green and swaying, brown tassels already visible and obviously tended by someone; fences of split timber, green hedges; lofty, star-leafed maples, fresh-looking road signs, a green-shingled steeple from which the sound of a bell came forth.

The lines in the sky widened, but the sky itself did not darken, as it usually did before a storm. So he drove on into the afternoon, until he reached the Dayton Abyss.

He looked down into the fog-shrouded canyon that had caused him to halt. He scanned to the left and the right, decided upon the left and headed north.

Again, the radiation level was high. And he hurried, slowing only to skirt the crevices, chasms and canyons that emanated from that dark, deep center. Thick yellow vapors seeped forth from some of these and filled the air before him. At one point they were all about him, like a clinging, sulphurous cloud, and a breeze came and parted them. Involuntarily then, he hit the brake, and the car jerked and halted and Greg moaned once more. He stared at the thing for the few seconds that it was visible, then slowly moved forward again.

The sight was not duplicated for the whole of his passage, but it did not easily go from out of his mind, and he could not explain it where he had seen it. Yellow, hanging and grinning, he had seen a crucified skeleton there beside the Abyss. *People*, he decided. *That explains everything.*

When he left the region of fogs the sky was still dark. He did not realize for a time that he was in the open once more. It had taken him close to four hours to skirt Dayton, and now as he headed across a blasted heath, going east again, he saw for a moment a tiny piece of the sun, like a sickle, fighting its way ashore on the northern bank of a black river in the sky, and failing.

His lights were turned up to their fullest intensity, and as he realized what might follow he looked in every direction for shelter.

There was an old barn on a hill, and he raced toward it. One side had caved in, and the doors had fallen down. He edged in, however, and the interior was moist and moldy looking under his lights. He saw a skeleton which he guessed to be that of a horse within a fallen-down stall.

He parked and turned off his lights and waited.

Soon the wailing came again and drowned out Greg's occasional moans and mutterings. There came another sound, not hard and heavy like gunfire, as that which he had heard in L.A., but gentle, steady and almost purring.

He cracked the door, to hear it better.

Nothing assailed him, so he stepped down from the cab and walked back a ways. The radiation level was almost normal, so he didn't bother with his protective suit. He walked back toward the fallen doors and looked outside. He wore the pistol behind his belt.

Something gray descended in droplets and the sun fought itself partly free once more.

It was rain, pure and simple. He had never seen rain, pure and simple, before. So he lit a cigarette and watched it fall.

It came down with only an occasional rumbling and nothing else accompanied it. The sky was still a bluish color beyond the bands of black.

It fell all about him. It ran down the frame to his left. A random gust of wind blew some droplets into his face, and he realized that they were water, nothing more. Puddles formed on the ground outside. He tossed a chunk of wood into one and saw it splash and float. From somewhere high up inside the barn he heard the sound of birds. He smelled the sick-sweet smell of decaying straw. Off in the shadows to his right he saw a rusted threshing machine. Some feathers drifted down about him, and he caught one in his hand and studied it. Light, dark, fluffy, ribbed. He'd never really looked at a feather before. It worked almost like a zipper, the way the individual branches clung to one another. He let it go, and the wind caught it, and it vanished somewhere toward his back. He looked out once more, and back along his trail. He could probably drive through what was coming down now. But he realized just how tired he was. He found a barrel and sat down on it and lit another cigarette.

It had been a good run so far, and he found himself thinking about its last stages. He couldn't trust Greg for awhile yet. Not until they were so far that there could be no turning back. Then they'd need each other so badly that he could turn him loose. He hoped he hadn't scrambled his brains completely. He didn't know what more the alley held. If the storms were less from here on in, however, that would be a big help.

He sat there for a long while, feeling the cold, moist breezes; and the rainfall lessened after a time, and he went back to the car and started it. Greg was still unconscious, he noted, as he backed out. This might not be good.

He took a pill to keep himself alert and he ate some rations as he drove along. The rain continued to come down, but gently. It fell all the way across Ohio, and the sky remained overcast. He crossed into West Virginia at the place called Parkersburg, and then he veered slightly to the north, going by the old Rand McNally he'd been furnished. The gray day went away into black night, and he drove on.

There were no more of the dark bats around to trouble him, but he passed several more craters and the radiation gauge rose, and at one point a pack of huge wild dogs pursued him, baying and howling, and they ran along the road and snapped at his tires and barked and yammered and then fell back. There were some tremors beneath his wheels as he passed another mountain and it spewed forth bright clouds to his left and made a kind of thunder. Ashes fell, and he drove through them. A flash flood splashed over him, and the engine sputtered and died, twice; but he started it again each time and pushed on ahead, the waters lapping about his sides. Then he reached higher, drier ground, and riflemen tried to bar his way. He strafed them and hurled a grenade and drove on by. When the darkness went away and the dim moon came up, dark birds circled him and dove down at him, but he ignored them and after a time they, too, were gone.

He drove until he felt tired again, and then he ate some more and took another pill. By then he was in Pennsylvania, and he felt that if Greg would only come around he would turn him loose and trust him with the driving.

He halted twice to visit the latrine, and he tugged at the golden band in his pierced left ear, and he blew his nose and scratched himself. Then he ate more rations and continued on.

He began to ache, in all his muscles, and he wanted to stop and rest, but he was afraid of the things that might come upon him if he did.

As he drove through another dead town, the rains started again. Not hard, just a drizzly downpour, cold-looking and sterile—a brittle, shiny screen. He stopped in the middle of the road before the thing he'd almost driven into, and he stared at it.

He'd thought at first that it was more black lines in the sky. He'd halted because they'd seemed to appear too suddenly.

It was a spider's web, strands thick as his arm, strung between two leaning buildings.

He switched on his forward flame and began to burn it.

When the fires died, he saw the approaching shape, coming down from high above.

It was a spider, larger than himself, rushing to check the disturbance.

He elevated the rocket launchers, took careful aim and pierced it with one white-hot missile.

It still hung there in the trembling web and seemed to be kicking.

He turned on the flame again, for a full ten seconds, and when it subsided there was an open way before him.

He rushed through, wide awake and alert once again, his pains forgotten. He drove as fast as he could, trying to forget the sight.

Another mountain smoked, ahead and to his right, but it did not bloom, and few ashes descended as he passed it.

He made coffee and drank a cup. After awhile it was morning, and he raced toward it.

## — XI —

He was stuck in the mud, somewhere in eastern Pennsylvania, and cursing. Greg was looking very pale. The sun was nearing midheaven. He leaned back and closed his eyes. It was too much.

He slept.

He awoke and felt worse. There was a banging on the side of the car. His hands moved toward fire-control and wing-control, automatically, and his eyes sought the screens.

He saw an old man, and there were two younger men with him. They were armed, but they stood right before the left wing, and he knew he could cut them in half in an instant.

He activated the outside speaker and the audio pickup.

"What do you want?" he asked, and his voice crackled forth.

"You okay?" the old man called.

"Not really. You caught me sleeping."

"You stuck?"

"That's about the size of it."

"I got a mule team can maybe get you out. Can't get 'em here before to-morrow morning, though."

"Great!" said Tanner. "I'd appreciate it."

"Where you from?"

"L.A."

"What's that?"

"Los Angeles. West Coast."

There was some murmuring, then, "You're a long way from home, mis-ter."

"Don't I know it.—Look, if you're serious about those mules, I'd appreci-ate hell out of it. It's an emergency."

"What kind of?"

"You know about Boston?"

"I know it's there."

"Well, people are dying up that way, of the plague. I've got drugs here can save them, if I can get through."

There were some more murmurs, then, "We'll help you. Boston's pretty important, and we'll get you loose. Want to come back with us?"

"Where? And who are you?"

"The name's Samuel Potter, and these are my sons, Roderick and Caliban. My farm's about six miles off. You're welcome to spend the night."

"It's not that I don't trust you," said Tanner. "It's just that I don't trust anybody, if you know what I mean. I've been shot at too much recently to want to take the chance."

"Well, how about if we put up our guns? You're probably able to shoot us from there, ain't you?"

"That's right."

"So we're taking a chance just standing here. We're willing to help you. We'd stand to lose if the Boston traders stopped coming to Albany. If there's someone else inside, he can cover you."

"Wait a minute," said Tanner, and he opened the door.

The old man stuck out his hand, and Tanner took it and shook it, also his sons.

"Is there any kind of doctor around here?" he asked.

"In the settlement—about thirty miles north."

"My partner's hurt. I think he needs a doctor." He gestured back toward the cab.

Sam moved forward and peered within.

"Why's he all trussed up like that?"

"He went off his rocker, and I had to clobber him. I tied him up, to be safe. But now he doesn't look so good."

"Then let's whip up a stretcher and get him onto it. You lock up tight then, and my boys'll bring him back to the house. We'll send someone for the Doc. You don't look so good yourself. Bet you'd like a bath and a shave and a clean bed."

"I don't feel so good," Tanner said. "Let's make that stretcher quick, before we need two."

He sat up on the fender and smoked while the Potter boys cut trees and stripped them. Waves of fatigue washed over him, and he found it hard to keep his eyes open. His feet felt very far away, and his shoulders ached.

Someone was slapping his leg.

He forced his eyes open and looked down.

"Okay," Potter said. "We cut your partner loose and we got him on the stretcher. Want to lock up and get moving?"

Tanner nodded and jumped down. He sank almost up to his boot tops when he hit, but he closed the cab and staggered toward the old man in buckskin.

They began walking across country, and after awhile it became mechanical.

Samuel Potter kept up a steady line of chatter as he led the way, rifle resting in the crook of his arm. Maybe it was to keep Tanner awake.

"It's not too far, son, and it'll be pretty easy going in just a few minutes now. What's you say your name was anyhow?"

"Hell," said Tanner.

"Beg pardon?"

"Hell. Hell's my name. Hell Tanner."

Sam Potter chuckled.

"That's a pretty mean name, mister. If it's okay with you, I'll introduce you to my wife and the youngest as 'Mister Tanner'. All right?"

"That's just fine," Tanner gasped, pulling his boots out of the mire with a sucking sound.

"We'd sure miss them Boston traders. I hope you make it in time."

"What is it that they do?"

"They keep shops in Albany, and twice a year they give a fair—spring and fall. They carry all sort of things we need—needles, thread, pepper, kettles, pans, seed, guns and ammo, all kind of things—and the fairs are pretty good times, too. Most anybody between here and there would help you along. Hope you make it. We'll get you off to a good start again."

They reached higher, drier ground.

"You mean it's pretty clear sailing after this?"

"Well, no, But I'll help you on a map and tell you what to look out for."

"I got mine with me," said Tanner, as they topped a hill, and he saw a farm house off in the distance. "That your place?"

"Correct. It ain't much further now. Real easy walkin'—an' you just lean on my shoulder if you get tired."

"I can make it," said Tanner. "It's just that I had so many of those pills to keep me awake that I'm starting to feel all the sleep I've been missing. I'll be okay."

"You'll get to sleep real soon now. And when you're awake again, we'll go over that map of yours, and you can write in all the places I tell you about."

"Good scene," said Tanner, "good scene," and he put his hand on Sam's shoulder then and staggered along beside him, feeling almost drunk and wishing he were.

After a hazy eternity he saw the house before him, then the door. The door swung open, and he felt himself falling forward and that was it.

## – XII –

Sleep. Blackness, distant voices, more blackness. Wherever he lay, it was soft, and he turned over onto his other side and went away again.

When everything finally flowed together into a coherent ball and he opened his eyes, there was light streaming in through the window to his right, falling in rectangles upon the patchwork quilt that covered him. He groaned, stetched, rubbed his eyes and scratched his beard.

He surveyed the room carefully: polished wooden floors with handwoven rugs of blue and red and gray scattered about them, a dresser holding a white enamel basin with a few black spots up near its lip where some of the enamel had chipped away, a mirror on the wall behind him and above all that, a spindly looking rocker near the window, a print cushion on its seat, a small table against the other wall with a chair pushed in beneath it, books and paper and pen and ink on the table, a hand-stitched sampler on the wall asking God to Bless, a blue and green print of a waterfall on the other wall.

He sat up, discovered he was naked, looked around for his clothing. It was nowhere in sight.

As he sat there, deciding whether or not to call out, the door opened, and Sam walked in. He carried Tanner's clothing, clean and neatly folded, over one arm. In his other hand he carried his boots, and they shone like wet midnight.

"Heard you stirring around," he said. "How you feeling now?"

"A lot better, thanks."

"We've got a bath all drawn. Just have to dump in a couple buckets of hot, and it's all yours. I'll have the boys carry it in in a minute, and some soap and towels."

Tanner bit his lip, but he didn't want to seem inhospitable to his benefactor, so he nodded and forced a smile then.

"That'll be fine."

". . . And there's a razor and a scissors on the dresser—whichever you might want."

He nodded again. Sam set his clothes down on the rocker and his boots on the floor beside it, then left the room.

Soon Roderick and Caliban brought in the tub, spread some sacks and set it upon them.

"How you feeling?" one of them asked. (Tanner wasn't sure which was which. They both seemed graceful as scarecrows, and their mouths were packed full of white teeth.)

"Real good," he said.

"Bet you're hungry," said the other. "You slep' all afternoon yesterday and all night and most of this morning."

"You know it," said Tanner. "How's my partner?"

The nearer one shook his head, and, "Still sleeping and sickly," he said. "The Doc should be here soon. Our kid brother went after him last night."

They turned to leave, and the one who had been speaking added, "Soon as you get cleaned up, Ma'll fix you something to eat. Cal and me are going out now to try and get your rig loose. Dad'll tell you about the roads while you eat."

"Thanks."

"Good morning to you."

"'Morning."

They closed the door behind them as they left.

Tanner got up and moved to the mirror, studied himself.

"Well, just this once," he muttered.

Then he washed his face and trimmed his beard and cut his hair.

Then, gritting his teeth, he lowered himself into the tub, soaped up and scrubbed. The water grew gray and scummy beneath the suds. He splashed out and toweled himself down and dressed.

He was starched and crinkly and smelled faintly of disinfectant. He smiled at his dark-eyed reflection and lit a cigarette. He combed his hair and studied the stranger. "Damn! I'm beautiful!" he chuckled, and then he opened the door and entered the kitchen.

Sam was sitting at the table drinking a cup of coffee, and his wife who was short and heavy and wore long gray skirts was facing in the other direction, leaning over the stove. She turned, and he saw that her face was large, with bulging red cheeks that dimpled and a little white scar in the middle of her forehead. Her hair was brown, shot through with gray, and pulled back into a knot. She bobbed her head and smiled a "Good morning" at him.

"'Morning," he replied. "I'm afraid I left kind of a mess in the other room."

"Don't worry about that," said Sam. "Seat yourself, and we'll have you some breakfast in a minute. The boys told you about your friend?"

Tanner nodded.

As she placed a cup of coffee in front of Tanner, Sam said, "Wife's name's Susan."

"How do," she said.

"Hi."

"Now, then, I got your map here. Saw it sticking out of your jacket. That's your gun hanging aside the door, too. Anyhows, I've been figuring and I think the best way you could head would be up to Albany and then go along the old Route 9, which is in pretty good shape." He spread the map and pointed as he talked. "Now, it won't be all of a picnic," he said, "but it looks like the cleanest and fastest way in—"

"Breakfast," said his wife and pushed the map aside to set a plate full of eggs and bacon and sausages in front of Tanner and another one, holding four pieces of toast, next to it. There was marmalade, jam, jelly and butter on the table, and Tanner helped himself to it and sipped the coffee and filled the empty places inside while Sam talked.

He told him about the gangs that ran between Boston and Albany on bikes, hijacking anything they could, and that was the reason most cargo went in convoys with shotgun riders aboard. "But you don't have to worry, with that rig of yours, do you?" he asked, and Tanner said, "Hope not," and wolfed down more food. He wondered, though, if they were anything like his old pack, and he hoped not, again, for both their sakes.

Tanner raised his coffee cup, and he heard a sound outside.

The door opened, and a boy ran into the kitchen. Tanner figured him as between ten and twelve years of age. An older man followed him, carrying the traditional black bag.

"We're here! We're here!" cried the boy, and Sam stood and shook hands with the man, so Tanner figured he should, too. He wiped his mouth and gripped the man's hand and said, "My partner sort of went out of his head. He jumped me, and we had a fight. I shoved him, and he banged his head on the dashboard."

The doctor, a dark-haired man, probably in his late forties, wore a dark suit. His face was heavily lined, and his eyes looked tired. He nodded.

Sam said, "I'll take you to him," and he led him out through the door at the other end of the kitchen.

Tanner reseated himself and picked up the last piece of toast. Susan refilled his coffee cup, and he nodded to her.

"My name's Jerry," said the boy, seating himself in his father's abandoned chair. "Is your name, mister, really Hell?"

"Hush, you!" said his mother.

"'Fraid so," said Tanner.

"... And you drove all the way across the country? Through the Alley?"

"So far."

"What was it like?"

"Mean."

"What all'd you see?"

"Bats as big as this kitchen—some of them even bigger—on the other side of the Missus Hip. Lot of them in Saint Louis."

"What'd you do?"

"Shot 'em. Burnt 'em. Drove through 'em."

"What else you see?"

"Gila monsters. Big, technicolor lizards—the size of a barn. Dust Devils—big circling winds that sucked up one car. Fire-topped mountains. Real big thorn bushes that we had to burn. Drove through some storms. Drove over places where the ground was like glass. Drove along where the ground was shaking. Drove around big craters, all radioactive."

"Wish I could do that some day."

"Maybe you will, some day."

Tanner finished the food and lit a cigarette and sipped the coffee.

"Real good breakfast," he called out. "Best I've eaten in days. Thanks."

Susan smiled, then said, "Jerry, don't go an' pester the man."

"No bother, Missus. He's okay."

"What's that ring on your hand?" said Jerry. "It looks like a snake."

"That's what it is," said Tanner, pulling it off. "It is sterling silver with red glass eyes, and I got it in a place called Tijuana. Here. You keep it."

"I couldn't take that," said the boy, and he looked at his mother, his eyes asking if he could. She shook her head from left to right, and Tanner saw it and said, "Your folks were good enough to help me out and get a Doc for my partner and feed me and give me a place to sleep. I'm sure they won't mind if I want to show my appreciation a little bit and give you this ring," and Jerry looked back at his mother, and Tanner nodded and she nodded too.

Jerry whistled and jumped up and put it on his finger.

"It's too big," he said.

"Here, let me mash it a bit for you. These spiral kind'll fit anybody if you squeeze them a little."

He squeezed the ring and gave it back to the boy to try on. It was still too big, so he squeezed it again and then it fit.

Jerry put it on and began to run from the room.

"Wait!" his mother said. "What do you say?"

He turned around and said, "Thank you, Hell."

"Mister Tanner," she said.

"Mister Tanner," the boy repeated, and the door banged behind him.

"That was good of you," she said.

Tanner shrugged.

"He liked it," he said. "Glad I could turn him on with it."

He finished his coffee and his cigarette, and she gave him another cup, and he lit another cigarette. After a time, Sam and the doctor came out of the other room, and Tanner began wondering where the family had slept the night before. Susan poured them both coffee, and they seated themselves at the table to drink it.

"Your friend's got a concussion," the doctor said. "I can't really tell how serious his condition is without getting X rays, and there's no way of getting them here. I wouldn't recommend moving him, though."

Tanner said, "For how long?"

"Maybe a few days, maybe a couple weeks. I've left some medication and told Sam what to do for him. Sam says there's a plague in Boston and you've got to hurry. My advice is that you go on without him. Leave him here with the Potters. He'll be taken care of. He can go up to Albany with them for the Spring Fair and make his way to Boston from there on some commercial carrier. I think he'll be all right."

Tanner thought about it awhile, then nodded.

"Okay," he said, "if that's the way it's got to be."

"That's what I recommend."

They drank their coffee.

## – XIII –

Tanner regarded his freed vehicle, said, "I guess I'll be going, then," and nodded to the Potters. "Thanks," he said, and he unlocked the cab, climbed into it and started the engine. He put it into gear, blew the horn twice and started to move.

In the screen, he saw the three men waving. He stamped the accelerator, and they were gone from sight.

He sped ahead, and the way was easy. The sky was salmon pink. The earth was brown, and there was much green grass. The bright sun caught the day in a silver net.

This part of the country seemed virtually untouched by the chaos that had produced the rest of the Alley. Tanner played music, drove along. He passed two trucks on the road and honked his horn each time. Once, he received a reply.

He drove all that day, and it was well into the night when he pulled into Albany. The streets themselves were dark, and only a few lights shone from the buildings. He drew up in front of a flickering red sign that said "BAR & GRILL," parked and entered.

It was small, and there was jukebox music playing, tunes he'd never heard before, and the lighting was poor, and there was sawdust on the floor.

He sat down at the bar and pushed the Magnum way down behind his belt so that it didn't show. Then he took off his jacket, because of the heat in the place, and he threw it on the stool next to him. When the man in the white apron approached, he said, "Give me a shot and a beer and a ham sandwich."

The man nodded his bald head and threw a shot glass in front of Tanner, which he then filled. Then he siphoned off a foam-capped mug and hollered over his right shoulder.

Tanner tossed off the shot and sipped the beer. After awhile, a white plate bearing a sandwich appeared on the sill across from him. After a longer while, the bartender passed, picked it up, and deposited it in front of him. He wrote something on a green chit and tucked it under the corner of the plate.

Tanner bit into the sandwich and washed it down with a mouthful of beer. He studied the people about him and decided they made the same noises as people in any other bar he'd ever been in. The old man to his left looked friendly, so he asked him, "Any news about Boston?"

The man's chin quivered between words, and it seemed a natural thing for him.

"No news at all. Looks like the merchants will close their shops at the end of the week."

"What day is today?"

"Tuesday."

Tanner finished his sandwich and smoked a cigarette while he drank the rest of his beer.

Then he looked at the check, and it said, ".85."

He tossed a dollar bill on top of it and turned to go.

He had taken two steps when the bartender called out, "Wait a minute, mister."

He turned around.

"Yeah?"

"What you trying to pull?"

"What do you mean?"

"What do you call this crap?"

"What crap?"

The man waved Tanner's dollar at him, and he stepped forward and inspected it.

"Nothing wrong I can see. What's giving you a pain?"

"That ain't money."

"You trying to tell me my money's no good?"

"That's what I said. I never seen no bill like that."

"Well, look at it real careful. Read that print down there at the bottom of it."

The room grew quiet. One man got off his stool and walked forward. He held out his hand and said, "Let me see it, Bill."

The bartender passed it to him, and the man's eyes widened.

"This is drawn on the Bank of the Nation of California."

"Well, that's where I'm from," said Tanner.

"I'm sorry, it's no good here," said the bartender.

"It's the best I got," said Tanner.

"Well, nobody'll make good on it around here. You got any Boston money on you?"

"Never been to Boston."

"Then how the hell'd you get here?"

"Drove."

"Don't hand me that line of crap, son. Where'd you steal this?" It was the older man who had spoken.

"You going to take my money or ain't you?" said Tanner.

"I'm not going to take it," said the bartender.

"Then screw you," said Tanner, and he turned and walked toward the door.

As always, under such circumstances, he was alert to sounds at his back.

When he heard the quick footfall, he turned. It was the man who had inspected the bill that stood before him, his right arm extended.

Tanner's right hand held his leather jacket, draped over his right shoulder. He swung it with all his strength, forward and down.

It struck the man on the top of his head, and he fell.

There came up a murmuring, and several people jumped to their feet and moved toward him.

Tanner dragged the gun from his belt and said, "Sorry, folks," and he pointed it, and they stopped.

"Now you probably ain't about to believe me," he said, "when I tell you that Boston's been hit by the plague, but it's true all right. Or maybe you will, I don't know. But I don't think you're going to believe that I drove here all the way from the nation of California with a car full of Haffikine antiserum. But that's just as right. You send that bill to the big bank in Boston, and they'll change it for you, all right, and you know it. Now I've got to be going, and don't anybody try to stop me. If you think I've been handing you a line, you take a look at what I drive away in. That's all I've got to say."

And he backed out the door and covered it while he mounted the cab. Inside, he gunned the engine to life, turned, and roared away.

In the rearview screen he could see the knot of people on the walk before the bar, watching him depart.

He laughed, and the apple-blossom moon hung dead ahead.

## — XIV —

Albany to Boston. A couple hundred miles. He'd managed the worst of it. The terrors of Damnation Alley lay largely at his back now. Night. It flowed about him. The stars seemed brighter than usual. He'd make it, the night seemed to say.

He passed between hills. The road wasn't too bad. It wound between trees and high grasses. He passed a truck coming in his direction and dimmed his lights as it approached. It did the same.

It must have been around midnight that he came to the crossroads, and the lights suddenly nailed him from two directions.

He was bathed in perhaps thirty beams from the left and as many from the right.

He pushed the accelerator to the floor, and he heard engine after engine coming to life somewhere at his back. And he recognized the sounds.

They were all of them bikes.

They swung onto the road behind him.

He could have opened fire. He could have braked and laid down a cloud of flame. It was obvious that they didn't know what they were chasing. He could have launched grenades. He refrained, however.

It could have been him on the lead bike, he decided, all hot on hijack. He felt a certain sad kinship as his hand hovered above the fire-control.

Try to outrun them, first.

His engine was open wide and roaring, but he couldn't take the bikes.

When they began to fire, he knew that he'd have to retaliate. He couldn't risk their hitting a gas tank or blowing out his tires.

Their first few shots had been in the nature of a warning. He couldn't risk another barrage. If only they knew. . . .

The speaker!

He cut in and mashed the button and spoke:

"Listen, cats," he said. "All I got's medicine for the sick citizens in Boston. Let me through or you'll hear the noise."

A shot followed immediately, so he opened fire with the fifty calibers to the rear.

He saw them fall, but they kept firing. So he launched grenades.

The firing lessened, but didn't cease.

So he hit the brakes, then the flame-throwers. He kept it up for fifteen seconds.

There was silence.

When the air cleared he studied the screens.

They lay all over the road, their bikes upset, their bodies fuming. Several were still seated, and they held rifles and pointed them, and he shot them down.

A few still moved, spasmodically, and he was about to drive on, when he saw one rise and take a few staggering steps and fall again.

His hand hesitated on the gearshift.

It was a girl.

He thought about it for perhaps five seconds, then jumped down from the cab and ran toward her.

As he did, one man raised himself on an elbow and picked up a fallen rifle. Tanner shot him twice and kept running, pistol in hand.

The girl was crawling toward a man whose face had been shot away. Other bodies twisted about Tanner now, there on the road, in the glare of the tail beacons. Blood and black leather, the sounds of moaning and the stench of burnt flesh were all about him.

When he got to the girl's side, she cursed him softly as he stopped.

None of the blood about her seemed to be her own.

He dragged her to her feet and her eyes began to fill with tears.

Everyone else was dead or dying, so Tanner picked her up in his arms and carried her back to the car. He reclined the passenger seat and put her into it, moving the weapons into the rear seat, out of her reach.

Then he gunned the engine and moved forward. In the rearview screen he saw two figures rise to their feet, then fall again.

She was a tall girl, with long, uncombed hair the color of dirt. She had a strong chin and a wide mouth and there were dark circles under her eyes. A single faint line crossed her forehead, and she had all of her teeth. The right side of her face was flushed, as if sunburnt. Her left trouser leg was torn and dirty. He guessed that she'd caught the edge of his flame and fallen from her bike.

"You okay?" he asked, when her sobbing had diminished to a moist sniffing sound.

"What's it to you?" she said, raising a hand to her cheek.

Tanner shrugged.

"Just being friendly."

"You killed most of my gang."

"What would they have done to me?"

"They would have stomped you, mister, if it weren't for this fancy car of yours."

"It ain't really mine," he said. "It belongs to the nation of California."

"This thing don't come from California."

"The hell it don't. I drove it."

She sat up straight then and began rubbing her left leg.

Tanner lit a cigarette.

"Give me a cigarette?" she said.

He passed her the one he had lighted, lit himself another. As he handed it to her, her eyes rested on his tattoo.

"What's that?"

"My name."

"Hell?"

"Hell."

"Where'd you get a name like that?"

"From my old man."

They smoked awhile, then she said, "Why'd you run the Alley?"

"Because it was the only way I could get them to turn me loose."

"From where?"

"The place with horizontal Venetian blinds. I was doing time."

"They let you go? Why?"

"Because of the big sick. I'm bringing in Haffikine antiserum."

"You're Hell Tanner."

"Huh?"

"Your last name's Tanner, ain't it?"

"That's right. Who told you?"

"I heard about you. Everybody thought you died in the Big Raid."

"They were wrong."

"What was it like?"

"I dunno. I was already wearing a zebra suit. That's why I'm still around."

"Why'd you pick me up?"

" 'Cause you're a chick, and 'cause I didn't want to see you croak."

"Thanks. You got anything to eat in here?"

"Yeah, there's food in there." He pointed to the refrigerator door. "Help yourself."

She did, and as she ate Tanner asked her, "What do they call you?"

"Corny," she said. "It's short for Cornelia."

"Okay, Corny," he said. "When you're finished eating, you start telling me about the road between here and the place."

She nodded, chewed, and swallowed. Then, "There's lots of other gangs," she said. "So you'd better be ready to blast them."

"I am."

"Those screens show you all directions, huh?"

"That's right."

"Good. The roads are pretty much okay from here on in. There's one big crater you'll come to soon and a couple little volcanos afterwards."

"Check."

"Outside of them there's nothing to worry about but the Regents and the Devils and the Kings and the Lovers. That's about it."

Tanner nodded.

"How big are those clubs?"

"I don't know for sure, but the Kings are the biggest. They've got a coupla hundred."

"What was your club?"

"The Studs."

"What are you going to do now?"

"Whatever you tell me."

"Okay, Corny. I'll let you off anywhere along the way that you want me to. If you don't want, you can come on into the city with me."

"You call it, Hell. Anywhere you want to go, I'll go along."

Her voice was deep, and her words came slowly, and her tone sandpapered his eardrums just a bit. She had long legs and heavy thighs beneath the tight denim. Tanner licked his lips and studied the screens. Did he want to keep her around for awhile?

The road was suddenly wet. It was covered with hundreds of fishes, and more were falling from the sky. There followed several loud reports from overhead. The blue light began in the north.

Tanner raced on, and suddenly there was water all about him. It fell upon his car, it dimmed his screens. The sky had grown black again, and the banshee-wail sounded above him.

He skidded around a sharp curve in the road. He turned up his lights.

The rain ceased, but the wailing continued. He ran for fifteen minutes before it built up into a roar.

The girl stared at the screens and occasionally glanced at Tanner.

"What're you going to do?" she finally asked him.

"Outrun it, if I can," he said.

"It's dark for as far ahead as I can see. I don't think you can do it."

"Neither do I, but what does that leave?"

"Hole up someplace."

"If you know where, you show me."

"There's a place a few miles further ahead—a bridge you can get under."

"Okay, that's for us. Sing out when you see it."

She pulled off her boots and rubbed her feet. He gave her another cigarette.

"Hey, Corny—I just thought—there's a medicine chest over there to your right. Yeah, that's it. It should have some damn kind of salve in it you can smear on your face to take the bite out."

She found a tube of something and rubbed some of it into her cheek, smiled slightly and replaced it.

"Feel any better?"

"Yes. Thanks."

The stones began to fall, the blue to spread. The sky pulsed, grew brighter.

"I don't like the looks of this one."

"I don't like the looks of any of them."

"It seems there's been an awful lot this past week."

"Yeah. I've heard it said maybe the winds are dying down—that the sky might be purging itself."

"That'd be nice," said Tanner.

"Then we might be able to see it the way it used to look—blue all the time, and with clouds. You know about clouds."

"I heard about them."

"White, puffy things that just sort of drift across—sometimes gray. They don't drop anything except rain, and not always that."

"Yeah, I know."

"You ever see any out in L.A.?"

"No."

The yellow streaks began, and the black lines writhed like snakes. The stonefall rattled heavily upon the roof and the hood. More water began to fall, and a fog rose up. Tanner was forced to slow, and then it seemed as if sledgehammers beat upon the car.

"We won't make it," she said.

"The hell you say. This thing's built to take it—and what's that off in the distance?"

"The bridge!" she said, moving forward. "That's it! Pull off the road to the left and go down. That's a dry riverbed beneath."

Then the lightning began to fall. It flamed, flashed about them. They passed a burning tree, and there were still fishes in the roadway.

Tanner turned left as he approached the bridge. He slowed to a crawl and made his way over the shoulder and down the slick, muddy grade.

When he hit the damp riverbed he turned right. He nosed it in under the bridge, and they were all alone there. Some waters trickled past them, and the lightnings continued to flash. The sky was a shifting kaleidoscope and constant came the thunder. He could hear a sound like hail on the bridge above them.

"We're safe," he said and killed the engine.

"Are the doors locked?"

"They do it automatically."

Tanner turned off the outside lights.

"Wish I could buy you a drink, besides coffee."

"Coffee'd be good, just right."

"Okay, it's on the way," and he cleaned out the pot and filled it and plugged it in.

They sat there and smoked as the storm raged, and he said, "You know, it's a kind of nice feeling being all snug as a rat in a hole while everything goes to hell outside. Listen to that bastard come down! And we couldn't care less."

"I suppose so," she said. "What're you going to do after you make it in to Boston?"

"Oh, I don't know. . . . Maybe get a job, scrape up some loot and maybe open a bike shop or a garage. Either one'd be nice."

"Sounds good. You going to ride much yourself?"

"You bet. I don't suppose they have any good clubs *in* town?"

"No. They're all roadrunners."

"Thought so. Maybe I'll organize my own."

He reached out and touched her hand, then squeezed it.

"I can buy *you* a drink."

"What do you mean?"

She drew a plastic flask from the right side pocket of her jacket. She uncapped it and passed it to him.

"Here."

He took a mouthful and gulped it, coughed, took a second, then handed it back.

"Great! You're a woman of unsuspected potential and I like that. Thanks."

"Don't mention it," and she took a drink herself and set the flask on the dash.

"Cigarette?"

"Just a minute."

He lit two, passed her one.

"There you are, Corny."

"Thanks. I'd like to help you finish this run."

"How come?"

"I got nothing else to do. My crowd's all gone away, and I've got nobody else to run with now. Also, if you make it, you'll be a big man. Like capital letters. Think you might keep me around after that?"

"Maybe. What are you like?"

"Oh, I'm real nice. I'll even rub your shoulders for you when they're sore."

"They're sore now."

"I thought so. Give me a lean."

He bent toward her, and she began to rub his shoulders. Her hands were quick and strong.

"You do that good, girl."

"Thanks."

He straightened up, leaned back. Then he reached out, took the flask and had another drink. She took a small sip when he passed it to her.

The furies rode about them, but the bridge above stood the siege. Tanner turned off the lights.

"Let's make it," he said, and he seized her and drew her to him.

She did not resist him, and he found her belt buckle and unfastened it. Then he started on the buttons. After awhile, he reclined her seat.

"Will you keep me?" she asked him.

"Sure."

"I'll help you. I'll do anything you say to get you through."

"Great."

"After all, if Boston goes, then we go, too."

"You bet."

Then they didn't say much more.

There was violence in the skies, and after that came darkness and quiet.

# — XV —

When Tanner awoke, it was morning and the storm had ceased. He repaired himself to the rear of the vehicle and after that assumed the driver's seat once more.

Cornelia did not awaken as he gunned the engine to life and started up the weed-infested slope of the hillside.

The sky was light once more, and the road was strewn with rubble. Tanner wove along it, heading toward the pale sun, and after awhile Cornelia stretched.

"Ungh," she said, and Tanner agreed. "My shoulders are better now," he told her.

"Good," and Tanner headed up a hill, slowly as the day dimmed and one huge black line became the Devil's highway down the middle of the sky.

As he drove through a wooded valley, the rain began to fall. The girl had returned from the rear of the vehicle and was preparing breakfast when Tanner saw the tiny dot on the horizon, switched over to his telescope lenses and tried to outrun what he saw.

Cornelia looked up.

There were bikes, bikes, and more bikes on their trail.

"Those your people?" Tanner asked.

"No. You took mine yesterday."

"Too bad," said Tanner, and he pushed the accelerator to the floor and hoped for a storm.

They squealed around a curve and climbed another hill. His pursuers drew nearer. He switched back from telescope to normal scanning, but even then he could see the size of the crowd that approached.

"It must be the Kings," she said. "They're the biggest club around."

"Too bad," said Tanner.

"For them or for us?"

"Both."

She smiled.

"I'd like to see how you work this thing."

"It looks like you're going to get a chance. They're gaining on us like mad."

The rain lessened, but the fogs grew heavier. Tanner could see their lights, though, over a quarter mile to his rear, and he did not turn his own on. He estimated a hundred to a hundred fifty pursuers that cold, dark morning, and he asked, "How near are we to Boston?"

"Maybe ninety miles," she told him.

"Too bad they're chasing us instead of coming toward us," he said, as he primed his flames and set an adjustment which brought cross-hairs into focus on his rearview screen.

"What's that?" she asked.

"That's a cross. I'm going to crucify them, lady," and she smiled at this and squeezed his arm.

"Can I help? I hate those bloody mothers."

"In a little while," said Tanner. "In a little while, I'm sure," and he reached into the rear seat and fetched out the six hand grenades and hung them on his wide, black belt. He passed the rifle to the girl. "Hang onto this," he said, and stuck the .45 behind his belt.

"Do you know how to use that thing?"

"Yes," she replied immediately.

"Good."

He kept watching the lights that danced on the screen.

"Why the hell doesn't this storm break?" he said, as the lights came closer and he could make out shapes within the fog.

When they were within a hundred feet he fired the first grenade. It arched through the gray air, and five seconds later there was a bright flash to his rear, burning within a thunderclap.

The lights immediately behind him remained, and he touched the fifty-calibers, moving the crosshairs from side to side. The guns shattered their loud syllables, and he launched another grenade. With the second flash, he began to climb another hill.

"Did you stop them?"

"For a time, maybe. I still see some lights, but farther back."

After five minutes, they had reached the top, a place where the fogs were cleared and the dark sky was visible above them. Then they started downward once more, and a wall of stone and shale and dirt rose to their right. Tanner considered it as they descended.

When the road leveled and he decided they had reached the bottom, he turned on his brightest lights and looked for a place where the road's shoulders were wide.

To his rear, there were suddenly rows of descending lights.

He found the place where the road was sufficiently wide, and he skidded through a U turn until he was facing the shaggy cliff, now to his left, and his pursuers were coming dead on.

He elevated his rockets, fired one, elevated them five degrees more, fired two, elevated them another five degrees, fired three. Then he lowered them fifteen and fired another.

There were brightnesses within the fog, and he heard the stones rattling on the road and felt the vibration as the rockslide began. He swung toward his right as he backed the vehicle and fired two ahead. There was dust mixed with the fog now, and the vibration continued.

He turned and headed forward once more.

"I hope that'll hold 'em," he said, and he lit two cigarettes and passed one to the girl.

After five minutes they were on higher ground again and the winds came and whipped at the fog, and far to the rear there were still some lights.

As they topped a high rise, his radiation gauge began to register an above-normal reading. He sought in all directions and saw the crater far off ahead. "That's it," he heard her say. "You've got to leave the road there. Bear to the right and go around that way when you get there."

"I'll do that thing."

He heard gunshots from behind him, for the first time that day, and though he adjusted the cross hairs he did not fire his own weapons. The distance was still too great.

"You must have cut them in half," she said, staring into the screen. "More than that. They're a tough bunch, though."

"I gather," and he plowed the field of mists and checked his supply of grenades for the launcher and saw that he was running low.

He swung off the road to his right when he began bumping along over fractured concrete. The radiation level was quite high by then. The crater was slightly more than a thousand yards to his left.

The lights to his rear fanned out, grew brighter. He drew a bead on the brightest and fired. It went out.

"There's another down," he remarked, as they raced across the hard-baked plain.

The rains came more heavily, and he sighted on another light and fired. It, too, went out. Now, though he heard the sounds of their weapons about him once again.

He switched to his right-hand guns and saw the cross hairs leap into life on that screen. As three vehicles moved in to flank him from that direction, he opened up and cut them down. There was more firing at his back, and he ignored it as he negotiated the way.

"I count twenty-seven lights," Cornelia said.

Tanner wove his way across a field of boulders. He lit another cigarette.

Five minutes later, they were running on both sides of him. He had held back again for that moment, to conserve ammunition and to be sure of his targets. He fired then, though, at every light within range, and he floored the accelerator and swerved around rocks.

"Five of them are down," she said, but he was listening to the gunfire.

He launched a grenade to the rear, and when he tried to launch a second there came only a clicking sound from the control. He launched one to either side and then paused for a second.

"If they get close enough, I'll show them some fire," he said, and they continued on around the crater.

He fired only at individual targets then, when he was certain they were within range. He took two more before he struck the broken roadbed.

"Keep running parallel to it," she told him. "There's a trail here. You can't drive on that stuff till another mile or so."

Shots ricocheted from off his armored sides, and he continued to return the fire. He raced along an alleyway of twisted trees, like those he had seen near other craters, and the mists hung like pennons about their branches. He heard the rattle of the increasing rains.

When he hit the roadway once again, he regarded the lights to his rear and asked, "How many do you count now?"

"It looks like around twenty. How are we doing?"

"I'm just worried about the tires. They can take a lot, but they can be shot out. The only other thing that bothers me is that a stray shot might clip one of the 'eyes.' Outside of that we're bullet-proof enough. Even if they manage to stop us, they'll have to pry us out."

The bikes drew near once again, and he saw the bright flashes and heard the reports of the riders' guns.

"Hold tight," he said, and he hit the brakes and they skidded on the wet pavement.

The lights grew suddenly bright, and he unleashed his rear flame. As some bikes skirted him, he cut in the side flames and held them that way.

Then he took his foot off the brake and floored the accelerator without waiting to assess the damage he had done.

They sped ahead, and Tanner heard Cornelia's laughter.

"God! You're taking them, Hell! You're taking the whole damn club!"

"It ain't that much fun," he said. Then, "See any lights?"

She watched for a time, said, "No," then said, "Three," then, "Seven," and finally, "Thirteen."

Tanner said, "Damn."

The radiation level fell and there came crashes amid the roaring overhead. A light fall of gravel descended for perhaps half a minute, along with the rain.

"We're running low," he said.

"On what?"

"Everything: Luck, fuel, ammo. Maybe you'd have been better off if I'd left you where I found you."

"No," she said. "I'm with you, the whole line."

"Then you're nuts," he said. "I haven't been hurt yet. When I am, it might be a different tune."

"Maybe," she said. "Wait and hear how I sing."

He reached out and squeezed her thigh.

"Okay, Corny. You've been okay so far. Hang onto that piece, and we'll see what happens."

He reached for another cigarette, found the pack empty, cursed. He gestured toward a compartment, and she opened it and got him a fresh pack. She tore it open and lit him one.

"Thanks."

"Why're they staying out of range?"

"Maybe they're just going to pace us. I don't know."

Then the fogs began to lift. By the time Tanner had finished his cigarette, the visibility had improved greatly. He could make out the dark forms crouched atop their bikes, following, following, nothing more.

"If they just want to keep us company, then I don't care," he said. "Let them."

But there came more gunfire after a time, and he heard a tire go. He slowed, but continued. He took careful aim and strafed them. Several fell.

More gunshots sounded from behind. Another tire blew, and he hit the brakes and skidded, turning about as he slowed. When he faced them, he shot his anchors, to hold him in place, and he discharged his rockets, one after another, at a level parallel to the road. He opened up with his guns and sprayed them as they veered off and approached him from the sides. Then he opened fire to the left. Then the right.

He emptied the right-hand guns, then switched back to the left. He launched the remaining grenades.

The gunfire died down, except for five sources—three to his left and two to his right—coming from somewhere within the trees that lined the road now. Broken bikes and bodies lay behind him, some still smouldering. The pavement was potted and cracked in many places.

He turned the car and proceeded ahead on six wheels.

"We're out of ammo, Corny," he told her.

"Well, we took an awful lot of them. . . ."

"Yeah."

As he drove on, he saw five bikes move onto the road. They stayed a good distance behind him, but they stayed.

He tried the radio, but there was no response. He hit the brakes and stopped, and the bikes stopped, too, staying well to the rear.

"Well, at least they're scared of us. They think we still have teeth."

"We do," she said.

"Yeah, but not the ones they're thinking about."

"Better yet."

"Glad I met you," said Tanner. "I can use an optimist. There must be a pony, huh?"

She nodded; he put it into gear and started forward abruptly.

The motorcycles moved ahead also, and they maintained a safe distance. Tanner watched them in the screens and cursed them as they followed.

After awhile they drew nearer again. Tanner roared on for half an hour, and the remaining five edged closer and closer.

When they drew near enough, they began to fire, rifles resting on their handlebars.

Tanner heard several low ricochets, and then another tire went out.

He stopped once more, and the bikes did, too, remaining just out of range of his flames. He cursed and ground ahead again. The car wobbled as he drove, listing to the left. A wrecked pickup truck stood smashed against a tree to his right, its hunched driver a skeleton, its windows smashed and tires missing. Half a sun now stood in the heavens, reaching after nine o'clock; fog-ghosts drifted before them, and the dark band in the sky undulated, and more rain fell from it, mixed with dust and small stones and bits of metal. Tanner said, "Good" as the pinging sounds began, and, "Hope it gets a lot worse," and his wish came true as the ground began to shake and the blue light began in the north. There came a booming within the roar, and there were several answering crashes as heaps of rubble appeared to his right. "Hope the next one falls right on our buddies back there," he said.

He saw an orange glow ahead and to his right. It had been there for several minutes, but he had not become conscious of it until just then.

"Volcano," she said when he indicated it. "It means we've got another sixty-five, seventy miles to go."

He could not tell whether any more shooting was occurring. The sounds coming from overhead and around him were sufficient to mask any gunfire, and the fall of gravel upon the car covered any ricocheting rounds. The five headlights to his rear maintained their pace.

"Why don't they give up?" he said. "They're taking a pretty bad beating."
"They're used to it," she replied, "and they're riding for blood, which makes a difference."

Tanner fetched the .357 Magnum from the door clip and passed it to her. "Hang onto this, too," he said, and he found a box of ammo in the second compartment and, "Put these in your pocket," he added. He stuffed ammo for the .45 into his own jacket. He adjusted the hand grenades upon his belt.

Then the five headlights behind him suddenly became four, and the others slowed, grew smaller. "Accident, I hope," he remarked.

They sighted the mountain, a jag-topped cone bleeding fires upon the sky. They left the road and swung far to the left, upon a well marked trail. It took twenty minutes to pass the mountain, and by then he sighted their pursuers once again—four lights to the rear, gaining slowly.

He came upon the road once more and hurried ahead across the shaking ground. The yellow lights moved through the heavens; and heavy, shapeless objects, some several feet across, crashed to the earth about them. The car was buffeted by winds, listed as they moved, would not proceed above forty miles an hour. The radio contained only static.

Tanner rounded a sharp curve, hit the brake, turned off his lights, pulled the pin from a hand grenade and waited with his hand upon the door.

When the lights appeared in the screen, he flung the door wide, leaped down and hurled the grenade through the abrasive rain.

He was into the cab and moving again before he heard the explosion, before the flash occurred upon his screen.

The girl laughed almost hysterically as the car moved ahead.

"You got 'em, Hell, You got 'em!" she cried.

Tanner took a drink from her flask, and she finished its final brown mouthful. He lit them cigarettes.

The road grew cracked, pitted, slippery. They topped a high rise and headed downhill. The fog thickened as they descended.

Lights appeared before him, and he readied the flame. There were no hostilities, however, as he passed a truck headed in the other direction. Within the next half hour he passed two more.

There came more lightning, and fist-sized rocks began to fall. Tanner left the road and sought shelter within a grove of high trees. The sky grew completely black, losing even its blue aurora.

They waited for three hours, but the storm did not let up. One by one, the four view-screens went dead and the fifth only showed the blackness beneath the car. Tanner's last sight in the rearview screen was of a huge splintered tree with a broken, swaying branch that was about ready to fall off. There were several terrific crashes upon the hood and the car shook with each. The roof above their heads was deeply dented in three places. The lights grew dim, then bright again. The radio would not produce even static any more.

"I think we've had it," he said.

"Yeah."

"How far are we?"

"Maybe fifty miles away."

"There's still a chance, if we live through this."

"What chance?"

"I've got two bikes in the rear."

They reclined their seats and smoked and waited, and after awhile the lights went out.

The storm continued all that day and into the night. They slept within the broken body of the car, and it sheltered them. When the storm ceased, Tanner opened the door and looked outside, closed it again.

"We'll wait till morning," he said, and she held his Hell-printed hand, and they slept.

## — XVI —

In the morning, Tanner walked back through the mud and the fallen branches, the rocks and the dead fishes, and he opened the rear compartment and unbolted the bikes. He fueled them and checked them out and wheeled them down the ramp.

He crawled into the back of the cab then and removed the rear seat. Beneath it, in the storage compartment, was the large aluminum chest that was his cargo. It was bolted shut. He lifted it, carried it out to his bike.

"That the stuff?" she asked.

He nodded and placed it on the ground.

"I don't know how the stuff is stored, if it's refrigerated in there or what," he said, "but it ain't too heavy that I might not be able to get it on the back of my bike. There's straps in the far right compartment. Go get 'em and give me a hand—and get me my pardon out of the middle compartment. It's in a big cardboard envelope."

She returned with these things and helped him secure the container on the rear of his bike.

He wrapped extra straps around his left bicep, and they wheeled the machines to the road.

"We'll have to take it kind of slow," he said, and he slung the rifle over his right shoulder, drew on his gloves and kicked his bike to life.

She did the same with hers, and they moved forward, side by side along the highway.

After they had been riding for perhaps an hour, two cars passed them, heading west. In the rear seats of both there were children, who pressed their faces to the glass and watched them as they went by. The driver of the second car was in his shirtsleeves, and he wore a black shoulder holster.

The sky was pink, and there were three black lines that looked as if they could be worth worrying about. The sun was a rose-tinted silvery thing, and pale, but Tanner still had to raise his goggles against it.

The pack was riding securely, and Tanner leaned into the dawn and thought about Boston. There was a light mist on the foot of every hill, and the air was cool and moist. Another car passed them. The road surface began to improve.

It was around noontime when he heard the first shot above the thunder of their engines. At first he thought it was a backfire, but it came again, and Corny cried out and swerved off the road and struck a boulder.

Tanner cut to the left, braking, as two more shots rang about him, and he leaned his bike against a tree and threw himself flat. A shot struck near his head and he could tell the direction from which it had come. He crawled into a ditch and drew off his right glove. He could see his girl lying where she had fallen, and there was blood on her breast. She did not move.

He raised the 30.06 and fired.

The shot was returned, and he moved to his left.

It had come from a hill about two hundred feet away, and he thought he saw the rifle's barrel.

He aimed at it and fired again.

The shot was returned, and he wormed his way further left. He crawled perhaps fifteen feet until he reached a pile of rubble he could crouch behind. Then he pulled the pin on a grenade, stood and hurled it.

He threw himself flat as another shot rang out, and he took another grenade into his hand.

There was a roar and a rumble and a mighty flash, and the junk fell about him as he leaped to his feet and threw the second one, taking better aim this time.

After the second explosion, he ran forward with his rifle in his hands, but it wasn't necessary.

He only found a few small pieces of the man, and none at all of his rifle. He returned to Cornelia.

She wasn't breathing, and her heart had stopped beating, and he knew what that meant.

He carried her back to the ditch in which he had lain and he made it deeper by digging, using his hands.

He laid her down in it and he covered her with the dirt. Then he wheeled her machine over, set the kickstand, and stood it upon the grave. With his knife, he scratched upon the fender: *Her name was Cornelia and I don't know how old she was or where she came from or what her last name was but she was Hell Tanner's girl and I love her.* Then he went back to his own machine, started it and drove ahead. Boston was maybe thirty miles away.

## — XVII —

He drove along, and after a time he heard the sound of another bike. A Harley cut onto the road from the dirt path to his left, and he couldn't try running away from it because he couldn't speed with the load he bore. So he allowed himself to be paced.

After awhile, the rider of the other bike—a tall, thin man with a flaming beard—drew up alongside him, to the left. He smiled and raised his right hand and let it fall and then gestured with his head.

Tanner braked and came to a halt. Redbeard was right beside him when he did. He said, "Where you going, man?"

"Boston."

"What you got in the box?"

"Like, drugs."

"What kind?" and the man's eyebrows arched and the smile came again onto his lips.

"For the plague they got going there."

"Oh. I thought you meant the other kind." "Sorry."

The man held a pistol in his right hand and he said, "Get off your bike."

Tanner did this, and the man raised his left hand and another man came forward from the brush at the side of the road. "Wheel this guy's bike about two hundred yards up the highway," he said, "and park it in the middle. Then take your place."

"What's the bit?" Tanner asked.

The man ignored the question. "Who are you?" he asked.

"Hell's the name," he replied. "Hell Tanner."

"Go to hell."

Tanner shrugged.

"You ain't Hell Tanner."

Tanner drew off his right glove and extended his fist.

"There's my name."

"I don't believe it," said the man, after he had studied the tattoo.

"Have it your way, citizen."

"Shut up!" and he raised his left hand once more, now that the other man had parked the machine on the road and returned to a place somewhere within the trees to the right.

In response to his gesture, there was movement within the brush.

Bikes were pushed forward by their riders, and they lined the road, twenty or thirty on either side.

"There you are," said the man. "My name's Big Brother."

"Glad to meet you."

"You know what you're going to do, mister?"

"I can really just about guess."

"You're going to walk up to your bike and claim it."

Tanner smiled.

"How hard's that going to be?"

"No trouble at all. Just start walking. Give me your rifle first, though."

Big Brother raised his hand again, and one by one the engines came to life.

"Okay," he said. "Now."

"You think I'm crazy, man?"

"No. Start walking. Your rifle."

Tanner unslung it and he continued the arc. He caught Big Brother beneath his red beard, and he felt the bullet go into him. Then he dropped the weapon and hauled forth a grenade, pulled the pin and tossed it amid the left side of the gauntlet. Before it exploded, he'd pulled the pin on another and thrown it to his right. By then, though, vehicles were moving forward, heading toward him.

He fell upon the rifle and shouldered it in a prone firing position. As he did this, the first explosion occurred. He was firing before the second one went off.

He dropped three of them, then got to his feet and scrambled, firing from the hip.

He made it behind Big Brother's fallen bike and fired from there. Big Brother was still fallen, too. When the rifle was empty, he didn't have time to reload. He fired the .45 four times before a tire chain brought him down.

He awoke to the roaring of the engines. They were circling him. When he got to his feet, a handlebar knocked him down again.

Two bikes were moving about him, and there were many dead people upon the road.

He struggled to rise again, was knocked off his feet.

Big Brother rode one of the bikes, and a guy he hadn't seen rode the other.

He crawled to the right, and there was pain in his fingertips as the tires passed over them.

But he saw a rock and waited till a driver was near. Then he stood again and threw himself upon the man as he passed, the rock he had seized rising and falling, once, in his right hand. He was carried along as this occurred, and as he fell he felt the second bike strike him.

There were terrible pains in his side, and his body felt broken, but he reached out even as this occurred and caught hold of a strut on the side of the bike and was dragged along by it.

Before he had been dragged ten feet, he had drawn his SS dagger from his boot. He struck upward and felt a thin metal wall give way. Then his hands came loose, and he fell and he smelled the gasoline. His hand dove into his jacket pocket and came out with the Zippo.

He had struck the tank on the side of Big Brother's bike, and it jetted forth its contents on the road. Twenty feet ahead, Big Brother was turning.

Tanner held the lighter, the lighter with the raised skull of enamel, wings on either side of it. His thumb spun the wheel and the sparks leapt forth, then the flame. He tossed it into the stream of petrol that lay before him, and the flames raced away, tracing a blazing trail upon the concrete.

Big Brother had turned and was bearing down upon him when he saw what had happened. His eyes widened, and his red-framed smile went away.

He tried to leap off his bike, but it was too late.

The exploding gas tank caught him, and he went down with a piece of metal in his head and other pieces elsewhere.

Flames splashed over Tanner, and he beat at them feebly with his hands.

He raised his head above the blazing carnage and let it fall again. He was bloody and weak and so very tired. He saw his own machine, standing still undamaged on the road ahead.

He began crawling toward it.

When he reached it, he threw himself across the saddle and lay there for perhaps ten minutes. He vomited twice, and his pains became a steady pulsing.

After perhaps an hour, he mounted the bike and brought it to life.

He rode for half a mile and then dizziness and the fatigue hit him.

He pulled off to the side of the road and concealed his bike as best he could. Then he lay down upon the bare earth and slept.

## — XVIII —

When he awoke, he felt dried blood upon his side. His left hand ached and was swollen. All four fingers felt stiff, and it hurt to try to bend them. His head throbbed and there was a taste of gasoline within his mouth. He was too sore to move, for a long while. His beard had been singed, and his right eye was swollen almost shut.

"Corny. . . ." he said, then, "Damn!"

Everything came back, like the contents of a powerful dream suddenly spilled into his consciousness.

He began to shiver, and there were mists all around him. It was very dark, and his legs were cold; the dampness had soaked completely through his denims.

In the distance, he heard a vehicle pass. It sounded like a car.

He managed to roll over, and he rested his head on his forearm. It seemed to be night, but it could be a black day.

As he lay there, his mind went back to his prison cell. It seemed almost a haven now; and he thought of his brother Denny, who must also be hurting at this moment. He wondered if he had any cracked ribs himself. It felt like it. And he thought of the monsters of the southwest and of dark-eyed Greg, who had tried to chicken out. Was he still living? His mind circled back to L.A. and the old Coast, gone, gone forever now, after the Big Raid. Then Corny walked past him, blood upon her breasts, and he chewed his beard and held his eyes shut very tight. They might have made it together in Boston. How far, now?

He got to his knees and crawled until he felt something high and solid. A tree. He sat with his back to it, and his hand sought the crumpled cigarette pack within his jacket. He drew one forth, smoothed it, then remembered that his lighter lay somewhere back on the highway. He sought through his pockets and found a damp matchbook. The third one lit. The chill went out of his bones as he smoked, and a wave of fever swept over him. He coughed as he was unbuttoning his collar, and it seemed that he tasted blood.

His weapons were gone, save for the lump of a single grenade at his belt.

Above him, in the darkness, he heard the roaring. After six puffs, the cigarette slipped from his fingers and sizzled out upon the damp mold. His head fell forward, and there was darkness within.

There might have been a storm. He didn't remember. When he awoke, he was lying on his right side, the tree to his back. A pink afternoon sun shone down upon him, and the mists were blown away. From somewhere, he heard the sound of a bird. He managed a curse, then realized how dry his throat was. He was suddenly burnt with a terrible thirst.

There was a clear puddle about thirty feet away. He crawled to it and drank his fill. It grew muddy as he did so.

Then he crawled to where his bike lay hidden and stood beside it. He managed to seat himself upon it, and his hands shook as he lit a cigarette.

It must have taken him an hour to reach the roadway, and he was panting heavily by then. His watch had been broken, so he didn't know the hour. The sun was already lowering at his back when he started out. The winds whipped about him, insulating his consciousness within their burning flow. His cargo rode securely behind him. He had visions of someone opening it and finding a batch of broken bottles. He laughed and cursed, alternately.

Several cars passed him, heading in the other direction. He had not seen any heading toward the city. The road was in good condition and he began to pass buildings that seemed in a good state of repair, though deserted. He did not stop. This time he determined not to stop for anything, unless he was stopped.

The sun fell farther, and the sky dimmed before him. There were two black lines swaying in the heavens. Then he passed a sign that told him he had 18 miles farther to go. Ten minutes later he switched on his light.

Then he topped a hill and slowed before he began its descent.

There were lights below him and in the distance.

As he rushed forward, the winds brought to him the sound of a single bell, tolling over and over within the gathering dark. He sniffed a remembered thing upon the air: it was the salt-tang of the sea.

The sun was hidden behind the hill as he descended, and he rode within the endless shadow. A single star appeared on the far horizon, between the two black belts.

Now there were lights within shadows that he passed, and the buildings moved closer together. He leaned heavily on the handlebars, and the muscles of his shoulders smouldered beneath his jacket. He wished that he had a crash helmet, for he felt increasingly unsteady.

He must almost be there. Where would he head once he hit the city proper? They had not told him that.

He shook his head to clear it.

The street he drove along was deserted. There were no traffic sounds that he could hear. He blew his horn, and its echoes rolled back upon him.

There was a light on in the building to his left.

He pulled to a stop, crossed the sidewalk and banged on the door. There was no response from within. He tried the door and found it locked. A telephone would mean he could end his trip right there.

What if they were all dead inside? The thought occurred to him that just about everybody could be dead by now. He decided to break in. He returned to his bike for a screwdriver, then went to work on the door.

He heard the gunshot and the sound of the engine at approximately the same time.

He turned around quickly, his back against the door, the hand grenade in his gloved right fist.

"Hold it!" called out a loudspeaker on the side of the black car that approached. "That shot was a warning! The next one won't be!"

Tanner raised his hands to a level with his ears, his right one turned to conceal the grenade. He stepped forward to the curb beside his bike when the car drew up.

There were two officers in the car, and the one on the passenger side held a .38 pointed at Tanner's middle.

"You're under arrest," he said. "Looting."

Tanner nodded as the man stepped out of the car. The driver came around the front of the vehicle, a pair of handcuffs in his hand.

"Looting," the man with the gun repeated. "You'll pull a real stiff sentence."

"Stick your hands out here, boy," said the second cop, and Tanner handed him the grenade pin.

The man stared at it, dumbly, for several seconds, then his eyes shot to Tanner's right hand.

"God! He's got a bomb!" said the man with the gun.

Tanner smiled, then, "Shut up and listen!" he said. "Or else shoot me and we'll all go together when we go. I was trying to get to a telephone. That case on the back of my bike is full of Haffikine antiserum. I brought it from L.A."

"You didn't run the Alley on that bike!"

"No, I didn't. My car is dead somewhere between here and Albany, and so are a lot of folks who tried to stop me. Now you better take that medicine and get it where it's supposed to go."

"You on the level, mister?"

"My hand is getting very tired. I am not in good shape." Tanner leaned on his bike. "Here."

He pulled his pardon out of his jacket and handed it to the officer with the handcuffs. "That's my pardon," he said. "It's dated just last week and you can see it was made out in California."

The officer took the envelope and opened it. He withdrew the paper and studied it. "Looks real," he said. "So Brady made it through . . ."

"He's dead," Tanner said. "Look, I'm hurtin'. Do something!"

"My God! Hold it tight! Get in the car and sit down! It'll just take a minute to get the case off and we'll roll. We'll drive to the river and you can throw it in. Squeeze real hard!"

They unfastened the case and put it in the back of the car. They rolled down the right front window, and Tanner sat next to it with his arm on the outside.

The siren screamed, and the pain crept up Tanner's arm to his shoulder. It would be very easy to let go.

"Where do you keep your river?" he asked.

"Just a little farther. We'll be there in no time."

"Hurry," Tanner said.

"That's the bridge up ahead. We'll ride out onto it, and you throw it off— as far out as you can."

"Man, I'm tired! I'm not sure I can make it. . . ."

"Hurry, Jerry!"

"I am, damn it! We ain't got wings!"

"I feel kind of dizzy, too. . . ."

They tore out onto the bridge, and the tires screeched as they halted. Tanner opened the door slowly. The driver's had already slammed shut.

He staggered, and they helped him to the railing. He sagged against it when they released him.

"I don't think I—"

Then he straightened, drew back his arm and hurled the grenade far out over the waters.

He grinned, and the explosion followed, far beneath them, and for a time the waters were troubled.

The two officers sighed and Tanner chuckled.

"I'm really okay," he said. "I just faked it to bug you."

"Why you—!"

Then he collapsed, and they saw the pallor of his face within the beams of their lights.

# — XIX —

The following spring, on the day of its unveiling in Boston Common, when it was discovered that someone had scrawled obscene words on the statue of Hell Tanner, no one thought to ask the logical candidate why he had done it, and the next day it was too late, because he had cut out without leaving a forwarding address. Several cars were reported stolen that day, and one was never seen again in Boston.

So they re-veiled his statue, bigger than life, astride a great bronze Harley, and they cleaned him up for hoped-for posterity. But coming upon the Common, the winds still break about him and the heavens still throw garbage.

After World War III, Jan-Michael Vincent has to battle blood-hungry giant scorpions as well as George Peppard in *Damnation Alley.*

In *Enemy Mine*, Willis Davidge (Dennis Quaid) and Jeriba Shigan (Louis Gossett, Jr.) are enemies at first, but friends in the end.

# Enemy Mine

## BARRY LONGYEAR

---

**Enemy Mine**
Director: *Wolfgang Peterson*
Screenplay: *Edward Khmara*
Producer: *Stephen Friedman*
Music: *Maurice Jarre*
Special Effects: *ILM*
Cast: *Dennis Quaid, Louis Gossett Jr.*
Released by: *20th Century-Fox*
1985, 108 Minutes. Color.

---

*EDITOR'S NOTE: "Enemy Mine" was originally published in the November/December 1979 issue of Isaac Asimov's Science-Fiction Magazine. The author, Barry Longyear, subsequently revised the story for inclusion in a collection entitled, Manifest Destiny (published 1980 by Berkeley Books). The work included in this edition is the revised and expanded version from Manifest Destiny.*

The Dracon's three-fingered hands flexed. In the thing's yellow eyes I could read the desire to have those fingers around either a weapon or my throat. As I flexed my own fingers, I knew it read the same in my eyes.
"*Irkmaan!*" the thing spat.
"You piece of Drac slime." I brought my hands up in front of my chest and waved the thing on. "Come on, Drac; come and get it."
"*Irkmaan vaa, koruum su!*"
"Are you going to talk, or fight? Come on!" I could feel the

spray from the sea behind me—a boiling madhouse of white-capped breakers that threatened to swallow me as it had my fighter. I had ridden my ship in. The Drac had ejected when its own fighter had caught one in the upper atmosphere, but not before crippling my power plant. I was exhausted from swimming to the grey, rocky beach and pulling myself to safety. Behind the Drac, among the rocks on the otherwise barren hill, I could see its ejection capsule. Far above us, its people and mine were still at it, slugging out the possession of an uninhabited corner of nowhere. The Drac just stood there and I went over the phrase taught us in training—a phrase calculated to drive any Drac into a frenzy. *"Kiz da yuomeen, Shizumaat!"* Meaning: Shizumaat, the most revered Drac philosopher, eats *kiz* excrement. Something on the level of stuffing a Moslem full of pork.

The Drac opened its mouth in horror, then closed it as anger literally changed its color from yellow to reddish-brown. *"Irkmaan, yaa stupid Mickey Mouse is!"*

I had taken an oath to fight and die over many things, but that venerable rodent didn't happen to be one of them. I laughed, and continued laughing until the guffaws in combination with my exhaustion forced me to my knees. I forced open my eyes to keep track of my enemy. The Drac was running toward the high ground, away from me and the sea. I half-turned toward the sea and caught a glimpse of a million tons of water just before they fell on me, knocking me unconscious.

*"Kiz da yuomeen, Irkmaan, ne?"*

My eyes were gritty with sand and stung with salt, but some part of my awareness pointed out: "Hey, you're alive." I reached to wipe the sand from my eyes and found my hands bound. A straight metal rod had been run through my sleeves and my wrists tied to it. As my tears cleared the sand from my eyes, I could see the Drac sitting on a smooth black boulder looking at me. It must have pulled me out of the drink. "Thanks, toad face. What's with the bondage?"

*"Ess?"*

I tried waving my arms and wound up giving an impression of an atmospheric fighter dipping its wings. "Untie me, you Drac slime!" I was seated on the sand, my back against a rock.

The Drac smiled, exposing the upper and lower mandibles that looked human—except that instead of separate teeth, they were solid. *"Eh, ne, Irkmaan."* It stood, walked over to me and checked my bonds.

"Untie me!"

The smile disappeared. *"Ne!"* It pointed at me with a yellow finger. *"Kos son va?"*

"I don't speak Drac, toad face. You speak Esper or English?"

The Drac delivered a very human-looking shrug, then pointed at its own chest. *"Kos va son Jeriba Shigan."* It pointed again at me. *"Kos son va?"*

"Davidge. My name is Willis E. Davidge."

*"Ess?"*

I tried my tongue on the unfamiliar syllables. *"Kos va son Willis Davidge."*

*"Eh."* Jeriba Shigan nodded, then motioned with its fingers. *"Dasu, Davidge."*

"Same to you, Jerry."

*"Dasu, dasu!"* Jeriba began sounding a little impatient. I shrugged as best I could. The Drac bent over and grabbed the front of my jump suit with both hands and pulled me to my feet. *"Dasu, dasu, kizlode!"*

"All right! So *dasu* is 'get up.' What's a *kizlode?"*

Jerry laughed. *"Gavey 'kiz'?"*

"Yeah, I *gavey.*"

Jerry pointed at its head. *"Lode."* It pointed at my head. *"Kizlode, gavey?"*

I got it, then swung my arms around, catching Jerry upside its head with the metal rod. The Drac stumbled back against a rock, looking surprised. It raised a hand to its head and withdrew it covered with that pale pus that Dracs think is blood. It looked at me with murder in its eyes. *"Gefh! Nu Gefh, Davidge!"*

"Come and get it, Jerry, you *kizlode* sonofabitch!"

Jerry dived at me and I tried to catch it again with the rod, but the Drac caught my right wrist in both hands and, using the momentum of my swing, whirled me around, slamming my back against another rock. Just as I was getting back my breath, Jerry picked up a small boulder and came at me with every intention of turning my melon into pulp. With my back against the rock, I lifted a foot and kicked the Drac in the midsection, knocking it to the sand. I ran up, ready to stomp Jerry's melon, but he pointed behind me. I turned and saw another tidal wave gathering steam, and heading our way. *"Kiz!"* Jerry got to its feet and scampered for the high ground with me following close behind.

With the roar of the wave at our backs, we weaved among the water- and sand-ground black boulders until we reached Jerry's ejection capsule. The Drac stopped, put its shoulder to the egg-shaped contraption, and began rolling it uphill. I could see Jerry's point. The capsule contained all of the survival equipment and food either of us knew about. "Jerry!" I shouted above the rumble of the fast-approaching wave. "Pull out this damn rod and I'll help!" The Drac frowned at me. "The rod, *kizlode*, pull it out!" I cocked my head toward my outstretched arm.

Jerry placed a rock beneath the capsule to keep it from rolling back, then quickly untied my wrists and pulled out the rod. Both of us put our shoulders to the capsule, and we quickly rolled it to higher ground. The wave hit and climbed rapidly up the slope until it came up to our chests. The capsule bobbed like a cork, and it was all we could do to keep control of the thing until the water receded, wedging the capsule between three big boulders. I stood there, puffing.

Jerry dropped to the sand, its back against one of the boulders, and watched the water rush back out to sea. *"Magasienna!"*

"You said it, brother." I sank down next to the Drac; we agreed by eye to a temporary truce, and promptly passed out.

My eyes opened on a sky boiling with blacks and greys. Letting my head loll over on my left shoulder, I checked out the Drac. It was still out. First, I thought that this would be the perfect time to get the drop on Jerry. Second, I thought about how silly our insignificant scrap seemed compared to the insanity of the sea that surrounded us. Why hadn't the rescue team come? Did the Dracon fleet wipe us out? Why hadn't the Dracs come to pick up Jerry? Did they wipe out each other? I didn't even know where I was. An island. I had seen that much coming in, but where and in relation to what? Fyrine IV: the planet didn't even rate a name, but was important enough to die over.

With an effort, I struggled to my feet. Jerry opened its eyes and quickly pushed itself to a defensive crouching position. I waved my hand and shook my head. "Ease off, Jerry. I'm just going to look around." I turned my back on it and trudged off between the boulders. I walked uphill for a few minutes until I reached level ground.

It was an island, all right, and not a very big one. By eyeball estimation, height from sea level was only eighty meters, while the island itself was about two kilometers long and less than half that wide. The wind whipping my jumpsuit against my body was at least drying it out, but as I looked around at the smooth-ground boulders on top of the rise, I realized that Jerry and I could expect bigger waves than the few puny ones we had seen.

A rock clattered behind me and I turned to see Jerry climbing up the slope. When it reached the top, the Drac looked around. I squatted next to one of the boulders and passed my hand over it to indicate the smoothness, then I pointed toward the sea. Jerry nodded. *"Ae, gavey."* It pointed downhill toward the capsule, then to where we stood. *"Echey masu, nasesay."*

I frowned, then pointed at the capsule. *"Nasesay?* The capsule?"

*"Ae,* capsule *nasesay. Echey masu."* Jerry pointed at its feet.

I shook my head. "Jerry, if you *gavey* how these rocks got smooth"—I pointed at one—"then you *gavey* that *masu*ing the *nasesay* up here isn't going to do a damned bit of good." I made a sweeping up and down movement with my hands. "Waves." I pointed at the sea below. "Waves, up here." I pointed to where we stood. "Waves, *echey*."

"*Ae, gavey.*" Jerry looked around the top of the rise, then rubbed the side of its face. The Drac squatted next to some small rocks and began piling one on top of another. "*Viga*, Davidge."

I squatted next to it and watched while its nimble fingers constructed a circle of stones that quickly grew into a dollhouse-sized arena. Jerry stuck one of its fingers in the center of the circle. "*Echey, nasesay.*"

The days on Fyrine IV seemed to be three times longer than any I had seen on any other habitable planet. I use the designation "habitable" with reservations. It took us most of the first day to painfully roll Jerry's *nasesay* up to the top of the rise. The night was too black to work and was bone-cracking cold. We removed the couch from the capsule, which made just enough room for both of us to fit inside. The body heat warmed things up a bit; and we killed time between sleeping, nibbling on Jerry's supply of ration bars (they taste a bit like fish mixed with cheddar cheese), and trying to come to some agreement about language.

"Eye."

"*Thuyo.*"

"Finger."

"*Zurath.*"

"Head."

The Drac laughed. "*Lode.*"

"Ho, ho, very funny."

"*Ho, ho.*"

At dawn on the second day, we rolled and pushed the capsule into the center of the rise and wedged it between two large rocks, one of which had an overhang that we hoped would hold down the capsule when one of those big soakers hit. Around the rocks and capsule, we laid a foundation of large stones and filled in the cracks with smaller stones. By the time the wall was knee high, we discovered that building with those smooth, round stones and no mortar wasn't going to work. After some experimentation, we figured out how to break the stones to give us flat sides with which to work. It's done by picking up one stone and slamming it down on top of another. We took turns, one slamming and one building. The stone was almost a volcanic glass, and we also took turns extracting rock splinters from each other. It took nine of those endless days and nights to complete the walls, during which waves came close many times and once washed us ankle deep. For six of those nine days, it rained. The capsule's survival equipment included a plastic blanket, and that became our roof. It sagged in at the center, and the hole we put in it there allowed the water to run out, keeping us almost dry and giving us a supply of fresh water. If a wave of any determination came along, we could kiss the roof goodbye; but we both had confidence in the walls, which were almost two meters thick at the bottom and at least a meter thick at the top.

After we finished, we sat inside and admired our work for about an hour, until it dawned on us that we had just worked ourselves out of jobs. "What now, Jerry?"

"*Ess?*"

"What do we do now?"

"Now wait, we." The Drac shrugged. "Else what, *ne?*"

I nodded. "*Gavey.*" I got to my feet and walked to the passageway we had built. With no wood for a door, where the walls would have met, we bent one out and extended it about three meters around the other wall with the opening away from the prevailing winds. The never-ending winds were still at it, but the rain had stopped. The shack wasn't much to look at, but looking at it stuck there in the center of that deserted island made me feel good. As Shizumaat observed, "Intelligent life making its stand against the universe." Or, at least, that's the sense I could make out of Jerry's hamburger of English. I shrugged and picked up a sharp splinter of stone and made another mark in the large standing rock that served as my log. Ten scratches in all, and under the seventh, a small *x* to indicate the big wave that just covered the top of the island.

I threw down the splinter. "Damn, I hate this place!"

"*Ess?*" Jerry's head poked around the edge of the opening. "Who talking at, Davidge?"

I glared at the Drac, then waved my hand at it. "Nobody."

"*Ess va* 'nobody'?"

"Nobody. Nothing."

"*Ne gavey*, Davidge."

I poked at my chest with my finger. "Me! I'm talking to myself! You *gavey* that stuff, toad face!"

Jerry shook its head. "Davidge, now I sleep. Talk not so much nobody, *ne?*" It disappeared back into the opening.

"And so's your mother!" I turned and walked down the slope. *Except, strictly speaking, toad face, you don't have a mother—or father. "If you had your choice, who would you like to be trapped on a desert island with?"* I wondered if anyone ever picked a wet freezing corner of Hell shacked up with a hermaphrodite.

Half of the way down the slope, I followed the path I had marked with rocks until I came to my tidal pool that I had named "Rancho Sluggo."

Around the pool were many of the water-worn rocks, and underneath those rocks, below the pool's waterline, lived the fattest orange slugs either of us had ever seen. I made the discovery during a break from house building and showed them to Jerry.

Jerry shrugged. "And so?"

"And so what? Look, Jerry, those ration bars aren't going to last forever. What are we going to eat when they're all gone?"

"Eat?" Jerry looked at the wriggling pocket of insect life and grimaced. "*Ne*, Davidge. Before then pickup. Search us find, then pickup."

"What if they don't find us? What then?"

Jerry grimaced again and turned back to the half-completed house. "Water we drink, then until pickup." He had muttered something about *kiz* excrement and my tastebuds, then walked out of sight.

Since then I had built up the pool's walls, hoping the increased protection from the harsh environment would increase the herd. I looked under several rocks, but no increase was apparent. And, again, I couldn't bring myself to swallow one of the things. I replaced the rock I was looking under, stood and looked out to the sea. Although the eternal cloud cover still denied the surface the drying rays of Fyrine, there was no rain and the usual haze had lifted.

In the direction past where I had pulled myself up on the beach, the sea continued to the horizon. In the spaces between the whitecaps, the water was as grey as a loan officer's heart. Parallel lines of rollers formed approximately five kilometers from the island. The center, from where I was standing, would smash on the island, while the remainder steamed on. To my right, in line with the breakers, I could just make out another small island perhaps ten kilometers away. Following the path of the rollers, I looked far to my right, and where the grey-white of the sea should have met the lighter grey of the sky, there was a black line on the horizon.

The harder I tried to remember the briefing charts on Fyrine IV's land masses, the less clear it became. Jerry couldn't remember anything either—at least nothing it would tell me. Why should we remember? The battle was supposed to be in space, each one trying to deny the other an orbital staging area in the Fyrine system. Neither side wanted to set foot on Fyrine, much less fight a battle there. Still, whatever it was called, it was land and considerably larger than the sand and rock bar we were occupying.

How to get there was the problem. Without wood, fire, leaves, or animal skins, Jerry and I were destitute compared to the average poverty-stricken caveman. The only thing we had that would float was the *nasesay*. The capsule. Why not? The only real problem to overcome was getting Jerry to go along with it.

That evening, while the greyness made its slow transition to black, Jerry and I sat outside the shack nibbling our quarter portions of ration bars. The Drac's yellow eyes studied the dark line on the horizon, then it shook its head. "*Ne*, Davidge. Dangerous is."

I popped the rest of my ration bar into my mouth and talked around it. "Any more dangerous than staying here?"

"Soon pickup, *ne?*"

I studied those yellow eyes. "Jerry, you don't believe that any more than I do." I leaned forward on the rock and held out my hands. "Look, our chances will be a lot better on a larger land mass. Protection from the big waves, maybe food . . ."

"Not maybe, *ne?*" Jerry pointed at the water. "How *nasesay* steer, Davidge? In that, how steer? *Ess eh* soakers, waves, beyond land take, *gavey? Bresha*," Jerry's hands slapped together. "*Ess eh bresha* rocks on, *ne?* Then we death."

I scratched my head. "The waves are going in that direction from here, and so is the wind. If the land mass is large enough, we don't have to steer, *gavey?*"

Jerry snorted. "*Ne* large enough, then?"

"I didn't say it was a sure thing."

"*Ess?*"

"A sure thing; certain, *gavey?*" Jerry nodded. "And for smashing up on the rocks, it probably has a beach like this one."

"Sure thing, *ne?*"

I shrugged. "No, it's not a sure thing, but, what about staying here? We don't know how big those waves can get. What if one just comes along and washes us off the island? What then?"

Jerry looked at me, its eyes narrowed. "What there, Davidge? *Irkmaan* base, *ne?*"

I laughed. "I told you, we don't have any bases on Fyrine IV."

"Why want go, then?"

"Just what I said, Jerry. I think our chances would be better."

"Ummm." The Drac folded its arms. "*Viga*, Davidge, *nasesay* stay. I know."

"Know what?"

Jerry smirked, then stood and went into the shack. After a moment it returned and threw a two-meter long metal rod at my feet. It was the one the Drac had used to bind my arms. "Davidge, I know."

I raised my eyebrows and shrugged. "What are you talking about? Didn't that come from your capsule?"

"*Ne, Irkmaan.*"

I bent down and picked up the rod. Its surface was uncorroded and at one end were arabic numerals—a part number. For a moment a flood of hope washed over me, but it drained away when I realized it was a civilian part number. I threw the rod on the sand. "There's no telling how long that's been here, Jerry. It's a civilian part number and no civilian missions have been in this part of the galaxy since the war. Might be left over from an old seeding operation or exploratory mission . . ."

The Drac nudged it with the toe of his boot. "New, *gavey?*"

I looked up at it. "You *gavey* stainless steel?"

Jerry snorted and turned back toward the shack. "I stay, *nasesay* stay; where you want, you go, Davidge!"

With the black of the long night firmly bolted down on us, the wind picked up, shrieking and whistling in and through the holes in the walls. The plastic roof flapped, pushed in and sucked out with such violence it threatened to either tear or sail off into the night. Jerry sat on the sand floor, its back leaning against the *nasesay* as if to make clear that both Drac and capsule were staying put, although the way the sea was picking up seemed to weaken Jerry's argument.

"Sea rough now is, Davidge, *ne?*"

"It's too dark to see, but with this wind . . ." I shrugged more for my own benefit than the Drac's, since the only thing visible inside the shack was the pale light coming through the roof. Any minute we could be washed off that sandbar. "Jerry, you're being silly about that rod. You know that."

"*Surda.*" The Drac sounded contrite if not altogether miserable.

"*Ess?*"

"*Ess eh 'surda'?*"

"*Ae.*"

Jerry remained silent for a moment. "Davidge, *gavey* 'not certain not is'?"

I sorted out the negatives. "You mean 'possible,' 'maybe,' 'perhaps'?"

"*Ae,* possiblemaybeperhaps. Dracon fleet *Irkmaan* ships have. Before war buy; after war capture. Rod possiblemaybeperhaps Dracon is."

"So, if there's a secret base on the big island, *surda* it's a Dracon base?"

"Possiblemaybeperhaps, Davidge."

"Jerry, does that mean you want to try it? The *nasesay?*"

"*Ne.*"

"*Ne?* Why, Jerry? If it might be a Drac base—"

"*Ne! Ne* talk!" The Drac seemed to choke on the words.

"Jerry, we talk, and you better *believe* we talk! If I'm going to death it on this island, I have a right to know why."

The Drac was quiet for a long time. "Davidge."

"*Ess?*"

"*Nasesay* you take. Half ration bars you leave. I stay."

I shook my head to clear it. "You want me to take the capsule alone?"

"What you want is, *ne?*"

"*Ae*, but why? You must realize there won't be any pickup."

"Possiblemaybeperhaps."

"*Surda*, nothing. You know there isn't going to be a pickup. What is it? You afraid of the water? If that's it, we have a better chance—"

"Davidge, up your mouth shut. *Nasesay* you have. Me *ne* you need, *gavey?*"

I nodded in the dark. The capsule was mine for the taking; what did I need a grumpy Drac along for—especially since our truce could expire at any moment? The answer made me feel a little silly—human. Perhaps it's the same thing. The Drac was all that stood between me and utter aloneness. Still, there was the small matter of staying alive. "We should go together, Jerry."

"Why?"

I felt myself blush. If humans have this need for companionship, why are they also ashamed to admit it? "We just should. Our chances would be better."

"Alone your chances better are, Davidge. Your enemy I am."

I nodded again and grimaced in the dark. "Jerry, you *gavey* 'loneliness'?"

"*Ne gavey.*"

"Lonely. Being alone, by myself."

"*Gavey* you alone. Take *nasesay*; I stay."

"That's it . . . see, *viga*, I don't want to."

"You want together go?" A low, dirty chuckle came from the other side of the shack. "You Dracon like? You me death, *Irkmaan.*" Jerry chuckled some more. "*Irkmaan poorzhab* in head, *poorzhab.*"

"Forget it!" I slid down from the wall, smoothed out the sand, and curled up with my back toward the Drac. The wind seemed to die down a bit and I closed my eyes to try and sleep. In a bit, the snap, crack of the plastic roof blended in with the background of shrieks and whistles and I felt myself drifting off, when my eyes opened wide at the sound of footsteps in the sand. I tensed, ready to spring.

"Davidge?" Jerry's voice was very quiet.

"What?"

I heard the Drac sit on the sand next to me. "You loneliness, Davidge. About it hard you talk, *ne?*"

"So what?" The Drac mumbled something that was lost in the wind. "What?" I turned over and saw Jerry looking through a hole in the wall.

"Why I stay. Now, you I tell, *ne?*"

I shrugged. "Okay; why not?"

Jerry seemed to struggle with the words, then opened its mouth to speak. Its eyes opened wide. "*Magasienna!*"

I sat up. "*Ess?*"

Jerry pointed at the hole. "Soaker!"

I pushed it out of the way and looked through the hole. Steaming toward our island was an insane mountainous fury of white-capped rollers. It was hard to tell in the dark, but the one in front looked taller than the one that had wet our feet a few days before. The ones following it were bigger. Jerry put a hand on my shoulder and I looked into the Drac's eyes. We broke and ran for the capsule. We heard the first wave rumbling up the slope as we felt around in the dark for the recessed doorlatch. I just got my finger on it when the wave smashed against the shack, collapsing the roof. In half a second we were underwater, the currents inside the shack agitating us like socks in a washing machine.

The water receded, and as I cleared my eyes, I saw that the windward wall of the shack had caved in. "Jerry!"

Through the collapsed wall, I saw the Drac staggering around outside. *"Irkmaan?"* Behind him I could see the second roller gathering speed.

*"Kizlode,* what'n the Hell you doing out there? Get in here!"

I turned to the capsule, still lodged firmly between the two rocks, and found the handle. As I opened the door, Jerry stumbled through the missing wall and fell against me. "Davidge . . . forever soakers go on! Forever!"

"Get in!" I helped the Drac through the door and didn't wait for it to get out of the way. I piled in on top of Jerry and latched the door just as the second wave hit. I could feel the capsule lift a bit and rattle against the overhang of the one rock.

"Davidge, we float?"

"No. The rocks are holding us. We'll be all right once the breakers stop."

"Over you move."

"Oh." I got off Jerry's chest and braced myself against one end of the capsule. After a bit, the capsule came to rest and we waited for the next one. "Jerry?"

*"Ess?"*

"What was it that you were about to say?"

"Why I stay?"

"Yeah."

"About it hard me talk, *gavey?"*

"I know, I know."

The next breaker hit and I could feel the capsule rise and rattle against the rock. "Davidge, *gavey 'vi nessa'?"*

*"Ne gavey."*

*"Vi nessa* . . . little me, *gavey?"*

The capsule bumped down the rock and came to rest. "What about little you?"

"Little me . . . little Drac. From me, *gavey?"*

"Are you telling me you're *pregnant?*"

"Possiblemaybeperhaps."

I shook my head. "Hold on, Jerry. I don't want any misunderstandings. Pregnant . . . are you going to be a parent?"

"*Ae*, parent, two-zero-zero in line, very important is, *ne?*"

"Terrific. What's this got to do with you not wanting to go to the other island?"

"Before, me *vi nessa, gavey? Tean* death."

"Your child, it died?"

"*Ae!*" The Drac's sob was torn from the lips of the universal mother. "I in fall hurt. *Tean* death. *Nasesay* in sea us bang. *Tean* hurt, *gav  '?*"

"*Ae*, I *gavey*." So Jerry was afraid of losing another child. It was almost certain that the capsule trip would bang us around a lot, but staying on the sandbar didn't appear to be improving our chances. The capsule had been at rest for quite a while, and I decided to risk a peek outside. The small canopy windows seemed to be covered with sand, and I opened the door. I looked around, and all of the walls had been smashed flat. I looked toward the sea, but could see nothing. "It looks safe, Jerry . . ." I looked up, toward the blackish sky, and above me towered the white plume of a descending breaker. "*Maga* damn *sienna!*" I slammed the hatch door.

"*Ess*, Davidge?"

"Hang on, Jerry!"

The sound of the water hitting the capsule was beyond hearing. We banged once, twice against the rock, then we could feel ourselves twisting, shooting upward. I made a grab to hang on, but missed as the capsule took a sickening lurch downward. I fell into Jerry, then was flung to the opposite wall, where I struck my head. Before I went blank, I heard Jerry cry *"Tean! Vi tean!"*

*. . . the lieutenant pressed his hand control and a figure—tall, humanoid, yellow— appeared on the screen.*

*"Dracslime!" shouted the auditorium of seated recruits.*

*The lieutenant faced the recruits. "Correct. This is a Drac. Note that the Drac race is uniform as to color; they are all yellow." The recruits chuckled politely. The officer preened a bit, then with a light wand began pointing out various features. "The three-fingered hands are distinctive, of course, as is the almost noseless face, which gives the Drac a toadlike appearance. On average, eyesight is slightly better than human, hearing about the same, and smell . . ." The lieutenant paused. "The smell is terrible!" The officer beamed at the uproar from the recruits. When the auditorium quieted down, he pointed his light wand at a fold in the figure's belly. "This is where the Drac keeps its family jewels—all of them." Another chuckle.*

"That's right, Dracs are hermaphrodites, with both male and female reproductive organs contained in the same individual." The lieutenant faced the recruits. "You go tell a Drac to go boff himself, then watch out, because he can!" The laughter died down, and the lieutenant held out a hand toward the screen. "You see one of these things, what do you do?"

"KILL IT . . ."

. . . I cleared the screen and computer sighted on the next Drac fighter, looking like a double x in the screen's display. The Drac shifted hard to the left, then right again. I felt the autopilot pull my ship after the fighter, sorting out and ignoring the false images, trying to lock its electronic crosshairs on the Drac. "Come on, toadface . . . a little bit to the left . . ." The double cross image moved into the ranging rings on the display and I felt the missile attached to the belly of my fighter take off. "Gotcha!" Through my canopy I saw the flash as the missile detonated. My screen showed the Drac fighter out of control, spinning toward Fyrine IV's cloud-shrouded surface. I dived after it to confirm the kill . . . skin temperature increasing as my ship brushed the upper atmosphere. "Come on, dammit, blow!" I shifted the ship's systems over for atmospheric flight when it became obvious that I'd have to follow the Drac right to the ground. Still above the clouds, the Drac stopped spinning and turned. I hit the auto override and pulled the stick into my lap. The fighter wallowed as it tried to pull up. Everyone knows the Drac ships work better in atmosphere . . . heading toward me on an interception course . . . why doesn't the slime fire? . . . just before the collision, the Drac ejects . . . power gone; have to deadstick it in. I track the capsule as it falls through the muck, intending to find that Dracslime and finish the job . . .

It could have been for seconds or years that I groped into the darkness around me. I felt touching, but the parts of me being touched seemed far, far away. First chills, then fever, then chills again, my head being cooled by a gentle hand. I opened my eyes to narrow slits and saw Jerry hovering over me, blotting my forehead with something cool. I managed a whisper. "Jerry."

The Drac looked into my eyes and smiled. "Good is, Davidge. Good is."

The light on Jerry's face flickered and I smelled smoke. "Fire."

Jerry got out of the way and pointed toward the center of the room's sandy floor. I let my head roll over and realized that I was lying on a bed of soft, springy branches. Opposite my bed was another bed, and between them crackled a cheery campfire. "Fire now we have, Davidge. And wood." Jerry pointed toward the roof made of wooden poles thatched with broad leaves.

I turned and looked around, then let my throbbing head sink down and closed my eyes. "Where are we?"

"Big island, Davidge. Soaker off sandbar us washed. Wind and waves us here took. Right you were."

"I . . . I don't understand; *ne gavey*. It'd take days to get to the big island from the sandbar."

Jerry nodded and dropped what looked like a sponge into a shell of some sort filled with water. "Nine days. You I strap to *nasesay*, then here on beach we land."

"Nine days? I've been out for nine days?"

Jerry shook his head. "Seventeen. Here we land eight days . . ." The Drac waved its hand behind itself.

"Ago . . . eight days ago."

"*Ae.*"

Seventeen days on Fyrine IV was better than a month on Earth. I opened my eyes again and looked at Jerry. The Drac was almost bubbling with excitement. "What about your *tean*, your child?"

Jerry patted its swollen middle. "Good is, Davidge. You more *nasesay* hurt."

I overcame an urge to nod. "I'm happy for you." I closed my eyes and turned my face toward the wall, a combination of wood poles and leaves. "Jerry?"

"*Ess?*"

"You saved my life."

"*Ae.*"

"Why?"

Jerry sat quietly for a long time. "Davidge. On sandbar you talk. Loneliness now *gavey.*" The Drac shook my arm. "Here, now you eat."

I turned and looked into a shell filled with a steaming liquid. "What is it, chicken soup?"

"*Ess?*"

"*Ess va?*" I pointed at the bowl, realizing for the first time how weak I was. Jerry frowned. "Like slug, but long."

"An eel?"

"*Ae*, but eel on land, *gavey?*"

"You mean 'snake'?"

"Possiblemaybeperhaps."

I nodded and put my lips to the edge of the shell. I sipped some of the broth, swallowed and let the broth's healing warmth seep through my body. "Good."

"You *custa* want?"

"*Ess?*"

"*Custa.*" Jerry reached next to the fire and picked up a squareish chunk of clear rock. I looked at it, scratched it with my thumbnail, then touched it with my tongue.

"Halite! Salt!"

Jerry smiled. "*Custa* you want?"

I laughed. "All the comforts. By all means, let's have *custa.*"

Jerry took the halite, knocked off a corner with a small stone, then used the stone to grind the pieces against another stone. He held out the palm of his hand with a tiny mountain of white granules in the center. I took two pinches, dropped them into my snake soup and stirred it with my finger. Then I took a long swallow of the delicious broth. I smacked my lips. "Fantastic."

"Good, *ne?*"

"Better than good; fantastic." I took another swallow, making a big show of smacking my lips and rolling my eyes.

"Fantastic, Davidge, *ne?*"

"*Ae.*" I nodded at the Drac. "I think that's enough. I want to sleep."

"*Ae*, Davidge, *gavey.*" Jerry took the bowl and put it beside the fire. The Drac stood, walked to the door and turned back. Its yellow eyes studied me for an instant, then it nodded, turned and went outside. I closed my eyes and let the heat from the campfire coax the sleep over me.

In two days I was up in the shack trying my legs, and in two more days Jerry helped me outside. The shack was located at the top of a long gentle rise in a scrub forest; none of the trees was any taller than five or six meters. At the bottom of the slope, better than eight kilometers from the shack, was the still-rolling sea. The Drac had carried me. Our trusty *nasesay* had filled with water and had been dragged back into the sea soon after Jerry pulled me to dry land. With it went the remainder of the ration bars. Dracs are very fussy about what they eat, but hunger finally drove Jerry to sample some of the local flora and fauna—hunger and the human lump that was rapidly drifting away from lack of nourishment. The Drac had settled on a bland, starchy type of root, a green bushberry that when dried made an acceptable tea, and snake-meat. Exploring, Jerry had found a partly eroded salt dome. In the days that followed, I grew stronger and added to our diet with several types of sea mollusk and a fruit resembling a cross between a pear and a plum.

As the days grew colder, the Drac and I were forced to realize that Fyrine IV had a winter. Given that, we had to face the possibility that the winter would be severe enough to prevent the gathering of food—and wood. When dried next to the fire, the berrybush and roots kept well, and we tried both salting and smoking snakemeat. With strips of fiber from the berry-bush for thread, Jerry and I pieced together the snakeskins for winter clothing. The design we settled on involved two layers of skins with the down from berrybush seed pods stuffed between and then held in place by quilting the layers.

We agreed that the house would never do. It took three days of searching to find our first cave, and another three days before we found one that suited us. The mouth opened onto a view of the eternally tormented sea, but was set in the face of a low cliff well above sea level. Around the cave's entrance we found great quantities of dead wood and loose stone. The wood we gathered for heat; and the stone we used to wall up the entrance, leaving only space enough for a hinged door. The hinges were made of snake leather and the door of wooden poles tied together with berrybush fiber. The first night after completing the door, the sea winds blew it to pieces; and we decided to go back to the original door design we had used on the sandbar.

Deep inside the cave, we made our living quarters in a chamber with a wide, sandy floor. Still deeper, the cave had natural pools of water, which were fine for drinking but too cold for bathing. We used the pool chamber for our supply room. We lined the walls of our living quarters with piles of wood and made new beds out of snakeskins and seed pod down. In the center of the chamber we built a respectable fireplace with a large, flat stone over the coals for a griddle. The first night we spent in our new home, I discovered that, for the first time since ditching on that damned planet, I couldn't hear the wind.

During the long nights, we would sit at the fireplace making things— gloves, hats, packbags—out of snake leather, and we would talk. To break the monotony, we alternated days between speaking Drac and English, and by the time the winter hit with its first ice storm, each of us was comfortable in the other's language.

We talked of Jerry's coming child.

"What are you going to name it, Jerry?"

"It already has a name. See, the Jeriba line has five names. My name is Shigan; before me came my parent, Gothig; before Gothig was Haesni; before Haesni was Ty, and before Ty was Zammis. The child is named Jeriba Zammis."

"Why only the five names? A human child can have just about any name its parents pick for it. In fact, once a human becomes an adult, he or she can pick any name he or she wants."

The Drac looked at me, its eyes filled with pity. "Davidge, how lost you must feel. You humans—how lost you must feel."

"Lost?"

Jerry nodded. "Where do you come from, Davidge?"

"You mean my parents?"

"Yes."

I shrugged. "I remember my parents."

"And their parents?"

"I remember my mother's father. When I was young we used to visit him."

"Davidge, what do you know about this grandparent?"

I rubbed my chin. "It's kind of vague . . . I think he was in some kind of agriculture—I don't know."

"And his parents?"

I shook my head. "The only thing I remember is that somewhere along the line, English and Germans figured. *Gavey* Germans and English?"

Jerry nodded. "Davidge, I can recite the history of my line back to the founding of my planet by Jeriba Ty, one of the original settlers, one hundred and ninety-nine generations ago. At our line's archives on Draco, there are the records that trace the line across space to the racehome planet, Sindie, and there back seventy generations to Jeriba Ty, the founder of the Jeriba line."

"How does one become a founder?"

"Only the firstborn carries the line. Products of second, third, or fourth births must found their own lines."

I nodded, impressed. "Why only the five names? Just to make it easier to remember them?"

Jerry shook its head. "No. The names are things to which we add distinction; they are the same, commonplace five so that they do not overshadow the events that distinguish their bearers. The name I carry, Shigan, has been served by great soldiers, scholars, students of philosophy, and several priests. The name my child will carry has been served by scientists, teachers, and explorers."

"You remember all of your ancestors' occupations?"

Jerry nodded. "Yes, and what they each did and where they did it. You must recite your line before the line's archives to be admitted into adulthood as I was twenty-two of my years ago. Zammis will do the same, except the child must begin its recitation"—Jerry smiled—"with my name, Jeriba Shigan."

"You can recite almost two hundred biographies from memory?"

"Yes."

I went over to my bed and stretched out. As I stared up at the smoke being sucked through the crack in the chamber's ceiling, I began to understand what Jerry meant by feeling lost. A Drac with several dozens of generations under its belt knew who it was and what it had to live up to.

"Jerry?"

"Yes, Davidge?"

"Will you recite them for me?" I turned my head and looked at the Drac in time to see an expression of utter surprise melt into joy. It was only after many years had passed that I learned I had done Jerry a great honor in requesting his line. Among the Dracs, it is a rare expression of respect, not only of the individual, but of the line.

Jerry placed the hat he was sewing on the sand, stood and began.

*"Before you here, I stand, Shigan of the line of Jeriba, born of Gothig, the teacher of music. A musician of high merit, the students of Gothig include Datzizh of the Nem line, Perravane of the Tuscor line, and many lesser musicians. Trained in music at the Shimuram, Gothig stood before the archives in the year 11,051 and spoke of its parent Haesni, the manufacturer of ships . . ."*

As I listened to Jerry's singsong of formal Dracon, the backward biographies—beginning with death and ending with adulthood—I experienced a sense of time-binding, of being able to know and touch the past. Battles, empires built and destroyed, discoveries made, great things done—a tour through twelve thousand years of history, but perceived as a well-defined, living continuum.

Against this: I, Willis of the Davidge line, stand before you, born of Sybil the housewife and Nathan the second-rate civil engineer, one of them born of Grandpop, who probably had something to do with agriculture, born of nobody in particular. . . . Hell, I wasn't even that! My older brother carried the line; not me. I listened and made up my mind to memorize the line of Jeriba.

We talked of war:

"That was a pretty neat trick, suckering me into the atmosphere, then ramming me."

Jerry shrugged. "Dracon fleet pilots are best; this is well known."

I raised my eyebrows. "That's why I shot your tail feathers off, huh?"

Jerry shrugged, frowned, and continued sewing on the scraps of snake leather. "Why do the Earthmen invade this part of the galaxy, Davidge? We had thousands of years of peace before you came."

"Hah! Why do the Dracs invade? We were at peace too. What are you doing here?"

"We settle these planets. It is the Drac tradition. We are explorers and founders."

"Well, toad face, what do you think we are, a bunch of homebodies? Humans have had space travel for less than two hundred years, but we've settled almost twice as many planets as the Dracs—"

Jerry held up a finger. "Exactly! You humans spread like a disease. Enough! We don't want you here!"

"Well, we're here, and here to stay. Now what are you going to do about it?"

"You see what we do, *Irkmaan*, we fight!"

"Phooey! You call that little scrap we were in a fight? Hell, Jerry, we were kicking you junk jocks out of the sky—"

"Haw, Davidge! That's why you sit here sucking on smoked snakemeat!"

I pulled the little rascal out of my mouth and pointed it at the Drac. "I notice your breath has a snake flavor too, Drac!"

Jerry snorted and turned away from the fire. I felt stupid, first because we weren't going to settle an argument that had plagued a hundred worlds for over a century. Second, I wanted to have Jerry check my recitation. I had over a hundred generations memorized. The Drac's side was toward the fire, leaving enough light falling on its lap to see its sewing.

"Jerry, what are you working on?"

"We have nothing to talk about, Davidge."

"Come on, what is it?"

Jerry turned its head toward me, then looked back into its lap and picked up a tiny snakeskin suit. "For Zammis." Jerry smiled and I shook my head, then laughed.

We talked of philosophy:

"You studied Shizumaat, Jerry; why won't you tell me about its teachings?"

Jerry frowned. "No, Davidge."

"Are Shizumaat's teachings secret or something?"

Jerry shook its head. "No. But we honor Shizumaat too much for talk."

I rubbed my chin. "Do you mean too much to talk about it, or to talk about it with a human?"

"Not with humans, Davidge; just not with you."

"Why?"

Jerry lifted its head and narrowed its yellow eyes. "You know what you said . . . on the sandbar."

I scratched my head and vaguely recalled the curse I laid on the Drac about Shizumaat eating it. I held out my hands. "But, Jerry, I was mad, angry. You can't hold me accountable for what I said then."

"I do."

"Will it change anything if I apologize?"

"Not a thing."

I stopped myself from saying something nasty and thought back to that moment when Jerry and I stood ready to strangle each other. I remembered something about that meeting and screwed the corners of my mouth in place to keep from smiling. "Will you tell me Shizumaat's teachings if I forgive you . . . for what you said about Mickey Mouse?" I bowed my head in an appearance of reverence, although its chief purpose was to suppress a cackle.

Jerry looked up at me, its face pained with guilt. "I have felt bad about that, Davidge. If you forgive me, I will talk about Shizumaat."

"Then I forgive you, Jerry."

"One more thing."

"What?"

"You must tell me of the teachings of Mickey Mouse."

"I'll . . . uh, do my best."

We talked of Zammis:

"Jerry, what do you want little Zammy to be?"

The Drac shrugged. "Zammis must live up to its own name. I want it to do that with honor. If Zammis does that, it is all I can ask."

"Zammy will pick its own trade?"

"Yes."

"Isn't there anything special you want, though?"

Jerry nodded. "Yes, there is."

"What's that?"

"That Zammis will, one day, find itself off this miserable planet."

I nodded. "Amen."

"Amen."

The winter dragged on until Jerry and I began wondering if we had gotten in on the beginning of an ice age. Outside the cave, everything was coated with a thick layer of ice, and the low temperature combined with the steady winds made venturing outside a temptation of death by falls or freezing. Still, by mutual agreement, we both went outside to relieve ourselves. There were several isolated chambers deep in the cave; but we feared polluting our water supply, not to mention the air inside the cave. The main risk outside was dropping one's drawers at a wind chill factor that froze breath vapor before it could be blown through the thin face muffs we had made out of our flight suits. We learned not to dawdle.

One morning, Jerry was outside answering the call, while I stayed by the fire mashing up dried roots with water for griddle cakes. I heard Jerry call from the mouth of the cave. "Davidge!"

"What?"

"Davidge, come quick!"

A ship! It had to be! I put the shell bowl on the sand, put on my hat and gloves, and ran through the passage. As I came close to the door, I untied the muff from around my neck and tied it over my mouth and nose to protect my lungs. Jerry, its head bundled in a similar manner, was looking through the door, waving me on. "What is it?"

Jerry stepped away from the door to let me through. "Come, look!"

Sunlight. Blue sky and sunlight. In the distance, over the sea, new clouds were piling up; but above us the sky was clear. Neither of us could look at the sun directly, but we turned our faces to it and felt the rays of Fyrine on our skins. The light glared and sparkled off the ice-covered rocks and trees. "Beautiful."

"Yes." Jerry grabbed my sleeve with a gloved hand. "Davidge, you know what this means?"

"What?"

"Signal fires at night. On a clear night, a large fire could be seen from orbit, *ne?*"

I looked at Jerry, then back at the sky. "I don't know. If the fire were big enough, and we get a clear night, and if anybody picks that moment to look . . ." I let my head hang down. "That's always supposing that there's someone in orbit up there to do the looking." I felt the pain begin in my fingers. "We better go back in."

"Davidge, it's a chance!"

"What are we going to use for wood, Jerry?" I held out an arm toward the trees above and around the cave. "Everything that can burn has at least fifteen centimeters of ice on it."

"In the cave—"

"Our firewood?" I shook my head. "How long is this winter going to last? Can you be sure that we have enough wood to waste on signal fires?"

"It's a chance, Davidge. It's a chance!"

Our survival riding on a toss of the dice. I shrugged. "Why not?"

We spent the next few hours hauling a quarter of our carefully gathered firewood and dumping it outside the mouth of the cave. By the time we were finished and long before night came, the sky was again a solid blanket of grey. Several times each night, we would check the sky, waiting for stars to appear. During the days, we would frequently have to spend several hours beating the ice off the wood pile. Still, it gave both of us hope, until the wood in the cave ran out and we had to start borrowing from the signal pile.

That night, for the first time, the Drac looked absolutely defeated. Jerry sat at the fireplace, staring at the flames. Its hand reached inside its snakeskin jacket through the neck and pulled out a small golden cube suspended on a chain. Jerry held the cube clasped in both hands, shut its eyes, and began mumbling in Drac. I watched from my bed until Jerry finished. The Drac sighed, nodded, and replaced the object within its jacket.

"What's that thing?"

Jerry looked up at me, frowned, then touched the front of its jacket. "This? It is my *Talman*—what you call a Bible."

"A Bible is a book. You know, with pages that you read."

Jerry pulled the thing from its jacket, mumbled a phrase in Drac, then worked a small catch. Another gold cube dropped from the first and the Drac held it out to me. "Be very careful with it, Davidge."

I sat up, took the object, and examined it in the light of the fire. Three hinged pieces of the golden metal formed the binding of a book two-and-a-half centimeters on an edge. I opened the book in the middle and looked over the double columns of dots, lines, and squiggles. "It's in Drac."

"Of course."

"But I can't read it."

Jerry's eyebrows went up. "You speak Drac so well, I didn't remember . . . would you like me to teach you?"

"To read this?"

"Why not? You have an appointment you have to keep?"

I shrugged. "No." I touched my finger to the book and tried to turn one of the tiny pages. Perhaps fifty pages went at once. "I can't separate the pages."

Jerry pointed at a small bump at the top of the spine. "Pull out the pin. It's for turning the pages."

I pulled out the short needle, touched it against a page, and it slid loose of its companion and flipped. "Who wrote your *Talman*, Jerry?"

"Many. All great teachers."

"Shizumaat?"

Jerry nodded. "Shizumaat is one of them."

I closed the book and held it in the palm of my hand. "Jerry, why did you bring this out now?"

"I needed its comfort." The Drac held out its arms. "This place. Maybe we will grow old here and die. Maybe we will never be found. I see this today as we brought in the signal fire wood." Jerry placed its hands on its belly. "Zammis will be born here. The *Talman* helps me to accept what I cannot change."

"Zammis, how much longer?"

Jerry smiled. "Soon."

I looked at the tiny book. "I would like you to teach me to read this, Jerry."

The Drac took the chain and case from around its neck and handed it to me. "You must keep the *Talman* in this."

I held it for a moment, then shook my head. "I can't keep this, Jerry. It's obviously of great value to you. What if I lost it?"

"You won't. Keep it while you learn. The student must do this."

I put the chain around my neck. "This is quite an honor you do me."

Jerry shrugged. "Much less than the honor you do me by memorizing the Jeriba line. Your recitations have been accurate, and moving." Jerry took some charcoal from the fire, stood, and walked to the wall of the chamber. That night I learned the thirty-one letters and sounds of the Drac alphabet, as well as the additional nine sounds and letters used in formal Drac writings.

* * *

The wood eventually ran out. Jerry was very heavy and very, very sick as Zammis prepared to make its appearance, and it was all the Drac could do to waddle outside with my help to relieve itself. Hence, wood gathering, which involved taking our remaining stick and beating the ice off the dead standing trees, fell to me, as did cooking.

On a particularly blustery day, I noticed that the ice on the trees was thinner. Somewhere we had turned winter's corner and were heading for spring. I spent my ice-pounding time feeling great at the thought of spring, and I knew Jerry would pick up some at the news. The winter was really getting the Drac down. I was working the woods above the cave, taking armloads of gathered wood and dropping them down below, when I heard a scream. I froze, then looked around. I could see nothing but the sea and the ice around me. Then, the scream again. "Davidge!" It was Jerry. I dropped the load I was carrying and ran to the cleft in the cliff's face that served as a path to the upper woods. Jerry screamed again; and I slipped, then rolled until I came to the shelf level with the cave's mouth. I rushed through the entrance, down the passageway until I came to the chamber. Jerry writhed on its bed, digging its fingers into the sand.

I dropped on my knees next to the Drac. "I'm here, Jerry. What is it? What's wrong?"

"Davidge!" The Drac rolled its eyes, seeing nothing; its mouth worked silently, then exploded with another scream.

"Jerry, it's me!" I shook the Drac's shoulder. "It's me, Jerry. Davidge!"

Jerry turned its head toward me, grimaced, then clasped the fingers of one hand around my left wrist with the strength of pain. "Davidge! Zammis . . . something's gone wrong!"

"What? What can I do?"

Jerry screamed again, then its head fell back to the bed in a half-faint. The Drac fought back to consciousness and pulled my head down to its lips. "Davidge, you must swear."

"What, Jerry? Swear what?"

"Zammis . . . on Draco. To stand before the line's archives. Do this."

"What do you mean? You talk like you're dying."

"I am, Davidge. Zammis two-hundredth generation . . . very important. Present my child, Davidge. Swear!"

I wiped the sweat from my face with my free hand. "You're not going to die, Jerry. Hang on!"

"Enough! Face truth, Davidge! I die! You must teach the line of Jeriba to Zammis . . . and the book, the *Talman*, gavey?"

"Stop it!" Panic stood over me almost as a physical presence. "Stop talking like that! You aren't going to die, Jerry. Come on; fight, you *kizlode* son-ofabitch . . ."

Jerry screamed. Its breathing was weak and the Drac drifted in and out of consciousness. "Davidge."

"What?" I realized I was sobbing like a kid.

"Davidge, you must help Zammis come out."

"What . . . how? What in the Hell are you talking about?"

Jerry turned its face to the wall of the cave. "Lift my jacket."

"What?"

"Lift my jacket, Davidge. Now!"

I pulled up the snakeskin jacket, exposing Jerry's swollen belly. The fold down the center was bright red and seeping a clear liquid. "What . . . what should I do?"

Jerry breathed rapidly, then held its breath. "Tear it open! You must tear it open, Davidge!"

"No!"

"Do it! Do it, or Zammis dies!"

"What do I care about your goddamn child, Jerry? What do I have to do to save you?"

"Tear it open . . ." whispered the Drac. "Take care of my child, *Irkmaan*. Present Zammis before the Jeriba archives. Swear this to me."

"Oh, Jerry . . ."

*"Swear this!"*

I nodded, hot fat tears dribbling down my cheeks. "I swear it. . . ." Jerry relaxed its grip on my wrist and closed its eyes. I knelt next to the Drac, stunned. "No. No, no, no, no."

*Tear it open! You must tear it open, Davidge!*

I reached up a hand and gingerly touched the fold on Jerry's belly. I could feel life struggling beneath it, trying to escape the airless confines of the Drac's womb. I hated it; I hated the damned thing as I never hated anything before. Its struggles grew weaker, then stopped.

*Present Zammis before the Jeriba archives. Swear this to me. . . .*

*I swear it. . . .*

I lifted my other hand and inserted my thumbs into the fold and tugged gently. I increased the amount of force, then tore at Jerry's belly like a madman. The fold burst open, soaking the front of my jacket with the clear fluid. Holding the fold open, I could see the still form of Zammis huddled in a well of the fluid, motionless.

I vomited. When I had nothing more to throw up, I reached into the fluid and put my hands under the Drac infant. I lifted it, wiped my mouth on my upper left sleeve, and closed my mouth over Zammis's and pulled the child's mouth open with my right hand. Three times, four times, I inflated the child's lungs, then it coughed. Then it cried. I tied off the two umbilicals with berrybush fiber, then cut them. Jeriba Zammis was freed of the dead flesh of its parent.

I held the rock over my head, then brought it down with all of my force upon the ice. Shards splashed away from the point of impact, exposing the dark green beneath. Again, I lifted the rock and brought it down, knocking loose another rock. I picked it up, stood and carried it to the half-covered corpse of the Drac. "The Drac," I whispered. *Good. Just call it "the Drac." Toad face. Dragger. The enemy. Call it anything to insulate those feelings against the pain.*

I looked at the pile of rocks I had gathered, decided it was sufficient to finish the job, then knelt next to the grave. As I placed the rocks on the pile, unmindful of the gale-blown sleet freezing on my snakeskins, I fought back the tears. I smacked my hands together to help restore the circulation. Spring was coming, but it was still dangerous to stay outside too long. And I had been a long time building the Drac's grave. I picked up another rock and placed it into position. As the rock's weight leaned against the snakeskin mattress cover, I realized that the Drac was already frozen. I quickly placed the remainder of the rocks, then stood.

The wind rocked me and I almost lost my footing on the ice next to the grave. I looked toward the boiling sea, pulled my snakeskins around myself more tightly, then looked down at the pile of rocks. *There should be words. You don't just cover up the dead, then go to dinner. There should be words.* But what words? I was no religionist, and neither was the Drac. Its formal philosophy on the matter of death was the same as my informal rejection of Islamic delights, pagan Valhallas, and Judeo-Christian pies in the sky. Death is death; *finis;* the end; the worms crawl in, the worms crawl out . . . *Still, there should be words.*

I reached beneath my snakeskins and clasped my gloved hand around the golden cube of the *Talman.* I felt the sharp corners of the cube through my glove, closed my eyes, and ran through the words of the great Drac philosophers. But there was nothing they had written for this moment.

The *Talman* was a book on life. *Talman* means "life," and this occupies Drac philosophy. They spare nothing for death. Death is a fact; the end of life. The *Talman* had no words for me to say. The wind knifed through me, causing me to shiver. Already my fingers were numb and pains were beginning in my feet. Still, there should be words. But the only words I could think of would open the gate, flooding my being with pain—with the realization that the Drac was gone. *Still . . . still, there should be words.*

"Jerry, I . . ." I had no words. I turned from the grave, my tears mixing with the sleet.

*   *   *

With the warmth and silence of the cave around me, I sat on my mattress, my back against the wall of the cave. I tried to lose myself in the shadows and flickers of light cast on the opposite wall by the fire. Images would half-form, then dance away before I could move my mind to see something in them. As a child I used to watch clouds, and in them see faces, castles, animals, dragons, and giants. It was a world of escape—fantasy; something to inject wonder and adventure into the mundane, regulated life of a middle-class boy leading a middle-class life. All I could see on the wall of the cave was a representation of Hell: flames licking at twisted, grotesque representations of condemned souls. I laughed at the thought. We think of Hell as fire, supervised by a cackling sadist in a red union suit. Fyrine IV taught me this much: Hell is loneliness, hunger, and endless cold.

I heard a whimper, and I looked into the shadows toward the small mattress at the back of the cave. Jerry had made the snakeskin sack filled with seed pod down for Zammis. It whimpered again, and I leaned forward, wondering if there was something it needed. A pang of fear tickled my guts. What does a Drac infant eat? Dracs aren't mammals. All they ever taught us in training was how to recognize Dracs—that, and how to kill them. Then real fear began working on me. "What in the hell am I going to use for diapers?"

It whimpered again. I pushed myself to my feet, walked the sandy floor to the infant's side, then knelt beside it. Out of the bundle that was Jerry's old flight suit, two chubby three-fingered arms waved. I picked up the bundle, carried it next to the fire, and sat on a rock. Balancing the bundle on my lap, I carefully unwrapped it. I could see the yellow glitter of Zammis's eyes beneath yellow, sleep-heavy lids. From the almost noseless face and solid teeth to its deep yellow color, Zammis was every bit a miniature of Jerry, except for the fat. Zammis fairly wallowed in rolls of fat. I looked, and was grateful to find that there was no mess.

I looked into Zammis's face. "You want something to eat?"

"*Guh.*"

Its jaws were ready for business, and I assumed that Dracs must chew solid food from day one. I reached over the fire and picked up a twist of dried snake, then touched it against the infant's lips. Zammis turned its head. "C'mon, eat. You're not going to find anything better around here."

I pushed the snake against its lips again, and Zammis pulled back a chubby arm and pushed it away. I shrugged. "Well, whenever you get hungry enough, it's there."

"*Guh meh!*" Its head rocked back and forth on my lap, a tiny, three-fingered hand closed around my finger, and it whimpered again.

"You don't want to eat, you don't need to be cleaned up, so what do you want? *Kos va nu?*"

Zammis's face wrinkled, and its hand pulled at my finger. Its other hand waved in the direction of my chest. I picked Zammis up to arrange the flight suit, and the tiny hands reached out, grasped the front of my snakeskins, and held on as the chubby arms pulled the child next to my chest. I held it close, it placed its cheek against my chest, and promptly fell asleep. "Well . . . I'll be damned."

Until the Drac was gone, I never realized how closely I had stood near the edge of madness. My loneliness was a cancer—a growth that I fed with hate: hate for the planet with its endless cold, endless winds, and endless isolation; hate for the helpless yellow child with its clawing need for care, food, and an affection that I couldn't give; and hate for myself. I found myself doing things that frightened and disgusted me. To break my solid wall of being alone, I would talk, shout, and sing to myself—uttering curses, nonsense, or meaning-less croaks.

Its eyes were open, and it waved a chubby arm and cooed. I picked up a large rock, staggered over to the child's side, and held the weight over the tiny body. "I could drop this thing, kid. Where would you be then?" I felt laughter coming from my lips. I threw the rock aside. "Why should I mess up the cave? Outside. Put you outside for a minute, and you die! You hear me? Die!"

The child worked its three-fingered hands at the empty air, shut its eyes, and cried. "Why don't you eat? Why don't you crap? Why don't you do any-thing right, but cry?" The child cried more loudly. "Bah! I ought to pick up that rock and finish it! That's what I ought . . ." A wave of revulsion stopped my words, and I went to my mattress, picked up my cap, gloves, and muff, then headed outside.

Before I came to the rocked-in entrance to the cave, I felt the bite of the wind. Outside I stopped and looked at the sea and sky—a roiling panorama in glorious black and white, grey and grey. A gust of wind slapped against me, rocking me back toward the entrance. I regained my balance, walked to the edge of the cliff, and shook my fist at the sea. "Go ahead! Go ahead and blow, you *kizlode* sonofabitch! You haven't killed me yet!"

I squeezed the wind-burned lids of my eyes shut, then opened them and looked down. A forty-meter drop to the next ledge, but if I took a running jump, I could clear it. Then it would be a hundred and fifty meters to the rocks below. *Jump*. I backed away from the cliff's edge. "Jump! Sure, jump!" I shook my head at the sea. "I'm not going to do your job for you! You want me dead, you're going to have to do it yourself!"

I looked back and up, above the entrance to the cave. The sky was darkening and in a few hours night would shroud the landscape. I turned toward the cleft in the rock that led to the scrub forest above the cave.

I squatted next to the Drac's grave and studied the rocks I had placed there, already fused together with a layer of ice. "Jerry. What am I going to do?"

*The Drac would sit by the fire, both of us sewing. And we talked.*

"You know, Jerry, all this," I held up the Talman, *"I've heard it all before. I expected something different."*

*The Drac lowered its sewing to its lap and studied me for an instant. Then it shook its head and resumed its sewing. "You are not a terribly profound creature, Davidge."*

*"What's that supposed to mean?"*

*Jerry held out a three-fingered hand. "A universe, Davidge—there is a universe out there, a universe of life, objects, and events. There are differences, but it is all the same universe, and we all must obey the same universal laws. Did you ever think of that?"*

*"No."*

*"That is what I mean, Davidge. Not terribly profound."*

*I snorted. "I told you, I'd heard this stuff before. So I imagine that shows humans to be just as profound as Dracs."*

*Jerry laughed. "You always insist on making something racial out of my observations. What I said applied to you, not to the race of humans. . . ."*

I spat on the frozen ground. "You Dracs think you're so damned smart." The wind picked up, and I could taste the sea salt in it. One of the big blows was coming. The sky was changing to that curious darkness that tricked me into thinking it was midnight blue, rather than black. A trickle of ice found its way under my collar.

"What's wrong with me just being me? Everybody in the universe doesn't have to be a damned philosopher, toad face!" There were millions—billions—like me. More maybe. "What difference does it make to anything whether I ponder existence or not? It's here; that's all I have to know."

*"Davidge, you don't even know your family line beyond your parents, and now you say you refuse to know that of your universe that you can know. How will you know your place in this existence, Davidge? Where are you? Who are you?"*

I shook my head and stared at the grave, then I turned and faced the sea. In another hour, or less, it would be too dark to see the whitecaps. "I'm me, that's who." But was that "me" who held the rock over Zammis, threatening a helpless infant with death? I felt my guts curdle as the loneliness I thought I felt grew claws and fangs and began gnawing and slashing at the remains of my sanity. I turned back to the grave, closed my eyes, then opened them. "I'm a fighter pilot, Jerry. Isn't that something?"

*"That is what you do, Davidge; that is neither who nor what you are."* I knelt next to the grave and clawed at the ice-sheathed rocks with my hands. "You don't talk to me now, Drac! *You're dead!*" I stopped, realizing that the words I had heard were from the *Talman*, processed into my own context. I slumped against the rocks, felt the wind, then pushed myself to my feet. "Jerry, Zammis won't eat. It's been three days. What do I do? Why didn't you tell me anything about Drac brats before you . . ." I held my hands to my face. "Steady, boy. Keep it up, and they'll stick you in a home." The wind pressed against my back, I lowered my hands, then walked from the grave.

I sat in the cave, staring at the fire. I couldn't hear the wind through the rock, and the wood was dry, making the fire hot and quiet. I tapped my fingers against my knee, then began humming. Noise, any kind, helped to drive off the oppressive loneliness. "Sonofabitch." I laughed and nodded. "Yea, verily, and *kizlode va nu, dutschaat.*" I chuckled, trying to think of all the curses and obscenities in Drac that I had learned from Jerry. There were quite a few. My toe tapped against the sand and my humming started up again. I stopped, frowned, then remembered the song.

> Highty tighty Christ almighty,
> Who the Hell are we?
> Zim zam, Gawd Damn,
> We're in Squadron B.

I leaned back against the wall of the cave, trying to remember another verse. *A pilot's got a rotten life/ no crumpets with our tea/ we have to service the general's wife/ and pick fleas from her knee.* "Damn!" I slapped my knee, trying to see the faces of the other pilots in the squadron lounge. I could almost feel the whiskey fumes tickling the inside of my nose. Vadik, Wooster, Arnold— the one with the broken nose—Demerest, Kadiz. I hummed again, swinging an imaginary mug of issue grog by its imaginary handle.

> And, if he doesn't like it,
> I'll tell you what we'll do:
> We'll fill his ass with broken glass,
> and seal it up with glue.

The cave echoed with the song. I stood, threw up my arms and screamed. "Yaaaaahoooooo!"

Zammis began crying. I bit my lip and walked over to the bundle on the mattress. "Well? You ready to eat?"

"Unh, unh, weh." The infant rocked its head back and forth. I went to the fire, picked up a twist of snake, then returned. I knelt next to Zammis and held the snake to its lips. Again, the child pushed it away. "Come on, you. You have to eat." I tried again with the same results. I took the wraps off the child and looked at its body. I could tell it was losing weight, although Zammis didn't appear to be getting weak. I shrugged, wrapped it up again, stood, and began walking back to my mattress.

"Guh, weh."

I turned. "What?"

"Ah, guh, guh."

I went back, stooped over and picked the child up. Its eyes were open and it looked into my face, then smiled.

"What're you laughing at, ugly? You should get a load of your own face."

Zammis barked out a short laugh, then gurgled. I went to my mattress, sat down, and arranged Zammis in my lap. "Gumma, buh, buh." Its hand grabbed a loose flap of snakeskin on my shirt and pulled on it.

"Gumma, buh, buh to you, too. So, what do we do now? How about I start teaching you the line of Jeriban? You're going to have to learn it sometime, and it might as well be now." The Jeriban line. My recitations of the line were the only things Jerry ever complimented me about. I looked into Zammis's eyes. "When I bring you to stand before the Jeriba archives, you will say this: 'Before you here I stand, Zammis of the line of Jeriba, born of Shigan, the fighter pilot.'" I smiled, thinking of the upraised yellow brows if Zammis continued, *"and, by damn, Shigan was a helluva good pilot, too. Why, I was once told he took a smart round in his tail feathers, then pulled around and rammed the* kizlode *sonofabitch, known to one and all as Willis E. Davidge . . ."* I shook my head. "You're not going to get your wings by doing the line in English, Zammis." I began again:

*"Naatha nu enta va, Zammis zea does Jeriba, estay va Shigan, asaam naa denvadar. . . ."*

For eight of those long days and nights, I feared the child would die. I tried everything—roots, dried berries, dried plumfruit, snakemeat dried, boiled, chewed, and ground. Zammis refused it all. I checked frequently, but each time I looked through the child's wraps, they were as clean as when I had put them on. Zammis lost weight, but seemed to grow stronger. By the ninth day it was crawling the floor of the cave. Even with the fire, the cave wasn't really warm. I feared that the kid would get sick crawling around naked, and I dressed it in the tiny snakeskin suit and cap Jerry had made for it. After dressing it, I stood Zammis up and looked at it. The kid had already developed a smile full of mischief that, combined with the twinkle in its yellow eyes and its suit and cap, made it look like an elf. I was holding Zammis up in a standing position. The kid seemed pretty steady on its legs, and I let go. Zammis smiled, waved its thinning arms about, then laughed and took a faltering step toward me. I caught it as it fell, and the little Drac squealed.

In two more days Zammis was walking and getting into everything that could be gotten into. I spent many an anxious moment searching the chambers at the back of the cave for the kid after coming in from outside. Finally, when I caught it at the mouth of the cave heading full steam for the outside, I had had enough. I made a harness out of snakeskin, attached it to a snake-leather leash, and tied the other end to a projection of rock above my head. Zammis still got into everything, but at least I could find it.

Four days after it learned to walk, it wanted to eat. Drac babies are probably the most convenient and considerate infants in the universe. They live off their fat for about three or four Earth weeks, and don't make a mess the entire time. After they learn to walk, and can therefore make it to a mutually agreed upon spot, then they want food and begin discharging wastes. I showed the kid once how to use the litter box I had made, and never had to again. After five or six lessons, Zammis was handling its own drawers. Watching the little Drac learn and grow, I began to understand those pilots in my squadron who used to bore each other—and everyone else—with countless pictures of ugly children, accompanied by thirty-minute narratives for each snapshot. Before the ice melted, Zammis was talking. I taught it to call me "Uncle."

For lack of a better term, I called the ice-melting season "spring." It would be a long time before the scrub forest showed any green or the snakes ventured forth from their icy holes. The sky maintained its eternal cover of dark, angry clouds, and still the sleet would come and coat everything with a hard, slippery glaze. But the next day the glaze would melt, and the warmer air would push another millimeter into the soil.

I realized that this was the time to be gathering wood. Before the winter hit, Jerry and I working together hadn't gathered enough wood. The short summer would have to be spent putting up food for the next winter. I was hoping to build a tighter door over the mouth of the cave, and I swore that I would figure out some kind of indoor plumbing. Dropping your drawers outside in the middle of winter was dangerous. My mind was full of these things as I stretched out on my mattress watching the smoke curl through a crack in the roof of the cave. Zammis was off in the back of the cave playing with some rocks that it had found, and I must have fallen asleep. I awoke with the kid shaking my arm.

"Uncle?"

"Huh? Zammis?"

"Uncle. Look."

I rolled over on my left side and faced the Drac. Zammis was holding up its right hand, fingers spread out. "What is it, Zammis?"

"Look." It pointed at each of its three fingers in turn. "One, two, three."

"So?"

"Look." Zammis grabbed my right hand and spread out the fingers. "One, two, three, *four, five!*"

I nodded. "So you can count to five."

The Drac frowned and made an impatient gesture with its tiny fists. "Look." It took my outstretched hand and placed its own on top of it. With its other hand, Zammis pointed first at one of its own fingers, then at one of mine. "One, one." The child's yellow eyes studied me to see if I understood.

"Yes."

The child pointed again. "Two, two." It looked at me, then looked back at my hand and pointed. "Three, three." Then he grabbed my two remaining fingers. *"Four, five?"* It dropped my hand, then pointed to the side of its own hand. "Four, five?"

I shook my head. Zammis, at less than four Earth months old, had detected part of the difference between Dracs and humans. A human child would be— what—five, six, or seven years old before asking questions like that. I sighed. "Zammis."

"Yes, Uncle?"

"Zammis, you are a Drac. Dracs only have three fingers on a hand." I held up my right hand and wiggled the fingers. "I'm a human. I have five."

I swear that tears welled in the child's eyes. Zammis held out its hands, looked at them, then shook its head. "Grow four, five?"

I sat up and faced the kid. Zammis was wondering where its other four fingers had gone. "Look, Zammis. You and I are different . . . different kinds of beings, understand?"

Zammis shook his head. "Grow four, five?"

"You won't. You're a Drac." I pointed at my chest. "I'm a human." This was getting me nowhere. "Your parent, where you came from, was a Drac. Do you understand?"

Zammis frowned. "Drac. What Drac?"

The urge to resort to the timeless standby of "you'll understand when you get older" pounded at the back of my mind. I shook my head. "Dracs have three fingers on each hand. Your parent had three fingers on each hand." I rubbed my beard. "My parent was a human and had five fingers on each hand. That's why I have five fingers on each hand."

Zammis knelt on the sand and studied its fingers. It looked up at me, back to its hands, then back to me. "What parent?"

I studied the kid. It must be having an identity crisis of some kind. I was the only person it had ever seen, and I had five fingers per hand. "A parent is . . . the thing . . ." I scratched my beard again. "Look . . . we all come from someplace. I had a mother and father—two different kinds of humans—that gave me life; that made me, understand?"

Zammis gave me a look that could be interpreted as "Mac, you are full of it." I shrugged. "I don't know if I can explain it."

Zammis pointed at its own chest. "My mother? My father?"

I held out my hands, dropped them into my lap, pursed my lips, scratched my beard, and generally stalled for time. Zammis held an unblinking gaze on me the entire time. "Look, Zammis. You don't have a mother and a father. I'm a human, so I have them; you're a Drac. You have a parent—just one, see?"

Zammis shook its head. It looked at me, then pointed at its own chest. "Drac."

"Right."

Zammis pointed at my chest. "Human."

"Right again."

Zammis removed its hand and dropped it in its lap. "Where Drac come from?"

Sweet Jesus! Trying to explain hermaphroditic reproduction to a kid who shouldn't even be crawling yet! "Zammis . . ." I held up my hands, then dropped them into my lap. "Look. You see how much bigger I am than you?"

"Yes, Uncle."

"Good." I ran my fingers through my hair, fighting for time and inspiration. "Your parent was big, like me. Its name was . . . Jeriba Shigan." Funny how just saying the name was painful. "Jeriba Shigan was like you. It only had three fingers on each hand. It grew you in its tummy." I poked Zammis's middle. "Understand?"

Zammis giggled and held its hands over its stomach. "Uncle, how Dracs grow there?"

I lifted my legs onto the mattress and stretched out. Where do little Dracs come from? I looked over to Zammis and saw the child hanging upon my every word. I grimaced and told the truth. "Damned if I know, Zammis. Damned if I know." Thirty seconds later, Zammis was back playing with its rocks.

Summer, and I taught Zammis how to capture and skin the long grey snakes, and then how to smoke the meat. The child would squat on the shallow bank above a mudpool, its yellow eyes fixed on the snake holes in the bank, waiting for one of the occupants to poke out its head. The wind would blow, but Zammis wouldn't move. Then a flat, triangular head set with tiny blue eyes would appear. The snake would check the pool, turn and check the bank, then check the sky. It would advance out of the hole a bit, then check it all again. Often the snakes would look directly at Zammis, but the Drac could have been carved from rock. Zammis wouldn't move until the snake was too far out of the hole to pull itself back in tail first. Then Zammis would strike, grabbing the snake with both hands just behind the head. The snakes had no fangs and weren't poisonous, but they were lively enough to toss Zammis into the mudpool on occasion.

The skins were spread and wrapped around tree trunks and pegged in place to dry. The tree trunks were kept in an open place near the entrance to the cave, but under an overhang that faced away from the ocean. About two thirds of the skins put up in this manner cured; the remaining third would rot.

Beyond the skin room was the smokehouse: a rock-walled chamber that we would hang with rows of snakemeat. A greenwood fire would be set in a pit in the chamber's floor; then we would fill in the small opening with rocks and dirt.

"Uncle, why doesn't the meat rot after it's smoked?"

I thought upon it. "I'm not sure; I just know it doesn't."

"Why do you know?"

I shrugged. "I just do. I read about it, probably."

"What's read?"

"Reading. Like when I sit down and read the *Talman.*"

"Does the *Talman* say why the meat doesn't rot?"

"No. I meant that I probably read it in another book."

"Do we have more books?"

I shook my head. "I meant before I came to this planet."

"Why did you come to this planet?"

"I told you. Your parent and I were stranded here during the battle."

"Why do the humans and Dracs fight?"

"It's very complicated." I waved my hands about for a bit. The human line was that the Dracs were aggressors invading our space. The Drac line was that the humans were aggressors invading their space. The truth? "Zammis, it has to do with the colonization of new planets. Both races are expanding and both races have a tradition of exploring and colonizing new planets. I guess we just expanded into each other. Understand?"

Zammis nodded, then became mercifully silent as it fell into deep thought. The main thing I learned from the Drac child was all of the questions I didn't have answers to. I was feeling very smug, however, at having gotten Zammis to understand about the war, thereby avoiding my ignorance on the subject of preserving meat. "Uncle?"

"Yes, Zammis?"

"What's a planet?"

As the cold, wet summer came to an end, we had the cave jammed with firewood and preserved food. With that out of the way, I concentrated my efforts on making some kind of indoor plumbing out of the natural pools in the chambers deep within the cave. The bathtub was no problem. By dropping heated rocks into one of the pools, the water could be brought up to a bearable—even comfortable—temperature. After bathing, the hollow stems of a bamboolike plant could be used to siphon out the dirty water. The tub could then be refilled from the pool above. The problem was where to siphon the water. Several of the chambers had holes in their floors. The first three holes we tried drained into our main chamber, wetting the low edge near the entrance. The previous winter, Jerry and I had considered using one of those holes for a toilet that we would flush with water from the pools. Since we didn't know where the goodies would come out, we decided against it.

The fourth hole Zammis and I tried drained out below the entrance to the cave in the face of the cliff. Not ideal, but better than answering the call of nature in the middle of a combination ice storm and blizzard. We rigged up the hole as a drain for both the tub and toilet. As Zammis and I prepared to enjoy our first hot bath, I removed my snakeskins, tested the water with my toe, then stepped in. "Great!" I turned to Zammis, the child still half dressed. "Come on in, Zammis. The water's fine." Zammis was staring at me, its mouth hanging open. "What's the matter?"

The child stared wide-eyed, then pointed at me with a three-fingered hand. "Uncle . . . what's that?"

I looked down. "Oh." I shook my head, then looked up at the child. "Zammis, I explained all that, remember? I'm a human."

"But what's it *for?*"

I sat down in the warm water, removing the object of discussion from sight. "It's for the elimination of liquid wastes . . . among other things. Now, hop in and get washed."

Zammis shucked its snakeskins, looked down at its own smooth-surfaced, combined system, then climbed into the tube. The child settled into the water up to its neck, its yellow eyes studying me. "Uncle?"

"Yes?"

"What *other things?*"

Well, I told Zammis. For the first time, the Drac appeared to be trying to decide whether my response was truthful or not, rather than its usual acceptance of my every assertion. In fact, I was convinced that Zammis thought I was lying—probably because I was.

Winter began with a sprinkle of snowflakes carried on a gentle breeze. I took Zammis above the cave to the scrub forest. I held the child's hand as we stood before the pile of rocks that served as Jerry's grave. Zammis pulled its snakeskins against the wind, bowed its head, then turned and looked up into my face. "Uncle, this is the grave of my parent?"

I nodded. "Yes."

Zammis turned back to the grave, then shook its head. "Uncle, how should I feel?"

"I don't understand, Zammis."

The child nodded at the grave. "I can see that you are sad being here. I think you want me to feel the same. Do you?"

I frowned, then shook my head. "No. I don't want you to be sad. I just wanted you to know where it is."

"May I go now?"

"Sure. Are you certain you know the way back to the cave?"

"Yes. I just want to make sure my soap doesn't burn again."

I watched as the child turned and scurried off into the naked trees, then I turned back to the grave. "Well, Jerry, what do you think of your kid? Zammis was using wood ashes to clean the grease off the shells, then it put a shell back on the fire and put water in it to boil off the burnt-on food. Fat and ashes. The next thing, Jerry, we were making soap. Zammis's first batch almost took the hide off us, but the kid's getting better . . ."

I looked up at the clouds, then brought my glance down to the sea. In the distance, low, dark clouds were building up. "See that? You know what that means, don't you? Ice storm number one." The wind picked up and I squatted next to the grave to replace a rock that had rolled from the pile. "Zammis is a good kid, Jerry. I wanted to hate it . . . after you died. I wanted to hate it." I replaced the rock, then looked back toward the sea.

"I don't know how we're going to make it off planet, Jerry—" I caught a flash of movement out of the corner of my vision. I turned to the right and looked over the tops of the trees. Against the grey sky, a black speck streaked away. I followed it with my eyes until it went above the clouds.

I listened, hoping to hear an exhaust roar, but my heart was pounding so hard, all I could hear was the wind. Was it a ship? I stood, took a few steps in the direction the speck was going, then stopped. Turning my head, I saw that the rocks on Jerry's grave were already capped with thin layers of fine snow. I shrugged and headed for the cave. "Probably just a bird."

*   *   *

Zammis sat on its mattress, stabbing several pieces of snakeskin with a bone needle. I stretched out on my own mattress and watched the smoke curl up toward the crack in the ceiling. Was it a bird? Or was it a ship? Damn, but it worked on me. Escape from the planet had been out of my thoughts, had been buried, hidden for all that summer. But again, it twisted at me. To walk where a sun shined, to wear cloth again, experience central heating, eat food prepared by a chef, to be among . . . people again.

I rolled over on my right side and stared at the wall next to my mattress. People. Human people. I closed my eyes and swallowed. Girl human people. Female persons. Images drifted before my eyes—faces, bodies, laughing couples, the dance after flight training . . . what was her name? Dolora? Dora?

I shook my head, rolled over and sat up, facing the fire. Why did I have to see whatever it was? All those things I had been able to bury—to forget—boiling over.

"Uncle?"

I looked up at Zammis. Yellow skin, yellow eyes, noseless toad face. I shook my head. "What?"

"Is something wrong?"

Is something wrong, hah. "No. I just thought I saw something today. It probably wasn't anything." I reached to the fire and took a piece of dried snake from the griddle. I blew on it, then gnawed on the stringy strip.

"What did it look like?"

"I don't know. The way it moved, I thought it might be a ship. It went away so fast, I couldn't be sure. Might have been a bird."

"Bird?"

I studied Zammis. It'd never seen a bird; neither had I on Fyrine IV. "An animal that flies."

Zammis nodded. "Uncle, when we were gathering wood up in the scrub forest, I saw something fly."

"What? Why didn't you tell me?"

"I meant to, but I forgot."

"Forgot!" I frowned. "In which direction was it going?"

Zammis pointed to the back of the cave. "That way. Away from the sea." Zammis put down its sewing. "Can we go see where it went?"

I shook my head. "The winter is just beginning. You don't know what it's like. We'd die in only a few days."

Zammis went back to poking holes in the snakeskin. To make the trek in the winter would kill us. But spring would be something else. We could survive with double layered snakeskins stuffed with seed pod down, and a tent. We had to have a tent. Zammis and I could spend the winter making it, and packs. Boots. We'd need sturdy walking boots. Have to think on that . . .

It's strange how a spark of hope can ignite, and spread, until all desperation is consumed. Was it a ship? I didn't know. If it was, was it taking off, or landing? I didn't know. If it was taking off, we'd be heading in the wrong direction. But the opposite direction meant crossing the sea. Whatever. Come spring we would head beyond the scrub forest and see what was there.

The winter seemed to pass quickly, with Zammis occupied with the tent and my time devoted to rediscovering the art of boot making. I made tracings of both of our feet on snakeskin, and, after some experimentation, I found that boiling the snake leather with plumfruit made it soft and gummy. By taking several of the gummy layers, weighting them, then setting them aside to dry, the result was a tough, flexible sole. By the time I finished Zammis's boots, the Drac needed a new pair.

"They're too small, Uncle."

"Waddaya mean, too small?"

Zammis pointed down. "They hurt. My toes are all crippled up."

I squatted down and felt the tops over the child's toes. "I don't understand. It's only been twenty, twenty-five days since I made the tracings. You sure you didn't move when I made them?"

Zammis shook its head. "I didn't move."

I frowned, then stood. "Stand up, Zammis." The Drac stood and I moved next to it. The top of Zammis's head came to the middle of my chest. Another sixty centimeters and it'd be as tall as Jerry. "Take them off, Zammis. I'll make a bigger pair. Try not to grow so fast."

Zammis pitched the tent inside the cave, put glowing coals inside, then rubbed fat into the leather for waterproofing. It had grown taller, and I had held off making the Drac's boots until I could be sure of the size it would need. I tried to do a projection by measuring Zammis's feet every ten days, then extending the curve into spring. According to my figures, the kid would have feet resembling a pair of attack transports by the time the snow melted. By spring, Zammis would be full grown. Jerry's old flight boots had fallen apart before Zammis had been born, but I had saved the pieces. I used the soles to make my tracings and hoped for the best.

I was busy with the new boots and Zammis was keeping an eye on the tent treatment. The Drac looked back at me.

"Uncle?"

"What?"

"Existence is the first given?"

I shrugged. "That's what Shizumaat says; I'll buy it."

"But, Uncle, how do we *know* that existence is real?"

I lowered my work, looked at Zammis, shook my head, then resumed stitching the boots. "Take my word for it."

The Drac grimaced. "But, Uncle, that is not knowledge; that is faith."

I sighed, thinking back to my sophomore year at the University of Nations—a bunch of adolescents lounging around a cheap flat experimenting with booze, powders, and philosophy. At a little more than one Earth year old, Zammis was developing into an intellectual bore. "So, what's wrong with faith?"

Zammis snickered. "Come now, Uncle. *Faith?*"

"It helps some of us along this drizzle-soaked coil."

"Coil?"

I scratched my head. "This mortal coil; life. Shakespeare, I think."

Zammis frowned. "It is not in the *Talman.*"

"He, not it. Shakespeare was a human."

Zammis stood, walked to the fire and sat across from me. "Was he a philosopher, like Mistan or Shizumaat?"

"No. He wrote plays—like stories, acted out."

Zammis rubbed its chin. "Do you remember any of Shakespeare?"

I held up a finger. " 'To be, or not to be; that is the question.' "

The Drac's mouth dropped open; then it nodded its head. "Yes. Yes! To be or not to be; that *is* the question!" Zammis held out its hands. "How do we *know* the wind blows outside the cave when we are not there to see it? Does the sea still boil if we are not there to feel it?"

I nodded. "Yes."

"But, Uncle, how do we *know?*"

I squinted at the Drac. "Zammis, I have a question for you. Is the following statement true or false: What I am saying right now is false."

Zammis blinked. "If it is false, then the statement is true. But . . . if it's true . . . the statement is false, but . . ." Zammis blinked again, then turned and went back to rubbing fat into the tent. "I'll think upon it, Uncle."

"You do that, Zammis."

The Drac thought upon it for about ten minutes, then turned back. "The statement is false."

I smiled. "But that's what the statement said, hence it is true, but . . ." I let the puzzle trail off. Oh, smugness, thou temptest even saints.

"No, Uncle. The statement is meaningless in its present context." I shrugged. "You see, Uncle, the statement assumes the existence of truth values that can comment upon themselves devoid of any other reference. I think

Lurrvena's logic in the *Talman* is clear on this, and if meaninglessness is equated with falsehood . . ."

I sighed. "Yeah, well—"

"You see, Uncle, you must first establish a context in which your statement has meaning."

I leaned forward, frowned, and scratched my beard. "I see. You mean I was putting Descartes before the horse?"

Zammis looked at me strangely, and even more so when I collapsed on my mattress cackling like a fool.

"Uncle, why does the line of Jeriba have only five names? You say that human lines have many names."

I nodded. "The five names of the Jeriba line are things to which their bearers must add deeds. The deeds are important—not the names."

"Gothig is Shigan's parent as Shigan is my parent."

"Of course. You know that from your recitations."

Zammis frowned. "Then I *must* name my child Ty when I become a parent?"

"Yes. And Ty must name its child Haesni. Do you see something wrong with that?"

"I would like to name my child Davidge, after you."

I smiled and shook my head. "The Ty name has been served by great bankers, merchants, inventors, and—well, you know your recitation. The name Davidge hasn't been served by much. Think of what Ty would miss by not being Ty."

Zammis thought a while, then nodded. "Uncle, do you think Gothig is alive?"

"As far as I know."

"What is Gothig like?"

I thought back to Jerry talking about its parent, Gothig. "It taught music, and is very strong. Jerry . . . Shigan said that its parent could bend metal bars with its fingers. Gothig is also very dignified. I imagine that right now Gothig is also very sad. Gothig must think that the line of Jeriba has ended."

Zammis frowned and its yellow brow furrowed. "Uncle, we must make it to Draco. We must tell Gothig the line continues."

"We will."

The winter's ice began thinning, and boots, tent, and packs were ready. We were putting the finishing touches on our new insulated suits. As Jerry had given the *Talman* to me to learn, the golden cube now hung around Zammis's neck. The Drac would drop the tiny golden book from the cube and study it for hours at a time.

"Uncle?"

"What?"

"Why do Dracs speak and write in one language and the humans in another?"

I laughed. "Zammis, the humans speak and write in many languages. English is just one of them."

"How do the humans speak among themselves?"

I shrugged. "They don't always; when they do, they use interpreters—people who can speak both languages."

"You and I speak both English and Drac; does that make us interpreters?"

"I suppose we could be, if you could ever find a human and a Drac who want to talk to each other. Remember, there's a war going on."

"How will the war stop if they do not talk?"

"I suppose they will talk, eventually."

Zammis smiled. "I think I would like to be an interpreter and help end the war." The Drac put its sewing aside and stretched out on its new mattress. Zammis had outgrown even its old mattress, which it now used for a pillow. "Uncle, do you think that we will find anybody beyond the scrub forest?"

"I hope so."

"If we do, will you go with me to Draco?"

"I promised your parent that I would."

"I mean, after. After I make my recitation, what will you do?"

I stared at the fire. "I don't know." I shrugged. "The war might keep us from getting to Draco for a long time."

"After that, what?"

"I suppose I'll go back into the service."

Zammis propped itself up on an elbow. "Go back to being a fighter pilot?"

"Sure. That's about all I know how to do."

"And kill Dracs?"

I put my own sewing down and studied the Drac. Things had changed since Jerry and I had slugged it out—more things than I had realized. I shook my head. "No. I probably won't be a pilot—not a service one. Maybe I can land a job flying commercial ships." I shrugged. "Maybe the service won't give me any choice."

Zammis sat up, was still for a moment; then it stood, walked over to my mattress, and knelt before me on the sand. "Uncle, I don't want to leave you."

"Don't be silly. You'll have your own kind around you. Your grandparent, Gothig, Shigan's siblings, their children—you'll forget all about me."

"Will you forget about me?"

I looked into those yellow eyes, then reached out my hand and touched Zammis's cheek. "No, I won't forget about you. But, remember this, Zammis: you're a Drac and I'm a human, and that's how this part of the universe is divided."

Zammis took my hand from his cheek, spread the fingers and studied them. "Whatever happens, Uncle, I will never forget you."

The ice was gone, and the Drac and I stood in the wind-blown drizzle, packs on our backs, before the grave. Zammis was as tall as I was, which made it a little taller than Jerry. To my relief, the boots fit. Zammis hefted its pack up higher on its shoulders, then turned from the grave and looked out at the sea. I followed Zammis's glance and watched the rollers steam in and smash on the rocks. I looked at the Drac. "What are you thinking about?"

Zammis looked down, then turned toward me. "Uncle, I didn't think of it before, but . . . I will miss this place."

I laughed. "Nonsense! This place?" I slapped the Drac on the shoulder. "Why would you miss this place?"

Zammis looked back out to sea. "I have learned many things here. You have taught me many things here, Uncle. My life happened here."

"Only the beginning, Zammis. You have a life ahead of you." I nodded my head at the grave. "Say good-bye."

Zammis turned toward the grave, stood over it, then knelt to one side and began removing the rocks. After a few moments, it had exposed the hand of a skeleton with three fingers. Zammis nodded, then wept. "I am sorry, Uncle, but I had to do that. This has been nothing but a pile of rocks to me. Now it is more." Zammis replaced the rocks, then stood.

I cocked my head toward the scrub forest. "Go on ahead. I'll catch up in a minute."

"Yes, Uncle."

Zammis moved off toward the naked trees, and I looked down at the grave. "What do you think of Zammis, Jerry? It's bigger than you were. I guess snake agrees with the kid." I squatted next to the grave, picked up a small rock, and added it to the pile. "I guess this is it. We're either going to make it to Draco, or die trying." I stood and looked at the sea. "Yeah, I guess I learned a few things here. I'll miss it, in a way." I turned back to the grave and hefted my pack up. "*Ehdevva sahn, Jeriba Shigan.* So long, Jerry."

I turned and followed Zammis into the forest.

* * *

The days that followed were full of wonder for Zammis. For me the sky was still the same, dull grey, and the few variations of plant and animal life that we found were nothing remarkable. Once we got beyond the scrub forest, we climbed a gentle rise for a day, and then found ourselves on a wide, flat, endless plain. It was ankle deep in a purple weed that stained our boots the same color. The nights were still too cold for hiking, and we would hole up in the tent. Both the greased tent and suits worked well, keeping out the almost constant rain.

We had been out perhaps two of Fyrine IV's long weeks when we saw it. It screamed overhead, then disappeared over the horizon before either of us could say a word. I had no doubt that the craft I had seen was in landing attitude.

"Uncle! Did it see us?"

I shook my head. "No, I doubt it. But it was landing. Do you hear? It was landing somewhere ahead."

"Uncle?"

"Let's get moving! What is it?"

"Was it a Drac ship, or a human ship?"

I cooled in my tracks. I had never stopped to think about it. I waved my hand. "Come on. It doesn't matter. Either way, you go to Draco. You're a noncombatant, so the USE forces couldn't do anything, and if they're Dracs, you're home free."

We began walking. "But, Uncle, if it's a Drac ship, what will happen to you?"

I shrugged. "Prisoner of war. The Dracs say they abide by the interplanetary war accords, so I should be all right." *Fat chance*, said the back of my head to the front of my head. The big question was whether I preferred being a Drac POW or a permanent resident of Fyrine IV. I had figured that out long ago. "Come on, let's pick up the pace. We don't know how long it will take to get there, or how long it will be on the ground."

Pick 'em up; put 'em down. Except for a few breaks, we didn't stop—even when night came. Our exertion kept us warm. The horizon never seemed to grow nearer. The longer we slogged ahead the duller my mind grew. It must have been days, my mind gone numb as my feet, when I fell through the purple weed into a hole. Immediately, everything grew dark, and I felt a pain in my right leg. I felt the blackout coming, and I welcomed its warmth, its rest, its peace.

"Uncle? Uncle? Wake up! Please, wake up!"

I felt slapping against my face, although it felt somehow detached. Agony thundered into my brain, bringing me wide awake. Damned if I didn't break my leg. I looked up and saw the weedy edges of the hole. My rear end was seated in a trickle of water. Zammis squatted next to me.

"What happened?"

Zammis motioned upward. "This hole was only covered by a thin crust of dirt and plants. The water must have taken the ground away. Are you all right?"

"My leg. I think I broke it." I leaned my back against the muddy wall. "Zammis, you're going to have to go on by yourself."

"I can't leave you, Uncle!"

"Look, if you find anyone, you can send them back for me."

"What if the water in here comes up?" Zammis felt along my leg until I winced. "I must carry you out of here. What must I do for the leg?"

The kid had a point. Drowning wasn't in my schedule. "We need something stiff. Bind the leg so it doesn't move."

Zammis pulled off its pack, and kneeling in the water and mud, went through its pack, then through the tent roll. Using the tent poles, it wrapped my leg with snakeskins torn from the tent. Then, using more snakeskins, Zammis made two loops, slipped one over each of my legs, then propped me up and slipped the loops over its shoulders. It lifted, and I blacked out.

I was on the ground, covered with the remains of the tent, and Zammis was shaking my arm. "Uncle? Uncle?"

"Yes?" I whispered.

"Uncle, I'm ready to go." It pointed to my side. "Your food is here, and when it rains, just pull the tent over your face. I'll mark the trail I make so I can find my way back."

I nodded. "Take care of yourself."

Zammis shook its head. "Uncle, I can carry you. We shouldn't separate."

I weakly shook my head. "Give me a break, kid. I couldn't make it. Find somebody and bring 'em back." I felt my stomach flip, and cold sweat drenched my snakeskins. "Go on; get going."

Zammis reached out, grabbed its pack, and stood. The pack shouldered, Zammis turned and began running in the direction that the craft had been going. I watched until I couldn't see it. I faced up and looked at the clouds. "You almost got me that time, you *kizlode* sonofabitch, but you didn't figure on the Drac . . . you keep forgetting . . . there's two of us . . ." I drifted in and out of consciousness, felt rain on my face, then pulled up the tent and covered my head. In seconds, the blackout returned.

"Davidge? Lieutenant Davidge?"

I opened my eyes and saw something I hadn't seen for four Earth years: a human face. "Who are you?"

The face, young, long, and capped by short blond hair, smiled. "I'm Captain Steerman, the medical officer. How do you feel?"

I pondered the question and smiled. "Like I've been shot full of very high-grade junk."

"You have. You were in pretty bad shape by the time the survey team brought you in."

"Survey team?"

"I guess you don't know. The United States of Earth and the Dracon Chamber have established a joint commission to supervise the colonization of new planets. The war is over."

"Over?"

"Yes."

Something heavy lifted from my chest. "Where's Zammis?"

"Who?"

"Jeriba Zammis; the Drac that I was with."

The doctor shrugged. "I don't know anything about it, but I suppose the Draggers are taking care of it."

Draggers. I'd once used the term myself. As I listened to it coming out of Steerman's mouth, it seemed foreign: alien, repulsive. "Zammis is a Drac, not a Dragger."

The doctor's brows furrowed, then he shrugged. "Of course. Whatever you say. Just you get some rest, and I'll check back on you in a few hours."

"May I see Zammis?"

The doctor smiled. "Dear, no. You're on your way back to the Delphi USEB. The . . . Drac is probably on its way to Draco." He nodded, then turned and left. God, I felt lost. I looked around and saw that I was in the ward of a ship's sick bay. The beds on either side of me were occupied. The man on my right shook his head and went back to reading a magazine. The one on my left looked angry.

"You damned Dragger suck!" He turned on his left side and presented me his back.

Alien Earth. As I stepped down the ramp onto the USE field in Orleans, those were the first two words that popped into my head. Alien Earth. I looked at the crowds of USE Force personnel bustling around like so many ants, inhaled the smell of industrial man, then spat on the ramp.

"How you like, put in stockade time?"

I looked down and saw a white-capped Force Police private glaring up at me. I continued down the ramp. "Get bent."

*"Quoi?"* The FP marched over and met me at the end of the ramp.

"Get bent." I pulled my discharge papers from my breast pocket and waved them. *"Gavey* shorttimer, *kizlode?"*

The FP took my papers, frowned at them, then pointed at a long, low building at the edge of the field. *"Continuez tout droit."*

I smiled, turned and headed across the field, thinking of Zammis asking about how humans talk together. And where was Zammis? I shook my head, then entered the building. Most of the people inside the low building were crowding the in-processing or transportation-exchange aisles. I saw two bored officials behind two long tables and figured that they were the local customs clerks. A multilingual sign above their stations confirmed the hunch. I stopped in front of one of them. She glanced up at me, then held out her hand. *"Vôtre passeport?"*

I pulled out the blue and white booklet, handed it over, then stood holding my hands as I waited. I could feel the muscles at the back of my neck knot as I observed an old anti-Drac propaganda poster on the wall behind her. It showed two yellow, clawed hands holding a miniature Earth before a fanged mouth. Fangs and claws. The caption read: "They would call this victory" in seven languages.

*"Avez-vous quelque chose à déclarer?"*

I frowned at her. *"Ess?"*

She frowned back. *"Avez-vous quelque chose à déclarer?"*

I felt a tap on my back. "Do you speak English?"

I turned and saw the other customs clerk. My upper lip curled. *"Surda; ne surda. Adze Dracon?"*

His eyebrows went up as he mouthed the word "Drac." He turned to the other clerk, took my passport from her, then looked back at me. He tapped the booklet against his fingertips, then opened it, read the ident page, and looked back at me. "Come with me, Mister Davidge. We must have a talk." He turned and headed into a small office. I shrugged and followed. When I entered, he pointed toward a chair. As I lowered myself into it, he sat down behind a desk. "Why do you pretend not to speak English?"

"Why do you have that poster on the wall? The war is over."

The customs clerk clasped his hands, rested them on the desk, then shook his head. "The fighting is over, Mister Davidge, but for many the war is not. The Draggers killed many humans."

I cocked my head to one side. "A few Dracs died, too." I stood up. "May I go now?"

The customs clerk leaned back in his chair. "That chip on your shoulder you will find to be a considerable weight to bear on this planet."

"I'm the one who has to carry it."

The customs clerk shrugged, then nodded toward the door. "You may go. And good luck, Mister Davidge. You'll need it."

"Dragger suck." As an invective the term had all of the impact of several historical terms—Quisling, heretic, fag, nigger-lover, all rolled into one. Ex-Force pilots were a drag on the employment market, with no commercial positions open, especially not to a pilot who hadn't flown in four years, who had a gimpy leg, and who was a Dragger suck. Transportation to North America, and after a period of lonely wandering, to Dallas. Mistan's eight-hundred-year-old words from the *Talman* would haunt me: *Misnuuram va siddeth;* Your thought is loneliness. Loneliness is a thing one does to oneself. *Jerry shook his head that one time, then pointed a yellow finger at me as the words it wanted to say came together. "Davidge . . . to me loneliness is a discomfort—unpleasant, and a thing to be avoided, but not a thing to be feared. I think you would prefer death to being alone with yourself."*

Mistan observed: "If you are alone with yourself, you will forever be alone with others." A contradiction? The test of reality proves it true. I was out of place on my own planet, and it was more than a hate that I didn't share or a love that, to others, seemed impossible—perverse. Deep inside of myself, I had no use for the creature called "Davidge." Before Fyrine IV there had been other reasons—reasons that I could not identify; but now, my reason was known. My fault or not, I had betrayed an ugly, yellow thing called Zammis, as well as the creature's parent. *"Present Zammis before the Jeriba archives. Swear this to me."*

*Oh, Jerry . . .*

*Swear this!*

*I swear it . . .*

I had forty-eight thousand credits in back pay, and so money wasn't a problem. The problem was what to do with myself. Finally, in Dallas, I landed a job in a small book house translating manuscripts into Drac. It seemed that there was a craving among Dracs for Westerns: "Stick 'em up *naagusaat!*"

*"Nu geph*, lawman." Thang, thang! The guns flashed and another *kizlode shaddsaat* bit the dust.

I quit.

I finally called my parents. *Why didn't you call before, Willy? We've been worried sick . . . Had a few things I had to straighten out, Dad . . . No, not really . . . Well, we understand, son . . . it must have been awful . . . Dad, I'd like to come home for a while . . .*

Even before I put down the money on the used Dearman Electric, I knew I was making a mistake going home. I felt the need of a home, but the one I had left at the age of eighteen wasn't it. But I headed there because there was nowhere else to go.

I drove alone in the dark, using only the old roads, the quiet hum of the Dearman's motor the only sound. The December midnight was clear, and I could see the stars through the car's bubble canopy. Fyrine IV drifted into my thoughts, the raging ocean, the endless winds. I pulled off the road onto the shoulder and killed the lights. In a few minutes, my eyes adjusted to the dark and I stepped outside and shut the door. Kansas has a big sky, and the stars seemed close enough to touch. Snow crunched under my feet as I looked up, trying to pick Fyrine out of the thousands of visible stars.

Fyrine is in the constellation Pegasus, but my eyes were not practiced enough to pick the winged horse out from the surrounding stars. I shrugged, felt a chill, and decided to get back in the car. As I put my hand on the door-latch, I saw a constellation that I did recognize, north, hanging just above the horizon: Draco. The Dragon, its tail twisted around Ursa Minor, hung upside down in the sky. Eltanin, the Dragon's nose, is the homestar of the Dracs. Its second planet, Draco, was Zammis' home.

Headlights from an approaching car blinded me, and I turned toward the car as it pulled to a stop. The window on the driver's side opened and some-one spoke from the darkness.

"You need some help?"

I shook my head. "No, thank you." I held up a hand. "I was just looking at the stars."

"Quite a night, isn't it?"

"Sure is."

"Sure you don't need any help?"

I shook my head. "Thanks...wait. Where is the nearest commercial spaceport?"

"About an hour ahead in Salina."

"Thanks." I saw a hand wave from the window, then the other car pulled away. I took another look at Eltanin, then got back in my car.

Nine weeks later I stood before the little gray man who ran Lone Star Pub-lishing, Inc. He looked up at me and frowned. "So, what do you want? I thought you quit."

I threw a thousand-page manuscript on his desk. "This."

He poked it with a finger. "What is it?"

"The Drac bible; it's called the *Talman*."

"So what?"

"So it's the only book translated from Drac into English; so it's the explanation for how every Drac conducts itself; so it'll make you a bundle of credits."

He leaned forward, scanned several pages, then looked up at me. "You know, Davidge, I don't like you worth a damn."

I shrugged. "I don't like you either."

He returned to the manuscript. "Why now?"

"Now is when I need money."

He shrugged. "The best I can offer would be around eight or ten thousand. This is untried stuff."

"I need twenty-four thousand. You want to go for less than that, I'll take it to someone else."

He looked at me and frowned. "What makes you think that anyone else would be interested?"

"Let's quit playing around. There are a lot of survivors of the war—both military and civilian—who would like to understand what happened." I leaned forward and tapped the manuscript. "That's what's in there."

"Twenty-four thousand is lot for a first manuscript."

I gathered up the pages. "I'll find someone who has some coin to invest in a sure thing."

He placed his hand on the manuscript. "Hold on, Davidge." He frowned. "Twenty-four thousand?"

"Not a quarter-note less."

He pursed his lips, then glanced at me. "I suppose you'll be Hell on wheels regarding final approval."

I shook my head. "All I want is the money. You can do whatever you want with the manuscript."

He leaned back in his chair, looked at the manuscript, then back at me. "The money. What're you going to do with it?"

"None of your business."

He leaned forward, then leafed through a few more pages. His eyebrows notched up, then he looked back at me. "You aren't picky about the contract?"

"As long as I get the money, you can turn that into *Mein Kampf* if you want to."

He leafed through a few more pages. "This is some pretty radical stuff."

"It sure is. And you can find the same stuff in Plato, Aristotle, Augustine, James, Freud, Szasz, Nortmyer, and the Declaration of Independence."

He leaned back in his chair. "What does this mean to you?"

"Twenty-four thousand credits."

He leafed through a few more pages, then a few more. In twelve hours I had purchased passage to Draco.

* * *

Six months later, I stood in front of an ancient cut-stone gate wondering what in the Hell I was doing. The trip to Draco, with nothing but Dracs as companions on the last leg, showed me the truth in Namvaac's words: "Peace is often only war without fighting." The accords, on paper, gave me the right to travel to the planet, but the Drac bureaucrats and their paperwork wizards had perfected the big stall long before the first human step into space. It took threats, bribes, and long days of filling out forms, being checked and rechecked for disease, contraband, reason for visit, filling out more forms, refilling out the forms I had already filled out, more bribes, waiting, waiting, waiting . . .

On the ship, I spent most of my time in my cabin, but since the Drac stewards refused to serve me, I went to the ship's lounge for my meals. I sat alone, listening to the comments about me from other booths. I had figured the path of least resistance was to pretend I didn't understand what they were saying. It is always assumed that humans do not speak Drac.

"Must we eat in the same compartment with the *Irkmaan* slime?"

"Look at it, how its pale skin blotches—and that evil-smelling thatch on top. Feh! The smell!"

I ground my teeth a little and kept my glance riveted to my plate.

"It defies the *Talman* that the universe's laws could be so corrupt as to produce a creature such as that."

I turned and faced the three Dracs sitting in the booth across the aisle from mine. In Drac, I replied: "If your line's elders had seen fit to teach the village *kiz* to use contraceptives, you wouldn't even exist." I returned to my food while the two Dracs struggled to hold the third Drac down.

On Draco, it was no problem finding the Jeriba estate. The problem was getting in. A high stone wall enclosed the property, and from the gate I could see the huge stone mansion that Jerry had described to me. I told the guard at the gate that I wanted to see Jeriba Zammis. The guard stared at me, then went into an alcove behind the gate. In a few moments, another Drac emerged from the mansion and walked quickly across the wide lawn to the gate. The Drac nodded at the guard, then stopped and faced me. It was a dead ringer for Jerry.

"You are the *Irkmaan* that asked to see Jeriba Zammis?"

I nodded. "Yes. Zammis must have told you about me. I'm Willis Davidge."

The Drac studied me. "I am Estone Nev, Jeriban Shigan's sibling. My parent, Jeriba Gothig, wishes to see you." The Drac turned abruptly and walked back to the mansion. I followed, feeling heady at the thought of seeing Zammis again. I paid little attention to my surroundings until I was ushered into a large room with a vaulted stone ceiling. Jerry had told me that the house was four thousand years old. I believed it. As I entered, another Drac stood and walked over to me. It was old, but I knew who it was.

"You are Gothig, Shigan's parent."

The yellow eyes studied me. "Who are you, *Irkmaan?*" It held out a wrinkled, three-fingered hand. "What do you know of Jeriba Zammis, and why do you speak the Drac tongue with the style and accent of my child Shigan? What are you here for?"

"I speak Drac in this manner because that is the way Jeriba Shigan taught me to speak it."

The old Drac cocked its head to one side and narrowed its yellow eyes. "You knew my child? How?"

"Didn't the survey commission tell you?"

"It was reported to me that my child, Shigan, was killed in the battle of Fyrine IV. That was over six of our years ago. What is your game, *Irkmaan?*"

I turned from Gothig to Nev. The younger Drac was examining me with the same look of suspicion. I turned back to Gothig. "Shigan wasn't killed in the battle. We were stranded together on the surface of Fyrine IV and lived there for a year. Shigan died giving birth to Jeriba Zammis. A year later the joint survey commission found us and—"

"Enough! Enough of this, *Irkmaan!* Are you here for money, to use my influence for trade concessions—what?"

I frowned. "Where is Zammis?"

Tears of anger came to the old Drac's eyes. "There is no Zammis, *Irkmaan!* The Jeriban line ended with the death of Shigan!"

My eyes grew wide as I shook my head. "That's not true. I know. I took care of Zammis—you heard nothing from the commission?"

"Get to the point of your scheme, *Irkmaan.* I haven't all day."

I studied Gothig. The old Drac had heard nothing from the commission. The Drac authorities took Zammis, and the child had evaporated. Gothig had been told nothing. Why? "I was with Shigan, Gothig. That is how I learned your language. When Shigan died giving birth to Zammis, I—"

"*Irkmaan,* if you cannot get to your scheme, I will have to ask Nev to throw you out. Shigan died in the battle of Fyrine IV. The Drac Fleet notified us only days later."

I nodded. "Then, Gothig, tell me how I came to know the line of Jeriba? Do you wish me to recite it for you?"

Gothig snorted. "You say you know the Jeriba line?"

"Yes."

Gothig flipped a hand at me. "Then, recite."

I took a breath, then began. By the time I had reached the hundred and seventy-third generation, Gothig had knelt on the stone floor next to Nev. The Dracs remained that way for three hours of the recital. When I concluded, Gothig bowed its head and wept. "Yes, *Irkmaan,* yes. You must have known Shigan. Yes." The old Drac looked up into my face, its eyes wide with hope. "And, you say Shigan continued the line—that Zammis was born?"

I nodded. "I don't know why the commission didn't notify you."

Gothig got to its feet and frowned. "We will find out, *Irkmaan*—what is your name?"

"Davidge. Willis Davidge."

"We will find out, Davidge."

Gothig arranged quarters for me in its house, which was fortunate, since I had little more than eleven hundred credits left. After making a host of inquiries, Gothig sent Nev and I to the Chamber Center in Sendievu, Draco's capital city. The Jeriba line, I found, was influential, and the big stall was held down to a minimum. Eventually, we were directed to the Joint Survey Commission representative, a Drac named Jozzdn Vrule. It looked up from the letter Gothig had given me and frowned. "Where did you get this, *Irkmaan?*"

"I believe the signature is on it."

The Drac looked at the paper, then back at me. "The Jeriba line is one of the most respected on Draco. You say that Jeriba Gothig gave you this?"

"I felt certain I said that; I could feel my lips moving—"

Nev stepped in. "You have the dates and the information concerning the Fyrine IV survey mission. We want to know what happened to Jeriba Zammis."

Jozzdn Vrule frowned and looked back at the paper. "Estone Nev, you are the founder of your line, is this not true?"

"It is true."

"Would you found your line in shame? Why do I see you with this *Irkmaan?*"

Nev curled its upper lip and folded its arms. "Jozzdn Vrule, if you contemplate walking this planet in the forseeable future as a free being, it would be to your profit to stop working your mouth and to start finding Jeriba Zammis."

Jozzdn Vrule looked down and studied its fingers, then returned its glance to Nev. "Very well, Estone Nev. You threaten me if I fail to hand you the truth. I think you will find the truth the greater threat." The Drac scribbled on a piece of paper, then handed it to Nev. "You will find Jeriba Zammis at this address, and you will curse the day that I gave you this."

We entered the retard colony feeling sick. All around us, Dracs stared with vacant eyes, or screamed, or foamed at the mouth, or behaved as lower-order creatures. After we had arrived, Gothig joined us. The Drac director of the colony frowned at me and shook its head at Gothig. "Turn back now, while it is still possible, Jeriba Gothig. Beyond this room lies nothing but pain and sorrow."

Gothig grabbed the director by the front of its wraps. "Hear me, insect: If Jeriba Zammis is within these walls, bring my grandchild forth! Else, I shall bring the might of the Jeriban line down upon your pointed head!"

The director lifted its head, twitched its lips, then nodded. "Very well. Very well, you pompous *Kazzmidth!* We tried to protect the Jeriba reputation. We tried! But now you shall see." The director nodded and pursed its lips. "Yes, you overwealthy fashion follower, now you shall see." The director scribbled on a piece of paper, then handed it to Nev. "By giving you that, I will lose my position, but take it! Yes, take it! See this being you call Jeriba Zammis. See it, and weep!"

Among trees and grass, Jeriba Zammis sat upon a stone bench, staring at the ground. Its eyes never blinked, its hands never moved. Gothig frowned at me, but I could spare nothing for Shigan's parent. I walked to Zammis. "Zammis, do you know me?"

The Drac retrieved its thoughts from a million warrens and raised its yellow eyes to me. I saw no sign of recognition. "Who are you?"

I squatted down, placed my hands on its arms and shook them. "Damn it, Zammis, don't you know me? I'm your Uncle. Remember that? Uncle Davidge?"

The Drac weaved on the bench, then shook its head. It lifted an arm and waved to an orderly. "I want to go to my room. Please, let me go to my room."

I stood and grabbed Zammis by the front of its hospital gown. "Zammis, it's me!"

The yellow eyes, dull and lifeless, stared back at me. The orderly placed a yellow hand upon my shoulder. "Let it go, *Irkmaan.*"

"Zammis!" I turned to Nev and Gothig. "Say something!"

The Drac orderly pulled a sap from its pocket, then slapped it suggestively against the palm of its hand. "Let it go, *Irkmaan.*"

Gothig stepped forward. "Explain this!"

The orderly looked at Gothig, Nev, me, and then Zammis. "This one—this creature—came to us professing a love, a *love*, mind you, of humans! This is no small perversion, Jeriba Gothig. The government would protect you from this scandal. Would you wish the line of Jeriba dragged into this?"

I looked at Zammis. "What have you done to Zammis, you *kizlode* sonofabitch? A little shock? A little drug? Rot out its mind?"

The orderly sneered at me, then shook his head. "You, *Irkmaan*, do not understand. This one would not be happy as an *Irkmaan vul*—a human lover.

We are making it possible for this one to function in Drac society. You think this is wrong?"

I looked at Zammis and shook my head. I remembered too well my treatment at the hands of my fellow humans. "No. I don't think it's wrong . . . I just don't know."

The orderly turned to Gothig. "Please understand, Jeriba Gothig. We could not subject the Jeriba line to this disgrace. Your grandchild is almost well and will soon enter a reeducation program. In no more than two years, you will have a grandchild worthy of carrying on the Jeriba line. Is this wrong?"

Gothig only shook its head. I squatted down in front of Zammis and looked up into its yellow eyes. I reached up and took its right hand in both of mine. "Zammis?"

Zammis looked down, moved its left hand over, and picked up my left hand and spread the fingers. One at a time Zammis pointed at the fingers of my hand, then it looked into my eyes, then examined the hand again. "Yes . . ." Zammis pointed again. "One, two, three, *four, five!*" Zammis looked into my eyes. "Four, five!"

I nodded. "Yes. Yes."

Zammis pulled my hand to its cheek and held it close. "Uncle . . . Uncle. I told you I'd never forget you."

I never counted the years that passed. Mistaan had words for those who count time as though their recognition of its passing marked their place in the Universe. Mornings, the weather as clear as weather gets on Fyrine IV, I would visit my friend's grave. Next to it, Estone Nev, Zammis, Ty and I buried Gothig. Shigan's parent had taken the healing Zammis, liquidated the Jeriba line's estate, then moved the whole shebang to Fyrine IV. When told the story, it was Ty who named the planet "Friendship."

One blustery day I knelt between the graves, replaced some rocks, then added a few more. I pulled my snakeskins tight against the wind, then sat down and looked out to sea. Still the rollers steamed in under the gray-black cover of clouds. Soon the ice would come. I looked at my scarred, wrinkled hands, then at the grave.

"I couldn't stay in the colony with them, Jerry. Don't get me wrong; it's nice. Damned nice. But I kept looking out my window, seeing the ocean, thinking of the cave. I'm alone, in a way. But it's good. I know what and who I am, Jerry, and that's all there is to it, right?"

I heard a noise. I crouched over, placed my hands upon my withered knees, and pushed myself to my feet. The Drac was coming from the colony compound, a child in its arms.

I rubbed my beard. "Eh, Ty, so that is your first child?"

The Drac nodded. "I would be pleased, Uncle, if you would teach it what it must be taught: the line, the *Talman;* and about the life on Friendship."

I took the bundle into my arms. Chubby three-fingered arms waved at the air, then grasped my snakeskins. "Yes, Ty, this one is a Jeriban." I looked up at Ty. "And how is your parent, Zammis?"

Ty shrugged. "It is as well as can be expected. My parent wishes you well."

I nodded. "And the same to it, Ty. Zammis ought to get out of that air-conditioned capsule and come back to live in the cave. It'll do it good."

Ty grinned and nodded its head. "I will tell my parent, Uncle."

I stabbed my thumb into my chest. "Look at me! You don't see me sick, do you?"

"No, Uncle."

"You tell Zammis to kick that doctor out of there and to come back to the cave, hear?"

"Yes, Uncle." Ty smiled. "Is there anything you need?"

I nodded and scratched the back of my neck. "Toilet paper. Just a couple of packs. Maybe a couple of bottles of whiskey—no, forget the whiskey. I'll wait until Haesni, here, puts in its first year. Just the toilet paper."

Ty bowed. "Yes, Uncle, and may the many mornings find you well."

I waved my hand impatiently. "They will, they will. Just don't forget the toilet paper."

Ty bowed again. "I won't, Uncle."

Ty turned and walked through the scrub forest back to the colony. I lived with them for a year, but I moved out and went back to the cave. I gathered the wood, smoked the snake, and withstood the winter. Zammis gave me the young Ty to rear in the cave and now Ty had handed me Haesni. I nodded at the child. "Your child will be called Gothig, and then . . ." I looked at the sky and felt the tears drying on my face. ". . . And then, Gothig's child will be called Shigan." I nodded and headed for the cleft that would bring us down to the level of the cave.

# Air Raid

## JOHN VARLEY

**Millennium**

Director: *Michael Anderson*
Screenplay: *John Varley*
Producer: *Douglas Letterman*
Music: *Eric Robertson*
Special Effects: *ILM*
Cast: *Kris Kristofferson, Cheryl Ladd, Daniel J. Travanti*
Released by: *20th Century-Fox*
1990, 108 Minutes. Color.

I was jerked awake by the silent alarm vibrating my skull. It won't shut down until you sit up, so I did. All around me in the darkened bunkroom the Snatch Team members were sleeping singly and in pairs. I yawned, scratched my ribs, and patted Gene's hairy flank. He turned over. So much for a romantic send-off.

Rubbing sleep from my eyes, I reached to the floor for my leg, strapped it on and plugged it in. Then I was running down the rows of bunks toward Ops.

The situation board glowed in the gloom. Sun-Belt Airlines Flight 128, Miami to New York, September 15, 1979. We'd been looking for that one for three years. I should have been happy, but who can afford it when you wake up?

Liza Boston muttered past me on the way to Prep. I muttered back, and followed. The lights came on around the mirrors, and I groped my way to one of them. Behind us, three more people staggered in. I sat down, plugged in, and at last I could lean back and close my eyes.

They didn't stay closed for long. Rush! I sat up straight as the sludge I use for blood was replaced with supercharged go-juice. I looked around me and got a series of idiot grins. There was Liza, and Pinky and Dave. Against the far wall Cristabel was already turning slowly in front of the airbrush, getting a caucasian paint job. It looked like a good team.

I opened the drawer and started preliminary work on my face. It's a bigger job every time. Transfusion or no, I looked like death. The right ear was completely gone now. I could no longer close my lips; the gums were permanently bared. A week earlier, a finger had fallen off in my sleep. And what's it to you, bugger?

While I worked, one of the screens around the mirror glowed. A smiling young woman, blonde, high brow, round face. Close enough. The crawl line read *Mary Katrina Sondergard, born Trenton, New Jersey, age in 1979: 25.* Baby, this is your lucky day.

The computer melted the skin away from her face to show me the bone structure, rotated it, gave me cross-sections. I studied the similarities with my own skull, noted the differences. Not bad, and better than some I'd been given.

I assembled a set of dentures that included the slight gap in the upper incisors. Putty filled out my cheeks. Contact lenses fell from the dispenser and I popped them in. Nose plugs widened my nostrils. No need for ears; they'd be covered by the wig. I pulled a blank plastiflesh mask over my face and had to pause while it melted in. It took only a minute to mold it to perfection. I smiled at myself. How nice to have lips.

The delivery slot clunked and dropped a blonde wig and a pink outfit into my lap. The wig was hot from the styler. I put it on, then my pantyhose.

"Mandy? Did you get the profile on Sondergard?" I didn't look up; I recognized the voice.

"Roger."

"We've located her near the airport. We can slip you in before take-off, so you'll be the joker."

I groaned, and looked up at the face on the screen. Elfreda Baltimore-Louisville, Director of Operational Teams: lifeless face and tiny slits for eyes. What can you do when all the muscles are dead?

"Okay." You take what you get.

She switched off, and I spent the next two minutes trying to get dressed while keeping my eyes on the screens. I memorized names and faces of crew members plus the few facts known about them. Then I hurried out and caught up with the others. Elapsed time from first alarm: twelve minutes and seven seconds. We'd better get moving.

"Goddam Sun-Belt," Cristabel groused, hitching at her bra.

"At least they got rid of the high heels," Dave pointed out. A year earlier we would have been teetering down the aisles on three-inch platforms. We all wore short pink shifts with blue and white stripes diagonally across the front, and carried matching shoulder bags. I fussed trying to get the ridiculous pill-box cap pinned on.

We jogged into the dark Operations Control Room and lined up at the gate. Things were out of our hands now. Until the gate was ready, we could only wait.

I was first, a few feet away from the portal. I turned away from it; it gives me vertigo. I focused instead on the gnomes sitting at their consoles, bathed in yellow lights from their screens. None of them looked back at me. They don't like us much. Our fat legs and butts and breasts are a reproach to them, a reminder that Snatchers eat five times their ration to stay presentable for the masquerade. Meantime we continue to rot. One day I'll be sitting at a console. One day I'll be *built in* to a console, with all my guts on the outside and nothing left of my body but stink. The hell with them.

I buried my gun under a clutter of tissues and lipsticks in my purse. Elfreda was looking at me.

"Where is she?" I asked.

"Motel room. She was alone from 10 P.M. to noon on flight day."

Departure time was 1:15. She cut it close and would be in a hurry. Good.

"Can you catch her in the bathroom? Best of all, in the tub?"

"We're working on it." She sketched a smile with a fingertip drawn over lifeless lips. She knew how I like to operate, but she was telling me I'd take what I got. It never hurts to ask. People are at their most defenseless stretched out and up to their necks in water.

"Go!" Elfreda shouted. I stepped through, and things started to go wrong.

I was faced the wrong way, stepping *out* of the bathroom door and facing the bedroom. I turned and spotted Mary Katrina Sondergard through the haze of the gate. There was no way I could reach her without stepping back through. I couldn't even shoot without hitting someone on the other side.

Sondergard was at the mirror, the worst possible place. Few people recognize themselves quickly, but she'd been looking right at herself. She saw me and her eyes widened. I stepped to the side, out of her sight.

"What the hell is . . . hey? Who the hell. . . ." I noted the voice, which can be the trickiest thing to get right.

I figured she'd be more curious than afraid. My guess was right. She came out of the bathroom, passing through the gate as if it wasn't there, which it wasn't, since it only has one side. She had a towel wrapped around her.

"Jesus Christ! What are you doing in my—!" Words fail you at a time like that. She knew she ought to say something, but what? *Excuse me, haven't I seen you in the mirror?*

I put on my best stew smile and held out my hand.

"Pardon the intrusion. I can explain everything. You see, I'm—" I hit her on the side of the head and she staggered and went down hard. Her towel fell to the floor. "—working my way through college." She started to get up so I caught her under the chin with my artificial knee. She stayed down.

"Standard fuggin' *oil!*" I hissed, rubbing my injured knuckles. But there was no time. I knelt beside her, checked her pulse. She'd be okay, but I think I loosened some front teeth. I paused a moment. Lord, to look like that with no make-up, no prosthetics! She nearly broke my heart.

I grabbed her under the knees and wrestled her to the gate. She was a sack of limp noodles. Somebody reached through, grabbed her feet, and pulled. *So long, love! How would you like to go on a long voyage?*

I sat on her rented bed to get my breath. There were car keys and cigarettes in her purse, genuine tobacco, worth its weight in blood. I lit six of them, figuring I had five minutes of my very own. The room filled with sweet smoke. They don't make 'em like that anymore.

The Hertz sedan was in the motel parking lot. I got in and headed for the airport. I breathed deeply of the air, rich in hydrocarbons. I could see for hundreds of yards into the distance. The perspective nearly made me dizzy, but I live for those moments. There's no way to explain what it's like in the pre-meck world. The sun was a fierce yellow ball through the haze.

The other stews were boarding. Some of them knew Sondergard so I didn't say much, pleading a hangover. That went over well, with a lot of knowing laughs and sly remarks. Evidently it wasn't out of character. We boarded the 707 and got ready for the goats to arrive.

It looked good. The four commandos on the other side were identical twins for the women I was working with. There was nothing to do but be a stewardess until departure time. I hoped there would be no more glitches. Inverting a gate for a joker run into a motel room was one thing, but in a 707 at twenty thousand feet . . .

The plane was nearly full when the woman that Pinky would impersonate sealed the forward door. We taxied to the end of the runway, then we were airborne. I started taking orders for drinks in first.

The goats were the usual lot, for 1979. Fat and sassy, all of them, and as unaware of living in a paradise as a fish is of the sea. *What would you think, ladies and gents, of a trip to the future? No? I can't say I'm surprised. What if I told you this plane is going to—*

My alarm beeped as we reached cruising altitude. I consulted the indicator under my Lady Bulova and glanced at one of the restroom doors. I felt a vibration pass through the plane. *Damn it, not so soon.*

The gate was in there. I came out quickly, and motioned for Diana Gleason—Dave's pigeon—to come to the front.

"Take a look at this," I said, with a disgusted look. She started to enter the restroom, stopped when she saw the green glow. I planted a boot on her fanny and shoved. Perfect. Dave would have a chance to hear her voice before popping in. Though she'd be doing little but screaming when she got a look around . . .

Dave came through the gate, adjusting his silly little hat. Diana must have struggled.

"Be disgusted," I whispered.

"What a mess," he said as he came out of the restroom. It was a fair imitation of Diana's tone, though he'd missed the accent. It wouldn't matter much longer.

"What is it?" It was one of the stews from tourist. We stepped aside so she could get a look, and Dave shoved her through. Pinky popped out very quickly.

"We're minus on minutes," Pinky said. "We lost five on the other side."

"Five?" Dave-Diana squeaked. I felt the same way. We had a hundred and three passengers to process.

"Yeah. They lost contact after you pushed my pigeon through. It took that long to re-align."

You get used to that. Time runs at different rates on each side of the gate, though it's always sequential, past to future. Once we'd started the snatch with me entering Sondergard's room, there was no way to go back any earlier on either side. Here, in 1979, we had a rigid ninety-four minutes to get everything done. On the other side, the gate could never be maintained longer than three hours.

"When you left, how long was it since the alarm went in?"

"Twenty-eight minutes."

It didn't sound good. It would take at least two hours just customizing the wimps. Assuming there was no more slippage on 79-time, we might just make it. But there's *always* slippage. I shuddered, thinking about riding it in.

"No time for any more games, then," I said. "Pink, you go back to tourist and call both of the other girls. Tell 'em to come one at a time, and tell 'em we've got a problem. You know the bit."

"Biting back the tears. Got you." She hurried aft. In no time the first one showed up. Her friendly Sun-Belt Airlines smile was stamped on her face, but her stomach would be churning. *Oh God, this is it!*

I took her by the elbow and pulled her behind the curtains in front. She was breathing hard.

"Welcome to the twilight zone," I said, and put the gun to her head. She slumped, and I caught her. Pinky and Dave helped me shove her through the gate.

"Fug! The rotting thing's flickering."

Pinky was right. A very ominous sign. But the green glow stabilized as we watched, with who-knows-how-much slippage on the other side. Cristabel ducked through.

"We're plus thirty-three," she said. There was no sense talking about what we were all thinking; things were going badly.

"Back to tourist," I said. "Be brave, smile at everyone, but make it just a little bit too good, got it?"

"Check," Cristabel said.

We processed the other quickly, with no incident. Then there was no time to talk about anything. In eighty-nine minutes Flight 128 was going to be spread all over a mountain whether we were finished or not.

Dave went into the cockpit to keep the flight crew out of our hair. Me and Pinky were supposed to take care of first class, then back up Cristabel and Liza in tourist. We used the standard "coffee, tea, or milk" gambit, relying on our speed and their inertia.

I leaned over the first two seats on the left.

"Are you enjoying your flight?" Pop, pop. Two squeezes on the trigger, close to the heads and out of sight of the rest of the goats.

"Hi folks. I'm Mandy. Fly me." Pop, pop.

Half-way to the galley, a few people were watching us curiously. But people don't make a fuss until they have a lot more to go on. One goat in the back row stood up, and I let him have it. By now there were only eight left awake. I abandoned the smile and squeezed off four quick shots. Pinky took care of the rest. We hurried through the curtains, just in time.

There was an uproar building in the back of tourist, with about sixty percent of the goats already processed. Cristabel glanced at me, and I nodded.

"Okay, folks," she bawled. "I want you to be quiet. Calm down and listen up. *You*, fathead, *pipe down* before I cram my foot up your ass sideways."

The shock of hearing her talk like that was enough to buy us a little time, anyway. We had formed a skirmish line across the width of the plane, guns out, steadied on seat backs, aimed at the milling, befuddled group of thirty goats.

The guns are enough to awe all but the most foolhardy. In essence, a standard-issue stunner is just a plastic rod with two grids about six inches apart. There's not enough metal in it to set off a hijack alarm. And to people from the Stone Age to about 2190 it doesn't look any more like a weapon than a ball-point pen. So Equipment Section jazzes them up in a plastic shell to real Buck Rogers blasters, with a dozen knobs and lights that flash and a barrel like the snout of a hog. Hardly anyone ever walks into one.

"We are in great danger, and time is short. You must all do exactly as I tell you, and you will be safe."

You can't give them time to think, you have to rely on your status as the Voice of Authority. The situation is just *not* going to make sense to them, ño matter how you explain it.

"Just a minute, I think you owe us—"

An airborne lawyer. I made a snap decision, thumbed the fireworks switch on my gun, and shot him.

The gun made a sound like a flying saucer with hemorrhoids, spit sparks and little jets of flame, and extended a green laser finger to his forehead. He dropped. All pure kark, of course. But impressive.

And it's damn risky, too. I had to choose between a panic if the fathead got them to thinking, and a possible panic from the flash of the gun. But when a 20th gets to talking about his "rights" and what he is "owed," things can get out of hand. It's infectious.

It worked. There was a lot of shouting, people ducking behind seats, but no rush. We could have handled it, but we needed some of them conscious if we were ever going to finish the Snatch.

"Get up. Get *up*, you *slugs!*" Cristabel yelled. "He's stunned, nothing worse. But I'll *kill* the next one who gets out of line. Now *get to your feet* and do what I tell you. *Children first! Hurry*, as fast as you can, to the front of the plane. Do what the stewardess tells you. Come on, kids, *move!*"

I ran back into first class just ahead of the kids, turned at the open restroom door, and got on my knees.

They were petrified. There were five of them—crying, some of them, which always chokes me up—looking left and right at dead people in the first class seats, stumbling, near panic.

"Come on, kids," I called to them, giving my special smile. "Your parents will be along in just a minute. Everything's going to be all right, I promise you. Come on."

I got three of them through. The fourth balked. She was determined not to go through that door. She spread her legs and arms and I couldn't push her through. I will *not* hit a child, never. She raked her nails over my face. My wig came off, and she gaped at my bare head. I shoved her through.

Number five was sitting in the aisle, bawling. He was maybe seven. I ran back and picked him up, hugged and kissed him, and tossed him through. God, I was beat, but I was needed in tourist.

"You, you, you, and you. Okay, you too. Help him, will you?" Pinky had a practiced eye for the ones that wouldn't be any use to anyone, even themselves. We herded them toward the front of the plane, then deployed ourselves along the left side where we could cover up the workers. It didn't take long to prod them into action. We had them dragging the limp bodies forward as fast as they could go. Me and Cristabel were in tourist, with others up front.

Adrenalin was being catabolized in my body now; the rush of action left me and I started to feel very tired. There's an unavoidable feeling of sympathy for the poor dumb goats that starts to get me about this stage of the game. Sure, they were better off, sure they were going to die if we didn't get them off the plane. But when they saw the other side they were going to have a hard time believing it.

The first ones were returning for a second load, stunned at what they'd just seen: dozens of people being put into a cubicle that was crowded when it was empty. One college student looked like he'd been hit in the stomach. He stopped by me and his eyes pleaded.

"Look, I want to *help* you people, just . . . what's going *on?* Is this some new kind of rescue? I mean, are we going to crash—"

I switched my gun to prod and brushed it across his cheek. He gasped, and fell back.

"Shut your fuggin' mouth and get moving, or I'll kill you." It would be hours before his jaw was in shape to ask any more stupid questions.

We cleared tourist and moved up. A couple of the work gang were pretty damn pooped by then. Muscles like horses, all of them, but they can hardly run up a flight of stairs. We let some of them go through, including a couple that were at least fifty years old. *Je*-zuz. Fifty! We got down to a core of four men and two dropped. But we processed everyone in twenty-five minutes.

The portapak came through as we were stripping off our clothes. Cristabel knocked on the door to the cockpit and Dave came out, already naked. A bad sign.

"I had to cork 'em," he said. "Bleeding Captain just *had* to make his Grand March through the plane. I tried *everything.*"

Sometimes you have to do it. The plane was on autopilot, as it normally would be at this time. But if any of us did anything detrimental to the craft, changed the fixed course of events in any way, that would be it. All that work for nothing, and Flight 128 inaccessible to us for all Time. I don't know sludge about time theory, but I know the practical angles. We can do things in the past only at times and in places where it won't make any difference. We have to cover our tracks. There's flexibility; once a Snatcher left her gun behind and it went in with the plane. Nobody found it, or if they did, they didn't have the smoggiest idea of what it was, so we were okay.

Flight 128 was mechanical failure. That's the best kind; it means we don't have to keep the pilot unaware of the situation in the cabin right down to ground level. We can cork him and fly the plane, since there's nothing he could have done to save the flight anyway. A pilot-error smash is almost impossible to Snatch. We mostly work mid-airs, bombs, and structural failures. If there's even one survivor, we can't touch it. It would not fit the fabric of space-time, which is immutable (though it can stretch a little), and we'd all just fade away and appear back in the ready-room.

My head was hurting. I wanted that portapak very badly.

"Who has the most hours on a 707?" Pinky did, so I sent her to the cabin, along with Dave, who could do the pilot's voice for air traffic control. You have to have a believable record in the flight recorder, too. They trailed two long tubes from the portapak, and the rest of us hooked in up close. We stood there, each of us smoking a fistful of cigarettes, wanting to finish them but hoping there wouldn't be enough time. The gate had vanished as soon as we tossed our clothes and the flight crew through.

But we didn't worry long. There's other nice things about Snatching, but nothing to compare with the rush of plugging into a portapak. The wake-up transfusion is nothing but fresh blood, rich in oxygen and sugars. What we were getting now was an insane brew of concentrated adrenalin, super-saturated hemoglobin, methedrine, white lightning, TNT, and Kickapoo joyjuice. It was like a firecracker in your heart; a boot in the box that rattled your sox.

"I'm growing hair on my chest," Cristabel said, solemnly. Everyone giggled.

"Would someone hand me my eyeballs?"

"The blue ones, or the red ones?"

"I think my ass just fell off."

We'd heard them all before, but we howled anyway. We were strong, *strong*, and for one golden moment we had no worries. Everything was hilarious. I could have torn sheet metal with my eyelashes.

But you get hyper on that mix. When the gate didn't show, and didn't show, and *didn't sweetjeez show* we all started milling. This bird wasn't going to fly all that much longer.

Then it did show, and we turned on. The first of the wimps came through, dressed in the clothes taken from a passenger it had been picked to resemble.

"Two thirty-five elapsed upside time," Cristabel announced.

"Je-zuz."

It is a deadening routine. You grab the harness around the wimp's shoulders and drag it along the aisle, after consulting the seat number painted on its forehead. The paint would last three minutes. You seat it, strap it in, break open the harness and carry it back to toss through the gate as you grab the next one. You have to take it for granted they've done the work right on the other side; fillings in the teeth, fingerprints, the right match in height and weight and hair color. Most of those things don't matter much, especially on Flight 128 which was a crash-and-burn. There would be bits and pieces, and burned to a crisp at that. But you can't take chances. Those rescue workers are pretty thorough on the parts they *do* find; the dental work and fingerprints especially are important.

I hate wimps. I really hate 'em. Every time I grab the harness of one of them, if it's a child, I wonder if it's Alice. *Are you my kid, you vegetable, you slug, you slimy worm?* I joined the Snatchers right after the brain bugs ate the life out of my baby's head. I couldn't stand to think she was the last generation, that the last humans there would ever be would live with nothing in their heads, medically dead by standards that prevailed even in 1979, with computers working their muscles to keep them in tone. You grow up, reach puberty still fertile—one in a thousand—rush to get pregnant in your first heat. Then you find out your mom or pop passed on a chronic disease bound right into the genes, and none of your kids will be immune. I *knew* about the para-leprosy; I grew up with my toes rotting away. But this was too much. What do you do?

Only one in ten of the wimps had a customized face. It takes time and a lot of skill to build a new face that will stand up to a doctor's autopsy. The rest came pre-mutilated. We've got millions of them; it's not hard to find a good match in the body. Most of them would stay breathing, too dumb to stop, until impact.

The plane jerked, hard. I glanced at my watch. Five minutes to impact. We should have time. I was on my last wimp. I could hear Dave frantically calling the ground. A bomb came through the gate, and I tossed it into the cockpit. Pinky turned on the pressure sensor on the bomb and came running out, followed by Dave. Liza was already through. I grabbed the limp dolls in stewardess costume and tossed them to the floor. The engine fell off and a piece of it came through. I grabbed the cabin. We started to depressurize. The bomb blew away part of the cockpit (the ground crash crew would read it—we hoped—that part of the engine came through and killed the crew: no more words from the pilot on the flight recorder) and we turned, slowly, left and down. I was lifted toward the hole in the side of the plane, but managed to hold onto a seat. Cristabel wasn't so lucky. She was blown backwards.

We started to rise slightly, losing speed. Suddenly it was uphill from where Cristabel was lying in the aisle. Blood oozed from her temple. I glanced back; everyone was gone, and three pink-suited wimps were piled on the floor. The plane began to stall, to nose down, and my feet left the floor.

"Come on, Bel!" I screamed. That gate was only three feet away from me, but I began pulling myself along to where she floated. The plane bumped, and she hit the floor. Incredibly, it seemed to wake her up. She started to swim toward me, and I grabbed her hand as the floor came up to slam us again. We crawled as the plane went through its final death agony, and we came to the door. The gate was gone.

There wasn't anything to say. We were going in. It's hard enough to keep the gate in place on a plane that's moving in a straight line. When a bird gets to corkscrewing and coming apart, the math is fearsome. So I've been told.

I embraced Cristabel and held her bloodied head. She was groggy, but managed to smile and shrug. You take what you get. I hurried into the restroom and got both of us down on the floor. Back to the forward bulkhead, Cristabel between my legs, back to front. Just like in training. We pressed our feet against the other wall. I hugged her tightly and cried on her shoulder.

And it was there. A green glow to my left. I threw myself toward it, dragging Cristabel, keeping low as two wimps were thrown head-first through the gate above our heads. Hands grabbed and pulled us through. I clawed my way a good five yards along the floor. You can leave a leg on the other side and I didn't have one to spare.

I sat up as they were carrying Cristabel to Medical. I patted her arm as she went by on the stretcher, but she was passed out. I wouldn't have minded passing out myself.

For a while, you can't believe it all really happened. Sometimes it turns out it *didn't* happen. You come back and find out all the goats in the holding pen have softly and suddenly vanished away because the continuum won't tolerate the changes and paradoxes you've put into it. The people you've worked so hard to rescue are spread like tomato surprise all over some goddam hillside in Carolina and all you've got left is a bunch of ruined wimps and an exhausted Snatch Team. But not this time. I could see the goats milling around in the holding pen, naked and more bewildered than ever. And just starting to be *really* afraid.

Elfreda touched me as I passed her. She nodded, which meant well-done in her limited repertoire of gestures. I shrugged, wondering if I cared, but the surplus adrenalin was still in my veins and I found myself grinning at her. I nodded back.

Gene was standing by the holding pen. I went to him, hugged him. I felt the juices start to flow. *Damn it, let's squander a little ration and have us a good time.*

Someone was beating on the sterile glass wall of the pen. She shouted, mouthing angry words at us. *Why? What have you done to us?* It was Mary Sondergard. She implored her bald, one-legged twin to make her understand. She thought she had problems. God, was she pretty. I hated her guts.

Gene pulled me away from the wall. My hands hurt, and I'd broken off all my fake nails without scratching the glass. She was sitting on the floor now, sobbing. I heard the voice of the briefing officer on the outside speaker.

"... Centauri 3 is hospitable, with an Earth-like climate. By that, I mean *your* Earth, not what it has become. You'll see more of that later. The trip will take five years, shiptime. Upon landfall, you will be entitled to one horse, a plow, three axes, two hundred kilos of seed grain ..."

I leaned against Gene's shoulder. At their lowest ebb, this very moment, they were so much better than us. I had maybe ten years, half of that as a basketcase. They are our best, our very brightest hope. Everything is up to them.

"... that no one will be forced to go. We wish to point out again, not for the last time, that you would all be dead without our intervention. There are things you should know, however. You cannot breathe our air. If you remain on Earth, you can never leave this building. We are not like you. We are the result of a genetic winnowing, a mutation process. We are the survivors, but our enemies have evolved along with us. They are winning. You, however, are immune to the diseases that afflict us ..."

I winced, and turned away.

"... the other hand, if you emigrate you will be given a chance at a new life. It won't be easy, but as Americans you should be proud of your pioneer heritage. Your ancestors survived, and so will you. It can be a rewarding experience, and I urge you ..."

Sure. Gene and I looked at each other and laughed. *Listen to this, folks. Five percent of you will suffer nervous breakdowns in the next few days, and never leave. About the same number will commit suicide, here and on the way. When you get there, sixty to seventy percent will die in the first three years. You will die in childbirth, be eaten by animals, bury two out of three of your babies, starve slowly when the rains don't come. If you live, it will be to break your back behind a plow, sun-up to dusk. New Earth is Heaven, folks!*

God, how I wish I could go with them.